DRUID

Book Three of the Druid Chronicles

J. Paige Dunn

Steel & Magic
5 Elements Press
Jonesboro, AR

Druid: Book Three of the Druid Chronicles
http://www.druidchronicles.com

Steel & Magic
a division of 5 Elements Press
Jonesboro, AR

Quantity discounts available to organizations, schools, and libraries.
Contact: 5elementspress@gmail.com

Editions ISBN
Print: 978-1-940882-05-5
eBook: 978-1-940882-06-2

Dunn, J. Paige
Druid: book three of the druid chronicles

Cover design by Leah Kay Suttle
http://www.leahsuttle.com

Model: Jason Aaron Baca
Photographed by Portia Shao
http://jasonaaronbaca.deviantart.com/

Prior novels of The Druid Chronicles

Traveler

Warrior

.

for Matt

Because everybody loves Bacon

Acknowledgements

Many thanks to my beta readers: Matt, Jessica, Ashley, Shannon, and John. If this book is great, it's because of their feedback, and if it not, it's all me. It's great to have friends who are "just friends," but it's even more amazing when they bring remarkable talent to the table.

Remarkable photographer Marc Santos helped me through the agony of choosing the perfect photo for the cover. To see Marc's brilliant, original, and dramatic photography, find him on the web: http://www.marcsantosphotography.com and on Instagram: @pixmarc.

A huge thank you to Leah Kaye Suttle, the marvelous graphic designer who helps bring my books to life. She really does all the work, y'all. All I do is tell her how many pages and offer a few color suggestions. She literally creates something out of nothing, and it's always beautiful. I am continually amazed at her talent and artistic ability, and she outdid herself on this one. You can see more of her work at: http://www.leahsuttle.com/

My husband Edward shouldered the financial burden of our family so that I could quit work and focus on school. I didn't tell him that it was also so I could finish this book, but he probably knew that anyway. I could not have designed a kinder, more generous, or more loving person to spend my life with.

I have to mention one more special person: Dusty. Anytime I felt like giving up, or when I despaired of ever finishing this book, or when I was convinced it was utter crap, I think of you. You may not realize it, but you motivate me to keep going. Just like Davis, you never give up, and you never give in. You are an inspiration to me, and for that, I thank you.

All the greatest things are simple,
and many can be expressed in a single word:

Freedom

Justice

Honor

Mercy

Duty

Hope.

~ Winston Churchill ~

Contents

Chapter 1 – Raw Power

Some are born great, some achieve greatness,
and some have greatness thrust upon them.
~William Shakespeare~

After all I had been through, I wondered exactly what my place was in the world, and what else the gods had in store for me. I had Traveled south with Angie, managing to arrive at White Oak Grove with both our skins intact, only to suffer insult, injury, and a beating that would mar my body for the rest of my life. It had all been done to fulfill the desires of ArchDruid Sebrina Silvermist, made possible by the acquiescence of Liam Everlight, and to be perfectly honest, with the consent of the entire citizenry of the grove.

I had received unexpected assistance from Padraig Everlight, Danica Harris, and the training masters of the grove, but it hadn't been enough. Helping Wolfric and Onóra escape the ArchDruid's clutches had sealed my fate. If not for Duncan Everlight's formidable healing ability, I would be dead. As it was, Angie thought I *was* dead.

The earth druid and I had both ended up in former ArchDruid Connor Shitozaki's sanctuary for those sons of the grove whose mothers had not taken away their gods-given magic but had sent them to him for safety. It didn't have a name before our arrival, but Duncan referred to it once as "Sanctuary" during dinner in the mess hall, and the name had stuck.

The gifts of elemental fire and earth had been bestowed upon

1

me by the gods on Beltaine, and while I had originally thought that I would soon be able to return to the grove and reclaim my chosen, the difficulty of learning to actually *use* those magical gifts stopped me in my tracks. While I had successfully managed to light the bonfire and keep it going all night at Midsummer, the magical ability I possessed was raw power. My understanding of elemental magic was almost purely theoretical. I had grasped the concept of using my will to control the elements of earth and fire, but putting it into practice was more difficult than I'd expected.

The former ArchDruid was a fire elementalist, and he schooled me in calling fire in the mornings. In the afternoon, Duncan gave me instruction on moving earth. Their teaching methods were like night and day – or perhaps a better comparison would be that they were like stone and flame.

Connor Shitozaki was hot-tempered, loud and active, yelling both insults and encouragement, giving demonstrations of how fire could be manipulated. His displays of skill attracted the attention of the rest of the Finns. They often quit their own practice and gathered around to watch, at least until he sent them away with a verbal barrage regarding their laziness, ineptitude, and general worthlessness.

Duncan Everlight was calm and quiet. We spent a lot of time sitting on the ground "feeling the earth" and engaging in meditation exercises. It reminded me of the times my father would take me into the fields of Jonesboro, talking to me about the quiet life of the world and the plants and animals it supported, and a bunch of other things that I ignored.

I was a kid. It was boring.

Now, as an adult… it was *still* boring.

Whereas Shitozaki's point of focus was that the energy of fire had to be summoned from within and thrust forward to be manipulated, Duncan's lessons involved getting into the heart of the earth, listening to its language, and learning how to request its cooperation.

Without elemental fire, earth magic would have given me the ability to heal. While healing would have come in handy, the tradeoff of having two elements more than made up for it. I recognized the intrinsic worth of elemental earth. It could give me an awareness of the world farther than I could see, warn me of

2

approaching enemies, and provide protection. However, I preferred fire because I could appreciate its more martial applications. It was interesting, alive, and dangerous. Earth wasn't, and I didn't pick it up quite as quickly.

I admit it. I was a deadhead where earth was concerned. Fire was just too interesting, alive, and dangerous. I tried to focus on earth, but my mind kept wandering back to the dancing flames. Shitozaki noticed that I wasn't progressing (Duncan was reporting back to him), and so he made a point to emphasize just how important it was to develop that element as well.

It was thus that I found myself standing with my sword in my hand, opposite Duncan, who had no weapon at all. This was such an obvious trap that I was instantly nervous. I had seen what the earth druid could do with his magic, and it was impressive. We hadn't even begun to spar, but I already had beads of sweat on my upper lip. I tried to wipe it away unobtrusively.

"Go," said Shitozaki.

I advanced on Duncan with hesitation. I didn't want to hurt him. At least that's what I told myself. In truth, I knew that the earth druid was a legend where elemental magic was concerned. Shitozaki would never have put Duncan against me without a weapon unless he was utterly confident that the earth druid didn't need one.

"Attack him, dammit!" Shitozaki snapped. "Stop mincing around like a fairy in a toadstool ring. Hit him with the sword."

I took a deep breath and lunged at Duncan, but the ground was no longer steady under my feet. The ground bumped up under my feet, throwing me off balance. Then it rose up between us, swept toward me in an earthen wave, and knocked me off my feet. I tried to roll, but again the ground would not cooperate. This time a huge chunk of dirt thrust upward beneath me, and split in half. The two halves began to rise and fall at irregular intervals so that I could not anticipate the next movement.

I tried to delve into the earth with my consciousness, but I had been so lazy about my lessons with Duncan that it was hopeless. I couldn't find enough balance – mental or physical – to control either my body or the earth beneath it. I managed to roll off the uneven chunks and regain my feet, then charged Duncan again. He somehow anticipated my move and threw up a wall of solid dirt. I

3

slammed into it full tilt and fell flat on my back, the breath knocked from my lungs and my sword sent spinning away.

"I yield!" I said when I could gasp out a breath.

"I don't think so," said Shitozaki grimly. He gave Duncan a sharp nod, and the next thing I knew, the wall of dirt collapsed, burying me. The earth beneath my back dissipated and I sank into it, swallowed whole. There was moist dirt in my eyes, nose, and mouth. It was compressing my chest. I panicked, and a rush of intense heat surrounded me. With a scream of defiance that took my last breath, I willed the earth off my body. Propelled by a massive ball of flame and superheated air, dirt exploded upward and away in a shower of dry clods and burning embers. Spitting to clear my mouth, I squinted my stinging eyes at Duncan and snarled.

"Hold!" said Shitozaki.

Duncan took a step back, his serious eyes never leaving my face. I was furious and wanted to kill him.

"Stand down, Davis. *Now*."

I glared at the master and coughed out some dirt.

"Go for a swim and get cleaned up."

I stomped over to get my sword and turned away from them.

"And Davis?"

I stopped but refused to look at him.

"Be ready to work tomorrow," he said. "Let's not do this again."

Without acknowledging his command, I stalked back to the barracks for clean clothes and a towel. I was still steamed when I reached the riverbank. I stripped and threw my filthy clothes on the ground, then stepped into the chilly water.

"By Zeus, Davis," I heard Seth say.

I didn't know he had followed me, but it was no surprise. Seth had been my shadow since I had arrived in Sanctuary.

"What?" I snapped.

He nodded his head toward the water, and I noticed it was boiling about my hips. Steam rose from its surface.

Steamed, indeed.

I took a few deep breaths to calm myself. Then I took about a hundred more.

"You realize what he's doing, don't you?" Seth asked.

"Yes. He's trying to get me to want to work with earth."

"Yes, because you've been lazy."

I shot him a look. "Who told you that?"

"*He* did."

"Quakes, does *everyone* talk about me behind my back? What's so wrong with concentrating on one thing at a time? Can't I just play with fire for a while?"

Seth laughed, and I couldn't help but grin.

"He's in a hurry," Seth said after a moment.

"Why? It's not like we're going anywhere."

"I'm not so sure about that. He seems to think it's urgent for you to master your elements as quickly as possible."

I frowned. "That is just not fair. Everybody else here has had *years* to get used to their magic. I've had three weeks!" Frankly, I thought I had made great strides in learning to control fire in that amount of time. Granted, I didn't have much finesse, but it went where I wanted and did what I wanted, and I hadn't even burnt up anything important.

"Nobody ever said it was fair."

Stifling a sigh at the air elementalist's inexorable logic, I said, "I just think that if I knew why it was so important, then maybe it would make things easier." I soaped my hair, scrubbing to get the dirt out of my scalp. Damn Duncan and his dirt. It would have been easier if my hair hadn't gotten so long. Attending to my personal appearance had been the last thing on my mind since being separated from Angie. My hair had grown fast; it was nearly down to my shoulders, a reminder of how long we had been apart. I wondered if she would even recognize me.

Seth crossed his arms over his chest. "So if you knew that someone is coming to kill you tomorrow, it would be easier to work harder?"

"If someone was coming to kill me tomorrow, I'd spend today relaxing."

"Exactly."

I ducked, rinsing my head. I thought about it and decided he was making a little bit of sense. I came up and began to scrub my skin clean. "So you think Shitozaki believes something is coming, but he doesn't want us to slack off because…?"

"Because he wants us at our best."

"I don't think we have to worry about them much. Most of the Finns have magic."

"So do the elders of the grove – and they have a *lot* more experience than we do when it comes to using it in combat."

"Do you really think they'll be up to fighting after being discouraged from using their own magic for so long?" I asked. "Don't you think they'd be a little rusty?"

Seth gave me a cynical look. "Would you stop using magic just because someone discouraged you from doing so?"

There he went, making sense again. I found it a little irritating.

"I still don't think it's fair," I said.

"Is it fair that Dermot lost his father? Is it fair that the rest of us were forced to leave our home? Is it fair that Conall and the other nulls were altered and denied the gift bestowed upon all druids by the Shining Ones?" Seth shook his head and gave me a look that said I should know better than to whine about anything where my magic was concerned.

He was right, but I wasn't finished complaining. "It's like training at the grove all over again, having to master things in weeks or months that others have been training at for years."

"Don't you want to be the best?"

I sighed. "At this point, I'd settle for being competent."

"What about revenge?" he said, gesturing to my back. I felt vaguely surprised and considered it. Was I still vengeful? I didn't feel vengeful.

"I just want Angie back," I said. "Other than that, I don't care about them one way or the other."

"I think *I'd* want revenge."

"I don't see where it would help at this point."

"Might make you feel better."

Somehow I didn't think that killing a several hundred people would make me feel better. Not even having Sebrina dead would help. Having Angie with me was the only thing that would make me feel better.

Gods, I missed her. It had been nearly half a year since I had seen her last. Ever since I had come into my elements, I wanted nothing more than to sit and talk with her about it. I needed to share the experience with her, hear her opinions. Maybe she could help me focus and work harder. More like as soon as I saw her, I'd forget about fighting and magic entirely and lose myself in her exotic green eyes.

"I'm sorry, Davis, I didn't mean to upset you." Seth was looking at me with a concerned expression on his face.

I waved a hand at him, shaking off the sadness and loneliness. "I'm clean enough. Let's get out of here."

"What are you going to do?"

"I guess I'm going to go meditate and listen to the earth."

* * *

"But I've only been an elementalist for six weeks!" I protested. "*And* I've had to learn two elements at once!"

"Don't give me that bullshit." Shitozaki looked stern. "When a man possesses two elements and is dramatically better in one than the other, it means one thing only – that he is neglecting one of them. And that, my friend, is an insult to the gods."

Connor Shitozaki nagged me almost every day about my "subpar manipulation of earth magic." I could understand his frustration since working with fire had come so easily to me. I only had to reach inside, draw out the eager flames, and point them in a direction. While it required conscious thought to keep it under control or pull it back, channeling it was instinctive. Fire was *easy*.

Earth was not. I'd never been good with sitting still, and the meditation required to commune with the earth mother was nigh intolerable. Even so, I truly was trying hard to master the art of earth-moving. It was just *tough*.

Hands on my hips, I scowled back at him. "Look, I spend just as much time working with earth as I do with fire."

"Then maybe you should spend more time in the dirt."

"Earth isn't like fire. It's not something I can force. Even Duncan would tell you that." Unfortunately, the earth druid was not present to do so.

"That is neither here nor there," said Shitozaki. "The power you have developed with elemental fire over the past six weeks far outstrips the ability of any druid I've ever seen, myself included. It stands to follow that your earth magic should be at that level as well." He paused. "Look, Davis, I'm a fire druid. I completely understand the attraction of throwing a screaming fireball, but it is earth that will be your defense after you toss that fireball. There is nothing defensive about fire magic, and you *must* be able to defend yourself."

Unable to hide my frustration, I huffed and looked away. I had never been much of one for defense; taking offensive action was always my first choice.

"Are we clear on this?" Shitozaki asked.

"Yeah. I understand."

"Good." He clapped me on the shoulder and left the barracks. I let out a frustrated groan and flopped onto my bunk.

"Don't let him get to you," said Seth, who was sitting on his own bed and sharpening his enormous *zweihänder*. Like at the grove, the longsword, a blade that required two hands to wield, was the weapon of choice for all the Finns. Dermot, being the smallest and skinniest of our number, was simply amazing with one. He had extremely fast reflexes and footwork as fluid as water. He often joked that while the rest of us might overpower him, we'd have to catch him first.

The air elementalists held an advantage because their magic provided a natural shield. Granted, it took quite a bit of focus to maintain a shield during a sword fight, but they enjoyed the ability to move it about easily, as well as see through it. In addition, they could also augment their strength by using air, permitting swifter strikes and more powerful blows.

"That's easy for you to say," I grumbled, wishing I was an air elementalist because then I wouldn't have to play in the mud anymore. Shitozaki wasn't the only one giving me a hard time about not learning earth magic quickly. I, too, thought I should have had it mastered by now. I had even started going barefoot all the time, thinking that it might help me stay connected to the mother the way Duncan always was. My problems with earth were especially annoying to me because fire was no trouble at all; it was like I had been born to wield it.

I had only lost control of it on a couple of occasions, the first of which was in response to several of the Finns openly doubting that I'd actually fallen in the volcano. I hadn't felt like climbing to the top that day, so I had created a split in the volcanic rock, underestimating the amount of pressure that had built up in there. As soon as I opened the gap, lava had sprayed out the side of the mountain, washing over me in a wave. Finns were running in all directions to avoid the liquid death pumping from the rock like blood from a severed limb. No one had been seriously hurt, and valuable lessons were learned all around. The individuals involved learned not to question the veracity of my word, while I received another lesson emphasizing how clumsy my control over earth was.

The second time I'd failed to keep it my elemental fire in check involved Conall (as many conflicts seemed to be). Once again he had been hacking at the ground with a scythe, completely butchering the crops he was supposed to be harvesting. When I told him that he was mucking it up and needed lessons in swinging a scythe, he got mad and slung it away. I don't think he had intended for the unwieldy tool to actually hit me, but it had sliced open my calf when I turned to evade it. Pain combined with sudden anger elicited a burst of uncontrolled elemental fire that set half the field ablaze. The tool shed, behind which Conall had taken cover, had exploded in a rain of fiery splinters.

After that, most of my training with elemental fire went off without a hitch – probably because Shitozaki began taking me farther away from the Finns' settlement to practice. I started quite a few forest fires initially but soon learned to pull back on my more destructive element and apply an appropriate amount instead of releasing everything I had all at once. My latest endeavors included finding new and interesting ways to set things on fire, to see what would burn (everything) and how long I had to apply magic to get it to do so (usually not very long). Shitozaki taught me the traditional druid fire attacks, but throwing fireballs and raising firewalls got boring after a while. To combat boredom and avoid being accused of laziness, I played around with seeing just how big or small I could make fireballs. He seemed mildly interested but dismissed the tiny ones – what I had dubbed "fire darts" – as of little worth. True, they wouldn't kill anything, but throwing a dozen of them in someone's face would definitely distract them.

I also set out to discover if fire was truly only useful in offensive situations, or if perhaps it had a defensive aspect as well. Inspired by Seth's air shields, I came up with the idea that maybe a firewall could be used defensively and had Shitozaki and the Finns attack me through it. The master's fireballs passed through it at first, but I was soon able to absorb his flame within it. He'd looked a bit stunned the first time I stole his fire but then waved it off as useless, saying that one druid couldn't be hurt by another druid's fire anyhow.

I enlisted Fenris, a spirit elementalist, to help explore the limitations of a wall of dancing flame. With each of us standing on either side of it, he cast a variety of spirit orbs and bolts while I stood at the edge and watched them go through the blaze. Duncan stood with me, while Seth and Dermot watched on the other side. The magic zipped by so quickly that I wanted more than one pair of eyes to judge. I also wanted them there in case my own hopes for success clouded my judgement.

We expanded our experimentation to include water balls hardened to the consistency of ice, as well as Seth's air punch. The wall boiled water and had no effect on air other than superheating it. In the end, we all agreed that there was no defending against spirit with fire.

Spirit was the element that concerned me the most. I had discovered firsthand how debilitating it could be the time I had tried to stop Angie from attacking Darryn Darkmane. After the fourth or fifth time he'd attempted to murder me, she had decided to return the favor. When I grabbed her arm to keep her from killing him, the shock had thrown me backward and rattled my brain. Spirit magic hurt like the dickens.

The memory of that pain combined with my own failed experiments convinced me of the absolute necessity of learning to defend myself with elemental earth. If nothing else, I needed to be able to raise some sort of earthen defense in a split second and without ten minutes of meditation beforehand. With this goal in mind, Duncan and I got back to work.

His method of teaching me earth magic frequently involved quite a bit of fire magic. He had me find rocks in the soil, melt them, and bring them up to the surface. After that, I would either let them cool back into rocks or spend time manipulating the molten substance. I spent quite a bit of time forming generic shapes like circles and squares, then moved on to making little statues of trees, people, and animals. True, they were of a stylized form and not very realistic, but anyone could easily identify them. The earth druid had never trained anyone else, but I figured he was doing the best he could. Having me learn to manipulate earth by melting rocks or forming obsidian had been a stroke of genius, but I still had a long way to go before I was as competent as he.

I wasn't the only one having difficulties with elemental magic. Dermot was having issues of his own. While he had made steady advances in the spring, the development of his magical skills had stalled with the coming of summer. He was still working hard, but as I was caught up in my own training, I had next to no time to help him. Without anybody to train him properly, or even give him feedback, he repeatedly came up against frustrating obstacles as he tried to learn to manipulate water.

"Give it up, water boy. You'll always suck."

It was Conall, tormenting Dermot yet again. I sat up and looked across the barracks. The water elementalist had brought in a bucket of water and was trying to practice, but Conall kept disrupting his concentration. In spite of the verbal abuse he received, I'd never once heard Dermot belittle Conall for having no magic of his own. It showed an admirable amount of restraint on the young water elementalist's part – especially considering how impulsive he was. Pointing out Conall's almost nonexistent magic would have been hitting below the belt, but such retaliation might have been understandable under the circumstances. Even now, with Conall practically in his face, Dermot was steadfastly ignoring him. I would have punched him long before, regardless of Shitozaki's rule against fighting.

"Can't you do anything better than make the water swirl around?" Conall asked.

"Yes," said Dermot, focusing intently on the water in the bucket. Three tiny tendrils of water appeared over its rim.

"Good, because this is boring as shit. Do something else."

"I am not here to entertain you."

"What the hell is that?" the blonde said.

"Water vines," said Dermot. "Davis suggested that I try thinking of water as though it's a plant since I'm already good at working with plants."

"Magicking plants," said Conall. "That will be *very* useful in a fight."

"Our magic is for healing the world. Not fighting," the water elementalist replied.

Conall snorted. "Tell that to the ArchDruid when she comes to murder us in our sleep."

She won't murder you, I thought, clenching my jaw so the words could not escape. Pointing out that he was safe from Sebrina and her sycophants because he'd been magically neutered would have been unforgivably cruel.

"Leave him alone, Conall."

He backed up a step and crossed his arms over his chest. "Oh, so you're all big and bad now that you have magic?"

"No, but I'm still the leader of your training group and if there's something going on that causes a disruption, I'm going to end it."

"Oh yeah, what are you going to do? Make me do pushups? Kick me out of tomorrow's training session?"

"If I have to."

Conall had become increasingly antisocial and belligerent over the past several weeks. I had a feeling it was because I was no longer a null. Not only did I have magic, but it was *fire*, an element that was imminently desirable in Shitozaki's eyes. He and I were the only two among the Finns who could wield it. I, however, still believed as Angie did – that magic was a gift of the gods given to us to heal the world.

It was yet another reason I was frustrated by how slowly I was learning to work with earth. I could see limitless possibilities for repairing the places nearby, such as the decimated city across the river. That kind of damage would take a whole grove full of druids a lifetime to repair. It may have been why using earth as a defense in battle was coming slower to me than it could have. In addition, I knew that Duncan's personal focus as a druid was in serving Danu, the Earth Mother. What better way to serve than to repair the damage wrought by our ancestors?

I understood Conall's jealousy. I was an outsider who had been granted elemental power that had been denied to a child of the grove. If you looked at it a certain way, you might deduce that the gods had intervened to give me magic, but they hadn't done a thing for him. Were our situations reversed, I might have been resentful, too.

However, while I was grateful that the Shining Ones had chosen to bestow this priceless gift upon me, I certainly hadn't fallen in the volcano intentionally. Not only that, but I didn't see Conall running around in thunderstorms trying to get hit by lightning in hopes of receiving full elemental magic. Still, I pitied him, enough that I cut him more slack than anybody ever in my life in tolerating his smart mouth and piss-poor attitude.

I sighed. "Could we just… not do this for once? Just for one day, let's all get along and not try to annoy each other?"

"I annoy you?" he said. "Forgive me, please, Master Davis, for daring to exist in the same realm as you."

"That's not what I mean, and you know it," I said, feeling my temper start to burn. I had to be careful; like all fire elementalists, a rise in my temper could result in a rise in the environmental temperature, not to mention other unintended and explosive reactions. With a conscious effort, I pulled the heat in the room back into my Well.

Conall gave me an incredulous look. "Did you just make it *cold* in here?"

Quakes. I'd pulled too much heat from the air.

"That'll come in handy later this summer," rumbled Seth, still calmly running his whetstone over the edge of his sword.

"Pulling the heat out of the air so nobody will know how you feel?" Conall taunted. "Anybody with eyes can see you're pissed."

"And anybody with ears knows why," muttered Dermot. The vine-like tendrils of water had risen higher, thickening and twining about each other like a braid. It was an impressive amount of control, especially considering the tension in the room.

"You know what I think of your opinion?" Conall kicked the water bucket, dumping the contents all over Dermot's bed. The water elementalist's face flamed red, and he jumped to his feet with clenched fists.

"Come at me, water boy!" Conall taunted. "Show me what you got!"

The water soaking the bedding coalesced into a mass and then shot out and hit Conall in the face. His head snapped back like he'd been hit with a hammer, blood spraying from his nose. I winced when his head thumped on the wooden floor, but he'd already lost consciousness. Silence fell in the barracks as the amazed Finns first regarded Dermot, shifted their gazes to Conall, and then back to Dermot.

13

Seth raised an eyebrow. "Well, would you look at that?"

His anger spent, Dermot fidgeted, looking worried. "Master Shitozaki is going to be furious," he said.

"Somehow, I doubt that," I said. "I mean, that was one volcanic hit. He might very well be impressed."

"Not that anybody's going to tell him," added Seth.

Dermot grinned and directed the water out of his bed and back into the bucket. Seth and I picked up Conall and laid him on his own bed. Harbin and Basil, ever on the lookout for opportunities to practice their healing arts, looked him over and proceeded to stop the bleeding and repair his fractured face.

"He'll be fine by morning," Harbin reassured me.

"Do us all a favor and make sure he sleeps till then," I said.

One thing was clear: I didn't need to worry about Dermot's development as a water elementalist anymore. He had things well under control.

Chapter 2 – The Earth Below

Never let formal education get in the way of your learning.
~ Mark Twain ~

I stood at the base of the volcano, ready to summon my magic. It was there that I felt more in touch with both of my elements. Since the calm, quiet earth was too tame to hold my attention, Duncan had suggested that I practice here. I hiked a few yards until I reached a hot spot, closed my eyes, and reached out my mind to it, the way he had tried to show me before, feeling the heat and the light just below the surface of the pitted rock. Beyond sight lay the power of the gods: the power to destroy, and the power to create. I stood on hallowed ground, my presence made possible only by my gods. Barely aware of moving, I sank to my knees, arms held apart in supplication. I whispered prayers to Danu and Dagda for guidance.

The sharp rocks over the hot spot parted, cracking and crumbling as a small fissure opened. Steam bathed my face, and I sought out the magma boiling below. The heat intensified as it rose to my call, and I opened my eyes to see it twine about my hand and arm in a curl of vermilion velvet. It was beautiful.

Someone has come, said the rocks, and I recognized what I used to think of as my "sixth sense," now vastly stronger. Duncan said it was called *seeking*. I had been accessing the element of earth all along, never even suspecting it might be magic.

"If you can do that, why can't you earthmove?"

I turned to see the earth druid hiking up the volcano, the sharp rocks smoothing out and detritus scattering at his approach.

"It's different. This is alive."

"The earth is alive."

"Not like this."

He considered a moment, casting a wary eye on the magma pit, then crossed his ankles and sank to the ground in an elegant motion, brown robes rippling around him. We sat together, just feeling the earth, in tune with the volcano. It sounded stupid, communing with dirt and rocks and extreme heat. It *felt* stupid, too.

"Let's do something," I said. My attention span for meditation had not improved.

"Move the earth just beyond the volcano's base," Duncan suggested.

I turned my attention to the rocky base, where there were no hot spots and the rocks seemed less alive. I could still sense the life in it even though it was somnolent without the fire to quicken it.

"Turn it over."

Still in mental alignment with the gods and the ground, I extended my will, and after a few minutes of intense focus, a chunk of earth flipped. Duncan had the nerve to look surprised. Just for that, a minute later I turned over another one, and then another, flipping square after square of dirt for twenty yards. It gave me a headache and sweat dripped down my neck, but I pretended it hadn't taken that much effort. Duncan wasn't fooled. The barest of smiles crossed his lips and vanished.

"That was well done, but you're working much too hard at this," the young earth druid said. "Try not to force it."

I took a deep breath and then let it out, puffing my cheeks in frustration. How could I will the earth to move without forcing it? With fire, I brought it forth and directed it wherever I wanted. It was simple, and it was easy. Being told to exert my will, but not be commanding while doing so was contradictory.

"That's impossible," I grumped. "Earthmoving makes me feel like Cú Chulainn trying to climb the Bridge of Leaps." In the story my father had told me, the bridge was enchanted and had bucked the legendary hero off it multiple times before he got pissed off enough to bring on his heroic fervor, which enabled him to take great leaps like a salmon to cross the bridge.

Duncan laughed out loud. "At least you're not as arrogant as he was."

"It's not funny."

"Has Angie ever seen you pout like this?"

"I don't pout, so *no*."

He laughed again. I scowled at him.

"You need to relax," he said.

"I can't relax. Not with Shitozaki referring to me as the human lightning rod all the time."

"As though he himself was immune to an attack by elemental spirit." Duncan snorted. "No matter what he says, you *have* been making progress."

"It's just that... fire is so *easy*. I picked it up so fast!"

"All dualists have a preference for one element over the other," he said. "Everyone knows that."

"I didn't know that." It was yet another thing that I had missed because I'd been raised outside of druid culture.

"The former ArchDruid has been remiss in his instruction, then." The earth druid pursed his lips in disapproval. "You must stop comparing the two."

"I don't see how I can." I had my doubts about whether Shitozaki had been remiss. It was far more likely that he had withheld the information deliberately to make me work harder.

"Are your left hand and right hand the same?" he asked. "No, they are not. You eat with your right hand. You hold a sword in your right hand. If you had to do those things with your left hand, you would find it difficult. True?"

"True." While the hand-and-a-half sword could be used with either one or both hands, the left mainly provided extra power or control. "But I can throw a tomahawk with either and still hit a bullseye."

"And you obtained that skill how?"

"Practice. Lots of it." I had spent hours upon hours perfecting my aim with the tomahawks.

"How much more did you have to practice with your left hand?"

"At least three throws with the left for every one with the right," I said.

Duncan nodded as if that was the answer he had expected to hear. "So, it took at least three times the effort."

"At least."

"Very well," he said. "Think of it this way: your right hand is the element of fire." He raised his right hand. "And your left hand is the element of earth." He raised his left hand and then placed it flat on the ground. "From this moment on, simply accept the fact that mastering the ability to move earth will take three times as long as mastering fire, and therefore, you will have to practice three times as much."

Oh, joy.

"This could take a really long time," I said. "Shitozaki's not going to be happy about that." On top of him making my life miserable, it was disheartening to consider the extra months that Angie and I would be separated. Returning to the grove before I could defend myself, however, was like painting a target on my chest and daring Sebrina to shoot a spirit bolt at it.

Duncan grimaced. "Connor Shitozaki's expectations are unrealistic. The Earth Mother moves at her own pace and does things in her own time," he said. "I sincerely doubt that the impatience of one fire druid has any effect upon her at all." He paused. "Allowing him to talk me into overwhelming you with earth magic was a mistake. For that, I apologize. I never should have agreed to that."

"So, what, am I supposed to just ignore him?"

Duncan raised an eyebrow. "Have you not ignored him every other time you thought he was wrong?"

"Yes, but this is *magic*. He knows way more about it than I do."

"The topic is irrelevant, Davis," he said, sounding indignant. "No outside force can motivate you more than what is inside your heart. *You* know you are trying your hardest. *You* know you are doing your best. Stop listening to Connor Shitozaki!"

He rose and dusted off his hands.

"Where are you going?" I asked.

"Swimming. It's hot."

"You're leaving me here to practice alone?"

"No. You're going, too," he said. "We're done for today."

* * *

While he let me slack off that day, Duncan had meant it when

18

he said I'd be practicing with elemental earth three times as much as fire. For the entire next week, I spent less than an hour a day wielding fire and six hours working with earth. The upside to this was that the first five hours was spent handling molten rock, and the last hour solid earth.

During the second week, my time with hot rocks was decreased by an hour; I was to focus on earth alone for two hours. I spent progressively less time in my comfort zone, but the general order of practice did not vary. First came fire, then lava, and then earth.

During the third week, I hit a stall.

"Close your eyes," Duncan said. "Feel the mother supporting you. Danu is the goddess of fertility, growth, and abundance. Permit her to help you grow and develop your elemental ability. She is the goddess of inspiration, intellect, and wisdom. Listen to her teaching and meditate on it. Allow your consciousness to flow into her, and let hers flow into you."

"I hate meditating."

"Don't think of it as meditating. Think of it as relaxing after a hard day's work."

"This *is* a hard day's work. If I was relaxing, I'd have a beer in my hand."

He sighed.

"Sorry. I know you're trying to help," I said. "If I had even a tenth of your patience, I might be able to meditate."

He chuckled. "I *am* aware of how much you dislike sitting still."

His words were meant to comfort, but instead, I felt shame. Was I an unruly child with no self-control? It reminded me of one of my father's frequent sayings: *Discipline is the difference between what you want now and what you want most.*

What I wanted most was to be with Angie again, something that would never happen if I didn't master elemental magic. I'd already figured out that saying Duncan was favored by Danu was just one of those lies that people told themselves to excuse their own laziness and lack of discipline. Duncan Everlight hadn't become a master swordsman without a lifetime of practice, and he wasn't considered the greatest earth druid since the Fracture because he was lazy. Yet here I was, making excuses for my own ineptitude. I turned to Duncan with the intention of confessing and found him regarding me intently.

"Perhaps I have erred in my teaching methods."

"How do you figure?"

"It has occurred to me that I have been trying to train you the way my own father trained me. However, it seems likely that there are nuances of druidry of which you are unaware, simply because you were not raised in the grove."

Like the fact that dualists were typically stronger in one of their two elements, but I wasn't letting myself off the hook that easily.

"That shouldn't matter," I said. "I was raised to honor the Shining Ones, the Ancestors, and the Nature Spirits. My parents told me the stories of the gods and taught me to perform ritual and gave sacrifices. What else is there?"

He smiled. "*Magic*, Davis. You were raised in an environment completely devoid of magic." He paused. "Unfortunately, I don't know how to rectify the situation."

"I don't think you can," I said. "Maybe the best thing is for me to ask more questions when I don't completely understand something, rather than just glossing over it with the assumption I'll get it eventually."

"Is that what you've been doing?"

"Well, yeah. As a Traveler, I didn't have to have an in-depth understanding of laws and customs of all the towns I've visited. I just had to learn enough to stay out of trouble."

He looked dismayed. "In that case," he said, "I believe we will have to start over."

So we did.

* * *

The upside of going back to basics was that Duncan had told Shitozaki that he was backing up and going over more basic lessons, so the bad-tempered former ArchDruid was no longer riding my ass about my magical skills or lack thereof. The downside was that the information he was providing was *really* basic and included lectures on the mythology and nature of individual gods, as well as the science and composition of dirt and rocks. Luckily, my father had managed to cram a wealth of information on dirt, soil, and other basic geologic facts into my head. After testing my knowledge by quizzing me throughout the first week of our new training schedule, Duncan decided it was safe to move on to the topics that revolved around the element and deity most important to us at present: Danu.

"Remember, like a human mother, Danu cares for us and wants to give us all we need and fulfill our desires, but she does not tolerate demands or rude behavior."

I snorted. "My mother was too focused on what *she* wanted for me to care about what I wanted for myself."

Duncan's face lit up. "That is why my allegory of the earth as a mother does not work for you! You lack faith in her willingness to help you!"

I opened my mouth to refute his statement, then closed it again. After thinking about it for a minute or two, it made sense. My mother and I had been at odds for years, ever since I had stated my intention to leave Jonesboro and become a Traveler. From that moment on, she'd been relentless in trying to convince, cajole, or guilt me into settling down there. Not once had she made any real effort to understand me, always brushing my reasons aside as selfish or childish.

"What do you suggest?"

"Think of the earth mother as an ally. A partner, if you will. Like Angie."

"You want me to think of a bunch of dirt and rocks the same way I think of Angie?"

"I want you to connect with your element the way you would with her if you needed help with something," Duncan said. "Would you treat her like a servant or a stranger?"

"Of course not."

"Would you demand her assistance or try to coerce her into doing what you wanted?"

"Absolutely not." That's exactly what she would say, too, if I was stupid enough to try it.

"Why not?"

I snorted. "You know what she's like." Angie was strong-willed; nobody bossed *her* around. Those who tried found out how quickly those exotic green eyes could take on a feral appearance.

He suppressed a smile. "Pretend I don't."

"If Angie didn't refuse outright, I'd probably have to work harder to make her help than if I did all the work myself." I said.

Oh.

This time, the earth druid *did* smile.

"Now," he said, "when you engage with the Earth Mother, communicate your feelings of respect, of amity, of camaraderie. Let your needs be known. Instead of demanding assistance, simply... ask for help. Would Angie ever refuse your request for help?"

"Never."

"Neither will your element." He gestured toward the crack in the rock. "Try here. Call the lava to you again."

I closed my eyes and grounded myself, reaching for the energy that swirled beneath the somnolent rock. It was unthinkable to disregard its power; impossible not to be awestruck by its intensity. I was humbled by the favor shown me by the gods that had given me this power, privileged to be here. A wave of heat washed over me, and I opened my eyes to see a thin feeler of lava wavering in front of me like a snake.

"Feel the connection to the earth," Duncan murmured, taking my hands in his. A tingle of magic ran up both arms and into my chest, making me gasp. "Just be present. Be here. Be one with us."

While my body didn't move, a sensation of descending washed over me. Ever so gradually, I felt my mind begin to merge with a dark, primordial consciousness too massive to comprehend. Even though it held me with great gentleness, I felt like it might swallow me whole, and that my very person would be subsumed into the vastness of the world. My heart began to race, and my breathing quickened until I felt the life energy of someone young, someone lighter and warmer than the ancient darkness.

"I'm here," Duncan tightened his fingers around mine. "Don't be afraid."

I breathed a sigh of relief, relaxing once more.

"Keep holding on, but rise a little higher," he said. "Come back to the surface, but stay just below it."

I drifted upward, following his lead.

"Now, very slowly, open your eyes."

I did, expecting to feel disoriented but instead filled with an awareness of exactly where I was. Not only that, but I knew where *everything* on the volcano was, from the squirrels at its base and the bugs creeping about in the scree to the hawk that landed on its peak. Duncan rose and helped me to my feet, then released one of my hands and directed my attention back to the place I'd been working some weeks before at the foot of the volcano. He made a small gesture with his fingers, causing a square yard of rock to churn up and down, the way he had when Shitozaki had set us against each other.

"Do that," he said. "Just one square."

I visualized what I wanted to happen, the single square of earth churning up and down. The urge to grab it and force it to move gripped me and my whole body tensed.

"Breathe," said Duncan. "Relax. Don't demand. *Ask.*"

As soon as the muscles in my shoulders began to unknot, the small square of ground began churning. It felt joyful and alive, and I laughed at its eager response.

"Good! Now more. Extend your reach. Say hi to the neighbors." There was laughter in his tone.

A stretch of ground came up and began churning at my request, crunching like the teeth of a rock giant. I doubled the area and then tripled it. Now that I understood how to speak to the earth and had developed a connection with it, earthmoving was *so* much easier. It hadn't been the lethargy of the earth at all, but my mindset toward it. I had decided it was boring; no wonder it hadn't been willing to work with me. Now that I had demonstrated a genuine appreciation, it was alive and eager, looking for more to do.

Duncan released my hand, withdrawing his elemental magic from the terrain as he did so. I felt it slip away like sand through my fingers.

"Now raise a wall."

I formed the wall in my mind, gave the image to the churning ground, and watched as a pillar of rocky earth thrust upward from the first churning square. Another one rose beside the first, then another and another until a twenty-foot-long wall stood firm at the base of the volcano.

"Outstanding!"

Startled, I snapped my head around to see Master Shitozaki standing behind us with his hands on his hips. My concentration broken, the earthen wall collapsed in a wave, filling the air with dust. I coughed and waved my hand in front of my face, trying to breathe clean air. Duncan coughed and spit, but was otherwise unbothered. Master Shitozaki raised his hands and released great gouts of flame that cleared the air around him, then shook his head at me.

"I take it back." He scowled. "You need more practice."

"Ignore him," Duncan murmured.

"But I *do* need more practice." I turned my mind back to my element, embracing the rich darkness of earth once more.

* * *

Summer was over before I could work with earth to Master Shitozaki's satisfaction, but still he insisted that in no way was I ready to face off with Sebrina (or anyone else, for that matter). I was frustrated but remembering the way she had sent a posse of druids after Wolfric and Onóra convinced me not to leave. In addition, the tyrannical ArchDruid was unlikely to let Angie go. She had been vehemently opposed to any of the younger generation pairing up in dyads in the traditional way, but in defiance Angie had sent her fetch – a spirit animal – out on a journey to find the partner chosen for her by the Ancestors. That partner had turned out to be someone who lived some hundred and fifty miles away.

Me.

Such a journey required travel over rough roads and across rivers with downed bridges, through territories infested with bandits, thieves, robbers, and rapists. And so Angie had waited five more years, watching through her the eyes of her spirit animal and waiting for an opportune moment. When she insisted on being allowed to seek out her chosen, the ArchDruid had offered her an ridiculous bargain that required her to give up her offensive and defensive elements – spirit and air – as the price for receiving permission to make the journey, with only the element of water at her command. Thankfully, her father and uncle had accompanied her on the trip north, keeping her safe.

Now that she thought I was dead, she had no reason to leave her family. If we were to be reunited, it was up to me to return to that horrible place where my back had been flayed by twenty lashes and where I'd suffered for days on end until Duncan had rescued me. There was little chance of getting to Angie without resorting to subterfuge or some sort of confrontation. My heart pounded and my hands shook every time I began thinking seriously about returning to White Oak Grove, but it was something I could not ask anyone else to risk their lives for.

Missing Angie fiercely and afraid that she would think of me less and less with every passing day, I drove myself relentlessly. I was the first Finn awake and the last one abed. I tried to use earth magic in each task of the day, constantly searching for opportunities to increase my skill. The fear of losing her forever and my renewed efforts to master earth magic kept my fear of returning to the grove at bay.

As crops were already planted and growing, there was no need to plow. However, they did need watering, so Dermot and I worked together to build an aqueduct from a nearby stream. It was constructed completely of dirt and rocks and collapsed once I let the magic go. The rest of the earth elementalists and most of the Finns with elemental water joined us the next day, recognizing a good opportunity to stretch their magical muscles.

We built a brand new channel every day, each one a little wider and a little longer, until we could support an entire system from the big river to our fields. The last one we constructed was so elegant and efficient that I hauled rocks from all around Sanctuary and melted them into a permanent aqueduct made of stone and covered in thick volcanic glass.

I still wasn't satisfied. While my various construction projects expanded my earth-moving abilities, I made little improvement in using earth for defensive purposes. The concept that earth magic was for healing people and repairing pre-Fracture damage was firmly lodged in my mind. I simply could not countenance such a wholesome element being used in the presence of violence. The only good part about it was that Shitozaki stopped hounding me about working harder.

Duncan and I tried sparring with swords to see if that might help. Any earthen barrier I put up would be relatively fixed in place, and would usually require me to stop fighting long enough to take cover by dropping into a squat and pulling a wave of dirt up over my head. The Finns referred to this tactic as "turtling." It was good protection, but I didn't like it because it required giving up sight of the enemy. Duncan said that I should be relying on the earth to inform me of an enemy's whereabouts. I did rely on it, the same way I had when I was Traveling, but I still wanted to *see*.

The most effective training was when Shitozaki came up with the brilliant idea of having people attack me at random times throughout the day. No matter if I was practicing with magic, engaged in swordplay, or doing farm chores, any of the Finns would approach and try to "kill" me. They were only permitted to use unsharpened training swords to attack, and I was only allowed to use earth to defend myself. If I was hit, I had to do whatever chore they didn't want to do that day.

It worked. Knowing I could be attacked at any moment made me spend more time thinking of various earth-moving possibilities, like starting with a thin defensive wall instead of a thick one; or, dropping to a squat so I could raise a thick wall more quickly. Once, when Fenris and I were walking through the fields, he spun toward me, sword in hand and screaming like a madman. Startled by the spirit energy sparking from his blade, I thought *Help!* and a hole in the ground appeared beneath me. I dropped into it and looked up to see it closing over my head, yet still providing me with air to breathe and enough space to move comfortably. I hadn't known such a thing was even possible.

It was then that Duncan's teachings about the Earth Mother finally sank in.

She *wanted* to help me and keep me safe.

Using earth to protect myself wasn't about violence; it was about *avoiding* violence. After overcoming that last mental obstacle, everything became easier.

When I mentioned it to Duncan, he looked delighted. "Of course Danu wants to help you," he said with a smile. "But that is a lesson only *she* could teach you, for you can only learn with your heart—" He tapped my chest. "—and not with your head."

* * *

A few days later, I told the master I was ready to go. He disagreed and advised me to stay. I nearly went anyway, but something stopped me. I tried to tell myself that his advice made sense and that I was smart for listening to it, but it was fear that

26

truly held me back. I stayed with the Finns and continued to work on both swordplay and magic. Duncan disappeared for parts unknown the week after Lughnasadh and I didn't know when he would return. Even if he didn't want to go to White Oak Grove with me to get Angie, I still wanted to tell him good-bye.

And so it was that I was still with the Finns a few weeks before Mabon when Shitozaki announced his plan for furthering our education.

"When I was a young man, a part of our duties was to protect those who could not protect themselves," he said. "Druid dyads worked to repair the damage of the Rebirth everywhere they went, but they spent almost as much time working with people." As he walked about the great hall and spoke, I could almost see the ArchDruid he used to be.

Seth and I looked at each other. "It's true," he said.

"I know," I replied. "I've met some of the people in the surrounding towns and villages. They still remember how the druids used to keep the bandits in check." I wondered if Chasity's people in Lone Oak were still holding out in their stockade town and if the folk at Lake Pickthorne were still safe in their forest.

The master continued. "It's a travesty that we stopped patrolling the lands in which we dwell." He paused, dark eyes traveling over each man seated in the hall. "Seeing as how you all have made great strides in swordsmanship, I think it's high time we rectified that situation."

"Are we going somewhere?" I asked, frowning. I still needed more practice with earth magic and had every intention of going back to the grove for Angie well before Yule – with or without Shitozaki's approval. Traveling would cut into my training time.

"We'll be heading out in a few days," he said. "Make sure your horses are sound and your tack is in good order. We leave as soon as Duncan returns."

I didn't have a horse. Not anymore. Steel had been left behind in White Oak Grove just like everything else I owned, except my weapons. Over the next couple of days, I watched as the others obediently followed Shitozaki's orders, moving in and out of the barn, trimming their horses' hooves, and polishing and repairing tack. I felt a pang of loss. The grulla stallion was one in a million; I felt I'd never see his like again. The sadness was tempered by the thought that maybe this meant I could stay behind and practice magic. I quit looking at them and went back to sharpening my sword.

"Davis, why the hell haven't you been to the barn yet?" Shitozaki demanded.

"I don't have a horse."

"Oh, well, if you thought you were going to laze around while the rest of us are off saving the world, think again," he said. "Last stall on the northeast side."

Apparently, I *wasn't* going to stay behind and practice magic. Driven more by curiosity than anything, I moved deep into the gloom of the barn. It was a long structure with doors to the east and west, and a high ceiling with haylofts over the stalls. Entering from the east side, I looked to my right, where a familiar black face poked his head over the stall door and whickered at me. Smiling in delight, I reached out and stroked his smooth neck, letting him nuzzle my chest.

"How...?" I didn't know what question I wanted to ask first.

"How should I know?" Shitozaki snapped. Unaware that he'd followed me, I turned to see him watching me with a satisfied look on his face. The look vanished so quickly that I might have imagined it.

"Stupid thing just showed up," he continued. "Rutting stallions, can't do a damn thing with 'em."

I turned back to Steel, feeling tears start to burn. It was a ridiculous reaction, but I'd lost so much that getting my horse back was a true blessing. Duncan must have been privy to Shitozaki's plan to send us out because only he had the knowledge and skill to risk trespassing on grove lands to retrieve the grulla stallion.

He had also remembered Steel's tack, I noted with pleasure. I liked that saddle; it was really comfortable. I wondered how in the world he had managed to get *that* out of the grove. Shaking my head in wonder, I ran my hand down Steel's face and over his nose, feeling the soft skin and tickling whiskers.

"Heya, old man," I said. "Feel like going for a ride?"

* * *

The next few days flew by in a flurry of activity. While most of the Finns were involved in preparing supplies for the journey,

Duncan and I spent most of our time working with the soil and the second harvest crops alongside our pure water elementalists: Dermot, Nêreus, Mohinder, and Galen. The master had announced that he expected us to Travel for several weeks, and with that in mind, we used magic to delay the harvest. Instead of becoming ripe by Mabon, it would instead be ready just before Samhain. We'd have a lot of work to do before the first frost, but at least the fruit, vegetables, and grains wouldn't rot in the fields.

I was finishing up packing my saddlebags when Master Shitozaki came into the barn.

"Quit messing around! Everybody is ready but you."

"Good morning, Master," I said, continuing to take my time. I had ceased to be fazed by his edginess. His impatience was either a fire druid trait or an act. Perhaps he just enjoyed seeing people jump at his command, but I wasn't jumping at *anyone's* order. Not anymore. I picked up the saddle blanket and slid it from Steel's withers to his back, noting the faded brown stain. It was my blood from when I'd shot during my journey south with Angie; I had never been able to get it all out. Shaking off the memory, I tacked Steel up and led him from the stall.

"How are you, Davis?" the master asked.

Something in his tone made me meet his gaze. His eyes were narrowed as if evaluating me, all traces of impatience gone.

"Fine," I said. "Right as rain."

He nodded. "Where are you thinking about heading?"

"I figured you'd tell us where you wanted us to go," I replied.

"No thoughts of going back to the grove?"

I was so taken aback that I couldn't respond for a moment.

"You told me I wasn't ready," I said. Finally having admitted the truth to myself, *I* knew I wasn't ready. Earth and fire magic aside, contemplating my return to White Oak Grove still made my heart race, even if my hands no longer shook.

"That doesn't mean you'll actually heed my advice."

Given my history of butting heads with the master on certain issues – the water elementalists, for example – I could see why.

"I plan to go back for Angie around Yule," I admitted.

"Why then?"

"It gives me the maximum time to work with my elements before my year and a day is up."

"Your year and a day?"

"You told me that when someone dies, they usually wait a year and a day before choosing a new partner." I couldn't say what I really meant – before she put aside her love for me in favor of finding someone new.

"Angelina already has a new partner," he said, frowning slightly. "I told you that."

The bad-tempered, hard-hearted, foul-mouthed fire druid had informed me of this the day I had woken up in a ramshackle cabin in the middle of nowhere. Niall Ashcroft, the man ArchDruid Sebrina had wanted to be Angie's partner, had sworn an oath binding himself to her.

"That doesn't mean I've been replaced," I replied.

"Ah. You mean you want to go back before she finds a new *lover*," he said. "That's a different matter."

While it may have been a "different matter" for the rest of the druids, loving each other was what bound Angie and me together as much as our bond as chosen did. Angie had carved it upon each of our palms, casting a spell with spirit, blood, and earth, as a symbol of our fidelity and devotion to one another. I massaged the oath mark beneath its protective leather wrapping, feeling the warmth there.

Shitozaki continued: "Either way, I'm glad you'll be staying a bit longer. And I'll do what I can to make sure you have the opportunity to get her back."

"You will?"

"I swear it," he said. "Chosen should not be kept so long from one another."

I was stunned that he supported my decision, and wondered if maybe it was because I *had* followed his counsel. The fact of the matter was that my newfound magical skill was still growing and developing, and though I missed Angie something awful, I knew that it was a terrible idea to return to the Grove before I was ready. The last thing Angie needed was to see me return, only to watch me die shortly after.

"I hesitate to mention this since it might give you cause to mount your horse and depart immediately for the grove, but I'm certain you are already a full druid," Shitozaki said.

"Is that possible?" I asked, realizing a split second how stupid that sounded. The usual order of things was to receive one's initial magic, usually at age seven. At age fourteen there was a dramatic increase in elemental power, with the development of maturity and the ability to channel magic directly from the gods at age twenty-one. Duncan had been a full druid as soon as he had come into his magic at the tender age of seven. It wasn't too far-fetched to think that I could have come into the fullness of power at the age of twenty-one.

"The Shining Ones are mighty and capable of great things," he said. It sounded like an automatic response from a spiritual leader. He waved his hand irritably, as though annoyed that he'd forgotten he wasn't ArchDruid anymore. "Never mind that," the master said. "Honestly, I don't think an elementalist could have survived falling in a pool of magma. Have you ever been tired after a whole day of using magic?"

"Sure, isn't everybody?" After a day of blade training, farming, and magic practice, all I wanted to do was stuff my face and sleep like a log.

"Right, right, right. But did you ever feel like you had run out of magic?"

I thought about it. "No."

"As hard as you've been pushing yourself, if you were only an elementalist, you'd have run out of earth magic, at least," he said. "Since you're a druid, the others will look up to you. They'll seek guidance from you. Of course, they've done so for quite some time. Even when you were a null."

I wondered if there was some other point to this conversation. Shitozaki was not in the habit of conversing without purpose. The master wanted something from me.

"We won't all be riding together," he said. "I've decided to split up the Finns, the same way we did at the beginning. Half will come with me. I'd like you to lead the other half."

I almost asked why he wasn't putting Seth or Duncan in charge, but he'd just told me why. While Duncan was a full druid, he had never once taken the initiative to lead. Seth was a great fighter and a superior elementalist, but he wasn't a druid.

"All right."

Shitozaki took a deep breath. "I didn't come to this decision lightly," he said. "These boys were given into my care, and I take that responsibility seriously. Keep them safe."

"I will."

He smiled and thumped my shoulder. "That's what I like about you, Davis. You don't give me any of that fucking bullshit about doing your best. Gods, I hate that."

I couldn't help chuckling. "Where do you want us to go?"

"Wherever you want. Except for White Oak Grove and the 'Ville, of course. I want you to get them some experience, not get them killed."

"So this isn't just about policing the druid lands," I said.

"It is, and it isn't."

"Killing two birds with one stone?"

"I've always hated that expression, but yes."

It reminded me of Padraig Everlight, who also disliked the saying. More than once over the past few months, I'd thought that if Padraig could be convinced to leave White Oak Grove and join the Finns, he could teach me to use earth and fire better than anyone. I had nearly asked Shitozaki to send Angie's uncle a message on any number of occasions to let him know that Duncan and I were here, but the earth druid himself had made no such request or showed any interest in reuniting with his father. I also refrained because I understood that if the message fell into the wrong hands, not only would the two of us be at risk, but all the Finns who had sought sanctuary with Shitozaki.

"Anything else?" I asked.

"Be back by Samhain."

"We will be," I said.

If I had my way, we'd be back well before then. I never Traveled during the winter months, always returning home in the autumn. Shitozaki might not like it, but I'd probably have my group back quite a bit earlier to ensure that we had a good harvest and that it was properly brought in.

"Excellent!" he said. "Let's get out there before they decide to leave without us."

Chapter 3 – On the Road Again

Not all those who wander are lost.
~ J.R.R. Tolkien ~

"The master has informed me that we'll be splitting into two groups," I announced after garnering the Finns' attention. I nearly told them to divide up as we had before, but that would have left me with all the water and earth elementalists, and only a few with air or spirit. Shitozaki would need his own folks who could find water and heal wounds, just as my group would need spirit and air elementalists to provide us with ranged attacks and defense as necessary.

I divided everybody up by elements and assigned them to one of two groups, making allowances for those who were brothers. I took the five Fitzpatrick brothers: Ciaran, Eian, Declan, Tristan, and Galen, which gave me a nice mix of elemental spirit, air, and water. Mohinder, Jasvinder, and Narinder Chaudhri also had this going for them, so I took them, too. The Chaudhris worried me a bit, but I figured if their mother had managed to keep their names straight enough to discipline them and call them to supper, then I would also manage.

Half the water and earth elementalists went with me, and half went with Shitozaki. I wasn't happy about it and neither were they, but it was way each group would be balanced. The two extra Finns went with him, making his group thirty-seven, while I took thirty-four. Because Duncan was coming with me, I assigned most of the practiced healers to the other group. I suppose I was guilty of

33

picking favorites because I also chose Seth and Dermot to come with me. And the gods alone knew why, but I also picked Conall.

"That is the smallest horse I have ever seen," Seth rumbled when I maneuvered Steel beside his mount. Dermot, sitting astride a leggy blue roan named Kelpie, made a show of leaning way over to look at him as if my horse were a tiny thing on the ground.

"Not everybody needs to ride an elephant," I said.

He grinned. Seth's horse was a huge stallion named Bucephalus. He was black as night with a flowing mane and tail, and feathered hair around his feet. Even amongst the typically large druid horses, it stood taller than the rest. It reminded me of Niall Ashcroft's horse Charger. Which reminded me of Niall. Which reminded me that he was now Angie's sworn protector. I pushed the thought away, reminding myself that she was dedicated to druid traditions and that it had not yet been a year and a day.

Master Shitozaki trotted up on his horse, Incitatus. Both he and Seth had named their steeds after horses from their hearth cultures: Shitozaki from the Roman and Seth from the Greek. The master reined in his feisty white stallion and made the following announcement:

"Training is officially over," he said. "As you know, we're going on patrol. I see Davis has already split you into two groups…" His gaze traveled over each of them. To my surprise, he did not frown at my choices but instead nodded approval.

"I'll be leading one, and as you have probably guessed, Davis will be leading the other." There were murmurs following this announcement, and the sounds of horses shifting and snorting as they caught their riders' excitement. "After all, hearing you all talk about Davis' road-traveling stories is what gave me the idea to send you out."

While I had told a few stories around the campfire, I'd kept them limited to the time before I had met Angie. It was too painful to speak of our times together; it only served to remind me of what I had lost. However, it was nice to finally relate some of the tales that previously I'd kept to myself, as they were unfit for children or my parents.

"Twenty years ago, druids kept this entire area cleared of bandit activity so the towns and villages around could live in peace," the master continued. "The bandits have gotten out of hand

34

since then, and that is not acceptable." There were hoots and calls of appreciation.

"We're going to remind them who they're dealing with. We're going to remind them that *we* are the protectors of the earth." The cheers were louder now. Shitozaki drew his sword and raised it high in the air; several Finns followed suit.

"Let's ride!" he cried, sheathing his sword and spurring his horse into a gallop. His half of the Finns followed as they headed east, parallel to the river, whooping and hollering as they went.

I looked at my half of the Finns. My Finns looked back at me. Surprisingly, they all looked ready. Not one person wore the doubtful expression that I had expected to see.

As Steel champed at the bit, I reined him about and started west, leading my Finns at a sedate pace.

"So where are we going?" Seth asked.

"No idea."

Dermot's horse trotted up between ours, bumping them both. "Can we go on the Road?" he asked excitedly.

I figured we could take whatever roads looked interesting for a couple of weeks and then retrace our steps on the return home. Surely we could find some kind of trouble to get into in that time period.

"Sure," I said. "Let's go on the Road."

* * *

I quickly discovered that traveling with thirty-four other people was a complete hassle. From simple things like cooking meals and cleanup to more complex tasks like setting up and breaking camp, it all took more time than when I journeyed alone.

Dealing with Conall was a chore that brought its own special brand of misery. He complained about everything – the humidity, his saddle, hunger, thirst, sleeping on the ground, and boredom. If I hadn't had to deal with the rest of the annoyances, I could have ignored him as usual. As it was, I wanted to stuff a gag in his mouth and tie him on his horse. Halfway through the first day, I told him to ride in the back where I wouldn't have to listen to him. He glared at me, reined his horse sharply, and trotted to the rear. Seth gave me a look of gratitude and sighed in relief. Duncan didn't say anything, but his expression lightened a little when

Conall left. Dermot turned around and started making faces at him, so I made him ride in back, too.

Since the grove was back east, and the big river was south of Sanctuary, I decided to go somewhere between north and west. We only came across the remnants of one ancient highway, but it was enough to make an impression. The Finns murmured to each other upon seeing such a thing for the first time, with most dismounting to examine it more closely. All the earth elementalists did, running their fingers over the cracked concrete.

We rode during the day, camping in the early afternoon to eat, allow the horses to graze, and set snares to catch game. In spite of Conall's constant worry about food, we never went without. Keeping hydrated was no problem, thanks to the water elementalists. As usual, the humidity was high, permitting them to siphon water directly from the air and into our canteens. When there were lakes or streams, they purified the water as they collected it.

On the third day of the trip, we arrived on the periphery of the 'Ville. I wasn't happy about having stumbled upon it, either – if we could see them, then they could see us as well. Even from half a mile away, we could see that the city was ringed with an enormous wall of concrete, stone, and metal. I could not imagine a more inhospitable looking place. The tops of a few buildings could be seen over the wall, crumbling with decay, windows shattered and missing, and walls peppered where chunks of concrete had fallen away.

Shitozaki had wanted us to keep an eye out for bandits, but he had expressly forbidden going to the city, and for once I was in complete agreement with him. The problem was that my only point of reference for it had been "north," which I had deduced meant north of White Oak Grove. In reality, it was northwest of the grove and due north of Sanctuary. I guided my little group west, hoping to escape notice.

It didn't work.

After midnight that night, a small group of thieves encroached on our camp. They were silent and stealthy, carrying knives that glinted in the dim light of our dying fire. I know this because I was awake – and the rest of the Finns with me. In my excitement, I released *way* too much elemental fire, causing the dying embers of our small campfire to develop into a pillar of fire three feet thick that shot forty feet into the air. One thief had been standing too close, and half his body was instantly cindered. The others shouted in alarm and scrambled to get away, but we surrounded them and cut them to bits. Thirty-five against eight wasn't a fair fight, but on the Road, there's no such thing.

If you're unlucky and stupid, you die.

If you're smart and your luck holds, you live.

It's as simple as that.

"Hey, Davis?" Dermot said.

"Yeah?"

"Um, the trees are on fire."

I looked up. Sure enough, the pillar of fire had torched the tree branches hanging overhead. Red-orange flickers had begun to spread across the treetops. Stretching my hand toward the canopy overhead, I backed the blaze back down and extinguished it. Left uncontrolled, it could have become much worse, spreading along the treetops into a bigger crown fire.

The sound of someone vomiting brought my attention back to the Finns. It was Mohinder, one of the water elementalists, and he was followed by Martin, an earth elementalist. I glanced around at the faces of the rest of the Finns. Those two may have been the only ones to vomit, but there were plenty of others who looked like they wanted to follow suit.

"What should we do with the bodies?" Seth asked.

"I'll bury them," volunteered Duncan. "Siorus, you can help me." The two earth elementalists got to work, lowering the corpses deep into the ground and covering them over with dirt.

Knowing I had used magic to kill turned my stomach a little. While I had no compunction about blowing someone away with my trusty Ithaca 37 shotgun, this seemed different. My element was a gift from the gods; was it really right that I use it in this manner? Then again, would it serve any purpose to rein it in if I lost my life in the process? Should I do without magic and allow others to die in doing so?

Now I understood how Angie had felt when she had used water magic to kill the bandit who had abducted her in the forests between Kingston and Jonesboro. Thinking back on the arguments I'd used to make her feel better, they seemed empty and pedantic.

"Break camp," I called to the others. "We need to move."

I had rolled up my own blankets and was headed for my horse when Conall appeared.

"What!" he demanded. "Without any sleep? We've been through a fight, and now we get no rest?"

I didn't consider what had just happened a real fight. "We can't sleep here because more bandits might come. Or they might come back. We don't know that they're all dead."

I bridled Steel and began to saddle him. My horse wasn't any happier than anybody else about having such a brief period of rest.

"Of course they're all dead! It would be insanity to attack a much larger force with anything less than everything they had."

"They weren't planning on attacking, Conall. They were merely going to rob us. Odds are good that they left a scout in the bushes – a scout who will run as fast as he can to carry tell the tale of fire-breathing druids who are headed to attack the 'Ville."

"We're not attacking anything!"

"You think they're going to care what the truth is? Thieves and murderers make up their own truths." I mounted my horse. He snorted and shook his head, swishing his tail with an annoyance that matched my own. "If you want to sleep here, Conall, go ahead. But be prepared to wake up in Valhalla."

"If I die in my sleep, I won't *go* to Valhalla," he said through clenched teeth.

"In that case, you might want to saddle your horse."

The rest of my little band had already saddled their horses and were ready to ride. Conall stomped away and took his sweet time tacking Twister up. My jaw clenched in frustration, but after a moment I made myself relax. It was useless to get angry just because he was being difficult. He was *always* difficult. I took a few deep breaths before giving the signal to move out. Conall wasn't in his saddle yet, but he would be by the time we all got going.

We rode for a few hours and then set up camp in a copse of sparse trees that provided cover along the lines of something being better than nothing. We'd moved into an area that was rather barren, composed of grasslands or just scrub brush. Steel grazed while I removed his tack and ran a brush over his back, making a mental note to check him over more thoroughly in the morning. I wrapped myself in a blanket, rested my head on the saddle, and fell asleep almost instantly.

* * *

The bandits caught up with us two days later. We'd stopped at a small lake to water the horses and refill our canteens when about fifty of them arrived, all mounted and well-armed. I'd expected them to show up eventually, but the fact that they didn't shoot first and ask questions later came as a surprise. Thankfully, my band of Finns had been up a while already and had spent a couple of boring hours in the saddle. From the tension in the air, I could tell they were spoiling for a fight.

"Ho, there!" the lead man called, guiding his horse ahead of the rest. "I'd like a word with you gentlemen if you don't mind."

"Not at all," I said, visually searching the group for firearms and seeing pistols at hips, shotguns in saddle holsters, and rifle barrels sticking up over shoulders. "What can I do for you?"

"Not to put too fine a point on it, we'd like you to get off our land," the man said in a congenial tone. "You boys are a little too far off the reservation for our comfort."

"The reservation?" I asked. I'd read about reservations in some history books I'd scavenged, and my mother had told me stories of how her ancestors had been forced to live there. I didn't know any still existed.

He cleared his throat. "Your grove."

"Ah." I nodded. "I see."

His use of the term *reservation* seemed to insinuate that not only had the 'Ville granted the druids of White Oak Grove the right to continue living there but that they also viewed druid territory as finite and their power as limited. It didn't bode well for them.

"We ain't out here to start a fight," he continued. "This is just a friendly warning, so don't take no offense."

"None taken," I said, making myself relax. I leaned back a bit in the saddle. "We were just out riding. Didn't realize this territory was claimed, seeing as how there are no fences or boundary markers."

"Well, now... In the interest of honesty and cooperation between our two peoples, I admit that we don't quite have full ownership at this time. However, our esteemed leader President Jackson has set his sights on expanding our boundaries and bringing the surrounding towns under the protection of our noble republic."

I nodded as though accepting his statement as the natural order of things and ignored Seth's concerned frown. My understanding of Master Shitozaki's directive was that we were to engage anyone who was actively oppressing or threatening defenseless individuals or communities. I was all too happy to mix it up with thieves, robbers, and even bandits when innocent or helpless people needed assistance, but I wasn't in the habit of picking fights with strangers without cause. This didn't seem to be this time or place to engage a group of bandits, seeing as how they had approached us peaceably.

"Alrighty then," I said. "Thank you kindly for the heads-up. We'll be on our way now."

"I appreciate your attitude," the bandit leader said. "Things have been a little tense around here since we lost a patrol down around our southern border about this time last year." He paused. "You wouldn't know anything about that, would you?"

This time last year, I'd been stirring up all kinds of trouble in the grove. Some had been intentional and some not, like the time I rode north with Niall Ashcroft and his little weasel Darryn Darkmane to demonstrate how effective the firepower of my Ithaca 37 shotgun was against some unsuspecting bandits. One thing had led to another and Niall had severed a man's arm to protect Darryn after he'd refused to give them his horse. I ended up shooting the rest to save our skins, and then the weasel had come up behind me, running me through with his sword. If Liam Everlight hadn't sent Duncan to watch my back, I'd be dead.

"Can't say I do," I said, ignoring Duncan's incredulous frown, as though he couldn't believe I'd declare such a complete and utter falsehood. It made me wonder if poker was unheard of among druids because not one of them had a decent poker face.

"Right," said the bandit leader, obviously unconvinced.

"Sorry I couldn't be any help," I said. "We'll be going now."

I reined Steel about and pointed his nose south, inwardly cringing at having to show my back to a bunch of armed bandits. After a moment, the Finns reluctantly followed. I kept my gaze forward until a niggling itch made me turn around to make sure they were all behind me. I wasn't at all sure they'd obey me like they did Shitozaki but relaxed a bit when I saw everyone had fallen into line.

All except for one.

Conall had been relegated to the back of bunch again after he'd gotten on my nerves early in the day, and instead of following the rest of the Finns, he was facing the bandit leader.

"Take the lead," I told Seth and circled back around. I'd use Steel to herd Twister back into the bunch if I had to; the little stallion pinned his ears back and bared his teeth at the other horse as if reading my intention. The dapple grey responded in kind and refused to budge – just like his rider.

"What are you doing?" I asked in a low voice.

"What if those towns aren't interested in your protection?" Conall asked the bandit leader, ignoring my question.

"It doesn't matter," I said. "It's not our concern."

"That's not what the master said," Conall retorted.

I cut him off before he could say anything more. "I know what he said. Let's go."

"No."

"Better mind, boy," said the bandit leader. "You don't want to be causing problems for your ArchDruid."

"That bitch can go to Hel." Conall spat. He reined Twister away from Steel and over to the bandit leader. "What happens if those towns don't want your 'protection'?" The challenge in his tone was unmistakable.

A backward glance told me that the Finns had halted and Seth was riding back, presumably to help move Conall along.

The bandit leader leaned on his saddle horn and squinted at him. "Well now, that ain't your concern," he said. "Is it?"

"As druids, it is our solemn duty to heal the earth and protect those who cannot protect themselves," Conall said. "Therefore, it *is* my concern."

The man smiled, and it was not at all nice. "The way I figure, if you ain't got no magic, boy, then you ain't no druid. *Therefore*," he continued in a mocking tone, "it *ain't* none of your business."

I stifled a groan. He could not have said anything more likely to guarantee an escalation of the situation. He was needling Conall for the simple reason that he believed he could do so without repercussion. Young men from the grove had no magic and were therefore defenseless against firearms, which is why I had agreed to teach gunnery to the altered warriors of the grove a year ago. They were chickens in a coop, and this man and his posse were foxes waiting to eat them.

Conall's face flushed with anger and he clenched his fists. Behind me, there was angry muttering that suggested the Finns would be all too happy to show this jackass what real druids were made of.

"You know nothing of druids," Conall snarled and hit the bandit leader with a tiny spirit bolt. It had taken him at least a full minute to summon it, and he was out of magic as soon as it left his hand. It probably hurt but did little real damage. That didn't stop the rest of the bandits from drawing their weapons while their leader cussed a blue streak.

There was no getting out of this without a fight. In my peripheral vision, I caught Seth's questioning glance and gave him a quick nod.

It was enough.

"*Tyr!*" Conall cried, reaching back for the spear strapped to his saddle and raising it high. "*Til Valhall!*"

Fenris spurred his horse forward from the middle of the Finns with an answering cry: "*Til Valhall!*"

The Fitzpatrick brothers began to chant, "*Hoo-rah! Hoo-rah! Hoo-rah!*" and the rest of the Finns picked up the chant until what started as scattered yells swelled into a thunderous war cry. The sounds of rifles and shotguns cocking were nearly drowned out by their raised voices. The bandit leader was waving his arms and yelling at his men to stand down, for *he* had a treaty to honor.

We weren't from White Oak Grove and didn't.

"*Til Valhall!*" Conall cried again, his face red with rage.

"*Til Valhall!*" the Norse Finns, who made up a third of our number, answered back.

Hoo-rah! Hoo-rah! Hoo-rah! Hoo-rah! Hoo-rah! Hoo-rah!

Chills ran over my flesh as the air pulsed around me. Hot blood pounded through my veins as the war chant vibrated through my chest and stirred my spirit, inviting me to join the Finns as they sang their hymn of promised destruction.

"*Til Valhall!*" Conall bellowed, veins protruding in his neck.

"Til Valhall!" roared the Norsemen, thrusting their spears high in the air. The silken ring of steel rang as the Finns drew their weapons, the high notes a harmony that rose in crescendo over the throaty war song.

Hoo-rah! Hoo-rah! Hoo-rah! Hoo-rah! Hoo-rah! Hoo-rah!

"Oden owns you all!" Conall screamed and threw the spear. His fervor seemed to have lent him strength at the expense of aim, for it sailed over the bandit posse and landed behind them. I couldn't believe he missed; the bandit leader was right in front of him.

"Fire!" bellowed the bandit leader as the Finns charged. A guttural roar rose from thirty-five throats, giving voice to the heart's cry of those who had been denied their place in the world, discarded as though they were of little worth. Their savage howl for justice rose and fell in waves over the rumble of pounding as the Finns called to their patron gods.

"Shields!" thundered Seth. Some of the air elementalists got their shields up, but just as many bullets zipped through the Finns and found targets as were blocked by solid air. There were high-pitched pings bullets striking solidified air, after which they ricocheted in all directions. Cries of pain rose in counterpoint to the war cry. Their injuries only served to whip the Finns into a frenzied rage, and they pressed the attack without fear or hesitation.

The bandits changed tactics, firing pistols as they wheeled their horses to the left and right. At first, I thought they were turning to run, but they split into three groups. Two of the three moved to encircle us, while the last held position, firing their weapons to try and pin us down. In mere seconds, we'd be caught in a vicious crossfire. None of it, however, stopped or even slowed the Finns' mad charge.

Only Seth, Duncan, and surprisingly, Madoc, remained at my side. Apparently, he was the only null with the sense to know he couldn't defend himself from a ranged attack.

"We have to call them back!" Seth shouted over the din.

I couldn't have pulled them back even if I tried. My command consisted of thirty-four young men who had been slighted and denied their rights as druidic people for most of their lives. Their passions had been pent up far too long, and that aggression had lain in wait for a target such as this. Now that they had one – and one who had been complicit in the grove's schemes to deny them magic, at that.

The Finns were out for blood.

The bandits were on either side of us, every one of them aiming to kill.

I'd never wanted my shotgun so badly.

A third of the bandit posse was circling about in a flanking maneuver. Hoping everybody survived their injuries long enough for the earth elementalists to heal them, I turned my horse around to address the flanking bandits and began to unleash a ravaging stream of fireballs into their path. The front-runners were either thrown or distracted as their mounts reared and bucked. Fighting with their mounts did them no good, for the horses' fear of fire was greater than their fear of whips or spurs. Their horses spun about and fled as herd instinct took over. Only a few of the flanking bandits were injured or dead, trampled by the panicked horses, but I'd ended the immediate threat.

Turning back to the main fight, I saw lightning streaking from Fenris' extended fingers, aiming for any bandit who raised a gun to fire again. Any man or woman unfortunate enough to be caught reloading was cut down mercilessly. The close combat was preventing the bandits from using their rifles effectively, but shotguns – and especially pistols – were still in use. Even so, the close quarters restricted them since, like me, they did not want to hit their own people. They tried to pull back and regroup to regain the advantage of firing at range, but the Finns pressed them hard and did not allow it. Those with pistols were still able to fire, but as soon as their chambers were empty, they died. However, my group was allowing itself to be divided, with the battle separating into two fronts. The Finns were about to be pulled apart, no doubt to be drawn into a dangerous chase.

"Seth! Get over there, throw up some shields, and keep our guys together! Madoc, you watch his back!"

Seth spurred his big, black horse toward the group on the left. Madoc followed. I spun Steel to face the group on the right. Duncan looked at me uncertainly, but Dermot reined his horse about and followed without question. Conall galloped up from out of nowhere, his mount drawing alongside my own. I glared at him.

I wanted to kill him for getting us into this mess.

I launched fireballs wherever I could do so without hurting any of my own people. Both fire and spirit could be cast fifty or sixty yards; however, accuracy dropped off dramatically between twenty and thirty yards, depending on the skill of the caster. With practice, a really skilled fire or spirit elementalist could increase his range even further by lobbing elemental magic in an arc like an arrow shot from a bow, but the accuracy still left something to be desired. Unlike spirit orbs, fireballs tended to unravel around the twenty-five-yard mark, depending on the size. The larger the fireball, the farther it could travel and still maintain enough heat and power to be effective; small ones fizzled out sooner. Even a loose fireball was good for a distraction and could scatter a group of enemies. Unfortunately, of all the tactics Master Shitozaki had shown me, none of his teachings had included instruction on how to avoid hitting one's comrades in the thick of battle. I was severely limited in how much elemental fire I could cast, for fear of burning one of the Finns.

The bandit leader fell back to the rear, breaking away at a gallop. I didn't know if he was saving his own skin or going for reinforcements, but couldn't take the risk of him doing either.

"Stop him!" I yelled to Duncan.

Conall responded instead. He bent forward in the saddle, sword in hand, urging Twister into a gallop. Sending a man without magic behind enemy lines was not what I had in mind, but it was too late now. He raced around the mass of fighters in hot pursuit of the bandit leader. When one of the riflemen on the outskirts turned and took aim at his back, I threw a small, fast, fireball. It struck the rifle and exploded the ammo inside, and the rifleman screamed and threw it away from him.

If I could do that with one firearm, I could destroy them all – provided I could get a clear shot. Circling the second group of bandits, I made a "pistol" with my right hand: thumb up, index finger extended, and the other fingers tightly tucked. Aiming at those enemies on the outermost edge of the fighting, I sent tiny fireballs screaming toward them that either set the gunpowder on fire and caused their firearms to explode or melted the ammunition in the barrels, rendering the weapons inoperable.

Chester appeared behind me, guiding his horse in tight and

dispatching several of the disarmed bandits. Still unable to break into the dense pack of horses and combatants, I threw handfuls of fire darts into the faces of the nearest cluster, causing their horses to spook. A few bolted away from the fight, and I was able to throw bigger fireballs. Riderless horses galloped madly away from the fighting and the fire. I didn't know that Dermot had fallen off my tail until he came around the opposite side of the free-for-all and passed me, whooping loudly. I spun Steel about to follow the reckless water elementalist as his horse weaved in and out of the edge of the battle. Wielding his sword with only his left hand, he circled the group counter-clockwise, slashing at any bandit within reach.

As for the rest, the Finns either downed the bandits with spirit magic or skewered them on their blades. Once the gunmen on my side had been eliminated, I looked around to find that Seth had pulled the other half of the Finns together in a defensive posture. Several were lying on the ground while a few of the earth elementalists tended to their injuries. Together with Alexandros, Jasvinder, Phelan, Skylar, Wyatt, and Ishkur, he was keeping them protected. Wyatt's face was blood-spattered, and Ishkur had a blood-soaked sleeve, but they were both still on their feet.

None of the elementalists with spirit were launching a counter-attack, and I figured out that they had formed a protective dome. While that might have been beneficial under a barrage of arrows, it was completely unnecessary against firearms. Bullets traveled in straight lines. Not realizing this, they were trapped within a defense of their own making while bandits circled around the dome. From my Travels with Angie, I knew that air shields could be destroyed by bullets. Seth and the others were sitting ducks.

I formed up what Finns I could find in the mayhem and informed them of my hastily created plan. Luck was with me, for the five Fitzpatrick brothers had stuck together and had only minor injuries. In addition, the five of them were all masters of their elements as well as being adept swordsmen. Ciaran and Tristan were both dualists who could control elemental air, and also water and spirit, respectively. Twins Eian and Declan wielded elemental air with a skill that ranked right up there with Seth's. Galen had struggled with his element like all the Finns with elemental water, but while Duncan had been teaching me to earthmove, Dermot had been teaching both his fellow pure water elementalists and the dualists everything he had discovered and taught himself. I split our small group further, keeping five with me and sending five with Duncan.

"You should take the twins," Duncan said.

"No. We're the hammer. You're the anvil. You need the shielding."

I chose to bring Ciaran and Tristan with me for their air shielding ability, along with Barak for shielding backup. However, the real reason I wanted Tristan and Barak was for their ability to attack with spirit – which is why I also took Ridley and Westley. Along with my fire magic, we would be the hammer of attack, throwing the fireballs, spirit orbs, and lightning bolts that would drive the bandits into Duncan's group.

Eian and Declan would go with Duncan to create rock-solid air shields. I also ordered Ingvar to stay with him, either to stop the bandits or shake the earth beneath their feet as needed. Working together, they would be the anvil upon which the bandits were smashed, while Dermot and Galen watched their backs.

With our groups still together, we galloped for the protective dome of air, using it as cover until dividing into the prearranged groups and riding around the curvature of the dome. The bandits milled around uncertainly, not knowing which way to go. As I'd hoped, most of them turned and headed for Duncan's bunch, deciding he was an easier target than someone who could shoot fireballs from his fingers.

They couldn't have been more wrong.

Eian and Declan's horses slid to a stop as they put up a thick wall of air to shield against the bullets that were already flying. Behind them, Duncan slid off his horse and dropped down on one knee, followed by Ingvar. Both earth elementalists planted their palms on the ground and sent a temblor through the earth that caused the bandit horses to stumble. A few enemies were unseated and thrown violently to the ground, where they were trampled by those that followed.

I lost sight of them as my group passed on the other side of the air dome. Tristan and Ciaran held up their air shields until the bandits had turned away from us. Once they dropped the shields, we bombarded the bandits with screaming fireballs and bursting spirit orbs. Panic ensued when the bandits came up against the Fitzpatrick twins' invisible barrier of air just opposite Seth's protective dome. Our enemies were hemmed in between spirit magic on one side and rapidly rising earthen walls on the other.

Seth's Finns dropped half their dome but retained the wall opposite the Fitzpatrick brothers to protect the wounded. Taking a cue from my group, Jasvinder, Solon, Narinder, and Phelan began their own barrage of spirit magic. In the quick glimpses I could get of individual Finns, they seemed to be holding their own in spite of their lack of experience with guns and the wounds they had received. I snapped a quick look at the lake, just in case anyone had gotten separated.

Galen was splashing into the lake, running to escape a trio of bandits trying to trample him with their horses. Dermot was already there, standing in knee-deep water with blood dripping off the blade of his sword. I wondered why he was trying to fight right-handed until I saw more blood soaking the sleeve of his left arm. Teeth bared in a defiant rictus, he faced the five bandits surrounding him. I took off toward them at a gallop.

"You want me?" he screamed. "Come get me!"

Five great gouts of water shot up from the surface of the lake and formed into tentacles that waved menacingly in the air. The bandits scrambled backward, but there was nowhere to run. The snakelike projections shot forward around Dermot's body to twine around them, and they screamed in terror as they were dragged over the lake and pulled beneath its glossy surface. More tentacles burst forth from the surface of the lake, driving deep into the furiously raging battle. His chest heaved with the effort of directing so much magic in so many directions, but he never stopped.

Galen joined him, and soon the air was filled with terrifying shapes from the watery depths, amorphous grasping arms that tore the bandits apart. They grabbed bandits at random, tossing them high in the air or drawing them deep into the lake. I tried to duck beneath the mindless grasping limbs, but one grabbed me about the waist, yanked me out of the saddle, and dangled me upside-down over the lake.

If there's one thing that should be understood, it's that fire and water don't mix. Given enough time, I might be able to command the earth at the bottom of the lake, but it was highly unlikely that I could wrest the sodden mud from the control of water before I drowned.

"Dermot!" I screamed, waving my arms to get his attention. He paused in his rampage, looked around. I screamed his name again, and he looked up. I saw surprise flash across his face – right before he dropped me in the water. Thankfully it was only hip deep. I thumped rather hard on the bottom, but that was much preferable to being dragged to the depths by merciless tentacles and drowned.

By the time I managed to wade out of the lake, the fighting had ended. I slogged over to Dermot and Galen.

"I'm sorry," Dermot said. His face was paler than usual, and he swayed on his feet. I helped him onto the shore and made him sit down. "I lost my head."

"Don't worry about it," I replied. "You did good. Let me see your arm."

I had to cut his sleeve off, for any movement of his left arm caused Dermot excruciating pain. Not only did he have a bullet in his shoulder, but two more were buried in his left bicep. The one that alarmed me the most was the graze across his temple, however. Two inches to the right, and he'd have been killed.

It hit me with stunning clarity that Shitozaki had sent a seventeen-year-old kid into dangerous territory with a bunch of warriors who were just as green as he was. I wrapped the bloody shirtsleeve around Dermot's bicep, glancing around for Duncan.

"Where is Duncan?" I asked, wrapping the makeshift bandages around his arm to stanch the bleeding.

"Over there," said Galen.

"Well, get him over *here*."

I hadn't seen the earth druid because he had been on his knees healing someone else. He finished and hastened to attend to Dermot.

"If you control the pain and bleeding, I'll dig out the bullets," I said, drawing my filleting knife. Dermot looked horrified.

"Why don't you draw them out with magic?" Duncan suggested.

"Can't you do that?"

He shook his head. "I can't work metal."

Up to that point, I didn't think there was anything he couldn't do.

"I can try," I said.

"Try?" squeaked Dermot. "What do you mean try?"

"Would you rather he used the knife?" the earth druid asked, laying hands on his shoulder. The water elementalist winced but started to relax in a few seconds as the healing magic coursed into him, relieving his pain.

"Shoulder first," Duncan said. "Think of it like *seeking*. Connect with the metal and draw it to you."

Pressing my fingertips to the flesh around the wound, I concentrated and quickly located the slug. It shot out of Dermot's shoulder with a gush of blood and struck my palm before falling to the ground. As Duncan healed that wound, I untied the makeshift dressing around Dermot's arm and had the bullets out in the blink of an eye.

"Damn," the water elementalist said as Duncan healed his arm. "You're like a human magnet, Davis."

"All earth-fire druids can work metal," Duncan said.

"Duh. All druid blacksmiths have earth and fire." Dermot retorted. "I just didn't know they could call metal to them like I can with water."

"You need a new shirt," I said.

"Nah. This is cool. Now I can show off my biceps!" Baring his teeth in a ridiculous grimace, he flexed both arms. From the size of them, I deduced that he possessed a wiry strength that allowed him to wield his sword one-handed.

"Most impressive," the earth druid said in a wry tone. Dermot grinned.

Duncan rejoined the other earth elementalists in triaging the wounded and treating the most serious injuries first. I assisted them by extricating bullets. Half of the earth elementalists had suffered gunshot wounds. Yiorgos had been trying to drag an unconscious Fenris to safety when he was shot twice in the leg. Martin had taken a bullet to the neck while tending to Nêreus, who had broken both his arms after being knocked off his horse. Warwick and Halldor had taken only minor injuries but were both were almost completely drained of magic after performing life-saving healings on the other severely injured Finns, including Skylar, whose section of the dome had failed under a barrage of gunfire.

It was bad enough that so many of my guys had suffered harm in the fight, but losing the earth elementalists was the worst. Without them, minor injuries would be severe, and severe injuries would be fatal. Over half of the Finns had come to harm, and I wasn't happy about that at all. Some had only been grazed by bullets, but several would be dead if not for our earth healers, Duncan in particular. To make matters worse, nearly all the Finns were dangerously low in elemental magic. Of the few that weren't, none had an inner Well more than half full.

I prayed that no other bandit patrols were within hearing distance of the fight, or we would be in serious trouble. One man alone – or even a few – could find a hidey-hole to rest in, but a large group like mine was constantly at risk of being discovered.

"You'd better dry off," said Seth, as I finished helping Yiorgos with Jasvinder, who had a bullet lodged in his right shoulder blade. Mohinder was the only water elementalist with plenty of magic left, so I asked him to help out. He removed the water from my clothing, and I was dry in moments.

"I gotta get Dermot to teach me how to do that," Mohinder said, gazing out over the now calm surface of the lake and the bodies floating there. I shuddered a little.

"You okay?" Seth asked.

"Yeah," I said. "Remind me never to piss Dermot off."

Chapter 4 – Knight of Pentacles

I think leadership's always been about two main things:
imagination and courage.
~ Paul Keating ~

Siorus was missing, and I couldn't remember when I'd seen him last. Quickly finishing my head count, I discovered that three others were also missing: Chester, Madoc, and Rob – all altered Finns. My gaze traveled over the field of corpses and I prayed to Danu that none of the four were there.

"Listen up!" I shouted. "Chester, Madoc, Rob, and Siorus are missing! Start searching the bodies! Find them!"

All who had been involved in the hammer-and-anvil maneuver split up and scrambled to examine the faces of the fallen, rolling the bodies as necessary. I wanted to breathe a sigh of relief that the forty-plus corpses were all enemies, but there were probably six bandits unaccounted for along with my four Finns. Then I remembered Conall, who had run off in pursuit of the bandit leader but had not yet returned.

I'd lost five men.

Quakes.

I dropped to one knee to perform a *seeking*. Though my perception was sharp, I had not yet developed a respectable range. I glanced at Duncan, but he was still tending to Martin.

Seth jogged over to me. "Conall's gone, too."

"I know. He went after the bandit leader."

"What was he thinking?"

"I didn't want him to get away, but I expected Duncan to go after him, not Conall."

"We should make sure he's all right," Seth insisted. "Ingvar!" he shouted. "Take the Fitzpatrick brothers with you and start searching for Siorus and the others." The six men took off at a run. "I'll get our horses, and we'll go look for Conall."

"Don't bother," Dermot said.

Seth frowned at him. "We are brothers-in-arms. You may not like him, but we are *not* leaving him behind!"

"All I meant was that we didn't need to look for him." The water elementalist wore a wounded expression. "See? He's back."

Sure enough, Conall rode back and leading the bandit leader's horse, its saddle empty. Even though this whole fiasco was Conall's fault, I was grateful that he was unharmed.

"I take it you caught him?" I asked.

Conall reached into one of his saddlebags and drew out a man's head. Gripping it by the hair, he tossed it in my direction. It sailed through the air with a spray of blood, bounced once, and rolled to a stop at my feet.

"That's disgusting!" Dermot said, with a huge grin on his face that indicated he was anything but disgusted.

"Well done," I said.

"I didn't do it for your approval," Conall said. "I did it for the glory of Asgard and my place in Valhalla."

"Norsemen," Seth muttered under his breath.

"I heard that," Conall said. "And you'd better step it up if you want a place in the Elysian Fields."

The air elementalist scowled at him.

"Hey! Davis!"

Hearing Declan's call, I turned to see him, his brothers, and Ingvar some two hundred yards away. The air elementalist was pointing at a group of riders farther away yet.

"We found them!" His voice boomed across the distance, amplified by elemental air.

"Oh, thank the gods," I said, heaving a sigh of relief. Even though the day had turned to chaos, I couldn't help smiling, for we'd made it through the first fight with everyone alive. Conall was back from his suicide mission, and Siorus, Madoc, Chester, and Rob were dismounting from their sweaty, lathered, and exhausted horses.

"Where have you been?" I asked, trying not to sound like my mother and failing miserably.

"Chasing bandits," said Chester. "Remember the ones that tried to flank us? They almost got away."

Rob nodded. "They ran like the Furies were after them."

"We never would have caught them without Siorus," Madoc said. "He tried to slow them down with earthquakes, but we still couldn't catch them. Then he made this massive – I don't know what to call it, an earth wave maybe – that picked them all up and flipped them backward. You should have seen it!"

"All I want to see is some food and the inside of my eyelids," Siorus said with a tired smile. "I'm tapped out." His hands were shaking, evidence that he wasn't exaggerating how little magic remained in his Well. It reminded me of the time Angie had wrested an entire weather system free of grove control, freeing it to bring much-needed rain to the drought-stricken town of Lone Oak. Afterward, her whole body had been shaking and weak because it had taken every bit of magic she had possessed.

"All right, get some rest. Eat some dried fruit first, though. It'll help." I clapped him on the shoulder. "Good work, guys."

Unfortunately, not even those drastically low in magic could rest as much as they needed to right now. We had to clean up the mess and get the hell out of Dodge. I gave instructions for the Finns to gather the fallen in preparation for burial.

"Why?" asked Conall. "Leave the bastards to rot."

"*Ewww,*" said Dermot, making a face.

"That's a bad idea," said Seth.

"Really?" Conall challenged. "What's bad about it?"

"The spread of disease, for one thing," I said. "There's a reason people bury or cremate their dead."

He shrugged. "It's not our land, and they're not our people."

"Disease doesn't care where your loyalty lies," Seth said.

I wondered at what point he had stopped being my shadow and started being my supporter. Was it when we started this journey? Or was it when he had joined my training group?

"We should leave them here as a message," said Conall. "It'll make the rest of them think twice before they choose to take us on again."

"They don't even know who we are," said Dermot.

"Exactly. They think we're from the *grove*," Seth replied. "If word of this gets back to the 'Ville, they'll think this was an attack by their allies."

"Good," Conall said. "That'll keep 'em confused."

"No, *not* good," Seth snapped. "All they have to do is communicate with White Oak Grove, and as soon as the ArchDruid learns it wasn't any of her people, it won't take long for her to figure out that it's *us*."

"So?" Conall said. "Shitozaki knew the risk and sent us out here anyway."

"Yes, with stern instructions to stay away from both the grove *and* the 'Ville!"

"Who else could we possibly run into out here?" Conall shot back. "He *knew* we'd run into bandits. That means he either knows people know about us, or that he doesn't care if people find out."

I had been under the impression that Sebrina was unaware of Shitozaki's sanctuary, but perhaps only its location was unknown to her. After all, seventy teenage boys couldn't just disappear without notice, even if they had left over a span of several years. White Oak Grove wasn't *that* big.

"That can't be true," Seth argued. "He's spent too much time and energy keeping us hidden and safe!"

"He also said that training is over," I said, interrupting their argument. "I hate to say it, but I think he's is right."

"All he meant was that our formal training was over," the air elementalist insisted. "This is still training. It's just… real-world training." He looked around at the torn earth littered with the bloody corpses of men and horses as if he didn't quite believe his own words.

"There's no such thing as real-world training," I said, realizing another reason Shitozaki had put me in charge. Seth had no experience beyond the confines of druid lands and had a tendency to rationalize most everything. "The only training is how fast you learn when you survive whatever tries to kill you, and the learning curve is steep." I gave Conall a pointed look. "Which is why we are *not* going to spend this whole trip picking fights with bandits."

"Is that not why Master Shitozaki sent us out here?" Conall asked, spreading his arms wide. "To inform the rabble that druids are once again a force to be reckoned with?"

He was a fool if he thought that even all the Finns together – three druids, sixty-three elementalists, and six nulls – were any sort of match for the hundreds and possibly thousands of people who called the 'Ville home.

"That may have been his intention, but we're not out here to lock horns with the 'Ville," I said. "We could have walked away today with nobody hurt and the bandits none the wiser. Instead, half our earth elementalists were injured today, two of them seriously. That cannot be allowed to happen again."

Conall's eyes narrowed, and I held up a hand to forestall the inevitable tirade. "I'm not saying that anyone here is more important than anyone else, but the ability to heal is a valuable asset and one that we're not likely to survive without," I said. "So from now on, *I* decide who, when, and where we fight."

Duncan joined us, hands tucked into the sleeves of his brown robes, bringing with him a sense of peace and serenity that helped settle the rising passions of others. If he caught wind of the tension, he gave no sign.

"We have gathered the bodies of the fallen," he said. "They are ready for cremation."

"I still say we leave them," Conall said.

"Leaving a pile of corpses would only spur the 'Ville to hunt us more earnestly, and in greater numbers," said Seth.

"Good!" Conall said. "Bring it on!"

He couldn't possibly mean that. He was an altered druid armed with only a sword, and he wanted to take on bandits with firearms?

"The master only meant for us to patrol. If we get into some skirmishes, that's to be expected, but what you're talking about sounds a lot like war," I said.

"I *am* talking about war," he replied. "That gods-forsaken city is one of the reasons we've been denied our heritage!"

While my ill-fated trip with Darryn and Niall had brought me to draw the same conclusion, I had not thought it to be common knowledge.

Seth shook his head. "The ArchDruid made that deal after the mothers began altering their sons. It was several years before she figured out that the grove would be vulnerable to bandits if only half its citizens had magic."

"You think I give a shit about that?" Conall snapped. "I don't have magic. They're involved. End of story."

"What are you going to do?" Dermot smirked. "Kill everybody who had anything to do with it?"

The hate in Conall's blue eyes was all the answer anyone needed, and several thoughts assailed me at once:

I wished he was with Shitozaki instead of me.

I was glad he'd been altered – and ashamed for even thinking such a thing – because someone with magic would be very difficult to restrain in this situation.

I hoped his thirst for revenge would not ramp up everyone else's lust for blood. In the name of all that was green and good in the world, how had this escalated so quickly?

What would Connor Shitozaki do in this situation? I wondered. Probably would tell Conall to sit down, shut up, and follow orders. The master ruled with an iron fist and brooked no argument, but I didn't have that kind of authority.

Duncan turned to me. "Ingvar, Siorus, and I are ready to bury the bodies whenever you are ready," he said, as though he hadn't heard a word of the argument.

Conall took two steps and got in Duncan's face. "We're *not* burying the fucking bodies!" he said through clenched teeth.

Regarding him evenly, the earth druid replied, "Leaving such a blemish would be an affront to the mother."

"I don't give a shit—"

"About the gods?" Duncan interrupted. "About Jörth, consort of Odin and mother of Thor?"

"I give honor to Odin by killing my enemies."

"And who do you honor by leaving them to rot and putrefy?"

With his eyes locked with Duncan's, Conall clenched his fists. For several long seconds, the only sound was the breath from his heaving chest.

"We are the protectors of the earth," Duncan said softly. "Druids were given magic by the Shining Ones to repair and restore the land – not ruin it further."

"I have no magic," Conall growled.

Duncan placed a hand on his shoulder. "As you pointed out not so long ago," he said, "you are still a druid."

The angry Norseman threw off his hand, shoved past Seth and me, and stalked away, but not before I saw a flash of naked expression on his face: raw sorrow and yearning.

It made me grateful that I'd been raised without magic, around people who had no idea that magic even existed. Just living at White Oak Grove for half a year had made me wish that particular gift had been given to me. I couldn't imagine spending my whole life knowing my mother had allowed someone else to bully her into taking away something so precious, something that came from the Shining Ones in their ethereal realms. It made me thankful that my own mother was a fiery and strong-willed woman unlikely to be swayed by outside pressure from anyone.

"I don't mean to question your decision," Seth murmured, interrupting my thoughts, "but I wonder if perhaps he should have gone with the master."

I didn't have an answer.

But I did have an idea.

"Seth, you and Dermot get all the other air and water elementalists – oh, and the dualists without spirit magic – and tell them I said to gather up the firearms and ammunition," I ordered, my eyes still on Conall's departing back.

"You want us to rob the dead?"

"Yeah. Get the gun belts and holsters, too."

Dermot asked, "Is this something you've done before? When you were on the Road?"

That's when I noticed his uneasy expression and Seth's furrowed brow. Even Duncan was looking at me askance.

"Every time," I said. "Have the spirit elementalists strip the bodies of their gear. Get the saddles and saddlebags, too."

Only a fool passed up food, clothing, and usable gear. It wasn't like the bandits were going to need it anymore.

* * *

"Go lower."

The earth elementalists had formed a circle around the bodies of our slaughtered enemies. Being the only druids present, Duncan and I did most of the actual work, but the other six earth elementalists were present for the learning experience. We lowered the earth upon which the bodies lay a good five or six feet down, where I could cremate them without starting a prairie fire. Just burying them in a mass grave was inadequate if we didn't want anyone to find or identify them. Besides, I had a feeling that the amount of elemental fire I was about to unleash would be difficult to contain on an open plain.

The Finns with elemental water, earth, and air packed away the collected ammunition and unloaded the few weapons that remained intact. Some of the Finns with spirit magic had gotten a little bent out of shape over having to deal with corpses, bags, and gear rather than collecting weapons, but I didn't want to run the risk of them igniting a pile of ammunition with an errant spark. To help smooth things over, I had worked with them on the grisly chore. Pistols were crammed into saddlebags, while shotguns and rifles were tied to the saddles of the captured bandit horses. I was the only one who knew how to unload a firearm and didn't have time to sort it all out, so the ammunition had been haphazardly dumped into in whatever bags were available and tied onto the saddles of two bandit horses.

"That's fine. Everybody back up."

I reached down deep for the fire and sent it forth into the mortal remains of our enemies. People generally believed that human bones burnt to ash. In my experience, this was not the truth. On one of my Travels, I had worked with a mortician for room and board in a town that had suffered a plague, assisting with grave-digging and, more frequently, cremations. After a body was burned – a process which took two or three hours – the bones were brittle enough to be crushed into powder and small pieces. These were placed in an urn or another special container, which could then be scattered per the wishes of the deceased or the living.

We didn't have that kind of time, and I wasn't constrained by the need to use natural accelerants or combustible material. The flames of my elemental fire blazed with such intensity that the thirty dead bandits and a dozen horses – including four of ours – were incinerated, turned to blackened char in under an hour. A pillar of smoke against the bright blue sky was certain to bring unwanted attention, so the air elementalists worked to keep the greasy grey mass low to the ground, billowing and boiling just above the pit.

When the fire died down, the air elementalists filtered out the soot, ash, oils, and tar, allowing the pollutants to drop into the pit while the clean air flowed away. Duncan, Siorus, and Ingvar covered the cremation site with fresh, living earth. The dirt was soon was leveled and smoothed out by the three earth elementalists, but it still marred the landscape. Both the battle and the earth-moving had obliterated all traces of ground vegetation in the area.

"Can I help?" asked Dermot, stepping forward.

"Sure." I watched as he knelt, touched the ground, and closed his eyes. He remained still longer than I expected, and I was about to whistle for Steel when I noticed the green tips of grass poking through the freshly turned earth. In just a few minutes, a field of ankle-high, lush, green grass had effectively camouflaged the area. Dermot, his face flushed with either excitement or effort, rose to his feet and smiled with satisfaction.

"That was volcanic," I said, clapping him on the shoulder. "Well done."

"Thanks," he said, looking pleased.

The four Finns who had lost their mounts in the fight had chosen the best-looking bandit horses, finding they liked the bigger, heavier saddles like the one I used on Steel. The rest of us mounted our own horses, with several leading the ones we'd captured as we headed west. All the spirit elementalists were up front, with the earth and water elementalists in the middle, the air elementalists next, and the air/water elementalists Ciaran and Skylar trailing at the back and leading the pack ponies. If something happened, the air elementalists as a group could shield those at the front, while Ciaran and Skylar could protect themselves with air and channel water onto any fiery outbreak.

I rode in the back behind the ammo ponies to keep an eye on heat levels so I could prevent an explosion before it occurred. Seth rode on my right and Dermot on my left, with Duncan and Conall following. The water elementalist wasn't displaying his usual disregard for danger, however, for the cap was off his canteen. I didn't know what he had in mind in case of an ammunition explosion, but he knew his element better than I did.

As we departed the area, excited conversations were being passed back and forth, rehashing the fight and exclaiming over individual acts of bravery, strength, and skill. With those closest to me, however, there was a different sort of conversation.

"What are you going to do with all the guns and ammu?" Dermot asked, changing the subject.

"Ammo," I said.

"Ammo," he repeated. "So what are you going to do with it?"

"We have a pretty well-rounded group, magically speaking," I said. "*But*, about a third of us have either no defense or ranged attacks. It leaves us vulnerable."

"So you're saying we're useless?" said Conall.

"I'm not saying that at all. I'm saying that anybody without the ability to make a shield needs a ranged attack," I replied. "There's not much I can do about shields, but what I *can* do is give you some range."

"What are you going to do, let me borrow some of your fire magic?"

"That," I said, "is *exactly* what I'm going to do."

We made camp early, and I quickly sorted through the various weapons we had acquired from the now-deceased bandits. While I was pretty sure that former ArchDruid Connor Shitozaki would have frowned mightily upon my idea, I also thought that he would applaud my ingenuity – especially if it kept everybody alive. I kept my own counsel on the matter, allowing the Finns to speculate at will.

Duncan knew what I was about, but then again, he'd seen me at it before when I'd been made the gunnery master. I put Seth in charge of sorting out the rifles and Dermot in charge of the pistols. Both air and water elementalists got to work organizing the ammunition by caliber, while those with spirit were given the responsibility of completing camp chores.

I myself collected the shotguns and gathered together the six altered Finns. Duncan tagged along, squatting on his heels to watch. We didn't have a lot of time, so they were going to get a crash course in field-stripping and cleaning their new weapons. Unfortunately, none of them was an Ithaca. There were other good makes, though, such as Remington, Winchester, Mossberg, and a single Benelli. There were a few pump-action shotguns, but most were the more reliable breech-loaders.

"*This* is your brilliant idea?" Conall said. "What happened to giving us fire magic?"

"It's a kind of magic," I said, not put off in the least by his derisive tone. He'd never experienced what a shotgun was capable of in his own hands, but like the altered warrior trainees of the grove, he'd come to appreciate it soon enough.

"*Guns* are magic?" said Uri. Beside him, Regnar looked equally skeptical.

"Give the man a chance to explain," Madoc said. Rob and Chester nodded agreement.

"So," I said, spreading out a piece of oilcloth, "We survived by the skin of our teeth today." Starting with the Benelli, I double-checked that each of the scatterguns was unloaded and placed them on the oilcloth.

"I didn't think today went so terribly," said Uri, frowning.

"You didn't get shot," said Madoc.

"There were a number of things that went wrong today," I said. "First and foremost, we shouldn't have let the bandits divide us." I handed the Benelli to Conall, who looked surprised to be the first. "It was only luck that we ended up with half the air elementalists on each side. If they'd all been on one side, the water elementalists and everyone without magic on the other side would probably be dead."

Regnar and Uri took their matching Remingtons and shared an uncertain look.

"Also, I never, ever, *ever* want to see our healers take fire like they did today." I handed Winchesters to Madoc, Rob, and Chester, keeping a Mossberg for use as a demonstration.

"Firearms will not shield us," said Madoc, running his fingers over the wooden stock of his shotgun.

"No, but they'll put you on even footing with the bandits."

To a man, the altered druids gave me looks of skepticism, doubt, and outright disbelief.

"Duncan, help me demonstrate? Just stay where you are."

I walked a few paces away and then turned to face him. Forming the shape of a pistol with my hand, I took aim at him with my index finger.

"I have a gun, and Duncan doesn't. If he can't get underground fast enough, what's going to happen?"

"He'll get shot," said Madoc.

"Or killed," said Uri.

"Exactly."

"What would happen if he had a pistol of his own?"

Mimicking my stance, Duncan aimed his "pistol" back at me.

"You'll both die," said Uri.

"Or you'll both miss," said Regnar.

"Whoever shoots first stays alive," said Conall.

I nodded. "All those things are possible. But really, who's just going to stand there and be a target?"

"You seem to be saying that if we have guns, the bandits aren't going to shoot us," Rob said.

"Not at all. They'll still try to kill you, but why make it easy for them?" I replied. "It's harder to aim with precision when you've got bullets flying back at you." I let them absorb that for a few seconds before continuing.

"Thanks to our friends from the 'Ville, you each now have a shotgun, which is also known as a scattergun." I dug a shell out of my pocket and had them pass it around. "That shell has two things in it: gunpowder and shot. When the shell is fired, about a dozen of these lead balls go shooting out the barrel in a cone-shaped spray pattern. That spread dramatically increases your chances of hitting your target."

The unmagicked Finns ran their hands over the metal and wood of their weapons, testing out their weight. Madoc, Rob, and Chester exchanged quick, eager grins while Uri and Regnar contemplated their weapons with renewed interest and respect.

"Aiming is important with any firearm, but a scattergun is more forgiving. If an enemy is in range, he's likely to be wounded if not killed outright."

Madoc nodded. "If injured, an enemy might be dissuaded from further attack."

"It's possible, but I wouldn't count on it. If you're in a gunfight, you shoot to kill, and you keep shooting until your opponent is dead or you're out of ammo. Otherwise, you'll be the one who ends up dead." The six altered Finns pondered this in silence, but I didn't give them long to think about it. "The kill range is about thirty-five yards, which is a little farther than I can throw an effective fireball. And as you now know, it's also *much* faster."

"When do we get to shoot?" Conall asked.

"You all need to practice, but unfortunately we can't use live ammunition because it would bring every bandit in three square miles down on us in a heartbeat. For another, we'd use up every bit of ammo here. So, you're going to learn to use them by dry firing."

"Dry firing?" Chester asked.

"Firing without ammunition," I said. "It's considered somewhat dangerous because you should always assume your weapon is loaded and treat it as such. However, we know that everyone else is back there—" I jerked my thumb toward the rest of the Finns, who were sorting out pistol and rifle rounds a hundred feet behind us. "And we'll just be aiming at some trees."

We practiced dry firing the shotguns until it was too dark to see the trees, after which I showed them how to clean each type of weapon. We had plenty of solvent, oil, and patches, for every single bandit had thoughtfully brought a gun cleaning kit to the battle. They even had wire brushes, brass rods, and slotted patch holders. Some of the altered Finns rigged the bandits' shotgun holsters to the druid-style saddles. They sorted and divvied up the ammunition, mostly 12- and 20-gauge shells, and practiced loading and unloading. As it turned out, each of them had enough for a small pouch on his belt. I didn't have time to work with anyone else on firearm usage, but that could wait until tomorrow.

* * *

I organized the Finns into groups of five and dubbed them *pentacles*. All but one had a mix a mix of elementalists and a gunman. Except for mine, each one was led by an earth elementalist, for the sole reason that they tended to be more grounded, slow to anger, and were less likely to act impulsively.

Having long since proven that he wanted no part of leadership, Duncan stayed with me. Seth became my official second-in-command, so having him in another pentacle was out of the question. As our youngest member, Dermot needed looking after more than anyone, a job my conscience would not allow me to delegate. Conall became our gunman even though he and the young water elementalist were frequently at odds, mostly because I would have felt guilty about saddling anyone else with him.

The groupings weren't perfect. The pentacles weren't as

64

balanced as I'd have liked, top-heavy in some elements and lacking in others. Ideally, there would have been a fire elementalist in each group, but since I was the only one, the Finns who had little or no control over an element would be their fire – *gunfire*.

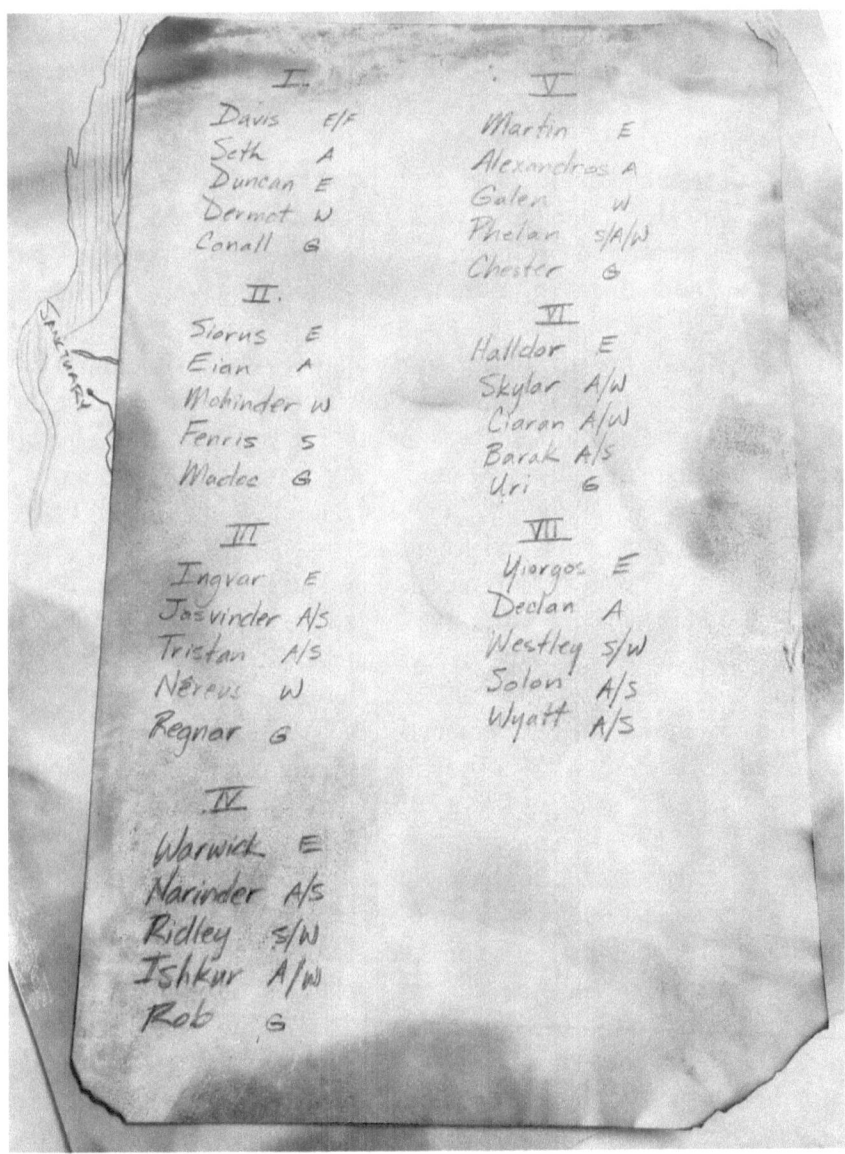

As for tactics, the air elementalists' primary function was to shield; they were also to attack when it was safe to do so. Those with elemental earth were to keep the enemy off-balance and to heal. Water elementalists were to use water to attack if we were near some, and swords or guns if we weren't. After the way Dermot and Galen had turned the tide of battle at the lake, no one questioned the combat value of elemental water anymore. None of them had good aim, but at least they'd make our enemies keep their heads down. Elemental spirit was for offense only, as no one knew of any other purpose it might serve. My group was different, of course, as we had no spirit magic. With my elemental fire, we didn't really need it.

I ordered the members of each pentacle to ride together, eat together, and sleep together. Twins Eian and Declan weren't happy about being separated – none of the Fitzpatrick brothers were – but once I explained my reasoning, they didn't complain. There weren't enough firearms for all the Finns, which caused some grumbling from the guys with spirit magic. A few of them were openly resentful until Phelan, the only Finn with three elements, pointed out how ridiculous it was that they were jealous of a bunch of air blowers, dirt stompers, and water boys, not to mention a bunch of nulls. It was rude and condescending, which I didn't like, but it got the point across so I let it pass.

All in all, it was a pretty good plan, and part of me was eager to try it out in a fight. One unexpected benefit was that Conall stopped complaining about everything. He took to the Benelli shotgun like a duck to water and was enthusiastic about assuming the role of gunman for our pentacle.

After everyone with a firearm received some basic training with it, I let each of them fire a couple of rounds each. It was one thing to know how to shoot; it was something else to feel the kick and adjust one's stance and aim. Live fire practice was a risk, as the pistols could be heard a mile away, and the shotguns three times that, if not farther. The air elementalists tried thickening the air around us, but the one and only pistol shot we tried nearly deafened everybody. I was glad we didn't try it with shotguns first. We didn't have enough time or ammunition for anyone to practice targeting properly, but the air elementalists found they could use their magic to guide a bullet as it fired. I reasoned that even if they couldn't hit anything, just knowing we had guns would make the enemy more cautious.

After most everyone had settled down for the night, Seth

expressed some concern about continuing the patrol: "I know you've created the pentacles for survivability, and I admire your dedication to following the master's orders," Seth said. "But I wonder if it would not be more prudent to return home and inform him of the reality of the situation."

"The thought has crossed my mind," I said. "The bandit patrols seem to be spread far apart, but I don't want to take the risk of running into two in a row."

He nodded, catching my drift. "Most everyone was severely drained of magic after that battle. I doubt we could survive back-to-back encounters."

"We're going to lose people if that ever happens," I said. "So you agree we should head back?"

"Head back?" broke in Conall. "Not on your life."

"I'm not saying we should go home and stay there forever. I'm saying we should go home until everybody can hit what they're aiming at. Then, when springtime comes, we can come back in full force."

"No," he said. "I'm not going home."

I lowered my voice. "Conall, I don't want anybody to die, but if we stay out here, that's exactly what will happen."

I expected an argument, but he seemed to consider my words.

"What if Shitozaki won't let us come back out?"

"I'd like to see him try and stop me."

"He's stopped you from going back for your chosen."

I didn't know how to respond.

"Davis hasn't gone back for her because he isn't ready," Seth said, saving me. Then he threw me to the wolves again. "The master knew he was blindly making decisions based on emotion rather than intellect."

"He said that to you?" I asked.

"Ah, no. Not in so many words."

"I think what Seth's trying to say is that *he* thought you were blinded by emotion." Conall snorted. "Typical air elementalist."

Seth let out a long exhale. "I'm sorry, Davis. I meant no offense."

I couldn't very well hold it against him. Love and longing had motivated me to leave Shitozaki's haven, but it was my own fear had held me back.

"None taken," I said. "I'll tell you what, Conall. Even if Shitozaki doesn't want us to leave in the spring, I'll go out with whoever wants to."

"What if I'm the only one who wants to go?" he asked.

"I'm sure you won't be the only one," Seth said.

Conall waited.

"I will go with you even if it is only the three of us."

"You, me, and Seth?" He sounded disgusted.

"No. You, me, and Angie. I'm going back to get her at Yule."

"And if she doesn't want to come?"

That would never happen, but I knew a challenge when I heard one.

"I guess it'll be just you and me, then."

* * *

Seth convinced me to continue west rather than turning south so that we could shake any bandits off our trail. It wouldn't do to have them follow us and discover Sanctuary. It seemed like a good idea, right up until it brought us within spitting distance of what could only be a stronghold of the expanding Republic of Jackson. It was high noon, and we were in the middle of open grassland bordered by forests when we came upon a section that had been completely stripped of trees. Standing in the middle of the barren area was what looked like a fort, complete with a sturdy timbered wall.

While it was true that trees were sacred to druids, we still used wood on occasion. Usually, it was from deadfall. On the rare occasion when a tree had to be felled, we cast for a positive omen beforehand and gave the nature spirits an offering afterward. Silence fell over the Finns. They brought their horses to a halt, trying to grasp the scene before them. A group of men worked to stack logs up in long wagons pulled by draft horses while two-man teams worked with crosscut saws as the logging continued unrestrained. There was no respect for the nature spirits here.

"They're cutting down all the trees!" Dermot said in a small voice.

"We need to move," I said, urging Steel into a trot.

"But Davis..."

"Move, people!" I ordered, urging Steel into a canter. "That fort can hold way more bandits than we can handle!" Snapped out of their shock, the Finns spurred their horses.

"They might just think we're just one of their patrols," said Seth.

"Unless they don't have any out," I said, never taking my eyes off the fort. My pentacle dropped to the rear while the others continued onward so I could be sure no one was paying us any attention. I had just begun to relax when the palisade gates opened and what looked like a small army poured out to take us on. I couldn't estimate how many horses there were until they'd left the fort, but it was definitely more than either patrol we'd run into so far.

"Going west over open territory doesn't seem like such a great plan anymore," said Conall, shucking his Benelli out of its saddle holster. The fastest route wasn't always the safest, but forests didn't always allow enough room for horses to pass through, even on game trails.

"Turn north and head for the trees!" I yelled. "Run!"

The crack of rifle fire chased us, the bullets whizzing by much too close to have been fired from horseback. Riflemen at the fort were taking potshots while their posse chased us down. If we could make it the half-mile to the trees, we might have a fighting chance.

The Finns in front of us surged forward, their long-legged druid horses carrying us swiftly toward a wooded area just north of us. The pentacles jostled each other a bit, and I saw that the Fitzpatrick brothers with elemental air had maneuvered their horses to the back to shield their pentacles from bullets. Noting the brothers' coordinated movements, Seth followed suit to cover our pentacle, with Narinder and Alexandros following suit for theirs.

"Keep going!" I yelled, splitting off from them and slowing Steel enough to make a wide turn. The little grulla stallion moved out into a comfortable gallop, completely unfazed when I stretched forth my hand and set fire to the grasslands in a wide swath that ran between us and the approach of both bandit groups. As sharp rifle reports filled my ears, I turned him sharply and headed in the other direction, creating another wall of fire between us. The enemy was growing closer, but I risked creating another barrier of fire, bending low over Steel's neck as he thundered over the plain.

Racing north in a zigzag pattern, I loosened the reins, giving the stallion his head as we ran straight for the woods. When I arrived, the rest of the Finns had spread out within the small stand of trees; surprisingly, they had stuck together in their assigned groups. Arrayed in a defensive semicircle, the pentacles stood at the ready with rifles and spirit magic, prepared to cut down the advancing enemy. There was something else we could do, however.

"Duncan!" I yelled, dismounting and slapping Steel's haunches. The stallion snorted and trotted deeper into the woods, looking for the rest of his herd. "Everybody with earth control, up front with me!"

Hearing my call, the earth druid raced to my side with the others close behind. After giving out hasty instructions, I dropped to the ground at the edge of the woods with Duncan kneeling about ten feet on my right. The rest of the earth elementalists spread out along the tree line, spacing themselves evenly. Siorus, Warwick, and Halldor went to the east, on my left, while Yiorgos, Ingvar, and Martin moved west, to Duncan's right. The earth began to pulsate beneath our hands, waking slowly to our request for aid. Small, rapid vibrations became bigger, wider pulses until the grassland between us and the bandits was rolling in undulating waves. The earthquake reached full force just in time, slamming into the bandit company approaching from the south. Running hard and fast over a plain covered with thigh-high grass and patches of raging fire, they didn't notice the rise and fall of the earth until it was too late. Screams of horses, men, and women reached our ears as the ground twisted beneath their feet, breaking legs and necks. We didn't have time to create multi-directional waves, but taking out half or even a third of the attackers could make all the difference in surviving this day.

The air elementalists came forward with their rifles as the earth elementalists backed off to rejoin their pentacles, conserving their magic for the inevitable healing that would later be needed. By *seeking*, I found that those bandits unaffected by the earthquake had headed east and were now turning back to attack us. I whistled to get everyone's attention and pointed out the direction they should shoot. Kneeling beside Seth, I kept a hand on the ground to gauge the firing distance. While we were beyond the bandits' rifle range, they were within ours – for not only could the air elementalists use magic to perfect their aim, they could *push* the bullets farther and faster. I gave Seth a thumbs-up, signaling the range was good.

"*FIRE!*" he roared, and fourteen rifles filled the air with loud pops, followed by the click-and-slide of chambering more rounds.

"Their frontrunners are down," announced Conall, looking through the spyglass we'd acquired in the last battle.

"Keep an eye on the south, too, in case the earthquake didn't take all of them out."

"Understood." He watched intently through the spyglass, yet never once took his left hand off the Benelli. My own hands itched for the weight of my Ithaca 37. I had given the Mossberg to Dermot, thinking it would serve him better than a pistol. The air elementalists fired again, with Conall confirming eleven more enemies down.

"Eleven?" I asked.

"One of their horses stumbled," he said grimly. "Lucky bastard."

Twenty-five kills was outstanding for a group of green riflemen. It would have been far different without magic, but we were greatly outnumbered and needed whatever advantage we could get. I lobbed fireballs high in the air to get the most distance, setting fire to the grass in an attempt to create an obstacle.

Bullets began whizzing by overhead, striking tree trunks and zipping through leaves as the bandits came into normal rifle range.

"Shields!" called Seth.

Another salvo from the bandits went pinging off the air shields, bullets ricocheting in all directions. The air elementalists quickly dropped shields and returned fire, taking down another three bandits before raising them again. I couldn't fault them for missing half their targets; switching focus from defense to offense was tough, and the precise timing required only increased the difficulty. They couldn't drop the air shields too soon, or we'd be riddled by enemy bullets. Until the shields were down, however, we couldn't return fire.

Seth's timing and precision were exact, so he shouted when to fire and when to shield. The next round of shots downed four bandits, and the one after that, five. I estimated that they had cut the eastern group down almost by half.

Then they were upon us, firing with shotguns and pistols. One bandit girl had a bow and was rapid-firing arrows with a vengeance. A small fireball burned her bow to ash in her hands, and a second set her quiver on fire. Her terrified horse wheeled about and galloped madly away from the fight, which caused me some relief. Even when it was in self-defense, I hated killing women.

While the bandits had mobility, we had cover. Of the two, I preferred the latter, as it permitted me to launch fireballs from behind the tree trunks. The pentacles met the bandits at the tree line, effectively using the trunks for cover as they returned fire with a barrage of spirit orbs along with bullets and scattershot. One brave soul dismounted and darted in among the trees, only to be cut down by Conall's shotgun.

I heard more and more empty clicks as the Finns ran out of ammunition. Once they ran out of shells, they were forced to switch to swords and their limited supply of elemental magic. The pentacles pulled back gradually, drawing together beneath the protection of the air elementalists' shields. They intermittently sought out those with elemental earth for quick healing as needed, then attacking the bandits in rapid, brief strikes before falling back again. When it came to maneuvering in a forest, the bandits were no match for druid-born sons raised among the trees. Our numbers now roughly equal to the enemy, and they pressed their attack. I grew increasingly frustrated at my inability to use fire magic to full effect, but if I wasn't careful, I'd roast my own people.

"Davis! From the west!"

At Conall's yell, my head snapped around and yes – several riders had avoided the earthquake by circling west and were running up behind us. I opened my mouth to shout at Skylar and Alexandros, the two riflemen nearest me, when I heard a distant *crack* of a rifle, followed in quick succession by two more shots. Someone had begun shooting from the cover of the nearby forest. Already three enemies had fallen from their saddles, picked off with deadly accuracy. It confused the southern group, taking their attention off us and set them to milling about, looking for the shooter.

It was just the diversion we needed.

"Shift to the left!" I yelled. "Push them back into the open!"

Fenris sent thin fingers of forked lightning streaking through the woods, shocking the foremost group of enemies senseless. The Finns set upon them with swords, hacking and slashing. Encouraged by his example, the others with spirit magic took turns popping up from the underbrush, zapping the bandits, and disappearing again. I joined them as best I could, tossing fireballs overhead, hoping the flames at the bandits' feet would drive them back. With my attention riveted on the fight in front of me, I didn't see the shotgun-wielding bandit come at me from the side until I was looking down both barrels. Bright green vines shot out of the underbrush, wrapping around his ankles, and yanked him out of sight. His scream of fear ended with a gurgle. Dermot appeared seconds later, blood dripping from the tip of his sword.

"Thanks," I said.

The violence intensified when we surrounded the bandits but lasted only a few minutes more. The battle had ended not a moment too soon, for we were completely out of ammunition, the air elementalists were spent, and the spirit elementalists nearly so. Few of the Finns were without injury, but all were alive and most still standing.

Westley had been shot in the thigh and was bleeding profusely in spite of Yiorgos' attention. Duncan took over and had the bleeding stopped in moments, using the opportunity to give further instruction on healing. Out of ammunition and possessing only water and spirit magic, Ridley hadn't been able to defend against a shotgun blast to the chest, but Warwick had gotten to him just in time. Though the multiple wounds were serious, the earth healer had laid hands on Ridley seconds after he was injured, saving his life. I pulled out the bullets one at a time, and Warwick healed him enough to seal the wounds and stop the bleeding. There were several others with serious wounds, but each pentacle's earth elementalist had rapidly treated and healed them, sometimes just enough to keep them from dying. As a result, they too were low in elemental magic.

Once stabilized, the casualties could wait while Duncan tended each of them in turn, beginning with the most serious. As a druid, there was no limit to the amount of healing magic he could provide, other than his own natural human need for food and sleep. I assisted him with removing buckshot and rifle slugs, and then moved among the pentacles, checking on everyone personally until I ended up back with my own.

Dermot looked tired but was relatively unharmed. His clothing was splattered with blood, but only bore scratches on his face and arms. He looked comfortable holding the Mossberg in the crook of his arm. Seth was exhausted, sitting on the ground with his back against a tree with a rifle across his lap. His dark complexion was an ashy grey, and his hands were shaking from elemental overuse. Like all elementalists, he had only the magic natural to him, that which was contained within his Well, and Seth was tapped out.

"Here, eat this," I said, digging in a pouch at my hip and handing him a package of dried fruit. "Drink some water, too. It'll help." He nodded and obediently ate and drank, then leaned his head back and closed his eyes.

Rising, I turned to Conall.

"He doesn't look so good," he murmured.

"I know." I didn't like the dull look of Seth's eyes, either.

"I didn't realize how bad using a lot of magic could be," Conall said.

"Running out is actually what does it," I said. "Kinda like running out of ammo for your gun."

"Except he'll be fine after some food and rest, but I never will."

"Yeah." Inwardly I cringed, fearing the return of bitter, angry Conall, and just when I'd started to like the new one. We stood there in silence for a few moments.

"He looks awful," Conall said. "I think I'd rather run out of shells."

I couldn't help but chuckle and clapped him on the shoulder.

"Keep an eye on him, will you?"

"Sure."

"Hey, Davis!" someone called.

Leaving Seth in Conall's care, I strode to the edge of the wood with Dermot following close behind. Phelan was standing there with his hand on the hilt of his sword, watching the grassland intently.

"Listen," he said.

Loud barking came from the wood adjacent to our refuge, and a big, furry dog appeared. He bounced around, barking madly, running toward us and then back again as if encouraging someone to come out and play. Without thinking about it beforehand, I whistled, earning a skeptical look from Phelan. The dog galloped straight to us and gamboled about barking happily. He was big and noisy, with wiry dark grey fur and a friendly light in his eye.

"Easy there," I said, getting him settled down enough to rub him behind the ears. "That's a good boy."

"What's a dog doing out here alone?" Phelan asked, eyeing it suspiciously. He was right to be wary, for a dog alone in the wilderness was likely to be vicious or rabid. As pack animals by nature, if a dog was not with its person, it was likely to be with a group of other dogs. However, this dog was neither vicious nor rabid and was clearly happy to be in the company of people.

"That's the biggest dog I've ever seen," said Phelan.

"He's almost as big as Davis' horse," Dermot said. "Wonder where he came from?" He bent to pet the dog, who wriggled in pleasure and proceeded to lick the entirety of the water elementalist's face.

"Looks like it isn't alone after all," said Phelan, nodding in the direction of the nearby trees from whence the dog had come. As he spoke, I felt the air ripple as he raised an air shield. The hair on my arms stood up as he summoned spirit magic in preparation for an attack. As much fighting as he'd done, I was surprised he had anything left.

Walking toward us was a tall girl with a willowy figure, clad in tan pants and a blue shirt with a backpack hanging from her shoulders. A large floppy hat covered her dark brown tresses. One hand carried a rifle, its strap dangling, while she raised the other in greeting. Another big dog – this one fawn-colored – accompanied her. I felt a huge smile spread across my face.

It was Kam Stone.

Chapter 5 – A Familiar Face

The report of my death was an exaggeration.
~ Mark Twain ~

"You can drop your shield," I told Phelan, ignoring his surprised expression as I went around it. The big dog followed, tongue hanging out the side of his mouth, then ran past me and to the brown-eyed girl.

Not wanting to appear threatening, I stopped halfway across the field and allowed her to come to me. Raising my hand in greeting, I couldn't keep the stupid smile off my face. Nor could I resist calling out to my fellow Traveler.

"Kam!" I called.

She stopped in her tracks, dark brown eyes wide and her lips parted slightly.

"Davis?"

"Heya!"

She quickly crossed the distance between us and stopped before me with a look that was part incredulous and part delighted. Tuiren sat quietly wagging her tail, and the other dog leapt about, barking a few times before plopping down in the long grass beside her.

"I don't believe it!" Kam said. She reached out and briefly touched my face, then threw her free arm around my neck, hugging me close. It took me by surprise, for we'd never shared more than a handshake before, but her next statement clarified why she had felt the need.

"You're *alive!*" she whispered fiercely. "They said you were dead!"

I pulled back so I could see her face.

"They who?"

"The druids."

"You went to the grove?"

She smiled. "I said I'd come visit you and Angie, didn't I?"

"Yes, you did," I replied. "When were you there?"

"Less than a month ago. When I asked about you, they said that you were dead and Angie was gone. What happened?"

Her words hit me like a ton of bricks.

"Angie is gone?"

"You didn't know?"

I shook my head. "Who said Angie was gone? Where? When did she leave?" I fired off the questions without giving her time to answer.

"A woman named Nualla told me Angie left with the others."

"What others?"

"She said a third of the grove's population had left just before my arrival, her own son among them."

Of course Niall would have gone with Angie if he'd sworn an oath to protect her. I felt my stomach clench.

"Did she say where they went?"

Kam shook her head. "She said they were going to settle somewhere else and form a new grove, but she didn't know where."

I should have gone back for Angie.

I should have told Shitozaki no.

"Davis, are you okay?"

Something earth-shattering must have occurred at White Oak Grove if a third of its population had chosen to abandon home and heritage to seek a new life. Niall had left his own mother. If Angie had left the grove, then it was likely that Padraig had gone with her. I wondered what decision Liam Everlight had made. Had he accompanied his family, or stayed with the ArchDruid? I told myself that she was safer away from Sebrina's tyranny, but it didn't make me feel much better.

How would I ever find her?

"Davis." Kam shook my arm. "What happened to you?"

I glanced behind me, where Dermot and Phelan were waiting, before turning back to her. "That," I said, "is a very long story."

We returned to the relative safety of the woods, where I was pleased to see that Seth's condition had improved a little. I introduced her to him, Conall, and Dermot. Duncan was still attending to the last few Finns who had been wounded.

Kam looked about curiously. "I didn't know druids used firearms."

"We don't, usually," I said, trying to push Angie to the back of my mind. It should have been easy since she always seemed to be there, but it wasn't. Seeing Kam again made me keenly aware of Angie's absence.

"For that matter, I didn't know you were a druid."

"Coincidentally, neither did I."

"Part of that long story, I assume."

"Yes. But to answer your question, we've had to improvise to deal with the bandits."

She nodded. "That's why I'm still down here. I've been trying to get home, but they show up every time I turn north or east."

"We can help you get home," said Dermot.

Seth gave him a stern look. "The master told us to be back by Samhain."

"We might be able to do both," said Conall, spreading out a piece of vellum. On it was drawn a crude map, with symbols I recognized for hills, mountains, trees, lakes, and rivers. Unfamiliar lettering marked various places along a dotted line.

"It's not exactly to scale, but this is approximately where we are." He pointed to the end of the dotted line, marked with an arrow and something that looked like a backward letter Z.

"What do those symbols mean?" Kam asked.

He pointed to the arrow. "This is *Teiwaz*, which means victory. I put that wherever we won a fight," Conall said. He pointed to the backward Z.

"This is *Eihwaz*, meaning safety. Those are the places we've camped." He slid his finger toward the right, eastward to our position, and tapped another rune, a letter H with a slanted line connecting the sides.

"*Hagalaz*," he said. "Disruption."

"That would be the 'Ville, then," I said. He nodded.

"We're almost past it now," said Dermot, peering over my shoulder. "Getting the rest of the way should be no problem."

"We're out of ammunition," Conall said. "Remember?"

"Yeah, but we haven't stripped the bandits yet."

Kam frowned. "You haven't *what*?"

I winced. "We collect guns and ammo after each battle."

She frowned. "You make it sound like you're fighting a war."

"I'm trying not to," I said grimly. "Honestly, we're headed for home. Things have gotten a little more dicey than I'm comfortable with."

She sat back, and her dark eyes traveled over the rest of the Finns, who had gathered around to listen. "What *are* all of you doing out here?"

"Learning to kill," Conall answered, rolling up his map. "We've gotten pretty good at it, too."

Kam gave me a look that said: *What have you gotten yourself into?*

"That's not really why we're out here."

"Yes, it is," said Seth. "Master Shitozaki sent us out to gain some combat experience."

Dermot said, "We're getting blooded." He grinned.

"And bloody as well," said Kam, touching my temple lightly. I hissed at the sting and ducked away. She showed me her hand, my blood staining the tip of her index finger.

"That hurt," I said.

"You got shot in the head," said Dermot.

I carefully traced the bullet graze along my skull, from the temple to just above my ear. "Probably that bandit with the shotgun."

"Oh, the one I tangled with the vines?"

"Yeah. That one."

Kam frowned, rubbing my blood between her thumb and fingertip. "Why do you need combat experience?"

"For when the grove druids come hunting us," Seth replied seriously. "Not everyone here has magic."

"I thought all druids had magic?"

"We do," said Dermot. "Unless a bunch of fucking assholes decide to take it away. Which they did. So now some of us don't."

Noticing Conall looking at him with an inscrutable expression, the water druid added, "Sorry, I didn't mean to call your mother an asshole."

Conall shrugged. "I've called her worse."

Dermot nodded, then reached out and patted him comfortingly on the shoulder. I don't know who was more surprised, me or Conall. After all the grief our altered companion had given him, the water elementalist still chose to treat him with compassion and understanding.

Kam frowned. "Why would anyone take magic away from their own children?" she asked.

"Because they were afraid that all the boy babies were augmented with extra elements," Dermot replied.

"What does that mean?"

Conall said, "The former ArchDruid had the fantastic idea that druids should try and share their elements with one another, and when that didn't work, they tried experimenting on babies."

Kam looked horrified.

"That is *not* what happened!" snapped Seth. "He never intended for anyone actually *try* it—"

"That doesn't make him any less responsible," Conall shot back. "People died because of him. Most of our generation doesn't have magic, because of him."

"How was he supposed to know people would experiment with such a theory?" Seth returned hotly.

"Oh, I don't know. Maybe because we're *druids*? Because there's nothing we like better than seeing if our theories and philosophies can become reality?"

Duncan intervened before their argument could escalate further. "It wasn't like Connor Shitozaki announced his idea to the entire grove. He mentioned it to a few close friends."

"How do you know that?" Conall said, his eyes narrowing.

"I overheard my father and uncle talking about it." Duncan paused. "It was only when the first child was born, possessing legitimate water magic and augmented spirit magic—"

"You mean it *worked*?" I interrupted.

"The transfer of spirit magic was successful, but it came at a terrible price. The boy was born with all the spirit magic a full druid could possess, and electrocuted his mother shortly after he was born."

"What happened to the baby?" Kam asked. The others startled; in the heat of their argument, they had forgotten she was there.

Duncan seemed to be considering his words carefully. "His magic was suppressed so that the healers could safely examine him. He had terrible physical defects that were… incompatible with life."

"So much for Shitozaki's brilliant idea," muttered Conall.

"The master was a scapegoat!" Seth said. "He never actively encouraged anyone to try augmenting their unborn children with extra elements, and he certainly never contributed personally!"

Conall ignored him. "Long story short," he continued, "Shitozaki was exiled from the grove twenty years ago, and the new ArchDruid decided she didn't want boys to have magic anymore."

"Why only boys?" I asked.

"Because the augmentation was only attempted on boys," he replied.

"How many were there?"

"Only a few," Duncan replied. "Father's chosen was one of them."

"Yes, but Sebrina decided to have *all* the boy babies altered, just in case someone was lying," Conall said.

Duncan said, "My father said that she told everyone it was because someone could have augmented their children without their knowledge. That's how so many people were tricked into altering their unborn sons."

"Liars see lies everywhere," the Norseman said bitterly. "And so all our lives have been ruined by the two of them."

"If you hate him so much, why have you stayed in Sanctuary so long?" Seth snapped.

"Because as far as I'm concerned, he owes me."

"So that's why he's so concerned about an attack from the grove," I said, putting it all together. "Since they didn't want any of us to have magic and most of us do, then the logical conclusion is that they'll come after us when they find out about it."

There was an uncomfortable silence in which Seth and Conall continued to glare at each other. Dermot squirmed uncomfortably, while Duncan remained placid as ever. Thankfully, Kam broke the silence.

"None of that explains why Davis has magic," she said.

"Several druid dyads left the grove rather than submit to Sebrina's policy of altering all the boys," Seth said. "The master thinks Davis is the child of one of those dyads."

"Does he now?" I said, stifling my irritation that no one thought to inform me of this.

"In all fairness, so does my father," said Duncan. Since the rest of the Finns had quietly gathered around to listen to their discussion, I chose not to reveal just how annoyed I was with both of them.

Kam then turned to me. "You didn't have magic the first time we met, did you?"

"No."

"But you do now?"

Dermot hooted. "Boy, does he ever! Did you see the all that grass on fire out there?"

"Yes, I did." Kam glanced at him, then returned her gaze to me. "That was your magic? You can control fire?"

"And earth," I said, nodding.

"So what else can druids do? Magically, I mean."

Seth answered, "We can control earth, air, fire, water, and spirit, either alone or in various combinations."

"Spirit?" she asked.

"Spirit is the energy within all living things…" he began.

"It's lightning," I interrupted.

Seth frowned. "It is more than merely lightning. Spirit is that which animates us. All living things are infused with spirit, to varying degrees. Only when it is present in large amounts can someone bring it forth from within and manipulate it at will."

"Anyone care to demonstrate?" I asked, looking around. "Phelan?"

He came forward and crouched between Kam and me. He held his open palm out to her, then closed it into a fist and said "Abracadabra," which made the rest of the Finns laugh. His fingers slowly opened to reveal a marble-sized spirit orb resting in his hand.

Kam's face lit up in wonder and amazement. She reached out to touch the orb, quickly yanking her fingers back when it shocked her.

"Oh!" she exclaimed, then giggled. She looked up at him. "So you control the element of spirit?"

"Actually, I have been given the gifts of spirit…" The orb winked out. "Air…" He waved his hand slightly, and a breeze blew through her long, dark hair. "And water," Phelan said. He made a "come here" gesture, and a narrow tube of water emerged from Dermot's canteen, undulated briefly before Kam's wondering eyes, then returned to its container.

"Hey, that's mine!" exclaimed Dermot.

"Cap your canteen next time," Phelan smirked.

"I don't *have* to cap my canteen," Dermot shot back. He leaned over to Kam. "*I* am a water elementalist, and I am *way* better at it than he is." With a slight gesture that was more for show than any aid in focusing his will or improving his concentration, Dermot caused slender green vines to rise from the ground. The greenling stems wove around each other, creating a basket of sorts, then joined together at the top and burst into a riot of colorful orange trumpet creepers. She laughed in delight.

I rose to my feet and clapped to get everyone's attention. We'd had enough of a break and needed to get things cleaned up before nightfall.

"All right, guys. Earth and water, collect the guns and ammo. Everybody else… You all know what to do." Seth started to rise, but I stopped him. "You stay put," I ordered. "That goes for anybody else who overextended themselves elementally today."

There was some grumbling about having to pull cleanup duty after such a rough fight, but the rest of the Finns did as I had instructed.

"What about the ones out there?" Conall asked, gesturing to the grasslands where so many of our enemies had died in their valiant effort to murder us.

"I'll take care of it," I said, and whistled for Steel.

"I'll come with you," Conall said.

We mounted our horses and were about to head out when Kam touched my knee. "Is there anything I can do to help?" she asked.

While she was certainly no stranger to dealing death herself, I shook my head. There was no need to subject her to the mass casualties we had inflicted.

"Stay here. You'll be safe with the Finns," I said. "We'll move out soon." The inevitable discussion of whether we'd be going north or south could wait until after our scavenging was complete.

* * *

The Finns voted almost unanimously to help Kam Stone get home. While we could have brought her home with us, she insisted that it was important for her to return and that her family needed her. I was going to let her ride double with me until Dermot brought her a quiet black gelding that had belonged to one of the bandits.

"Can you ride?" I asked.

"I prefer to walk, but I have a feeling we need to hurry."

She commanded the dogs to heel, and I gave her a leg up. She was settling comfortably in the saddle just as Steel halted beside me. He shook his head, tossing the thick black forelock down over his eyes. I swung aboard and ordered Warwick's pentacle to take the lead. Everyone knew where north was, and if I called a direction change, they would be able to make the proper adjustment.

Our deceased enemies had generously provided us with plenty of ammunition and fresh foodstuffs. While I was pleased with the resupply, the abundance of both food and ammunition present in their saddlebags was sobering. Each group of raiders had been supplied with enough dried fruit, nuts, and jerky for days, and maybe even weeks. They'd been loaded for bear, too.

My guess was that it was a coincidence and that they hadn't been gunning for us. They had probably been making preparations to find a town in need of their "protection." We might have come along at just the wrong time. Regardless of their purpose, it was likely that the tale of the disappearance of over a hundred people and horses would get back to their President Jackson. Somebody would put two and two together and come up with an opposing force, and the 'Ville would be gearing up for a search-and-destroy mission in short order.

The lead pentacle switched after an hour, with Martin's group moving up to take point. The earth elementalist cantered ahead, followed by Alexandros, Galen, and Chester. Phelan, trailing well behind them, moseyed his horse alongside Kam's gelding and smiled at her. He stayed there until she smiled back, then clucked to his mare and cantered to the front with his pentacle.

"I think he likes you."

"I think he's out of luck."

"Oh, ouch. Nobody tell him how quickly he was rejected."

"His ego will be crushed," Seth observed in a dry tone.

"You say that like it's a bad thing," Conall replied.

"Tell me what happened to you and Angie," Kam said, "and I promise not to tell him."

I sighed, even though I'd known that she would ask eventually.

"You don't want to talk about it."

"It's just... ugly." I shook my head. "The whole story, start to finish."

"You don't talk about Angie much," Kam said. "Are you giving up on her?"

"No. It's just...complicated."

I *had* stopped talking about Angie. Not that I had been particularly talkative in the first place. The problem was that once I started talking about her, I couldn't get her out of my head. I would lie in bed sleepless for hours, then when I fell asleep, I would dream about her. About *us*. It made for lonely nights, not to mention awkward and uncomfortable mornings. I couldn't talk about that with Kam, though, or anyone else for that matter. I rubbed my jaw, feeling reluctant to scratch the surface of barely healed emotional wounds.

"Sometimes it helps to talk," she said, reminding me of the day we'd met. The caravan in which Angie and I were traveling had been attacked by highwaymen and she had been kidnapped. I had run through the surrounding woods in search of her, only finding her because of the bond between us – the bond between chosen. Even though I hadn't accepted her declaration that we were destined to be together forever, it had guided me to her.

When I had returned with Angie, many of the caravan folk had been suspicious, some going as far as to accuse me of colluding with thieves. Even though she didn't know me, Kam Stone had argued on my behalf until they had backed down. She had even tried to get a visibly distressed Angie to talk about her ordeal and help remove the weight from her shoulders, so to speak. I was no more inclined to discuss my feelings today than Angie was then but Kam had walked over a hundred miles to visit us at the grove. The least I could do was give her an explanation.

"I'm not a storyteller like you," I said, "but since you've come so far to find me, you deserve to hear what really happened."

"We'll ride on ahead so you two can talk," said Seth. He and Duncan clucked to their horses, joined a second later by Conall. Dermot followed reluctantly, wearing an expression of disappointment.

"You don't have to go," I said. If anyone deserved to hear the whole sordid tale, it was my friends. The tale of how we'd met might be embarrassing for Angie, so I began where we'd parted ways with Kam – in Jonesboro. I also told them about the fight with Trainer in the street, which was followed the fight with my mother in the house, which was followed by my parents arguing for the rest of the night.

Kam chuckled. "You sure get in a lot of fights."

"You think that's funny?"

"No." She gave me an apologetic smile. "But it's nice to know that other people have screaming matches with their mothers, too."

"I wasn't screaming. *She* was screaming." As far as hot tempers went, my mother could give Connor Shitozaki a run for his money. "Okay, so maybe I was yelling a little. Mostly I was wishing I was still small enough to fit in the crawl space under the house."

She laughed, and I began to relax. I skipped visiting Grandmother, glossed over passing through the crossroads at Cash, and barely made mention of all the times we were attacked between there and Searcy. I talked about Sinclair quite a bit, mostly for Kam's benefit.

"You actually met an old, *retired* Traveler?"

"It *was* pretty amazing."

"What's so special about meeting an old blind guy?" Dermot asked.

"Most Travelers don't live that long," I said.

"It's dangerous because we Travel alone," Kam added. "Granted, I carry a rifle and pistols and have Tuiren to protect me, but they're only good against people or wild animals. Things like breaking your leg or drinking bad water will leave you weak and defenseless. When you're stuck in one place, you quickly run out of food and ammunition."

"Movement is life," I said.

"Movement *is* life," Kam agreed.

"Searcy was bad," I said after relating the hair-raising account of rescuing Angie from being burned at the stake. "But it turned out well. That's where I picked up this guy." I patted Steel's neck. "He's saved my life more times than I can count."

Dermot leaned over. "Yeah, almost as many times as *I* have."

"You've saved me twice," I said.

"That's more times than you can count, right?"

"Get outta here," I laughed. Deciding to include a few more details, I described how I'd spoiled the ambush on the south side of Searcy, and also how I'd gotten myself shot because I'd been distracted by the way Angie's hips swayed in the saddle. Seth merely chuckled at this, but Dermot and Conall laughed themselves silly. It was the first time I'd ever heard Conall laugh.

I told them how the witches of Ward had saved my life, and how I'd decided that a romantic relationship with Angie was a bad idea, which seemed to pique Duncan's interest. He shook his head when I described how jealous she'd been. Like the witches, jealous behavior was simply not acceptable among druids. I described the dancing and music at the summer solstice and left it at that.

"Wait a minute!" Dermot said before I could continue with meeting the people fishing at Lake Pickthorne. "You didn't tell us what happened with Angie at Midsummer!"

"Nor will I," I said, unable to keep a smug smile off my face.

"Mind your own business, scrub," Conall said, not unkindly.

Dermot pretended to pout.

I gave the story-telling a break when we stopped for lunch, walking amongst the pentacles to make sure everyone was all right. After riding fast and fighting hard yesterday, men and horses alike deserved to have the day off today, but it wasn't in the cards. That southern fort would be missing their raiders right about now and eventually someone would be out to look for them – and for us. If we were very lucky, we'd have a couple days to travel unchallenged. We might even make it north of the bandit city before they figured out where we were. After seeing Kam Stone safely on her way with directions to Ward, we could swing back around to the west and give the 'Ville a nice, wide berth, hopefully avoiding further encounters with bandits and arriving home by Samhain.

After our midday break, I resumed the story, limiting the description of the trip from Lake Pickthorne to Lone Oak as "a pain in the ass." I gave more details about the little stockade town that believed in guns but not gods, and the terrific thunderstorm Angie had whipped up that filled their wells to overflowing.

"I remember that storm!" Kam exclaimed. "My family said they hadn't heard thunder all summer long. After the wells went dry, we had to haul buckets from streams farther and farther away." She smiled, remembering. "When the storm rolled in, we all ran outside and played in the rain like children! My brother rolled in the mud with the hounds!"

"After helping defend Lone Oak from the bandit attack, the rest of our trip to the grove was uneventful," I said. "Without a doubt, it was the toughest trip I've ever made, but living in White Oak Grove made it pale in comparison."

"Was it really that bad?" Kam asked.

"In all honesty, the only thing that made it different from the Road was that nobody was shooting at me," I said.

"That doesn't sound so terrible," said Dermot.

"No, it doesn't," Duncan said, speaking up for the first time. "Until you take into consideration that his barracks mates never pulled their punches like we do during training."

"Ouch!" Dermot said, wincing.

The earth druid wasn't finished. "And, there was the time that Niall and Darryn jumped him in the street and beat him to a bloody pulp with training swords."

"Those knuckleheads? With *training* swords?" said Conall. "Please tell me it was steel, at least." It shouldn't have surprised me that he knew them, but it did.

"Nope, they were wood."

"And they *still* kicked your ass?"

"Well, they *did* break both my arms and knock me unconscious first," I said. "Luckily, Duncan found me and took me to the only other earth druid in the grove who was willing to heal me."

"Why didn't *you* just heal him?" Conall asked.

"A young man who openly displays his elemental abilities in the grove is not allowed to remain there long," the earth druid replied.

"Why did you stay?" Seth asked. "We would have welcomed you at any time."

"For my father, mostly." Duncan paused. "And also for a few others whose magic was still a secret."

"Did you know about Wolfric?" I asked.

He nodded. "I know about them all."

"Who else *was* there?"

"Other than Wolfric, the only ones with whom you were acquainted were Haamid Parks and Lin Overholt."

"*Lin?!?* You're joking!" Then I remembered the offhanded comment Lin had made to Wolfric the day we'd met, something about how Wolfric would be tied to the whipping post long before he himself was. At the time I'd thought it an exaggeration of the punishment meted out in the grove.

"He is an air elementalist."

"So *that's* how he survived Sebrina's attack."

Duncan shook his head. "He couldn't reveal himself, even in defense."

"Then how did he survive?"

"Liam managed to deflect much of the spirit bolt and used his own magic to keep Lin alive." He paused. "To his credit, my uncle kept Lin's secret, right along with covering up the ArchDruid's transgression."

Seth looked offended. "Do you mean to tell me that the ArchDruid attacked a citizen of her own grove and was allowed to remain in office?"

"Things are pretty messed up there," I said. "Or were." I glanced at Kam. That was her story to tell.

"When you finish telling your story, I'll tell everyone mine," she promised. I took that as a signal to continue. They'd all been through similar training, so I skipped all of it except for when Padraig Everlight had given me my sword.

Dermot whistled.

"No wonder you're so attached to it," said Seth. He had tried to get me to use a *zweihänder* several times, saying I was strong enough and needed the reach, but I had steadfastly refused. The greatsword was as much a part of me now as the Ithaca 37 shotgun had been. I tried to hit the high points of my time in White Oak Grove, but the fact of the matter was that it had been an eventful six months. It took the rest of the afternoon to include the rest of it, mostly centering on the High Holy Day festivities such as the jousting tournament, the elemental duel between Angie and Onóra after the much more civilized magic demonstration by the younger elementalist girls.

"By the way, Dermot, that's when I saw your sister demonstrate her skill with elemental water. What's her name again? Something that starts with A?"

"Ariadne," he said. "She's not so great, but she sure thinks she is."

"Reminds me of someone else I know," Conall muttered.

I continued my tale, and soon they were riveted by my account of the ritual at Samhain when I'd seen both the Celtic and Norse gods place their hands on Wolfric.

"I don't think I'd have gotten in the middle of that," Conall said, shaking his head. The Morrigan had made it clear that she wanted me to do something about it, and refusing her would have been poor form after all the times she had seen me through battle and still alive at the end. My narrative came to a close when Duncan and I began discussing how many times I'd nearly died.

"I thought it was only four." I thought back and counted on my fingers. "Let's see... The first when Darryn assaulted me with Niall, the second was when he stabbed me in the back..."

"And after you had *just* saved his life," Duncan said.

"The third time was... wait a minute. I forgot that he jumped me after dark another time before that."

"Gods, I hope you didn't let him give you another spanking," Conall muttered.

I grinned. "No, I whipped him good and then dropped him off with Danica Harris. She healed him and kept him asleep for the rest of the night. When he woke up, she told him he couldn't remember what happened because he slipped and hit his head."

Kam and the rest of the pentacle laughed, but Duncan gave me a frosty glare. "It *wasn't* funny."

"Well, maybe not at the time…" I couldn't help but chuckle. "Anyway, he also rigged the Yule tourney so I'd advance to the final rounds, and he tried to kill me with another training sword – it *was* steel that time, Conall – so that makes four times."

"He attempted to murder you *five* times," the earth druid insisted.

"The time he tried to shoot me doesn't count," I said. "I knew he was going to try something. That's why I didn't give him real shotgun shells."

"What about the time he drew steel on you in the forest just after Yule?"

I shrugged. "That was when Wolfric and Onóra were escaping."

"And?"

"And as we've all learned on our little jaunt, a man with a sword is no match for a man with a gun."

The earth druid sighed in exasperation. "Just because you were able to foresee, prevent, or fend off an attack, it does not nullify the fact that he wanted to murder you!"

He had me there.

"That would make it six times that Darryn tried to kill me, then."

There was a pause, after which Duncan quietly added, "Seven."

I gave him a look that said: *Shut the hell up right now.*

Duncan responded with a mutinous glare.

There was an uncomfortable silence while I stared him down, after which he turned away, scowling off into the distance.

Seth cleared his throat and broke the awkward silence. "And it was aiding in your friends' escape that motivated the ArchDruid to punish and exile you?"

"Yes." I was finished with storytelling for today, and maybe forever.

"You don't have to talk about that," Kam interjected.

"There isn't much more to tell. My memories are pretty sketchy between then and when I woke up and met Shitozaki."

"You must have thought it was a nightmare," quipped Dermot.

Seth gave him a stern look. "Very funny."

"Thanks!" the water elementalist said. "I thought so, too."

"Is that why people at the grove think you're dead?" Kam asked.

I glanced at the earth druid, but he wasn't finished ignoring me. Duncan and I had never discussed the events following my flogging, poisoning, and subsequent illness, and it occurred to me that I still didn't know exactly what had happened. That was something between Duncan and me, though – something none of the others needed to know.

"They think I'm dead because that's what we want them to think."

"Why?"

It was Seth who answered. "It was to keep him safe. Nobody goes looking for a dead man."

"But what about Angie?"

I rubbed my left palm, feeling the warmth of the oath mark beneath the leather wrappings. "I'm going back for her as soon as we get back to Sanctuary."

Kam nodded. "It's a good thing you have magic now." She paused. "Speaking of, when did it manifest?"

"At Midsummer."

"So you only acquired magic after leaving the grove."

"A most fortunate stroke of luck," Seth observed.

"That's no lie," agreed Conall.

It had occurred to me that I could have developed elemental magic at any point during my stay at the grove. ArchDruid Sebrina would surely have had me killed in a most spectacular manner. She might even have convinced Liam Everlight to do it.

"So Angie doesn't know?" Kam asked.

"No."

When we stopped for the night, I created a semi-circle of small campfires and then elevated a small chunk of earth for Kam to sit on while she delivered her news of the grove. Tuiren sat beside her, calm and poised, while Hector, the big puppy, flopped onto the ground on Kam's other side.

Fondling Tuiren's ears, she said, "As I'm sure you all know by now, Davis and I have met before. Travelers are getting rather scarce these days, so it's always a pleasure to meet another one." She smiled at me. "We met on the road about a year and a half ago. I was returning home with my sister and her husband, who had been forced out of the town where they had settled." She paused. "That's another long story, and one I will save for different day. On this particular morning, however, Tuiren woke me in the early dawn, warning me that things were not as they should have been…"

Kam spun an exciting yarn about the bandit attack. However, since she didn't know what had happened after the raiders kidnapped Angie and I'd run off into the forest to find her, I picked up the tale. Mostly I told the story because it demonstrated how the bond between partners worked in a dyad, which was information the rest of the Finns would need to know – at least, they'd need it if they ever managed to join with their own chosen, which I hoped they would. I also reported exactly how Angie had rescued herself, for the benefit of everyone with elemental water.

"Impressive," said Nêreus. "Horrifying, but impressive."

"Angie must be quite adept at manipulating her element," said Seth.

Before I could answer, Phelan said, "That's a given. The Everlights have always had big magic and the willingness to use it."

"Now wait a minute," I said. "She's worked hard to master her elements."

"If we excel at magic and swordplay, it is because we work at it," Duncan said, looking miffed. "Whether it be with swords or magic, we train every day."

"I thought you couldn't use magic in the grove," said Conall.

"Prior to Davis' arrival, the times I spent there were infrequent and brief," the earth druid replied. "Father made it very clear to me that the ArchDruid would only ignore my existence as long as I did not display my ability to use elemental magic."

Conall raised an eyebrow. "So Davis shows up and all of a sudden you have a mad desire to hang out in the grove again?"

"It became evident to me early on that neither my father nor my cousin was being particularly diligent regarding his safety,"

Duncan said. He sounded peeved. "*Somebody* had to keep him alive."

Another reason was that Duncan had developed a romantic interest in me, but like other parts of the story, that was between us. Besides, we had hashed it out, and the matter was settled.

"I'm sorry," Kam broke in. "Did you say Angie is your cousin?"

"She is."

"Oh." She frowned.

"Is that a problem?" the earth druid asked.

Kam looked apologetic. She lowered her voice. "No, it's just that the rest of my story won't make you very happy. But surely you've already told him, Davis."

"Oh, quakes." I had forgotten to tell Duncan about his family leaving the grove for parts unknown when he should have been the first to know. Introducing Kam to the rest of the Finns, getting the bodies cleaned up, making plans, and collecting supplies and ammunition had completely put it out of my head.

"I'm sorry, man, I should have told you sooner."

"Told me what?" he asked warily.

I lowered my voice. "Angie left the grove weeks ago with a bunch of others. Nobody knows where they are or where they were going." Some friend I was. "I'm sorry. I should have told you immediately."

"Did my father go with her?" There was only concern in Duncan's eyes. Selfishly, it made me glad that earth elementalists were slow to anger and the least likely of people to take offense.

"I don't know. I would assume so."

"Who else went? How many?"

"Kam says Nualla told her about a third of the grove—"

"Nualla." Duncan's tone was laced with loathing. "You would put trust in *her* word?"

"No. But I can't see her lying about her own son leaving."

"*Niall* left the grove?" His dark eyes darted back to Kam.

"She didn't mention any names," she said. "I asked about Angie, and she only said that a third of the grove's people had left, including her own son."

"As though she had only one son," Duncan muttered under his breath.

94

"Our families disowned us when we left the grove," Conall replied in response to my questioning look. I really wanted to know which one of the Finns was Nualla's other son, but neither of them was forthcoming with that information.

The Finns were patiently waiting, so I said, "Kam, go ahead and tell everybody else. Please."

She nodded. "When we parted ways in Jonesboro, I promised to Travel south and visit Angie and Davis at the grove…"

I tuned out the rest of her narrative and just sat there with my elbows on my knees and my head in my hands until she was finished. Only when the others were engaged in animated conversation did I lift my head and look at Duncan.

"Duncan, I'm sorry."

He cocked his head, puzzled. "That is the third time you have apologized. Why?"

"Because I didn't tell you sooner. Because Kam told me Angie was gone, and all I could think about was that I'm never going to find her again!" I ran my fingers through my hair. "I didn't even think about you losing your whole family!"

"We have been dealing with quite a few challenges since leaving the camp," he said. "We've all been focused on keeping fed and staying alive, but you have shouldered the lion's share of the burden. That is enough to distract anyone."

"That's no excuse for thoughtlessness."

Duncan placed a hand on my shoulder. "Is there anything at all I could have done with this information twenty-four hours ago?"

"No, but they're your family, and you deserved to know! What if we can't find them? What if you never see them again?"

"Oh, Davis, have you learned nothing?" His look of concern changed to one of fond amusement.

"What's that supposed to mean?"

"Davis. We are earth druids. If there is anyone capable of finding them, it is you and I."

I shook my head. "With all due respect to you, magic, and the gods, you just don't realize how enormous a task that is. We're talking hundreds of miles. Maybe thousands. We could be searching for years."

His only response was to chuckle.

"What are you laughing at? This is not funny!"

"Do you honestly think my family would abandon me?" he asked. "No. Even if my father and uncle have chosen to depart the land of their forebears, they will not settle far from it."

He was making sense, and it helped settle my worried soul.

"Besides," he said, "do you not think it likely that those who left may very well have the goal of joining the ones they have lost?" With a grand gesture, he swung one arm wide, as if to encompass all the Finns.

I hadn't stopped to consider such a thing. Duncan was right; I had been fully absorbed in the day-to-day provisioning and survival of those for whom I had accepted responsibility.

"If they've left White Oak Grove," Duncan said, "they may be searching for us even now." He smiled. "Do not forget my cousin's all-encompassing and possessive love for you."

Just that fast, I felt terrible again. Angie thought I was dead, I'd waited too long to go back for her, and now I might never find her. There was a flash of regret in his eyes, followed by a look of compassion that I wasn't sure I deserved.

"We *will* find them," he said. "As soon as we return from our journey with the Finns, we will go looking for my family. And when we find them, Angie will be there, too."

Chapter 6 – Reciprocity

If the Gods gave me the power to bring about
positive change in this world, then it is my responsibility
to honor that gift and exercise that power.
~ J.D. "Hobbes" Hickey ~

"Davis! Rider!"

The next morning, all the horses were saddled in preparation for departure, but only the members of my pentacle were mounted up. I turned Steel and walked him over to where Fenris was standing watch. Seth came with me on Bucephalus. Duncan, Conall, and Dermot trailed behind. Taking the spyglass from the spirit elementalist, I put it to my eye and saw a lone rider on a dun horse. Something was off about the pair, but I couldn't quite put my finger on it.

Passing it to Seth, I asked, "What do you think?"

"Could be a scout," he said. "Maybe a quarter-mile away. Maybe less." He passed the spyglass to Conall, who took a brief look and passed it back to me. I watched as the horse stopped short, danced around in a circle, and then leapt forward and took off running.

"He spotted us!" Conall cried. "Get him!"

"Wait!" I yelled, but he had already taken off with Dermot right behind him. I was glad they were getting along better, but damned if the water elementalist hadn't started to do everything the Norseman did.

Swearing under my breath, I urged Steel into a fast gallop. His

97

body lengthened with each stride until we had caught up and then passed the pair. The dun horse was galloping flat out, its rider's long coat flapping wildly, but didn't maintain its lead for more than a minute. We ran them down, got a little bit ahead, and angled in to cut them off. Steel pinned back his ears and snapped at the dun horse, which shied away and swerved back around toward a rapidly approaching Kelpie and Twister.

I had planned to try and grab the dun's reins, but it wore neither bridle nor saddle. The rider jerked his head up in alarm at the others approaching. His hood flew back, revealing bold red hair and a familiar, young-looking face.

It was Ahearn.

"Hold!" I shouted, trying to wave Dermot and Conall off. The four horses nearly collided as they came together in a cluster. Conall jumped down and yanked Ahearn off his horse in a flash.

"HOLD!" I roared. "Let him go!"

Still gripping Ahearn's shirt, Conall froze mid-punch. "Are you crazy?" he snapped. "If we let him go, he'll run back and tell them where we are!"

"No, he won't," I said. "Let him go."

Conall shoved the witch away from him. Ahearn stumbled but managed to keep his feet, and when he straightened, we were facing each other. His eyes widened in shock, and I raised my hands, palms facing outward in a gesture of reassurance when he leapt at me with a snarl.

"Whoa!" I cried, backing up. "Ahearn! It's me! It's Davis!"

Conall pounced on him again, pinning the witch's arms tightly behind his back. The red-haired witch tried to fight, but the Norseman was bigger, stronger, and more vicious. When Ahearn continued to struggle, Conall put him in a chokehold and forced him to his knees. Seth and Duncan finally arrived but stayed mounted.

"You *know* this man?" the Norseman asked.

"Curse you!" Ahearn yelled at me. "How could you *do* this?"

"I didn't know it was you! I would never have run you down otherwise."

"Rogue!" the witch spat. "Scoundrel! Let me *go*!"

Dermot looked at Conall. "Yep. Sounds like they know each other."

"Quakes, Ahearn! Calm down, and we'll turn you loose!"

"Liar!" he shouted. "We helped you, and *this* is how you repay us?!"

I couldn't have been more confused. Seth looked askance at me, and I held up a hand to forestall any questions until the witch calmed down.

"We *trusted* you, and you *betrayed* us!" Ahearn glared up at me.

"What are you talking about?"

"Just kill me and get it over with! I'll *die* before telling you where the coven is!"

"I am *not* going to kill you, and I *already* know where the coven is!" I shouted back, exasperated. His eyes widened, and his body started to shake with fury and terror.

"What coven?" Conall barked.

"The one in Ward! The one I told you about yesterday."

"*Betrayer!*" shouted Ahearn, his face twisted in an ugly sneer. "Did you lead them to us yourself, Davis, or did you just draw them a map?!"

"What is he talking about?" Conall demanded.

"I don't know!" I shouted back, exasperated.

"*Liar!*" Ahearn screamed. His face was as red as his hair, and his neck was corded with strain. "Bandits *stole* our home and *murdered* our people, and *druids helped them do it!*"

"What?" It came out as a whisper. Louder, I said, "Who helped them?"

"*DRUIDS!*"

Stunned with disbelief, I went down on one knee before him.

"Ahearn, I would *never*—"

"It was *druids* riding side by side with bandits when they came to demand that we give up our home and lands, and it was *druid magic* that shielded those murderers when we tried to defend ourselves!" Ahearn said, sweat and tears running down his face. "They stood and watched as our elders were slaughtered and our people captured!"

My blood ran cold, and I swallowed hard.

"How did druids come to be there that night? Can you explain *that* to me, Davis? Can you explain to me why the protectors of the earth stood by and did nothing while our fathers were gunned down trying to protect us?"

"No," I said. "But I swear to you that no one here had anything to do with it. If I had known such a calamity would befall your people, I would have done everything in my power to stop it."

"My home was ransacked by bandits and druids just weeks ago, and here I find you in the company of druids, miles and miles from where you are supposed to be!" Ahearn locked gazes with me, his voice shaking. "How can I believe you?"

"Let him go," I said to Conall, never looking away from the witch's eyes.

"Davis—"

"*Now*."

The Norseman released him, stepping back a couple of paces with his hand on the hilt of his sword. I knelt before Ahearn.

"I swear by my ancestors that I had nothing to do with the attack on Ward," I said. "So I do swear, and may the sky fall on my head, the sea rise up to drown me, and the earth swallow me whole if I lie."

Convincing Ahearn that we weren't involved in the capture of Ward turned out to be easier than convincing Seth to help the coven. The Finns quietly listened to the young witch tell his story of how raiders from the 'Ville had ventured north to Ward, seizing the coven's land and livestock in a violent attack and driving the witches out into the chill autumn night.

"They attacked after midnight," Ahearn said. "The protective wards woke us when they crossed our border, but their numbers were too great. We ran, mostly mounted bareback, riding double or even triple. The older folk guarded the rear so the younger ones and children could escape."

"Why didn't you fight back?" asked Fenris. "With magic, I mean."

"We're a peaceful coven," replied Ahearn quietly. "Our bows are for hunting. Our magic is for growing things, for health and for healing. We worship the Lord and Lady by living in harmony with the seasons and the land, and by celebrating the gifts given to us through their generosity."

"Rhiannon?" I said, afraid to hear the answer.

"Safe," Ahearn replied. "For the moment."

"Thank the gods," I said, heaving a sigh of relief that the High Priestess hadn't been captured or killed. "And Brennan?" Though all the adults in the Ward had a hand in raising their children, High Priest Brennan was Ahearn's natural father.

"He fell."

"I'm sorry."

"One less father to watch over me," he said, sadness in his eyes. A solemn heaviness came over me, and I wished I had been there to help prevent it. Brennan had been a kind and generous man.

Seth asked, "How long ago was this?"

"Weeks ago," said Ahearn.

"I didn't know there were still witches around," Dermot said. "My dad used to tell me stories of the ones he and Mom sometimes met before us kids were born."

"Like most places close to the 'Ville, we try to keep a low profile," Ahearn replied. "Until just recently we had cordial relations with druids, however."

"We were all born in the grove, but everyone here was either driven out or sent away for safety," Duncan said. "Except Davis, of course." Though I dreaded a rehash of his argument with Seth, it didn't happen.

"Some of us left because we chose to," Conall said, meaning the altered Finns. Ahearn frowned. "Why would they cast you out?"

"We have magic," said Dermot. "The ArchDruid doesn't like young men to have magic."

"To be more exact," Seth put in, "*most* of us have magic, but a few of our number have suffered the grievous loss of their gods-given ability and decided to leave the grove because of it. Those are the ones of whom Conall speaks."

Ahearn looked appalled. "I'd leave, too. What sort of wretched people would take magic away from their sons?"

"The same people who treat with bandits to murder innocent people and steal their land," Conall said darkly. He turned to me. "We have to help them."

I nodded. "We will."

"Davis, we need to talk about this," Seth said. Undoubtedly, he was thinking of our deadline to return by Samhain.

"No, we don't."

"Escorting Kam is one thing, but committing to protecting an entire coven is something else," Seth argued. "We've had a difficult enough protecting ourselves."

Ahearn looked up. "Someone has attacked you?"

Dermot nodded. "Bandits."

Conall added, "That's where we got the guns."

"I will not abandon them," I replied in a tone that brooked no argument. As second-in-command, he had an obligation to remind me of our obligations to Master Shitozaki, and frankly, the rest of the Finns could do what they wanted. I was going to help the coven even if I had to do it alone. I was indebted to them for their kindness, generosity, and protection when Angie and I needed a safe place to stay. Seth's countenance clouded with anger, but further support came from an unexpected source – Conall.

"Good," the Norseman said. "I hate working the harvest."

"That's because you swing a scythe like a blind man with one arm and one leg," Dermot said.

Conall eyed him. "So you'd rather spend your time digging up potatoes than rescuing people and killing bandits?"

"Of course not!" the water elementalist said. "This is more fun."

"Just how far away is Ward?" Seth asked, frowning in concern.

"At least twenty miles as the crow flies," Ahearn replied.

"We can do it," I said.

"That would mean cutting through the heart of the 'Ville's territory," said the witch, shaking his head. "It's too dangerous. We'd have to go around."

"If we do this, we'll be lucky to make it home by Yule," Seth protested.

"If we escort them to Ward and help them get their home back, we'll be lucky to make it home by *spring*," Conall said, sounding immensely pleased by the possibility. "Maybe even summer."

Seth scowled at him. "You are *not* helping."

Conall smirked at him. "Were you expecting me to?"

While I respected Seth's desire to respect the master and follow orders, I couldn't understand how that obligation was more important to him than helping people. These were people who shared our beliefs, to a large extent. And even if they didn't, I would still feel obligated to assist. What kind of man would I be if I turned my back on people helpless to protect themselves?

"I, too, will help," Duncan said, rising and drawing his sword. Holding the blade in his open palms and proffering it with outstretched arms, he dropped to one knee before Ahearn.

"My cousin related to me the account of how your people aided her when Davis was badly wounded, and how you provided them a place of safety. By our traditions, she owes your people reciprocity for their hospitality, but since my cousin is not here, I offer my blade for your protection and my skill with healing for anyone who might need it."

After such a noble demonstration of druidic virtue, whatever argument Seth had prepared to further his case died on his lips. One by one, individuals and then full pentacles mimicked the earth druid's actions, indicating their desire to help.

* * *

My heart sank when I saw the ragged remains of the coven's once-vibrant community, sitting in a disheveled despondence that was evident even at a distance. They huddled close to one another against the biting wind in a small copse of trees – a negligible shelter on the open plain. It was nothing that could keep out the rain and cold. It was nothing that would enable them to survive the winter.

A glance at Seth revealed that the scowl he'd worn for the entire eight-mile ride had been replaced by an expression of horror and compassion. The tension that had camped out in my gut since morning finally eased, along with my concern over his moral character. Like most air elementalists, he was ruled by logic and intellect; it was a relief to find there was compassion for strangers within him also.

"Look!" called Conall, pointing northwest of the pitiful camp. A group of bandits crested the hill overlooking the coven's camp. They paused, yelling and brandishing their weapons, then spurred their horses over the top. Ahearn brought his bow into play, loosing arrows at the bandits as his horse wheeled away toward the witches' rude camp.

"Form up! Air shields front!" I roared. "*Attack!*"

Drawing my blade, I bent low over Steel's neck as he leapt into a fast gallop. As one, the Finns put heels to horse and drew ringing steel with a growing roar of vengeance. The pentacles sorted themselves into a rough wedge formation as we raced straight toward the enemy, my own at the apex. Casting a shield of elemental air to protect us, Seth led the charge, all trace of reluctance gone. Conall and I rode echelon left and right just behind him, with Dermot and Duncan following. The air elementalists at the head of each pentacle raised their own shields against the enemy bullets. Each pentacle's shield overlapped with that of the one laterally behind him, either to the left or the right depending on which side of the formation they rode. Thunder rolled across the land as the horses' hooves pounded the hard-packed earth.

A cry of dismay rose up from the beleaguered encampment, pierced by shrieks of terror as they perceived themselves beset on both sides. Adults frantically grabbed children to pull them out of harm's way. Realizing that we would not reach them first, I threw a huge fireball at our enemies, launching it over the top of Seth's shield. My ability to manipulate magic I'd already cast was improving; as soon as the fireball exploded on the ground, a six-foot-high wall of flame spread out in a burning rush along their front line. The bandit horses skidded to a stop, whinnying and rearing in fear. We raced past the witches' camp, coats and cloaks flapping in the wind, sharp metal flashing in the light of the setting sun. We plowed into the enemy at full tilt, holding the wedge pattern and splitting their disorganized raid group right down the middle.

The air shields were no longer as effective in this situation, but our gunmen helped encourage the enemy to keep their heads down. All those with shotguns were aligned on the outsides of the wedge and had begun blasting away as soon as we'd broken through their ranks. The enemy's confusion allowed us to set up in a defensive diamond pattern, with the earth elementalists in the center to shake the ground and keep our opponents off balance. I kindled a wall of fire to our rear, primarily to keep the bandits off it, but also to dissuade them from approaching the witches.

While the others were busy shooting, launching spirit orbs,

and causing earthquakes, I tried tossing fireballs. After nearly hitting a couple of the Finns, I changed to a more controllable casting. Directing two separate bodies of elemental fire required more focus than I was capable of providing, so I built up the heat of the existing firewall and willed it to encircle the entire battleground. Using earth magic to pinpoint the location of friend and foe alike, I commanded it to blaze inward upon the enemy flanks and rear. Great gouts of flame swept over the raiders, burning flesh and setting hair and clothing alight. With each rapid burst, ammunition cooked off in random pops and bangs, followed by shouts of alarm. My fire magic was helping, but it wasn't working fast enough to end the fight. What I needed was a wall of flame that could be driven right through them lengthwise, instead of these narrow lines.

"Seth!" I yelled. "Raise a shield!"

He did what I wanted, but gave me a questioning look as he did so.

"Come with me to the front! I want to try something!"

"*Now?*" he asked, accompanying me without hesitation in spite of his obvious misgiving.

"I have an idea!" Creating a ten-foot-long, two-foot-thick wall of raging fire, deep red at the base and rising to shades of clear orange at the top, I pointed and said, "Push *that!*"

"What?" He looked at me like I was crazy.

"Make a shield and push the fire with it!"

Even though he didn't understand my end goal, Seth focused on the blaze and shoved a wall of air toward it, grunting loudly with effort. I concentrated on raising the temperature and maintaining intensity as it *whooshed* across the battleground.

While I'd been sure that my casting would work, I'd had no idea just how effective it would be. The firewall progressed through the raid group, flaring with brilliant light as clothing, hair, and leather ignited. Raiders to either side steered clear of comrades with heads alight like candles, filling the air with their screams.

"By the gods!" Seth exclaimed.

"Again! Bigger!" I yelled for Eian and Declan, who abandoned their pentacles to help. If this worked as well as I intended, their pentacles wouldn't need them for much longer. Grabbing Conall and Dermot, I pushed them to the back and ordered them to get everyone else behind a protective shield while Seth told the twins what to do. I gave instructions to make the shields much wider along the front. Calling on the limitless fire magic inside me, I channeled an inferno that stretched across the killing ground.

Caught up in the beauty and power of the roaring flames, I fed them elemental fire until the red at the base became clear, brightening to a brilliant orange and then vivid yellow at the crest. I was so enamoured of the sight that I forgot to give any orders.

"*Push!*" roared Seth, snapping me out of my reverie.

The firewall surged forward under the magic impulsion of the three air elementalists, sweeping through the raid group and incinerating everything that moved. Dark shapes flared to bright lights as living beings combusted and burned like giant torches. Part of me cringed on the inside, but only a small part, for those marauders had murdered folks who had never done them harm. The witches of Ward Coven had been good to me, and I was going to do everything in my power to make sure that they never suffered such ill-treatment again.

When it was over, the crown of the hill was black and smoking. Only heaps of crumbling bone and ash remained.

"Regroup your pentacles!" I shouted. "Check to see who's wounded and take care of them."

I started to follow my own order, but Seth pulled me aside.

"What happened to you?" he demanded, keeping his voice low.

I didn't have to ask what he meant.

"I don't know," I said. "I was just... mesmerized."

The light of comprehension showed on his face.

"I know what that is," he said. "Fire druids have to be careful not to get so wrapped up in their magic that they lose control." He paused, dark eyes earnest. "You must be vigilant, Davis. You've spent all your time learning to bring fire forth and increase it. You have little experience with backing it down, and a fire druid out of control is *extremely* difficult to stop."

There had been a moment when the lovely, dancing flames had called out to me, and I had wondered what it would be like to set the world on fire. I nodded, feeling a bit shaken.

"If that ever happens, make sure you take me down."

106

"I can't kill you!" he protested, visibly horrified.

"I didn't say *kill* me!" I said, appalled. "Just stab me in the leg or have Phelan shock me or something. Gods, Seth! Kill me?" It shook me to the core by the fact that he considered a fire druid out of control as something so dangerous that it warranted murder to stop. "Bring it down a notch, will you?"

He rolled his eyes. "Of *course* I would try less lethal methods first," he said. "But I stand by what I said: you must be vigilant."

"Trust me, I will be." *Especially after this conversation.*

"Looks like we don't have to clean up the bodies this time," said Dermot, walking up with Conall.

"We're not going to be collecting any ammunition, either," grumped Conall, giving me a scowl.

"Protecting people is more important," I said.

"Kinda hard to protect people without any ammo," Conall grumped. Dermot nodded agreement. I ignored them both. Ammunition popped off or melted at nearly half of that fire's lowest temperature; there wasn't much I could do about that.

"They've got a point," Seth said. "Maybe we could work on pushing around superheated air instead."

Or we could let Conall do it for us by letting him run his mouth, I thought. He was better since acquiring a shotgun, but that didn't mean being around him was all wine and roses.

"I see that look," Seth chided. "No one is criticizing you."

"Oh, no?" I raised an eyebrow at him. "Look, I'm just trying to keep everybody alive and in one piece. I'm doing it the best way I know how. It's not always going to be pretty."

I stalked off to check on the rest of the Finns. Stopping by Siorus' pentacle, I found Eian standing behind Duncan, watching him heal Mohinder. The water elementalist had suffered a gunshot wound to his left side, just above the hip. The bleeding had already stopped, and the flesh knit together before our eyes. Mohinder stood up, stretched this way and that, then thanked Duncan and went to find his horse.

"That," I said to Duncan, "was volcanic."

He rose, giving me a curious look. "You've seen me heal before."

"I've experienced *being* healed, which is not quite the same thing," I said. "I think I prefer watching you heal somebody else."

He chuckled and shook his head.

"Is he the last?" I asked, meaning the last wounded man to be healed.

"He is."

"We should go check on the witches, then."

We tromped down the hill to the ragtag encampment, leading our horses so we wouldn't frighten those we'd come to help. Handing my reins over to Dermot, I proceeded to the witches' camp with Seth and Duncan. I found the High Priestess striding toward us as her people parted to let her pass. Her face was wan and grief-stricken, and her dress was spattered with mud, but she still carried herself with dignity.

"Blessings on you and your men," she said in her rich, throaty voice. "The Lord and Lady have blessed us with your presence this day. You have been an aegis of protection for us, and we owe you a debt for your kindness." She was dirty, and her red hair was tied back in a tangled ponytail, but her grey eyes were clear.

I threw back my hood. "You owe me nothing," I said. "Consider it repayment of the debt I owe you."

The High Priestess of Ward Coven stared at me in disbelief, then let out a wordless cry and threw her arms around me. It was not what I'd come to expect from Rhiannon, but she'd been through a lot. I held her while she gathered her composure. She stepped back, still holding onto my arms as though unwilling to let go.

"You are *most* welcome here, Davis – you *and* your companions. I only wish we had food to share." She wrung her hands in distress.

"Don't worry about that. We'll take care of it."

I returned to the Finns and gestured to Eian and Declan. The twins were the best bowmen – and riflemen – of the group.

"You two see if you can bring down a deer. Eian, you go west. Take Siorus with you to help find game. Declan, you and Yiorgos go northwest. Ingvar, who's your best shot? Jasvinder? Fine, grab him and go north. Halldor go northeast with Skylar—"

"Skylar is tapped out," he said. "I'll take Barak."

"Fine," I said. "Oh, one more thing – nobody goes east or south for any reason. Got it?" They all murmured acknowledgement of my orders and departed.

Martin and Warwick approached me next. "What do you want us to do?" Warwick asked.

"Warwick, take your pentacle to set snares. Use magic if you have to. These people are hungry." He gave me a sharp nod, spoke briefly with his guys, and the five rode away.

"Martin, I'd like you to help Duncan." The earth druid was already moving among the witches and tending to any physical ailments they might have. When he left, I looked around for Seth and found him right behind me, as always.

"Seth, set a perimeter guard alternating air, spirit, and guns," I said. "It probably won't be even, but do your best."

"I'm on it," he said, striding to the edge of the witches camp. From there I could hear him bellowing the names of the other Finns he wanted.

"What about me?" Galen asked.

Dermot waved his hand, blurting, "There's a stream nearby! Galen, Nêreus, and I can go fishing!"

"All right, but take Westley and Solon with you." Westley was one of our two spirit/water dualists, while Solon possessed spirit and air. The water elementalists needed no help catching fish; I was sending the dualists along for safety.

Everyone that wasn't injured or low on magic had been given an assignment, leaving me with Skylar and Mohinder. They needed to rest, but the witches were in worse shape than any of the Finns.

"All right, you two," I said to them. "Start going through all our supplies and see if there are any potatoes or carrots for soup or stew."

"We have a bunch of apples," said Mohinder. "Can I give them to the children?"

"I'm sure they'd like that," I said. "Bring them back with the rest."

They hiked back to the horses and set to work going through saddlebags without complaint. Watching the Finns hustle to help others when they themselves were tired from fighting made my chest tight with warmth and feeling. Not one had argued about his assignment; not one had protested that giving the witches our food would leave us without.

No leader could ever have been more proud.

Meat was plentiful that night. Since I had given them permission, those that were able used magic to call the animals into snares or lure them into bow or rifle range. It wasn't fair or sporting, but I wasn't about to let women and children go hungry. Several small piles of wood were gathered in a large circle, and I went around lighting them one by one. Wanting the fires to last throughout the night, I commanded them to burn hot but consume the wood slowly. I wasn't sure if it would work, but it couldn't hurt to try. I tried to ignore the "oohs" and "ahhs" when the merry flames erupted, but couldn't help winking at the children.

We washed away the remnants of battle in the stream Dermot had discovered, going a pentacle at a time while the deer and some rabbits roasted on a spit. Half the venison was cut into large chunks so it would take less time to cook, and the other half was cut into roasts and laid on the coals. The rabbits were done first, and the children were soon fed and tucked into warm blankets.

Ahearn showed back up with Kam in tow, her two Irish wolfhounds at heel. "Did you forget someone?" he asked, thumbing at the Traveler behind him.

"Of course not," I said. "Kam can take care of herself."

"You didn't have to leave her alone."

"I didn't. She has Tuiren."

Before Ahearn could protest further, Kam said, "I was fine. Once I found a good place to shoot, all I needed was Tuiren to watch my back and enough rifle rounds to take out some bad guys." She smiled and gave me a wink.

"Davis, where is Angie?" Rhiannon asked.

I hesitated, not wanting to discuss our situation in public.

"Ahearn, would you mind showing me where I could bathe in private?" Kam asked.

"You don't want to wash in the stream?" he asked.

"The water's a little too chilly," she said. The witch nodded understanding.

"I know a place," he said, leading her away.

When they had gone, Rhiannon said, "I was right about the grove, then."

"Obviously." My gestured encompassed both the ragged camp and her beaten people, victims of grove politics and bandit conquest. I had expected her to ask about Angie, but it wasn't any easier for the expecting.

Rhiannon's jaw tightened. "She abandoned you."

"No, she didn't."

"*You* abandoned *her*?" Her eyes narrowed. "Did she change her mind and start working with the ArchDruid again? Is she involved in this?"

I shook my head. "She thinks I'm dead." Rhiannon drew in a sharp breath. I put up a hand to forestall the lecture I was sure she was about to give. "I know. You warned us, and we didn't listen. A lot of bad things happened, and there were events beyond our control. She may have been naïve, but I was stubborn. None of this is her fault, and I'll not have anyone blaming her."

"She practically dragged you to that grove, Davis," Rhiannon said in a scolding tone.

"I went willingly."

After a pause, she said, "You still love her, don't you?"

"Of course I do."

The High Priestess's fond smile held more than a touch of melancholy and very little mirth. She touched my cheek softly.

"I hope the Goddess brings her back to you, Davis. But I fear for your brave and noble heart."

I met her gaze evenly. "At least I know she is alive and safe."

She dropped her gaze, and I took her hands in mine. "I am so very sorry for your loss. Brennan was a good man."

"I mourn him deeply," she said, closing her eyes. "But we will meet again in the Summerlands."

"So be it," I replied.

The witches enjoyed a relaxing evening of precious safety, while the Finns cooked and washed up afterward. Duncan had cooked a thin soup from leftover rabbit, a few chunks of deer, and the vegetables that he had saved in his saddlebags. This was given to the sick and those with delicate stomachs. The men I'd sent to hunt had also brought back wild potatoes, carrots, and leeks. The Finns were hungry after the fight, but not one of us ate before the people of the coven.

"You must be hungry," Rhiannon said, handing me a bowl of soup and a stick of roasted deer meat before seating herself beside me. I noticed that she had bathed and brushed her hair.

"Have you eaten?"

"As much as I can hold," she said, patting her belly. "I don't know what we would have done if you and your men hadn't shown up."

"Y'all can't stay out here, that's for sure. You're defenseless, and winter is coming."

"Shall we just waltz back to Ward and politely request that those ruffians give us our home back?" she asked tartly.

"A polite request wasn't really what I had in mind." I wiped juice from my chin.

"Oh? Just what did you have in mind?" There was a sardonic light in her grey eyes; watching her people endure this hardship had given her a bitter edge, one that I hoped to take away.

"We could demand rudely," said Dermot, reaching over for a chunk of meat on a skewer. Conall nodded agreement.

"We could build a defensive wall around your lands," I said. "After we drive them out, of course."

"The construction of such a barrier could take weeks to complete," said Duncan, his eyes laden with meaning. We didn't have weeks if we wanted to return the Finns home and start our search for his family.

"We can't stay inside forever, anyway," Rhiannon said. "As much as I love our home, I would rather relocate than be trapped within a confined area."

"If there were no bandits, you wouldn't have to worry about it," Conall said.

"That goes without saying," Seth said with a snort.

"I'm so glad you agree," the Norseman said. "Because the obvious solution is to eradicate them."

"Excuse me?" Seth said. "Exactly how do you plan on going about that Herculean task?"

"By destroying their city," he replied. "The best defense is a good offense."

"Ordinarily I would agree with you," I said, "but as we've had quite a bit of difficulty fighting individual bands and raiding parties, I don't think we stand a chance against an entire city of bandits with an arsenal at their disposal."

"Hear, hear," agreed Seth.

"We haven't had quite a bit of difficulty," Conall retorted.

"We've had a few minor injuries."

"Gunshot wounds aren't minor injuries."

He shrugged. "They are while we have healers around. No limbs have been lost, and nobody has died."

"Knock on wood," I said, while Ahearn and Rhiannon quickly made matching gestures mimicking horns to ward off evil. Interestingly enough, both Kam and Seth reached inside their shirts, bringing out nearly identical amulets. Each amulet was a royal blue disk with concentric circles of black, white, and light blue in varying widths and a black dot in the center. Upon seeing Kam's amulet, Seth smiled broadly at her and gave her a cordial nod. It must have been a Greek thing, or he wouldn't have had one, and I wondered if she, too, honored the gods of Olympus.

"We don't even know how many soldiers they have, or how big the city is," Seth argued. "They could have thousands."

"Remember when some of the guys didn't believe Davis could control the volcano and he opened up the base of it and proved it?" Conall said.

"Thank for reminding me," I grumbled.

"All I'm saying is that if you can tear open the outer walls of a volcano, then opening up an underground magma chamber and flooding the 'Ville in a sea of lava is not outside the realm of possibility."

Rhiannon's jaw dropped, her expression mimicked by Ahearn, Dermot, and Kam. Seth and Duncan, however, fixed disapproving gazes on our bloodthirsty friend. My concern was that there might be unfriendly ears listening to this conversation. We were fresh out of a fight, and I had no desire to engage the enemy anytime soon. Protecting the witches and keeping the Finns alive while being hunted by tenacious raiders was a logistical nightmare.

"Conall…"

"Don't 'Conall' me. You can do it."

"You don't know that!" I said. "Besides, there's no telling what—" I broke off, remembering Seth's warning to guard myself against losing control. I couldn't think of anything more likely to hypnotize me with magical lust than what Conall was suggesting.

"No telling what you might be capable of?"

"No. I was going to say that there's no telling what might happen. Besides, Master Shitozaki gave me explicit orders to stay away from the 'Ville."

"And of course you've always done whatever he wants." Conall fixed me with a challenging stare. I wanted to think his suggestion was the brainchild of an angry man who blamed an entire city for the crime of taking his magic away, but the fact of the matter was that his sullenness had mostly gone by the wayside, leaving in its place calm rationality that was occasionally punctuated with passionate intensity.

"I follow the orders that make sense to me," I said. "While the 'Ville has grown into a threat that should be addressed, a small group with only two druids, twenty-seven elementalists, and six gunmen are *not*, in my opinion, ready to deal with such a threat at this time."

Surprisingly, he listened, and after a moment gave me a nod of acquiescence. "Some other time, then."

"Right," I said, not agreeing at all. "Some other time."

"Yeah," Dermot muttered. "Like *never*." In response to the funny looks he received, the water elementalist became defensive.

"What? Never is a time."

Rhiannon chuckled, followed by Ahearn and Kam, which helped the tension begin to dissolve.

"Aren't you a clever fellow!" she said, smiling warmly at the youngest Finn. "Thank the Lord and Lady, you are correct. Never is most definitely a time."

Dermot beamed.

"In fact," she continued, turning her grey gaze upon me, "the present is also a time. And as the saying goes, 'there is no time like the present,' Davis, so why don't you tell me the story of how you acquired elemental magic?"

I wanted to groan but suppressed the urge.

"Just to make things clear," I said. "I did *not* have magic when Angie and I were in Ward. I never even suspected that such a thing was possible."

"Oh, I know that," she laughed. "You're far too honest for such a deception." She paused. "Your young lady, however…"

I frowned. "What about her?"

"Let's just say that when Angie does find out about your magic, I don't think she'll be terribly surprised."

"What's that supposed to mean?"

"It means I'm sure she suspected you were of druid stock all along."

Master Shitozaki had said something similar. It made sense, for why would the fetch of a powerful elementalist have chosen someone who lacked magical ability?

"So... How did your abilities manifest, and when?" Rhiannon asked.

Keeping it intentionally brief, I relayed the story of how I fell into the volcano and didn't die. Kam – who hadn't heard that part – gasped and clapped both hands over her mouth, her brown eyes wide. It made me wish the fall had been due to something other than my own clumsiness.

"So you've only possessed fire magic since Beltaine, but you are already this powerful?" the High Priestess asked.

Always ready to help me out, Conall said, "He has earth magic, too."

This time, I did sigh.

"Then you have truly been blessed by the gods," said Rhiannon. "No wonder our harvest was so abundant last year."

Heat crawled up my neck as I grasped that she was referring to the manner in which Angie and I had blessed the coven's fields. When she skipped over an explanation of how *that* had occurred, I considered myself blessed indeed.

"How common is it to have two elements?" she asked.

Seth explained. "Most people only have one. About twenty percent have two, and somewhere between five and ten percent have three."

"Angie is gifted with three elements if I remember correctly."

"She is," I said.

"The first druid to possess three elements was an Everlight," Duncan said. "My father wields fire and earth as Davis does. Angie gets her elemental ability from my uncle, who also possesses spirit, air, and water."

Rhiannon's brow furrowed momentarily as she pieced the relationships together.

"Duncan is Angie's cousin," I said, annoyed that I'd forgotten to mention it sooner.

"I was adopted into the Everlight family," he said. "I possess one element only, that of earth."

"Don't make it sound like that." To Rhiannon I said, "Duncan's abilities are remarkable. Not only can he move earth and do things like stop earthquakes, but he is a truly talented healer."

"It is only because of my deep respect for Danu, the earth mother," he said quietly.

Rhiannon smiled. "And because of her love for you, I am sure."

He acknowledged her words with an elegant nod.

Her eyes grew sharp when they found me again. "I am very interested to hear how you ended up away from the grove with Angie's cousin, but not Angie herself."

Duncan and I exchanged a glance, his expression patient and asking without really asking. Mine, I'm sure, looked tired and resigned.

"Fine. You tell the story. I've already told it once this week."

"Very well."

"Just... leave out that one thing. Please."

Duncan raised an eyebrow, and I could almost hear his thoughts: *Of all the things that happened to you, that is the thing you consider to be the worst?*

Having shit smeared over my back when I was tied down on a cot?

Yeah.

Without a doubt, it was the most degrading thing that had ever happened to me in my whole life.

"Forgive me, High Priestess, for not going into detail, but Davis has suffered greatly at the hands of druids," he said. "It was as if the grove as an entity had conspired to heap upon him as much distress and pain as it could within the brief period in which he dwelled with us."

This was not the story I had expected. Although I opened my mouth a couple of times to interject something, I ended up closing it each time without speaking.

"Suffice it to say," he continued, "that even though he consistently displayed a noble and heroic character, the ArchDruid manufactured a reason to have him brutally flogged—"

"*What?*" Rhiannon whispered. Kam looked distressed.

"—after which an enemy poisoned him, even though he'd

shown the man mercy numerous times." He paused, looking down. "It is an action I deeply regret. I never should have left you that night."

"I told you to go."

"I went because I was afraid," he said. "And you nearly died because of my cowardice."

"You are *not* a coward." I was so dumbfounded by his statement that I struggled for words for several seconds. "Who stuck around the grove even though it was dangerous? *You* did. Who followed me when I left with Niall and Darryn to give the shotgun demonstration? *You* did. Who hid Onóra so Sebrina and her bootlickers couldn't find her? *You* did."

"Those were only small things," he said with a dismissive wave of his hand.

"Coming back to get me wasn't," I said. "Hauling my nearly-dead and unconscious carcass out of there and risking being caught was no small thing."

"It was the least I could do to make up for our failures – mine, and those of the rest of my family."

"We all do the best we can, Duncan," Rhiannon said kindly. "We all have moments when we wish we'd been braver, faster, stronger, or more clever. Those moments do not exist to drag us down or to keep our eyes on the past. Those moments exist so that we learn from them and grow in wisdom." Rhiannon leaned over and placed her hand on his. "If you do not forgive yourself your human mistakes, you can do neither. Let it go, beloved of the Earth Mother."

Duncan bowed his head deeply in acknowledgement of her wisdom, and the High Priestess leaned back to regard us all. She was silent for a few long moments. Then she turned again to me.

"What do you intend to do?"

"Go back for Angie, hopefully by Yule."

"And in the near future?"

"Win Ward back for you."

"We won't be home by Samhain," said Conall in a mocking singsong tone.

Rhiannon shot him an imperious glare. "That is quite enough childishness from you, young man."

I think we were all surprised when he wilted under the power of the High Priestess' gaze – and a little bit gratified, as well.

He cleared his throat, straightening his shoulders. "Master Shitozaki *will* be angry if we're not back on time."

"Probably," I said. "But it's the right thing to do."

"Davis…" Seth began.

"I know," I said. "I know. But if Shitozaki was standing here right now, what decision do you think he would make?"

The air elementalist sighed. "He'd say that we are the protectors of the earth. He'd stay to protect the witches and make sure they got their home back."

Former ArchDruid or not, I wasn't so certain that Connor Shitozaki would have done anything of the sort, regardless of the speeches he'd made about protecting the earth and her people in our great hall. What I did know was that Seth held our master in very high regard and that *he* believed Shitozaki would have taken that action. My friend might be annoyed with me later, but the master's fury would most definitely overshadow it.

"Exactly."

"Even if you do succeed," Rhiannon said quietly, "once you're gone we'll never be able to keep it."

"One thing at a time, High Priestess," I said. "One thing at a time."

Chapter 7 – The Oracle

I can control my destiny, but not my fate.
Destiny means there are opportunities to turn right or left,
but fate is a one-way street.
I believe we all have the choice as to whether we fulfill our destiny,
but our fate is sealed.
~ Paulo Coelho ~

After a few days of guarding the witches, I noticed a subtle change in the Finns. They sat a little straighter in their saddles. Their eyes were brighter, and they held their heads higher. There was more dignity in their bearing and more confidence in their posture. To a man, the Finns embraced their new role as protectors, not only of the earth, but also of the defenseless and the weak. We had truly become an aegis, their shield against danger.

Having the opportunity to repay the generosity and protection that the witches had shown to me was an honor. I was happy to do it, but our snail's pace was driving me *crazy*. If I thought that traveling with thirty-four other men was difficult and annoying, traveling with them plus the coven was a nightmare. It wasn't that the witches whined or grumbled; quite to the contrary, they endured all hardships without complaint.

The sheer number of stops, even if they were brief rest breaks, only served to irritate me more. Camp had to be broken, meals had to be cooked, pregnant women and small children needed frequent breaks to relieve themselves, food had to be gathered, camp pitched, and supper cooked when we stopped, with everything to start over again the next day.

We had collected a goodly-sized herd of horses from the bandits, but there were still many people who had to walk. Many of the witches alternated days of walking with days of riding, sometimes riding double with a child. This allowed them some rest but did not allow us to cover more ground each day. The Finns wanted to offer up their own mounts but I wouldn't allow it. If the bandits showed up, there would be no time for dismounting and remounting. Anything that delayed our counterattack could cost lives.

Shitozaki expected us back by Samhain, just three weeks away. While that would have been enough time to see Kam Stone safely north of the 'Ville and back home, it was now impossible. Until I experienced what traveling with women and children was really like, I had thought it plenty of time to get to Ward at least. Now, I wasn't so sure. We couldn't leave the witches alone until after we dealt with the bandit threat, and this, I was fairly certain, would take until winter was upon us.

The rest of the Finns might think I wasn't worried about Connor Shitozaki, but nothing could be further from the truth. It wasn't so much that I feared his temper; it was breaking my word to him that I disliked. If I wanted to split hairs, the only promise I'd made was to bring everyone back alive. However, I knew for a fact that Shitozaki would be more than a little put out when we did not make it back as ordered.

"You're scowling again," said Seth.

I sighed and tried to relax, rolling my shoulders. The last thing I wanted was for anyone to think I resented the job we'd taken on.

"What's bothering you?" he asked.

"Just thinking about the master," I said. "Do you think he might come looking for us?"

From the look on Seth's face, it was evident that he hadn't considered that possibility. "I hate to say it, but that does seem likely," he said.

"Now you know why I was scowling."

"We do need to pick up the pace," he said. "It's getting cold sooner than expected. I think we're in for an early winter."

The weather had been unpredictable and often violent since the Fracture. Winter brought storms of snow and ice more often

120

than not, which is why I had always spent the season in my parents' home. Traveling in knee-deep snow was not my idea of a good time, and an early winter meant bitter cold and heavy snows.

"Phelan is our only triple threat," I said. I had water and air elementalists aplenty, but none of them had any experience with the complex magic required to manipulate the weather. For that matter, neither did he. Now, if Angie had been with us... I cut off that line of thought. Thinking about how much she could help us – how much she could help *me* – just made me miss her all the more.

"A triple threat is required in building a thunderstorm, but not for winter weather," Seth observed. "Air and water are all that are needed."

"Hm."

"And while I have every confidence that we could work together with the water elementalists to learn weather-working, we need to conserve our magic for fending off the marauders from the 'Ville," said Seth.

"That's true." I looked around, making a quick scan of the surroundings and checking on everyone. "I just wish we could go faster."

"The witches are exhausted from living on the run with little food and no rest," Seth said. "It would be cruel to ask them to exert themselves further."

"There must be some way..." I caught sight of Ahearn across the sea of people, walking ahead of his dun filly while three small children rode. Something about them sparked the beginnings of an idea.

"How many horses do we have?"

"We started out with thirty-five and acquired about ten bandit horses, more or less."

"Let's go find out how many the witches have."

Reining Steel and Bucephalus away from the main body, we cantered to the rear and turned toward the west, again slowing to a walk when we reached Ahearn. I dismounted and began leading the little grey stallion so I could converse with the horsemaster more easily.

"Merry meet, Davis," he said. "What's up?"

"How many horses do you have?" I asked.

"Less than twenty, out of a herd of a hundred." He grimaced.

121

"Why do you ask?"

"I'm trying to figure out a way to get us moving faster somehow," I said. "We're sitting ducks out here."

Ahearn nodded. "If the bandits don't get us, the cold will." He peered at the cloud-covered sky.

"Exactly." I paused, doing some mental math. Out of the ninety-something inhabitants of Ward, thirty percent had been murdered by bandits, captured, or simply lost as they fled from danger. Of the remaining survivors, half were small children or teenagers. There were no babies.

One had been born too early a week before we found them.

He didn't make it.

I tried not to think about what might have happened to any other babies – or their mothers. In the areas I had Traveled, bandits were notorious for capturing people during raids and keeping them as slaves. There was no reason to believe these brigands were any different. Every night, when darkness covered us all, the muffled sobs of grieving men, women, and children could be heard throughout the camp as they mourned their lost loved ones. I didn't know which would be worse, knowing someone I loved was dead or thinking they might be alive and enslaved.

"Did you have something in mind?" Ahearn asked, breaking my train of thought.

"I'm thinking about having everyone ride double."

"That would overwork the horses," he said. "Yours are bigger, but they'd still wear out fast. They'd be unsound in no time, either from being back sore, foot store, or just plain exhausted."

"What if we only rode double every other day?" I asked. Pain and injury we could handle if we had to, but magic couldn't fix overworked and underfed.

"You want them to bear two riders one day, and then your men all day the next?" He shook his head. "If they have to carry two riders all day, then the next day *everyone* would have to walk."

I glanced back at the children on his dun filly. "We can't ask the little ones to walk all day. That's too much."

Seth, who had been listening to our debate, said, "Why not have everyone walk in the morning when it's cooler? The exercise will help everyone stay warm, and the children can ride when they get tired. Then after lunch, we can double up."

Ahearn and I exchanged a look.

"Also, given the ratio of people to mounts, not all the horses will have to carry two riders every day," Seth continued.

Air elementalists and their logic. What would I have done without it?

"Once the kids are up, they don't have to *stay* up," Ahearn said. "They're kids, they recover fast. They could be on and off horses all day long."

"That just might work," I said.

When we stopped for the night, I gathered my companions and discussed the strategy for increasing our speed. The Finns were pleased to hear it, which made me proud of them all over again. They were putting themselves at risk by protecting others and were still eager to give additional assistance. We discussed the details for walking and riding double in pentacles, as well as the quickest and safest way to remove our passengers if bandits showed up. For her part, Kam had been walking as soon as our journey with the witches had begun, and had given up her black gelding to Britta, a pregnant woman with a young son.

"You know, we wouldn't have to do any of this stuff if we destroyed the 'Ville and killed all the bandits," said Conall, helping Cinna down from his horse. I'd noticed the auburn-haired witch riding with him more often than not.

"I would have to have an extremely good reason for attacking a bandit stronghold," I said. Especially with women and children in tow.

"You mean like helping people live free from tyranny?"

That was hitting below the belt. If there was anyone who cherished his freedom and wanted others to share in it as well, it was me. The anger I felt must have been reflected in my expression, because Cinna deftly took Twister's reins out of Conall's hands and led the stallion away, escaping the brewing confrontation.

"I'm not doing it."

"You won't destroy a city full of greedy, low-down, no-good, dirty thieves, rapists, and murderers? Even if it means that all the surrounding towns and the people in them could be free?" he asked. "Even if it means they never have to live in fear again?

Because that's what it would mean if the 'Ville was destroyed."

"I'm *not* doing it," I said. "Quakes, Conall! Next thing I know, you'll be planning how to destroy the grove."

"Now *that* is a fantastic idea. I'll start working on a plan for that next." He gave me a savage grin.

"Enough!" said Seth. "The master gave us an explicit command, and we are going to obey it."

"Of course you would say that. If Shitozaki needed to take a piss, you'd hold his dick for him."

I'd seen the air elementalist irritated a time or two, but I'd never seen him mad. He rounded on Conall with balled-up fists and a muscle jumping in his jaw. Before he was about to throw a punch, I stepped between them. It may not have been the smartest thing to do, but I couldn't afford to have them come to blows over mere words.

"You've just earned yourself first watch tonight," I told Conall.

"First watch!"

"And latrine duty."

"Latrine—! For how long?"

"Until I say otherwise." I crossed my arms over my chest, daring him to say anything else. I could think of several dirty jobs to give him. I'd done plenty of them myself as a Traveler, and I couldn't have cared less whether he missed out on some private time with the auburn-haired witch. She was probably the motivation for his whole tirade.

Conall stormed away with a curse.

The High Priestess endorsed Seth's plan to travel faster wholeheartedly. Once everyone else had bedded down for the night, she and Spencer, the acting High Priest, began working out a plan for deciding who would ride with whom.

After banking all the fires to glowing coals that cast more heat than light, I stretched out on my blanket and gazed up at the stars. The fires would die out eventually after I fell asleep, but Conall and whoever else was keeping watch could stoke them as needed.

Kam Stone appeared out of the darkness and spread her blanket beside mine before sitting on it. "Your idea is wonderful," she said. Tuiren curled up at her feet, and she rubbed the dog's ears fondly. Hector plopped down between us, licked my hand, then laid his hand on his paws. I rubbed his head, and he thumped his tail happily.

"It was a Seth's idea," I replied.

"Nothing at all would have happened if you hadn't tried to solve the problem."

"I'm just trying to get us to Ward as quickly as possible."

I heard her chuckle softly. "Are you so eager to fight again?"

"Just the opposite. I want to get them to a safe place before we're forced to fight again."

Kam stretched out on her left side, propping her head on her hand to look at me. "Do you feel responsible for *everyone* here?"

I thought about that for a minute. The Finns *were* my responsibility. Master Shitozaki had tasked me with their guidance and care, and I had accepted that duty. Even though Rhiannon was the leader of the witches, I had taken on the burden of protecting them. She had entrusted me with their safekeeping, and I would do everything in my power to make sure they were untouched by any enemy, whether it be bandits, starvation, or the cold. Still, I was not responsible for every single person here.

"No," I said, "not everyone."

"Ah," she said. "There are people here who don't need you?"

"Just one."

"Truly? And who might this special creature be?"

"You," I said.

There were a few seconds of silence before she spoke again.

"I think I'll take that as a compliment."

"Why would you think it otherwise?" I asked, frowning. If she had decided to take it as a compliment, that meant she had also considered it might be an insult. "You're a Traveler, and from what I've seen, an expert marksman with that rifle. You don't need anybody to take care of you, Kam. You can take care of yourself."

"You thought I needed you when you said the Finns would see me safely north of the 'Ville."

"By my reckoning, we *are* north of the 'Ville," I said. "Honestly, I wonder if you wouldn't be better off alone at this point."

"Why is that?" she asked quietly.

"I just feel like I have a big ole' bulls-eye painted on my back. That's why we need to move faster. It's only a matter of time before the bandits find us again."

"Aren't the earth elementalists erasing our tracks?"

"They are, but this is enemy territory. We could be spotted by a scout, or stumble upon a raiding party."

"Do you *want* me to leave?"

"Want you to? No, of course not," I said. "I enjoy your company."

"Good." I could hear the smile in her voice. "Because I'd like to stay with you a while longer."

* * *

It took a couple of days to sort out who was riding with whom and on what horses. We practiced rapid dismounts and remounts in the afternoons, deciding that the witches could dismount on the off side of the horses as the Finns mounted on the usual side. Luck was with us over the next few days; no bandits attacked, and we were able to drill uninterrupted.

I made everybody practice about twenty times a day, and I'm pretty sure they hated me for it. Rhiannon backed me up when her people complained about being tired, so they probably hated her, too. It wasn't like we were asking pregnant women to jump on and off horses. In fact, the older witches never complained; it was the teenagers and the ones our age that were whining. The Finns were especially unhappy because after they had ditched their passengers, I made them practice forming up into pentacles. Ahearn wasn't delighted with the extra work the horses were doing, either. When he complained about it, I told him that they'd have plenty of rest and time to graze after the bandits killed us all. It was harsh, but I was tired of the griping.

"Bandits north!" I shouted, swinging aboard Steel. Kam, who had been riding him, slipped off the other side and ran to the outer edge of the caravan. Whistling to her dogs, she knelt with her rifle up and aimed north, where my imaginary bandits were supposed to be. By the time I had both feet in the stirrups and the grulla stallion had reached a gallop, all the Finns were on their mounts and headed north at a fast pace, forming up in a wedge with my pentacle at the head. Raising my right hand to signal a stop, everybody slowed and halted, then stood still while I turned around to inspect them. My pentacle was together if a little disorderly. I trotted Steel around to look at everyone else. All the other pentacles were grouped correctly, with air elementalists at the fore, spirit in the middle, and earth and water at the rear. Overall, the wedge formation looked straight. Returning to the apex of the wedge, I halted beside Seth. I could almost hear our guys holding their collective breath.

"What do you think?"

"Looks good," he said.

"I think so, too." I raised my voice, along with my fist in the air, shouting, "Good job! You've got it down!"

They whooped and cheered, and we hustled back to where we had deposited our charges. I kicked off my left stirrup so Kam could put her foot in it, then held out my hand. She smiled broadly, dark eyes sparkling, and allowed me to pull her up. Caught up in the collective good mood, Tuiren and Hector bounced around barking excitedly, and we both laughed. The Finns passed the good news on to the witches, who began clapping and singing and dancing for joy. Catching sight of Rhiannon shaking her head at them with a fond smile, we cantered over to the High Priestess. I expected Kam to dismount as soon as we stopped, but she stayed put, her arms comfortably around my waist.

"For a bunch of exhausted people, they sure have a lot of energy, don't they?" I said, watching Cinna dance back to Conall's horse and mount up behind him again.

"Sometimes all the refreshment we need is a reason to celebrate," Rhiannon said. "Why don't we camp here tonight?"

It was rather early in the day, but everyone had worked hard, both walking all morning and practicing mounts and dismounts for half the afternoon. Also, it seemed like a suitable spot to stop. We were on the outer edge of a rectangular clearing that was bordered on the other three sides by trees. In the center of the clearing was a pond that looked big enough for everyone to have a bath and small enough for me to heat the water up quickly and easily.

"*That* is a volcanic idea," I said. "What I'd really like to do is grab a shotgun and do some hunting." A flock of geese winged its way overhead, honking as they flew south.

"I, too, would rather hunt than ask the animals to sacrifice themselves for us," the High Priestess said. "But then again, is it ever a fair contest?"

I winked and said, "I guess that depends on who's doing the hunting."

It was good to hear her full, throaty laugh. Gods knew that none of the Ward people had many reasons for merriment since being forced out of their home. Still, they were as happy and optimistic as anybody could be in their situation.

We set up camp in the shelter of the trees, and our cavalcade began their assigned chores. The water elementalists got busy siphoning water from the pond, filtering the impurities out, and refilling all the canteens. Half of the earth elementalists moved out to the corners of the clearing, ostensibly to keep watch, but probably to meditate. They were welcome to it. Several of the witches grabbed their bows and headed in various directions looking for game. The Fitzpatrick brothers took their primitive bundle bows and headed out of the clearing and away from the trees, talking amongst themselves and gesturing at the sky. While I would have liked to go hunting with them, I was no good at archery, and guns were too noisy.

Witches and Finns worked together to unsaddle the horses, brushing the sweat from their coats and checking their feet and legs for warmth or swelling. Our mounts might mean the difference between life and death, so we checked them thoroughly every morning and every night. The healers tended to them if they even looked like they might be getting lame or sick. Kam helped me take care of Steel, combing his mane and tail while I gave his coat a good brushing. He was getting furrier by the day, and he'd catch a chill from all the sweat that built up under his saddle if it didn't dry quickly. The woven wool saddle pad helped, but the plucky little fellow was still working hard. I took an apple that I'd been saving from one of his saddlebags and cut it up, feeding them to him a slice at a time. He gobbled them down, then gave me an applesauce-slobber kiss.

"Blech," I said, shoving him away. "Go on, old man. You're off duty for the rest of the day. He tossed his head, thick black forelock falling over his eyes, and ambled off to drink from the pond.

"I'm no fan of riding, but he *is* really pretty," Kam said.

"Getting that horse is one of the best things that's ever happened to me," I said.

"So what's next on your agenda?" she asked.

"I was thinking about helping with supper," I said.

"You're not going to burn it, are you?" she teased.

"Oh, *very* funny," I said. "I'll have you know that I am an excellent cook."

"That's rare in a man."

"Are you kidding? Every one of these guys can cook. There aren't any women in Sanctuary."

"What! None?"

"No, and even if there were, we'd still cook and wash dishes afterward. Druids are pretty egalitarian as far as things like cooking and chores go."

Kam nodded. "As far as I can tell, the witches are, too."

We tried to help with supper and setting up camp, but the witches only let me light the cooking fires before shooing me away. The little kids were rolling around in the grass with Hector, so Kam left him there to play with them.

"Well, what now?" I wondered aloud.

"We could scout the forest," Kam suggested. "See how far east it goes."

"Good idea." We hiked across the clearing and headed into the woods. Whether by chance or shared thinking, we stopped talking until we were well within the trees and the noise of camp had faded behind us. Soon the only sounds to be heard were the rustling of tree branches in the wind, Tuiren snuffling about, and the autumn leaves crunching under our feet.

We walked for a good half hour before coming to the edge of the woods, both hanging back for several minutes before leaving the shelter of the trees. Tuiren sat quietly at Kam's feet, casually looking about with her tongue hanging out. If there were any bandits about – or anybody at all – the dog would have been noticed them. Even though she was relaxed, I dropped to one knee, brushed the fallen leaves aside, and placed my palm on the ground. Closing my eyes, I breathed deep of the chilly autumn air, feeling the quiet earth awaken to my touch. It took only a few minutes to develop a rapport with the unfamiliar territory, and I stretched out with earth magic to see how far I could *seek*.

"We seem to be alone," I said, rising and dusting my hands.

"Tuiren already knew that." Kam's tone was gently teasing.

"I know she did," I said, reaching out to pet the Irish wolfhound. "It's just easier to perform a *seeking* away from the others."

"Too much noise?"

"Something like that."

We turned and started back the way we'd come, more relaxed now that we knew there were no enemies hiding in the forest waiting to kill us in our sleep.

"It's nice walking with someone who knows when to talk and when not to," I said.

"Oh?" Kam arched a delicate eyebrow.

"Yeah. I mean, Seth and Duncan are good to scout with, but Dermot and Conall would have been yakking or bickering the entire way."

"I take it they haven't been out in the world much."

I snorted. "They haven't been out in the world at all."

"This journey must be really eye-opening for them," Kam said. "For all the Finns, I mean."

It had been pretty eye-opening for me, too. I'd guessed that the 'Ville was a decent-sized town, but now that I'd seen the very large raiding parties that had come after us, it had dawned on me that the bandit city could very well have a population of thousands. No wonder the druids of White Oak Grove were worried about being overrun.

"Don't be surprised if the Finns want to stay in Ward with the witches," Kam said, distracting me from grim imaginings of ten thousand brigands on the march.

"Stay with the witches?" Honestly, I hadn't thought about it, but now that she'd mentioned it, the stewpot of my mind decided to stir that idea around a bit and let it simmer awhile.

"It just seems logical," she said. "The Finns are strong but don't seem to have much of a home. The witches have a home, but not the strength to keep it."

"I'm pretty sure Shitozaki isn't going to go for that," I said.

"Why not? Wouldn't you all be safer if you were farther away from the grove?"

We'd be farther from the druids, but closer to the bandits. That proximity, however, would be less of an issue once all the elementalists became full druids in their twenty-first year. My gut told me that Connor Shitozaki would hate the idea anyway.

"I get this funny feeling that he'd rather live in a place populated entirely by druids," I said.

"When I was there, they did seem a bit…"

"Bigoted? Arrogant? Xenophobic?"

She laughed. "I was going to say *standoffish.*"

"That's putting it mildly," I said. "But there's no iron-clad precedent for it. While I was in the grove, I read some journals written by a woman during the Fracture—"

"During the Fracture?" Kam interrupted, her brown eyes wide.

"It's true. There's no mistaking it. She wrote detailed accounts of what it was like to live through the earthquakes, weather the storms, and run from the volcanic eruptions." I turned to her, laying a hand on her arm. "Did you know that there was a short ice age after all the volcanic activity?"

"No!" Kam exclaimed. "Wow. I would *love* to get my hands on a book like that."

"You like to read?"

"When it's cold, it's the best thing you can do in front of a roaring fire."

"Second best, maybe," I said, thinking of the times Angie and I had made love in front of the fire. It made my chest ache with longing.

"Is that right?" Kam's glance was flirtatious.

"Uhh…" I felt my face get hot. "Sorry, that just slipped out. I hope I didn't offend you."

"Don't worry about it." She chuckled. "So do you own a lot of books?"

"By most people's standards, we do. I've added a few dozen over the years." When I was a teenager, my favorite hobby had been risking my neck crawling through the ruins of old buildings. It started out as a way to get away from everyone, but after I found a few books in phenomenally good condition, it turned into a near-obsessive search for them.

"My folks have quite a collection," I said. "It's a good size, but nothing compared to the library of the grove."

"I'm surprised they even let you in the door," Kam said.

"They didn't. Padraig – Duncan's father – used to smuggle books out for me. I read as many as I could. It used to irritate

Angie sometimes."

"She didn't want you to read?"

"Our times together were brief and infrequent because of our training schedules," I said. "It wasn't an issue after we moved into our own house."

"I see."

"Anyway, Jayne Pierce – that's the author – wrote the story of how White Oak Grove was settled. And while they might think otherwise, the grove *wasn't* settled entirely by druids."

"Really."

"Jayne herself was not a druid. Her chosen was a druid, but she was a Buddhist. She also had an adopted son, who was something called 'Baptist,' but I don't know what that is."

"It's a Triune sect," Kam said, pressing her lips together like she was trying not to laugh.

"Are you sure about that?"

"Positive. There's a sect of Baptists in Harrisburg." She grinned. "It's probably the dominant religious sect in Jonesboro, but you never bothered to ask."

"Damn right I never bothered to ask," I grumbled.

"Speaking of bigoted..." Kam said, playfully bumping me with her shoulder.

"Yeah, yeah." She was right, but I had plenty of bad experiences to back up my prejudices. Mulling over it, I had to admit that no one in Jonesboro had abused me until that awkward business with Sarah. In addition, I had met plenty of Triune people who were both kind and generous, like the Hayworths and Missus Michaelson, the caravan boss' wife.

Kam said, "So what you're telling me is that the original grove was settled by a druid, a Buddhist, and a Triune?"

"Oh, no, there were lots of others. Witches, atheists, some people called 'Hindu' and others called 'Catholic'..."

Kam chuckled.

"So, even though the druid *ideals* prevailed – like the Nine Virtues, and cherishing knowledge and valuing scholarship, along with the way rituals are conducted – all those people with different beliefs learned to live and work together in peace."

"It's amazing how people can sometimes—" Kam started.

I never got to hear what she was going to say because Tuiren barked sharply at her and blocked her path. The Traveler girl frowned, looking apprehensive. Tuiren pressed against her legs, whining. I'd never seen the dog do anything so peculiar.

"I need to rest for a while," Kam said, easing herself down to the leaf-strewn ground. "Go on back to camp without me."

"What, and leave you here alone?" I squatted beside her.

She smiled, but it never touched her eyes. "I'll be fine."

Something was off about this situation, from the dog's behavior to Kam's insistence on being left alone.

"Please, Davis, go on without—" Her words cut off and her head was flung back as her whole body went rigid. She stopped breathing, and her eyes had rolled back in her head as she collapsed onto the forest floor.

"Kam!"

I reached out to touch her shoulder but was stopped by a low and menacing growl. Glancing to the right, I was treated to a view of Tuiren's gleaming fangs, mere inches from my face. The dog was as big as a pony and probably weighed as much as I did, and I had no desire to test the strength of her jaws. Like any sane person, I pulled my hand back – *slowly* – then dropped my eyes and hunched my shoulders to appear as non-threatening as possible until she stopped growling. I waited in that posture for a minute or two more, then glanced up to make sure that the Irish wolfhound had put her sharp teeth away. From the uncomfortable squatting position, I eased back to sit on the ground, where I stayed as still and quiet as possible.

Kam sat bolt upright, gasping. Relief flooded through me. Even though I didn't know what was going on, I *did* know she needed to breathe. Tuiren was a good protector, but even the best dog could be stupid at times, having only canine intelligence and instinct to guide it.

"Oh, good, you're—"

The words died in my throat when Kam turned her head and looked at me with glowing golden eyes that no human should ever possess. There was no recognition in them, and the expression on her face had become cold and haughty. I was nothing under the weight of that gaze, a mortal man who could be crushed as easily as I would crush a bug beneath my boot heel. As disturbed as I was at that point, my alarm only escalated when she started to speak in a voice that wasn't her own:

> *Son of Tara, heed my words –*
> *Though flesh be whole and blood unshed*
> *Though steel be sharp and fire's flame bright*
> *The lion will fall, struck by Zeus' hand,*
> *Unshielded from the eagle's strike.*
> *Beware the grey wraith, the spirit walker.*
> *Bargain well with the immortal and the dead.*

A chill raced up my spine, my scalp prickled, and the hair on the back of my neck stood on end. Stricken with near panic, a wave of hot sparks burst around me. I scrambled backwards, kicking up leaves and sticks from the forest floor. Running like hell would have been my next course of action if Kam hadn't fallen over unconscious. As it was, I stayed frozen for several minutes with my breath coming in harsh pants and my heart thundering in my chest.

Rational thought finally returned, and I carefully scooted close to her again, mindful of both the giant dog and the terrifying sun god that might choose to reveal itself in her eyes again. I bent over Kam to make sure a pulse still beat in her neck, then watched the slow rise and fall of her chest. I was no healer, but it looked like she'd had some kind of fit or seizure just prior to being gripped by some sort of evil magic.

After living most of my life in a mundane environment, I had no idea what kind of magic might have affected Kam in such a way. I'd only recently discovered that magic was a real and tangible force, so wild thoughts of other fantastic powers and beings raced through my mind. That magic could have been wrought by a wizard, or enchanter, or even the fae for all I knew. I cast a quick glance around, looking for toadstool rings. This area was fairly flat, and the fae lived under hills, but that didn't mean there weren't other nature spirits around.

The Irish wolfhound's unwavering gaze told me that I wouldn't be allowed to move the Traveler girl. The dog and I watched over her together for the next hour. I was tempted to leave and get help, but I was afraid that I'd come back to find her dead or gone. There may not have been any bandits around, but there were plenty of other predators – lions and tigers among them.

I wondered why no one had come looking for us. The sun was setting and the temperature had begun to drop. We'd been gone for almost two hours; you'd think the Finns might have gotten worried. Just when I started to think that maybe I *should* go for help, Tuiren whined and nudged her master's shoulder with her nose. Kam's eyes fluttered open. Thankfully, they were her usual dark brown color. Even though she was awake, I could tell she wasn't all there from her unfocused gaze.

"Are you all right?" I asked. Her dark brown eyes found mine, then widened dramatically. Kam sat bolt upright, throwing her arms around me. I tensed, ready to bolt, but I made myself stay put.

"Don't go!" she cried. "Please don't go!"

"I'm not going anywhere," I said. "I won't leave you."

She was shaking and had a death grip on my neck. While it wasn't choking me, the panic that had prompted such a reaction it was alarming. I'd never seen Kam afraid before and held her close in the hope that it would calm her down. Her rapid breathing slowed after a minute or two, giving way to big, shuddering breaths. Her arms began to relax, and she pulled away.

"I'm sorry," she said in a tremulous voice. "I didn't mean to startle you."

Startled wasn't the word for it. I'd been scared spitless, but I wasn't about to tell *her* that.

"It's all right," I lied. "I was just worried about you."

"I try not to let anyone see me like that."

"This has happened before?"

She nodded, hugging her knees to her chest. "Have you been cursed?" I asked, wondering if Rhiannon could unravel a curse.

Kam made a noise that was half laugh, half sob. "Sometimes it feels that way."

"So it's not a curse?" I asked. "Or an evil spell?"

"No."

I was disheartened by this news but tried not to show it.

"It's not as bad as it seems," Kam said.

Do you even know what you looked like? I nearly blurted but somehow managed to hold my tongue. It took a few seconds, but I finally thought of something appropriate to say.

"Does this happen a lot?"

"No. Usually just a few times a year."

Being incapacitated like that was nothing to take lightly. On one hand, I admired her courage and determination to Travel in spite of this affliction. On the other hand, it was dangerous and foolhardy, if she only had a few seconds' warning before having a fit. If a stranger had seen those glowing eyes, he'd have shot her on impulse. Even if he had run away instead – as I had nearly done – she'd been unconscious for an hour afterward, rendered completely vulnerable.

Unless the magic protected her somehow. I looked at Tuiren, wondering if perhaps the big dog's warning growl had been to protect me also. I shoved the thought away.

"Look, I'm not one to tell other people how to live their lives…" I began.

"Then don't," Kam said. "I've heard it all before."

"Isn't it kind of dangerous? Traveling alone?"

"I'm not alone. I have Tuiren," she said, rising and dusting off the seat of her pants. She wobbled unsteadily, and I grabbed her elbow. She quickly found her balance, and I let go. I had a feeling that she was upset with me staying and watching over her, but what else was I supposed to do? Even if I'd known about the convulsions ahead of time, I still wouldn't have been able to leave. I'd never have left her alone anywhere, ever.

"What if it happens when you're attacked?"

"It doesn't."

Her tone had a note of finality, as though she had a rock-solid assurance of the fact. I stood there a moment, debating whether to pursue the matter further and decided against it. While we were friends, every Traveler had boundaries that were not to be crossed. This was Kam's private business, and I had no right to meddle in her affairs. I hated it when people tried to tell me what I couldn't do; clearly, she felt the same. Hypocrisy in the guise of caring was still hypocrisy, so I let the matter drop.

"Do you feel up to walking back?" I asked, not knowing what else to say. Kam shook her head and just stood there with her head bowed, staring at nothing, and holding onto Tuiren's shoulder for support. Something was going on with her, but after what I'd just experienced, I was willing to wait. As troubled as I was over it, it had to be far worse for her. Finally, she turned and looked at me, meeting my eyes with what seemed to be a tremendous effort.

"I don't share this aspect of myself with outsiders," she began. Her use of the term "outsider" was like a slap in the face. It made me take a step back, both mentally and physically. The word held extremely painful memories for me, and I couldn't help the reaction. Only the fact that I respected her as a friend and fellow Traveler kept me in place.

"I don't mean that in a bad way," Kam said, noticing the look on my face. "I just mean people outside my... tribe."

That didn't make it sound any better to me. As a Traveler, she should know better – all Travelers were outsiders, no matter where they went, even in their own places of origin.

"I'm sorry," she said. "I know that's insulting, but I don't know how to say it any other way. I need to tell you something about what just happened, but I'm afraid of how you'll react."

I wasn't in the habit of uttering meaningless platitudes or reassurances about how I would or would not react – especially not after someone had insulted me. It was too close to lying outright, and I valued honesty. So I just stood there and waited.

Kam paused and took a deep breath. "I have visions."

"I beg your pardon?" That was definitely not what I had expected to hear.

"I see the future. And sometimes I give prophecies."

I stared at the Traveler girl in disbelief.

"What you saw... what just happened to me... is a part of my family heritage, just like elemental magic is part of your druid heritage. My ancestors moved to the United States from Greece generations ago, but they continued to worship the old gods – the Gods of Olympus," Kam explained.

"Oh," I said, no longer feeling like the earth was about to drop out from under my feet. This was familiar territory. This I could handle.

"Seth worships the Olympians, too," I said.

She gave me a sad smile. "It's not quite the same. Druids may worship the old gods, but it's within a different context, for we are Hellenismos." It seemed like a subtle distinction to me, but I stayed quiet and let her continue.

"My family has carried on all the old traditions, celebrating the festivals, making sacrifices to the gods, practicing divination…" She paused. "One of my ancestors foretold the coming of the Fracture. That's how we survived – because we were *ready*."

"That's… remarkable."

"She also predicted that after the Fracture, Apollo's oracle – what used to be called the Oracle at Delphi – would be reborn and that her arrival would be heralded by an earthquake that would crack the floor of the temple but not destroy it."

"Your family has a *temple*?"

She nodded. "My great-great-great-grandfather was a builder. He studied the building methods of the ancient Greeks, and made a smaller-scale model of the Temple of Apollo at Delphi."

"And nobody noticed?"

"Of course people noticed. Back before the Fracture, no one had any privacy at all. He was old by the time he started the actual construction, so people just thought he was crazy. His sons told all their neighbors that they were building a temple to appease a senile old man, so nobody questioned it further."

It was a stroke of genius. I'd read enough pre-Fracture books to know that her ancestors never would have had a moment's peace if their neighbors had thought they were building a functional temple for worshiping the Greek gods of antiquity.

"Somehow the temple stayed standing throughout all the upheaval as the old world died," Kam continued. "It stayed in one piece until the day I was born. On the Seventh of February, as I was entering the world, the whole town shook from the most devastating earthquake since the Fracture. When I was took my first breaths, cracks appeared in the temple floor, running deep into the ground." She paused, taking a deep breath.

"I was dedicated to Apollo and given into his service that very day. From now until the day I die, or until my successor is ready, I am the Priestess of Apollo, the Oracle at Delphi reborn."

The fact that I did not question her claim spoke volumes about the kinds of experiences I'd had since leaving Jonesboro with Angie. It was still a lot to wrap my mind around, but I caught on quickly.

"So you just saw the future?"

"Yes. I enter a trance state beforehand," she said. "Usually it only happens after lengthy preparation, when I'm sitting in the temple." She paused. "It's only lately that it's been unpredictable."

"Is that how you knew your sister and her husband were in trouble in Hardy?"

"Yes."

"Are you ever wrong?"

She bit her lips, and for a moment I thought she might cry. After blinking her eyes rapidly a few times, she shook her head.

"Never," Kam said.

"That gives you quite an advantage."

"An advantage?"

"Sure. If you can see when bad things are about to happen, you can work to avoid them."

She shook her head. "It doesn't work that way. The future cannot be changed. The Fates make sure of it."

"I don't believe in fate."

She pressed her lips together. "I have to apologize, Davis, for misleading you."

"That's okay." I doubted she'd been dishonest about anything important. She couldn't very well go around telling everybody that she could see the future. There were too many unscrupulous people in the world who would take advantage of her gift for their own personal gain.

"No, it is *not* okay!" she snapped. "I'm not a liar, and I especially don't lie to people I care about!"

"I just figured it was related to being an oracle," I said. "So, yeah, it's okay."

She looked down at her feet. "I didn't Travel all this way on a whim. I didn't just get up one morning and decide to pay you and Angie a visit. I had a vision of you being beaten and killed that was more vivid and more *real* than any other." She paused, meeting my eyes again. "I'm sorry I didn't get there sooner, Davis. I could have saved you so much suffering."

"Harrisburg *is* a long way from White Oak Grove," I said.

"I would have had plenty of time if my family hadn't tried to keep me from going," she said. "I had the visions over and over again. I watched you die a dozen different ways." Kam rubbed her eyes as if trying to erase the memories. "I'm only supposed to receive visions once a month because it takes so much out of me.

Even though foretelling so much was exhausting, but I couldn't stay away from the temple for fear that I'd miss something."

"But we were little more than strangers," I said.

"That's what I kept telling myself," she replied. "All my life, I never once questioned my position as Oracle, or even thought about deviating from my destiny – until I met you."

I caught myself rubbing the oath mark, feeling the scar warm and tingle with magic.

"I'd never journeyed so far from home before because I had to go back for the ritual and give the prophecy every month," Kam continued. "I never felt alone, until I saw the way you were with Angie. It made me wonder how things would be if..." She swallowed hard. "If I'd met you first."

My stomach sank.

"But... being a priestess of Apollo means I belong to *Apollo,*" Kam said. "As long as I am his Oracle, there can be no one else."

The muscles in my shoulders relaxed when I realized she wasn't going to profess her undying love. While I had thought about Kam from time to time, I'd never regretted accepting Angie's invitation to accompany her, to fight by her side, to be her chosen.

"So your family preferred that you stay home instead of trying to warn me," I said, relaxing. "Honestly, I can't say I blame them." I suspected that her sister had relayed to the rest of the family the hours and hours that Kam and I had spent together, walking and talking. It didn't take a genius to figure out that the Stone tribe didn't want their long-awaited and precious oracle to go running off into the wilderness to find a man she barely knew.

Her dark eyes flashed with anger. "It doesn't matter what anyone else *prefers*. I am the Oracle of Apollo and a grown woman. I should be allowed to make my own decisions!"

I nodded. I was the last person to criticize anyone for wanting that. "So what happened?"

"My family finally let me leave because they were afraid that overusing the gift was going to kill me. And even if it didn't, going without food and sleep surely would have." Her face fell. "And after everything I've been through, it doesn't even matter!"

"What do you mean?" I asked, with absolute certainty that I knew *exactly* what she meant.

"I'm sorry, Davis. The vision I just had was about *you*."

Of course.

I sighed.

Kam Stone's pronouncement probably should have elicited a more dramatic response from me, or given rise to trepidation at least, but after looking death in the face a dozen times in the last two years, I really wasn't all that apprehensive. Granted, I had no idea what any of it meant, surely I could figure it out with her help.

"We should head back to camp," I said.

"I'm so sorry, Davis," Kam whispered.

"Why are you apologizing? Am I going to die because of you?"

"No, but—"

"Then you don't have anything to apologize for." I sounded grumpier than I should have, for she was clearly distraught. I started walking, leaving her no option but to keep up or be left behind.

"I feel guilty anyway. People aren't supposed to hear what is foretold about them."

"Then who listens to your prophecies?"

"The tribal elders," she said. "I used to have a close friend who stayed with me and acted as my attendant, but after hearing one of my prophecies, she left and refused to come back."

"What happened to her?"

"She died by her own hand."

I stopped and turned around. "She *killed* herself?! Quakes, Kam, what did you see?"

"I saw her in my place as the oracle, but everything she said was a lie."

"So it didn't come true."

"What?"

"If she's dead, Kam, then the prophecy about her wasn't true," I said. "Kind of like how you saw me die a dozen times."

"And then some," she said, sounding depressed.

"And yet I'm still here."

"I don't think that's going to happen this time."

"What's different this time?" I said.

"You *heard* the prophecy."

"Wouldn't that make it *less* likely to come true?" I asked, as though a prophecy from a god was the equivalent of hearing someone's birthday wish after they'd blown out the candles.

"You don't understand," she insisted. "My attendant didn't hear the one about becoming a false oracle. She heard the one about her suicide."

I still wasn't convinced.

"Did you see her do it?"

"No!" Kam stumbled over a root; I stopped and caught her arm to steady her, then looked her in the eye.

"Then how do you know she wasn't murdered?" I asked.

"Why would anybody do that?"

"Because you saw her as a lying oracle and somebody wanted to make sure it didn't happen."

Kam stared at me. "I had no idea you were so cynical."

"One man's cynicism is another man's realism."

"Oh, and a pessimist, too?"

"You're the one foretelling my doom."

"This is *not* funny, Davis!" Kam stomped her foot, reminding me of Angie, and I noticed that I was still holding her arm. Drawing my hand away, I nodded in the direction of the camp.

"Come on," I said. "It's getting dark."

"I don't want to talk about this around other people," she said, sounding miserable.

"We can talk on the way. And it would help if you told me what you *saw* because what you *said* didn't make much sense."

"Was it poetic?"

"More like a riddle."

"Oh." She swallowed. "If it's a riddle, you're supposed to figure it out."

She could tell me I was going to die, but not give me any details. Nice.

"Don't look at me that way," Kam said. "I'm not supposed to tell you anything at all."

"Then why did you?"

"Because seeing you alive after watching you get hit by a lightning bolt was such a shock!"

That explained the part about being *struck by Zeus' hand.*

"No pun intended, I'm sure."

Kam clapped her hands over her mouth.

142

I started walking again, and my brain immediately tackled the prophetic riddle. There was no doubt that *Son of Tara* was a reference to my Celtic hearth culture, which had originated on the other side of the world. Tara was where the gods lived after coming to Ireland.

Zeus' weapon of choice was a thunderbolt – lightning – which could kill me without spilling a drop of blood, and from which neither my sword nor elemental fire would shield me. That would make me the lion – maybe because I was born under the sign of Leo?

I had no idea what the *eagle's strike* or the *grey wraith* might be. They didn't seem terribly important anyway. The obvious explanation for the prophecy was meant that Sebrina would find out I was alive and try to kill me again.

It wasn't entirely unexpected.

I stopped and looked back at Kam, who was fighting tears.

"Will it be soon?"

"I think so."

"Can you at least tell me if I'll see Angie again?"

She shook her head and looked away.

How could she tell me I was going to die and then not tell me if I'd see the one person who was most important to me before it happened? Heat began to radiate off my skin, and I opened my mouth to yell at her, but then I noticed how she was shaking.

Tuiren barked sharply, and Kam's knees buckled. Barely managing to catch her before she fell, I remembered that giving a prophecy took a physical toll. I was still angry, but I couldn't leave her alone like this. Scooping her up, I carried her back to the camp, glad that the long hours of calisthenics and swordplay had made my arms and back strong. The earth gave me aid, smoothing my path, but even so, it was quite a hike.

When we exited the forest, we were surrounded by concerned people all demanding to know what had happened. Rhiannon shooed them all away, knowing that the earth healers could handle this.

"She tripped and hit her head," I said, handing the Traveler girl over to Seth, who took her gingerly. He led the way to where they'd placed our belongings and laid Kam on her blanket. I worked my aching shoulders and back, stretching out the tight muscles.

Duncan ran gentle fingers over her scalp, feeling for a knot, then looked at me with a slight frown. Kam wasn't injured, and he could tell. I gave him the barest shake of my head, and he responded with a nod that was hardly more than a tuck of the chin.

"She will be well by morning," the earth druid pronounced after laying his hand on her forehead for a few moments. I draped another blanket over her, and Tuiren curled up by her mistress, dark eyes watchful. Lying at her feet, even boisterous Hector was subdued.

"Sorry, man," Conall said. "If we'd thought something was wrong, we'd have come to check on you."

"We've been gone for hours!" I said, keeping my voice down so as not to waken Kam. "Where were you?"

They exchanged guilty looks.

"We were giving you privacy," Seth said delicately.

"Privacy? For what?"

"When you left with Kam, we rather thought you might be—"

"We were hoping you'd get laid," Dermot interrupted. "You've been a little tense lately."

"He's always a little tense," said Conall.

"Exactly," said Dermot.

Duncan snorted.

They'd thought I was off having a romantic interlude with Kam when in reality she was foretelling my death. I started to laugh. I couldn't help it.

"So… you're not mad?" asked Dermot.

"No, I'm not mad," I said. "How could I be mad with volcanic friends like you?" I threw my arms over his and Conall's shoulders. "Let's go get some supper."

When night had fallen and everyone else was settled, I took a walk around the camp. Around, and around, and around. After the third or fourth, or maybe even the fifth time, Seth joined me.

"You should be sleeping," I said.

"So should you."

"I don't think I can."

"Does your restlessness have anything to do with what happened with Kam in the woods?"

I stopped and looked at him. "She told you?"

"No, she's still asleep."

I started walking again.

"You want to talk about it?" he asked.

"I'm not sure I should."

"Might make you feel better."

"It might, but is it right to divulge someone else's private business, just to make myself feel better?" I sighed heavily.

"That is a predicament." He paused. "Are there aspects that would not violate Kam's privacy?"

I considered. "Yes."

"Perhaps you could share those parts."

"Sometimes in the near future, I'm going to be struck by lightning and killed."

Seth stopped in his tracks. "I rather think that trumps anyone's right to privacy!" he said. "What happened?"

"What do you know about Apollo and the Oracle at Delphi?"

"One legend has it that Apollo himself led a group of people from Crete to the location where he wanted his shrine to be built. Another legend says a goat herder observed one of his goats behaving strangely near some cracks in the earth, and when he went near it, he experienced the presence of Apollo and began having visions."

"Visions of the future?" I asked.

"Yes, but also the past," Seth said. "As the years went on, priests and priestesses were chosen to serve at the temple, and eventually it became just the priestesses who were chosen to act as oracles." He gave me a funny look. "This is not something I expected to be on your mind."

"That makes two of us."

His eyebrows went up. "*Kam Stone* is a priestess of *Apollo*?"

"Not just *a* priestess. *The* priestess."

He whistled. "I never thought I'd ever meet a Pythia."

"A what?"

"A Pythia. It's the official title of Apollo's oracle. Or was."

"Apparently it is again," I said. "She said she was *the* oracle."

Seth nodded. "And as such, she belongs to Apollo and no one else," he said. "It is just as well that you have no romantic intentions towards her."

"Yeah, well, I'm not sure I'd want to be with someone who has foreseen my death over a dozen times."

"I cannot fault you for that. What was the prophecy, exactly?"

I told him, and then he had me repeat it five or six more times.

"I understand most of it," I said. "I think I'm the lion, and being 'struck by Zeus' hand' seems to mean lightning."

"The 'eagle's strike' refers to Zeus as well. He often took the form of an eagle when visiting mortals." He paused. "The part about bargaining might have something to do with Charon, the ferryman."

"The ferryman?"

"Charon takes the dead spirits across the River Styx, to the underworld." Seth paused. "I don't think he would take you, though. You don't have any money."

"Volcanic. What about the 'grey wraith'?"

"I'm not sure..." Seth rubbed his beard thoughtfully, reminding me of Padraig. "I suppose it could be a shaman."

"A spirit healer?"

"A shaman is more than a spirit healer. It is said that not only do they speak with spirits, but also have the ability to travel through the spirit realms." He paused. "Of course, it could also mean a necromancer. They can talk to spirits, too."

"I wonder if that means I'll talk to him before I'm dead, or after?"

Seth frowned. "That isn't funny."

"Do you see me laughing?"

He shook his head. We started walking again, making another complete circuit around the camp before speaking again.

"I do not think we should share this with anyone else," Seth said.

"Agreed."

Chapter 8 – Slow Burn

Freedom is never really won.
You earn it and win it in every generation.
~ Coretta Scott King ~

Kam Stone left the next day.

I assumed it was because of the prophecy and couldn't blame her. What do you say to somebody after you've foretold their death? What do you do when a friend is going to die and you can't do anything about it?

You leave so you don't have to witness it, apparently.

I let her go without argument, but I couldn't help watching her disappear into the distance with her loyal Tuiren and the rambunctious Hector. It was better for us to be apart – to avoid temptation if nothing else. I'd be lying if I said I wasn't tempted, especially after she'd admitted that meeting me had made her question her fate in life.

Kam was a priestess dedicated to Apollo – *a god* – chosen by him through a prediction decades before she'd been born. Knowing the capricious and sometimes jealous nature of gods, it wouldn't have surprised me to learn that Apollo had sent her all those visions of me dying to convince her that I was not worth abandoning her duty.

I was devoted to Angie, bound to her by oath and by choice. To remind myself of it, I had only to rub my left palm and feel the magic there. It didn't matter if I died before seeing Angie again or not; I would remain true to her.

We druids take our oaths seriously.

There was nothing I could do about the future, so I tried to focus on the present. This was made slightly more difficult by Seth's constant presence. It was because an air shield could block a lightning strike, but it was highly unlikely that any of our spirit elementalists would intentionally hit me with a spirit bolt. That left the possibility of accidents, of course, but I'd go crazy if I started worrying about things like that.

While Seth had initially been my shadow in the early months with Shitozaki, he'd started giving me more space since my dramatic dive into the volcano. That changed after telling him about the prophecy, but since he was a member of my pentacle and had a history of being stuck to my ass, I don't think anyone noticed his renewed hovering but me.

Kam had been gone a week, we were getting close to Ward, and we still hadn't come across any bandits. There was some speculation that we'd come so far north of the 'Ville that our enemy had given up on their pursuit. I wasn't so sure about that; it felt more like the calm before the storm. My gut told me that the enemy was biding his time, rounding up more people, horses, guns, and ammunition before coming to finish us off once and for all. Seth once voiced the opinion that they could very well be waiting in Ward for our arrival. We discussed the various possibilities with Rhiannon, but we kept our speculations to ourselves. There was no need to alarm anyone else over conjecture.

We were still carrying out the plan of walking with the horses in the morning and riding double in the afternoons. I made everybody practice discharging their passengers and getting into combat formations at least once a day. Steel was not a large horse so I didn't ride double often, but occasionally I was called upon to put a child on the back of my saddle. I gave them strict instructions each time, reminding them of what they were supposed to do – dismount on the off side and seek cover or their mothers, and preferably both. The children all happily agreed, and usually spent the rest of the day chattering endlessly about puppies, kittens, ponies, flowers, the sky, clouds, their friends, and when they ran out of things to talk about, they asked a million questions. I was not accustomed to the company of children, and so the constant stream of talk tended to annoy me. So far, I had managed to keep this fact to myself.

Seth, on the other hand, seemed quite pleased to be traveling with the coven, due in no small part to sharing his horse (and his bed) with a different witch every night. While the witches had been through a difficult time, they seemed to find comfort in the Finns' company. After having been sequestered with Shitozaki with no female company whatsoever for years, the Finns were delighted to accept their invitations. I was the odd man out, so our snail's pace bothered no one but me.

I admit to being envious. Not that I wanted a witch in my bed; I could have had one. Several had asked, I had politely declined, and eventually, they quit asking. It was Angie that I missed, that I wanted, and that I dreamed of every single night. Prior to meeting up with the coven, I had dreamed of her occasionally but had been too tired to dream at all most of the time. Now we were traveling at a slow and easy pace, and we were surrounded by women. And so my dreams had increased, both in frequency and intensity. It was making me irritable.

Sullen and angry, elemental fire pulsed around the edges of my vision. I wanted to let it out, as though destroying something would calm the tumult of anger and resentment inside. It was a familiar feeling from the past, one that had dogged me throughout childhood and adolescence when things weren't going my way. My father had always lectured me on keeping my temper and controlling my emotions. My mother had often sent me outside to cut firewood.

We had no need of firewood, but I needed to move, to fight... or at least tear something up. When the caravan had set up camp for the night, Seth was the first thing I found.

"You okay?" he asked, eyeing me cautiously.

"I need to blow off some steam."

His expression brightened, and he grabbed his sword belt and buckled it on, following me a small distance outside the camp. Dermot followed us, munching on an apple.

"With elements, or without?" Seth asked.

"You with, me without."

He raised an eyebrow. "You sure?"

"You don't want him to burn you, do you?" Dermot said.

"Not particularly." Seth's tone was dry.

"Practicing with sharpened steel is risky enough," I said. "You can block with air." Shielded by his element, Seth would be safe from any blows I might manage to get past his guard.

"You could use earth."

"I just want to hit something, okay?"

"Very well."

We stood apart from one another, swords at the ready. Dermot untied a bandanna from his neck and let it dangle from his hand between us.

"On my mark," he said. "Three, two, one – *go!*" He jerked the bandanna away, hopping backwards on one foot.

Seth and I hadn't sparred since leaving Sanctuary. We had been fighting or running from bandits for weeks, and there had been no time for practice. We charged at each other, swords meeting with a crash of metal. He parried my strike with his two-handed broadsword and then brought it around again; I ducked so I could keep my head. I had forgotten how fast he was with the huge weapon. The air rang with the clash of bright steel as we traded blows. He came at me with that infamous overhand slash, but I threw up a guard and rolled away. I regained my feet and jammed a backhand thrust to his midsection, just missing by inches. I could feel the point of my blade slide across the invisible wall of air and swing away from his body. I reversed the blade, again ducking a cut that should have separated my arm from my shoulder, and spun about. The edge of my sword hit the side of his neck with a crack and bounced off.

"Whoa!" Seth cried, grabbing his neck.

"Are you hurt?"

"No."

"*Good,*" I said and lunged at him again. We fought for several minutes more, until we were both grunting with effort. Sweat poured down my face and neck, and my arms trembled with fatigue.

"Break!" called Dermot, waving his bandanna.

I wasn't ready to quit, but I backed away and sheathed my sword. "Want to go next?" I asked the water elementalist.

"*I* don't have an air shield," he said, shaking his head and giving me a look that said I was insane for even suggesting such a thing.

"So you can work with elements," Seth suggested.

I hesitated. I wasn't concerned about using earth against anyone, but playing with fire could get someone seriously hurt.

"After all, we now have an audience." Seth winked. I glanced at the edge of the camp and noted that half the coven and most of the Finns had turned out to watch us practice. Wonderful.

"Fine."

"Only if we go by the lake," said Dermot.

"Only if you promise not to drown me," I replied. We walked the short distance to the lake, and Dermot took off his boots, rolled up his pant legs, and walked out into the water.

"You're going to freeze to death in there."

"I'm stronger in the water. The same as you are when touching the earth."

"You need to be stronger?"

"I'm going up against you, aren't I?"

As powerful as my fire magic was, I couldn't argue with that. Seth gave us the signal to go, and I waited for Dermot to attack. He also waited for me to attack. I snorted and tossed off a few fire darts at him.

"Ow! Ow, ow, ow!" He danced around, slapping at the embers until a rough wave splashed over him and soaked him from head to toe. His face turned red when some of the witches giggled. There was a determined look in his eyes, and two snakelike projections shot out of the water and headed straight for me. I called to the fire and blasted each of them to steam with small fireballs. Next, he called four tendrils of water, and I turned each of them to steam as well.

"Come on, Dermot, you can do better than that," Conall called. "Kick his ass!"

Dermot's hazel-green eyes narrowed. The surface of the lake churned angrily, bubbling and hissing. I took an involuntary step backward, drew my sword, and sent fire racing along its length. Over a dozen water serpents thrust into the sky, writhing against the stark backdrop before focusing in on me. Breathing hard, Dermot sent all of them at me at once.

I dodged the first one, slashed the second with my flaming sword, then raised my left hand and sent out a stream of fire that cut through several of the watery arms, causing their remains to splash down on our heads. They only lengthened and attacked me again, growing from the body of the lake. I held my ground as they came at me, whipping and lashing. Fireball after fireball, I blasted one after another into steam. I was just finishing off the last one when something cold and wet wrapped around my ankle and yanked me into the air. I let out a wild yell, and fire went everywhere.

Dermot also hollered. I caught a glimpse of him swatting at embers again, but his creation held me tight. He immediately called to the water again, and his water snakes came at me with a vengeance. Hanging upside down, I shot fire bolts and fireballs, but still the cold, slimy things kept coming. After several minutes there were fewer and fewer of them. I was still hurling an abundance of elemental fire and accidentally vaporized the tendril that held me in the air. I fell with a surprised yell and a loud splash.

Dermot walked over and gave me a hand up. "There's no way I could beat you."

"You could always drown him," Conall said helpfully.

He grinned. "Yes, but he asked me not to."

Seth approached. "You're not even close to being out, are you?"

"No." Truth was, I felt just as full of fire as when we started.

"Good," said a voice behind me.

Duncan.

Inwardly I groaned, but outwardly... well, outwardly I groaned, too.

"You need the practice."

"I don't really feel like meditating right now."

"Very well," he said and knocked me off my feet. Knowing I was in trouble, I rolled away from the churning earth, tossing little fire darts at Duncan in an attempt to distract him. He dodged them, and that second or two gave me the opportunity to touch the earth. He had already claimed it for what felt like miles in all directions. I grabbed the piece under his feet and thrust it upward to throw him back. At least, it was *supposed* to throw him back. He merely stepped backward onto another piece of earth and gave me a reproving look for being dumb enough to try that trick. He took back control of all the earth in the area, ripped open a hole under my feet, and covered it over as I dropped to the bottom.

I sat in my hole and sighed. I was tired, but most of my bad mood had been sweated away. So I sat in my little hole, called a flame, and tried to quiet my thoughts. Bare seconds later, Duncan ripped back the earth over my head.

"Davis!" he shouted. I frowned at the panicked look on his face.

"What?"

Seeing me sitting with the flickering flame, his worried look turned to one of disgust.

"*Now* you meditate," he grumbled, throwing the blanket of earth back over me.

When I finished my meditation (which admittedly was not very long by Duncan's standards), I climbed out of the hollow space in the ground. There was no sign of my brief and embarrassing battle with Duncan. With the exception of my hole, he must have repaired the damage to the earth. Like a *good* earth druid, I thought grumpily and proceeded to replace the earth where I had been sitting. Someone had left my pack, along with a bar of soap.

Very funny.

I grabbed the soap and headed to the lake. Stripping to the skin, I stuck a toe in the water; it was ice cold. There was no way I was jumping into that. Kneeling on the bank, I thrust my fist into the chill water and called fire. No fire came, of course, but the temperature rose. I stepped into the warm spot, and let the heat suffuse through my body and into the water.

I wondered exactly how much magic I would have to expend to reach my limit. I wondered if I could warm up the whole lake. Not hot; I didn't want to kill the fish. Just… warm. I lathered up with the soap, scrubbing the dirt out of my hair. Everyone kept as clean as they could on the trip, but with the days growing shorter and the temperature steadily dropping, no one wanted to take their clothes off for long – unless they were getting into their blankets with a warm and willing partner, of course. I finished bathing and dried myself with a burst of heat, then went to find something to eat.

Ahearn, Weylin, Cinna, Conall, Dermot, and twins Riordan and Tiernan were engaged in an animated discussion that ceased abruptly when I approached.

"What?"

"Nothing," said Conall.

"That definitely means it's something," I said, ladling venison stew into a bowl. It was especially true if Weylin and the twins were involved, not to mention Dermot.

"You're right," he said. "It isn't nothing, but it is a subject that you've made clear isn't open for debate."

"Still cooking up plans for attacking the 'Ville, eh?" I asked.

"You don't think it's a good idea?" asked Ahearn.

"Do you?"

"Of course. If we eliminate the enemy, we eliminate the threat."

His use of *we* caught my attention, as did the nods of agreement from the other witches present. I wondered if Rhiannon knew how they felt but replied as I had before.

"While wiping out the bandits would definitely solve a problem, I think it's a bigger job than we're equipped to handle."

"From what I've seen of your magic, I can't imagine anyone standing up to you," said Ahearn. Cinna nodded agreement.

"I'm also a druid," I said.

"You're *all* druids," said Weylin.

We actually had two druids and twenty-seven elementalists, but a discussion of semantics was not something I had any interest in today. To my surprise, Conall proceeded to explain the difference between a druid and an elementalist. It was far more informative and educational than I could have done. In fact, he explained it better than anyone else I'd ever heard, and this time I actually understood the finer details. Conall's altered state was cruel on any given day, but somehow hearing him teach witches about druids made it seem worse.

"So everybody but Davis and Duncan might run out of magic in a fight?" Weylin asked with a frown of concern.

"I used over half my magic dueling with Davis," said Dermot.

"People usually get their full druid magic at age twenty-one," Conall said.

"Some of you have quite a while before that happens," Ahearn said.

"Unfortunately," Dermot said with a frown.

"Even so, I doubt there is anything we can't handle, given enough guns and ammunition," Conall said.

"I don't know about that," I said.

"We've done fine so far."

"A lot of that has been sheer luck," I said.

"Come on, Davis," Conall said, rolling his eyes.

"He might have a point," said Seth, joining us.

I gave him a look that said, *A little support, please?*

"I'm not saying we should go on Conall's suicide mission, and I still don't agree with attacking the 'Ville," he hastened to add. "But perhaps you should consider the possibility that we're all still alive and in one piece because of superior leadership and combat ability."

Conall nodded, and I didn't know whether to be grateful or scared that he and Seth were in accord about something.

"I don't think you've come close to your limits with fire magic," Seth continued, thinking aloud.

"That may be true, but I'd rather not test my limits standing in the heart of the 'Ville surrounded by people who want to kill me."

"Also a good point."

"Speaking as someone who lives in the shadow of said bandit city, it would be a blessing to have them gone, once and for all," said Riordan.

Tiernan nodded. "They're nothing but a plague and a nuisance," he said. "They've been that way since the Fracture, and it's only gotten worse."

"You can't protect us forever," said Cinna, speaking for the first time. She gave Conall a worried look, and he squeezed her hand. Was the auburn-haired witch the reason he'd brought up attacking the 'Ville again? Had he actually *chosen* Cinna even though they'd only known each other for a couple of weeks? Was he thinking of staying with the coven or planning to bring her home with us?

"Cinna is right," said Seth, drawing my attention back to the debate. "We can't stay with the coven forever. Even if we could, eventually the bandits will come after us with everything they have."

"And leave their city undefended?" Conall shook his head.

As well-armed and numerous as the raiding parties have been, it seemed obvious to me that not only would the bandit city be defended by their entire fighting force, but that they would have a huge arsenal at their disposal with which to wage war. It would be much better if they were forced to come to us, and I said so.

"Agreed," Seth said. "That is why it's preferable to fight them away from their base of operations."

"I'd rather not fight them at all," I said. "I'm not sure we could defeat them even if we had all the magic-users in the grove." If Sebrina Silvermist had believed her population of experienced druids could resist a bandit invasion, she would not have made a treaty with them.

"Everything is possible with magic," Cinna said.

"Not everything," Conall replied.

*　*　*

I scouted alone the next day. Seth and Duncan didn't like it, but they gave me the space I needed. I was frustrated at our slow pace and constantly worried about being attacked with no way to spend the energy and vent my anger – until I found sign of what appeared to be a bandit patrol, that is.

Dismounting to study the ground, I noted they were headed south, towards the 'Ville. The tracks were fresh. Estimating there to have been forty or fifty raiders, alarm shot through me as I become aware of how close they had gotten to the caravan of witches and druids. I surmised that the group was either a patrol that had spied us out and was returning to the 'Ville to report on our location, or it was a random posse hoping to get in good with them or make a trade for information on our location.

Either way, I couldn't allow that to happen. I was not going to stay stuck out here in the middle of nowhere and do nothing while the enemy tracked and hunted us like prey. There was no time to go back to let the Finns know my plans, or I'd lose any chance of catching up to them.

It took me all day, and the sun was setting when I spotted the raid group, towards a home they'd never see again. The bandits were slumped in their saddles as if they'd been riding hard all day long, their long black shadows stretched across the grassland. Dismounting, I jogged up behind the group until I was close enough to see the whites of their eyes – if they'd been facing me, that is – and sent a five-foot wall of fire streaking across the dry, brittle grass to encircle them. The alarmed shouts of men and women combined with the frightened whinnies of their mounts as they milled about looking for an escape. The shouts changed to screams as I dropped the earth down a couple of feet. I didn't really want to hurt the horses, so I opened a gap in the flames wide enough for one horse to exit at a time. The first horse to jump out of the sunken circle carried his rider about thirty feet, a distance I imagined was far enough to make him heave a sigh of relief at making his escape. His relief was short-lived, for he didn't survive the fireball that knocked him off his galloping horse.

Two other horses had cleared the ring of fire, so I launched two more fireballs in quick succession, taking out their riders as well. The remaining bandits in the ring began to fire shots in random directions, but they weren't shooting at me yet, so I ignored them. They'd be less likely to shoot if they were fighting each other to get out, so I opened up another gap in the firewall. Seconds later, a horse leapt out from each opening, followed rapidly by two more. I tossed fireballs at the lead riders and then fired off a couple of firebolts, twin arrows of fire that would have allowed them to target me if they hadn't been so desperate to get out of the pit that had sunk just a little bit lower.

After a brief struggle and several gunshots, four horses with riders emerged from the pit, while two riderless animals made their escape. Firebolts turned the four into flaming, screaming demons that were rapidly ejected from their mounts. I tossed little fireballs at the galloping horses before they got too far, herding them back toward the northeast and away from the 'Ville. The people remaining in the pit either couldn't see what was happening to their comrades or didn't care. Group after group dared breach the ring of fire, and by the time the sun had set, they were all dead, the campfires of their fallen bodies slowing turning to ash. I briefly considered cleaning up and dumping them all in the pit, but decided I just didn't care that much. Leveling out the pit, I turned to the nice little herd of horses that I'd rounded up. A few well-placed fireballs had them spooked again and running northeast. With any luck, they'd end up near the coven's caravan, where Ahearn could round them up.

I whistled for Steel and mounted.

Time to see what other trouble I could stir up.

It was getting darker, and the moon wasn't up yet, so Steel and I kept to an easy walk, still heading southeast. As luck would have it, I stumbled upon what appeared to be a small outpost, enclosed within a wall constructed of heavy timbers.

Steel was probably hungry and would appreciate some supper. I dug a hole just outside the palisade, unbuckled my sword belt, and removed my tell-tale black druid robe. Wrapping it around the sword, I deposited both in the hole, filling it with dirt and replacing the grass so no one would be able to tell it had been disturbed. Taking up the reins, I led Steel to the outpost gates and was about to knock when I noticed a cast-iron bell with a tattered bit of rope attached. Absently pondering the likelihood of bandits receiving casual visitors and thinking it would be nice to have my shotgun, I rang the bell until somebody unbarred the gates. Just for fun, I kept on ringing it until the gates were wide open and the gatekeeper started cussing me.

"Stop that racket, goddammit!" he shouted. "Who the hell do you think you are?"

"Name's Davis," I said, leading Steel inside and heading for a decent-sized barn. It that just happened to be the first building to the left of the entryway. Smelling fresh hay, the grulla stallion's nostrils flared, and he marched toward the barn with a purpose. A quick glance about the outpost revealed four men ranging from early twenties to late thirties, leaning on the wall of what appeared to be either a barracks or a saloon, watching us with casual interest.

"And just where do you think you're going?" the gatekeeper demanded.

"My horse is hungry," I said, allowing said horse to drag me along by the reins. The first stall on the right was empty, with fresh bedding and a nice big bale of hay. Of the eight stalls, seven of them were occupied. I put Steel in the empty one.

"You can't come in unless you say the password!" snapped the gatekeeper, trailing behind me.

"And yet here I am," I said, opening the stall door without bothering to look at him. I slipped off Steel's bridle and went eagerly into the stall.

"You youngsters always think you can walk all over me, but I was running slaves when you were still shitting your pants!" The gatekeeper's face was tomato red and veins popped out at his temples. "You'll tell me that password right now, or I'll put a bullet in your brain and take a piss in the hole!"

He drew a pistol, and I threw a tomahawk.

He died. I didn't.

I wasn't much on pistols, but I couldn't pass up on taking his Colt revolver. Especially when it was one-half of a matched set. Relieving the old coot of his gun belt, I fastened it about my hips, then opened the cylinder of each revolver, checked the bullets, and swung it closed again. I retrieved my tomahawk from the gatekeeper's neck, wiped it clean, and tucked it in my belt. Drawing one of the Colts and concealing it alongside my thigh, I exited the barn.

"The boss is gonna be pissed when he finds out you killed Mad Dog," one of the young men said.

"Guess I can't let that happen." I shot him once and put a bullet into another one with the second revolver. The first man hit the ground, screaming and clawing at the dirt, while the other one dove behind a nearby wagon. The third fell backwards through the door of the saloon and slammed the door closed. The fourth drew a shotgun; I smiled when I saw it and tossed a swarm of fire darts at him, followed by a couple of bullets. He died distracted. The first bandit I'd shot at had stopped moving, so I set the wagon on fire to flush out the other one. He must have been too close to it because he ran screaming down the street, trailing flames in his wake. I put him out of his misery before extinguishing the wagon and a few random fires, then went to collect the shotgun.

It wasn't an Ithaca 37, but in all my time as a Traveler, I'd never seen another one. It reminded me that I wouldn't see mine again, either, which pissed me off all over again. Fortune smiled on me just at that moment, providing me with a handful of bad guys to kill while I was still standing behind the scorched trail wagon. They shouted in alarm and filled the air with the clicking and clacking of rounds being chambered and hammers being cocked.

A few small but well-placed fireballs had them diving for cover before even one got off a shot. My newly-acquired shotgun took care of the rest. A corner of the barn caught fire, but I quickly put it out. The building beside it also began to burn, and I let it that one go. Hopefully, the gunfire coupled with the blaze would flush any other bandits out of hiding. The place stayed quiet, so I waved my hand at the burning building, commanding the fire to abandon it and leap to the roof of the next one.

It occurred to me that there might be valuable supplies in any of the structures, and with six extra horses available, I could carry quite a lot back to the coven. The thought of depriving the tyrant city of both horses and supplies made me feel all warm and fuzzy inside, and the notion that I'd be killing two birds with one stone pleased me immensely.

Hearing the door behind me creak open, I spun on my heel, leveling the shotgun, and froze – not because it was a woman, for there were plenty of vicious female bandits. It wasn't the woman's disheveled state, either, because that meant nothing in and of itself. It wasn't the shank she held or the blood that coated her hands as if she'd dipped them in a basin of it.

I froze because I recognized her.

"Maeve."

"Davis?"

Her voice was low and sounded raw, as though she'd spent a lot of time screaming recently. There was something else that was different about her, something that couldn't be attributed to the blood or her disheveled appearance, but I couldn't put my finger on it.

I nodded. "It's me."

Dirty, fear-filled faces appeared in the darkened doorway behind her, barely visible in the dim light. "May I come in?"

She nodded, eyes darting about as she backed in through the door. Closing it behind me, I looked the place over. There was a bar on one side of the room, and an upstairs loft with rows of straw pallets. Half a dozen women cowered in the semi-darkness. Clearly, drinking alcohol wasn't all this building was used for, and the room got a little hot before I got my temper under control.

"Did they bring everyone from Ward here?" I asked.

"I don't know." Maeve's expression was stony. "When we were captured, they tied us together and made us march blindfolded. We've not been allowed outside since we've been here."

Another brave soul came forward. I recognized her as a witch

160

named Aurelia. She had sung and played the guitar at the Summer Solstice celebration that Angie and I had attended. It seemed like forever ago.

"We tried to talk to each other to keep in touch, but they started whipping and beating us for it. We stopped trying after—"

"Aurelia." Maeve's voice was still quiet, but it had a firmness that no one could ignore.

"You've no cause to be ashamed," said Aurelia. "You were so brave…"

"And it did me no good whatsoever."

"They made an example of you," I said.

Maeve did not answer.

It was her nose, I decided. When last I'd seen her, it was straight and narrow. Now it was crooked with a knot on the bridge. Her skin was dark and dusky, and the faded yellow bruising beneath both eyes was difficult to see in the dimness, even when you knew what you were looking for.

"Are you hurt?"

Maeve raised an eyebrow that clearly suggested I might be an idiot.

"What I mean is – can you ride?"

"I'd join the Wild Hunt if it meant getting out of here," she replied.

Of the six women I'd found, four were witches from Ward – Maeve, Aurelia, Katarina, and Elin. The other two were strangers to me. I left them where they were and began systematically searching the remaining buildings for suitable clothing. They'd only been allowed to wear short dresses made of thin cotton, and all I could think of was the Big Bad Wolf telling Little Red Riding Hood: *The better to eat you with, my dear*.

Truth be told, I had to get out before I accidentally set the building on fire. I hadn't been this enraged since those people had tried to burn Angie at the stake in Searcy. Part of me was glad that I'd already killed everyone else in the outpost, but the other part of me wished I hadn't so I could burn them alive.

The search for clothing and supplies helped me focus on something else so that my anger would subside. My first objective was the building beside the… I wasn't going to call it a whorehouse. Prostitution was a respectable profession in which people got paid. What had been done to Maeve and the others was an outrage, an unforgivable and violent assault on their bodies and minds. Thinking about it didn't diminish my anger in the slightest, so I stopped and took a few deep breaths before entering the building. I wasn't any less angry, but I probably wouldn't burn it down.

Probably.

There were six bunkbeds, each with a chest at its foot, as well as a wardrobe at the back of the room. I lifted each of the chest lids, giving the contents a cursory examination. There were basic clothing pieces and personal items; the witches might find something suitable. Turning to the wardrobe, I opened it to find a whole slew of leather duster coats, all lined with shearling. Now *that* was a find. An identical building stood across from this one, and I soon discovered it was a barracks, too. There were only a few coats left in this wardrobe, however. The others were likely full of bullet holes and soaked with blood now. The second group of enemies I'd killed must have run out without their coats. There was plenty of clothing remaining in the chests, so we were good to go on that score.

The fourth building was the mess hall, with only enough room for a dozen people. It had a nice, warm fire going in a generously-sized hearth. The table was set with plates, cups, and eating utensils, but no food had yet been served. The delicious smell of roast chicken greeted me as I entered the kitchen. Five platters were laid out, but only four of them held golden-brown hens on a bed of potatoes. The fifth platter contained only potatoes; the fifth bird was lying on the hearth, covered in ashes. I'd interrupted them just as they'd been about to eat supper.

The women will just have to eat it for them, I thought, a vicious smile spreading across my face. Poking my nose into the larder, I discovered enough food storage that it made me wish there were more horses so we could take it all with us. Mentally calculating how much we might be able to take, I left and opened the door to the first building I'd set afire. While I'd already put out the fire, but thick, black smoke still poured out. I launched a four-foot fireball and smashed a huge hole in the back wall. A chill late-autumn wind streamed around my body and through the building, taking the smoke with it.

What I saw inside nearly made me run for cover. There were several dozen wooden crates marked "Ammunition – Keep Away from Fire." In the time it took my heart to beat twice, I had sucked every bit of heat out of the room. It was only sheer dumb luck that the ammo hadn't cooked off while I was tossing fireballs willy-nilly. Once my heart had settled into something approaching a normal speed, I looked over the walls, lined with gun racks. It reminded me of the shotgun storage back at my gunnery range in White Oak Grove. A closer inspection revealed sawdust on the floor, indicating that the racks were a recent addition to the building. The amassed weaponry and ammunition made me think hard about the possibility of taking it back to the caravan. Clearly, the bandits had brought it in the now-scorched wagon. Only, there hadn't been any draft horses in the barn. Just the six horses similar in build to my own.

Interesting, that. Counting the five men who'd been just inside the gate, plus the other six who'd run to investigate the gunfire, the outpost was at least five horses short – and that was only if old Mad Dog hadn't had a horse of his own and never left the outpost, which was doubtful.

So maybe there was a corral outside with a few more horses in it. I went back to Maeve and the others, showed them the trunks and wardrobe in the closest barracks, and left them to their inspection of the available fashion options while I wandered outside the palisade to look for more horses.

A large corral was connected to the other side of the barn by a gate in the thick timber wall. The four draft horses I'd suspected of being present were there, along with several other saddle horses. It seemed odd to have so many horses here when there wasn't space in the barn for them. In fact, the whole place had the look of being crammed with more than it had been designed to hold, evidenced by the many rifles and shotguns, multiple crates of ammunition, the heavily stocked larder, and barracks buildings with so many bunkbeds there was barely room to stand between them.

It was possible that this outpost's original purpose had been of a practical nature, a way station for scouts and outriders perhaps, but all the evidence within pointed to its new mission of territorial expansion. They had taken Ward to the northeast and were building forts to the southwest. Just how far was the Republic of Jackson spreading?

"Are you going to bring the horses in or just stand there scowling at them?"

I turned and hardly recognized Maeve, now dressed in blue jeans, a pale yellow shirt, black boots, and one of the shearling-lined leather duster coats. In addition, she was wearing a floppy wide-brimmed hat that reminded me of the one Kam Stone wore. She looked good. Well, maybe not *good*, but better, anyway.

"Did you ever hear the slavers talk about other attacks?"

She nodded. "They talked about attacking several townships, bragging about how many people they'd killed."

I swore under my breath.

"They told us we would never see our loved ones again, and that our homes now belonged to the Republic of Jackson," she continued. "Maybe it was just boasting, but they claimed to have captured hundreds."

It seemed likely that my guesses regarding the size of the 'Ville's population were accurate. Capturing towns and enslaving hundreds of people would have required a workforce of thousands. I wondered just how far the bandits had ranged and how many towns and villages they'd captured.

"I was afraid of that," I said. "Let's go back inside."

She nodded and walked alongside me, just out of arm's reach.

Couldn't say I blamed her.

The others were standing around in the middle of the outpost when we returned. I knew that Maeve and Aurelia were in their late twenties or early thirties, and if I judged correctly, Katarina and Elin were in their late teens. The two women I didn't know appeared to be somewhere in the middle. I shut and barred the gates, and was about to suggest that we all have supper, but Maeve spoke before I could.

"As you may have gathered, I am acquainted with our rescuer," she looked at me, and while she didn't smile, there was a warmth in her rich, hazel eyes. "His name is Davis, and you can trust him." The other three witches nodded acknowledgement, but the other two women exchanged an uncertain look.

"Davis, this is Anne," Maeve walked over and gestured to a skinny woman with ash blonde hair. "And this is Ruth." Ruth had dark, frizzy hair and skin that was a shade or two darker than Angie's.

"Pleased to meet you," I said automatically, then added: "I wish it was under better circumstances." It was horribly inadequate, but there wasn't anything even remotely acceptable about this situation.

"Davis is going to help us," Maeve said.

I nodded. "That's right. I found more horses in a corral outside, along with some draft horses to pull that wagon," I said, glad that I hadn't burned it up completely. "I'm thinking that we need to sit and make some plans for getting out of here, but not on an empty stomach."

"Do you want us to cook supper for you?" Anne asked timidly.

"Do I...?" I was momentarily at a loss for words. "No, of course not. Besides, the bandits did it for us. There's plenty in the kitchen."

"Are you sure no one's in there?" she whispered.

"Positive." She couldn't have missed the dead bodies sprawled all over the place, so she must not have known exactly how many bad guys had occupied the outpost. "Shall we?"

The ladies followed me to the mess hall, then looked around nervously. I wasn't one to stand on ceremony, so I fetched the chicken platters two at a time, warmed them up, and put them on the table. When I went back for more, Maeve followed. She started to pick up a bowl of green beans, but I stopped her.

"Hang on a second," I said. "Those are cold." I took the bowl and focused my intent and energy upon it, warming both it and the vegetables. She gave me a funny look.

"What are you doing?"

"Warming it up."

"With your bare hands?"

I looked at her, vaguely surprised. Had they not seen me tossing fire hither and yon during the fight? An instant later, I realized that their prison had been without windows.

"I, um..." Why was it so difficult for me to tell people about my magic? "As it turns out, I am a druid. And I have magic."

Maeve stared. "What kind of magic?"

"Elemental fire," I said. "And earth."

"Since when?"

"Since Beltaine."

"That isn't very long."

"True, but I've worked hard to become proficient with it," I said. "Grab one of those other chicken platters, and I'll just warm everything up at the table."

"Better do it in here. Anne and Ruth are Triune, and they think magic is evil. Well, Anne does. As many times as I've healed Ruth, I don't think she cares anymore. Anne won't let me touch her, though."

"They can think what they like." I started to walk away, but she put a hand on my arm. I stopped and listened while she quietly explained that the two were from a place called Cypress Creek, which was almost due north of the 'Ville. Unlike the attack on Ward Coven, who had been alerted by magic, *all* the men had been slaughtered and the babies and very young children taken away from their mothers, who were taken as slaves along with girls and boys over the age of ten.

"Anne lost her children, and they both lost husbands," Maeve said. "They've wasted away with grief." She held onto my arm long enough to let that sink in. I closed my eyes, unable to imagine going through such anguish. I couldn't imagine losing Angie, much less her *and* a child.

"Anne won't eat if she knows it's been touched by magic," she added.

I nodded, moved by her compassion. Maeve had been through everything the others had, suffered the same pain, the same insults, the same repeated violation of her body, yet she was still able to focus on the needs of others. I handed her the now-steaming bowl of green beans, and she carried it to the table. Once the gravy bowl and platter of corn on the cob were hot, I brought them out and set them on the table. I sliced up the chickens and served each of the women while they helped themselves to the potatoes and vegetables. My pleasure in eating the meal that our enemies had prepared for themselves was diminished somewhat, but I still felt some satisfaction that their victims were being nourished by it. Not one ounce of food touched my plate until everyone else had taken at least a bite, but I still managed to eat half a chicken myself. The hall was warm and cozy, and nobody said much more than "Pass the potatoes" until our bellies were full.

Maeve got up and refilled her cup from the beer barrel in the kitchen, but remained standing instead of returning to her seat. "I have a lot of questions, and I imagine you all do, too," she said. "Since Aurelia, Elin, Kat, and I already know Davis, I think it's only right to give Ruth and Anne equal footing." She turned toward the Triune women. "When I said you could trust Davis, I meant it. Partly because I already know him to be a good and honorable man, and partly because he is a Traveler."

Anne kept her gaze downcast, but Ruth stared at me like I'd sprouted a second head.

"I thought there weren't no more Travelers," she said.

"We're getting pretty thin on the ground," I replied. "There aren't many of us left these days."

"You must be very brave to go through Republic territory alone," she said.

"Oh, I'm not alone," I said. "I mean, I'm alone right now, but I'm actually Traveling with… a rather large caravan. I was out… scouting when I stumbled across the outpost."

Lying was definitely not one of my strengths. I'd almost said I was Traveling with the *coven*. I most certainly had not been out scouting unless looking for trouble could be referred to in that manner. It would be more accurate to say I was hunting, or more truthfully, that I'd been looking for someone upon which to unleash my wrath.

"Do you mean to say that you killed *all* them slavers by yourself?" Ruth's dark eyes were huge.

I shifted uncomfortably. "Well…"

"All of them but one," Maeve said, referring to the one whose throat she'd cut. I raised my glass to her in a solitary, wordless toast.

"No wonder you're not afraid to go it alone," said Katarina.

"Still, you're lucky you missed the raid group that left just this afternoon," said Elin, shuddering. "There were at least fifty." Katarina reached out and took her hand.

"That *is* lucky," I said, thinking that the group obviously hadn't missed *them*. Viciously, I decided that being trapped in a hole and allowed the false hope of escape so that I could burn them alive one or two at a time was well deserved. While slaughtering

167

them wasn't the most honorable thing I'd ever done in my life, I couldn't bring myself to regret it now. Not to mention that Ward and Cypress Creek had been invaded and plundered by a raid group like that. If it was the same group of forty-plus bandits that I'd massacred, I could well understand why Anne had been worried that more of them might be in the mess hall. I pushed away that train of thought before it pissed me off again.

"You said you had some questions?" I asked, mostly to help them get their minds off what they'd suffered and focus on something else.

"I do," Maeve said, gracefully seating herself once more. "I just… I don't know where to start."

"While I haven't been to Cypress Creek," I began, somewhat apologetically, "I do have news of Ward."

The witches sat up straight, all wide-eyed and wearing expressions displaying mixed feelings of hope and fear.

"We ran across Ahearn—"

"Ahearn!" The four witches exclaimed.

"Is he well?" Maeve asked.

"He's fine. Most of the your people escaped the attack and are alive and well," I said. "They make up most of the caravan I mentioned."

Aurelia cried out with joy, Katarina and Elin reached for one another, clasping hands and bursting into sobs. Maeve put her hand over her mouth, her hazel eyes welling with tears.

"Thank the Lord and Lady, they survived!" she whispered. Raising her head, her eyes sought mine. "Rhiannon?"

"She is also well."

"Oh, thank the goddess!" she exclaimed. However, she must have seen something in my expression, because she then asked, "What is it?"

"Brennan fell," I said.

"Who is protecting them while you're away?" Aurelia asked.

"Oh, uh, I'm traveling with about thirty other men," I said, giving Maeve a significant look so she would be sure to understand that I meant other *druids*. "We're well-armed and have gained quite a bit of experience fighting bandits in recent weeks."

"What of the others?" Elin exclaimed. "What of the rest of our men?"

I rattled off as many of the male witches as I could remember, realizing all over again how few were over the age of twenty, with none past thirty-five. The older men – and no few of the older women – had stayed behind to fight the invaders, knowing their lives would be the price paid to give the rest of the coven time to escape.

"Do you know Killian?" Elin asked. "He's my brother."

I nodded. "He's with them."

"What about Heath?" Katarina asked. "Do you know him or Cullen?"

"Heath is alive," I said. "But Cullen isn't with them. I'm sorry." No one knew for sure whether the missing ones were dead or enslaved; we only knew they were lost. Elin covered her hand with her mouth, while Katarina buried her face in Elin's shoulder, sobbing.

"Cullen is her brother," Maeve said quietly.

"Killian will be a brother to both of us," Elin said, putting her arms around her friend. I looked away, feeling wretched.

"Davis." I felt a gentle hand on my shoulder. I hadn't heard Maeve's chair move or her footsteps, Katarina's wailing was so loud. "It's not your fault."

"That doesn't make me feel any better," I said roughly. I stood up, resisting the urge to shove my chair back.

"I'm going to start loading the wagon," I said. "Try to get some rest. We leave at daybreak."

Before closing the door behind me, I cast a long look back at them. Maeve and Ruth had gone to support Katarina with Elin, embracing them both and sharing their grief with tears of their own. Aurelia went to sit by Anne, whose shoulders shook as she silently wept.

No one should ever have to go through what they had, but in spite of everything they'd suffered, these women still had a sensitivity to another's grief, had retained the kindness of heart to show compassion.

I was humbled, uplifted, and depressed, all at the same time.

Mostly, though, I was incensed.

Conall was right.

The 'Ville had to be destroyed.

Chapter 9 – Liberty

*Enslave the liberty of but one human being
and the liberties of the world are put in peril.*
~ William Lloyd Garrison ~

Returning to the building where I'd discovered the weapons cache, I closed the door behind me so none of the ladies could see what I was about. While I'd wanted them to rest for the journey, Maeve and the other witches were set on helping. The four of them ransacked the rest of the outpost for every last bit of clothing, bedding, tools, rope, and any other supplies that might prove useful. Even Anne and Ruth got involved, plundering the kitchen and larder.

I lit the lanterns mounted on the walls, channeling magic to improve their illumination. It allowed just enough light to see by, and breaking open the heavy wooden crates of firearms and ammunition was just the thing for helping me work out my anger. The bandits had helpfully left a clawed hammer atop one of the crates, and I began unpacking. Once all the crates had been unstacked and their lids removed, I discovered an impressive stockpile of long guns and ammunition.

Putting my hands on my hips, I surveyed the loot. I'd never seen so many firearms in one place before. A closer inspection of the rifles in each crate revealed them to be identical, and appeared to be brand spanking new. I cracked open the crates of shotguns and pistols and found the same thing. None of the guns had been manufactured before the Fracture. Clearly, the Republic of Jackson had developed a method of mass-producing both firearms and the various types of ammunition they required.

Even if we hadn't needed it, I would have taken it all just to keep it out of the hands of the enemy. While the crates and straw packing were the best way to transport the weaponry, the heavy crates were added weight we could do without. The supplies and munitions had to have been delivered in multiple wagons, but we only had one. It was a nice, big trail wagon with a bed that was eleven feet long and three feet wide with four-foot-high sides, but it wouldn't hold everything.

After checking each shotgun and rifle to make sure they were unloaded, I carried them outside and leaned them against the sides of the wagon. There were so many that long guns were stacked two deep on both sides of it. There were no barrels of powder or shot. Nor was there a press for refilling shells. It was telling that the outpost had been supplied with only finished ammunition. The fact that it was being manufactured elsewhere, probably in the 'Ville, and transported here told me that our enemies were gearing up for a major offensive.

If there were more outposts like this one, spaced out around the perimeter of the 'Ville, it meant the bandits could ride out light, load up, and be out invading towns in short order. We needed to know if there were more forts like this to the northeast between the 'Ville and Ward. If there were, it would be a simple matter for the bandits to flank us, trapping us between two groups of enemies. Even if we surprised the interlopers and took Ward back, a group of little enemy stations like this could keep up a constant stream of attacks.

Forty rifles and ten shotguns would even things up a little when we challenged the bandits for possession of Ward, but the ammunition wouldn't last forever. Would druid magic be enough to fend them off? Had I made a wrong choice in escorting the witches home? Should I have taken them back to Sanctuary?

While I stood there obsessing over possible future events, Anne and Ruth showed up with heavy armloads of canned goods. We packed them into the now-empty rifle crates, and I shoved them under the driver's seat. They repeated the process several times until twelve full crates sat stacked under the seat.

"Is that everything?" I asked. It didn't seem like much for a post supporting twelve people, much less forty or fifty more.

Ruth shook her head. "There are big bags of flour, rice, and beans – things like that."

"How big?"

She considered. "The flour, rice, and oats, about fifty pounds each, I think. The beans, cornmeal, and sugar are smaller."

That was a lot. "How many of each?"

"Three or four."

I looked at the wagon, which was now nearly half-full from front to back. There were several inches of space above the crates, however, and it occurred to me that a person could take cover from gunfire by lying flat atop the crates.

"We can stack the bags on top of the crates," I said. "I'll carry them for you."

"No need for that," said Ruth. "Lord knows we've carried weights heavier than that before." Anne nodded agreement. Before returning to the mess hall for another load, she stopped and touched one of the rifles.

"Can you use a rifle?" I asked.

"Yes, sir," she replied.

"Any good with it?"

"I done plenty of huntin'," she said. "My family never went hungry, neither. Even if it was just squirrels."

I looked at Ruth. "How about you?"

"I can shoot the eyes out of a gnat at fifty paces," she said, her expression challenging me to contradict her.

Suppressing a smile, I said, "That's good to know. Feel free to pick out whatever you want. Rifle shells are in that stack of boxes over there." I nodded at the stack of cubes by the off-side front wheel.

Anne took the rifle she'd touched and grabbed three pouches of rounds. Climbing up the side of the trail wagon, she placed them on the driver's bench and propped her rifle against it. Ruth handed up her own weapon and another three pouches of rounds, which Anne put on the other side of the driver's bench. They both dusted their hands and returned to the mess hall.

Amazed all over again by their resilience, I stood there thinking for a few moments, until Katarina and Elin brought up a stack of thick woolen blankets. They dumped them on the wagon's tailgate and went back to the barracks for more. The ladies would probably be mortified, but the long guns needed to be wrapped in something to transport them, and those blankets would do nicely. I spread one out, folded it lengthwise, and laid one of the rifles on it, rolling it up so that the metal was completely covered, then repeated the process until I had a blanketed bundle of rifles. Tucking it up against the rifle-crates-turned-food-crates, I repeated the process several more times until I had seven tidy rolls of rifles and two rolls of shotguns. Placing the blanket rolls in the wagon, I took the bags of flour and rice from Anne and Ruth as they brought them out, layering them atop the blanket rolls. Once we were finished, the long guns were secure, and there were soft bags of flour and rice upon which the ladies could sit if they desired.

Maeve had said she'd ride, but that didn't mean she was physically up to it, and maybe the others weren't either. And even though Anne and Ruth seemed to have claimed the driver's bench for their own, I considered having them ride in the back with their rifles. If they were as good as they claimed, they'd be invaluable in the event of an attack.

After the food, weapons, linens, supplies, and extra clothing were loaded in the wagon, there was just enough room for the cubed boxes of ammunition. I was glad there weren't any barrels of gunpowder; it would have been a fire hazard. Even though I could manipulate fire and heat, I didn't want to deal with a barrel of gunpowder ignited by a stray bullet in the middle of a firefight. There was also the possibility that my fire magic could get out of hand while my attention was divided between causing earthquakes, throwing fireballs, and shooting. It wasn't that I thought I'd lose control; rather, something near a target or targets might catch fire and accidentally spread. I didn't plan on stopping the wagon for *anything,* so it wasn't likely to happen, but it didn't hurt to plan for the contingency.

Since leaving the slave-house, not one of the women returned to it or even looked in its direction. They had bedded down together in the barracks beside the mess hall, but it wouldn't be surprising if they hadn't slept a wink. I managed to sleep for only a few hours before waking at the grey light of dawn.

With my hatchets, sword, a pistol, and a shotgun, I was loaded for bear and ready to hunt. Because I couldn't wear my sword with them, I had traded the dual pistols obtained from the late Mad Dog for a single-pistol gun belt and holster. It still felt awkward, but I could draw either weapon quickly with my right hand. Shrugging on a calf-length black leather duster I'd found, I stepped outside the barracks across from the mess.

The women were dressed and ready, an air of quiet alertness about them. Before going to bed, I had discovered that two of the crates – which I'd thought to contain ammunition – actually held several pistols, tucked into holsters on gun belts with bullets already present in the loops. Each woman took a belt and buckled it on at my urging. I showed each of them how to load a bullet into a revolver, then let them load the other five.

"We don't have time for me to teach you to shoot," I said. "So don't use the pistols unless someone is so close you can't miss."

All the witches but Maeve looked uncomfortable just holding their pistols, but if each of us was packing both a pistol and a long gun, a small group of bandits might think twice about taking us on.

"Also: Don't aim at anybody that you don't plan to shoot," I said, helping Elin holster her pistol. "Everybody got that?" They all nodded.

"Let's get the horses ready, then." I went to the barn, leaving Maeve, Aurelia, Anne, and Ruth working together to hitch the four draft horses to the wagon. I was standing in the tack room trying to guess which saddle fitted what horse when Katarina and Elin came in and quickly sorted it all out. We tacked up the extra horses from the corral in addition to the seven in the barn. Luckily there were halters available for the ones that wouldn't be ridden, so we tucked their bridles into old feed bags and tied them to the horn of each saddle. There were too many horses to tie to the wagon, so I was counting on herd instinct to keep them together on the journey.

"So, who's riding in the wagon?" I asked, leading Steel and a black mare with a spotted rump like Scarlet's.

"I'll drive," Elin said. She climbed onto the driver's bench and picked up the reins.

"I'll ride shotgun, then," said Ruth, following her up. "Anne, you want to cover the rear?"

"I can do that."

Katarina climbed into the back with Anne and sat on one of

the sacks of rice. Maeve took the reins of the black spotted mare from me, while Aurelia chose a chestnut gelding. I mounted Steel, thinking that the only upside to their captivity was that they'd been well-fed. Their muscle tone had been preserved and the more severe physical injuries – like Maeve's broken nose – were more or less healed. The emotional ones, however…

Those were going to take a while.

* * *

We set off in a northeasterly direction. My reasoning was that if we headed straight for Ward, then we would soon cross paths with the caravan. It had taken me a full day's ride to reach the outpost, but I hadn't been traveling in a straight line. I figured that we'd meet up with the caravan by evening tomorrow at the latest.

The four draft horses were powerful but ponderous, leaving me plenty of time to do a little scouting. Making quarter-mile circles around the wagon once every hour or two, I never left sight of it except once, when I returned to the outpost and burned it to the ground.

Thanks to the pitch the Republic builders had used to coat the palisade logs to protect them from rot, the whole place went up like a torch. I may have used more magic than necessary, for the flames were white at the tips, and the entire place was reduced to ashes in minutes. Like the raid group I had destroyed the day before, I left the evidence for our enemies to find. Burying the outpost was a waste of time. They would surely see the smoke and investigate, but I could not allow them to keep such a valuable asset.

Late in the afternoon on the second day, I could tell we were getting close. Duncan and the other earth druids had covered their tracks, but the earth mother recognized our kinship and generously shared their location and heading with me. Then she told me something else: we were being followed, and they were fast coming upon us.

"We're getting close," I said, turning to check behind us.

"How close?" asked Maeve, mimicking my movement. On our journey with the witches, we'd learned that they, too, used elemental magic – just not quite in the same way. A witch could use any element he or she wanted but usually specialized in one, based on the principle that practice makes perfect. Becoming expert with all five elements would take a tremendous amount of time and energy, often precluding a full life with children or artistic pursuits.

It was one of the reasons the coven's relationships were not exclusive, and that the children were literally raised by their village. Rhiannon explained that if a woman became pregnant and preferred having the freedom to advance her magical practice over parenting, others took on the responsibility of any child she bore. From what I'd seen, most were content to master one or two elements and still enjoy having a relationship and/or a family, contributing to the survival of the coven, and pursuing any personal interests in their spare time. Maeve, I'd learned, used earth to heal like Duncan.

"Not close enough," I said, then called to Katarina, who had taken a turn driving the wagon: "Whip 'em up! Get those horses moving!"

"But they've been pulling all day!" she protested. "Aren't we almost there?"

"Yes, and *so are they*!" Maeve yelled. She pointed behind us, to a dust cloud barely visible on the horizon.

Beside her on the driver's bench, Elin cried out in alarm. Katarina began slapping the reins and yelling at the team. I heard the draft horses snorting and the creak and jingle of their harness as they plunged forward. Their trot wasn't fast, but it was better than the slow plod they'd been doing. I was about to holler at Anne and Ruth to get their rifles ready, but they were already checking their weapons and rearranging bags of dry goods to give themselves stability in the now-jolting wagon.

"Aurelia!" Maeve yelled. "Get in front of the team so they'll follow!"

The singer gave her a wave of acknowledgement and her chestnut gelding sprinted ahead of the draft horses. The riderless horses followed, moving into a fast gallop. Responding to the movements of the herd, the draft horses' large hooves began to churn the ground in earnest, plunging forward first into a canter and then a lumbering gallop.

I pulled Steel back, turning him to face the oncoming threat. Black-tipped ears pricked forward, he set off at a gallop, rapidly closing the distance between us and our pursuers. He slid to a halt, and I dismounted. Dropping to one knee, I placed my palms flat on the ground, ready to unleash my elemental magic.

"What in the name of the Goddess are you doing?" Maeve shouted behind me. "You'll be trampled!"

I'd been so focused on the enemy ahead that I hadn't paid a lick of attention to what was behind.

"Get out of here!" I said. "You should be running with the others."

"I'm not leaving you out here to die a fool's death!" she snapped, jumping off her horse.

I snorted. "That won't happen."

"You're not invulnerable just because you have magic!"

"I'll be fine."

Maeve crossed her arms over her chest. "You haven't changed any."

Her words may have been intended as an insult, but they only served to encourage me. Somehow, her biting comment meant I hadn't left my true self behind in White Oak Grove. I was still a Traveler at heart. I was still committed to helping those who needed it. So what if I took risks sometimes? No one lived forever.

I resumed my kneeling pose, and the earth responded readily, already awakened to my touch. The power at the epicenter beneath our feet was immense. Behind me, Maeve gasped.

"Are you doing what I think you're doing?" she said.

"If you think I'm creating an earthquake, then yes."

I gave it another thrust of my own power, and the earth before us began to undulate in a one-hundred-eighty-degree arc, as though someone had dropped a heavy stone in the water beside a wall, causing the ripples to spread out forward and laterally. The swells of dirt grew ever taller as they spread out and away, heading for the raid group on our tail. The wagon's rear would be covered from east to west for several hundred feet. The groundswell had become five-foot-tall waves, but the raid group still kept coming.

"They're not stopping!" Maeve cried.

"They will."

The bandits were within approximately two hundred yards of us. Maeve dove for cover as rifle rounds zipped and whined around us, demonstrating that our enemies were well within firing range. I set fire to the next rough tremors, the tall flames designed to conceal our presence. Maybe the tall grasses had helped conceal the ground rolls, but the fire caught their attention, and in a matter of seconds both men and horses were scrambling to turn around and head the other way.

While the rolling waves traveled slowly in comparison to natural seismic activity, their amplitude and intensity were far greater. In addition, a real quake stopped once its energy had been spent, while mine increased in accordance with my will. Rippling lines of fire streaked away, carried by the rising and falling terrain; the screams of man and animal could be heard over the rumbling of the earth as it swept over them. The waves became like those on a stormy sea, and the earth was churned apart by its own brutal motion. At the apex of each choppy swell, elemental fire burned brightly, consuming everything in its wake.

Closing my eyes, I performed a *seeking*, using the earth's motion to enhance and extend my perception. Two other bands of marauders were coming up fast, hard on the heels of the one now fighting to escape. My initial plan had been to delay and defend, but I now knew it would never be enough. Whoever commanded the 'Ville was bent on conquest, and the appetites of those who followed his lead were whetted for both blood and material gain. Insatiable, they would never stop.

Time could never be turned back, and the injury Maeve and the others had suffered could never be entirely removed, but I could make sure that those who followed us never hurt anyone ever again. Over a hundred arcing lines of flame swept across the expanse of violently bucking earth, obliterating our enemies as though they were no more than rows of dried cornstalks standing lifeless in the fall. Channeling more elemental magic than I ever had before, I released a torrent of fire upon the surface of the churning earth in a brilliant typhoon of red, orange, and yellow, fueled by my undiminished wrath. Reveling in the swath destruction, I was captivated by its roaring hunger, feeling myself fed as it consumed all living things within its reach. The earth ceased its bucking and rolling, growing quiet as the blaze intensified. Scarlet flame brightened to a silken orange tipped in brilliant yellow, enthralling me and drawing me in. Hypnotized by its beautiful savagery, I opened wider the conduit through which magic flowed from the gods. Elemental fire poured forth from the Well of my soul in a torrent that engulfed the plain, creating a raging inferno as far as the eye could see. Someone called my name, but I heard it as if from a long way away. My mind was adrift, floating through the light and heat as the magic surged through me.

The ear-splitting roar of a gunshot yanked me out of it.

I jumped and spun around to find Maeve red-faced and sweating, the pistol in her hand aimed at the sky.

"Snap out of it!" she shouted. "We have to get out of here!"

We rode hard and fast to catch the trail wagon. Dealing with the bandits had taken less than thirty minutes, but the draft horses had been galloping. While they weren't fast, Katrina and Elin were likely to whip them until they dropped in their traces to keep from being taken as slaves again.

"Look!" Maeve cried, pointing ahead.

Vague, scattered mounds appeared in the distance, some large and some small. The first one we encountered turned out to be a dead man; the second, a dead horse, with more at regular intervals. No doubt they'd brought down by the sharp targeting skills of Ruth and Anne. I counted as we galloped past – two, then five, then seven. There was a gap where no bodies had fallen, and I feared the worst. The only good sign was that the trail wagon had left obvious traces of its passage. We followed the trail for another quarter mile, both our horses foamed and sweat-soaked from the swift pace.

"There it is!" Maeve cried.

The trail wagon had stopped. As we drew near, I could see Katarina and Elin were standing beside it, holding pistols at arm's length against a group of men in dark clothing. Anne and Ruth were standing in the back of the wagon still, their rifles trained on the strangers. Still heated with battle and fearful for the women's lives, I threw a screaming fireball. The men scattered, diving for the ground, and I threw another one. It smashed against an invisible object, flames scattering and harmlessly dissipating.

Only an air shield could block a fireball and break it up like that. I slowed Steel to a trot and then a walk; sides heaving and head down, he was only too happy to oblige. Maeve's mare raced ahead of me and slid to a stop near the rear of the wagon. She pulled her own pistol, aiming it at the small group of Finns.

"Don't you come any closer!" she shouted. "I'll kill every last one of you with my bare hands if I have to!"

"It's all right," I told her. "These are my guys. Everybody, put your weapons up." The Finns looked at each other, looked at me, and then holstered all their weapons: swords, rifles, shotguns, pistols, everything.

Everything but magic.

None of the women moved a muscle; it was going to take more than my words to convince them. As luck would have it, Conall's temper helped solve the problem.

"What the fuck are you doing throwing fireballs at us?!" he screamed, in complete disregard of the danger posed by the multiple firearms trained on him.

"I'm sorry!" I said. "I couldn't see!"

"You couldn't—" His face purpled with rage. "You're an *earth druid*, Davis! You don't *need* to see!"

"You expect me to do a *seeking* on the back of a galloping horse?" I fired back.

"I *expect* you to not be a fucking idiot!" he shouted, before storming away ranting about how he could not *believe* I'd just thrown a fireball at them, and how stupid could one person be?

"These are your friends?" Maeve said, giving me a hard look.

"Yeah," I said with a sigh. "These are my friends."

The women I'd rescued held their armed standoff at the wagon for at least a quarter of an hour in spite of my reassurance that it was safe to continue. Bored after about five minutes, the Finns followed Conall back to the caravan, bringing them news of our arrival. It wasn't until Rhiannon, Spencer, and Ahearn galloped up bareback that they finally put down their guns. After hugging each and every one of the women and welcoming Anne and Ruth, the High Priestess grabbed me in a fervent embrace and cried a little, thanking me over and over for bringing them back.

They'd gone through hell on earth, but she had, too. As leader of the coven, she was responsible for their well-being. She had to have known her lost ones were enduring great pain and suffering.

It made me stop and consider if she'd truly *known*, and not just in a general everybody-knows-bandits-do-bad-things-to-people

180

kind of way.

Back when we were on the road to White Oak Grove, Angie had done some kind of spirit magic that had allowed her to travel through the spirit realm in search of help. It was Rhiannon who had answered that desperate cry, and it made me wonder if she had done some spirit traveling herself in search of the missing members of her coven.

Supper, a bath, and my bedroll were all I wanted, but I had only just begun to take care of my exhausted horse when Seth showed up. Standing on Steel's other side, Dermot's eyes went wide when he saw the air elementalist. Then he ducked out of sight. I passed him the reins and motioned for him to lead the horse away before turning to face Seth. Standing in silence while he reamed me in front of everyone, I'd never seen him so furious.

"Where in the name of Zeus have you been?" he bellowed. "You've been gone for *three days*, Davis! Three!" He paused only long enough to take a breath. "You owe me an explanation for your reckless behavior! In fact, you owe *everyone* an explanation!"

A collective hush settled over the camp. Behind Seth, standing with his arms crossed over his chest and still irate at having to dodge a fireball, Conall glared at me. About half the Finns had encircled us, including all the other earth druids except Duncan. None of them looked happy.

"Look, I never intended to go rogue. I found the trace of a raid group that was too close to us for comfort," I said. The irritation and resentment radiating off Seth were replaced by an expression of concern and apprehension.

"What did you do?"

"I followed them."

"*What* did you *do*?"

I met his gaze unblinking. "Ambushed a raid group, killed all the bandits in the outpost where I found Maeve and the others, stole that trail wagon and loaded it with every weapon, bullet, and scrap of food that I could pilfer before burning the whole place down to the ground, and took out a few more raid groups on the way back."

"Sounds like a productive three days," Conall said, now radiating an air of approval.

"Are you *mad*?!" The air elementalist looked like he wanted to hit something. Probably me.

"I couldn't just leave them, Seth!"

"Stop!" He rubbed his temples. "Just… stop. Go back and tell me how everything happened – in order."

Behind him, Conall spoke up. "You can start by telling us how you took on a hundred bandits and lived to tell the tale."

"I'm… pretty sure it was more than that."

"How many more?" asked Seth.

"I don't know. I was pretty pissed off after finding out what Maeve and the others had been through."

"Humor me with your best estimate."

"There was a whole passel of them. I'm guessing each band had about as many raiders as what we've been facing."

"So… fifty?" Conall said.

I shrugged. "Plus the ten or eleven stationed at the outpost." While the women had informed me that the group of bandits passing through the outpost had numbered forty or fifty, I hadn't stopped to count the three others that had pursued the trail wagon, but it seemed likely that they had manpower equal to the first.

"You slaughtered two hundred bandits in three days?"

"Well, it wasn't all at once." I paused, thinking. "I came across the first group on the evening of the first day. And the other three were pursuing us, so I had to stop them before they reached the caravan."

They stared at me.

"I mean, the bandits were hot on our heels, and the women were in danger, so I was in a hurry. Besides, I wasn't just using fire. I used earth, too," I said, feeling uncomfortable under their scrutiny.

They stared at me some more.

"It wasn't like I took out all four raid groups at the same time," I said, fidgeting.

"No, you only took out three instead of four." Conall's tone was dry.

"Well, two of the three didn't show up until after I'd covered a goodly-sized area of the plains in big, rolling waves."

"How big?" Siorus asked, and I thanked the gods for his endless curiosity and pursuit of new and better ways to master earthmoving.

"Mm, four and a half feet high. Maybe five." I paused, thinking. "I could still see over them, so it had to be five or less. Oh, and I set the tall grass on fire, so it was kind of like a... burning ocean."

"Did you get lost in the flames again?" Seth asked. "And before you answer that, we saw the smoke."

"Ahh... Not for too long."

The air elementalist groaned.

"I can't imagine how you avoided getting shot," Conall said.

"The first group never saw me coming," I said. "I trapped them by making a kind of sinkhole with a wall of flame around it."

"You buried them alive? Nice."

"Not exactly."

"Burned them alive." Conall nodded approval. "Even better."

Seth swore under his breath.

I remembered about the bandit horses I'd loosed from that first group. Noticing Ahearn standing among the Finns, I asked, "Did any horses happen to make it up this way?"

Ahearn gave me a funny look. "Yeah. Twenty or so. Why?"

"Because I didn't kill most of the horses from the first group." I frowned. "I was hoping more of them would make it this far."

"Gods of Olympus," Seth breathed. I didn't think his reaction had anything to do with how he felt about the extra horses.

"I know. It wasn't very honorable."

"There's no such thing as a fair fight," Conall said. "Besides, they had the advantage of numbers. Only a fool would even consider honorable combat."

"I killed them in cold blood, Conall."

"What you did is known as a preemptive strike," said Seth. "It's a time-honored tactic."

"Good," I said. "Because I'll be doing a lot more of them in the future."

Seth's eyes narrowed. "What is that supposed to mean?"

"I'm going to destroy the 'Ville."

"*What!*" Seth's eyeballs almost popped out of his head. Conall gave me a look of disbelief and then threw his hands up in the air like my mother used to do.

"Wait just one minute. You said you didn't think we'd stand a chance against them!" the Norseman said.

We still didn't stand a chance against them, but my little jaunt had proven to me that *I* could take them apart a piece at a time. Being sneaky, devious, and ruthless were all qualities of an accomplished Traveler, and I had those traits in spades. One man was far more difficult to track than thirty-five – especially if that man was not only a Traveler but an earth druid as well.

"You also said you'd have to have a *really* good reason to attack the Republic," Conall said, his expression challenging.

I couldn't help but look at Maeve, sitting by the fire with Rhiannon, her head resting on the High Priestess' shoulder. Following my gaze, he shook his head and snorted in disgust.

"Oh, so now that somebody you know personally has been hurt, you're willing to try it."

"Yes. You were right, and I was wrong."

"You—" He was left speechless for a moment, probably for the first time in his life. Then: "Wisdom of Odin," he said in a tone of wonder. "By the gods, count me in! When do we leave?"

"What... How... *Have* you *lost* your *mind*?" Seth demanded. "This is *not* what Master Shitozaki sent us out here to do!"

"You're right. It's not. That's why I'm sending the rest of you back to Sanctuary after we get the coven to Ward." Unless the Finns decided to stay there, that was, but there wasn't much I could do about that.

"Wait. Just wait," he said, as if trying to wrap his mind around what I had just said. "Every time Conall has brought up attacking the 'Ville, your response has been that they are far more powerful and that we would be wiped out in such an attempt. You've said this consistently, so before any of us can support your decision, we need to know what happened out there to make you change your mind."

I was going to destroy the 'Ville whether he supported me or not, but out of respect for our friendship, I relayed what Maeve had told me about the bandits' boasting and what the women from Cypress Creek had experienced. Then I described the outpost, the barracks, the slave building, and how over half the horses were kept outside the palisade.

"That's odd," Seth said. "One would have expected them to keep all the animals inside."

"The barn only had stalls for eight horses."

"Hm."

His demeanor changed when I recounted finding the multiple boxes of firearms and the stacks and stacks of ammunition crates, his expression becoming sharper and more calculating.

"It sounds like they were provisioning and stocking for something bigger than just a raid," he said, rubbing his bearded chin. "I don't want to sound like a doomsayer, but if they've already conquered all the towns and villages, a munitions stockpile like that could only be for one thing – war."

I nodded. "Exactly."

"And that's why you now think we should attack the 'Ville?"

"No, that's why *I* am going to attack the 'Ville." I paused. "You are my friends, and I could not ask for better, but I can't allow any of you to risk your lives any more than you already have."

"You can't fight a war alone."

"Don't tell me what I can't do."

* * *

As an air elementalist, Seth's personality was largely on the intellectual side, making him rational, slow to anger, quick to make logical decisions, and disinclined to worry or panic. It seemed likely that his reaction and continuing anger was due to having leadership dumped in his lap. I was clean and fed and ready to sleep, but since I'd shirked my duty and left him holding the bag, I sought him out again.

He was standing on the outskirts of camp with his eyes fixed on the southern horizon.

"Want to talk about it?"

"I am unaware of any issues requiring discussion," he replied, his face stony.

"You could always yell at me some more."

He didn't respond.

"I heard the Finns gave you a rough time while I was gone."

"I had to order everyone to remain in camp to keep them from charging off after you," he said, finally looking at me. "Do you know what it's like to have a bunch of *earth elementalists* mad at you?"

I could well imagine. Earth elementalists were slow to anger, but once they got their dander up, no one held a grudge longer.

"People don't always like the orders they're given," I said. "The important thing is that they stayed."

"They didn't say out of respect for me *or* Master Shitozaki," he growled. "They stayed because of the *witches*."

"They stayed because they're committed to the task they've taken on and are honor-bound to see it through," I said. He snorted.

"Being in command isn't about making people do things they don't want to do, Seth. It's about helping them remember why they should – and you accomplished that."

"Because I refused to allow them to search for you, I was accused of being a power-hungry glory hound. Aspersions were cast upon my honor. They called me a coward and the master's bootlicker," he said.

"Then you deserve an apology from everyone who did so."

"Davis, the insults heaped upon me by others were *nothing* compared to my self-recrimination. Don't you see? *I* wanted to go find you, too!" he said. "Am I supposed to feel good about being a hypocrite?"

"It's only hypocrisy if your actions don't follow your words."

He shook his head. "You do not understand. I spent three whole days constantly questioning if I was doing the right thing and was never able to decide! Do you know what that's like?"

"Yeah," I replied quietly. "I do."

Realization hit him like a ton of bricks, and he swore quietly under breath, an entire string of invectives that would have done the master proud.

"Maybe they weren't really angry that I wouldn't let them search for you," Seth said. "Maybe they were angry because they feel safer with you here."

"They'll have to get over it," I said. "I promised Master Shitozaki that I'd bring everyone home alive, but eventually I'll have to pass that duty on to you." I paused. "Command of the Finns should have been yours all along, anyway."

The air elementalist looked away. "If it had been up to me, we would have already returned."

"There's nothing wrong with that."

"Isn't there? If the Fates hadn't led us here, what would have happened to the witches? Or Kam Stone? They'd have been

186

captured or killed, that's what!" he said. "That's what they think when they look at me. *I'm* the one who would have doomed the coven, and the fact that I was completely ignorant of their predicament means nothing."

"Don't let their opinions get under your skin, Seth. It's easy for someone to criticize until they're the one making the tough decisions."

"If you return to Sanctuary and let Master Shitozaki know what is happening up here, perhaps he'll decide to intervene."

"And maybe he'll decide to stay in hiding," Seth said, sounding disgusted. "We could accomplish as much by sending a single rider to deliver the message."

"It's too dangerous a journey for one person."

"One pentacle, then."

"I am going *alone*, Seth," I said firmly.

He let out a huff, shaking his head. *"The wise man does not expose himself needlessly to danger since there are few things for which he cares sufficiently; but he is willing, in great crises, to give even his life – knowing that under certain conditions it is not worthwhile to live."* He paused. "If I didn't know better, I'd think Aristotle was talking about you."

"I just want to be able to sleep at night," I said. "That's why I'm going alone."

Someone cleared his throat behind me. I turned to see Duncan standing with hands tucked into the sleeves of his robe and one eyebrow raised.

"Alone except for Duncan," I amended. Gods knew I'd probably need healing at some point, and it wasn't like I could stop him anyway.

"If he's going, so am I," said Conall, emerging from the shadows with Dermot following.

"Me, too," said Dermot.

I sighed. I wasn't going to win this battle. Not today, anyway.

Chapter 10 – A Murder of Crows

We know the road to freedom has always been stalked by death.
~ Angela Davis ~

The next morning, everyone wanted to see what we'd absconded with in the wagon. I dropped the tailgate, climbed up on it, and drew back the tarp to reveal the twelve crates marked AMMUNITION. There were scattered whistles among the Finns, and murmurs from the witches.

Weylin cocked his head to one side. "Did you happen to get any more guns to go with all that ammo?"

I nodded. "Forty rifles, ten shotguns, and an odd assortment of pistols."

"Ooh! I want a pistol!"

"A pistol is what you use to fight your way to your rifle," I said, quoting some ancient, nameless gunman who had definitely known what he was talking about.

Weylin frowned.

"Honestly, though, you'll be better off with a shotgun," I added, and his eyes lit up again.

Since they were the most excited about the new weapons and ammunition, I let Madoc, Rob, Chester, Uri, and Regnar take over unwrapping the bundles of rifles and passing out ammunition. The altered Finns could instruct the witches in gunnery as well as I could.

Duncan showed up and stood beside me, observing the activities in silence. While Seth had been livid at my disappearance and hadn't hesitated to let me know about it, the earth druid hadn't said a word or given a hint as to his feelings on the matter.

"I knew you would return," he said, answering my unspoken question.

Sometimes the man was downright spooky.

"I think maybe Seth wasn't so sure about that."

"I know you better than Seth does, or any of the Finns," he said. "I also remember what you did for Wolfric."

For probably the thousandth time I wondered what had become of Wolfric and Onóra. They had escaped the grove with help from Angie, Duncan, and me, but there was no way of knowing if they'd made it through the wild and woolly lands between White Oak Grove and Ward Coven. Ever since chancing upon the witches fleeing for their lives and struggling to survive in the rough country, I'd regretted telling Wolfric to head for Ward. Maybe they'd stopped in Lone Oak or another small township because the bandit activity had become too hot for them to continue on to Ward. I had to content myself with the thought that Wolfric was both smart and savvy. He'd see them both somewhere safe.

"Do you know what today is?" Duncan said.

"No."

"It's Samhain."

While the autumn festival was one of the more important ones during the wheel of the year, marking the beginning of the new year, when old things died to make room for the new. Lately, however, it had been my least favorite.

When I was sixteen, I'd spent the holiday in bed after Trainer had brutally beaten me because a girl had asked me to kiss her – and then had gone and spread the lie that I'd tried to take more than she was willing to give. That year it had marked the beginning of the loneliest period of my life, when nearly everyone had scorned me. I became a pariah in the only place I'd ever known. Sequestering myself within the confines of my family's land, I had steadfastly refused to put one foot past our borders for over two years, until the day I set out on the open road and fulfilled my dream of becoming a Traveler.

Last year, when I'd still been in White Oak Grove, Morgana had woven a scene of spirit and mist during the Samhain ritual, drawing me into a place that demonstrated just how thin the veil between worlds really was on certain nights of the year. While everyone else had seen the illusions the ancient druid priestess' elemental magic had woven of the Celtic god and goddess honored on that occasion – Donn, the Dark Ruler of the Land of the Dead, and the Morrigan, Queen of Battle and Magic – I alone had been favored with the Great Queen's attention.

While Morrigan was the name on my lips whenever I entered battle, no sane person would ever *want* her dark and burning gaze upon them, for she was as deadly as she was terrifying. But she had come down from her throne of mist and ice to offer me her battle spear – and a challenge. Not knowing what sort of trial I would be undertaking, I took the spear anyway. I still don't know how long her merciless and daunting gaze was the only thing in my awareness – until I snapped back to myself after the end of the ritual, standing alone in the crowd with my arm held stiffly before me and my first clenched as though I still held that spear.

Wolfric, my only other friend at the grove besides Duncan, had been under a very real threat to his life after revealing to everyone that he had not been altered. Manipulated by Onóra, the partner chosen for him by the ancestors and the gods, he had revealed his pure, undiminished fire magic. She had dared him to do so as a condition for accepting him as her chosen. Then, after he'd literally risked his life in an environment toxic to young men with elemental magic, she had run away because she herself was too cowardly to follow through. I watched as *four* gods governing battle and death had placed their hands upon his head and shoulders: Donn and the Morrigan from my Celtic hearth culture, and Odin and Freyja from the Norse pantheon that Wolfric revered. And then they'd looked at me.

It was at that moment when I had understood that the Shining Ones had placed Wolfric's life in my hands. My actions would determine whether he lived or died, and the Morrigan had given me her spear as a demonstration of support.

"The High Priestess has decided to stay here another night and perform a ritual to honor their dead," Duncan said, interrupting my ruminations.

"I don't think that's a very good idea," I said, thinking about how the forces of the 'Ville were still too close for comfort.

"I mentioned that it might not be safe," he replied. "She told me that they had already begun raising the energy to cast a circle."

While druids chose to placate potentially harmful spirits and powers by making offerings to them during our rituals, witches preferred to cast a circle of protection that would prevent any evil spirits, demons, trickster spirits, or what-have-you from disrupting their spellcasting and rituals. Call me faithless, but I didn't think casting a magic circle would keep out bandits *or* bullets.

"That's going to be one big circle," I said.

"Perhaps that is why they started this morning."

"Let's round up the rest of the earth elementalists," I said. "We're going to make a circle of our own."

"We are?"

I admit to a certain amount of pleasure in eliciting surprise from the unflappable earth druid.

"Yeah. An earth druid circle," I said. "We're going to make some waves."

One corner of Duncan's mouth curled up in a smile.

* * *

With the exception of the earth elementalists, the Finns celebrated Samhain with the witches. The eight of us of us were on guard duty. Siorus, Yiorgos, Ingvar, Warwick, Martin, and Halldor were now fully trained due to Duncan's insistence that each one fully master the ability to earthmove and heal. He had engaged in teaching them to fully develop their healing skills, and we had both worked with them on earthmoving. Duncan's teaching was the most valuable by far, as he'd been a druid since the age of seven, but my ability to think outside the box was useful, too. While I possessed the magical ability of a grove-raised druid, I didn't think like one. I had none of their preconceived notions of what could or could not be done with my elements.

As far as I was concerned, there *were* no limitations.

The evening sky was a soft grey that would soon give way to the obsidian darkness of the new moon rising. I couldn't blame Rhiannon for wanting to perform ritual magic on a night when the moon was new and the boundary between the middle realm and the Otherworld was sheer. The danger of attack by raiders was a very real threat, however, so the earth elementalists were spread out in a massive circle which encompassed that of the witches. Standing equidistant from one another, we were far enough apart that we would have had to shout to communicate, except that our elemental magics were connected through the body of the mother.

"Eight is a good number," Siorus remarked.

Everyone had nodded, understanding his meaning. Each of us stood at one of the cardinal points of the earth, mirroring the festivals and solstices on each spoke of the wheel of the year. I stood at the southernmost point of the circle, while Duncan was stationed at the southwest point. As we were the only full druids, it was best for us to be in the locations where the enemy was most likely to attack. Because of their alliance with White Oak Grove, we had to assume our enemies had to know that we would sense their approach and be ready when they attacked. Their best bet was to sneak in close and then charge in an attempt to overrun us before we could mount a response. It was a good night to try such a tactic, with the new moon providing cover of darkness and the night vision of their prey obscured by the three roaring bonfires in the middle of the witches' circle.

The ritual was in full swing when I felt a warning vibration from Duncan. I peered into the distance out of habit, a useless action since I could barely see my hand in front of my face. The buzzing intensified, so I went down on one knee and placed my hand upon the ground to perform a *seeking*, threading my fingers through the reedy grasses. I could feel the witches and Finns inside the protective circle, recognized each individual earth elementalist standing guard in the outer circle, but no one else. As I sat there wondering why Duncan would be warning me if there were no enemies attacking, the warning became a spike of alarm. My fingers swept over the ground, both acknowledging his message and brushing it away.

A shadowy pair of black leather boots with metal greaves caught me off-guard and drove all other thoughts out of my mind because, according to the earth mother, *no one was standing there*.

The unknown entity squatted beside me, and I found myself looking into eyes so pale they could have been carved from glacial ice, framed by thick, black lashes and featuring prominently in a face that was both lovely and fierce. A thick mane of blue-black hair was pulled back from her high forehead and tied with a length of sinew. Clad in black leather and fur, she wore braided leather bracers on her forearms and a sword belted at her waist. A twisted silver torc with the heads of snarling wolves at the ends gleamed above a breastplate as iron-grey as my horse's coat. Ravens, wolves, and skulls were interwoven with etchings of Celtic knotwork and spirals painted crimson.

At least, I assumed it was paint.

The Morrigan looked different from the last time I'd seen her, more solid – more *real*. She gripped a familiar black spear, its sharp silver point rising from leather bindings and raven feathers as if it would pierce the very sky.

No wonder Duncan was alarmed.

Gleaming with an unearthly pale light, the Morrigan reached out, touching my face with icy fingers. I jerked upright, impelled by the shock of seeing the goddess as much as in response to the pressure beneath my chin. Even standing, I was forced to look up at her, for she was close to six feet tall. As her eyes of ice-blue fire stared into my soul, all I could think of was my father's stories about the legend of Cú Chulainn and how the great Celtic warrior had failed to recognize her, even after she'd told him she was responsible for his many victories. When she told him that she would continue to assist for the small price of having his love, he had arrogantly told her he didn't need a woman's help in the arena of battle.

It hadn't gone over well.

"My Lady," I said, finally finding my voice. To hear it so clear and level was a surprise because my mouth was dry from the sheer terror that had caused adrenaline to pump throughout my body. My heart thundered in a chest that heaved with deep, rapid breaths. My legs shook so badly that it would have been no surprise to hear my knees knocking. In an attempt to collect myself, I clenched my fists to control their trembling and bowed deeply before her.

While Danu and Dagda were my patron god and goddess, I highly revered the Phantom Queen, goddess of magic and battle. I called upon her anytime I drew a weapon to fight, whether it be shotgun, sword, or elemental magic. I owed her my faithfulness, my piety… and reciprocity for all the fights I'd survived and the battles I'd won.

"Rise, warrior," she said in a voice as husky and rich as black velvet. "You may look upon me without fear."

Though she had given me permission to do so, I wasn't so sure I'd be able to look at her 'without fear,' but I raised my eyes to hers. While they were as cold and implacable as before, one corner of her red-stained lips quirked upward in a sardonic smile.

"Thank you, my Lady," I said, automatically giving her the traditional druid gesture of respect – knuckling my head, lips, and heart, and then sweeping my upward-turned palm toward her. "How may I serve you?"

"As you always have," she replied, sending a chill down my spine. "Ever am I drawn to places where battles are fought and men slain. Long has it been since I have seen a warrior fight with such courage and ferocity. Long has it been since the dead have numbered so many, in a single season, on such a small parcel of land."

Gazing toward the south, she gestured with the spear. "The shout of the warrior, the clash of swords, and the screams of the dying have drawn me to this mortal realm. The torn flesh and ruptured entrails of the dead are an enticement to my ravens, who feast upon the carrion. Drawn by the scent of the blood-drenched earth, my wolves hunt the battlefield, gnawing on the bones of the fallen."

She locked eyes with me again, and for long moments I could not breathe. The world began to grey, and my head began to swim before I remembered to inhale again.

"Long has it been since a champion has laid a legion of corpses at my feet," the Morrigan said, her glacial eyes glittering. "Will you accept my love and my aid?"

I was terrified to accept and terrified to refuse.

"Yes, my Lady." It was barely a whisper.

Her blood-red lips formed a sultry smile as she leaned in close and kissed me, her lips a chill softness upon mine. Reacting instinctively to danger, my fire magic burst forth; I only just managed to suppress it, surrounding us both with a ring of dancing flame.

"Would you warm me this night, my champion?" she asked in a voice of smoke and embers. I had no idea whether she meant my elemental fire, my body, or both. I only knew that whatever she wanted, it would be dishonorable – and unwise – to refuse.

"Aye, my Lady," I said. "If it please you."

The Morrigan grinned with a delight that was terrible to behold. I closed my eyes, no longer able to hide the heat and the trembling that were now more desire than fear. When she kissed me again, dread was replaced by an insatiable blaze of carnal hunger. A yearning to see her bare flesh came over me and in the next instant everything else was forgotten as her hot tongue slid across my lips and plunged into my mouth, ratcheting up my lust tenfold. For a goddess of death and destruction, she kissed like fertility was her domain. My breath quickened still more when I felt her hands take hold of my belt, tugging on it. The metallic slide of metal was barely audible over the rush of blood in my ears, and I forgot all about it when she bit my lip hard, drawing blood.

The goddess drew back, leaving me empty and wanting, but the chill hardness of my own steel, laid at the juncture of my neck and shoulder, kept me from reaching for her. Its razor-sharp edge vibrated slightly with each pounding beat of my heart. The Morrigan smiled slyly at me. There was nothing I could do to stop her. She was an immortal goddess whose element was earth. Cú Chulainn had wounded her, but he had been one of the Tuatha de Danaan... The animalism within me gradually subsided, but the fear did not return.

"Are you not afraid?"

"No, my Lady."

"Know you not that I can take your life with the flick of my wrist?" She almost sounded indignant. Unable to help myself, I smiled.

"My Lady, you need no blade to end my life." She increased the pressure ever so slightly, slicing open my skin. It served only to inflame me anew, even as warm blood trickled down my neck. "It is you, Great Queen, who have allowed me the privilege of being the victor and not the slain. It is because of you that I live and breathe." Emboldened, I stepped closer to her, feeling the blade bite deeper. "If my life is what you desire, then I give it to you freely, and with joy."

Blood flowed over my right shoulder, spilling down my arm and chest. As if drawn to the metallic scent, the Morrigan drew near once more, fluid and controlled like the prowl of a hunting wolf. I shuddered as her tongue traced down my neck, tenderly probing, delicately tasting. Her breath was frosty upon my skin, igniting as it spread along the wound. The pain did nothing to diminish my renewed ardor. I closed my eyes and tipped my head back, reveling in the erotic sensations. The shivers wracking my body had nothing to do with the chilly night air.

"My desire is that you continue to serve me in this realm," she whispered. Stepping back once more, she held my sword upright, and I watched as my life's blood oozed down its length.

"You are far more courteous than Cú Chulainn," she said, making me wonder if she had read my earlier thoughts. "As you have accepted my love, I will be true and lend you my aid. Forget not that I am death and magic, but also life. Behold, mortal warrior!"

The Morrigan sliced her own flesh, showing no sign of pain. Heedless of the blood dripping down her naked arm, she chanted in a guttural language. The hilt of the bastard sword turned dull and black, as though covered in coal dust. The darkness spread upward from there, turning the blade the same color grey as the goddess' breastplate. Scarlet lines etched into the metal, woven into spirals and knotwork patterns. Once it was completely transformed, the Phantom Queen exhaled through pursed lips, blowing her artic breath across its length, making it glitter as though coated with frost. Finished with her handiwork, she flipped the blade lengthwise, catching the end with her bare hand and offering me the hilt.

I took it without hesitation, my eyes traveling over the intricate designs crawling over the dark metal. There was the knotwork that I'd expected to see, with its stylized wolves and ravens, but there was more still. Misted shapes of warriors and horses ghosted across the surface of the metal, swirling within its deep grey confines beneath the coating of frost. It was no longer mundane steel, that was for sure.

"With this blade, your glory will shine, and you will be a hero among men. Your enemies will fall like wheat before the scythe so that I may collect the trophies of your victories." Her eyes held a wicked glint. "It will never need sharpening, nor will it bend or break, and even you will not be able to melt it, no matter how hot the fire within you burns."

"Thank you, my Lady!" I dropped to one knee.

"Rise, champion."

I obeyed immediately.

"I eagerly await your sacrificial offerings," said the Morrigan, who then gestured to the south with a broad sweep of her arm.

"Your prey awaits." She dissolved in a torrent of darkness, changing into a surging flock of crows, all cawing raucously as they winged away into the moonlit night.

A murder of crows.

Racing toward me from the south were innumerable enemies, dressed in black with faces smeared with soot. I stamped my foot to send the signal vibration through the ground to Duncan and the other earth elementalists. As planned, the earthen ring surrounding the protective magic circle began to thrust a shockwave outward; it occurred exactly as when I was defending the trail wagon with Maeve and the others – only this time the groundswell moved outward in every direction, creating concentric circles around the ritual site.

The original plan had been to hold a defensive stance and keep the bandits at bay until the ritual was complete, all night if need be. However, since the Phantom Queen had so generously laid an enchantment upon my sword, and since that weapon was meant to provide her with the trophies of battle, I could not in good conscience allow it to go to waste.

I smoothed a path through the violently bucking earth. Unable to proceed past the undulating terrain, our enemies took advantage of the easier route. As they set foot upon the path, I raised a wall of flame to conceal my presence. Then I sent seven-foot walls of flame racing in random zigzag patterns down the cone of calmed earth, separating the marauders and trapping them between fire and unstable ground. Feeling the next few enemies ahead, I dropped the nearest wall of elemental fire. Catching them off guard, I lopped off the first man's arm as he was raising his pistol to fire. He screamed and fell to his knees, clutching his arm. Behind and to either side of the first bandit, the other two stood facing away from me, rooted in fear of the blaze that had sprung up to cut off their only way of escape. I'd intended to maim him and then kill him after taking care of the other two, but my body moved of its own accord. Perhaps instinctively – or perhaps spurred by a certain goddess – the luminescent grey blade swung about and chopped his head clean off.

I'd witnessed beheadings a time or two and knew how durable the bones of a man's neck truly were. Even with someone tied motionless to a chopping block, an executioner using all his strength typically took two swings to separate a man's head from his shoulders and sometimes three or more. The ease with which the grey blade had sliced through muscle, sinew, and bone was literally staggering. I was thrown off balance by the extra force I'd put into the strike.

It was fool's luck that saved my life, for one of the remaining bandits had recovered from his shock, spinning about and rapid-firing dual pistols. One bullet grazed my skull in a red-hot line across my right temple while the rest whizzed by overhead. Using my existing momentum to propel myself forward, I tucked and rolled between the two remaining bandits. Pulling my sword arm in tight and directing the lethal blade away from my body, I rolled through the flames, calling them up thick and red-hot. Regaining my feet, I flung a handful of fire darts at the woman on the left to occupy her attention as I sprang up and drove the grey blade through the gunslinger's gut, slicing him from stem to stern. When I yanked it out, his entrails spilled upon the ground in a slimy, steaming heap. Blood spewed from his mouth and gushed from his chest, and the smell of hot iron filled my nostrils as it bubbled on the ground.

I turned to the woman with the shotgun, bringing the inferno with me. I took a few steps toward her as she stared with wide, terrified eyes. The acrid stink of fear and urine reached my nose when I stopped and leveled the grey blade, its point a bare inch from her naked throat. Petrified and shaking, she never made a move to raise her weapon. Sweat poured down her face and soaked her shirt.

The Morrigan, Queen of Battle and Chooser of the Slain, had called me her champion. She wanted blood and bones, and the mountains of slaughtered enemies I could bring her. She had placed an enchantment woven of magic and our mingled blood upon my sword. She had promised me assistance, and it was clear that with this blade I would be victorious over anyone who opposed me. I owed the goddess a debt, a reciprocal payment of all the times she had helped me against past enemies.

But I still could not bring myself to murder this woman.

I hated killing women, no matter the circumstance.

Lowering the blade, I said, "Just this once, I will let you live. If I ever see you again with a gun in your hands, I *will* kill you."

The shotgun fell to the ground, and tears fell from her eyes.

"You can go back to them if you want, but if I were you, I'd find myself a different line of work," I said. "I'm gunning for the 'Ville next. Warn them if you want, but that won't stop me from destroying it."

She shook her head wildly, sending sweat flying in all directions. Dousing the flames, I gave her safe passage. She ran as if a pack of the Morrigan's wolves were on her heels, shoving past the rest of the bandits until she was consumed by the night. They ignored her and came after me.

I smiled grimly, and the corridor of flame sprang up again, trapping the marauders once more.

The Morrigan would have trophies aplenty this night.

* * *

Dawn broke over the horizon some hours after the battle was over. The enemy had tried attacking from several points around our earth druid circle but had always returned to my corridor of death. Eventually, the survivors had run away, but I didn't have my horse and was too tired to give chase, anyway. Granted, the grey blade sliced through flesh and bone like a hot knife through butter, but I'd been awake for over twenty-four hours. My whole body ached.

Squatting to take a breather, I slapped the ground a couple of times to signal the other earth elementalists to cease provoking the earth and let it settle back down again. I was played out, but as soon as I saw Duncan's face, I knew I wouldn't be getting to sleep anytime soon. Siorus was the next to join us, followed by the rest of the earth elementalists in a group. None of them seemed to be tired, even after the long night, but I still wondered how many had completely expended their magic.

If they were all tapped out, that would be bad. We couldn't afford to have most of our earth elementalists out of juice for days on end. Duncan and I had virtually limitless power, but we were still only human and needed rest.

Each of them took notice of the cone-shaped swath of scorched earth that stretched for a hundred yards, but nobody asked about it or the dozens of corpses scattered across it. I wondered why until I noticed that some of them were so excited they couldn't sit still. I couldn't figure why they weren't falling-down tired after a whole night of channeling magic. Duncan appeared not to have noticed, probably because he looked as tired as I felt.

"How is it that six guys who look as tired as you do still have the energy to smile?" I asked, feeling grouchy and out of sorts.

"Well," said Siorus, grinning hugely. "We all became druids last night."

"Truly?" asked Duncan, looking delighted.

They all nodded, grinning like kids in a candy store.

"Praise the gods!" I said, feeling an immense weight lifted from my shoulders.

Siorus said, "If we hadn't held the earthen ring last night, I doubt any of us would be full druids today."

"Agreed," said Martin.

"Well, we *are* all of age," said Warwick.

"I'm not!" proclaimed Yiorgos. "I'm only eighteen."

"That's right," I said. "And Halldor and Ingvar are nineteen."

"Actually, I'm twenty," said Ingvar.

"Sorry," I said, chalking my memory's failure up to fatigue.

"Don't worry about it," he said with a laugh. "My birthday was two days ago. You missed the party."

"Aww, quakes," I said. "Now I'm really sorry."

Halldor elbowed Ingvar. "Don't tease him like that. We didn't have a party, Davis."

"I'm glad I didn't miss anything, then."

"Well, nothing but my birthday," Ingvar said.

Even though the eight earth elementalists – no, *druids* – had gotten no sleep last night, the caravan wasted no time breaking camp and moving on. I slept in the back of the trail wagon with the others, but only until noon. After the midday meal, I saddled up and rode Steel for the rest of the afternoon. I hurt pretty much everywhere by the end of the day. While the enchantment on my sword made it cut through enemies like they were made of air, it still weighed three pounds. Three pounds may not sound like much, but when you swing it hundreds of times, it takes a toll.

When we camped for the night, I dug a hole in the earth, sealed it watertight, and begged Dermot to fill it for me. He did, but only on the condition that he got to soak in the hot water, too. Of course, since he got to join, I couldn't very well deny the rest of my pentacle, so I made the "tub" larger. Thus, my nice, relaxing soak wasn't as tranquil as it should have been.

"So," Conall said, beginning the inevitable interrogation, "What in the nine hells happened out there last night?"

"There's really not that much to tell," I said.

"I rather doubt that," said Seth. "Warwick and Halldor both mentioned that it looked like you slaughtered the entire raiding party by yourself."

"I would like to know also," said Duncan, throwing me to the wolves. "You said we would only be defending."

I looked expectantly at Dermot.

"I couldn't care less what you were doing," he said. "I had sex with three witches last night, and my back is *killing* me."

Conall looked at him. "Together, or separately?"

Dermot grinned. "Yes."

"Fine," I said. I had no desire to hear about our youngest member's wild sexual escapades, especially since I wasn't having any. "I'll tell you what happened, but I want you to promise to keep it just among us."

Seth frowned. "You would keep something important from the High Priestess?"

"Or Master Shitozaki?" Conall added. It was a jab; he couldn't have cared less whether I discussed anything with Connor Shitozaki.

"If it was something that impacted the Finns or the coven, I would," I said, vaguely irritated. "This is personal."

"What could possibly be personal about slaughtering bandits?" Conall asked.

Duncan gave in and saved me. "You did receive my warning, didn't you?"

"I did, and it was a good thing you warned me." I paused. "It was weird, though. I couldn't even feel her through the earth, and she was standing right beside me, so I don't know how you even knew she was there."

Confusion crossed his features. "She who?"

"The Morrigan."

Duncan's dark eyes widened. "You saw the Phantom Queen again last night?!"

"You didn't?"

"No!"

"Then what was the warning about?"

"The bandits approaching. And why didn't you answer me back?"

"I did. Well, I didn't answer back, exactly, because I don't know *how*, but I kinda… made it go away."

"And you didn't think to answer?"

"Look, we haven't worked on communicating through the earth very much—"

"Perhaps not, but as I've told you many times, your element will interpret your intent—"

Dermot interrupted. "Excuse me. Can we get back to the part where Davis saw a *goddess*?"

Both Seth and Conall's heads snapped from Duncan to me, indicating that they weren't familiar with deities outside their own hearth cultures. I gave them the abbreviated version, skimping on the parts where the Great Queen had kissed me and relaying most of our conversation.

"By the gods!" Dermot said, awestruck. "You had sex with a goddess last night!"

"No, I did not."

"This is *exactly* like the story of the Morrigan and Cú Chulainn," Duncan said, looking flabbergasted.

"Except that Cú Chulainn was an idiot," commented Dermot.

"Davis, you *do* know that story, don't you?" the earth druid asked.

"Yes, I know the story."

"I don't," said Conall and Seth in unison.

"In short, Cú Chulainn met the Phantom Queen more than once, but on this specific occasion she asked him if he would accept her assistance *and* her love." Duncan gave me a significant glance that could have meant anything, but probably meant that he thought Angie was going to kill me when she found out about it.

"Cú Chulainn refused her offer and then further insulted the Morrigan by telling he did not need a woman to help him."

"That's never a good idea," said Conall. "Goddess or not."

"Indeed," said Duncan. "The goddess rescinded her offer and proceeded to bend her considerable will and magical ability to undermining him. Eventually, she orchestrated his death." He turned back to me. "Please tell me you told her yes. Please tell me you did not allow your devotion to my cousin to reject the aid of the goddess of battle and death."

Conall whistled.

"I did not refuse her," I said.

"If she offered you her love and you didn't refuse her, then that means you had sex with her," Seth said in a tone that suggested he did not quite believe what he was hearing.

"Davis dipped his wick in a goddess pool," Dermot said, his eyes shining with admiration. "I am in awe."

"I did *not!*" I snapped. "What does that even mean?"

Duncan interrupted before the water elementalist could explain. "You *must* have," he insisted. "The legends are quite clear on how the Morrigan operates. It was she who made love with Dagda so that he could defeat the Fomorians. Sex is how she confers her favor, and her blessing."

"She kissed me, nothing more," I said. "I did *not* have sex with her."

"You are positive that you did not refuse her?" Duncan pressed.

"Honestly, I don't think I could have."

"Well," said Seth. "She *is* a goddess."

"You lucky dog!" exclaimed Dermot. "Even if it was just a kiss. Not that I believe *that* for a second."

"Well, she also licked my neck," I admitted, omitting the fact that it was blood she was licking off my skin.

"Now that's what I'm talking about," Conall said.

There was quiet for a few moments, and I decided it was as good a time as any to get out of the tub and dry off.

"So what did she give you?" Conall asked once we were clothed again.

"Why do you think she gave me anything?"

"She promised you aid, and right now what we need the most

is help fighting the bandits." He shrugged. "I just figured she gave you a weapon or talisman or something of the like."

The others looked at me expectantly.

"She placed an enchantment on my sword," I admitted.

"Which one?" Dermot asked with a grin. Conall splashed him, and the water elementalist sent the wave right back, giggling.

"What kind of enchantment?" Duncan asked.

"The kind that makes it sharp enough to split hairs," I replied.

"Let's see it," said Seth.

Trying not to grimace as I knelt beside the earthen tub, I drew the grey blade out of the earth.

"Why did you bury it?" Seth asked.

"I'm afraid to leave it unattended," I said. "I don't know what will happen if anyone else touches it. Somebody might get hurt."

Unsheathing it, I revealed to them the cold grey steel with its crimson etching and black hilt. The whorls in the metal moved slowly within the blade, so slowly that I was probably the only one who even noticed.

Conall whistled again.

"Wow," said Dermot. "You kissed a goddess *and* got a badass sword."

Seth crossed his arms over his chest and frowned.

"What is it?" I asked.

"Reciprocity for such a gift could very well require a lifetime of service."

"If it helps me destroy the 'Ville," I said, "so be it."

Chapter 11 - Rescue

I had crossed the line. I was free;
but there was no one to welcome me to the land of freedom.
I was a stranger in a strange land.
~ Harriet Tubman ~

Since the caravan had six brand new earth druids brimming with power and eager to use it, Duncan and I took off alone to go scouting.

"How are you feeling today?" he asked. He had healed me the night before, and while I would not ordinarily have asked him to expend his magic on mere sore muscles, I needed to be in top form for the rest of this journey, not to mention retaking Ward and destroying the 'Ville.

"Right as rain," I said. "Although, I'd have preferred not to discuss the Morrigan with anybody but you."

"Do you not share all your thoughts with Seth?" Duncan asked.

I shook my head.

"Why not?"

"Because I already have someone to share all my thoughts with."

"But Angie is not here."

"I don't share all my thoughts with Angie, either."

"You don't?" he said. "But she is your chosen."

"She doesn't react well to certain things."

He was thoughtful for a few moments. With some hesitation,

he said, "Davis, I know you value independence and free thinking, but everyone needs someone to whom they can say anything."

"I do."

"But if not Angie or Seth, then who?" he asked, looking perplexed.

I gave him a funny look. "You." His expression said that he was having some difficulty accepting my response. "Look, even if I *don't* tell you everything, I know I *can*. No matter what sorts of harebrained ideas I come up with, you're not going to have a come-apart over it. Seth is very intellectual, and he has to think of a thousand reasons why something won't work before he can even consider that it might. Dermot is young, and while I enjoy his optimism and sense of adventure... he's a water elementalist. As for Conall, he's just..." I trailed off, unable to put the thought into words.

"Norse," Duncan supplied wryly.

"Exactly." I chuckled. "Besides, I've known you longer than anyone except for Angie. You're intelligent and thoughtful and passionate about things you believe in. Every day I learn something new from your devotion to the gods."

He looked away, shaking his head. "You give me too much credit."

"Everybody makes mistakes, Duncan. The difference is that you recognize when you've made one and then try to learn from it. That is real wisdom."

"Hm." Duncan shook his head in astonishment. "I never considered that I might be your *anam cara*."

"My what?"

"Did your parents not teach you this? It is an integral part of our Celtic heritage."

"Maybe they just called it something else. What is an... *anam cara*?"

"Someone who is not family, or spouse, or lover, but who is more than a friend. The literal translation is *soul friend*."

"No, they never mentioned anything like that." Down deep, that hurt. My mother had expected me to stay in Jonesboro, settle down, start farming, and raise a family. In that scenario, it was highly unlikely that I would ever meet anyone who might qualify as an *anam cara* – or ever even need one.

"This doesn't please you," Duncan said.

"What? No, it does," I said. "I'm just kind of pissed that my parents didn't think it necessary to teach me about it." I smiled at him. "I can't think of anyone I'd rather have as a soul friend."

Then I remembered the secret I'd been keeping from him – Kam's prophecy about my death.

"You're pensive again," he said.

"There's something I haven't told you, that I probably should have."

"Oh?"

"As it turns out, Kam Stone is an oracle of Apollo. *The* Oracle of Apollo, actually."

He nodded. "She told me."

"She did?"

"It was something of a necessity if I was to believe that she had genuinely foretold your death."

"You mean you've known all along?"

"Aye."

"And you never said anything?"

"I felt that you would bring it up when you were ready."

"Did Kam say why she was telling you?"

"Aye. She asked me to watch your back."

"Well, I'll be." So Kam Stone hadn't just left me to fend for myself against Zeus's striking eagle bolt of doom, and her departure wasn't because she had written me off. Maybe she had left because she really *was* faithful to Apollo.

Maybe I had been a temptation for her, too.

"So you believe her."

He shrugged. "While I do believe that Kam Stone's claim that she is the Oracle of Delphi, I do *not* believe her prophecy to be unassailable."

"*She* sure did. Why don't you?"

"Because she also told me that she's foreseen your death many times, in several manners and locations," he said. "This tells me that either her prophecies are not set in stone, or that you are protected. I assumed it was the latter, and that this protection came from one of the gods."

"Guess we know which one it is."

"Indeed."

Around mid-morning, Duncan picked up the trail of a small group of people. He estimated that they were a little under half a mile away and moving slowly. Now that Steel and Scarlet were nicely warmed up, we got them moving at a canter until we caught sight of our quarry. The arrogant bastards never once checked their back trail, and when we were close enough, we discovered why. They had cornered a pair of potential victims – one standing in defense of the other, who was pinned beneath a downed horse. Four of the six were still mounted, while the other two had dismounted to approach their intended victims on foot.

We acted in unison without a word, urging our horses into a fast gallop. Upon hearing their pounding hoofbeats, the six bandits turned to see us – two lone riders – bearing down on them.

They weren't afraid.

They should have been.

One pulled forth a longbow and fired a few arrows. He was a good shot, but I burned the arrows before they even got close to hitting either of us. He was joined shortly afterward by the other riders, firing rifles. I lobbed fireballs at each of their weapons, melting them and cooking off the ammunition inside. By the time the bandits had tossed their hot weapons aside, we were within melee range. I drew my sword and took the head of the first rider I encountered, followed by the head of the second rider on the backstroke. Steel wheeled about, and I cut down the last two mounted bandits, then started to look for the ones still on their feet. Duncan had killed three and was pulling his sword from a dead man's belly when the last one came at him with a knife. Pulling his blade free with a yank that sent blood droplets flying, he spun and gutted him. It was a dirty fight; bloody, messy, and murderous.

As I turned to check on the bandits' intended victims, a small fireball flew by my head. Surprised but ready for the next attack, I caught the second one. It seemed to shock the hooded elementalist standing before me, just long enough for me to decide that it was a woman. The next thing she launched was a firebolt, a burst of streaming flames that shot from her extended right hand. I caught that blast, too. A second later her elemental fire petered out and died. It seemed that attacking me had used her last bit of magic. She flung her arm downward in frustration and then drew a heavy knife.

"Stay back!" she warned in low tones. "I will kill you!"

There was something familiar about her voice, but I couldn't place it.

"We won't hurt you," I said. "We're here to help."

"No one from the grove wants to help us."

"I imagine not," I said, taking a step toward her and ignoring the wavering blade. "But we aren't from the grove."

Beneath the hood, she shook her head. "You're lying!"

Possibly this was a young elementalist who had departed the grove much in the same way as Wolfric and Onóra, against the ArchDruid's wishes. If that was the case, I was honor-bound to assist them in any way I could. First, though, I had to convince her to trust me. I drew back my hood, pushing my long shaggy hair out of my face.

"Davis," she breathed before I could introduce myself. Then: "Duncan!" when he also flipped back his hood.

"You know us?" I asked, nonplussed. She drew back her hood, revealing short black hair that had been raggedly cut, and hazel eyes sunken into a face sharpened by hunger. I don't know who was more shocked, me or her.

"Onóra." That meant that her fallen companion was—

"*Wolfric!*"

Ignoring her blade, I hastened to kneel by his side.

Duncan placed a hand on Wolfric's chest. "He lives," the earth druid said, and went to work tending him.

A sob of relief escaped Onóra's lips. She wavered on her feet, and I moved to take her arm for support; she was so unsteady that I feared she might fall.

"You're a fire elementalist?" she said, a trace of awe in her voice. "How is this possible? You had no magic before!"

"Fire and earth, actually," I said. "Just like you."

"He was blocked," Duncan said absently, still examining Wolfric's injuries. There were a lot of them. His blonde hair was matted and caked with dried blood, and his shirt was stained red where an arrow protruded from his right breast. Bloody froth dribbled between his lips, and I felt sure the arrow had punctured a lung. It was likely that he has also suffered multiple broken bones from the weight of the horse falling on him.

Her face pinched with worry, she said, "How will we ever get it off him?"

"Fortunately, we have just the magic for the job," I said, placing one palm on the ground. The earth responded to my call, rising up on either side of Wolfric to lift the horse off his inert body. As soon as there was a foot of space between him and the animal's corpse, I commanded the earth to move him out of danger while Duncan kept one hand on the fallen warrior's chest to prevent further harm. Wolfric's body gently slid across the grass, allowing me a good look at his legs. The left seemed to be okay, but jagged white bone protruded through torn and swollen flesh of his right thigh.

I had thought to throw him over a horse's back and take him back to the caravan so Duncan could heal him in a safer place, but it was obvious that Wolfric wouldn't survive it if we tried. His pelvis could be fractured, causing bleeding inside, or his back might be broken. He'd not thank us for saving his life if it meant never walking again.

Onóra sank to her knees beside her chosen, fear and hope warring in her gaunt features. I didn't want to leave them, either, as the possibility of bandits coming upon them was great. However, I also did not want to be out here trying to defend them with only one other druid to help. The two of us could handle fighting bandits if it came to that, but protecting two other people at the same time might require that we divide our concentration too much. Besides, we needed more hands if we were to get Wolfric back in one piece.

All I could think of was to send a signal, and the only thing I had to signal with was fire. Rising to my feet, I raised my fist into the air and began shooting fireballs into the sky, each about half a second apart. They sailed well above the distant treetops before bursting like fireworks in the chill air. I paused a couple of minutes and then repeated the action. After that, I sent a signal about every fifteen minutes, three fireballs punctuating the sky to guide whoever saw them to us. They revealed our position to anyone who saw them, but hopefully my pentacle would arrive before the enemy did. I figured that we could defend adequately against any enemies that turned up until then. It took them just over an hour, and they showed up on sweating, lathered horses.

"What happened?" Seth was dismounting before his horse had even stopped.

"Bandits," I said. "They were moving in for the kill when we intervened. This is Onóra and her chosen, Wolfric. I knew them at the grove." I turned to her next. "Onóra, these are our friends." In answer to her anxious expression, I said, "None of them are from the grove. We'll get Wolfric fixed up and take you both to safety."

"Safety? Is that what we're calling it now?" quipped Conall.

"It's safer than here," I said, giving him a warning look.

"Is that Wolfric Rask?" he asked.

"It is," I replied. "You know him?"

"Used to," he said. "I haven't seen him in years, of course. Why'd he leave the grove?"

"Sebrina found out he had magic."

"That trickster!" He snorted and shook his head. "He told me he'd been altered."

"You can hardly blame him," Onóra said in a reproving tone.

Wolfric slipped from unconsciousness into a restful sleep after Duncan's healing. Conall and Dermot rounded up the bandit horses, and Seth and I strapped the travois to one of them for transport back to the caravan. I helped Onóra mount up behind Duncan and then mounted my own horse. Seth, Dermot, and Conall took the reins of the remaining horses to bring them along.

As soon as we returned, we were surrounded by people wanting to know what had happened. When the members of my pentacle had responded to my signal, Rhiannon had ordered everyone to halt and set up camp even though it was only noon.

"You found more horses!" Rhiannon exclaimed, falling silent when she caught sight of the blood on my clothes. Then she noticed the body on the travois and the thin, tense girl riding with Duncan.

"What happened?"

"This is Onóra and her chosen, Wolfric. He was pinned beneath their dead horse when we found them, and she was about to be taken by bandits. They left the grove some months ago."

"What can I do for him?" the High Priestess asked, moving to assist as Seth and Conall untied the travois from my horse.

"Duncan healed him, but he needs a place to rest." I lowered my voice. "Onóra is the one who needs you the most. She looks as if she's had a hard time of it."

"Of course! Come here, darling, you look exhausted," Rhiannon said tenderly. Soon the elementalist girl was surrounded by a cluster of witches who led her away, crooning comfortingly to her.

"Bring her young man, too," the High Priestess ordered. "She will want to be close to him, I'm sure."

Seth and I hoisted the travois and toted Wolfric to a small makeshift tent. The witches brought buckets of water, which I warmed until they were steaming. The Finns left them to their work of tending to the bedraggled pair, knowing them to be in the best of hands. My pentacle and I went back to the horses to find Ahearn checking them over.

"These horses belonged to the bandits?" he asked.

"I figured we can never have too many."

We spent the next couple of hours removing their tack, then examining them for injuries, looking at hooves, teeth, and coats, and then groomed them thoroughly. Ahearn declared the newest members of the witches' herd to be healthy and sound, aside from being tired from hard riding. We looked over their tack next, noting that both saddles and bridles were in good repair. While supper was being cooked, we sat beside a small fire, cleaning and oiling the leather.

"So you knew them at the grove?" Seth was asking.

"Wolfric is my friend, and Onóra is one of Angie's."

"What are they doing out here?"

"Still running, I guess," I said, frowning. I'd have thought they would have made it farther than this, settled down into a peaceful life in a quiet town. "The ArchDruid didn't like it much when Onóra decided she wanted to be with her chosen instead of the one who had been picked out for her. When she left with Wolfric, Sebrina sent a posse to hunt them down."

"I'm surprised they weren't caught," said Dermot.

"Onóra's an earth-fire elementalist. Before they left, Duncan taught her to cover their tracks," I said. "And I might have led the masters to believe they went one way when they actually went another."

"You helped them escape," said Seth, his dark eyes sharp.

"Anyone would have done the same."

"I doubt that," said Conall.

I was saved from having to explain further by the return of the High Priestess. Seating herself gracefully, she looked at me with a caring and motherly expression. I wasn't fooled; an interrogation was about to begin.

"I thought you might like to know how your friends are doing," she said without preamble. "Of course you know Duncan healed the young man completely. All he needed was a bath and a warm bed. The young lady, however, is another matter. We have cared for her physical needs, but she is in quite a distressed emotional state." When I did not answer, she continued: "It would help if you could tell me what happened to them."

"They were attacked by bandits."

Her lips pursed in irritation. "That doesn't explain why two young druids were all alone in the wilderness, and on the verge of starvation from the looks of things."

"You've seen what the grove has become, High Priestess," I said, meaning the attack on Ward. "They were forced to leave the grove when the ArchDruid found out Wolfric had magic. I'm sure you can imagine the kinds of things they've been through."

"You're not going to tell me."

"It's not my place. If you want to know, ask her."

Rhiannon sighed and frowned. Of course, she had already asked, and the young elementalist must have chosen not to answer. I couldn't blame her. Who would want to admit to a perfect stranger that she had her hair chopped off as punishment? That their own people had hunted them? That if they were caught, Wolfric's life would have been forfeit?

No, that horror was not mine to tell.

"What are you going to tell Wolfric?" Seth asked when the High Priestess had gone.

"About what?"

"About why you left the grove."

"I'm not."

* * *

The next day we were breaking camp and discussing the best way to get Wolfric into the trail wagon when he woke up.

He did not get up in a good mood.

Dermot was first to notice, raising his head and craning his neck to see what was causing the sudden commotion. I wasn't concerned at first. Traveling was stressful for everyone, and the children frequently entertained themselves by playing pranks on the adults or scrapping with each other. It usually resulted in being yelled at by their mothers. Sometimes even the Finns got on to them.

"What?" I asked when he stood, attention riveted on the busy camp behind us.

"Something's going on in the healer's tent," he said.

There was a sharp cry of alarm, and a couple of witches came stumbling out of the tent.

"Looks like your friend's awake," Seth said.

"Grouchy bastard, isn't he?" remarked Conall.

"Definitely not a morning person," agreed Dermot, as Wolfric burst through the tent flaps. He was staggering and barely able to hold his sword, seemingly intent on killing everyone in range of his blade.

"At least he's not throwing fireballs," I said.

"Yet," said Conall.

"It'll be good to have another fire elementalist around," said Seth.

"I'd better handle this," I said. "Duncan, come with me. Everyone else stay here."

Most of the caravan kept their distance, except for a group of Finns that had made a protective semicircle around Wolfric to contain his magic and keep him from harming anyone. I noticed that Jasvinder and his brother Narinder, both air/spirit elementalists, were there along with the twins Eian and Declan. Warwick and Siorus were also present, ready to heal anyone who needed it. Seconds later, flames appeared in Wolfric's free hand. Duncan and I broke into a run just as he launched the fireball. I reached out and willed it to come to me. It made a sharp turn in its trajectory and burst harmlessly against my palm. We slowed to a walk and drew back our hoods before entering the protective circle.

A crazy light shone in Wolfric's eyes, and he stood in a defensive crouch, snarling like a wolf cornered by hounds. Even though he was barely able to stand on his own two feet, he was ready to lash out at the slightest provocation.

"Heya, Wolfric."

"Davis?" The sword tip lowered slightly.

"It's me."

"Who are these people?" The blade tilted upward again.

"Exiles from the grove," I said. "We call ourselves the Finns."

His keen blue eyes traveled over the assembled group of elementalists. He lowered the blade. "They have magic?"

"Most do."

"How did we get here? Onóra says we were attacked by bandits."

I nodded. "Duncan and I were out scouting when we came across their trail. You were hurt pretty bad."

Wolfric hesitated, eyes traveling over me, Duncan, the Finns, and the camp, which had returned to the business of packing up.

"It's a long story," I said. "Why don't we have some breakfast and I'll tell you all about it?"

* * *

I filled Wolfric in on Connor Shitozaki, the history of the Finns, what we were doing out here, and how we had come upon the coven after they'd been dispossessed of their home. He ate and listened, saying little. Onóra ate with him; I figured it was her second breakfast. They had both lost a significant amount of weight; it would take more than a few meals to set them to rights.

"Are you still being chased by the grove?" I asked.

"Not anymore," said Wolfric, shaking his head. "It's bandits that have been harassing us."

"Every time we got settled, whatever little town or village we were in was overrun, and we had to flee again," Onóra said. "They're everywhere!"

"They're expanding their territory," I said. "We've been attacked by them a few times, but so far we've managed to fight them off. You might want to stick with us for a while. It'll give you both a chance to rest."

It seemed the Wolfric was about to refuse when Onóra laid a thin hand on his shoulder. "The witches are very nice," she said. "I'm so tired of running. I'd like to stay."

Their eyes met, and I could tell she had convinced him; not

with words, perhaps, but with the thinness of her face and the frailty of her body. I remembered when Onóra Nightshade had been lovely; no doubt he did as well.

Wolfric nodded. "We are grateful for your hospitality."

As we rose from the meal, Rhiannon came over with Ahearn, who was leading two horses, a blaze-faced chestnut and a dark bay with a star.

"I didn't know if you would be leaving or staying with us," Ahearn said, "But I'd like you to have these horses. I raised and trained them myself." The horse master handed their reins to Wolfric, who appeared stunned by the unexpected generosity.

"My thanks," he finally managed. "I am in your debt."

The red-haired horsemaster smiled. "Well, by all rights the bandit horses that Davis brought back should belong to you. They need a little retraining, though, so this is actually a trade."

Onóra put her cheek against the nearest horse's blazed chestnut face, smiling softly at her chosen. "I told you they were nice."

Together, Ahearn and I introduced Wolfric to the High Priestess. He gave Rhiannon the sign of druidic respect, touching fingertips to his forehead and heart, before extending his hand to her.

"You honor us with your kindness and generosity," he said. "May Odin All-Father watch over you and Frigga grant you prosperity and fertility."

"Lord and Lady bless you both," replied Rhiannon, inclining her head graciously. "We are happy to have you."

Mother and son departed to lead the coven onward, leaving Wolfric and me to rejoin my pentacle. I tried to get Wolfric to ride in the trail wagon but he would have none of it. He seemed to have recovered sufficiently to walk without a limp, and even helped Onóra up onto her chestnut horse, so I figured he was well enough to ride. He walked companionably beside me, leading his bay until I reached my own horse. I claimed Steel's reins from Dermot, then mounted and made formal introductions. He could meet everyone else later; I was ready to be on the move. Upon meeting Dermot, Wolfric turned thoughtful.

"What's your name, again?"

"Dermot Stoddard," replied the redhead.

"I know you," said Wolfric. "I was friends with your brother Jason. You tried to follow us everywhere when you were little."

Dermot had a brother? I looked askance at him, noting that Seth did likewise. He had mentioned his sisters, but never a brother. Dermot's fingers tightened around his reins until the knuckles were white.

"And how was it that you escaped the ArchDruid's notice while my brother did not?" he replied testily.

"I was careful, while your brother was not," Wolfric replied. "Jason was extremely impulsive, even for a water elementalist. For that matter, you aren't old enough to be finished training. What are you, fifteen?"

"*Seventeen.*" The water elementalist sat hunched in his saddle, eyes fixed on an unseen point between his horse's ears.

"You bear the same scars as your brother, then?"

"No," Dermot said, refusing to look at him. "My mother sent me to Master Shitozaki to finish my training."

"Shitozaki," Wolfric repeated. "It must be interesting to train under an exiled ArchDruid."

"That's one word for it," Dermot muttered.

Wolfric continued as if he hadn't heard. "My father says he was insufferably arrogant, even for a fire druid."

Seth frowned, but from what little I knew of Adalwulf, I could well imagine him saying such a thing. The man was all honor and integrity, and he might very well think that anyone who acted out of some other motivation was overly prideful.

"So when did you leave the grove?" Wolfric asked me.

"Shortly after you did."

"That's good. I was afraid that the weasel would carry tales and get you into trouble," he said.

Darryn Darkmane had done exactly that, but I said nothing.

"It will be so good to see Angelina again," said Onóra, peering at the faces of the people who made up the caravan. "Where is she?"

I should have expected her to ask, but I still wasn't prepared for the question. "She's not here."

Wolfric reined his horse up short. Fortunately, my pentacle was riding at the rear of the caravan today. "What? Where is she?"

"Back at the grove."

"You *left* her?" There was no mistaking his accusing tone.

I met his angry gaze. "I didn't have a choice."

"You didn't have a—" He broke off. "There is *always* a choice."

I made no reply. My choice to help him leave the grove with Onóra was what had led to my separation from Angie, but it wouldn't be right to throw that in their faces.

"Did you at least try to go back for her?"

"No."

"But you have magic now."

"I came into my elements at Midsummer. It's taken a while to learn to use them."

"You should have tried anyway. It is your duty as her chosen."

"Even if I died in the attempt?" It was funny how these thoughts sounded so logical inside my own head when I was castigating myself, and how insane they sounded when spoken out loud.

"At least she would know you never gave up," he said, sounding disgusted. I had no reply to that. I knew that I hadn't given up, but most days it still felt like I had.

"You don't know what Davis has been through," said Seth. "He nearly died."

"I am your friend, Davis, but this is a matter of honor," said Wolfric. "It is only because you aided us in our escape last winter that I can still call you friend."

"Last winter?" said Seth. From his expression I could see him thinking hard, linking me helping them escape with my arrival on the Finns' doorstep a few weeks after Yule.

"How very noble of you," muttered Dermot, scowling.

"Especially since you're the reason he had to leave," said Seth, having put it all together. "And the reason he was unable to go back for Angelina."

"Seth—" I held up a hand to forestall him.

He shook his head. "No. You are a good friend to him in not mentioning the debt he owes, but I will not stand by while he berates you for a matter in which he himself bears some responsibility."

"What are you talking about?" said Wolfric.

"Unless I am mistaken, Davis was brought to us a few weeks

after your escape." He looked at Duncan. "Am I correct?"

Reluctantly, the earth druid nodded. "You are." At this, both Conall and Dermot caught on.

"What an ass," said the redhead, spurring his horse forward. Conall snorted and shook his head, following. Duncan's spotted mare trotted forward to join them, surprising me. I had thought if anyone was likely to understand Wolfric's position, it would be him.

Seth continued. "It's a pity don't know just how much a friend you have in Davis."

"Enough!" I snapped. I could see him struggling with wanting to tell Wolfric off, but also wanting to respect my wishes.

"Very well." Fixing Wolfric with a dark look, he said. "You would be wise to consider what sort of penalty an Outsider might suffer, should the ArchDruid discover that he aided a renegade fire elementalist in running away with a young lady." He held up a hand to forestall me when I opened my mouth to speak. "I will say no more on the matter."

Then he too moved his horse ahead in the group, leaving me alone with Wolfric and Onóra. I tried not to look at them or to see their concerned expressions. I expected him to press me for the truth, but he held his tongue. His honor would not allow him to inquire when I had so clearly declared my wish to keep the tale to myself.

After an hour or so of silence, Ahearn dropped back and began conversing with the newest members of our traveling party, telling the story of meeting the Finns in the middle of nowhere and how we had helped defend against multiple bandit attacks.

"Should you not have returned to your master already?" Wolfric asked me. "Winter is coming."

He was wrong about that. Winter was upon us.

"We were supposed to be back by Samhain," I admitted.

"You've missed your deadline."

"It's a good thing, too, or we'd all be dead," said Ahearn.

And so would both of you, I did not say.

"Connor Shitozaki's temper is legendary, even for a fire druid."

"Honor demands that I stay and protect those who cannot defend themselves," I said. "I'll deal with Shitozaki's legendary temper later."

* * *

The events of the past several days had distracted me, but Wolfric's harsh words were a reminder that I would not be able to return for her by Yule. Escorting the witches back to Ward had guaranteed that by the time we were reunited, a year and a day would have long since passed. She would move on with her life without me. There was no reason she shouldn't.

The conversations of the caravan flowed around me while I brooded by my pentacle's little fire. I didn't have a gun to clean, my knives and tomahawks were sharp, and my enchanted sword needed no attention. I could sheathe it bloody, and the next morning it would be as clean and sharp as if it had never seen use. Duncan sat cross-legged with his eyes closed, meditating, while Dermot shoveled stew in his mouth as fast as its heat would allow. Conall had finished sharpening his sword and had moved on to cleaning his Benelli. Seth was still running his whetstone over the edge of his *zweihänder* when he spoke.

"You seem disturbed, Davis."

"I'm fine."

His lips pressed together in disapproval. Ever since he'd grown a beard, he did dark and forbidding really well. I ignored it.

"Let it go, Seth."

"It isn't right," he said. "Wolfric had no right to speak that way to you. You should tell him what really happened."

Before I could reply, Conall intervened. "It's a matter of honor. Davis didn't mention it before, and certainly can't now."

"Why not?" Seth demanded.

"Well, *before* Wolfric told him off, Davis couldn't say anything because he doesn't want Wolfric to think he owes him."

"Wolfric *does* owe him," Seth growled. "It's reciprocity."

"True, but Davis is a Traveler, and Travelers are known for helping people with no expectation of repayment. It's against their moral code."

I looked at Conall. "How did you know that?"

"Shitozaki was bitching about you one day, about how you were more Traveler than druid, and I asked him to explain it to me." He paused. "It was enlightening."

"But you're a druid now, and reciprocity is one of our core values," said Seth. "It is why we perform ritual. It is why we make offerings to the gods."

"I don't expect reciprocity from people the same as I do the gods."

Dermot piped up. "The Morrigan does."

I couldn't argue with that. She had told me as much herself; if things stood otherwise between me and the Battle Queen, she'd not have enchanted my sword and claimed me as her champion. Was that a sign that Angie and I would not be reunited? Had the Morrigan chosen me because she had foreseen my future without her? My heart sank a little more.

"That's different," I said.

"All I am saying is that you assisted Wolfric in leaving the grove," Seth continued. "Therefore, he owes you a debt." He looked at Conall. "Wolfric *must* know this."

"I'm sure he does," Conall replied, scrubbing the barrel of his shotgun with the bore brush. "However, after he lambasted Davis for 'abandoning' his chosen, he announced that a continuation of their friendship was in payment for that debt, so in his mind, now they are even."

The debate had finally garnered Duncan's attention. Both the earth druid and the water elementalist's eyes flitted back and forth between Seth and Conall as if avidly watching a contest.

"But he doesn't know the whole story," Seth argued. "Davis nearly died helping him!"

"A fact that is now irrelevant." Conall's tone had a note of finality.

"I hardly think it is *irrelevant*—" Seth returned hotly.

"That is because you are Greek," Conall said, with a hint of condescension.

"Is that supposed to be an insult?" Seth growled, rising to his considerable height of six and a half feet, towering over Conall, longsword in hand. Seth was inarguably the biggest *and* the strongest of all the Finns, as well as being the best air elementalist of the group. Conall was needling him – as he did everyone – and I wondered how long it would take my second to figure that out.

"Why, did you take it as one?" Unconcerned, the Norseman continued running the solvent-soaked cleaning patches through the shotgun's barrel.

"If you meant it as such."

"Perhaps you perceive it as an insult because deep inside, you secretly wish you were Norse."

Dermot snorted and started to laugh. Duncan laughed quietly, and even I could not help chuckling. Realizing he'd been baited, Seth let out a breath of exasperation and sat back down.

"Conall, why don't you go see if Wolfric and Onóra need anything," I said. "Show them some of that famous Norse hospitality."

"Very well," he said, finished with his weapon. He quickly packed up his cleaning kit, put the shotgun back together, reloaded it, and headed off to the convalescent tent.

After a few moments, Seth said, "He got me. Again."

"Yes, he did." I grinned and punched him in the shoulder.

Seth huffed indignantly.

"If it makes you feel any better, it's been quite a while since he's gotten your goat."

"It doesn't." He looked at me, serious once more. "You truly have no objection to Wolfric's continued ignorance of the truth?"

"He'll find out eventually." I tapped my shoulder, indicating the whiplash scars crisscrossing my back. "I won't be able to hide it forever."

"Davis."

I looked up from my little fire to see Duncan squatting across from me. Preparing for bed, I was so wrapped up in my own thoughts that I hadn't noticed him approach.

"I've been thinking about the situation with Angie."

No matter how well I thought I knew the earth druid, it seemed he always had one more surprise for me. Something akin to hope kindled in my chest. "I'm listening."

"You can learn to create and release your spirit animal."

"What good will that do?"

"How did Angelina find you?"

"She sent..." I trailed off as realization struck. Sometimes I could be so dumb.

"Her fetch?" He smiled.

We practiced for three hours until I could produce a spirit

animal. I was sweating and exhausted at the end of it, but I had done it. Before me stood a huge golden lion. I reached out to run my fingers through its thick mane, but Duncan stopped me.

"Don't touch it, or else it will come back into you."

That made sense.

"One other thing," he said. "It is a spirit, and as such cannot be killed by mortal weapons. But it *can* be killed by magic."

"Good to know."

He placed a hand on my arm. "If *it* is killed by magic, *you* will die also. A spirit animal is literally a part of your spirit that is outside your body. This is why full druids rarely create one, much less release it into the world."

It was worth the risk. I knelt before the lion, gazing intently into its eyes. "Find Angie," I ordered. "Keep her safe."

Spirit animals had no ability to affect the physical environment, so I had no idea how it might keep her safe. Even so, I couldn't help wanting it to protect her from danger. The lion turned, sniffed the air, and bounded away, a gleaming gold shimmer in the darkness.

"Your magic will be slightly reduced," Duncan said. "But I don't think that will be a problem."

Chapter 12 – Vengeance

If you prick us do we not bleed?
If you tickle us do we not laugh?
If you poison us do we not die?
And if you wrong us shall we not revenge?
~ William Shakespeare ~

When we reached Ward, the High Priestess and I had an intense debate over battle plans. She and the more experienced witches wanted to fight. While I had no problem with women engaging in combat, I was adamant about refusing to involve those who were mothers of small children. So many of the coven's children had already lost their fathers that I couldn't stomach the thought of leaving them orphans. I was having enough trouble sleeping as it was.

Spencer, the acting High Priest, agreed with me and so Rhiannon relented. However, they both insisted that any coven members who were good archers participate. I agreed to this at Seth's urging, swayed by his argument that the witches should be involved in taking back their home.

As we crouched in the early darkness with Spencer and Ahearn, I could just barely see the sentries patrolling the coven's holding, walking back and forth between the buildings like ghosts. The wind soughed through the dead cornfield, rustling the dried leaves. The seemingly endless rows of dead cornstalks were still standing after the fall harvest, and an idea began to take shape.

"We could smoke them out," I said.

"This would be a whole lot easier if you just burned the whole place to the ground and the bandits with it," grumbled Conall.

Ahearn looked at him in alarm. His expression turned to anger, and his whisper was fierce. "This is our home!"

"Don't be stupid," Dermot said, frowning at Conall. "How do you expect to keep warm through the winter?"

"With my lovely lady." Conall grinned and waggled his eyebrows.

"Women aren't interested in such things when they're cold and hungry," Spencer retorted in a biting tone.

Seth snorted. "Neither are *men*." He gave the Norseman a look that said he was an idiot for even suggesting such a thing.

"Relax," said Conall. "I wasn't serious."

"That's good," I said, "because I doubt Cinna would appreciate hearing how little you value her home."

Spencer gave him one last scowl and turned to me. "We cannot afford to lose *anything*. Even the small buildings contain important tools and supplies."

"I won't burn any of the buildings."

"Then how are you going to make smoke?"

"By burning the cornfield."

"Davis, we planted it this far from the hall on purpose, so that smoke wouldn't get inside when we burned the dry stalks after the harvest," the High Priest said.

"He has a point," said Dermot. "It's too far away to make a real difference."

"Not with air elementalists to push it along," said Seth.

"Exactly."

"Ugh," said Ahearn. "Everything is going to stink."

"At least you'll have them," I replied.

Conall clapped Ahearn on the shoulder. "We'll just get the water boys to wash 'em afterward."

"Shut up, Conall," said Dermot, but it was a reflexive response without any real heat.

I sent Martin south to watch for bandit reinforcements, accompanied by Phelan to shield and attack should the need arise. Yiorgos went southwest with Solon. I'd have preferred to send more people to act as lookouts, but we needed them for the attack.

The assault to take back Ward began just before dawn. Silently we took down sentries before they could sound an alarm. There were far more than I had expected. The interlopers from the 'Ville were dug in, perhaps expecting such an attack.

Spencer ordered his archers to take concealed positions around the buildings that made up Ward proper. Conall and the other gunmen accompanied them in the event that they were forced into melee combat. Duncan gathered up the earth elementalists to act as fire control, taking Siorus and Ingvar with him in case any came close to the buildings. He assigned Halldor and Warwick to follow behind to make sure any stray sparks were extinguished. Their magic fully recovered, Onóra and Wolfric were to help me manage the fire line.

"What do you want *us* to do?" asked Dermot, meaning the water elementalists.

"Improvise," I said. He looked like he didn't care for that order much, but I couldn't figure out how to use them. With one fire elementalist, two earth-fire dualists, and five earth druids in attendance, there was no chance the blaze would get out of control. He wandered off to round up the other water elementalists, before heading out with the archers and gunmen.

"Do you plan to burn the entire field?" asked Seth, who had brought Eian, Declan, and Alexandros to help blow the smoke where we needed it.

"Might as well. More fuel for the fire."

The gods had blessed us with clear skies. When the red sun began to rise, we ignited the cornstalks. I summoned a line of fire half of the length of the cornfield. Wolfric and Onóra followed my lead, dividing the other half between them to preserve their limited stores of magic. Seth and the other air elementalists spread out along the line, holding the smoke low to the ground while pushing it slowly forward. Lying east of the town proper and with the air elementalists to corral the smoke low to the ground, the burning field was camouflaged by the brilliant winter sun.

The flames raced across the field with little impetus from us, licking greedily up the stalks and devouring the dried leaves and husks. The volume of smoke increased dramatically, and the air elementalists struggled to contain it. They called upon the dualists who had elemental air to help and with nine more Finns to assist, they kept the smoke compacted in a thick, grey, roiling mass close to the ground. We had burned over half of the field before the intruders sounded the alarm.

Bandits began pouring out of the hall and outbuildings, racing for water buckets and the nearby well. With an intimate knowledge of the best hiding places in Ward, Spencer's archers were able to unleash a storm of arrows with little risk of reprisal. They picked the bandits off as they ran around in a panic, and soon the village square in front of the great hall was littered with bodies bristling with arrows. Abandoning their firefighting mission, the interlopers began returning fire with pistols and rifles. The deep-throated roar of shotguns reached my ears as the gunmen came into play. Some of the air elementalists with rifles joined the firefight even as they continued to gather and direct the smoke. When the brigands realized they were dropping like flies, they retreated into the great hall.

Unnerved by close proximity to the enemy, Onóra had ceased using fire in favor of earthmoving. As we drew nearer to the buildings, she backed away to join Warwick and Halldor in the rear as they turned over the smouldering ashes like magical plows, covering their heat with the soil's coolness. Once we were freed from fire duty, Wolfric and I approached the coven proper – he with his long knives and I with the grey blade.

The air elementalists and dualists first directed the giant smoke cloud to encompass the great hall, forming an ashen dome. It settled over the hall with finality, completely blocking our view of the building. I wasn't too happy with that, but unless the enemy came out with guns blazing, they weren't going anywhere.

Turning to Wolfric and the earth elementalists, I said, "Tell everyone on the ground to back off to bow and rifle range. Gunmen are to move outside the village perimeter."

Moments later, the sound of an air shield shattering like glass was followed by rapid pistol fire, and a lone bandit charged out of the smoke, sputtering and coughing. An arrow shaft appeared in her throat, ensuring that she choked to death on her own blood instead of breathing in the life-giving air she so desperately needed. A few more emerged before the air shield was replaced, and were picked off by archers and riflemen alike.

No one else came through.

"Lift the dome," I told Seth. He relayed the order to the others, who transformed it into a rushing wind that dispersed the ash and soot back over the cornfield from whence it came. Once the air was clear, the destruction we'd wrought became evident. Bandit corpses littered the village square, lying in all manner of abnormal positions, bloodied and broken from trying to fight their way out. The others, lying on the front steps of the great hall and just beyond, bore no marks. They were the ones who had tried to shelter within the hall and who had waited too long to attempt escape. I suddenly felt sick to my stomach for condemning them to death by asphyxia.

Seth placed a hand on my shoulder.

"They came here and murdered peaceful people who never did them harm," he said. "And druids helped them do it."

"I know."

It was around mid-morning when the rest of the coven arrived, led by Rhiannon. By then we'd moved the bodies out of the square, laying them in neat rows. They arrived singing songs of praise, but the joyful noise died away when they saw the pile of bodies, and a solemn silence fell. The High Priestess dismounted and approached the pile of corpses, a mixture of horror and hate in her eyes.

"Get the trail wagon unloaded," she ordered Ahearn. "We'll use it to transport the bodies off our sacred land."

"There's no need," I said. "Stand back," I said. Seth, Alexandros, Eian, and Declan surrounded the pile with a wall of air. I took a deep breath, allowing the magic to build before channeling it out in a burst. The corpses were incinerated in a flash. In spite of the wall of air, a wave of heat exploded outward. The witches cringed. Some of the Finns did, too. Lacy ashes floated briefly on the morning breeze.

"Odin's beard!" exclaimed Wolfric.

"Lord and Lady, Davis!" Rhiannon said, shaking her head and waving the smoke from in front of her face. "Lord and Lady."

We had defeated the bandits. Ward was won.

Once the smoke and ash was been cleared a second time, druids and witches alike began setting the place to rights. Everyone set to dusting, sweeping, scrubbing windows, washing clothes and blankets, mucking out the barn, and herding the horses into the coven's pastureland. With the addition of the horses that had belonged to the occupying force, the coven's herd was even larger than before. And while the invaders hadn't husbanded the livestock as frugally as the coven did, there were still plenty of cows, sheep, pigs, and chickens.

Once the place was livable again, the witches got busy putting their lives back in order, which included harvesting what was available to put up for winter stores. The Finns pitched in wherever they could, mostly performing the usual autumn chores like planting winter vegetables and grasses, chopping wood, and hauling water. Of course, some things were easier for us than the coven members. Dermot, Nêreus, Galen, and Mohinder made quite a show of rolling several man-sized globes of water from the nearby lake and then filtering it before filling all the rain barrels, watering troughs, and topping off the well. The earth druids had two-thirds of the coven's nine hundred acres plowed in under a week, and everyone pitched in to scatter seed for the cold-weather crops.

Wolfric and Onóra continued to regain their physical strength, but she was still an emotional wreck and he was constantly on edge. Anne and Ruth wandered around the unfamiliar environment as though they were lost for the first couple of hours, but the now-familiar people of the coven soon roped them into the activities of daily life.

The great hall, which had seemed so large the first time I'd visited, now seemed small and cramped. Before our arrival, no one had slept there. Now we were all underfoot when it was time to bake bread, cook meals, and sweep floors. After gaining permission from Rhiannon and Spencer, I assembled the other earth druids and began designing an expansion, druid-style.

The High Priestess shook her head at my plan. "It'll crumble in the first earthquake."

"We can keep them at bay," I said.

"And when you're gone?"

"There are several witches here whose primary element is earth," Seth said. "Can they not be taught to still the ground?"

"Stopping an earthquake is never easy," said Duncan. "That is why we perform ritual and make sacrifices at altars around the grove – to keep the mother sleeping peacefully."

I nodded. "Like my father says, an ounce of prevention is worth a pound of cure."

Rhiannon smiled. "In that case, we might be able to manage an ounce or two."

At Duncan's suggestion, each earth druid worked with two or three witches, constructing altars dedicated to the Earth Mother. These were located at the four cardinal points of the compass and the four intercardinal directions, set in a protective ring around the main body of the village. While we druids honored the Shining Ones as individual gods and goddesses, the witches viewed them as many aspects of one God and one Goddess. Even so, the result was similar to what I'd expect in a druid grove: unique shrines honoring different goddesses. Each one, however, also bore the triple moon, which was not a symbol utilized by druids.

Three times a day, for seven days straight, we joined the witches at their altars to give offerings, perform rituals, or cast spells, whichever those involved preferred. By and large, we earth druids were present to sit in meditation, seeking the consciousness of the earth below in order to communicate our desire for a peaceful stillness. It helped that each of the witches was an accomplished practitioner of their craft. As it was part of their usual practice, they took to Duncan's meditation sessions much more readily than I had.

Convinced that marauders from the 'Ville could return at any time, I chafed at a week's delay in building. I was alternately bored and irritated with thirty minutes of sitting still, and spent most of the time telling the mother all my concerns. Once it was done, however, I eagerly dove into the construction of two long structures of twenty little apartments apiece. Each long building was attached to the rear of the great hall, transforming the U-shaped structure into an H.

Inside, the little rooms comfortably held a double bed and a washstand, and each one had an entire wall of square cubbyholes molded into it for storage. The earth witches helped, learning to manipulate their magic more like we did. Having them support dirt walls with magic was good practice for convincing the earth to lie still and quiet when it wanted to buck wildly. Once the buildings were complete, Duncan and I began throwing more challenging jobs at them, gradually increasing the difficulty level. By the time spring arrived and we departed, they would be able to hold the ground underneath all the structures of Ward and keep them from collapsing.

As we settled into a daily routine, I started to hear people expressing the hope that the 'Ville had given up on acquiring this bit of property. That was too good to be true. To hear Rhiannon tell it, the orchards produced so much fruit that the tree branches hung nearly to the ground, the lake's fish always took the baited hook, the sheep and goats reproduced like rabbits, and the cows always delivered healthy twins. It might have been a bit of an exaggeration, but the livestock *was* healthy and stout, especially the cows and horses. The fertility of lands and animals was due in large part to witchcraft, but the bandits didn't know that. All they knew was that this rich, fertile corner of the world was a prize too valuable to give up.

I figured that we had maybe another week of peace before we were on the defensive again. So while I was busy working with my hands helping set Ward to rights, my mind was even busier making plans for the future. While chopping wood, I pondered defensive structures. When helping cook supper, I thought about how much food we'd need to last the winter. As I accompanied Ahearn on his rounds of all the pastures to check on the livestock, I memorized the lay of the land. In addition, I also had the Finns drill with their swords every morning before breakfast and practice dry-firing firearms in the afternoon.

Having achieved our goal of regaining the coven's home, I was stumped as to how they might keep it in our absence. We could offer to take them back to Sanctuary with us, but I doubted they would leave – especially not without knowing what had happened to the coven members that were lost in the initial attack. To complicate matters, it was difficult to focus on any of it while Angie kept intruding on my thoughts.

I desperately wanted to go to her, desiring nothing more than to have her by my side again, but my conscience dictated that I remain and help the witches until they could defend themselves. She was safe with her family, wherever they were, while the people of Ward were in a precarious position. I couldn't leave them. Not yet.

231

It was quiet in the great hall when the High Priestess approached me after everyone else had gone to bed. The past several weeks had been so hectic and riddled with danger that I hadn't had five minutes of time alone. The hour or so I spent staring into the flames every evening was a much-needed respite. Even so, when I saw her troubled expression, I could not ignore it.

"Come sit," I said, patting the cushion on the bench beside me.

"You're inviting me to sit in my own hall?" she asked, arching an eyebrow.

"No, I'm inviting you to come share *my* fire," I replied with a wink.

She dropped her priestess façade and plopped down on the bench beside me. "If only that were true," she said. The light tone of her voice was belied by the attractive pout of her lips and the seriousness of her grey gaze.

"I think we have more important things to deal with," I said.

"You were a hard man to impress before, Davis," she said with a wan smile. "It's even harder now."

I nearly told her that she was wrong, but then I remembered how taken I'd been with Angie's exotic green eyes, bright smile, and creamy caramel skin. Maybe she was right.

"In all seriousness, I do need your help with something," she said.

"Of course. What do you need?"

"A private ritual space that is dark and without distraction."

"Were you thinking a small cob building like the ones we just put up? It wouldn't have to have windows."

"No, but it would have to have a door," she said ruefully.

I nodded. "And people would be constantly knocking on it."

"I was thinking more along the lines of going underground," she said. "I need to travel on the astral plane to find the rest of my people. For a journey like that, I need absolute, uninterrupted quiet, for at least an hour or two every day. Maybe longer, depending on the distance."

Rhiannon had mentioned her missing people several times, both during the journey and while setting Ward to rights, so it didn't surprise me one bit to find out that she had a plan to locate each and every one of them.

I nodded. "Underground I can do. Where do you want it?" I bent over to reach under the bench for my boots.

She looked surprised. "You want to do it now?"

"There's no time like the present."

We settled on hollowing out a space that was approximately the size of a horse's stall underneath the High Priestess' quarters. Other than the great hall and the new addition, the rest of the coven's quarters was unfamiliar territory. Rhiannon led me down one long, dark hallway to her room at the very end.

A few candles lit up as we entered her room, just enough for me to make out the few pieces of furniture: a desk and chair, wardrobe, and a full bed with a thick feather mattress covered by a bright patchwork quilt. I didn't allow myself to look at it too long.

"So this is where you do ritual?" I asked, nodding toward the center of the room, which was conspicuously empty.

She nodded. "It's too dark to see now, but there is a circle burnt into the floorboards."

Assuming as much, I hadn't moved farther than the doorway.

"It isn't active," she said. "When I've finished spellcasting, I always take out this little piece of the flooring." She fished a square of pine out of her dress pocket and handed it to me. It was marked with intricate designs of ivy and daffodils within a border of Celtic knotwork.

"This is beautiful work," I said.

"Brennan was quite skilled at woodburning," she said softly. "This circle was his gift to me when I became High Priestess."

"His death is a great loss," I said. "I'm sorry."

She took a deep breath and straightened her shoulders. "No, *I'm* sorry. You didn't come here for me to cry on your shoulder. We have work to do."

She pressed several boards before picking one and using her knife to pry it loose. Sheathing the blade, she pulled out several items from the opening, including some cloth bags and a couple of small wooden boxes with hinged lids. Clearly, the space beneath the flooring was a secret location for items that were magical, personal, or both. I averted my eyes as she put them away in another location.

"It will be a tight squeeze, but I think you'll be able to fit all right," Rhiannon said, dusting her hands.

Reaching into the space, my fingers tingled with the sensation of residual magic briefly before encountering the cool, dry earth a foot or so beneath the subfloor. Lying prone on the wood floor with both hands in the dirt below, I closed my eyes and let myself become immersed in its quiet stillness. It took a few minutes for the ground to accept me, for it was accustomed to Rhiannon's presence, and indeed, her mastery.

I visualized what I wanted, which was a space slightly smaller than her room; it wouldn't do to undermine the walls of the house. I compacted the new dirt walls until they were nearly the density of stone before hollowing out the necessary space, It was an adequate size, but a room of bare dirt floors and walls wouldn't do for a High Priestess.

I sat up, took off my boots and socks, swung my legs around, and put my feet through the space in the floor. "I'll be right back," I told Rhiannon and dropped through the opening. My shoulders nearly stuck, but I managed to squeeze through. Barefoot inside the earthen cavern, now I could really work. I shut my eyes again and reached down deep to where the bedrock slept. Channeling elemental fire and earth, I melting some of the bedrock into a pool of magma. Drawing it up into the space, I began lining the walls and floor with it. As soon as the floor was covered in molten rock, it surged to the four corners of the underground room and began climbing the walls.

"Davis?" Rhiannon called through the hole. "It's become quite hot in here. Is everything all right?"

"Sorry, I'll cool it off as soon as I can," I said. "You might want to open the windows, though."

"What exactly are you—" Her words cut off abruptly, and I looked back over my shoulder to see Rhiannon hanging upside down with her head and shoulders visible through the floor, her dark red hair drifting about in the hot air currents and her grey eyes wide with shock. It seemed that it was one thing to see me throwing fireballs and causing earthquakes, and something else entirely to see me standing ankle-deep in glowing orange lava. "Do you think the wood floor will be quiet enough?" I asked. "I can add a layer of stone beneath it if you like."

Rhiannon found her voice. "That's a good idea," she said faintly. "Leave room for a trap door, won't you?"

"I'll do that," I told her. "This won't take long."

She withdrew from the now-superheated space beneath the floor of her room, and I worked more quickly, spreading thin layers of molten rock across the walls and floor. Realizing that I had little experience with dispersing the heat of my fire magic, I was a little concerned that the wooden subfloor might burn from the close proximity to the hot rock. The wood was smoking a little and had turned a darker shade of gold. I could just imagine her reaction if I incinerated her room – not to mention her treasured magic circle – just because bringing up melted rocks was quicker and easier than relocating solid ones.

After drawing the heat from the rocks overhead down into the floor, I laid my hands on each wall and *pushed* the remaining heat away, spreading it out into the earth beyond. The temperature dropped as I dissipated the heat downward, through the surrounding layers of earth. With a chunk of ground to give me a boost, I squeezed back through the secret opening, returning to Rhiannon's room.

"If it's all right, I'd like to keep working on it," I said. "It's functional, but it isn't very pretty."

"I don't need pretty. I need quiet, and this will be perfect. Thank you, Davis."

"You're welcome." I started for the door. "I'd better head on to bed."

"You really did fall into a volcano, didn't you?" she said.

I sighed. "Yeah."

"I genuinely thought it was a story Dermot made up. He has *such* an imagination." She smiled apologetically.

"It serves him well when it comes to magic," I said, turning the knob and opening the door.

"Davis."

I stopped in the doorway and looked back, half-hoping and half-afraid she'd ask me to stay. I felt guilty at the thought, but now that we weren't running for our lives anymore, loneliness had begun to ride me hard.

"Want to see a pretty trick?" she asked, her grey eyes dancing.

"Sure."

With a wave of her hand, Rhiannon extinguished all the candles except the one beside the door on a narrow ledge that ran around the circumference of the room, except for the one bedside the door. My gaze followed the line of her hand and arm as she pointed to it, and then the next. A tongue of fire appeared on the next candle, and then the next, and the one after that, followed by a whole row of them flaring to life in rapid succession, running around the room until all four walls had been illuminated with what looked like a hundred candles.

"Volcanic," I said.

Rhiannon smiled. "You shouldn't flatter me. Especially since I'm sure you could have lit them all at once."

"More like I'd probably scorch the walls and set the roof on fire," I admitted. "I don't have that kind of fine control."

"Really," she said. "Perhaps it is an area in which I could tutor you, then."

It was a generous offer. "I'd like that. Thank you."

She laughed softly. "You're more than welcome."

"Did I say something funny?"

"I'm sorry, I didn't mean to laugh, or offend you."

"I'm not offended." *Yet.*

"You are such a unique individual," she said. "If anyone else had done the things you have for me and my people, they would assume that they were entitled to anything offered them. *You*, however, are so lacking in presumption that you are grateful for my offer."

"And that… amuses you?"

"No." She caressed my cheek. "It humbles me. Thank you again, Davis. For everything."

* * *

While I had taken note of Maeve's absence from Duncan's lessons in earth elementalism, I assumed that she either wanted to stick with her healing arts or needed some time alone to recover from her ordeal. Neither was true.

What she *was* doing was learning to shoot a rifle under Seth's tutelage. Apparently, she was just as skilled with air as she was with earth. That fact impressed me all by itself because no druid had ever possessed opposing elements like air and earth. I knew that from discussions with Padraig and from reading Jayne Pierce's handwritten histories.

236

"Very nice," I said after watching her pop the heads of three snowmen in a row at about two hundred yards. It was a clever idea for target practice, especially if you had an imaginative water elementalist who could shape them like real people and who loved to play in the snow.

"I'm a fair archer," she replied. "The principle isn't much different."

"Why the sudden interest?"

"When you head back out to rescue everyone else, I want to go."

While it was true that I'd given quite a bit of thought to getting their lost ones back, I hadn't mentioned it to anyone. And even though the High Priestess was busy locating them through magical means, we had kept that information to ourselves. All that the rest of the coven knew was that she was engaged in powerful workings and was not to be disturbed.

"What makes you think I'm going to do that?"

"Because you're going to destroy the 'Ville," she replied. "But you can't do that until you get the innocent people out first." Maeve put the rifle to her cheek once more and fired three rounds into the chest of each snowman. Then she looked at me. "Unless you're planning on sacrificing them, which I doubt."

Seth and Dermot looked at each other, then at me.

"I hadn't really gotten that far," I said. "We have to make sure Ward is safe first. Otherwise, we'll be bringing them back for nothing."

"I have an idea about that."

"Oh?"

Maeve nodded. "Rhiannon has a spell."

"A spell."

"Yes. In her Book of Shadows."

"What's a Book of Shadows?" Dermot asked.

"It's a witch's spellbook. It contains all the lore and learning a witch accumulates over a lifetime," Maeve replied. "As we achieve particular levels of training, we are allowed to examine the Book of Shadows of either the High Priest or High Priestess for a day and a night, and to copy anything we wish from it for our own Books."

"So you copied a spell that can help defend Ward?"

"No. *I* was always looking for healing spells, love spells, spells for wisdom and happiness and fertility – all that fluffy stuff." Maeve's voice was bitter. "But I've seen the one we need. It's a death spell. Some might even call it a curse."

I was speechless for a moment, unable to imagine Rhiannon, High Priestess of Ward Coven, performing any kind of magic that could be considered a *curse*.

"Don't look so surprised," Maeve said, reloading the rifle. "A High Priestess must master many types of spellcraft." She fired again, and a snowman's head exploded. "The question is: can you talk her into using it?"

Later that evening, I was trying to come up with a quick and feasible way to build a defensible wall around Ward, but something kept interfering with my focus. I thought it was the singing and chatter of the witches and the Finns relaxing after a hard day's work, but the distraction was worse when I stepped outside. Giving up, I sat cross-legged on the ground and sought the peace of the earth mother. Her wisdom came at me in a decidedly *un*peaceful rush, a dizzying array of vibrations and images created from sound waves. I'd never connected with Danu this quickly or easily before, and it overwhelmed me for several moments. It took that long for my mind to sift through the information and understand what she was saying to me.

The enemy comes.

I leapt to my feet, sprinting for the barn. When the attack came, I was mounted bareback and galloping past great hall as a group of Finns burst through the door and barreled down the steps. I thought I heard Seth calling my name, but I didn't stop. I had wasted too much time already. All I could do was buy the others time to grab their weapons and get ready to fight.

A raid group charged in from the west, heading straight for Ward. Had one of the former squatters escaped, carrying the tale of how it had been lost to the 'Ville? Were there regular communications that our counterattack had interrupted?

These ruminations lasted but a moment before all rational thought was gone, replaced by instinct and action. A quick burst of heat singed all the vegetation surrounding the western gate, creating a smokescreen to hide me from view for a few precious seconds. I raised both hands in the air and launched fireball after fireball in rapid succession, breaking up the enemy front line. Steel spun on his haunches, and we charged down the gap between the bandits and the coven, while I laid down a blazing firewall that neither man nor animal would dare approach.

Planning to encircle the whole village with the giant firewall, I turned my back to the bandits as we galloped east. The dancing yellow flames might be hot enough to turn any projectile into liquid slag, but that didn't mean they wouldn't hurt me. I wasn't sure if I could be injured by the melted speeding projectiles and this wasn't the best time to find out, but I was willing to take the risk to protect the others. Showing them my back was foolish, even while they were momentarily diverted, but I needed to see before I could place the fiery barrier. Otherwise, it might cut through the buildings and people I was trying to safeguard.

I remembered the corral behind the barn just before Steel soared over one fence, took three strides, and cleared the other. The firewall trailing behind me cut through the corral fencing, turning a thin slice of the railing of it to char. Thank the gods no animals were there; Ahearn would have killed me if any of his horses had been hurt.

A quick glance between the buildings on my left revealed that most of the air elementalists had surrounded the great hall and its new addition, joining their magics to cast a shield over it. I urged the grulla stallion ever faster until he stretched his neck out level with the ground, thick muscles bunching for even greater speed. As soon as the firewall was laid, its presence would allow me to engage the enemy without worrying about the safety of anyone in Ward.

Once I was back at the west end where I'd started, I caught sight of a group of Finns that had been trapped between the fire and the bandits. I was surprised that both Siorus' and Ingvar's pentacles had managed to run out that far in such a short amount of time. Both were hard pressed, with only air elementalist Eian and air/spirit dualists Jasvinder and Tristan to shield them from gunfire. Both dualists were alternately tossing spirit orbs and bolstering each other's shields. Mohinder and Nereus summoned water from their big canteens, using a couple of three-tentacled monsters to pluck enemy riders out of their saddles, or simply spear them through. The earth druids had hands on the ground and looked ready to rock the world on its axis, while Madoc and Regnar lay down cover fire for them as they were able.

Sensing the oncoming tremors, the bandit horses whinnied in fear, some rearing and fighting their riders. To spook them further, I sent volley after volley of fire darts into the surrounding aggressors, followed by great gouts of flame that made the enemy duck and dodge. Their horses went to bucking and bolted for safety; only a few of their riders managed to hang on. A low, hollow *boom-boom-boom* sounded as the ground erupted, heaving upward and then forward in undulating waves that knocked enemies off their feet and carried them away.

Another group had managed to whip their horses away from the rolling earth and was now turning to re-engage the two pentacles of Finns. I aimed one hand at the ground. Low, thin lines of sparks erupted beneath the enemy horses' feet, twisting and running like vines. The horses whinnied in alarm, refusing to go forward. A third group of marauders came onto the scene, plowing through the confused mass of frightened horses and angry riders. I launched fireballs and spooked their horses, but they knew we were drastically outnumbered and pressed the attack.

I dismounted and pressed both palms to the earth, feeling it waken to my touch. I would have to be very careful to affect only the bandits, so I focused on an imaginary border a few feet from Siorus' and Ingvar's pentacles. A moment later, their elemental magics joined with mine, allowing the three of us to coordinate our efforts. With a quick prayer to Danu, I envisioned the earth rippling beneath the enemy, leaving my men untouched, and unleashed the magic. The ground before me rose, gaining in strength and depth. A tidal wave of crumbling dirt and crushing rock swept over the remaining bandits. The air filled with the screams and shrieks of terrified and dying men and horses.

The groundswell quieted beneath my feet as I drew the grey blade and finished off those unlucky to have survived. A few begged for death, never knowing that the Morrigan would be along just before dawn to collect their heads as trophies. I hoped the Phantom Queen would not be too disappointed with the spoils of war this day. Most of them had been slain by magic and not by the sword.

I knelt again, *seeking* and finding no further threats.

"Anything?" I called, noticing the other two earth druids doing the same. All three shook their heads, and I called the fire back to me.

"That's it, then," I said. "Everyone all right?" There were murmurs and nods from the ten Finns. "Good. Go check on the others."

I remounted Steel and let him amble back to the village proper, where Seth promptly began chewing me out. Leading my horse back into the barn, I threw a blanket over his sweaty back so he wouldn't get chilled. Realizing that the air elementalist's tirade could take a while, I plopped down on a bale of hay to listen.

"You shouldn't have gone out there," he said, frowning. "What were you thinking? Are you *trying* to get yourself killed?"

"Why, was somebody throwing lightning around? Other than Jasvinder and Tristan, I mean."

Seth frowned. "The Oracle's prophecy is no laughing matter."

"Then why were you worried? *They* don't have magic." I pointed south, toward the 'Ville.

"We don't know that. They could have brought the same druids that helped take over Ward."

It was something I had not considered. "Sorry," I said. "Danu warned me and—"

"You've seen *another* goddess?" Seth interrupted.

"No, she was speaking to me through the earth. That's how I knew the attack was coming."

"How is it that Duncan didn't know about it?"

"He was, uhh... busy." I paid little attention to who was romancing whom as a general rule but had noticed the earth druid frequently enjoying the company of a witch named Erik. Erik's golden blond curls rivaled those of any woman, and his biceps were almost as big as Seth's. I was happy to see my friend taking pleasure in the company of another after being alone for so long.

"Maybe she was speaking so loudly to me because nobody else was paying attention."

"I see," said Seth, letting go of his aggravation. "In any case, you should have warned the rest of us."

"I was already outside, and my only thought was to keep the bandits out of the village. If they'd gotten any closer, they'd have been able to use the buildings for cover."

"That certainly would have led to an extended firefight."

"Exactly. And there were too many even for all seven pentacles."

"Too many for all seven pentacles, but not for one dualist," he said, giving me a sardonic look. His voice was heavily laden with irony, but clearly fighting alone was never going to be a problem for me.

"I hate fighting defensively," I said. "The whole time we were moving, I kept wishing we could just leave the coven somewhere safe so we could battle it out with the enemy and be done with it."

He nodded. "And now that we're here, it still isn't safe."

"I have to destroy the 'Ville to make sure the witches are safe, but I can't destroy it they actually are."

"Sometimes there aren't any easy answers," Seth said.

Just like always.

Chapter 13 – Defensive Tactics

*Those who profess to favor freedom, and yet deprecate agitation,
are men who want crops without plowing up the ground.*
~ Frederick Douglass ~

Yule was weeks away, but winter weather had set in already, bringing with it an early, heavy snowfall. It looked like I was stuck here until spring, and while I should have been dreading what Master Shitozaki would have to say to me after smouldering like a quiescent volcano all winter, I could only think of Angie.

In spite of the size and power of my fetch, I was unable to see through its eyes the way she had claimed to do with hers. It was a disappointment, to say the least, for I had no way of knowing if it had found her or if it was still searching. In addition, my Well of elemental fire was more than slightly reduced, with approximately one third invested into creating the spirit animal. It was only to be expected, seeing as how large my fetch had turned out to be. Thankfully, my ability with elemental earth was unaffected.

Since I had virtually limitless reserves of magic to draw upon, that meant making the adjustment of using smaller castings with greater frequency. I didn't tell anyone about the decrease I was experiencing and covered for it by mentioning that I was experimenting with different tactics, but I could tell that Duncan knew, or at least suspected. Sustaining it required a lot of magic, but I was fine with that; it was out there looking for Angie.

I trusted that it would find her, but the waiting was killing me. So when Seth suggested that we start regular patrols around the coven, I quickly agreed to it, even though it was growing colder by the day. I assigned pentacles to patrol on different days, with two going each day, one in the morning and one in the afternoon. There was some grumbling but not much. Now that the witches were settled and life was more or less back to normal, like as not they would find some useful chore for the Finns to perform that wasn't nearly as fun as the service they'd been providing on the journey.

Running regular patrols was the only way to keep the enemy from surprising us again. The morning after the attack I scribbled the names of the Finns in chalk upon a piece of slate, trying to figure out how to run morning and afternoon patrols in all four cardinal directions without exhausting both men and horses. Dermot was "helping" me, which meant he was sitting beside me drinking coffee and flirting with every witch who happened to saunter by.

Wolfric and Onóra showed up and seated themselves at the table opposite me, unconsciously mimicking each other's posture: backs straight, hands folded upon the table, expressions somber.

"What are you doing?" Wolfric asked.

"Trying to figure out how to keep this place safe," I replied, erasing the marks from the slate once again. The honest truth was that I just didn't have the manpower.

"Ward is not your responsibility, Davis," said Wolfric. "Your chosen is."

"That's what we came to talk to you about," Onóra said. "Angie needs you. She needs your protection, and you should be with her."

I was well familiar with the concept of chosen as they described it, which as far as I could tell had started with ArchDruid Sebrina. Historically, druid dyads hadn't worked that way. According to the journals of Jayne Pierce, the first dyads worked hand-in-hand, supporting and protecting one another as necessary. If there was one thing I was certain of, it was that Angelina Everlight didn't need protection – mine, or anyone else's.

"Did the two of you sleep through the attack yesterday?" Dermot interjected. "Because I didn't see either one of you charging out to help fight off that raid group."

Until that moment, Dermot hadn't spoken to Wolfric since their rescue. There was definitely some bad blood there, but the only thing I knew was that it concerned his older brother Jason. Since then, the usually affable water elementalist had either left the room when the Wolfric entered or pretended like he didn't exist.

The fire elementalist scowled and opened his mouth to respond, but I held up a hand.

"No one expects either of you to fight," I said. "Not after what you've been through."

"And no one should expect you to, either," Onóra insisted. "Not when Angie needs you."

"Why would she need him right now?" Dermot said with a frown. "*She's* not under attack by bandits."

"No one invited you to this discussion, Stoddard," Wolfric said.

"I was sitting here when it started, and I'll be here when it's finished," Dermot fired back. "If you wanted it to be a private conversation, you should have had it in private."

Wolfric shoved back from the table, with Onóra a half-second behind him. Disregarding the water elementalist, he stabbed a finger at me, saying, "I'm not letting this go, Davis. I'm right, and you know it."

I made no response as the dyad grabbed their coats and departed the great hall. Part of me agreed with him – I should have been by Angie's side all along, and I should have long since gone back for her.

"I can't believe my brother was ever friends with that guy," Dermot said, shaking his head. "Water and fire do not mix."

"Is that so?"

"Well... Except for me and that hot little fire witch over there." He grinned and slipped away from the table, taking his chicory coffee with him. His easy way with women was remarkable for one so young. The witches loved his tricks with water manipulation. Every evening, at least one person asked him to show off his talents, and Dermot proved that not only was he a master of water but that he was every bit as good with plants. The more cynical side of me wondered if the coven members were deliberately trying to breed druid magic into their own bloodlines, or if it was just an added benefit to having new sexual partners.

When Rhiannon appeared moments later, a witch named Luna left her place by the fire where she had been knitting and greeted the High Priestess with excited whispers. A delighted expression appeared on Rhiannon's face, and she took Luna's hands in hers. She gave her an excited hug and kissed her on the cheek before grabbing her coat and proceeding out the door.

I rose and followed her. "May I accompany you?"

"I'm just going to exercise my horse," she said. Rhiannon's daily ride was her time to get away from the hubbub of the great hall. I knew it was an intrusion but needed her input.

"If it's not inconvenient, I'd like to speak with you about something."

"Very well," she said. "You can help me groom and saddle her while we talk."

"I'd be happy to."

We walked to the barn, and I grabbed a hoof pick and started cleaning the feet of Rhiannon's white mare.

"I know you, Davis. You're curious but too polite to ask," she said when I'd finished the first hoof.

"I trust you to tell me when something concerns me," I replied.

"This does. Luna has just informed me that she is pregnant."

"I assure you, that does *not* concern me." I started on another hoof.

Rhiannon laughed. "Not you specifically, but one of the Finns, at least," she said. "And since they are your responsibility…"

"Her pregnancy becomes my concern," I said. "I don't mean to be rude, but does she know who the father is?"

"Does it matter?"

"It might to him."

"The children born here belong to all of us," Rhiannon said.

"I realize that, but I should think you would also be interested in what kind of magical ability you're breeding."

Her back straightened. "Is that your concern? That we are stealing druid magic?"

"What is freely given cannot be stolen," I said.

"Then what is your point?"

I tossed the hoof pick back into the bucket, picked up the curry comb, and started grooming the mare's heavy winter coat.

"Honestly, I'm just wondering how big of a problem this is going to be for me. My plate's pretty full right now."

246

Rhiannon crossed her arms over her chest. "Why would it be a problem for you at all? *You're* not having a baby."

"I'm not so sure that this is a good time for anyone to have a baby."

"It's too late to shut the barn door once the cows are out."

"Druids can control whether or not they become pregnant," I said. Angie had done so, as neither of us was ready to raise a child. Considering all that had happened in the last year and a half, it had been a wise decision.

"So can we, but that is neither here nor there." Rhiannon said. "Do you really think the Finns have given a single thought to that?"

Even if they had, they'd probably expect the witches to attend to their own reproductive status, just like druid women did. Unlike Ward, the children of the grove belonged to their individual mothers, so it was the women who held exclusive control over their choice to become pregnant or not. The Finns were a group of energetic young men in their sexual prime who had been deprived of the company of the fairer sex for far too long – some of them for several years. Now, finding themselves in association with women who seemed to view them as standing somewhere between heroes and demigods, they were enjoying every advantage the situation had to offer. Even the members of my little company who relished the touch of another man, like Duncan and Siorus, had no lack of romantic invitations.

"No, but I think they might when their lovers' bellies start to swell," I replied. We could forget asking the witches if they'd like to move south after all they'd been through to win back their home. There was an excellent chance that some of the Finns would want to stay and put down roots, however. Even though Connor Shitozaki would have a conniption over losing them, maybe it would be better if they did. If a person's parents determined a child's magical status, it was likely that at least some of these babies would possess druid magic. Thus, they would need older, experienced druids to teach them to use it. Or maybe the women could make sure their kids were all witches and not druids.

The fact of the matter was that druids and witches had similar feelings about the "ownership" of children, and I was probably the only one who expected paternity to be an issue. I sighed. It was one more burden on my overtaxed mind, but something I wouldn't have to deal until springtime.

"Clearly they aren't the only ones who have not considered the future," said the High Priestess. "Does the notion trouble you?"

"Only the part where I become responsible for protecting pregnant women and infants."

"You view the gift of new life as an added burden?" Her voice deepened with displeasure.

"Not if the coven was seeing to its own defense," I said, switching to the finishing brush and running it over the mare's snowy coat.

Rhiannon's tone turned frosty. "Are you implying that we have not carried out own weight? That we have not raised arms in our own defense?"

"Not at all," I said. "I'm just saying that the lion's share of Ward's protection comes from druid magic."

"Our magic is for growth and nurturing! It is not for combat and killing!" Rhiannon had not raised her voice, but spots of color had appeared on her cheeks.

"Neither is ours, but you don't seem to mind us using it for that purpose."

The High Priestess inhaled deeply, and for a moment I thought she was going to start yelling. If it hasn't been for the possibility that her horse might spook, she probably would have.

"If anyone else had said such a thing to me, I would throw him out of my hall," she said. "However, I must admit that you are right. Your druids have taken on most of the burden of defending my people and property, and without asking for anything in return."

"I'm sorry. I didn't mean to offend you," I said. "I just wanted to discuss how that can be changed. Like it or not, as long as we're here defending Ward, we can't go get your lost people."

"I bear some responsibility for neglecting to explain things sooner. A great deal of the coven's magic – mine in particular – is tied to the land. When we are away, the bond weakens."

"So you *can't* defend Ward." I slid the saddle pad onto the mare's back.

"Couldn't. Now that we have returned, Spencer and I have performed rituals to strengthen that bond once more, which will give us a more stable power base from which to draw."

I slung the saddle over the mare's back and set it down gently.

"Maeve mentioned that you have a spell that might be used for defense. She said it was death magic."

The High Priestess fell into a stony silence, struggling with anger once again. When she spoke again, it was in clipped tones.

"She should never have mentioned that. The content of a witch's Book of Shadows is sacred – and *secret*."

"She didn't say anything other than that. She also said that she herself didn't have it."

"I could banish her for this."

"Please don't do that. She's just trying to help."

She sighed. "Of course I would never do such a thing. Especially considering what she has so recently endured."

"So you'll use it?"

"I *have* been considering it," she admitted. "But it is not a defensive spell."

"Then why would she mention it?" If revealing the contents of the High Priestess' spellbook could be punished by exile, why had Maeve risked it?

"It's an immovable offensive spell, so the uneducated often assume it is used for defensive purposes," Rhiannon replied. "It cannot be used like one of your fireballs, for example, but it is just as lethal, if not more so. Strictly speaking, a defensive spell only protects, and does no harm."

"Ah. So what does it do?"

"It is a magic circle that encompasses a certain area, and any creature that crosses it dies instantly," she said.

"That sounds like just what we need," I said, starting to feel hopeful.

"Don't praise the gods just yet. There are significant drawbacks."

"Such as?"

"It kills indiscriminately."

"So, even those it's meant to protect will die if they cross through it."

"Hence my hesitation to employ such a barrier."

It was a huge drawback considering the risk to children and animals, but one that might be simply addressed by the construction of a high earthen berm. Simple did not mean easy, however, for the land it encompassed would be extensive.

"What if I can guarantee everyone's safety?"

She regarded me evenly. "If anyone else tried to promise me such a thing, I would chastise them for their foolishness. But if you promise me this, Davis, I have complete faith in your word."

No one had ever expressed such unshakeable faith in me before – not even Angie. It was humbling and eliminated any temptation to make it any less than one hundred percent perfect. If any plan we devised was not completely flawless, I would not recommend it to her.

"I have an idea, but I want to run it by Seth and Duncan first," I said. "What other problems are there?"

"It takes a great deal of power to cast, which Spencer and I do not have at this time. Also, it must be cast in the total darkness of the new moon."

"That's only two weeks away. Will that allow you time enough to build up the necessary power?"

"I believe so. However, once the spell is cast, it lasts for the duration of the moon cycle. It does not wane until the moon is new again."

That meant that, for a solid month, those inside the deadly magic circle were stuck in Ward, and whoever went on the rescue mission would be locked out. That was all right; I was used to being on my own, and so were the Finns.

"Twenty-eight days isn't much time to find all the garrisons, much less search them thoroughly." I tightened the cinch on her saddle.

"That would be true if you were reliant on mundane methods. I will have them all located by the time you depart."

"Conall has a map of our route so far," I said. "Maybe we can put our heads together and finish it out so you can mark the locations."

"An excellent idea." She took the reins and led the mare from the barn.

"I think this can work," I said, feeling cautiously optimistic.

"Keep in mind that each new moon lasts for only three days," Rhiannon said, mounting her horse. "We can keep the circle down from nightfall on the first day until nightfall of the second. We dare not leave Ward vulnerable to attack longer than that. If you do not return within that time, we will cast the circle anew on the second night."

Even though her expression and tone of voice were full of caution, I felt encouraged, for it opened up a few possibilities when before there were none. In a month's time, we could search several bandit outposts, return to Ward with what abducted members we'd found, and then go out for another month if we hadn't recovered them all. With our increased combat experience and a solid knowledge of where we were going, the bandits had no hope of standing against us, no matter how many there were. There was no way this plan could fail.

I would make sure of it.

* * *

I headed to the great hall the next morning with the small, leather-bound journal Rhiannon had given me. She herself used one to make sure that coven chores were meted out fairly. Mine was for keeping track of who went on patrol, when they did, and where they went. The pentacle led by Siorus was gearing up to go out in the cold and the snow, and I'd given them a few probably unnecessary last-minute instructions.

"We might want to think about sending more than two pentacles out per day," said Fenris, tossing his thick black hair out of his face. I nearly suggested that he cut it, until I remembered that mine was nearly as unruly.

"Why?" I asked. Seth had already suggested it, but I was curious to hear the spirit elementalist's thoughts on the matter.

"If we're only patrolling one area in the morning and one in the afternoon, then they could catch us by surprise in any of these other directions." He waved at on the map.

"With earth druids around?" Siorus looked skeptical. He disliked the cold and would have spent all day, every day by the hearth if given a chance.

"Having earth druids around didn't prevent the last attack," said Eian.

"Nobody was watching for it, either," said Mohinder.

If there was one thing I could count on, it was that the water elementalists would always back up the earth elementalists. It went

251

back to the first training group I'd taught, the ones who had been sick and tired of Shitozaki's haranguing and the attitudes of superiority demonstrated by the air and spirit elementalists. Having a common adversary had caused them to form a tight bond.

"That's true, but having more patrols will allow us to cover more area," said Madoc, the gunman of their pentacle. Interestingly enough, while the nulls had started out with a chip on their collective shoulders, they'd become the negotiators of each pentacle. Conall was the exception, of course. He didn't really have a bad attitude anymore, but he was more inclined to instigate an argument than mediate one, if only for the sake of his own entertainment.

I nodded. "Seth says more equals better as far as vigilance is concerned."

"We don't know much about this area," Fenris said, tracing his finger along a blank part of the makeshift map. I had copied it from Conall's and was trying to fill it out as much as possible before the new moon. As soon as Ahearn returned from checking on the herds, I was going to rope him into working on it with me. The horsemaster knew more about the area surrounding Ward than anyone.

"Y'all head on out," I said. "I'll think about this some more and see what I come up with."

Siorus and his group rose from the table and left the great hall. It had definitely been a good idea to put an earth elementalist in charge of each pentacle. Some of them, like Siorus, might be a little on the lazy side, but at least they weren't prone to galloping pell-mell into danger like a fire or spirit elementalist might. Also, now that they were all druids and experts at earthmoving *and* healing, I felt a lot better about sending each pentacle out alone.

When their departure, I flipped to the front of the journal where the members of each pentacle were listed by name and element. Figuring out a rotational schedule wasn't difficult, except that I also had to take into consideration how much the horses would be working. I didn't want my men *or* horses too tired to fight. During my musings, Duncan and Dermot joined me with steaming cups of chicory coffee and plates laden with scrambled eggs and bacon. Shortly thereafter, Conall showed up with Cinna, both grabbing coffees to help chase the sleepiness away before joining us. Stomach rumbling, I decided it smelled good and went to get some breakfast for myself.

Katarina and Heath were in charge of making breakfast that morning, and she handed me a plate laden with eggs, bacon, and a buttered biscuit as soon as I approached the hearth. Any time they were assigned culinary duties, they either brought me something to eat or had hot food loaded up and waiting when I went to get some. It seemed to be their way of thanking me for rescuing her, and it reminded me of my Traveling days when food and board were my rewards for helping people out or handling situations they themselves could not.

"You need to eat more," said Katarina. "You need to keep up your strength."

"You should never be too busy to eat," Heath added.

I thanked them and promised to stop skipping meals, fully aware that it was a promise I wasn't sure I could keep. They were right, but sometimes my longing for Angie created a gnawing in my belly that made eating unthinkable. When I got back to the table, Conall was sitting with his arm draped casually over around Cinna, with her head resting on his shoulder. It made me miss Angie with a fierce intensity. We'd had that closeness once; I wanted it back so bad I could taste it.

There was nothing I could do about it now, so I pushed the uncomfortable feelings and dug in. Not eating wouldn't bring us together sooner, and Katarina was right. I would be of no use to anyone if I was weak from hunger. Right now I needed to focus on hashing out a plan for protecting Ward during the two weeks until the new moon.

"If you think we need to patrol in two directions," said Duncan when I returned, "then perhaps we should patrol in four."

"That makes it unanimous, and if we had eight pentacles, we could do that," I said. "But we only have seven."

"Even if we did have eight, we'd still get pretty tired," said Dermot. "And riding hard every day would wear the horses out."

"True," I said. It wasn't like when we're just Traveling. A patrol moved faster to cover more ground in a shorter amount of time. We'd be expending more energy even if we didn't do any fighting.

"Maybe Ahearn would loan us some of the coven's horses,"

said Conall.

"You four have your heads together quite early this morning. What mischief are you up to?"

I looked up to see Rhiannon smiling down at us, Seth following after.

"Good morning, High Priestess," I said, then related the conversation I had earlier with Siorus' pentacle, mentioning Fenris' thoughts specifically. "We're trying to decide the best way to increase patrolling the area."

"We could talk to Ahearn about using some of the coven's horses," she said. Seth leaned over to look at my journal.

"That's what I said," Conall replied.

"He'll be the one to give you a final answer since he handles the livestock, but I don't think it will be a problem," she said. "We acquired so many horses on the way home that our herd is bigger than it was before."

Rhiannon reached over my shoulder and tapped the page where the Finns were listed. "It doesn't look like you have enough manpower for what you want to do, even with more horses."

"We don't," Seth rumbled.

She took a seat beside me, while Dermot moved down a little to make room for Seth. Spencer, who had been confirmed by the coven as their new High Priest, entered moments later, grabbed some food, and joined us.

"Hm," Rhiannon said, sipping her chicory coffee. "Borrowing mounts only solves half that problem. Why not include some of my people on your patrols?"

"We need more groups, not more people in each group," said Seth.

"I understand that, love," she said with a tolerant smile. "I am suggesting that you make new groups, with druids *and* witches."

"I don't know," I said. While the witches had been instrumental in taking back their holdings, the Finns had much more experience with fighting on the run. Taking the peace-loving witches along might get somebody hurt.

"Remember that this is our home," said Spencer. "We know the territory well."

"We don't have enough earth elementalists to *seek* on every patrol," Duncan said. "But most of the earth witches have become quite proficient at it."

"In the event that a group has no *seeking* ability, coven members can suggest likely spots where someone might hide," Rhiannon said.

"We may not be the most warlike of people," Spencer added, "but we are expert healers, and our archers rarely miss their targets."

"We'd need at least one earth elementalist and one spirit or fire elementalist in each group," said Dermot. "Plus either a gunman or a water elementalist. A coven archer and a healer would round out the group."

"That would work." Seth nodded approval. "Anne and Ruth have turned out to be crack shots with a rifle. Maeve has learned to shoot, so maybe the rest of the coven should, too."

"I am not certain I like that idea," said Rhiannon.

"I've already told some others that I would teach them," he replied.

"And you did not think to ask me first?"

"They're adults," Seth replied as if that settled the matter.

"Such technology was instrumental in bringing about the Fracture," she said. "I am reluctant to embrace it once again."

"Is it the fault of a thing if people choose to misuse it?" he asked.

The relentless logic of an air elementalist won out over Rhiannon's misgivings. She relented, saying she would give it some thought.

"We should utilize people with multiple elements as effectively as possible," I said, bringing them back into the discussion at hand. "Like Dermot said, there should be at least one offensive and one defensive magic user in each group."

If one member of a party possessed two elements, then even more elements could be brought on each patrol. For those with offensive and defensive magics, like spirit/air, fire/earth, and air/water, it would also offer the opportunity to use both modes of combat simultaneously. Phelan had it down pat, but all the dualists needed more practice switching between offensive and defensive combat, myself included.

"We should include Wolfric and Onóra in the patrols," Seth said. "With both of them having fire and her also having earth, we could send them with an archer and a healer, and have quite an effective pentacle, combat-wise."

"I'm not sure they're up to it yet, but I'll ask them," I said. "When and if they join us, they should go in all-druid parties until they're comfortable with how we operate."

The dyad had been on the run from either White Oak Grove druids or bandits for nearly a year, and the few weeks they'd had to recuperate wasn't nearly enough. It might be spring before they were physically up to the task, and while Wolfric might be ready for combat then, I had my doubts about whether Onóra would ever recover from the ordeal. She had been frightened and timid in White Oak Grove when her life *wasn't* in danger. Now she started at the smallest noise and jumped at shadows. She barely left the great hall, and when she did go outside, her dark eyes darted about in a constant search for threats.

"Make sure there's a water elementalist anywhere a group will be near a lake or stream," Conall said.

"Really?" Dermot said, giving him a look that was somewhere between suspicion and surprise.

"I never thought that water could be used in a fight," said Conall, "but nobody can dispute how effective your tentacle monsters are. And the snowmen for target practice? That was genius."

The water elementalist beamed. "Thanks."

"By the way," said the High Priestess. "After much consideration, Spencer and I have come to the decision that if you druids will continue to deal with our enemies in the field, we will handle our defense."

"With all due respect, that didn't work well before," Seth said.

She nodded. "That is true. Brennan and I made the mistake of thinking that an early warning would be enough to keep us safe. He paid for that mistake with his life, and I pay for that mistake every time I look upon the faces of the women who were abducted or hear a mother weeping for her lost child."

The air elementalist shifted uncomfortably in his seat. I gave him a look that said he should have known better than to open his mouth. He deserved to feel bad, especially since he'd spent the night in her bed. Air elementalists were excellent at rational thought and clear discourse, but sometimes came across as cold and unfeeling.

"Apologies," he said. "That was unkind of me."

"It's all right," Rhiannon said, patting his hand and letting him off the hook. "You said nothing I didn't already know."

Spencer spoke up, preventing an awkward silence. "Rhiannon and I have decided that the *Circitorium Fati* is indeed our best option for a magical defense at this time."

"Is that the death spell?" I asked.

"Yes it is," said Rhiannon. "The literal translation is 'curtain of death,' or perhaps, 'veil of doom'."

"While it is true that most of our magic is for healing and growing things," continued Spencer, "that is only because we wish to focus on the positive side of magic. We are no strangers to its negative side."

"That doesn't mean that positive magic is good, or negative magic is bad," Rhiannon added, anticipating my next question. "Positive merely means that we are bringing forth life and light, growing and healing. It is attractive, bringing actions to fruition. Negative magic is detractive – decomposition instead of growing, wounding instead of healing. Instead of giving life, it takes life away."

"That sounds pretty bad to me," I said.

"Is it bad when leaves fall from the trees in autumn?" the High Priestess said. "Is it bad when a wolf pack brings down a deer to feed its young? Is it bad when our spirits have left our bodies, and they decay and return to the earth?" She shook her head. "Life and death are all part of human existence."

"We will be ready to cast the *Circitorium Fati* at nightfall of the next new moon," said Spencer. "While the patrols keep the raiders at bay, the rest of us will ensure that there are enough food and other supplies for the month in which the spell is active, both for those who will remain in Ward and also for those that go on the search-and-rescue mission."

"What if they've been taken to the 'Ville?" Cinna asked.

"Then we go there and get them back," the High Priestess replied.

Conall sat up, suddenly alert. "We're actually going to attack the 'Ville?"

"*If* we need to," I said. "Primarily we're after the missing coven members, but we'll also free any people who were taken from the surrounding towns."

"And then we're going to attack?" he pressed.

I looked around the table, meeting the eyes of each member of my pentacle in turn. With the exception of Seth, each of them was ready and willing – if not eager – to go on the offensive. If liberty was to be preserved for all the free peoples of the land, the bandit city had to be destroyed.

"We'll see."

* * *

Discussing patrols with Wolfric and Onóra was not to be, for the fire elementalist and his chosen insisted on having it out with me about Angie. This time, however, Wolfric started out by trying to win Duncan over to his point of view. It was my misfortune that the conversation was taking place in the great hall when I came in from the morning patrol. Seeing the two together, Seth inclined his head toward the kitchen fire, where we sidled away to pour a couple of mugs of coffee.

"It was my father's original plan," I overheard Duncan tell Wolfric. "He knew it was too dangerous for Davis to stay at the grove, but he allowed himself to become embroiled in my cousin's grand plans to change the world." His tone was scathing.

"It needs to be changed," said Wolfric. "Nothing at the grove will ever change if people keep running away."

"You ran away."

"Yes, because of what they did to Onóra!"

The earth druid just looked at him.

"What?"

"You expect others to take risks, as Angie risked her own chosen, but are unwilling to take those risks yourself," Duncan finally said.

"Angie wasn't being hurt!"

"No, but Davis was."

Wolfric was silent for the space of a few breaths.

"You're on his side."

"I act as Danu leads me."

"How very convenient that your patron goddess led you to support a man who you obviously love."

258

"Of course I love him," said Duncan, unruffled. "We share a holy friendship."

Wolfric changed tactics. "So your father decided that the grove was too dangerous for Davis and made arrangements to send him to Shitozaki."

"Yes."

"And nobody thought to inform Angelina?"

"It would have been ill-advised."

"You don't trust your own cousin?" Onóra said. "She would never have told anyone!"

"She wouldn't have to," I said, interrupting their tiff. Duncan had already taken enough heat on my behalf, and I could speak for myself.

She spun about to face me. "What's that supposed to mean?"

"Angie's a terrible liar. Nobody would have believed I was dead if she'd been told I wasn't."

"You mean you agreed to this?"

"It wasn't something we discussed, no."

"But you didn't protest, either."

I recognized that snide tone of voice; Angie herself had used it often enough when we'd first met, in the days before Traveling with me and events on the road had knocked her off her high horse.

Duncan made an exasperated noise. "He was in no shape to make such a decision," he said. "It was *my* choice."

"But you *knew*!" Onóra cried. "And you did *nothing*!"

"Look, I didn't like it, but by the time I found out about it, there was nothing I *could* do," I said. When Master Shitozaki had informed me of Duncan's bold action, I could barely walk outside to take a piss.

"There was nothing you could do," she repeated. Her fists clenched and the room got a little hotter. "You could have sent a message! You could have gone back for her after your magic manifested!"

I opened my mouth to answer, but Duncan spoke first. "How can you even suggest such a thing after what Sebrina did to him?" The earth elementalist was slow to anger, but she'd gotten his dander up.

From the look on Wolfric's face, I could see that his delicate sense of honor had perked up at the earth druid's comment about what the tyrannical ArchDruid had done to me. Onóra, fixated on me, ignored them both.

"Not to mention that it would have put the rest of us at risk a well," Seth said. "The master expended a great amount of effort in creating a safe place for us, and even more over the years to make sure it stayed that way."

"So you were just willing to go along with Duncan and Connor Shitozaki's grand plans?" she said in a nasty tone. That tipped the scale for me; enough was enough. She'd been traumatized and was upset, but she was taking things too far.

"My willingness to go along with the plans of others served you well enough in the grove," I said, fuming. "This conversation is over." If I didn't get out of the great hall, I was going to burn it down. People were roasting in here as it was. Drawing the excess heat back into myself, I walked out the front door and stomped down the front steps. So much for a relaxing day after a hard ride.

I wanted to avoid conflict, but Onóra chased after me, in spite of Seth's warning to Wolfric that he should stop her. She leaned over the porch railing, gripping it tightly.

"Of course! Why bother going back for her when you could have a high old time gallivanting with your new friends!"

"Is that what you think?" I stopped in the middle of the street between the great hall and the barn, knee-deep in snow. Now I was pissed. "For your information, it took half the winter for me to get back on my feet. It was *Imbolc* before I could even pick up a sword again!"

"What about your *magic*?" she said, sneering. "You've had it for half a year and still you have done nothing for Angie!"

"That's enough!" Wolfric snapped, but she ignored him, too.

Now seething, I said, "I had to learn how to *use* it, Onóra! It's not just something you can pick up in a day or two."

She rolled her eyes. "If you cared about her at all, you would have already gone back for her!"

Incensed, I shot back, "She left the grove and I don't even know where she is! And if she *was* still there, wild horses couldn't drag me within a hundred leagues of that place! I will *never* go there again! Not for Angie. Not for *anyone*." I turned my back on her with the intention of going somewhere to cool off. Onóra Nightshade, however, was relentless.

"I never realized you were such a coward."

I froze.

A coward?

Something inside me snapped. What I felt inside was beyond fury - the legendary temper of a fire druid had risen up inside me and was about to blaze out of control.

"How dare you—" Duncan began, falling silent when I turned slowly around and faced Wolfric's chosen.

"A coward, am I?" Angie had told her friends about every single exciting thing that had occurred on our journey from Jonesboro to White Oak Grove. Onóra had struck below the belt, and I was going to hit her back *hard*.

"Very well. Let's review my cowardly deeds." I spoke quietly, but there was no masking the threatening tone. "Was it the time I ran through a pitch-black forest to rescue her from bandits? Or the time I took on a small army of witch hunters so she wouldn't be burned at the stake? The time I took a bullet and got back on my horse to make sure she got out of the woods safely?"

She clenched her fists, mouth twisted in a defiant snarl. "You were honor-bound to do those things!"

"Very well. What about the time I covered your tracks so no one would find you in the willow grove? Or when I gathered food and supplies for you and Wolfric? Oh, right. It was when I held Darryn and Niall at bay so *you* could run away."

Onóra's dark eyes were huge. She cast a panicky look to Wolfric for support, but the fire elementalist stood glaring off into the distance with his arms crossed.

"Hm, let's see, then. Was it when I stayed at the grove even after Darryn tried to kill me the first time? How about the second time? The time he ran me through with his sword? Oh, wait – *you* were already gone by the time that happened."

She backed up the steps, shaking her head as I approached.

"It must have been when I told the ArchDruid that I'd rather be whipped than leave the grove because banishment meant leaving Angie behind."

Unable to look me in the eye any longer, she bowed her head, her thin body trembling, but I was ruthless.

"You profess to be her friend, but it's clear to me that you don't know Angie at all. So let me tell you a few things about

Angelina Everlight. She is strong, she is brave, she is fierce, and she is a *warrior*," I said. "She doesn't *need* me to protect her, Onóra, because she is everything you are not."

She buried her face in her hands, shoulders shaking with silent sobs. Everyone was silent while the bitterly cold wind whipped our clothes around our bodies. The chill did not reach me, however.

Seth broke the silence first. "Davis."

"What?"

He cleared his throat. "You're, ah... You're steaming again."

I looked down. The snow that had coated my blue jeans and boots had melted, and the water was now rising off them as steam. The village square was completely cleared of snow and ice from the great hall to the barn. Not only was the ground dry when it should have been muddy, but it was also scorched. Every square inch of ground was burnt black, except for a thin border around the buildings.

It brought a sense of rationality back to me, and I became aware of my thundering heart and heaving chest. Forcing my fists to unclench, I turned in a slow circle, surveying the damage – or lack thereof. Nothing was damaged that could not be fixed.

At least I'd had that much self-control.

I stalked out to the fallow field the Finns had taken over for sword training, a trail of dry ground marking my path. The heat of my anger melted the surrounding snow, evaporating the moisture before it could saturate the dirt. I was going to have to walk a lot farther if I was going to cool off.

"Leave me alone, Seth," I called over my shoulder.

Instead of listening, the air elementalist jogged to catch up.

"I brought my sword," he said. "In case you want to spar."

Ordinarily, some strenuous physical activity was just what I needed to get over my ire, but this was something more. It was fury, and it left me feeling like a volcano ready to erupt.

"Not a good time."

He was silent for a moment. "Let's go for a hike, then," he said, and began to trudge forward through the nearly knee-deep snow.

"Let me go first," I said, exasperated.

"Sure."

"And shield yourself if things start to get hot."

"I will."

We hiked in silence for the rest of the afternoon, heading back to Ward just before supper. I'd missed lunch, and my stomach was growling loudly. Rhiannon and Spencer were waiting for us on the porch.

Waiting for *me*.

"It's pretty cold to be sitting around outside," I said.

"Are you all right?" Rhiannon asked.

I had expected an ass chewing, not this warm concern.

"I'm fine. I apologize for losing my temper. I'll fix this… later." I gestured to the charred earth.

"Do not trouble yourself," the High Priest said. "There are many here with the skill to repair it."

"Onóra, for one," said the High Priestess. "In fact, I've told her that the damage she caused is hers to repair."

"But I'm the one who did it."

"Oh, so you would have turned my front yard into charcoal all on your own, without Wolfric and Onóra's insensitive and arrogant harassment?"

"That doesn't matter," I said. "It was my lack of control that caused the damage." My father had instilled in me that I was the only one who could control my reactions to sadness, fear, or anger.

Rhiannon reached out and took my hands in hers. "Davis, what she did was akin to sticking a knife in your most vulnerable spot and twisting it to torture you. She's lucky she's still alive."

I pulled away. "I would never kill anyone over mere words."

"No, but I might." Her lips pressed together in anger a moment before her features smoothed into an expression of compassion once more. "Come in out of the cold. I'll make you some hot chocolate."

I relented and followed her up the steps.

"I have that list for you, Davis," said Spencer, handing me a piece of slate with names chalked on it in two columns.

"Thanks," I said, taking it and reviewing the names. It included the same teens and young adults who had helped us win back their home, as well as some of the older, more experienced healers. I handed it to Seth.

"It looks good," he said. "If we work on this over supper, we

263

can start running four patrols tomorrow morning."

It didn't take a genius to figure out that giving me the list was their way of distracting me. If I was focused on manpower and patrols, I wouldn't be thinking about Angie *or* Onóra, and I wouldn't burn Ward to the ground.

The hot chocolate was pretty tasty, too.

Chapter 14 – On Patrol

Those who expect to reap the blessings of freedom must,
like men, undergo the fatigue of supporting it.
~ Thomas Paine ~

Seth, Ahearn, Maeve, and I hammered out the Ward patrol schedule until we had a workable plan that did not overtax either man or beast. We tried to stick with organizing people in pentacles, but we wanted everyone to have a day off between rides whenever possible. As it stood, the schedule was so tight that it allowed too little time for rest.

"We'll split up into groups of four – we'll call them shields – and anybody left over can ride relief if someone is sick or injured." *Or if someone dies*, the cynical side of my brain added.

"Why shields?" asked Seth.

"Like a shield knot," said Maeve, referring to the protective embroidery that some of the witches had sewn onto their cloaks. Some of the Finns had done likewise, but what I had really been thinking was that the name represented our position as shields between Ward and the 'Ville.

"I like it," Ahearn said.

The Finns were not as enthusiastic at the meeting that night.

"Everybody here? Good," I said, then turned to Fenris. "Your idea of patrolling in multiple directions was a good one, so we're going to start running four groups on patrol, morning and afternoon."

The black-haired spirit elementalist looked dubious. "You said we didn't have enough people or horses. How are we going to do that?"

"We're adding witches to the patrols, and splitting up the pentacles."

"What do you mean we're splitting up our pentacles? I *like* my pentacle!" Madoc protested.

"So do we!" said Phelan, followed by a chorus of protests from just about every druid in the room. The hubbub went on for a few minutes before Seth decided he'd had enough and bellowed for silence.

Conall put his hands on his hips. "Did it even occur to you to ask what *we* thought about this plan?"

I tossed my journal onto the table in front of him. "It doesn't matter what you think. It doesn't matter what I think. We simply don't have the manpower. Besides, Ward does not belong to us, and by all rights, the witches should be able to help in seeing to their own protection."

"Why can't the witches just have their own pentacles, then?" asked Nêreus. That was a water elementalist for you, reacting with their hearts first instead of their brains. Fortunately, this tendency was matched by an equal passion and devotion to whatever project in which they were involved.

Ahearn rose, taking the floor. "We're not ready to go it alone," he said. "We need your expertise. We aren't accustomed to using our magic for combat, and you are. You have a lot more experience riding hard and fighting on the move. You know a lot more than we do about how bandits act and react."

Maeve stood up beside him. "Believe me, we *want* our own pentacles. We want to be able to defend ourselves. But most of us aren't ready to take on that responsibility, whether it be physically, mentally, magically, or all three."

Ahearn nodded. "We just need you to show us the ropes until we're able to handle things ourselves."

"Exactly," I said. "It was pretty much unanimous when we decided to safeguard the coven. Do you really want to throw them to the wolves now?"

"So it's only temporary," said Siorus. The guys in his pentacle, a tight-knit bunch, sat behind him in a semicircle. Their expressions told me that they backed their leader one hundred percent. If you'd ever told me that a Welsh earth druid, a Roman air elementalist, a Vedic water elementalist, a Norse spirit elementalist, and a Celtic null would become closer than brothers, I'd have had my doubts. Nevertheless, the men in each and every pentacle had demonstrated time and again that they felt the same, so I understood how they felt.

"Look, if makes any difference, I don't want to be separated from the guys in my pentacle, either," I said. "Not even Conall." Scattered laughter helped break the tension.

"Look, I can't make any promises because I can't see the future. But ideally, yes, it'll be temporary."

"Can we pick what witches we want in our group?" asked Conall.

I should have anticipated that question and was at a loss for a moment. Fortunately, Seth stepped in.

"You can do that so long as everyone in the group gets along," he said. "However, it's more advisable to take a friend rather than a lover. We can't afford to be distracted out there."

Reactions to his second statement among the druids and witches were mixed; there were several who frowned, but just as many nodded understanding.

"While it's important to get along with your shield-mates," I said, "it's more important to balance your magics and skill sets. Each shield is to be made up of two druids and two witches. First and foremost, every group is to have a healer. No exceptions. Second, you need at least one person who can attack at range, either with magic, a bow, or a gun. Third, each group needs some defense, and we have plenty of people with elemental air for that. Fourth, you need someone who either knows the territory or who can perform a *seeking* through the earth."

We had eight earth druids all experienced with *seeking*, and most of the earth witches were far better at *seeking* than earth-moving. Some could sense farther than Duncan. I chalked this up to the witches' power being tied to their land.

"We'll be sending four groups out, morning and evening. Each shield will cover the same territory every time so you can learn it well," Seth added. "Shields who have seekers will be alternated with those without. For example, if the northeast morning shield doesn't have someone who can *seek*, the northeast afternoon shield will."

"It certainly solves the manpower issue," said Fenris. "Do we have enough horses?"

"Davis has asked me to be in charge of the mount scheduling," Ahearn said. "So if anybody has a difficult horse or a problem with other people riding it, they need to let me know by this evening."

"I don't want anybody riding Steel," I said.

"Nobody wants to ride your pony anyway," Seth snorted.

"At least I don't need a ladder to get on him."

"I don't need a ladder."

"That's because you're ten feet tall and bulletproof." I clapped his shoulder. "One more thing before you all start grouping up," I said. "If it looks like you can't sort things out for yourselves, I'll will make the shield assignments myself. Any questions?" There were none, and I picked up my journal and held it in the air. "I've written all the available slots in here. Please make your final decisions before writing anything down. Meeting adjourned."

I withdrew to a corner of the great hall and commandeered a chair with a book I'd borrowed from Rhiannon on the history of Ward. It was the first opportunity I'd had to open it, so of course, someone interrupted. Since that someone was Maeve, I didn't really mind.

"I'd like to be in your shield," she said.

I smiled. "Sounds good to me."

She looked over her shoulder at the milling throng of people, then turned back to me and said, "I'm a bit surprised that you aren't being mobbed with potential companions."

"I don't think this plan has increased my popularity any. Nobody is happy about losing their pentacle."

"Yes, but one would think that patrolling with the most powerful magic-user in residence would be appealing."

I shrugged. That might have been the case before turning the front yard into a barbecue pit this morning, but probably not now. Duncan appeared and saved me from answering, but brought a problem of another kind.

"You and I should remain together," he said.

"I knew you weren't going to like this plan."

"You're right. I don't."

While my pentacle had been informed of the plan to deliver

the captured witches from imprisonment, and to protect Ward with what I had come to think of as the circle of death, the rest of the witches and Finns were as yet unaware. I gestured Duncan closer; predictably, Maeve leaned in, too.

"It's only for two weeks," I murmured. "On the new moon, we depart to find the lost citizens of Ward."

"She agreed to use the spell!" Maeve whispered.

"Yes, she did. Conditionally."

Duncan nodded, having been included in the plan to build a giant earthen wall around Ward.

"I want to go with you," she said.

I hesitated, having intended only to take the Finns.

"Davis," she insisted. "I *need* to go."

"You can ride with our pentacle," said the earth druid, meeting my irked expression with a placid air. "Our enemy has done her a great injustice. She has the right, as does anyone else who wishes to exact revenge."

"I think I liked you better when you didn't have any opinions," I grumped.

Duncan smiled.

"Fine," I told Maeve. "You can come."

* * *

Each day, four shields went out in the cardinal directions, turned clockwise, and patrolled a quadrant – the area of land between two directions. Each shield covered the same territory, alternating days with a second shield that did the same. In this way, each group could learn its region and pass on any changes or items of concern to the next.

Siorus' shield group came in just as a little boy began ringing the triangle announcing the midday meal. The shield consisted of himself as healer and scout, Madoc as gunman, archer Shannon, and Elin, who turned out to be skilled in the element of spirit. Once she'd had some lessons in casting spirit bolts and orbs from Fenris and Phelan, she'd become quite deadly. It seemed to have helped some in her recovery from the torment she'd suffered at the hands of the bandits.

They were first to return, like always.

"Are you sure you don't want to switch to the afternoon run?"

I asked the earth druid as he swung down from his horse.

"Positive," Siorus replied, wrapping his cloak more tightly around his body. "I'd just spend the whole morning dreading it. Then my whole day would be ruined instead of just half of it."

"At least this way the lazy bear can spend the rest of the day warming up by the fire," Madoc said, giving the earth druid a fond smile.

The shield members handed their reins over to the off-group, who saw to the care of horses, tack, and supplies. Tomorrow they would be riding, with Siorus' group attending to the chore. By Rhiannon's order, those who had been on patrol got to eat before everyone else.

"No sign of bandits," Siorus said. "I dismounted in several places to do some intensive *seeking* and didn't find anything that way, either."

"Good. Go get some grub. It's just chicken and dumplings for lunch, but Eian brought down a deer early this morning so there'll be roast venison for supper tonight."

"Praise the gods!" said Siorus, and gestured for Madoc to join him. They tromped up the stairs holding hands. No wonder the gunman had been so opposed to splitting up the pentacles. I didn't pay much attention to the personal affairs of others, but that might have been an error. Romantic entanglements could have a profound effect on how well my battle plans were carried out. The girls followed the druid pair, walking arm in arm and chatting quietly.

After lunch I went to the barn to saddle Steel and found Maeve and Ahearn already inside, saddling their own mounts.

"Have either of you seen Dermot?" I asked.

Ahearn pointed up at the hayloft. As if on cue, the sounds of giggling and rustling could be heard.

"Dermot!"

The water elementalist peeked over the edge of the loft, shirtless and with hay sticking out of his red hair. "Is it time to go already?"

"Yes, so get your ass down here."

"All right, all right! You don't have to be so pushy."

He disappeared for a few moments and then slid down the ladder with his shirt untucked and hair unruly.

"Do you even have your sword?" I asked. "Or your shotgun?"

"Um..." He looked around and patted his hips as if he expected either item to magically appear. "I'll be right back."

"And get your coat, too!" I yelled after him. "And your canteen! The big one!"

"I wondered why he wasn't leading a shield group like everyone else in your pentacle," said Ahearn.

"And now you know," said Maeve.

I lowered my voice. "Dermot's with me because I knew his mother and sisters while I was still at the grove. His father is dead, and his older brother was exiled. His family has been through enough, and I want to make sure they see him again."

"Brutal," said Ahearn. "How old is he?"

"I'll be eighteen in March," the water elementalist said, leading Kelpie into the barn. He still had hay in his hair, but other than that he was put together. "Beware the Ides of March!"

"Pisces," said Maeve. "How did I know?"

"Probably because, like all Pisces, I am a fantastic lover."

"Now that I wouldn't know," Maeve said dryly.

"Would you like to?" He waggled his eyebrows at her.

"With a man half my age? No."

There was a giggle from the hayloft. The healer was doing her best to stay aloof, but even her impenetrable stone walls could not stand against Dermot's eternal high spirits.

"You've been traveling through the wilderness and fighting bandits with a seventeen-year-old kid?" Ahearn said, looking at me like I was crazy.

"It's not like I could drop him off anywhere. Besides, there's no telling what kind of trouble he'd get into—"

Dermot finished saddling his horse in record time. "You're just grouchy because I'm getting laid and you're not."

Maeve let out an indignant huff. "Rude!"

I pinched the bridge of my nose. "Could we please just go?"

Heading south, we gave the horses a while to warm up, then alternately trotted and cantered until we were a good distance from Ward. As we slowed to a walk again, I closed my eyes and tried to connect to the earth while mounted. Either the snow or the frozen ground made it harder than usual, so I dismounted, used fire magic to clear a spot and dry the ground, then performed a *seeking*.

Dermot did likewise. He plopped down on his hands and knees in the snow, so focused on what he was doing that he didn't notice his horse stealing stray pieces of hay from his hair.

"What are you doing?" I asked.

"I'm *seeking* through the snow."

"You can do that?"

"I don't know. I just thought I'd try it."

Druids generally believed that the element of water was useless in combat, but time and again Dermot had proved them all wrong. He hadn't known he could make giant water tentacles until he'd actually tried it, so I was happy to allow him to experiment.

"There's something to the southwest," he said.

"I don't feel anything," I said, remounting Steel.

"Well, it's winter. Maybe the mother is sleeping deeply because of the cold." He pulled his hands out of the snow, blew on them, and put his mittens back on.

"It's possible," I said, wondering if perhaps the heavy snow was interfering. "Can you tell how many are out there?"

He shook his head. "No, but I can tell they're people."

"All right, then. Let's go check it out."

It was another quarter mile before I could sense them, too. By that point, Dermot had determined there were ten individuals with horses. We rode another half mile before we could see them, and we dismounted and continued on foot to remain unseen.

"Remarkable," said Ahearn.

"I hand-picked Dermot to come with us because he's the best water elementalist we have."

The water elementalist grinned hugely.

"*Don't* tell anyone I said that."

"Davis wants everybody else to think I'm a troublemaker so he can have me all to himself." He stripped off one furry mitten and knelt in the snow. "Definitely ten bandits out there."

"How do you know they're bandits?" Ahearn asked.

"Is there anybody else out here *but* bandits?"

"He's got a point," I said, squatting and placing one hand on the ground to get a feel for what we might be facing. The closer distance was better; in addition to sensing them through the earth, I could also tell they were sitting around a fire. Out of curiosity I tried touching the flames and found that I could.

"*Volcanic.*"

"Is that good or bad?" asked Maeve.

"Definitely good. I can feel their fire."

Dermot grinned at me. "We could have some fun with this, you know."

Fun was something we'd had very little of lately. We were at a safe distance, and the enemy was not aware of our presence, much less our location.

"Sure," I said. "Why not?"

Dermot whipped off his other glove and tossed it aside, plunging his hands deep into the snow. He leaned forward like a hunting hawk with a look of mischief on his face. "I just *love* snowmen, don't you?" Ten mounds of snow began to grow behind the bandits, forming into stocky, halfling-sized figures.

"They're kind of small, don't you think?"

"I don't want to run out of magic."

It was a reminder that he was still an elementalist and thus limited by the size of the Well within him. Dermot was so creative and his ability to manipulate of water so impressive that I tended to forget that limitation.

The bandits sat stock-still for several moments, until the snowy figures came to life, walking around them with stumpy steps. The bandits jumped to their feet, yelling and scrambling for their weapons. As if in response to the gunfire, the snowmen increased speed, first skipping and then running, weaving in and out of the enemy campsite like demented dwarves. Bullets punched through the snow bodies but did not damage them in any significant way. They did, however, injure one of their own people. She screamed in pain when struck by a stray bullet that had passed through the living snow.

"Tsk, tsk," said the water elementalist. "Somebody forgot to pay attention to what was behind his target."

"Let's move closer while they're distracted," suggested Ahearn, stringing his bow. Holding her rifle at the ready, Maeve nodded agreement. It was freezing, and we were only halfway through our patrol area, so I was all for finishing this quickly and getting back to the horses. We crept within range of the horse master's longbow, where he took cover behind a scraggly spruce tree. Since Dermot was busy with the snowmen, I piled up some snow to give Maeve some cover as she lay prone, and also as a prop for her rifle.

By this time the snow figures were *dancing* around the fire. The ten had merged into eight – to conserve magic, I assumed – and were now paired together to perform what looked like a promenade, followed by a circle to the left, an allemande, and a circle to the right. Having recovered from their shock, our enemies were now paying less attention to the snow dancers and had begun looking outward.

Looking for us.

They'd either seen or heard of us doing amazing things with magic, so it hadn't taken them long to figure out that druids might be behind the square dancing snowmen. It didn't matter, however. By the time the first one turned around, Ahearn had let an arrow fly, punching through his neck and sending bright red blood spurting over the nearest snowman. A second arrow followed, striking another in the gut. Maeve dropped the third one a split second later with her rifle, after which the rest of the bandits rapidly deduced our location. Horse master and healer each brought down two more that had stupidly remained standing with their guns out.

The five remaining enemies were on the ground piling up snow for cover. It would have been a good tactic if not for the water elementalist's creations. The snowmen fell apart, individual balls rolling about rapidly until they were much larger. Just as the bandits started taking pot-shots at us, the giant snowballs rolled over them, and the gunfire stopped.

Dermot stood up, dusting his hands with a look of satisfaction.

"Get down before you get shot," I said.

"Oh, they won't be doing any more shooting," he said.

"How do you know?"

He looked at me. "Have you ever built a snowman?"

"Of course, when I was a kid."

"Without help?"

"No, my dad helped." Realization dawned. "Because the balls for the chest and head were too heavy."

"Right."

"Can't they just kick the snowballs apart?" Maeve asked.

"Not while I'm holding them together."

We brushed the snow from our clothes and headed for the bandit campsite. The last five bandits had been crushed beneath snowballs that sat as high as my chest. Only their lower legs and feet were showing; one man's foot was still twitching.

"What now?" Ahearn asked.

"Now I burn and bury them," I said. "Dermot, move all the snow out of the way. If there are other bandits around, I don't want a blast of steam to give away our position."

"Gross," said the water elementalist, when the remains were revealed. The bones had been pulverized and the organs squashed to a bloody pulp. He and I collected the firearms, sliding them out of the mess and shaking off the gore. Ahearn's face became pale, and he walked away to whistle whistling up the horses.

"Guess I don't need to burn them," I said and removed my mitten again.

"Wait," said Maeve. "Let me try?"

"Sure."

She hadn't assisted in making the new earthen construction apartment buildings in Ward, so this was a good opportunity to practice earthmoving. Squatting to touch the earth, she closed her eyes and concentrated. After a few minutes, the ground began to sink, an inch or two at first, then more quickly, to a depth of about three feet.

"Very nice."

"Thank you." The witch opened her eyes and sat back, breathing rapidly. Whether it was from effort or excitement, I couldn't tell. She looked up at me with pride and wildness in her hazel eyes. A bitter smile played upon her lips while and her chin rose in satisfaction once she had covered the remains. In the face of someone I'd come to know as a healer, it was somewhat disconcerting to see.

Maeve wore that look often in the weeks that followed.

* * *

Provisioned, armed, and loaded for bear, the search-and-rescue party sat mounted on their horses, still and silent in the dead of night. There were fifteen witches accompanying us, plus one Triune – Ruth. I wasn't sure whether she was going because she hoped to find loved ones or to seek revenge, but it didn't matter either way. She had nerves of steel and was a crack shot with a rifle. I was glad to have her.

Maeve was another story. The healer-turned-warrior had grown more ruthless and vicious each time we engaged the enemy while on patrol. She was out to exact retribution, and nothing would satisfy but the blood of our enemies. Even so, she had remained sane and stable, and as yet had exhibited no risky behavior. While I had some concern that she might get crazy out there and put the rest of the group in jeopardy, I had no legitimate reason to leave her behind. Hopefully, the element of air would continue to rule her decision-making, and earth would keep her grounded.

Elin and Katarina, who also had been captured by raiders not so long ago, surprised me by volunteering for the mission. Elin's brother Killian insisted on coming with her, as did Shannon, her lover and the archer in Siorus' shield. Katarina was accompanied by her lover, Heath. The four expressed hope that they might find Cullen, her missing brother.

Rhiannon's eldest children also came with us. Archer and healer Cinna was never far from Conall's side, while Ahearn joined to manage the horses. Riordan, Tiernan, and Weylin were also along for the ride, for wherever the horse master was, they were usually not far behind. Like specters in the night, the Weird Sisters had appeared with their horses, joining our number without saying a word.

All eight earth druids and every single earthmoving witch had come together to create a wall of earth and stone that encircled all of Ward within a quarter-mile radius of the great hall. What would have taken the eight of us weeks was accomplished in only a few days with the substantial amount of magic the witches brought to bear. Twenty feet high and five feet thick, the wall only included about a tenth of their land holdings. Even so, it encompassed all the buildings, including the hay barn and livestock shed. After many of the sheep and cows had been slaughtered before winter, there was plenty of room for the rest to roam. More needed to go under the butcher's knife, for there wasn't enough feed to last through the winter, but that was a project left for those that remained behind.

I didn't dare leave Ward undefended until the magic circle

was raised, which meant a midnight departure. The High Priest and Priestess of Ward Coven were weaving their dark spell. As soon as the sun's light had vanished from the sky, they had begun walking along the outside of the wall and had nearly finished traversing its length. A ten-foot gap had been left in the wall, to be closed from the inside by earth witches. Everyone else had been sequestered within the great hall for safety. The ritual took several hours, during which we packed our saddlebags, tacked up the horses, and bundled up in layers of clothing. We'd been standing outside for half an hour, awaiting their arrival. Just as they approached the opening in the wall, a horse and rider appeared, racing through the gap just before Rhiannon and Spencer completed their circle and the spell with it.

The horse, a rangy dark bay with a star, slid to a halt outside the earthen wall just as Rhiannon and Spencer came together, closing their magical circle. Each holding an athame high, him inside the circle and her outside, they chanted in unison, words of power that were impossible to understand and immediately forgotten. Dark currents of magic filled the air between them, coalescing into an inky black curtain that rippled with hints of deep purple and midnight blue, giving off a faint, ethereal glow. Tiny sparks of actinic blue glimmered within the murky shadows of the curtain, revealing the elemental spirit used in its creation. As Rhiannon had said, it was not life-giving energy; rather, it was elemental spirit magic that siphoned the life from whatever came into contact with it, whether that be man or beast.

Seth leaned over in his saddle. "I still find it disturbing that they don't make offerings to the Outdwellers," he murmured.

Dermot and Conall shared a glance and then uncorked small flasks, pouring a little whiskey upon the ground surreptitiously before tucking them away again. The creation of a magic circle to keep out unwanted entities and powers had been unknown to us druids until the witches' ritual at Samhain. Instead of a protective ward to keep them out, we set aside peace offerings to the forces of Chaos, trickster spirits, the fae, or belligerent beings such as the Fomorians of Celtic lore, the frost giants of Norse legend, or the Titans who were overthrown by the gods of Olympus.

"It'll take more than ale and candy to appease these Outdwellers," I said, keeping my voice low. When dealing with the rapacious populace of the 'Ville, a conjured circle of death was exactly what was required to defend the Ward coven.

The High Priest and High Priestess lowered their blades and heaved twin sighs of relief. Rhiannon lowered the hood of her black cloak, revealing a face that was pale and wan. Spencer didn't seem to have the energy to do even that. His shoulders slumped, and he weaved as though it was an effort to remain on his feet. Aurelia put an arm around his shoulders to steady him.

"The spell is cast," said the High Priestess, her voice carrying clearly.

The High Priest collected himself. "Go with the blessing of the Lord and Lady. May the gods, spirits of nature, and the ancestors guide and protect you. Hunt the enemy. Destroy those who have brought harm to us, and bring our people home!"

"Blessed be," said the witches, while the druids intoned: "So be it."

Ahearn led her horse over and gave Rhiannon a leg up. I was concerned about her ability to ride through the night, but it was too late to do anything about it now. Spencer gave the order to close the earthen wall. The earth witches had raised it about a foot when the great hall door banged open and Onóra came running down the street, calling in desperation.

"Onóra, no!" Rhiannon shouted, one hand flung out in useless warning. Thankfully, the wall was up to three feet in height by the time she reached it. Spencer grabbed the young woman's arm to keep her from climbing the wall – and away from the undulating magic curtain.

"Wolfric!" Onóra cried. "Wait!"

The rider of the dark bay horse threw back the hood of his shearling coat, revealing the fire elementalist's scruffy blond head.

Rhiannon might be in charge on coven lands, but I was in command on the road. *I* decided who came along – and who did not. She did not appear the least bit surprised by Wolfric's appearance. Our gazes met and locked for a few seconds before she turned her horse and joined our posse.

"Come along, Wolfric," Rhiannon said, then called: "Go back inside, Onóra!"

Onóra continued wailing at the steadily rising wall. "Wolfric!" she cried. "*What are you doing?*"

"Good question," said Dermot, scowling at him. "What *are* you doing?"

"That's what I'd like to know." I said.

"It seemed like a nice night for a ride," the fire elementalist said, directing his reply at me. Dermot's eyes narrowed at the brush-off, and the cap of his big canteen flipped off with a *pop*.

"It was before *he* showed up," the water elementalist grumbled. The look I gave him quelled any further remarks. I had no intention of going easy on Wolfric.

Turning back to Wolfric, I said, "That doesn't mean you are welcome to join us." I'd made enough allowances for him already, and if the low murmurs behind me were any indication, the rest of the Finns agreed.

"It seemed to me that you could use another fire elementalist," he said. "And the High Priestess agreed."

"We don't need one bad enough to tolerate a malcontent," I said. "You have made your opinion of me and the choices I've made quite clear, and I have little faith that you will follow orders."

That man had the gall to look surprised. "I've come to help," he said. "Is that so hard to believe?"

"Wolfric, you may not think much of me, but you should know by now that I'm neither an idiot nor a fool. So if you're thinking to pester me about Angie for the next month, you can go straight to Hel."

My statement was followed by a hush as deep as the night was dark. Even Onóra, who had been steadily calling Wolfric's name, fell silent. Seth and Duncan wore twin expressions of open-mouthed surprise, while Conall and Dermot shared a look of approval. The rest of the Finns, having only seen me lose my temper once – and with this man's chosen – seemed to be holding their collective breath. Rhiannon wore a queenly look of disapproval but said nothing.

Wolfric took a deep breath, held it a moment, then let it out.

"I deserved that," he said. "Truly, though, I've come to help."

"You've shown no inclination to be of assistance before. Why now?"

"I don't suppose we could speak privately?"

"Since you've never given *me* that courtesy, no."

279

He straightened his shoulders and lifted his chin, ignoring his chosen's renewed caterwauling. "Because it is the right thing to do. Honor demands it."

"You can take your honor and shove it up your ass."

He gave a deferential nod of the head. "Very well." He dismounted and dropped to one knee in front of my horse.

"I owe you my life twice over, and I've no right to judge you. I beg your forgiveness for my thoughtless words."

I jumped off my horse and yanked him to his feet. "Stop that!"

"I beg your pardon?"

"I said shove it up your ass, not wave it like a flag in the street," I hissed. The ghost of a smile crossed his lips, and the renewed spark of life in his eyes did what his ridiculous groveling could not. I couldn't help but wonder if having a lethal magic barrier between him and his chosen was a factor.

"Apology accepted," I growled. "But as for the rest, you are my friend, and you owe me nothing."

His expression said that he didn't agree, but he didn't argue the point. "It has also occurred to me that by coming along, I can help you end this crusade so you can get back to Angie sooner," he said.

I frowned at him, and he raised his hands in surrender.

"That is all I will say on the matter. You have my word."

Having him along probably wouldn't end our mission sooner, but we could definitely use another fire elementalist.

"Get on your horse," I said. He gave me a sharp nod and remounted his horse with unmistakable eagerness.

I nodded at Seth and climbed back into Steel's saddle,

He called to the Finns: "Move on out!"

"*Noooo!*" Onóra wailed. "You *can't* go!"

He looked over his shoulder at his chosen, tearful and clinging to the top of the earthen wall with her fingertips. "You're safe here. I'll be back in a month."

"Don't leave me!"

"Go back inside, Onóra," he said and turned his back on her.

"*I hate you!*" she screamed at his retreating back. "I hate you, and I wish I'd never accepted you as my chosen!" She dropped from where she clung to the wall, the sound of her broken sobs fading behind the steadily rising barrier.

Wolfric heaved a sigh of relief.

"They don't *all* act like that, do they?" Dermot asked, sounding concerned.

"I hope not," the fire elementalist muttered.

Dermot turned to me. "Your chosen doesn't act like that, does she?"

Aware of the weight of Duncan's gaze, I was compelled to respond honestly. "Sometimes," I admitted.

"I doubt that," Wolfric said.

"She's never said she hated me, but she's yelled at me plenty."

"If having a chosen partner means putting up with *that*—" Dermot jerked his thumb back towards the wall. "—then I don't want one."

"Seeing as how you don't have a fetch yet," Seth said, with his merciless logic, "you don't need to worry about it."

The water elementalist snorted and looked away, but not before I caught a glimpse of his hurt and worried expression.

"Don't worry about it, man," said Conall. "Fetches and chosen are overrated. I'd rather pick my own companion any day."

Dermot perked back up.

"I rather think Conall might be right," said Wolfric, turning in his saddle to look back once more upon the empty main street of Ward. "I don't know what the Ancestors were thinking. Onóra is exhausting."

"She's been through a lot," I said, surprising myself. I wasn't sure if I'd stuck up for her to make him feel better, because I believed in druid dyads, or because it was true.

"That doesn't mean she needs to act like such a harpy. It's dishonorable."

Riding in front of us, Rhiannon turned around in her saddle.

"People react to emotional trauma in different ways," she said. "Some emerge stronger, as fighters. Others are shattered and require a long time to put themselves back together. We should not judge one another, for until we've traveled the same roads, we will never know if our feet will blister and crack, or become tough and callous from the journey."

"Don't blisters form callouses?" asked Dermot.

The High Priestess smiled at him. "Indeed they do, young man. Indeed they do."

Chapter 15 – The Wild Hunt

Injustice anywhere is a threat to justice everywhere.
We are caught in an inescapable network of mutuality,
Tied in a single garment of destiny.
~ Martin Luther King, Jr. ~

Thanks to the High Priestess' astral travels, we knew exactly where each missing member of Ward Coven was being held. Conall had marked them on the map he'd begun after leaving Sanctuary. At the time, I'd only considered the rune marks to be a way of recording the events of our journey. Now, however, the campsites might offer us future shelter, and each battle site gave us a reference point by which we might locate forts and garrisons. Each pentacle had its own copy of the map, just in we got separated.

The decision to begin attacking the bandit settlements farthest from the 'Ville had been a nearly unanimous one. Nobody wanted to get sandwiched between the inner ring of outposts and the outer ring of larger garrisons. Seth and Duncan had expressed some concern regarding attack from behind once our enemy discovered what we were up to. To my way of thinking, it was inevitable since the bandit city had essentially ringed itself with a buffer zone.

Rhiannon, Seth, Dermot, Ruth, and I lay prone in the cold, our position masked by a blind of snow and ice that the water elementalist had created. Our first target was the town of Cypress Creek, which lay about six miles from Ward as the crow flew. Ruth and Rhiannon had compared timeframes, and it turned out that Cypress Creek had been overtaken by raiders a month or two before they had invaded Ward. Riding easily through the moonless night, we'd reached it in under three hours.

"What do you think?" the High Priestess asked, passing the spyglass to me. I didn't need it but took a look anyway because it gave me time to think. The earth mother told me just about everything I needed to know. There were about a dozen buildings, with two huge stables located along the outer perimeter wall. I estimated the stables could house approximately seventy-five horses each. Assuming that there were people who staffed the garrison and that a third of the horses belonged to them, that still left a space for a hundred more horses. It wasn't too much of a stretch to figure that the garrison could accommodate two raid groups.

Passing the spyglass to Ruth, I said, "What's different?"

"There wasn't a wall before," she said. "But once we get rid of them outlaws, we'll sure as hell keep it."

"Good idea," Seth murmured.

"How many buildings were there originally?"

"Well, there's the trading post, the granary, three storerooms, the town hall, which also doubled as the church and school."

"What, no saloon?" Dermot asked in jest.

"Drinkin' ain't allowed," Ruth said. "At least not in public. No matter what people claimed, though, lots of 'em had hooch in their cellars."

"I'm surprised there's a trading post," said Seth.

"Just 'cause y'all druids like to keep to yourselves, that don't mean the rest of us do," Ruth said. "We're pretty self-sufficient, but a little town like Cypress Creek can't make everything it needs."

"Who did you trade with?"

"Mostly towns south and west of here."

"You didn't trade with Ward?"

"I've heard tell of people payin' Ward a visit if they needed some medicine for a sick child, but won't nobody own up to doin' it," Ruth said.

"Why not?" asked Dermot.

" 'Cause witches are evil Devil-worshippers." She snorted, clearly aware of the irony. Rhiannon echoed her snort, shaking her head.

"What's a devil?" asked Dermot.

"*The* Devil," Ruth corrected. "Satan, ruler of Hell, Liar and Father of Lies, Tempter, and Prince of this World."

"Hel's a goddess," he replied. "I don't think anybody rules over her."

"Hell is a place in the Triune religion," I explained. "They believe that when evil people die, they go to hell and suffer eternal torment in lakes of burning fire."

"They'd have to come up with something better than that for *you*," he said.

"Nice. Could we get back to discussing plans?"

"When would you like to attack?" asked Rhiannon.

"How about now?"

Our plan was simple: the Finns would do most of the fighting while the witches found and liberated their lost ones, along with anyone else who had been kidnapped and imprisoned. Leaving the horses with Ahearn, Katarina, and the Weird Sisters, we advanced to the eastern side of the garrison on foot with each pentacle's air elementalist standing at the fore to shield against gunfire. I fully expected there to be a lookout, but no alarm ever sounded.

"They're expecting us, right?" I asked Rhiannon.

"Perhaps not this soon, but I did tell them after the new moon."

"Right." I linked my fingers and cracked my knuckles before dropping into a crouch beside Duncan. "We'll have to put part of the wall back up later."

"Well, at least it won't be charcoal." The High Priestess' tone was dry, but there was a sparkle in her eye.

Together Duncan and I loosened the dirt around the eastern wall of the palisade. The frozen earth was a little resistant, but after a few pulses of heat, it finally acquiesced. Half of the air elementalists supported the wall and lowered it quietly to the ground. From the outside, it appeared to be constructed of solid logs, but they were actually sawn in half lengthwise to create a flat interior wall. Several horses, startled from sleep, came to snorting alertness. Discovering that the barrier between them and freedom was gone, they eagerly moved out, hooves thumping over the flat-backed wall. Mohinder, Barak, Galen, Nêreus, and Ridley moved among them, touching the first few horses, and soon the herd was off and running to where we'd left Ahearn with our own mounts.

Once the stalls were empty, we could see straight through to the center of the garrison. I raised my hand to signal a move forward when a light appeared in the stable.

"What in Sam Hill...?" came a voice, and the yellow glow of a lantern revealed an old man. Beside me, Maeve raised her rifle to her shoulder and took aim, but I grabbed the barrel and pushed it upward. She glared at me, and I shook my head. A rifle shot would bring the whole garrison running.

Someone loudly whispered: "Brother Hardy!"

Ruth was jogging toward the old man, her footfalls light upon the downed palisade wall. He turned sharply, swinging the lantern and casting crazy shadows on the walls.

"Who's there?" he hissed.

"It's me, Ruth Kavenaugh! Put out that light!"

"Ruthie? Heaven above! Where did you come from?"

"Never mind that now. Put that light out!"

Remarkably, the old man complied. After a hasty whispered conversation, Ruth brought him over and made introductions.

"Hardy Boyd is my next-door neighbor. Or was, anyway."

"Pleased to meet you, sir." I shook his hand.

"Ruthie tells me you're looking for your lost ones," the old man said.

"Yes, we are."

"I can take you right to 'em. You gonna liberate the town?"

"That's the plan."

"To God be the glory!" he said. "You'll have to get rid of them outlaws first, though."

"I figured as much. How many are there?"

He *tsked*. "You came at a bad time. There's over a hundred of them baddies right now." He paused, and a sly look crossed his face. "I hear tell somebody done burned down Fort Greystone and killt purty near fifty raiders after. You wouldn't happen to know anything about that, now, would you, young feller?"

"The fort burned after the raiders died, actually."

Hardy nodded. "I 'magine you'll handle this all right, then. There are five barracks buildings with twenty soldiers each, all up at the front, on the south side. Slave buildings are in the back corners – men on the northeast side and women on the northwest."

"How come you ain't locked up?" Ruth asked.

"Why, Ruthie, who'd lock up a harmless old man?" he replied with a wink that reaffirmed my own experience. Hardly anybody I'd met in my Travels was ever truly harmless.

"Ruth, you and Hardy go with Rhiannon and free the prisoners." She nodded and led him to the small group of witches.

"Halldor, Martin – you guys go with them," I said. "Wolfric, you go, too." They each gave me a nod and sprinted after the witches with their pentacles following.

"Are you sure about that?" Seth asked, watching them vanish in the inky darkness.

"There are only five barracks, and one pentacle for each should be sufficient." I said. "Air druids block the windows and doors so that nobody gets out. Let's go."

In addition to permitting us ingress, the stall doors would also provide cover. They weren't bulletproof, but the enemy would have a hard time aiming if they couldn't see us. The five remaining pentacles – and Maeve – entered the stalls, unlatching the doors quietly before continuing silently across the town square. They crept through the somnolent garrison, each taking charge of a barracks. Once each pentacle was in place and every exit secured, I set the first building on fire. Built of wood planks and treated with shellac and pitch to preserve and waterproof them, it went up like a torch. It was horrible and I hated doing it, but this method was safer for us *and* for those we were trying to rescue.

Terrified faces appeared in the windows, palms smacking the glass as they tried to break it and escape. Screams of terror and the hammering of fists upon doors roused first the people in nearby bandit quarters, and then the garrison staff. The spirit and earth elementalists stood ready to fight if necessary, but there was no violence from those who crept out to watch from the shadows.

I glanced at Seth and saw the horror in his eyes as he comprehended that it was his magic holding them prisoner as they burned. I thought he might back away from the gruesome task, but he never did. It was one of the reasons I had chosen the air elementalists for this. They were logical and would understand that *any* death we gave our enemies would be agonizing and that they would all die screaming, begging their gods for salvation.

It didn't make it any easier.

Opening the channel to my fire magic wide and unhindered, I increased the temperature to yellow-hot in the blink of an eye, incinerating all inside within minutes. Dermot had turned his face away and, seeing me notice, steeled himself and faced the burning building once more.

"Don't look," I said. No seventeen-year-old kid needed to see this, no matter how many people he himself had put to the sword. It was bad enough that he could still hear the screams. He nodded and turned his back on the inferno. "Keep an eye on him," I said to Conall. He nodded and joined Dermot in facing away from the destruction.

As I moved on to the next one, Duncan dropped the jumble of ash down deep into the ground. The earth druid's face remained placid and focused, but he rarely showed what he felt on the outside. I wondered if he truly agreed with my actions, or if he had put his conscience aside in order to follow my lead.

In front of the second building, I approached Tristan and Jasvinder.

"Can you two handle this?"

Neither was strictly an air elementalist, both having spirit as well, so I felt it necessary to ask. Tristan licked his lips before nodding, but Jasvinder shook his head.

"I'm sorry," he said. "Fighting them is one thing, but this…"

"I know," I said. "It's all right."

"I'll do it," said Seth from right behind me.

"You've already done one," I said.

"And you're doing them all. Let's get this over with."

The remaining four barracks buildings combusted and collapsed inward upon themselves even more quickly than had the first. There was a part of me which said that the people inside were evil and had done terrible things to the people of this town, Ward, and others, but the other part of me recognized that this was murderous retribution and would not be quiet about it. It spoke in my father's voice, but I'd ignored him many times in the past, hadn't I?

It wasn't so easy this time.

It was a dirty job, like so many other dirty jobs I'd done

because there was no one else to do them.

"I don't want to do this ever again," Seth said when we were through. "I'd rather risk my life in a fair fight."

"We have magic, and they don't. There will never be any such thing as a fair fight," I replied, putting a certainty in my voice that I did not feel inside. I knew what he meant, and part of me agreed with him, but I wasn't going to risk my people any more than I had to on this mission. I'd promised to bring the Finns back alive, and I was going to do just that. The lives of marauders, slavers, murderers, and rapists were nothing compared to the lives of my friends and those we'd sworn to protect.

"Duncan and I will handle the rest of this. Get the other pentacles together and start clearing out the buildings. I don't want anybody getting shot in the back."

"I'm on it." He started calling out orders, and the garrison staff who had been watching began to slip away into the darkness.

Duncan and I buried the last ruinous piles of char, turning the earth over to bring up clean soil while burying the remains deep. That's when I noticed Conall and Dermot, still standing together. Neither had joined in searching the remaining buildings. Sharing a look, Duncan and I moved over to join them.

"Are you two okay?"

"I should have watched," said Dermot, shaking his head. "I shouldn't have been a coward. I should have watched."

"You did the right thing, looking away. And you're not a coward."

"*You* didn't look away." He sounded disgusted. On his face was the desire to "man up" and be strong, warring with horror and sadness at the deaths of fellow human beings.

"There is no shame in valuing human life," said Duncan. "These people died a horrible death, but they were no innocents. Had we not stopped them, they surely would have gone on to harm others."

"I *know* that. That's why watching them burn up shouldn't bother me. They *deserved* to die."

"It's easier to kill somebody when they've already tried to kill you first," said Conall.

I sighed and placed a hand on Dermot's shoulder. "You're not heartless. Don't become heartless. Don't be like me."

"You're not heartless."

"Dermot, I've killed more people than the 'flu."

"But they all deserved it, right? I mean, they were always hurting somebody, or you were always trying to help somebody, right?"

"Yeah," I said.

At least, that's what I always told myself.

After a house-to-house search for any remaining bandits and the resultant, on-the-spot executions, we freed the townsfolk of Cypress Creek. Of the five female witches we rescued, two of them were only sixteen. When I found out how badly they'd been abused took away any remaining guilt regarding the manner in which I'd put our enemies to death. Those bastards deserved every moment of the agony and terror they had experienced and then some. Furious, I had to go walk around outside the palisade before I accidentally incinerated something.

When I got back, Rhiannon informed me that their investigation of the buildings revealed food storage and dry goods aplenty in a couple of the newly constructed buildings. It looked to be enough to see them through the winter, or perhaps a siege. Water would be a problem in the event of a siege, however, so Siorus and Martin went out with their pentacles to alter the flow of the nearby creek so that the town would have an uninterrupted water supply. Mohinder and Galen, their water elementalists, had become full druids shortly after retaking Ward and so had no trouble getting the job done in a few hours.

Ahearn brought most of the liberated horses back before we departed the town. I say *most* because, ever on the lookout for fresh quality breeding stock, he had asked if he might keep several of the horses. In addition, we needed five extra mounts for the coven members we had just liberated. Thrilled to have their freedom back, the townspeople happily gave the animals to him.

I only had two regrets about the destruction I'd wrought, the first being the loss of enemy firearms and ammunition. The townsfolk told us that the raiders always kept those items with them in the barracks.

The second was that people were afraid of me.

It wasn't overt or obvious. Nobody ran screaming at my

approach, but they didn't get close, either. The general tendency was to give me a respectful nod or ask me if I needed anything and then to back away to go about their business. Recognizing it for what it was, I asked Rhiannon to deal with the townsfolk.

It wasn't exactly a new experience, but prior to this it had been because of my collection of weapons and the speed with which I was ready to use. Now people were afraid because of what I *was* – a druid with fire magic. While I could put down my machetes, knives, and shotgun, the magic was a part of me. It bothered me more than I cared to admit, and by noon I'd escaped the confines of the town, seeking solace in the quiet of the slumbering earth.

"I brought you some supper," Ruth said, handing me a tin plate.

"Thanks," I said, reaching for it. A quick burst of elemental fire and it was piping hot.

"Welcome. And don't worry 'bout them in there."

"I beg your pardon?"

"The way they been treatin' you. Don't let it bother you none."

"I'm not."

"Mm-hmm, and that's why you're sittin' out here in the freezing cold all by your lonesome." She gave me a knowing look.

"I happen to be *seeking*," I said. "Somebody's got to keep watch for bandits." It wasn't a complete lie. I'd been doing just that, trying to extend the reach of my earth magic. Using fire magic at the same time to keep myself warm was an added challenge, but both tasks were really just to give me something to do.

"Whatever you say."

"I take my fair share of watches and guard duty."

"Of course you do. A good leader don't ask folks to do what he himself won't."

I shrugged, quit arguing, and started eating. Hot fried chicken, mashed potatoes and gravy, and steamed peas were too good to waste on stupid arguments that Ruth wouldn't believe anyway.

I wish Angie was here. I didn't know how she would have helped the way I was feeling. Mostly I'd have felt less alone.

"Just so you know, they ain't afraid of you because you burned them buildings down."

"Oh no?"

"Naw. They're skeered of you 'cause you're one of them Devil-worshippers that bathes in fire and eats brimstone." She put her fingers up on her head like horns and bared her teeth as a demon might. I couldn't help chuckling.

"You come on in out of the cold 'fore it gets dark."

"Yes, ma'am."

* * *

We left before dawn the next morning. Even though they'd been healed by my earth druids, I wasn't sure if the five rescued witches would be up to riding with us, but every single one of them was mounted and ready to go. Another surprise was Ruth showing up with her gear packed and her horse saddled.

"You don't have to come with us!" Rhiannon protested. "You have your home back now!"

"And I wouldn't have it, neither, if your people hadn't helped me," the Triune woman replied. "Y'all have done me a kindness, and I feel obliged to return the favor."

"You already helped us get our home back," Rhiannon said. "You owe us nothing."

"Beggin' your pardon, Priestess, but you ain't got all your folks back, and far as I can tell, most everybody who lived in my town is still here."

Rhiannon reached up and took Ruth's hand. "I am blessed and honored to have a friend like you at my side."

"It ain't nothin'." Cheeks reddening, Ruth ducked her head, but not before I caught a glimpse of her pleased expression.

Our next target was a placed called Watson, which Hardy Boyd had heard was an outpost to the southwest, approximately ten miles distant. It was a little closer to the 'Ville than I wanted to venture at that point, but there was a garrison in Faulkner due west of Cypress Creek, and it wouldn't be wise to attack it with even a small outpost at our backs. There were two other settlements nearby that were closer, Otto and Bailey Lake, but they were ghost towns now. Word had it that the people of both towns had joined together, putting up such resistance that every last man, woman, and child had been murdered.

"I bet you're not so sorry to have killed those bandits now," Maeve observed. On the other side of her, Ruth nodded agreement.

I wasn't, but heard myself say: "Two wrongs don't make a right."

"That sounds like something your father would say," Dermot commented.

"That was one of my mother's favorites, actually."

"*Gods*, it must have been miserable growing up at your house," Conall said.

"Who is to say that what we did here was wrong?" Seth said. "There is an appropriate time and place for vengeance."

"'Vengeance is mine, sayeth the Lord'," said Ruth. "But I figure He won't object too much if we help Him out with that a mite."

"The problem with revenge is that it usually escalates," I said. "I've been in places where the people have been skirmishing with the next village over for decades and can't even remember what started it all."

Seth nodded. "This situation could definitely escalate."

"It might," said Duncan.

"It *will*."

"Bring it on!" said Conall. "Those honorless dogs deserve every bit of what's coming to them." He looked at me. "And that's something that *my* father would have said."

Can't say I was surprised.

The ride took less than three hours. Leaving the main body of my force behind and out of sight, I took Wolfric, Seth, Dermot, and Maeve to scout the settlement up close, a job made easier by the fact that its occupants had left the front gates wide open. The layout appeared similar to the outpost where I'd found Maeve, Ruth, and the others.

"Looks like just an outpost. Of course, they could be using the same style of buildings for different purposes," I said, passing the spyglass over to Wolfric.

Dermot snorted. "'Just an outpost,' he says."

"Compared to a garrison like Cypress Creek, it *is* just an outpost."

"It would make sense to give each outpost exactly the same layout," Seth pointed out. "That way, no matter which place you'd been to, you'd always know where everything is kept."

"Agreed," Wolfric said. "So far, our enemies seem to be well-organized and efficient."

"When are we going in?" Maeve asked quietly, her eyes locked on the enemy outpost. I couldn't imagine what thoughts might be going through her head, looking at a replica of the prison where she'd been tortured.

"Whenever we feel like it," I said.

"Would it not be better to wait for nightfall?" Seth asked.

"Maybe, but I don't want to stand around trying to stay warm all day." The air was frigid, especially when the wind picked up.

"What's the plan?" Wolfric asked.

"I'm going to do exactly what I did when I helped Maeve and the others escape, except I'm going to take people dressed in the bandit coats we've acquired."

"They'll shoot you as soon as they see you," he said.

"Nah. They'll think we're just another patrol," I said.

"Not for long, they won't."

"We won't need that long," said Maeve, taking hold of her rifle and creeping backwards through the snow. Wolfric and Seth followed, leaving me alone with Dermot.

"So… are you going to let her be one of the seven?" Dermot asked.

"Yes, I am."

"I don't think you should let her. She's a little scary."

While I understood that he was referring to how cold-blooded she was in picking off her targets, it wasn't really a fair judgement. Just because she was dispassionate about her killing while the rest of us used righteous anger or rage to power through it, that didn't mean she was mentally unstable. He was young, though, and might not understand that.

"She's already wearing bandit clothes. It's not like I can ask her to give them to somebody else and leave her naked in the wintertime."

Dermot grinned. "One can always hope."

I ended up with a crew of ten because Duncan refused to stay behind. He insisted that we needed a healer since Maeve's focus was primarily on shooting these days. I also took Wolfric for extra fire damage; Seth, Eian, and Declan to shield with air; and two of the four pure water elementalists: Dermot and Nêreus. That left Conall as the only member of my own pentacle who wasn't

293

included, so I told him to grab his shotgun and a bunch of extra shells. He hadn't kicked up a fuss, but I didn't want anyone to think I was leaving him behind because he was a null. Nor did I want him to think I didn't need him, because what had started out as a rescue mission would likely turn into a war. I needed *everybody*.

I discussed my plan with Rhiannon, who directed a small group of witches and the remaining water elementalists to create a berm of snow and ice behind which everyone else with a rifle to cover us as we approached as well as pick off any enemies that tried to escape.

"You know, fire magic is good for more than just fireballs," Dermot was saying as my hand-picked group gathered. "Why don't you try casting a firewall like Davis does?"

"I know how to use my element," Wolfric said stiffly. "I don't need advice from *you*." He looked at me. "What are they even here for?" he asked, gesturing to the two water elementalists.

"They're good to have in a fight," I said. The town of Watson, now a bandit outpost, just happened to be situated on a peninsula in the shape of a teardrop. The open front gate lay across the narrow isthmus, with water bordering each side of it.

"*Water* elementalists?" Wolfric shook his head. "Maybe if you need somebody to plant crops after the rest of us finish taking the outpost."

"I'll be doing some planting, all right," Dermot said, "but it won't be crops." Nêreus let out an evil-sounding chuckle and they bumped fists.

We put on our borrowed bandit coats, mounted the new horses that we'd acquired from Cypress Creek, and made for the open gate. Seth had suggested that we ride those particular horses because the people in Watson might recognize them, lending us credibility and precious time with it.

"See?" Maeve murmured. "Everything's fine."

Then the palisade gates swung shut behind us.

"Shields!" I shouted as the clicks and clacks of cocking rifles and shotguns filled the air, but Seth and the twins had already put them up. Wolfric spun around and launched two fireballs at the bandits who had closed the gates and trapped us inside. Their hair and clothing ignited, and they ran away screaming.

"Duncan, bring the walls down!" I slapped both palms on the ground, and together we created a rolling wave of earth that jerked the timbers of the front gate out of their post-holes. They rumbled and clattered to the ground as bullets whined around us, pinging off the solid shields of air.

"Flush 'em out!" I told Wolfric. "But don't set any buildings on fire. We don't know where the captives are yet."

He began tossing fireballs, sending them arcing over the top of the shields to land between the buildings. As I could "see" where people were standing through my contact with the earth, I sent firewalls zigzagging through the outpost, chasing enemy combatants out into the open where Maeve and Conall could take them out at range.

"What pretty, sparkly fireballs," Dermot said, grinning at the Norse fire elementalist.

"Let me know when you do something useful," Wolfric snarled.

"Okay." Dermot and Nêreus split up, moving to opposite sides of the downed gate in a crouching run. Each water elementalist extended his arms out, performing a scooping motion as though he was about to lift a heavy weight. Two tentacle monsters with six arms each burst forth from the water surrounding the outpost, diving into the town like striking snakes. Some grabbed enemies and tossed them over the downed palisade wall, while others formed sharp points and pierced their bodies through before withdrawing to wave wildly in the air again.

The fight was over in minutes.

"Hey, fireballer!" Dermot shouted. "Was that useful enough?"

His face gone pale, Wolfric's jaw hung open.

"Don't get cocky," Seth admonished, pointing an authoritative finger at the water elementalist.

"Aww, Mom, I just want to have a little fun!"

"I think we're good," I said. "You can drop the shields." I had just turned to signal the all-clear to Rhiannon when the barn doors banged open and the roar of a shotgun drowned out all other sound. What felt like the world's biggest hammer slammed into my chest, knocking me backwards.

My chest a blaze of pain, I landed hard on the ground, gasping to breathe like a fish out of water. Wolfric incinerated the front of my coat and shirt so Duncan could slap his hands on my chest and keep me alive. Blood gushed from my neck and chest with every agonized beat of my heart.

The sky above swam in my vision while multiple tentacles from the two water monsters grabbed at the man who'd shot me, fighting over him like prey and lifting him high above us. His terrified eyes bulged in a face gone purple, his mouth opened wide in a soundless scream above the tentacle squeezing his neck. Gripping his arms and legs, they tore him to pieces, and blood splashed over the air dome. Chunks of flesh thudded down upon it and bounced off, while a steaming pile of entrails smacked wetly against it before slowly slithering down the sides. Seth and Eian had raised a protective dome so thick it refracted sunlight like a soap bubble, creating prismatic rainbows across its surface. Outside the dome, Conall slam-fired his Benelli, gunning down two more bandits that had appeared around the corner of a building.

"Davis!" Duncan gripped my shoulder tightly, shouting in a panicky voice: "I can't work metal! Push the bullets out!"

I can't breathe. At first, I didn't have the breath to speak, and then I could breathe again and didn't need to. My heart stuttered as I took a deep, searing breath and tried to focus on the bits of metal lodged in my chest.

Out, I commanded, but they only wiggled a little, resulting in even more excruciating pain. Exercising the last bit of willpower I had, I slapped my hand against my chest, causing every piece of the scattershot and shrapnel out simultaneously. As my flesh vomited out bits of foreign matter, my heart picked up that erratic rhythm again, propelling more blood out of my body and onto the frozen ground. I held my breath as it paused, breathed again when it raced ahead for a few beats.

And then it stopped.

Chapter 16 – Backlash

The boisterous sea of liberty is never without a wave.
~ Thomas Jefferson ~

I floated, suspended in an inky blackness completely devoid of sound or sensation but replete with the presence of the earth mother. She surrounded me, cradling my body against hers. I would have relaxed into her omnipresence but for the arrival of another equally powerful entity – the Phantom Queen.

Rise, champion! commanded the Morrigan.

Live, my son, crooned Danu, infusing me with power that nurtured my damaged body, the pulse of her rhythms stimulating my heartbeat. Infused with pure, life-giving elemental magic, my wounds closed and energy returned to my body. As the darkness faded, awareness returned, battering my consciousness with a cacophony of sound for which I was not prepared. People were yelling, crying, and screaming, and the winter sky overhead was blinding. One quiet whisper was louder than out all of it.

"Please," I heard Duncan whisper. "*Please.*"

With his head bowed and tears running down his face, he held my hand, repeating his plea again and again. I took my first deep breath, feeling the sweet, cold air revive me further. Sensation returned to my fingers and toes first. It was painful at first but soon subsided as blood flow returned to my extremities.

"Oh, gods, is he dead?" Dermot said, sounding panicked. "He can't be dead! Duncan, you can't let him die!"

"Come on," Conall put an arm around his shoulders to lead

him away, but he jerked free.

I squeezed Duncan's hand, still pressed against my chest and covered in bright red blood. His eyes flew wide with shock, and he gripped my arm. "This is not possible!" he whispered. "You were dead!"

"We are Danu's favored ones," I rasped.

He let out a shuddery breath and bent low with his forehead to the ground, shaking with renewed emotion as he whispered prayers of thanks.

"Davis, we need you! You can't die!" Dermot cried, dropping to his knees beside me and knocking a paralyzed Wolfric out of the way. "Oh, gods, he's not dead, is he? He can't die! He can't!"

With gritted teeth, I managed to growl, "Dermot. *Shut. Up.*"

The water elementalist sat back. "Oh. Oh, thank the gods." He heaved a sigh of relief and looked over his shoulder at Nêreus. "He's going to be all right."

The ground began to vibrate and what sounded like a hundred voices shouting a war cry filled the air. Letting my hand fall to the ground, I learned what intellect had already told me. The rest of the Finns had charged forward, swarming through the outpost and slaughtering all remaining enemies.

"Don't let me go to sleep," I tried to say, feeling the lassitude that came over me as Danu's magic relaxed my body and made my head swim.

Somebody had brought me inside one of the outpost buildings and cleaned me up. Lying there in that bed, all I wanted was just to be still and quiet for a few minutes. I wanted to enjoy the feeling of air in my lungs and just being *alive*. I sat up slowly and ran my hand over my naked chest, discovering that there wasn't a single scar. Nothing hurt, and the cold that had pervaded my limbs upon returning to life was gone except for my left hand. That was odd, but I decided to be grateful that nothing else was different. The door banged open, distracting me from it.

"You," I heard Maeve say, "are an idiot." She looked and sounded furious.

"Sometimes," I replied. "Is everybody okay?"

"Oh, sure! Everyone is just *wonderful* after watching you almost die this morning!"

"Why are you angry?"

"Because you tried to leave Duncan behind and he is the *only* reason you still live!"

The only reason I was alive was because the Morrigan still had a use for me and Danu had healed me, but it didn't seem like a good time to mention it.

"Hey, I had to get the scattershot out all on my own. That should count for something," I said, trying to lighten the mood.

It backfired.

Maeve pounced on me, pinning me to the bed. "Why do you insist on making such *stupid* decisions?!"

"I don't want him to get hurt!" I wheezed.

"He's hurting anyway! Do you think Duncan's life will be worth anything if you die?"

"He has his famil—*oof!*" She drove her knee into my chest.

"You didn't see his face after you passed out!"

"I didn't pass—"

"He was a wreck, Davis! He was groveling in the dirt with your blood all over his hands, sobbing like a helpless child!"

I vaguely remembered his tears, but it seemed so impossible. Duncan? The calm, quiet earth elementalist who rarely raised his voice? Who never became upset over anything? Crying?

"Duncan is like a brother to me," I protested. "I would never do anything to hurt him!"

"What about the rest of us?" She shook me hard. "*Everyone* was upset, you inconsiderate asshole! Do you think *any* of our lives will be worth anything if you die? Do you not know that if you die, this rescue mission is *over*?"

"What do you mean?"

"Do you *really* think Seth would keep going without you?" She demanded, then gave me no chance to respond. "No! He would make his apologies, promise to come back with more help, and go running back to that Master Shitozaki of his!"

I opened my mouth to protest and then closed it again because she was probably right.

"And then the forces of the 'Ville will sweep over the land like a flood of evil, leaving nothing for Seth and his master to find except charred ruins filled with our scorched bones!"

This isn't fair, I wanted to say. I hadn't asked to be given this responsibility. Yes, I had shouldered it, had borne the burden of leadership as best I could, but I wasn't perfect and had never claimed to be.

Life rarely fair, son, said my father's voice inside my head. *You take what cards you're dealt, and you play the game best you can.*

I looked at Maeve – really looked at her, from her angry, twisted mouth and heaving chest to her shaking hands and tear-shiny eyes filled with terror.

"Would you please get off me?"

She pressed her lips together and regarded me for uncomfortably long moments, her hazel eyes brimming with indignation and fear.

"Maeve. Please."

She did as I requested, jerking away and stumbling off the side of the bed. I sat up, swinging my legs over the side, and tried to take her hands in mine. She had been through enough trauma; I'd upset her and wanted to make her feel better.

"I won't apologize," she said, stepping away. "I've said what needed saying, and I have no regrets."

"Look, I didn't mean to scare anyone—"

"What you *meant* to do is irrelevant," she said. "I've grown rather fond of you. Just like everyone else, I suppose. I just didn't realize how much until I saw you lying on the ground covered in more blood than I've ever seen..."

"Maeve."

"Don't." She held up a hand. "I know how you feel about Angie. And I know how I feel about having any man touch me ever again. I don't even know why I said anything about it." She shook her head, straightened her shoulders, and marched to the door. "Don't you dare get yourself killed, Davis. Not until you see this through."

"Do you think I *like* getting shot?" I protested. "I don't want to die, but this is turning into a war, and I'm only one man!"

Maeve whirled around, fists clenched and curls flying.

"Not to us, you aren't! Don't you *understand*? You are the spirit of Odin, leading the Wild Hunt! You are the mighty arm of Dagda, dealing life and death with his club! You are the heart of Prometheus, giving fire to the human race!"

I was so stunned that I couldn't move or think.

"You may not feel like those things, but to Duncan and Dermot and all the other Finns, and Ahearn and Rhiannon and *me*…" She pressed a hand against her chest.

"To us, you *are* those things, and we *need* you."

* * *

Maeve wasn't the only unhappy person I had to contend with.

Wolfric was pissed, too. Or maybe he was just offended. It was hard to tell. I had barely gotten my boots on when he came to chew me out, but at least he didn't pin me down and sit on me.

"Why didn't you tell me?" he asked.

"Tell you what?"

"About the beating you took for me."

I scowled at him. "Who told you about that?"

"Who told me? Nobody had to tell me – Seth and Conall took off your shirt. They covered it up fast, but not before I saw the scars. How many lashes was it, Davis? Five? Ten?"

"Does it matter?"

"According to Seth, you nearly died from it. I'd say that's pretty important."

So my second had gotten his way after all. He had wanted Wolfric to know from the very beginning, and he'd picked this particular opportunity to indulge himself while I was unable to do anything about it.

"I was punished for stealing food."

"Food you took for us."

"Yes."

He shook his head, his expression reproachful. "You weren't beaten for stealing. It was because you helped Onóra and me escape."

"If it hadn't been for helping you, it would have been for something else, Wolfric. Padraig warned me time and again that the ArchDruid had it in for me."

"Did Sebrina not offer you the chance to leave?"

"She did."

"But you didn't want to leave Angelina."

"No, I didn't."

"How many lashes, Davis?"

"It doesn't—"

"*How many?*"

I sighed. "Twenty."

His righteous indignation drained away, along with the color in his face. After taking a moment to collect himself, he said, "Then I owe you a debt."

"You are my friend. You owe me nothing," I said for what felt like the thousandth time.

"Honor demands I set things right. Until then, I am unworthy of your friendship."

Gods, I thought. *How much worse could this day get?*

As it turned out, pretty quaking bad.

I sought out Duncan next – literally. He was nowhere to be found, either inside or outside the outpost. I had to find him using earth magic, and then I had to dig my way there. Enlarging the cramped space, I brought forth a small flame to illuminate our surroundings. In the darkness of an earthen womb, Duncan was sitting with his arms wrapped around his knees and his hood over his face.

"Maeve told me you were upset."

His only response was to draw in a deep breath, followed by a heavy exhalation.

"I came to apologize. I shouldn't have asked you to stay behind for that attack. You were right. I needed you close."

After a few moments, Duncan said, "I am glad we are neither lovers nor chosen."

I didn't know quite how to take that statement, so I said nothing. He was rarely that blunt so it might have seemed more of an insult than was intended. Even if he hadn't meant to offend, clearly something fundamental had changed between us.

"I never thought I would even think such a thing, much less say it aloud," he continued. "After what happened today, I nearly abandoned you and the others, but…"

My heart sank as I waited for him to finish, expecting that he did not want to leave without saying goodbye.

"Conall suggested that I meditate before making a decision."

"*Conall* said that?" It was out of my mouth before I could stop myself.

"Our friend is neither as thoughtless nor as foolhardy as he would have us believe. Or, perhaps he has acquired some wisdom during this journey, as I have."

I think we all have, I thought, feeing wretched.

Duncan finally slipped his hood back and looked at me. His eyes were red and swollen, and it hit me like a punch to the gut. Maeve hadn't exaggerated.

"I'm sorry." Pathetic apologies could not take away his pain, but they were all I had. I reached out to touch his hand, but he pulled it away, smoothly covering the action by tucking his hands into the sleeves of his robe as if to warm them. Only, it wasn't cold in his gloomy little lair, because I'd warmed it up.

"Dermot was distressed as well, but I think it was only because Seth chastised him," Duncan said, changing the subject.

"Chastised him for what?"

"For distracting you."

"Seth told him you would not have been injured, had he not been teasing Wolfric."

"I'd better go talk to him, then."

"There is one good thing about this situation," he said before I departed.

"What's that?"

"I no longer envy my cousin."

When I found Dermot, he was standing in front of his horse, holding his saddle. He wore a troubled expression, an emotion rarely seen on his young face. For all his stout heart, he was still just a kid, a seventeen-year-old boy that I'd dragged into my own personal crusade. And yet, there was no sign that he'd been crying. If the situation had been reversed, and Seth was blaming me for distracting Dermot and getting him hurt, I'm not so sure I'd have been all that stoic about it.

"Going somewhere?"

"Davis!" He smiled, his face brightening briefly before his brows knit together as he remembered that he was to blame for my injury. "Are you okay?"

I nodded. "I'm fine. Thanks to Duncan. Again." I wasn't sure what the earth druid had told the others about my miraculous recovery, but until I knew for sure, they could continue to assume he was responsible.

"He was really upset," Dermot said.

"He said you were, too."

"Oh, good, you've already talked to him."

It simultaneously warmed my heart and hurt it to know that even in the midst of his own troubles, Dermot had been worried about Duncan.

"I'm sorry," he said. "I know that's not good enough, but I really am."

I held up a hand. "It's not your fault."

"Yes, it is! Seth said that if I hadn't distracted you, you'd have known there were more bad guys around and you wouldn't have gotten shot."

"Dermot, you didn't distract me. I was careless. I should have done a *seeking* to make sure we'd gotten them all before telling Seth and Eian to drop the shields. Or I should have had Duncan do it. I just… forgot."

The excuse sounded lame even to me, and he looked skeptical. Honestly, I wasn't sure what had happened. I had the nagging suspicion that it might have been overconfidence on my part.

"I don't know," he said, looking down at the saddle. "Seth's pretty mad at me right now."

"I'm sure he's mad at me, too. So is Maeve. And Wolfric. And Duncan. I imagine that a certain High Priestess is just waiting to rake me over the coals, too."

"Are you *sure* I didn't distract you?"

"Positive," I said. "Honestly, Dermot, if you distracted me that much, I'd have died a hundred times by now."

Dermot grinned, and as if by magic, my day improved.

* * *

The sea of people in the crowded outpost tavern parted before me, with every one of the Finns either looking concerned about me or wondering who I was going to come down on. It must have been the look on my face, for I just stood there until it got deathly quiet and Seth finally figured out it was him I was staring at.

"Oh." His knees bumped the table, sending beer sloshing over the sides of several mugs. "I'm sorry. I didn't see you come in."

Nor had he come to check in with me at all since I'd been

awake, and he'd had plenty of time. If I was to judge by the looks of things, he'd been going over a map with a tableful of air elementalists. Planning the next attack? Or planning to run back to the master?

"Take a walk with me."

"Sure," he said, trying to sound casual in front of the others, but there was a rising tension in the set of his shoulders. "Of course."

I held my peace until the door closed behind us, then stopped and faced him.

"You really scared Duncan this morning—" he began.

"My friendship with Duncan is my business," I interrupted. "We're not out here to talk about me. We're out here to talk about you."

"Have I done something?"

"Dermot is not to blame for what occurred this morning."

"How can you say that? He was running his mouth and tormenting Wolfric from the very beginning."

While that wasn't something I'd openly encouraged, I *had* allowed it to continue, primarily due to Wolfric's open disdain of the water elementalists. I had commented on his verbalized prejudice against water a few times already since this mission began, but he just wasn't getting the message. Wolfric was a man who tried to do the right thing, governed by his family's strict code of honor – but my friendship with him hadn't blinded me to the fact that he was also narrow-minded and slow to change. If I didn't know better, I'd have thought he was an earth elementalist. Or maybe it was the natural arrogance of a fire elementalist.

"Name one fight we've been in that Dermot *hasn't* done something distracting," I said. "In fact, name even a single day."

"I'm not sure I can think of a single hour," Seth muttered darkly.

"Exactly." I shook my head. "We're not going to blame a boy for a man's failings."

His eyes narrowed. "You think *I'm* responsible?"

"No, I am," I said. "I'm the one who told you and Eian to drop the shields."

Seth relaxed a bit. "Well, everybody makes mistakes. You can't think of everything."

"Right. Which brings me to my next point: Did you even think of asking me if it was clear before you dropped them?"

"No, of course not."

"Why not?"

"Because you're in command."

"I may be the leader, but everybody makes mistakes, and I can't think of everything. Right?"

"Right..."

"But you're going to drop shields the moment I tell you to."

"Do you not want me to follow orders?"

"I want you to *think*. I do not want or need unquestioning obedience. You are rational, logical, and intelligent. That's what I need from you."

"I've questioned your decisions before."

"Yes, you have. But never when the bullets are flying. Never in a stressful situation." His brow furrowed as he thought that over. "I can't have you losing your head when things go wrong, Seth. Panic again like you did today—"

"I didn't panic!" he said hotly.

"That's not what I heard."

"Who said I panicked?"

"Only Rhiannon has spoken to me directly. The rest, I've only overheard the conversations of others in passing," I said. "You lost it. And then you yelled at Dermot and blamed him for my mistake."

"People yell at him all the time," Seth said dismissively.

"Not the members of his own pentacle. Not the leadership of this group." I paused. "When I finally found him this afternoon, he was saddling his horse. Who knows where he would have gone?"

"Back to Sanctuary, I would assume."

"If he made it that far."

"You're the one who's always making a point of how resourceful a water elementalist can be."

"Resourceful, yes. Imaginative, yes. Forward-thinking, no."

"If he chose to leave, then that is on *him*."

"No, that's on *me*. *I* am the one who promised Shitozaki that I'd bring everyone back alive. Not you."

Seth had no response to that.

"I'm not perfect, Seth. I'm not bulletproof, either, but I won't back down from a fight. It's reasonable to expect that I'll get hurt again. Most likely, every single one of us is going to know what red-hot bullet feels like before this is all over. I can't afford to have anybody panic in a bad situation, you least of all, and I have a feeling we're in for a lot of them. If it happens again, I'm making Conall my second."

"Conall!" The barest hint of derision was in his voice, and I could almost hear his unspoken thought: *An altered druid in charge?*

"As far as I can tell, Conall is the only one who kept his wits."

"Conall."

"You remember him – tall blond guy who walks around with a chip on his shoulder because he doesn't have any magic?" In other words, the only one who'd kept his head in a dire situation was also the only one who had any excuse at all to panic.

"I'm not sure rest of the Finns would accept him as your second," he said, as though choosing his words carefully. "Even if his attitude *has* improved."

Seth's loyalty to Master Shitozaki was rock solid, but I doubted the rest of the Finns felt that way. After all, under Shitozaki they'd spent their days working the fields or training to fight, totally isolated from the rest of the world. Under my leadership, they'd gotten to Travel, put those fighting skills to the test, and meet some wonderfully agreeable witches. Not only had they gotten a taste of what they were capable of, but they'd also tasted something else: *freedom.*

"If you'd been paying attention, you'd know that he hasn't been angry since he found out what that Benelli can do," I said.

"He's still cantankerous."

"Yes, he is. But more importantly, he's used to dealing with catastrophic situations without having to rely on anything more than his wits and his weapons."

In fact, *all* the nulls had settled down, and most of them were as dependable as the earth druids – so much so that nearly all the pentacles had an altered druid gunman as second-in-command. The only exceptions were Yiorgos, who didn't have a gunman, and my own. Granted, my pentacle was made up of individuals who didn't need much guidance. We all knew what we were doing, which allowed any one of us to keep an eye on the youngest and most troublesome Finn – Dermot.

Looking offended, Seth said tightly, "Is there anything else?"

"Yes. I want you to apologize to Dermot."

"I assume you want that apology made in front of everyone."

"Since you yelled at him in front of everyone, I think it's only fair."

"Fine."

* * *

"Here you are again," Ruth said. "If you think I'm gonna keep bringing you food because you're too stupid to come in out of the cold, then you've got another think coming."

"Thanks," I said, accepting the bowl of stew. "You don't have to do this. I can eat leftovers later."

"So whatcha doin' out here? Keeping watch again?" Her tone was dry.

"No, just thinking."

"I told you not to let them get to you," Ruth said.

"I didn't."

"I think you did. Otherwise, you wouldn't have let yourself get hurt."

"What's that supposed to mean?"

"I get it. You don't want to be different. It's completely understandable, but you *are* different. You're special. I can tell by the way all them other boys talk about you."

I snorted. If there was one thing life had taught me, it was that I was most certainly *not* special.

"You don't believe that."

"No, ma'am, I don't."

"Then why are you in charge?"

"Honestly, I'm not sure," I said. "I did all kinds of things that pissed Master Shitozaki off."

"Let me guess – not following orders? Marching to the beat of your own drummer? Doing what you thought was best?"

More like refusing to attend sword practice, refusing to engage in magic discrimination, and starting my own practice group.

"Something like that."

"Let me give you a valuable piece of advice, Davis. Stop worryin' about what other people think and just do your own thing."

"That's easier to say than do."

"Yeah, it is. When I was a girl, my momma used to tell me that I'd better quit wearing pants, ridin' horses, huntin' and fishin', or I'd never get a man to marry me."

"Sounds like you didn't need one."

Ruth smiled. "That might have been her point. But my daddy said that when the right one came along, he wouldn't care about how I dressed or what I did."

"And he was right."

"He surely was. I didn't get married 'til I turned twenty-six, though. I had plenty of suitors, but they was always promisin' to marry me even if I'd only quit doing just *one* of the things I enjoyed."

And once she had given one thing, it would have been easier to talk her into giving up the rest. That's why I had never given in to my mother's nagging. I did my chores and whatever other responsibilities I'd been given, but after that, my time was my own and I did as I pleased. As soon as I turned eighteen, I was off and Traveling the open road.

"Ironically enough, I met my Daniel while I was out huntin'. He broke a leg falling out of his deer stand. I rigged up a travois with his poncho and my blanket, and then I took him back into town all by my lonesome."

"Did you nurse him back to health?" I asked, even though I could guess the answer.

"Hell, no. I went straight back to the deer woods. Daddy had passed away by that time, and I had to put food on the table for Momma 'n me." She paused. "But he did come a-callin' after his leg healed up. We courted for a year, and then I agreed to be his wife – but only after I made him promise not to try and change me."

"Smart move."

"It was a smart move. But you're bein' dumb."

"You think I got shot because I don't want people to be scared of me?"

"I think that's part of it. But I also think you got shot because you want to be like the rest of your friends," Ruth said. "Problem is, you ain't like the rest of your friends. I ain't no druid, but even I can tell that."

She unwrapped a basket with two large cornbread wedges, handed me one and munched on the other. I ate my stew and cornbread and did some thinking. When we were both finished eating, we packed up and headed back for the outpost, where at some point during the day the front gates had been put back up.

"I've had people look down on me before," I said as we stopped outside the gates. "But I've never had anybody treat me the way the folk of Cypress Creek did the other day."

"That's called respect, Davis."

"It felt more like fear."

"So what? Those ain't your people. Don't matter a hill of beans what they think."

She was right. It was my own people I was worried about.

"I've never been a part of anything before," I admitted, our silent walk having given me time to think. "I don't want to lose that. I don't want to lose *them*."

"If what you can do with your magic scares them that bad, then you don't need 'em," Ruth said gently. "If they don't know you well enough by now to realize that they can trust you, then they ain't really your friends."

"My mother said something like that to me once when I was a kid. It didn't work out so well."

"The Holy Book has a passage that says 'When I was a child, I talked like a child, I thought like a child, I reasoned like a child. When I became a man, I put those childish ways aside'," Ruth said. "You ain't a kid anymore, Davis. Whether you like it or not, you got responsibilities."

I sighed, rubbing my still-cold left hand through its leather wrap. I couldn't help thinking that if Angie was here, I wouldn't be worried about any of this. As long as I had her love and acceptance, I wouldn't care.

But what if Angie is afraid? whispered an insidious voice. It was the one that used to keep me awake at night, telling me that she'd soon forget me and find another lover.

"It's time to put your childish ways aside," Ruth said. "'Cause right now, you got bigger problems than kids who won't play nice on the playground."

Chapter 17 – Discord

Things do not get better by being let alone. Unless they are
adjusted, they explode with shattering detonation.
~ Winston Churchill ~

Watson Outpost provided us with an unexpected gift: a map of the territories acquired by the Republic of Jackson. Every outpost and garrison was marked, and some thoughtful individual had made notations of distances and travel times between them. Conall had updated the map he'd made, along with those belonging to the other pentacles.

Seth, Rhiannon, Conall, Siorus, and I poured over the map and debated what to do with the freed citizens of Watson and Beryl while Duncan, Cinna, Ruth, and Maeve looked on. The liberated coven members would stay with us, of course. Even if it had been safe for them to travel alone, they couldn't get through the veil of doom surrounding Ward for another three weeks.

"Taking them to Cypress Creek adds two days to our journey," Seth said.

"We can spare the time," Conall said. "Even if we hit every single garrison and outpost surrounding the 'Ville, we'll still return to Ward with time to spare."

"Faulkner is the last place we need visit," Rhiannon said.

"It might be the last place *you* need to visit," he countered. "But there are other people out there who used to be free. People who are now slaves."

"I have no objection to helping liberate others," she said. "But

I must first think of my own. And this garrison—" She tapped Faulkner's location. "—is where they've taken our children."

"We can't drag children all over the country side and still fight a war," Siorus said.

"Who said anything about fighting a war?" Seth said. "This is a rescue mission."

The earth druid shrugged at Conall, a gesture that Seth would have to have been blind to miss. He visibly stiffened.

"The master did *not* send us out here to start a war."

"No, he didn't," Siorus said. "But how can we save some and not all? How can we turn our backs on those still enslaved?"

"We don't have to," said Seth. "After we liberate all of Rhiannon's people, we can ride south and inform the master of what has occurred and—"

"And nothing," Conall interrupted. "Shitozaki will never let us return. He's too busy hiding from the grove."

"He is *not* hiding!" Seth snapped "He has provided us a place of sanctuary, and I for one am grateful for it!"

"All right, settle down," I said. "You're both right."

"They *can't* both be right," murmured Siorus.

"Seth is right about Master Shitozaki providing a safe place for us, and Conall is right about him never allowing us to return," I said. "However, winter will soon be upon us, and it will be too cold to return—"

"That is an empty argument." The air elementalist made a chopping motion with one hand. "We are already traveling in the freezing cold. It's *snowing*."

"There has been some early snow, but it's hardly a blizzard," I said. "Even if we returned to Sanctuary before the heavy snows, we wouldn't make it back here until late spring, giving the 'Ville time to rebuild everything we've taken down."

Seth rolled his eyes. "They're going to build outposts in the middle of winter?"

"Why not?" said Conall. "They have hundreds of slaves to do the work for them."

Siorus nodded. "We have to take them out now, while they're weak."

"Oh, are they *weak* now?"

"They're weaker than they'll be in the spring," the earth druid replied.

"I don't like this," said Seth. "I don't. The master told us to return by Samhain. We are *way* overdue, and I see no indication that we'll be returning anytime soon."

"I thought you agreed with returning in the spring," I said.

"In principle, yes. To win Ward back and rescue her people, yes. But to wage war on an enemy that vastly outnumbers us? No."

Conall said, "So this doesn't have anything to do with Shitozaki's order. This is about you being afraid."

Seth surged to his feet. "I am not afraid! I just know that if we all die out here in this wasteland, then we have no hope at all of winning our own home back!"

Several seconds of shocked silence followed.

"I wondered if you'd ever admit that out loud," Conall said.

"Is that really what Master Shitozaki has in mind?" Siorus asked, visibly appalled.

"Of course! Isn't that what you want? Isn't that what we *all* want? Don't you want to go *home*?"

"I used to," said Siorus. "But not anymore."

"What do you mean?" Seth demanded.

"I don't have a fetch," the earth druid replied. "I've never had one. Madoc had one for maybe a month, and then it left, never to return. Neither of us even cares about fetches anymore. That's why we…" He paused, suddenly shy. "That's why we've sworn an oath binding us as chosen."

The table erupted in to handshaking, back-slapping, and offers of congratulations. Forgotten, Seth glowered.

"Where is Madoc?" I asked. "Why didn't you bring him?"

"I was invited to this meeting, and he was not."

"From now on, if you're invited, so is he," I said. "Madoc is your chosen and should be by your side."

"Are you sure?"

"Trust me; if Angie wasn't a hundred miles away, she'd be right here beside me." I pointed at the empty chair to my right. It was a thoughtless and unfortunate choice, as it was the chair that Seth had recently vacated.

"Thank you," Siorus said. "I'll bring him next time."

"The same goes for anybody else," I said. "Born chosen or sworn chosen, it doesn't matter."

"What about you?" Seth said, reclaiming the conversation by pointing at Dermot, who had entered shortly after the discussion had begun and who for once had stayed quiet.

"I do miss my family," he began, which elicited an expression of triumph on the air elementalist's face. It was short-lived.

"But no," Dermot said. "I don't want to go back to the grove."

"So you're just going to abandon them?" Seth said.

"Of course not! I was just thinking that they might like to..." Wearing the expression of a kid caught with his hand in a cookie jar, the water elementalist trailed off.

"Go on!" barked Seth. "Don't keep us in suspense."

"I was thinking they might like to live in Ward," Dermot said, his face reddening. "Forgive me, High Priestess, if that was presumptuous of me. I was waiting for a better time to ask your permission."

Touched, Rhiannon placed a hand over her heart. "Oh, sweet boy. Of course, we would welcome your family!"

"Really?" Dermot beamed.

Cinna nodded. "That goes for the rest of the Finns as well." She glanced at Rhiannon, who nodded. "We'd planned on inviting everyone to stay once the fighting is done."

"That would solve all our problems," Conall said. "The coven would have protection, and we'd have a home."

"We *have* a home!" Seth shouted. "*White Oak Grove!*"

At his outburst, Rhiannon nudged Cinna and indicated they should leave. Ruth and Maeve went also, followed a split second later by Siorus. The only people left at the table were the members of my pentacle: Duncan, Seth, Conall, Dermot, and myself. As the emotions continued to run high, I wondered if I would even have a pentacle in the morning.

"White Oak Grove isn't my home anymore," said Conall. "I didn't have to leave, but I wouldn't go back even if those people begged me to."

"Which they won't," inserted Dermot.

"'Those people'? They are *our* people!"

"Maybe they're *your* people," said Conall. "They ceased to be mine the day they took my magic away."

"What about your family?"

Conall's expression hardened. "I have no family. The only

314

people who are important to me are the ones who are right here. The ones who have fought by my side. The ones who have watched my back. The ones who don't give a flying fuck about whether I have magic or not." He looked right at me as he said it. "*These* are my people, and *this* is my family."

"Honestly, Seth," Dermot said with a puzzled frown, "I kinda expected you to feel the same."

"The only thing I feel is *loyalty*. Loyalty to the master and to the grove."

"Typical," Conall said.

"You owe him a debt," Seth said. "You have no magic and no reason to flee the grove. He didn't have to take in a—" He stopped speaking abruptly, receiving glares from the other Finns who happened to be in the tavern.

"A null?" Conall finished. "Go ahead, say it. I don't care anymore. So he gave me a place to live. Does that mean I'm indebted to him for the rest of my life?"

Seth dropped heavily into the chair beside me and began rubbing his temples. "No," he replied.

"How long does he expect us to stay with him?" Conall asked. "We have no chance of having a real life there. No chance of having families or homes of our own."

"That all would change once we return to the grove."

Conall snorted. "Does he really think we owe him so much that we should risk our lives making him ArchDruid again?"

"That's not what he wants," Seth said. "He wants to unify us so that we can be one grove and one druid people again."

"We're not the Lost Boys, Seth," said Conall. "We're all grown up, and we're handling the pirates just fine on our own. We don't need Peter Pan anymore."

"They don't want us, Seth," Dermot said. "They threw us away! Why would you want to go back?" There was no animosity in his tone; the water elementalist looked genuinely perplexed.

"Because *he* wasn't thrown away," said Conall. "He was sent."

"So?" Dermot asked. "My mom sent me, too."

"Yes, but *his* mother sent him to live with his *father*."

"Oh yeah," said the water elementalist. "I forgot."

"It's easy to forget," said Conall. "There's not much family resemblance."

"I'm sorry, what are we talking about?" I was utterly lost.

"Master Shitozaki is Seth's dad," Dermot said.

I couldn't help my reaction, which was to slowly turn my head and look at Seth with wide eyes and raised eyebrows. "Shitozaki is your father?"

He wouldn't meet my gaze. "Yes."

"Connor Shitozaki, screaming, swearing, pipe-smoking, former ArchDruid of White Oak Grove, is *your* father."

"Yes!"

"Just out of curiosity, at what point were you planning on informing me of this?" I asked.

"I didn't intentionally mislead you. It just never came up."

Conall and Dermot exchanged an incredulous look.

"You mean you didn't know?" Conall asked.

"No!" A few things started to make sense, though, like Seth's continual worry over how Shitozaki would react when we finally saw him again. His unquestioning compliance with my orders also made sense; if Shitozaki had demanded instant obedience from all of us, how much more so would he expect it from his own son?

"*Fuuuck*," said Dermot. "Some people thought he put you in charge just because you were Seth's friend."

In that case, it was surprising that they had followed me at all. Thinking back to all the times we'd been in imminent danger, every one of them would have been justified in mutiny, or at least tucking tail and running away.

"Well, being tight with Duncan Everlight didn't hurt your case any, either," said Conall.

"And here I was thinking it was all my exciting Travel stories," I said dryly.

"The scars, too," Duncan murmured. He'd barely spoken since yesterday but remained an ever-present, silent shadow. It had been uncomfortable for me since our talk in the dark womb of earth; I couldn't imagine it to be much better for him. I wondered how long things would be awkward between us.

"I'm sorry I wasn't more forthcoming," Seth said. "Sometimes it seemed like you already knew, so I assumed someone had mentioned it."

"Would you guys mind if…?" I turned to Seth. "Could we talk

privately? Outside?"

He heaved himself upright with a weighty sigh. "Great. Another ass-chewing."

"Davis chewed your ass about something?" Dermot's face was alight with glee. Conall elbowed him, shaking his head.

"Mind your own business," I told him, leading the way out.

Seth closed the door behind us. "Just get it over with," he said.

"I didn't bring you out here to yell at you," I said. "I want to apologize."

"Apologize? For what?"

"For brushing aside your concerns about not returning in time. Having your father pissed at you for something like that is a lot different than having your master angry. Fathers worry a lot more about the safety of their sons."

"I couldn't justify myself to you using that reasoning," Seth said. "My opinion shouldn't carry more weight because of who my father is."

"Maybe not, but I would have taken a son's concern for his father's feelings into consideration."

"I know you would. That's why I didn't bring it up, even though I thought you might not know," Seth said. "Alternatively, if you *did* know he was my father, I trusted that you'd already considered it before choosing a particular course of action."

"Fair enough," I said. "It also occurs to me that Shitozaki doesn't exactly encourage people to speak up or have opinions about his plans."

"No, he doesn't."

"So, perhaps I've been expecting something from you that you haven't been able to give."

"What do you mean?"

"How long have you lived with him? Six or seven years?"

Seth nodded.

"Well, if you've spent a third of your life getting hammered for asking questions and thinking independently, I can see where that would not predispose you to questioning orders."

"I think independently," he said, sounding a touch defensive.

"I've never doubted that for a second," I said. "But after being raised by *that* man? Quakes, Seth, I'm surprised you don't wait for somebody to tell you it's okay to change your socks!"

His affronted expression melted into sheepish grin. "I can see how you might think that," he admitted.

"So. Seth Shitozaki. It has a nice ring to it."

"It does, but that's not my name."

"It isn't?"

"No. I was given my mother's surname – Starseeker."

I stopped in my tracks. "Starseeker? What is your mother's name?"

"Nioba. Why?"

"I've met her."

"Have you? Was she well?"

"Right as rain," I said.

"How did you meet?"

"Interestingly enough, the same way I met Dermot's mother. And on the same day. Your mother was teaching Angie how to use elemental air, and his mother was teaching her to use water, both for non-combat purposes."

"Remarkable that the three of us are now friends," he said.

"What are the odds of that, I wonder?"

"Pretty good, if the Fates had anything to do with it," Seth replied.

* * *

What I had begun to think of as my command staff reconvened in an upstairs room of the tavern to finish the discussion of what our next move should be.

"So, the garrison at Faulkner is our next target," said Seth.

"After we take the rescued folks back to Cypress Creek," Conall said.

"Sounds like a plan," I said. "All right, good work everybody. Let's get some shuteye."

Chairs scraped the floor and maps rustled as people got up to leave.

"Davis, why do you keep rubbing your hand like that?" Rhiannon asked. Siorus, Madoc, Maeve, and Ahearn continued out the door and down the stairs, while the members of my pentacle paused at the door.

"Hm?" I put my hands back in my lap, having been unconsciously rubbing my cold left hand. It was mighty irksome, but I noticed it the most when I was sitting still.

"It's cold," I said. "It's been cold since... well, yesterday."

"You mean since you were restored to life by the Goddess."

The Goddess of the witches encompassed all goddesses, including the earth mothers of many different cultures.

"Yeah, that." I glanced at Duncan, but his placid gaze stayed firmly upon the High Priestess. He must have told her.

"While I'd like to tell you that you're lucky to have only that as a consequence of dying, it doesn't sit right with me the Goddess would heal you completely except for that one thing." She held out her hand. "May I see it?"

"Sure." I removed the leather wrap and held my hand out to her. She ran gentle fingers over each finger, the palms, and the backs of both my hands.

"It feels no different than the right."

"It does to me," I grumbled.

Rhiannon frowned. "Is it cold all over or just in one certain spot?"

"Well..." I closed my eyes and ran my right thumb over my palm, tracing a cold spot that seemed to run in a straight line across it. Opening my eyes, I saw that my thumb had been tracing the faint silver scar there – where Angie had sliced open my palm to bind us together.

The oath mark.

Until now, it had always been warmer than the surrounding skin and tingled with magic when I touched it. I sat back in the chair, thinking hard.

"Can you tell if a spell has been broken?" I asked, feeling my stomach start to churn.

"Sometimes," the High Priestess replied. "Often a broken spell will leave a residual trace of magic."

I held my hand out to her again. "Would you please check?"

Rhiannon raised an eyebrow. "It would help to know what sort of magical working I am looking for."

"It's uh... it's an oath. Between Angie and me."

"Angie cast this spell?"

"Yes."

"And what components or materials did she use?"

"Blood, spirit, and earth."

Behind her, Seth and Duncan exchanged a concerned look.

"Tell me the ritual she used."

"She cut my hand with a knife, and when the blood welled up, she sprinkled earth over it and infused it with spirit."

"She used the same ritual on herself? She cut her own palm and mingled earth with her blood and her spirit magic?" Rhiannon asked. "She swore an oath as well?"

"Yes."

"And what did she swear?"

"Honesty. And loyalty."

"And what did you swear?"

"It's... personal."

"Lord and Lady help me, Davis, you are trying my patience! If you want my help, you *will* tell me."

I sighed, knowing none of them were going to like what I had to say. Reciting the words like it was yesterday, I said, "I make my most solemn vow to stay by your side always and to love you to the exclusion of all others. I promise to protect you always, even if it means my death. So I do swear, and may the sky fall on my head, the sea rise up to drown me, and the earth swallow me whole if I break this vow."

Duncan's jaw dropped, and the disbelief in Seth's face could not quite hide the horror in his eyes. Dermot and Conall exchanged a wordless look that clearly said that I was quite mad.

Now that I knew about druid relationships, I understood their reactions. I wasn't stupid *or* oblivious. I had reflected a few times on what the oath would mean for my future if Angie and I were never reunited. I had simply decided to wait and see what happened, the same way I would have if we had not had a binding oath.

"Let me get this straight," Rhiannon said slowly. "You two entered a binding oath mingling your blood and elemental magics, on a night when the veil between worlds is thin and the intensity of the spellcasting would be exponentially magnified?"

"I didn't know anything about magic then! And I certainly didn't know I was an earth elementalist!"

"As we've discussed before, I'm quite sure Angie suspected."

"That is not the *worst* of it," said Duncan, standing abruptly.

"It's not?" Rhiannon raised an eyebrow at him.

"No! Not only did they do as you said, but Davis used the most powerful oath a Celtic druid can make!" The earth druid threw his hands in the air.

"Regardless, Angie should *never* have let you swear that," the High Priestess said.

"She didn't know what I was going to say."

"Why would you do this?"

I hesitated. "Because she was keeping secrets from me." It hadn't seemed like a selfish request at the time, but now I could see that it just might have been.

Rhiannon sat back in her chair, a knowing look in her eyes.

"Does this have anything to do with our conversation just before the Solstice?"

"Yes."

"About the way druids live, and what the grove is truly like?"

"Yes."

She took my hand again and was silent for a few moments.

"It's water under the bridge now," she said, releasing it.

"What do you mean?"

"Your oath is broken and no longer binding."

As I suspected. "Why did it break?"

"Davis, you *died*. All magic requires power of some sort to keep it alive. After the initial casting, magical workings such as this are generally maintained by one's life force. When it's gone, they unravel, and the spell breaks."

My heart sank. Nothing else linked me to Angie other than our bond as chosen, and we were too far apart to make any kind of meaningful connection through it. True, the oath mark had only been made evident by the small warmth it radiated beneath its leather wrap, but its presence had comforted me. Now there was nothing left to feel and nothing left to see. It was gone, just like Angie herself.

"You do realize that Angie will know the oath has been broken?" Rhiannon said.

I hung my head, overcome with certainty that Angie would think I had betrayed her trust. Not only would she know that she'd been lied to about my death, but she would also believe that I was unfaithful to her.

"Davis..." Seth said slowly, "if you are both bound by the

oath, and your chosen feels it break…"

"She'll hate me forever," I groaned, slumping in my chair. "I should have gone back for her sooner!"

"You don't get it, do you?" Rhiannon said, a note of ire creeping into her voice.

"She'll think I'm an unfaithful oath-breaker," I snapped. "I get it!"

"No, Davis!" she snapped. "She'll think you're *dead*!"

"She *already* thinks I'm dead!" I shouted.

"Actually," said Seth slowly, "now she'll know you weren't dead before and will believe you truly are now."

Dermot piped up. "Maybe she'll think you just got laid."

Quakes.

* * *

I slept little and dawn was a welcome sight. Morning broke grey and dreary, mirroring my mood. Picking up my tomahawks, I buckled their skinny belt about my hips and fastened the ties around each thigh. The heavier sword belt went over that, slung low on my left hip. I went down to the kitchen, warmed up the tavern's common room, and started a fire to make coffee. A quick perusal of the larder revealed plenty to feed us breakfast with enough left over to pack in our own saddlebags and those of the newest bunch of horses we'd acquired along with this outpost.

The same thoughts that had kept me up all night were still going round and round in my mind. What was Angie thinking right now? It would be so easy for grief to turn to anger, and then to hate because she had been misled. No, because she'd been lied to.

Because I *had* lied to her. As my father had said to be often enough as a child, a lie of omission was still a lie. So was deception, for that matter.

I was cooking bacon when the rest of my pentacle came downstairs. Seth and Conall exchanged an unreadable look, while Dermot poured himself some coffee and plopped down at the bar. Duncan came into the kitchen, surveyed the items I had laid out, and picked up a stick of butter. Cutting off a few chunks, he tossed them into the pan to melt, then began breaking eggs into it.

"Come on, Dermot," Conall said. "Let's go feed the horses."

"I'd rather feed myself."

"Horses first. You know how irritable Kelpie gets when you don't feed him on time."

"Yeah, yeah." Dermot took his mug and followed Conall out.

Seth took his place at the bar.

"Are you all right?" he asked.

"Well, I'm not dead, so I suppose that's something," I replied sarcastically. "On the other hand, Angie thinks I'm dead and a liar, so that spoils it a little bit."

Duncan regarded me somberly. "I know that you aren't happy about this," he said, "but it is for the best."

I made no reply. People always said that things were 'for the best' whenever you wanted something that they thought wasn't good for you.

"You don't need it," he added.

"As long as it was warm, I knew she was well. Now I have nothing," I said bitterly. "I can only imagine what she's feeling right now."

"We will be reunited again," he said. "You with your chosen, and I with my family."

It was little comfort. Gods only knew what Angie was thinking of me now, but I was sure it wasn't good. Not only would I have to explain to her why I allowed her to believe I was dead for so long, but now she would be brooding about why I hadn't come back, feeling betrayed, and grieving all over again.

"Of course, it will take longer than we originally planned," the earth druid added.

Chapter 18 – Bulletproof

Friends show their love in times of trouble, not in happiness.
~ Euripides ~

There were eight women who'd been enslaved to provide whatever services the itinerant forces from the 'Ville demanded when they visited Watson. Four of them were from Cypress Creek, and two were from a small town called Beryl, which they said had been destroyed when the Faulkner garrison was built. The other two were witches.

The broken oath had me feeling vindictive; if it weren't for the Republic of Jackson's mission of conquest, I would have been reunited with Angie by now. After we ransacked the Watson outpost, Wolfric and I burned it to the ground. The air elementalists condensed the twisting clouds of oily black smoke into a mass that barely floated above the ground. The earth druids dug a deep hole where the outpost had stood, and we left the smut buried there. Afterward, I asked the water elementalists cover the area in green grass and put a cluster of flowers in the middle, one for every enemy we had killed.

Let our enemies wonder why they hadn't seen the smoke.

Let them wonder when it had happened.

Let them wonder whether their people were dead or alive.

It was deeply disturbing that there was a tendency for the witches to have been used as sex slaves, while the rest were used for cooking and laundry and the like. That wasn't to say that the other women escaped rape and abuse, but the witches were the most cruelly used.

"It's because they resisted," said Rhiannon. "They fought and kept on fighting until they could fight no longer."

"They were made an example of." Like Maeve had been.

"Precisely."

I was already in a bad mood. The thought of people enslaved was more than enough to spark my anger, but such heinous acts made me rage inside and struggle to control the elemental fire burning within me. I'd never been keen on killing people before, viewing it as a necessary evil, and the change within me was disturbing. I couldn't very well fault the people of Cypress Creek for being afraid of me; lately, my own wrath was frightening. I wondered if the vengeful thoughts running through my mind had anything to do with the Morrigan, or perhaps the enchanted sword.

"I need you to do something for me," I said.

"Anything," Rhiannon replied, her brow furrowing slightly with concern. "What is it?"

"Ruth told me that I needed to quit holding back. To just release the magic, kill the bad guys, and not worry about what other people think."

She nodded. "She has much wisdom."

"Yeah, but she doesn't know how much devastation I can unleash." In fact, the reduction in power I'd experienced after creating a spirit animal was barely noticeable now. Maintaining the fiery lion seemed to take a negligible amount of magic, as though my inner Well had expanded to make up for the loss.

I swallowed, then cleared my throat. "I don't think anybody does."

"I see."

"I need someone who can pull me back if I go too far."

Rhiannon pursed her lips. "I'm not sure I can be that person for you," she said. "There is too great a desire for vengeance in my heart."

"We might have a problem, then. Fire druids sometimes get… lost in the flames. Mesmerized. It's happened to me before, and Seth told me I needed to be vigilant about not losing control. The last time it happened was after I found Maeve and the others, and the bandits were catching up to the trail wagon we stole."

"I see."

"I just don't want to become some kind of monster."

Her icy expression melted and was replaced by one of compassion, gently replying, "Vengeance aside, I still might not be the best choice."

"Yeah, well, the best choice isn't here and might never be," I said, unable to keep the bitterness out of my tone. I knew without the shadow of a doubt that Angie would be able to get through to me and bring me back to myself, no matter what. *If* she didn't hate me for allowing her to think I was dead and then having to grieve all over again after the oath broke, that is.

"She will understand, Davis," Rhiannon said.

I wasn't so sure about that.

I didn't say much on the ride that day, mostly staying ahead of everyone else. The rest of my pentacle lagged a little bit behind at what must have seemed a safe distance, giving each other concerned looks that I wasn't supposed to see. My depression revealed itself in barked orders, sharp retorts, and sullen silences. I knew that I was difficult to live with, but couldn't seem to shake the ill temper.

Even with the assurance of knowing the High Priestess would try to bring me back from the abyssal depths of my fire magic, I still worried about the depths to which I might sink. I thought it over, unsure of what more I could do to put my mind at ease other than confide in Duncan. The problem was that he'd barely spoken to me since I'd been shot. I didn't want to approach him, but desperation drove me to it. It was likely that he would refuse, but I had to ask.

"Can I talk to you?" I asked, hating how hesitant I sounded.

"Of course," he said, continuing to brush Scarlet's chestnut coat.

"I'm sorry to impose, but I don't know who else I can turn to."

"What is it?"

"Once we've finished our rescue mission and go on the offensive, I'm afraid that I'll get mesmerized and... lose control," I said, the words coming out in a rush. "I need somebody who can hold me back. Someone who can stop me." Earth was a natural firebreak; surely he could see that?

"I cannot do that for you," Duncan said.

My heart sank. It was clear that the events in the Watson outpost had severely damaged my friendship with him, perhaps beyond repair. It was just my luck to have lost my *anam cara* when I needed him the most.

"All right. I understand."

I started to turn away, but Duncan placed his hand on my arm, halting me. "I'm sorry," he said.

"It's been a rough trip. I'm sure you have your reasons."

"You misunderstand, Davis. I didn't mean that I wouldn't," he said. "I truly don't think I *can* counter your magic." He frowned slightly. "At least, not your elemental fire."

I looked down, digging in the dirty snow with the toe of my boot. Of course he had noticed. Everyone else probably had, too. I was a fool to think otherwise and could not imagine why this group of druids and witches continued to follow me.

"Everyone says that you are the most powerful earth druid ever born," I said at last. "There's no way I could be stronger than you are."

While Duncan and I were alike in that we'd both received full druid magic all at once rather than in stages occurring every seven years like everyone else did. He had been blessed with his magic in its entirety as a small child. Having turned nineteen back in the spring, he'd had over a decade to perfect his skill, while I'd had five months.

"People do say that, but there are others whose ability is equal or greater to mine. My father likes to tell stories about an old friend who he thought was the best earth druid since Jayne Pierce herself," he said with a small smile. "Honestly, though, we all share the same source and hold the same potential. The difference is how much effort we put into learning to wield our elemental magics."

I nodded, absorbing this. "Thanks for considering it, anyway."

"Davis, wait." He grabbed my arm again. "I *am* sorry."

"There's no need to apologize," I replied. "If you can't, you can't."

"It's not about that," he said. "I ask your forgiveness for the harsh things I said to you. It is not your fault that I could not—" He broke off, looking away.

"Oh." I had foolishly assumed that the romantic feelings he'd had for me had fallen by the wayside long ago. I had believed that our relationship for the past half year had been one of brotherhood and friendship. It was stupid, considering that I myself knew how hard it was to give up on loving someone, even when that someone who didn't love you back. Continuing our close relationship must have made it impossible for Duncan to let go.

"Oh," I said again, completely at a loss for words.

"This is *not* your fault," he said, squeezing my arm hard. "I and I alone am responsible for my feelings."

"I could have been a little less obtuse about it."

Duncan snorted. "While being chased by bandits and discovering what the ArchDruid's treaty has allowed to occur? After having your death foretold by the Oracle of Apollo? After rescuing the coven, taking back Ward, and embarking on this rescue mission? After meeting *the Morrigan*?" He shook his head. "Be reasonable."

Okay, so I'd been a little busy.

"It has been… difficult… to accept," he continued. "I love and admire you, but I can no longer deny that I am not well suited to sharing anything more than friendship with you. You behave recklessly, inviting danger and bringing doom upon your head."

Is that what everyone thinks? I wondered.

"That is what I came to understand after Watson," he continued. "But it took some time to sort it all out. I had just come to that conclusion when you found me, and I blurted the first thing that popped into my head. I regret that it was cruel."

"It was honest."

"Honest or not, I should never have said something so hurtful."

"Well, you did go off and bury yourself," I said. "That's what I get for cornering a bear in his den."

Duncan chuckled.

"If you two are finished kissing and making up, Seth wants to talk tactics again," Conall said.

Duncan turned slowly around, brow furrowed in a scowl that could have peeled paint off a barn. While I was forgiven, the wounds were still fresh. He threw Scarlet's grooming brush to the ground and headed for the center of camp, shouldering Conall aside as he did so. We watched him stalk through camp until he was well out of earshot.

"He's been a bit touchy lately," the Norseman murmured. "Maybe he wasn't as over you as we all thought."

"Recent events seem to have changed that," I said, picking up the brush.

* * *

My command staff made the decision to down two of Faulkner's walls at once and attack from those directions. The plan was based on the assumption that the garrison there was identical to the one at Cypress Creek. There would be no more attempts at gaining entrance from subterfuge.

"I think it's best if I'm at the vanguard," I said.

"The only problem with you at the van is that you don't have a shield," said Seth. Behind him, Siorus and Madoc nodded. The earth druid leaders of the other pentacles were also at the meeting, along with Rhiannon and Ahearn. Wolfric had invited himself, but no one objected to his presence, so I let him stay.

"I can shield with earth."

"It's difficult to raise earthen walls while advancing," Siorus said. "Very difficult."

"Difficult, but doable."

"It may require all of your concentration, though," Rhiannon said. "Will you be able to raise progressive shield walls and still attack effectively while constantly moving?"

Their skeptical looks mirrored my own feelings.

"Why don't you use a fire shield?" asked Dermot.

"Fire can't be used defensively," Wolfric said. He'd said little since announcing that we were no longer friends, but it seemed that he was determined to do something to pay back the debt he thought he owed me. Since he was helping, I decided to ignore his overly formal and standoffish behavior.

"Yeah, and everybody said water couldn't be used for offensive purposes, but they were all wrong about that, weren't they?" the water elementalist retorted.

"Davis has found a few defensive uses for elemental fire," Duncan said. "The time he surrounded Ward with a firewall was quite effective."

"It was," admitted Seth. "But we tested out fire shields like

Dermot is suggesting that a long time ago. It doesn't work."

"It didn't work against spirit magic, but that doesn't mean it won't work against bullets," Dermot said.

"Bullets can pass through flames intact," said Conall.

"Not if it's hot enough to melt them," the water elementalist insisted.

"Then Davis gets sprayed with extremely hot, melted brass and steel," Seth said drily.

"So? It won't burn him," said Dermot. "Besides, he can work metal."

Seth said, "It'll still hurt." He turned to Duncan, wearing a puzzled expression. "You can work metal, can't you?"

"No. Very few earth elementalists can. The ability to manipulate metal with magic is usually the domain of earth-fire druids."

The air elementalist frowned. "Then how did you get the bullets out when Davis got shot in Watson?"

"I didn't. He did it himself. I merely tried to keep him alive while he did so."

"Merely," muttered Conall.

"You know what he means," I said. We were usually careful not to talk about magic as though it were effortless or as easy as breathing. However, this wasn't the time for mollycoddling his delicate sensibilities regarding how people talked about their elemental ability.

Seth interrupted before the Norseman could interject another unnecessary and off-topic comment. "Do you mean to tell me that while you were lying on the ground in a pool of blood, you were using magic *to expel bullets from your own chest*?!"

"You don't have to make it sound so dramatic," Dermot said.

"It *was* dramatic," Wolfric said.

I slapped my thighs and rose. "Fire shield. Great idea. Let's try it." Anything to get out of this conversation.

We moved to the edge of our campsite so that any rounds fired would be projected away from it. I tried to raise a shield, envisioning something similar to what I thought an air elementalist might do. It didn't work. Any time I released the stream of fire from my fingers to the shield, it dissipated.

Dermot stepped forward. "Here, let me try."

"You're going to try to make a fire shield?" Wolfric said.

"Of course not. I want to see if I can do it with water."

Wolfric rolled his eyes. "Fire is *nothing* like water," he said.

Ignoring him, the water elementalist uncorked one of the two half-gallon-sized water bags hanging from his belt and brought forth a stream of water. It sinuously waved in the air, then slid outward in the shape of a rod. A spiral formed at the end of the rod, drawing in on itself, becoming tighter and tighter until it morphed into a solid circle. Dermot rapped on it with his knuckles, nodded once in satisfaction, and walked backward several yards, extending the rod as he did so. When he was out of he gave Conall a thumbs-up.

"Okay, Conall. Shoot it."

Scattershot pinged loudly against the shield, and a sound like splintering glass filled the air as cracks spiderwebbed across the water shield's surface. Dermot narrowed his eyes in concentration. The cracks began to vanish, leaving the shield smooth once again. Wolfric crossed his arms over his chest, looking impressed.

"It might be better if it was concave," Seth observed. "That way it could deflect bullets randomly back at the bandits."

"If you can make it concave, you can make a dome," said Madoc. Beside him, Siorus nodded.

"I'd be like a turtle in a shell!" Dermot exclaimed, dropping to all fours under his water shield, rearranging it so that it lay on his back. After a moment the shield began to droop, draping around his body. While he happily meandered around acting like a turtle, I tried his trick with the spiral, but the flames, constantly in motion by their very nature, didn't meld together well. It occurred to me that if I could make them spin like my mother's firecracker pinwheels on the Fourth of July, they might be a little more cohesive.

To my surprise, it worked. The elemental fire responded to my thoughts, flames of clear cherry and deep orange swirling against the surface of my palm.

"Put more fire into it," said Madoc. "And make it hotter."

I did as he suggested until I had a spinning disc of fire that was bright yellow in the center, transitioning into a clear orange and then bright red at the edges. It required that I keep pouring magic into it, but since I had an immense and limitless Well from which to draw, it took little effort beyond mental concentration and focusing my will.

"That looks great!" Dermot called. "Try shooting it, Conall!"

"Hold up," Seth said. "That won't prove anything. I'll put up an air shield so we can stand behind it and see what happens to the bullets."

I backed up to escape the ample range of Conall's shotgun, channeling a stream of elemental fire to maintain my connection with the pinwheeling flames while the others scrambled like excited puppies behind Seth's shield. You'd think they'd never been shot at while behind an air shield before.

"Ready when you are," I told Conall, then concentrated on maintaining the spinning, blazing disc and holding the temperature steady. The Norseman fired, brass sailing out the side of his shotgun, and the pellets sped through the fire. Metal rang against Seth's air shield, sticking to it in viscous globs. The guys behind it whooped and cheered.

"Do it again!" Dermot cried.

"More heat!" shouted Madoc.

Their cheerful enthusiasm was contagious. I grinned and cranked up the heat until the shield flared outward, its center flashing yellow-white as it broadened in diameter. The red flame-tips at the edges of the whirling turned a vibrant orange. Conall fired again, and this time the brass splattered against Seth's air shield and ran down it like raindrops, while the buckshot made fat splats and slid down more slowly.

"Again!" cried Dermot, followed by Madoc: "Hotter!"

Trying it again with a yellow vortex that was white-hot in the center, I had even better results.

"Look at this!" Seth exclaimed. "Some of the splatters are actually steaming! You've managed to completely melt them in the split-second they passed through the fire!"

Beside him, Wolfric leaned away and murmured something into Duncan's ear; the earth druid's response was an indifferent shrug that was meant to be interpreted as *I don't know*, but that probably meant *I don't care*. When they returned to watching, the fire elementalist's gaze was narrow with suspicion, while Duncan appeared unperturbed as usual.

"Do you think you can make it hotter still?" Seth asked.

"I can try," I said. "But I want to do it without your shield."

In for a penny, in for a pound, as my father used to say.

"That is a terrible idea," Duncan said.

"Probably, but I need to know if this will work before we're in the thick of battle again."

He sighed and turned to Siorus. "Get ready to keep Davis out Annwyfn," he grumbled. The other earth druid grinned at Duncan's reference to the Welsh Otherworld.

Seth kept his shield up but turned it so they could all shift position while I moved to where they'd been standing, facing the camp with my back to the wide world where the bullets wouldn't hit anything important. I took a deep breath and blew it out.

"Ready when you are, Conall."

He pulled the trigger, and the Benelli roared.

The whirling disc of fire flared a dazzling white, and I flinched. It was two or three seconds before I opened my eyes and realized that if anything was going to hit me, it already would have.

"Anything?" Seth asked, looking anxious. "Were you hit?"

I shook my head. "No." Standing thirty feet from the muzzle of Conall's gun, I should have been struck by *all* the scattershot.

Dermot strutted out from behind Seth's shield with his hands on his hips. "*I* am a genius." He turned back around to Wolfric, holding out one hand. "I told you none of them would hit. Pay up, fireballer!"

"Damned water elementalist," grumbled Wolfric, tossing him a shiny silver flask.

* * *

The garrison at Faulkner was huge compared to the one at Cypress Creek, encompassing two or three times the area. Its palisade wall was easily thirty feet high, broken into segments that were separated by square guard towers at intervals that I estimated to be a hundred yards apart. Even if the bad guys inside were only mediocre shots – which I doubted – they still had a good chance of hitting anything trying to scale their neighbor's tower.

We had planned to sneak up to the garrison walls and bring them down as we had at Cypress Creek. However, as we approached in the frosty predawn gloom, we discovered that the trees had been cleared in a three hundred yard radius around our target. In addition, the wall was lit by torches every few yards, casting illumination on the armed defenders patrolling at its top. Their elevated position was more than adequate to see by, during the daytime at least, which meant it was also just fine for shooting. The distance they'd allowed for the clearance also told me they had rifles with which to defend, so I had to assume those within could hit a target at three hundred yards.

"That's not a garrison," exclaimed Dermot. "That's a fucking castle!"

"This isn't good," Conall said, passing the spyglass to Seth.

"I think maybe they heard we were coming," the air elementalist said.

"I think maybe I'm gonna shit my pants," said Dermot.

"All right, everybody settle down," I said. "Remember what they say, the bigger they are, the harder they fall."

"Hey, fireballer, think you can throw a fireball and set that tower on fire from here?" Dermot said, pointing to the nearest one.

"I'm going to find out if I can throw *you* that far, if you don't quit calling me that," Wolfric said. There was no anger in his tone, and I wondered if his supposed debt to me was making him tolerate the constant teasing.

It was pretty cold, but I didn't know what to do yet, so I sat and thought about it while the sky lightened and fingers of sunlight crept across the land. As soon as the sunlight hit the garrison's eastern wall, the large gates in the southern wall opened just enough to allow a lone rider carrying a white flag to exit, then closed behind him once more. He rode out a couple hundred yards from the gates, well within rifle range of the two southern towers, and stopped. The white flag fluttered in the morning breeze.

"That is one ballsy bastard," Conall said, a note of admiration in his voice.

Duncan looked at me. "Tell me you're not going out there."

"I'm going out there."

I whistled for Steel. The sooner we got the witchlings back, the sooner we could move on to the next garrison. We didn't have time for a siege, and negotiating to get them back might save us some time.

The High Priestess rode up on her white mare. "Are you going

334

to speak with him?"

"Yep."

"I'm coming with you."

"I don't know if I can shield us both."

She regarded me with a cool expression, saying nothing.

"All righty, then," I said, and swung into Steel's saddle. We rode out in a triangle, Rhiannon and I riding side by side, and Duncan following behind.

"Too chickenshit to come alone, son?" the man with the flag said to me by way of greeting. "Or don't you know what a white flag means?"

"Neither," I said. "The lady and I share leadership."

"What about him?" he jerked his chin at Duncan.

Shitozaki's words, spoken to me what seemed like ages ago, sprang to mind: "The earth druid goes where he wishes."

"So you *are* druids."

"Not I," said Rhiannon. "I am a witch and the High Priestess of Ward Coven, which you people stole from us in September!" Her voice shook with anger.

"You got it back, though, didn't you?" His tone was challenging.

"The land and the buildings, yes. My people, *no*. You *murdered* my High Priest. You *stole* our *children*!" Rhiannon's grey eyes glittered with icy anger. "I want my people back, and I want them *now*."

"That's the thing, see. They ain't here. That's why I came out to have a chat with you fine folk."

The color drained from Rhiannon's face. "What!"

"President Jackson decreed that the children from all the surrounding villages be taken to the city for safekeeping. They'll be raised proper there, as citizens of the Republic of Jackson. Once they're grown, they'll be sent home as representatives in their home towns."

"I will *die* before I ever allow that to happen!" she snarled. An athame appeared in her hand. She wasn't close enough to kill him with the blade, but she could use it as a focus for an offensive spell.

"You might," he said. His fingers played over the butt of the pistol on his left hip.

A gunslinger. I should have known.

"Don't bother," I said. "You'll be dead before you can draw."

He snorted. "Son, you don't even have a gun."

I held up one hand, allowing a single tongue of flame to spring from the palm before moving to dance from finger to finger. His eyes followed the flame until I clenched my fist, extinguishing it.

"*Son*," I said, mocking him, "I don't need one."

"Well." He shifted in his saddle. "I didn't come out here to pick a fight, anyhow. I came to tell you there's no sense in attacking us since we ain't got what you want."

"We'll be the judge of that," I said, then looked at Rhiannon. Her face was twisted with rage. "We'll discuss it, and I'll be back to let you know."

Once we were out of earshot, we stopped. I said to Rhiannon, "We need to know if he's lying or not."

"He's not. I would be able to tell if he was."

"He's a gunslinger," I said. "In my experience, gunslingers are the best deceivers in the world." They had to be, just to survive. I'd never seen even one who acted like he could move quickly. They all spoke thoughtfully, looked around carefully, and moved like molasses ran in their veins instead of blood – until it was time to draw, that is.

"I'd rather not rely on the word of a brigand that there are no innocents inside," I said. "He could be lying just to keep us from attacking." I had every intention of destroying the garrison anyway. Removing as many assets as possible before running an incursion to get the witchlings back was only prudent.

"He didn't say there were no innocents inside," Duncan corrected. "He said they didn't have the witchlings."

"What do you want me to do?" Rhiannon asked.

"Can you travel the astral to find out for sure?"

"Here? In the middle of the wilderness?"

"Angie did it," I said. In an aside to Duncan, I said, "That time, *she* saved my life." He sighed and shook his head.

"*Maeve* saved your life that time," Rhiannon said.

"There wouldn't have been anything left to save if Angie hadn't gone looking for help. She traveled the astral under extreme duress while sitting on the side of the road," I said. "The point is, can you do it?"

"Of course I can do it!" she snapped. "I'll need an hour to prepare." She reined the white mare about and cantered away.

"We have all the time in the world, now," I murmured to her departing back, for I had a feeling the gunslinger was telling the truth.

Awaiting word from Rhiannon felt like two hours instead of one. Pushing through the front lines of the Finns, Cinna came to deliver the news.

"They're not here!" she gasped. "He's telling the truth. They took our children to the 'Ville!"

I had hoped the man's words a lie. I wasn't sure I could destroy this garrison and keep everyone alive, much less invade the 'Ville. Things would be so much easier if Seth would just take the Finns home.

Duncan and I returned to the gunslinger.

"I guess today's your lucky day," I told him.

"How d'ya figure?"

"I won't be burning that fort down around your ears today," I replied.

He snorted. "If you actually think your little war band can take us on, you've got another think coming."

"I *know* this little war band can take you on," I replied. "And if I even think you're going to send a posse out after us, I'll turn it right back around and provide a demonstration. Do we have ourselves an understanding?"

For several seconds, the gunslinger's eyes bored into me like the bullets he'd have loved to drill me with.

"We have an understanding," he finally said.

"Good."

Following Cinna, Duncan and I turned our horses when we heard someone shouting from the direction of the garrison.

"No! Don't leave us!" someone cried. A young man was running along the walkway inside the wall, waving his arms frantically. "Don't leave us! Please!" Heedless of the garrison guards moving toward him with guns drawn, he continued crying out, pleading for our aid. One of the guards slammed him in the gut with the stock of his rifle, and another shoved him over the wall. He landed with a sickening thud. Duncan jerked in startlement, his eyes wide in horror. I thought the man was surely dead, until a few moments later when he started screaming in pain.

Siorus bolted out from the front line as if he intended to rescue the fallen man. Madoc was hot on his heels, however, grabbing his arm and jerking him back. A commotion and a loud argument ensued.

"I'm not letting you get killed over some stranger!" Madoc yelled. "Be sane!" Siorus backed off with obvious reluctance, his eyes still upon the screaming man.

"Hold your positions!" I roared. It seemed to settle them some.

Conall rode out to meet me. "We should go get him!"

Duncan looked at him like he was crazy, but he ignored it.

"Think! He's been inside. He knows the layout!"

"The witchlings aren't even in there," Seth said. "We have no reason to attack." His statement drew looks of horror from several others – even Wolfric.

"How can you say that after what they just did!" Conall said, gesturing to where the helpless man lay.

"We have a responsibility to get our own people out first," Seth said. "And they are not in this garrison."

"Oh, are they not our people because they don't have magic?" Conall snapped. "Does *that* make them 'not our people'?! Does that make *me* 'not our people'?!"

"That's not what I mean, and you know it!" Seth shot back.

"Enough!" I shouted. "All of you shut up so we can go get him before somebody shoots him. Cinna, ride back and tell everybody else to mount up and get ready to move."

Seth wasn't happy about it, but he held an air shield to protect us from enemy gunfire while we ran to the bottom of the palisade wall and rescued the fallen man. It seemed that the people inside were serious about not starting a fight, for not one of them fired. Duncan knocked him out with a finger-tap on the forehead, after which we tossed him over the back of a spare horse and ran like crazy back to our camp in the woods. Yiorgos and Halldor healed the man's shattered left leg with remarkable quickness, and I gave the order to move out.

Siorus' pentacle took the lead while mine stayed in the rear to keep an eye out for enemy pursuit. I leaned on my saddle horn and examined the enormous structure. It would burn just as fast as the barracks in Cypress Creek and the outpost at Watson, but only if I could get within thirty yards of it. Since the Faulkner garrison was three times the size of the one at Cypress Creek, it would be reasonable to assume it had at least three times the number of defenders.

We would be outnumbered at least ten to one.

"We can't just leave!" Conall protested, interrupting my chain of thought. "What about the people still inside?"

"This is no longer our fight," Seth said.

Conall ignored him. "You said we were going to destroy the 'Ville!" He stabbed a finger at the garrison. "And *that* is a big part of it!"

"A *really* big part," muttered Dermot.

"Now is not the time," I said.

"They're likely to send a raid group after us," Wolfric said.

"Probably."

"The 'Ville is everything that we stand against!" The veins in Conall's neck and face were becoming prominent. "And you're just going to walk away?!"

"For now, yes."

"You said—"

"Quakes, Conall, could you just trust me for once?"

He fell into an angry silence, and I continued my ruminations on the probable capabilities of the Faulkner garrison in raising a defense. If they outnumbered us ten to one, theoretically they could man the walls with three hundred rifles. Not even shields of elemental air would be able to withstand that kind of barrage for long. A daylight offensive was completely out of the question. Even the cover of darkness would not provide adequate protection from rifle fire. Our use of spirit and fire would allow them to track us in the darkness, even if the garrison's own torches were extinguished.

We halted approximately a mile east of Faulkner. After giving the order to make camp, I sent Duncan back west with Halldor and Ingvar to watch our back trail, and sent Warwick and Martin to keep watch north and south. Next, I found Yiorgos and told him to wake the man who'd been tossed off the wall and pump him for information on the fort's layout. Within thirty minutes the earth druid had brought me a rough sketch of the garrison's layout, including barracks, armories, and stables. There was also an estimate of how many prisoners there were and their probable locations.

"He said they were locked here at night," said Yiorgos, pointing to an X on the map. Hopefully, knowing where the prisoners were would keep us from killing them by mistake.

"Excellent, thanks."

"Oh, and Davis? He says some of the captives are witches."

With our focus on getting the witchlings back, I'd forgotten about the adults. "Let me know if he tells you anything else."

Yiorgos nodded sharply and returned to his charge.

"All right, let's talk," I said as Seth, Conall, Dermot, Siorus, Madoc, Phelan, and Wolfric gathered around. Rhiannon, Ahearn, and Maeve represented the interests of the witches. Running my hand over the ground, I cleared an area of snow and then grabbed a stick to draw in the dirt. Quickly sketching out the garrison and its known defenses, I pointed to the location of the front gate.

"About what?" Conall said, sounding surly.

Little did he know that I was about to knock that chip on his shoulder right off.

"Taking down that garrison."

"You want to attack the garrison?" Seth asked. "But we have no reason to do so."

Rhiannon agreed. "What we *should* do is ride to the 'Ville and get our children back!"

I cleared another area of dirt, drawing a pentagon to represent the bandit city, along with a circle to represent us. The circle was smack dab in the middle between Faulkner and the 'Ville.

"Anybody see a reason now?" Silence fell. "I don't know about the rest of you, but I'd rather not be caught between that particular hammer and anvil."

"We all knew some risks would be required," the High Priestess said.

"Not stupid ones," said Siorus.

"Some of your people are still inside," I said, looking up at Rhiannon. "Did you know that?"

"Yes," was her thin-lipped reply. "Those within insisted that we rescue the children first."

"We wouldn't even make it halfway to the 'Ville before that entire garrison was turned loose to hunt us down," said Conall.

"We agreed that we should take out the farthest settlements first," Madoc said. "That decision was made before we left Ward."

Ahearn nodded. "I say we stick to the plan." Wolfric and Phelan nodded agreement.

"Very well," I said, turning back to my sketch. "There's only one way in or out, and that's through the front gates."

"Which would be suicide to attempt," Phelan said.

"We could go under the wall," Siorus suggested. "Of course, we'd have to tunnel underground for three hundred yards before going under it."

"We'd only be able to emerge two or three at a time at any one point," said Phelan, clearly uncomfortable with the idea of being underground for so long.

"We'd also be facing an enemy holding the high ground," said Conall.

Seth frowned. "This fort is as least three times the size of the one at Cypress Creek. That means they could have three times the number of raid groups."

"At least," Madoc said.

"Air shields won't stand up to that kind of gunfire," the air elementalist continued. "They'd be shattered in seconds."

I nodded. "Attacking after dark is our best option."

"What if we create a diversion?" Wolfric said. "Make them think we're attacking from a different direction."

"What're you gonna do?" said Dermot. "Set the towers on fire?"

"That's not a bad idea," I said, tapping the X with the stick and thinking hard. It was far from an ideal situation, but we were about to find out just how effective my fire shield really was.

Beneath the dim light of the crescent moon, I approached the front gates alone and on foot, my fire shield glimmering red and orange. Yellow sparks spun off the whirling blades of flame; it was guaranteed to attract notice. Halting a few yards from the front gate and well within range of the two front towers, I drew my sword. Flames licked at the frosted metal as they raced down its length.

The enemy reacted to my advance with mockery and insults, then began taking pot shots at me. I responded by turning up the heat. Bullets from both of the gate towers whizzed by on either side of my shield, but none penetrated it. The gunfire directed towards me intensified, but I had expanded my shield for more thorough protection. The orange-yellow spirals of flame instantly melted the bullets, while the rotational spin flung the hot metal away. Swinging my blazing sword in an outward arc, I sent a fireball flying toward the southeast corner of the fortress.

Now I had their full attention.

A chorus of voices rose in alarm as the tower went up like a torch, followed by thumping footsteps scrambling to escape. Concentrating hard on maintaining the integrity of the fire shield in my left hand, I flung a salvo of fireballs over the palisade. The last and biggest one crashed into the southwest tower, enveloping it in a wash of light and heat. The riflemen there panicked and dove headfirst over the wall, burning and screaming until they reached the ground.

Then they just burned.

To the north, a dozen fireballs rose into the night sky and arced outward like a fountain, igniting the rear guard towers. Wolfric, with Phelan to guard him, had successfully made his way to the fortress wall unseen.

Coated in pitch and shellac to preserve the wood, both the palisade and the platform atop which the guards patrolled ignited with a *whoosh*. The sound of booted feet pounding on the wood reached my ears as they tried to flee, followed by panicked screams and the thud of bodies hitting the ground. The entire top of the fortress wall was a roaring inferno, effectively ending the threat of death from above.

"Now!" I shouted.

Duncan popped out of the ground behind me, crouching low to remain protected by the fire shield. A fast rumble ripped through the earth, and the right-hand gate was jammed fast by a tidal wave of dirt and rocks. The left-hand gate was ripped from its hinges, falling inward. Cries of pain, howls of terror, and the sound of crunching bones were followed by the wooden echo of heavy boots as a small group of bandits mob leapt onto the downed wooden gate. I let them come to me in hopes that the rest would follow and ignore the Finns as they infiltrated the garrison.

Duncan and I set the ground around us to bucking, with only a narrow channel of smooth earth by which our enemies could progress. Emboldened by the fact that there were only two of us, they charged with a roar, a sea of enemies trying to surge through the gap. Four or five men could stand abreast in the gateway, but only two could approach via the channel. As the fire shield in my left hand deflected their gunfire, the sword in my right hand flickered out and drank deeply of their blood.

This was not the plan, however; I needed to get *in* there.

A blast of broiling heat and flame pushed them back through the doorway. Slashing and hacking, I cut my way into the garrison, leaving a trail of scorched and bleeding bodies in my wake. Duncan followed, then charged inside the fortress using rolling waves of dirt both as protective shield and blunt weapon. Every now and then he would vanish, dropping into the earth to avoid harm, only to reappear behind an enemy to skewer them with his longsword. As long as the bandits made a push to escape the flames, I held my position atop the downed gate. Even though I cut down all who approached, too many ran back inside in spite of the threat presented by the inferno.

Through the earth, I felt the rumble of approaching horses as the Finns raced around the fortress wall. Splitting up into three groups, they attacked from the north, east, and west. Uprooting the solid posts and tossing them aside, they rent gaping holes in the palisade and plunged inside, slaughtering the enemy with blades, guns, and magic. From the back of the garrison came the dragon's roar that was Wolfric's elemental fire, setting the northern and eastern walls of the garrison alight. Following his lead, I ignited the western wall. The wood turned to black char, filling the air with thick, oily smoke.

Trapped by fire on three sides and pressed by rampaging druids within, our prey redoubled their efforts to flee through the gate, trampling and sometimes slaying one another in their panic. Many had even ceased to fight, seeking only escape, but I allowed none to pass. The three groups of Finns slowly came together, crushing our enemies in an escapable crush of destruction.

When the fight was over, only one enemy was still standing: the gunslinger who had ridden out with the white flag. I had no idea why they brought him to me instead of killing him outright, but he was my problem now. I sighed and pivoted the sword in my hand until the blade rested on my shoulder.

"So you're going to kill me now?" the gunslinger said angrily.

"Wouldn't you, if the situation was reversed?"

He shook his head. "No. I'd hog-tie your sorry ass and send you back to your ArchDruid and let her deal with your lawless behavior."

"*My* lawless behavior? I'm not the one raping and pillaging my way across the countryside."

Murdering, yes. Raping and pillaging, no.

"I ain't ever raped nobody!" he spat.

"Can you say the same for the rest of your people?"

Glaring at me, he made no reply.

"My father was fond of saying that a man is judged by the company he keeps, so he'd best choose his companions wisely."

The gunslinger rolled his eyes. "Your daddy didn't make that up. George Washington said that." He paused, eyeing me. "Washington also said that few men have virtue to withstand the highest bidder. So what's your price?"

"My price?"

"Your people are already allied with us, but clearly you want something more. You're a clever commander, and I imagine President Jackson would like to have you on our side." The gunslinger paused. "So what do you want? Power? You could have a garrison like this of your very own, with five hundred men to command." He put his hands on his hips and surveyed the Finns. "That would be a damned sight better than this ragtag bunch."

"This ragtag bunch just mopped the floor with your garrison full of soldiers."

He glowered. "That's 'cause two hundred of them ain't here."

"Where are they?" Seth asked. He was thinking the same thing that I was; those extra soldiers could be on our backs at any time.

"They're the ones that escorted all the kids to the 'Ville," said the gunslinger.

"And after that?"

"I guess they received orders to go somewhere else," the gunslinger said. "I'm not in charge here, so I don't know."

Seth gave me a questioning look, and I shrugged in response.

"I doubt another two hundred soldiers would have made a difference," I said. They would have, but the enemy didn't need to know that.

"Fine, then," the gunslinger said. "You tell me what you want, and I'll deliver your message to President Jackson personally."

"Freedom," I said. "For everyone."

The gunslinger rolled his eyes. "You can't ask for that."

I swept the grey blade from its resting place on my shoulder, slicing through the man's neck in a single, fluid motion. Blood sprayed, and his head rolled several feet, another trophy for the Morrigan.

"Don't tell me what I can't do."

Chapter 19 – Trojan Horses

Genius is one per cent inspiration,
ninety-nine percent perspiration.
~ Thomas Alva Edison ~

"I will *not* go home without them!" Rhiannon cried. "I can't!"

"We're not," I said. "We won't."

If my children had been stolen away, I wouldn't rest until I'd gotten them back. And if I couldn't do it myself, I'd want someone to help me. Besides, these weren't null children we were talking about. These were witchlings with magical ability that would either be quashed by their evil captors or worse, fostered and used for evil deeds. To my way of thinking, there simply was no other option but to get them back.

I just wasn't sure how we were going to do it.

At least we'd managed to rescue Cullen and Toby, the last two adult witches who had been missing since the raid on Ward. There had been more, but the rest of the young men – and three of the young women – had been killed outright or tortured to death for their continued resistance. Katarina had rejoiced over her brother's return while weeping over his considerable wounds. It seemed that Cullen had caused quite a bit of trouble for his captors, which had resulted in multiple beatings. They had also blistered his neck and back with hot pokers. Duncan offered to do what he could to help, but so much of the damage had been done weeks ago. Like me, he would wear the scars for the rest of his life.

Assured that his wife Billé was safe back in Ward, Toby was

eager to join the war band in spite of his multiple bruises. "I'm more into making potions for love and fertility," he had said, "But I'm a fair hand at making poisons and explosive philters, too."

I didn't really think we'd need explosives or poison but told him to make a list of what he needed, and we'd see if gathering the components was feasible. Weylin, Tiernan, and Riordan had taken my words to heart, daring the upper levels of the ruined fort to find glass bottles, herbs, solvents, and whatever else they could find.

"Davis," Seth began, speaking slowly, "Please remember that the rescuing the witchlings will require invading a very large walled city whose citizens have proven to be heavily armed and willing to kill without hesitation."

Rhiannon rounded on him with her fists clenched. "Are you suggesting that we leave our children with those rapists and murderers?"

"Not at all," he said, holding up his hands in a placating gesture. "I'm saying that the tactics we used today probably won't work there. I'm saying that we could use some help."

"*From who?*" she shouted.

"These'uns might be willin' to help," Ruth said, indicating the hundred or so people we'd just set free with a nod of her head. "Or we could go back and pick up some folks from Cypress Creek."

The people we'd most recently liberated appeared as though they'd put up quite a bit of resistance to the bandit occupation. Even though they looked like they'd been decently fed, most of them bore signs of abuse that ranged from bruises and lacerations to broken bones. None of them looked up to fighting a winter war.

"I'm not sure more people and guns are the answer," Seth replied. I knew what he meant. He wanted to go back to Sanctuary and get the rest of the Finns.

"Here we go again," grumbled Conall.

"We're outnumbered and outgunned, but I'm not sure that more people are the answer, whether armed with guns *or* magic," I said. "We're talking about a major incursion here, which we are neither trained nor equipped to fight – even if we did have the rest of the Finns."

"How many more of y'all are there?" Ruth asked.

"Shitozaki has thirty-seven with him if I remember correctly."

Seth nodded. "That's right. Seventy-three total."

"Oh," Ruth looked crestfallen. "Davis is right, then. Even all y'all together wouldn't be near enough."

"We have to try!" demanded Rhiannon.

I reached out and took her hands in mine. "These are your children, and you don't want to lose them forever. I understand," I said. "But these are my men, and I don't want to lose them, either. We can't just charge into this without preparation."

Furious, she yanked her hands away and stormed off.

Tossing a small fireball, I lit our campfire, but that minor display of anger did little to relieve my frustration. I threw my blanket on the ground and dropped onto it heavily, staring into the flames and thinking. I hadn't expected the search-and-rescue mission to go off perfectly – far from it – but I hadn't counted on the enemy moving the kids to the 'Ville. It made me wonder if someone had escaped the attack on Watson to warn Faulkner that we were coming. Dropping the captives we'd rescued at Watson back at Cypress Creek had allowed them two whole days to load the witchlings up and drive them to the bandit city.

How were we supposed to get them back when they were in a huge city covering multiple square miles that was protected by walls of concrete and steel? How could we fight an enemy of thousands? How could thirty-five druids, most of whom were still elementalists, ever hope to match their firepower and live to tell the tale?

Answer: We couldn't.

We might be a war band, but there were too few of us to endure a long conflict. The Finns were tough, but still only human. We would have to stop fighting in order to eat and sleep, while the Republic of Jackson could just rotate in fresh troops to relieve the tired ones. Theoretically, with enough personnel, they could carry on the fight twenty-four hours a day. That effectively ruled out a direct confrontation, so I quit thinking about attacking the city and diverted my energy to other possibilities – the kind that only a Traveler would see.

Like breaking and entering.

Like sneaking and stealing.

Like assassination and kidnapping.

Now, I'd never assassinated or kidnapped anyone, and had certainly never taken anything for personal gain, but I'd picked a few locks to retrieve stolen property. I'd crept in through windows to deliver dire warnings to folks at gunpoint in the dead of night, like the time I'd paid a visit to an overly eager young man who kept pursuing his neighbor's daughter in spite of her refusal to court him. That was the sort of reasoning that we needed right now – that of the fox, rather than the lion.

"What are you thinking?" asked Duncan.

"If fighting isn't an option, then maybe subterfuge is."

"What are you going to do?" Conall said mockingly. "Offer to make peace and give 'em a Trojan horse?"

"I don't think they'd fall for that, Conall," Dermot said earnestly. "I mean, everybody knows that story."

"But what if..." Seth began, then shook his head. "Never mind, it's stupid."

"Spit it out," I said. "At this point, stupid might be smart."

"What if wasn't big or a horse?" he said. "What if it was small? Say, the size of slightly scorched trail wagon?"

"Might be a little cramped with all of us in one trail wagon," Conall said drily.

"No, it won't, because we won't be in it," Seth replied.

* * *

"But we can't get to the trail wagon," Ahearn said. "It's inside the *Circitorium Fati* protecting Ward. We didn't want the enemy to return and claim it again."

"Hm." I looked at Seth. "Any ideas?"

"Why don't we go look and see if *they* had any," he suggested, indicating the wrecked garrison. We'd left it in the same condition as when the fight was over – blood splashed across the inner walls and bodies piled up in the gateway. More lay haphazardly scattered about the inner streets, as though a giant had scooped up handfuls of corpses and tossed them amongst the buildings.

"Why don't I wander over and ask our new friends?" said Ruth. "Seems like they oughtta know."

"Good idea," I said. "I'll go with you."

As we walked to the other side of the camp, I took the opportunity to eyeball the Finns who had been injured. Just about everyone had been shot or stabbed, and Warwick had broken his leg falling down some stairs. Solon and Wyatt had gotten burned, but Yiorgos had fixed them up fast.

"Evenin', gents," she said, smiling warmly. "No need to get up. I ain't no lady," she added, as some of the former prisoners struggled to rise. She squatted down beside them, and I did the same. "This here is the leader of them boys that rescued y'all today. We were hopin' you could help us out with somethin'."

"Yes, sir!" said one young man. It was the one who had been tossed over the wall the day before, and who had provided us with a rough map of the garrison interior. "I owe you my life and my freedom. I'll help with anything you need."

"Thank you," I said. "What's your name?"

"James Reece, sir."

"You don't have to call me sir," I said. "My name's Davis."

"It's a pleasure," he replied. "What can I do for you?"

"Do you happen to know if there were any trail wagons in that fort?"

He nodded vigorously. "There sure are! Several, in fact."

"Can you show me where they are?"

"Sure can!" He eased himself up, favoring his left leg. "We can go now if you want."

Ahearn chose a gentle gelding for James Reece to ride so he wouldn't have to walk on his newly healed leg. The horsemaster joined us so he could evaluate the wagons and any harnessing. Riordan, Tiernan, and Weylin volunteered to help. Belatedly realizing that neither Ahearn nor any of the other witches was likely to tolerate the grisly scene well, I hollered for Wolfric to help me clear the bodies. The two of us rode ahead and burned them to ash before the others arrived.

"Your fire is a lot hotter than mine," Wolfric said after we'd cleaned up the bodies near the northern wall.

"It's because I'm a druid," I said, moving inside to cremate the rest. "I can channel more magic because I don't have to worry about running out."

Wolfric followed suit, saying, "I think it's more than that."

I hadn't mentioned my sworn service to the Morrigan in his presence, but it was likely that he had already heard of it. After all, my sword had been indelibly altered by the goddess on Samhain, and there was no hiding its darkened, dull grey color and blood-red etchings.

"What do you think it is?" I asked, heading back for the gap in the eastern palisade.

"I asked Duncan why your sword looks weird and he told me about your visit from a goddess. I think it's possible that she magnified your fire magic."

"That's what he thinks, too," I said.

"You took out a lot of people all by yourself at the gate."

"Bullets can't penetrate the fire shield, and the enchantment on my sword can cut through just about anything. Besides, Duncan was with me." I shook my head. "Part of me thinks it should be harder to kill people."

"Those people were trying to kill you," Wolfric reminded me. "And they've raped, enslaved, and murdered innocent people. Probably tortured them, too."

"They *did* torture people," said a voice behind us. We turned to see James Reece entering through the damaged wall along with Seth, Dermot, and Conall. Ahearn poked his head around the corner, looking about warily. Our assaults on Cypress Creek and Watson had taught him to look before he leaped.

"We cleared most of it out, Ahearn," I called. "You might want to avoid looking at the front gate, though." He nodded and slipped inside, followed by Weylin and twins Riordan and Tiernan.

"There's an honest-to-god torture chamber here," James Reece continued. He pointed to the northwest tower, now a blackened skeleton. "It was there."

"It had open windows," said Wolfric. "I only noticed because the other towers didn't."

James Reece nodded. "So we could hear the screams. My brother Mark died in there," he said. "Some nights I think I can still hear him screaming."

Everyone stopped and stared at him, so unbelievably calm as he revealed that bit of information.

"The coach house is this way," he said, leading us to a two-story building in the northeast corner of the fort. Like Cypress Creek, the stables were up against the northern and eastern palisade walls, which explained the building's placement at the rear of the garrison. Dermot, Tiernan, and the twins sprinted up the outside steps to check out the storage space above. Weylin stuck his head out the loft window and announced that it was chock full of saddles, bridles, harnesses, and other tack. The rest of us progressed to the large barn doors, which Seth and Conall pulled open, sliding them along their tracks to reveal *six* trail wagons.

As the others went inside the coach house, I turned to examine the stock in their stalls, snorting and restless after the return of fire to their domain. No draft horses were evident, so I wandered around to the north side of the building looking for them. Wolfric followed. Only a few feet below the scorched wood of the northern wall stood a row of oversized stalls that ran along the entire northern wall. Each one held a very large, very unhappy horse, for the stable roof had burned through in spots, allowing hot cinders to drop on the animals. All of them had several small scorch marks on their backs and rumps. Not surprisingly, their stall doors had boards with splintered wood and damaged latches. The surprising part was that the doors had held fast.

Wolfric whistled.

"We almost barbecued the horses that pull those wagons," I said.

"You mean *I* almost barbecued them."

When Duncan proceeded to the huge animals, they greeted him with bared teeth and flattened ears. I headed back to the coach house and called for Dermot.

"Yeah?" The water elementalist poked his head out the second story tack room window.

"I need you to go help Duncan with the draft horses. They're injured."

"You got it," he said, disappearing briefly before reappearing to thunder down the stairs and run over to the earth druid.

Shortly after, Seth exited the coach house. "Ahearn says that everything we need for all six coaches is here and that all the tack seems to be is in good repair."

The horsemaster stuck his head out the window above. "I'll have to inspect it more closely, the bandits seem to have taken excellent care of it."

James Reece looked up. "Actually, *I* took excellent care of it," he said. "Tack and horses both."

"Apologies," said Ahearn. "I won't insult you by examining it further."

I looked at Seth. "Looks like we got us some Trojan horses."

So far, we'd only heard bits and pieces of Seth's plan. I was still vague on a couple of points, like the part where the bandit city voluntarily opened its gates. Luckily, the former inhabitants of the garrison had left us another treasure: a detailed map of their area of conquest, which included the defensive walls surrounding the 'Ville and the locations of the gates that breached them.

"We should leave now," I said. "Before they have a chance to move the children again."

"I disagree," said Seth.

Rhiannon raised an eyebrow. "While I do not think they will leave the city, they could very well spread the children out in multiple buildings," she said. "That would make the task of finding them significantly more difficult, not to mention time-consuming and therefore more dangerous. As Davis has pointed out, time is not on our side."

"I understand that," he replied. "However, they surely know by now how quickly we can travel. We have to assume that they think we'll come after the children immediately, without destroying the garrison."

"Why do you say that?"

"The garrison's representative was sent out specifically to tell us the witchlings were no longer here," Seth said. "That means they know we're magic users. They probably know we're a mixed force of druids and witches."

"That doesn't mean they know what we can do," said Dermot.

"Oh, I think they're getting the idea." Conall smirked.

"How do you think we should proceed?" I asked, ready to get the ball rolling.

"Consider this," Seth began, "Davis burned the outpost where he found Maeve and the others – the one between the 'Ville and Cypress Creek. Then we used smoke to do away with the brigands in Ward. After that, we burned the barracks buildings in Cypress Creek, and followed that up by burning the outpost at Watson."

"Yeah, but nobody at the 'Ville knows we burned that outpost because they never saw the smoke," said Dermot.

"Right. But, the Faulkner garrison somehow found out about it, which made them decide to move the witchlings."

"Which means that 'Ville knows we destroyed the Watson outpost," I said.

"So, High Priestess," said Seth, "taking our known tactics into consideration, if you were a soldier of the Republic of Jackson, what would you expect to happen to this garrison?"

"I would expect you to burn it to the ground."

"Exactly. But we haven't done that yet."

"We made a pretty good start on it," said Wolfric, eyeing the scorched towers, from which black smoke was still rising into the heavily clouded sky.

"Are you saying you want us to destroy it completely and then leave?" I asked, warming to the idea.

Seth nodded. "Yes. But I also think that the wagons need to roll out just before that, as though some of the people from the garrison managed to escape."

"That disguise thing didn't work so well last time," Conall said.

"It'll work this time," Seth replied.

"How do you figure?"

"Because *this* time, the wagons will be running full speed for the 'Ville, yelling for help and begging to be saved from a bunch of bloodthirsty druids riding hot on their heels with guns blazing, spirit bolts flying, and fireballs exploding all around."

Dermot said, "Sounds like the perfect job for you, fireballer."

"It does," Wolfric returned. "Too bad you don't have one."

The water elementalist fell silent, looking perplexed.

"So we get a head start," Ruth observed. "Makes sense."

"How will we reach the children once we're inside?" I asked.

"This gate is the closest to the building where they have our children," Rhiannon said, tapping where the northern gate was drawn on the map. "I can travel the astral while in the wagon to confirm they're still in the same place when we get closer, but I doubt I'll be able to concentrate once the horses start galloping."

"That'll have to be good enough," I said. "How do you plan on getting from the gate to that building?"

Ahearn's smile was impish. "Panicked horses are nearly impossible to stop," he said. "Everybody knows that."

"What are you going to do after you have the kids?" I asked.

"If we put them all in one wagon," Cinna suggested, "we'd

only have to worry about getting one out."

Ahearn nodded. "If five wagons are left behind, I don't think they'll bother chasing *one* down."

"We'll need more than one," Rhiannon said.

Seth said, "You don't think we can get all twelve witchlings in one wagon?"

"We'll need at least three," she said.

"Why?" I asked, recognizing her pensive tone of voice.

"There are twelve of our own," said Rhiannon. "But they tell me there are others with them."

"How many others?"

"Approximately thirty."

"That'll take three wagons, all right," said Ahearn.

"Wait," I said. "Who do those extra kids belong to?"

"I don't know," Rhiannon replied. "But they're all captives."

"You're sure about that."

"Lindsey was quite emphatic about it."

"Lindsey?"

"She's the eldest of the group. It is she with whom I have been communicating on the astral."

"How old is Lindsey?" I asked, knowing I wasn't going to like the answer.

"She's ten."

Quakes.

Seth leaned forward in his chair. "We're relying on information from a ten-year-old child to plan this incursion?"

"We've been relying on her from the very beginning," Rhiannon said, evenly meeting his gaze. "She's quite clever."

"I don't know about anybody else, but I'm glad I didn't know about that before now," Conall said.

"I'm with you there," I said.

"What about an escape route?" asked James Reece.

"That's the hard part," said Seth, tapping his fingers on the table. "The best I've been able to come up with so far is that we follow the wagons into the city and wreak so much havoc that people forget all about them."

"In that case, we'll have to bring a *lot* of water," Dermot said.

"We could put water barrels in the wagons," Conall suggested.

"Excellent idea," I said. "Put a row of barrels in the back of each wagon. It can give those in the back some protection, as well as providing a ready source for water magic."

"Ha!" Dermot said. "I do too have a job – wreaking havoc!"

"Nobody causes mayhem like you do," said Wolfric.

"That's right," said Conall. "So you'd better thank the gods he's on *our* side."

"I most certainly do," I said before an argument could start.

Dermot beamed.

* * *

With Ahearn and Ruth instructing and sometimes assisting, the Finns learned how to hitch the draft horses to the trail wagons. Wolfric and I had cremated the rest of the bodies to make the garrison's environment tolerable, after which Seth, Siorus, Madoc, and Rob had begun repairs to the doors. It seemed foolish to fix the doors and then burn it down, but the fact of the matter was that we needed it for a little bit longer. If the Republic of Jackson got wind of what had happened here, they'd send a force to try and take it back. While I wasn't particularly worried about fighting them off, taking the time to do so would interfere with my plan to rescue the witchlings.

Not everyone was in favor of it, however.

"This is the *craziest* idea I've ever heard!" Maeve said. "It cannot possibly work!"

"Tell that to the Trojans," I said.

Maeve whirled around to face Rhiannon, who was hitching up a draft team of her own. "You can't possibly be considering this madness!"

"If you have a better idea, Maeve, I'm all ears."

Even for a fake attack, I needed every single Finn and witch at my side. We had six wagons and needed at least twenty-four people to man them. Each one needed a driver, someone to ride shotgun, another gun for defense in the back, and someone to mind the cargo: namely, the children we would be rescuing. Unfortunately, we didn't have enough able-bodied people for all six, and as yet I hadn't come up with a solution.

"It is not the first time that one of Davis' schemes has sounded like it sprang from the mind of a madman," Rhiannon replied without looking up from the leather straps she was buckling.

356

I frowned. "Thanks a lot."

"However..." She gave me a look of chastisement for interrupting. "Not once has he led us astray."

"Davis is reckless! This plan of his will only get us all killed – or worse, *enslaved*!"

The High Priestess set aside her work and approached Maeve, taking her hands. "You don't have to go," she said softly. "No one expects you to endure more than you already have. You have shown an exemplary amount of courage just by setting foot outside Ward again, not to mention picking up a gun and defending us."

Maeve angrily twisted away. "Don't you patronize me!" She stormed out of the coach house.

"We need her," I said.

Rhiannon returned to her work. "Not if she isn't capable of doing the job."

The wagons were ready. The teams of draft horses were hitched, the water barrels strapped in, and tarps tied down to hide what was inside. Anticipating a hard ride later, the Finns were taking the time to rest, as much as excited anticipation would allow, anyway. While Wolfric went to stoke the fires burning the garrison, Seth and I walked up and down the line of trail wagons, doing last minute checks to make sure everything was in order.

As I passed the first wagon, James Reece was gathering up the reins and checking the brakes to make sure it was secure.

"I'll ride with you, James Reece," said Ruth, climbing aboard his wagon.

"Uh, no offense, ma'am, but I'm not much good with a gun."

"That's all right, sugar," she replied with a smile, "I am."

I smiled to myself and heard Seth chuckle behind me. Rhiannon's wagon was next, with Ahearn sitting in the driver's seat, conversing with Toby, who was standing with his foot propped up on a wheel. Turning away from them, I spotted Conall pushing a big bag of shotgun shells onto the seat of Cinna's wagon and then climbing up into it.

"Conall! What are you doing?"

"I'm riding shotgun for Cinna."

"But I need you with me!"

He smiled, and for once it lacked its usual hint of cynicism.

"You know, I think you really mean that."

"Of course I mean it!"

"You don't need me, Davis," he said, settling in beside the auburn-haired witch. "You've got Wolfric."

"But..." *But he's not part of my pentacle*, I wanted to say.

"You don't need any of us, really," said Regnar, walking over to Weylin's wagon. "And the witches do."

"After all," said Rob, heading for Heath and Killian's wagon, "We have *way* more experience running and gunning than they do."

"*All* of you are going?" I said, mortified. "Madoc, you, too?"

"Siorus thinks I'll be safer up there," said Madoc, handing his shotgun to Ahearn before swinging aboard himself. Toby wandered around back to join Rhiannon.

"After all, you made us gunmen," called Uri, walking backward toward the farthest wagon in line. "So let us ride shotgun."

I opened my mouth to protest, but Seth stopped me.

"Let them go," he said.

"You're okay with this?!"

"We've ridden in shields before. They seem to work as well as pentacles."

"How can I keep everyone safe, if we're not together?"

"You can't," he replied. "Realistically, you never could."

He was right. I wasn't a healer and I couldn't cast a shield over multiple people like an air elementalist could. The best way to protect my people was by doing what I did best: making myself a target the enemy couldn't resist.

I stabbed a finger at Conall. "Don't get shot. And don't die!"

He just laughed and gave me a cocky salute.

"Don't worry," Cinna called with a smile. "I won't let him do anything stupid."

I continued down the line, repeating my admonishment to the rest of the altered Finns. Grinning and chuckling at my concern, they all promised not to get shot and die.

"You sound like a mother hen!" Conall yelled as the wagons began to roll. I flipped him the bird, and the gunmen laughed even harder.

"Move over!" someone snapped, and I saw Maeve toss a bag

over the tailgate of the farthest wagon, the one with Uri riding shotgun.

Riordan and Tiernan poked their heads out the back. "I thought you weren't coming," Tiernan said.

"*Somebody* has to make sure you two wildlings stay out of trouble," she said, passing up her rifle and then a sizeable box of ammunition. "Get out, Riordan!" she barked. "You're driving." He obediently jumped over the tailgate and started for the front of the wagon. Maeve noticed me watching.

"Don't just stand there staring, Davis," she shouted. "Go stir up some trouble or something!"

"How come he can get into trouble and not us?" Tiernan asked, frowning at her.

Maeve glared at me. "Because that's all *he* knows how to do."

I stood with Seth until the wagon train was well away, watching it growing smaller in the distance.

"They'll be all right," Seth assured me.

"How can you be so sure?"

"As many fights as we've been in, not one of them has been struck by an enemy bullet," he said.

"Sounds like you're tempting the Fates."

"Nah," he said. "I just know they're just used to ducking."

Chapter 20 – The Spirit of Odin

You don't know what you can get away with until you try.
~ Colin Powell ~

When the wagons were half a mile from the 'Ville, we charged at them from the northwest. I threw the first fireball, arcing it high overhead to signal a barrage of near-misses from the rest of the Finns. It crashed to the right of Rhiannon's wagon, and the horses increased speed, galloping for the closed gates.

The six Trojan horses shot forward with unexpected swiftness, even considering that each team was drawing a mostly-empty wagon. Their recent experience of being trapped in a stable with an inferno blazing around them, might have had something to do with it.

The riflemen in the back of the wagons flipped up the tarps and started shooting over our heads. Once each pentacle's air elementalist raised a protective shield, however, the air was filled with the pinging of bullets on hard air along with the sounds of sizzling spirit magic and roaring fireballs. Spurring our horses faster, we gained on the wagons until they were about a quarter mile from the bandit city's gates, which still had not opened.

Steel and I were among the first to reach the foremost wagons; though the druid-bred horses were taller and leggier, the muscular grulla stallion was quicker at a quarter-mile sprint and rapidly closed the gap. Those driving the front wagons – Ahearn and James Reece – were standing up, holding the mass of long reins in one hand while waving and shouting for help. As the Finns drew closer to the wagons, my druid gunmen began firing their shotguns, the bullets again blocked by air shields. A few of the Finns returned fire with rifles, aiming high over the wagons even though they probably didn't need to. They weren't used to aiming rifles from the backs of galloping horses, and their chances of hitting anything at all were poor.

My heart stopped when Conall crumpled to the floor beside Cinna, nearly falling off the side. Dermot cried out in dismay. The Norseman, his whole upper body dangling off the side of a wildly bouncing trail wagon pulled by panicked, racing horses, opened his eyes and gave us a thumbs-up.

As soon as I saw he was alive, I wanted to kill him.

The rest of my gunmen acted like they'd been shot and followed suit in quick succession, each one collapsing in an even more dramatic manner than the one previous. Uri flopped back onto the wagon tarp, somersaulted backward, and fell into the wagon bed. Only Ruth stayed where she was, rifle at the shoulder, steadily pinging away at our shields.

The gates finally opened and those within scrambled to get out of the way of the racing trail wagons. They tried to slam the gates shut and prevent our entrance, but Maeve stuck her head out the back of her wagon and pointed at the ground. It thrust upward in response to her command, knocking the gates asunder and flinging the gatekeepers aside. Thundering through the ruptured gates, the Finns split up as they raced through the streets. Yiorgos' pentacle and the shields led by Halldor and Siorus charged after the still-speeding wagons. Siorus' pentacle only had one elementalist who could cast offensive magic – Fenris – so I'd sent Wolfric with them. They followed under the pretense of pursuit, while their real purpose was to protect the witches and the children they were rescuing.

The rest of us were organized into shields whose sole purpose was to distract the bandits from our real mission. Whooping and hollering, we barreled down different streets, tossing fireballs and spirit magic every which way. First to catch up to the wagons but last to enter the bandit city, I observed the directions each shield took in case they went missing and we needed to go after them later. Ingvar and Martin's shields followed the wagons due south, as did mine, while Warwick's swung southeast across a wide, open area.

Siorus, Ingvar, and Yiorgos stuck to their assigned trail wagons like white on rice. Each group was positioned to the left of a particular wagon to make it look like they were herding the draft horses. Their target, a large pre-Fracture building, lay equidistant between the two paths in the hope that Warwick's deviation would draw the bandits' attention away from the place where the kidnapped children were kept. He and Ridley were the only full druids in their pentacle. Ridley was slated to fight offensively with spirit while Ishkur shielded with air, with Narinder to alternate between air and spirit as necessary. The three did not disappoint, lobbing spirit orbs and hurling spirit bolts to the front and sides as they galloped a block past the big building, turned a corner, and disappeared from sight.

Ingvar's shield, which contained water elementalist Nêreus and air/spirit dualists Jasvinder and Tristan, plunged through the northwestern gate alongside the very last trail wagon, following it through a hard right turn. I had a brief moment to admire how smoothly the two dualists switched off between shielding with air and attacking with spirit before they, too were gone.

Martin's shield veered away from the wagons' trail shortly after entering, moving to the northeast and down a parallel street. He now had another druid in his pentacle, our lone triple threat Phelan. I'd gone to bed the night before thanking the gods when he'd come to tell me he'd gotten his full magic. No other elementalist could match a triple threat when it came to versatility – not even one with earth and fire. Travelling on parallel streets, I could see them for a few blocks as we passed through intersections. Once they'd veered away, flashes of bright actinic light over the tops of buildings revealed their location.

Once the wagons and other groups of Finns were off on their respective missions, I made myself forget about them and turned my attention to garnering as much enemy attention as possible. The people we'd rescued from the Faulkner garrison had told us that the Republic forces were well aware that this ragtag little war band was led by a man who could shake the earth and incinerate buildings in the blink of an eye, so I was ready to set the place ablaze.

Dropping Steel's reins, I raised both hands and channeled a

steady stream of fire along the rooftops of the two-story buildings that lined the streets, occasionally shooting small fireballs through the upper story windows. Creating an inferno was not the object, for it was possible that slaves were living or working in those buildings. Even though I understood that some civilian casualties were inevitable, the last thing I wanted was to kill innocent people.

"Whoa! Look at that!" shouted Dermot, pointing to a giant white cylinder that rose two stories high. He was practically bouncing in his saddle at the sight of it.

"What is it?" Seth yelled back as he shielded us against a barrage of gunfire.

"A water tower!"

A quick seeking told me that we were almost due south of the big building holding the witchlings and other children. The wagons should have reached them by now, and the best way for us to help them was to draw the attention of the city defenders.

"Go-go-go!" I shouted.

When we reached the water tower, enemies poured from the doorways of several buildings that ringed the giant cylinder on three sides. Duncan made them stumble with a well-placed tremor, while Seth shielded us as we crowded up against the tower's skin. Their horses didn't like the close quarters, but the ever-willing Steel performed a beautiful side-pass and moved right up against it. I lay a hand on the brick exterior, causing it to crack and fall away before sending a burst of heat through the metal to melt any ice that might be inside.

"Get ready," I said to Dermot before commanding the metal to peel open. He took over from there, rubbing his hands together excitedly. A nightmarish shape emerged from the hole in the tank, pouring out smoothly as it climbing down the side. It had a head that looked like a cross between a wolf and a beaver, or maybe an otter. The spiked fins along its jaws first swept forward, then backward against its sinuous neck. Covered in ripples that resembled lustrous, thick fur, the creature had broad shoulders and an elongated body that terminated in a long, narrow tail that reminded me of an eel. Its four feet were disproportionately large for its sleek body, with webbing between toes that sprouted claws a lion would be proud to own. Three more identical water monsters surfaced from the tank, opening their jaws wide and hissing as they revealed mouths replete with razor-sharp fangs.

"Dermot!" Seth looked horrified. "What *are* those things?"

"*Dobhar-chú*," the water elementalist replied, a fiendish glint in his eye. "Sic 'em, boys!"

The hissing became excited, and the *Dobhar-chú* sprang from their perches on the water cylinder, racing toward our enemies with snakelike speed, their bodies undulating like lizards. The enemy shot at them but the bullets passed through the sea-wolf-bear-things and buried themselves in the dirt. The first man fell under the massive claws of one water monster, his feet swept out from under him and his throat torn open. It swung its bloody muzzle toward its next victim and panic ensued, filling the air with screams and unearthly hissing. They tried to escape by running back inside the buildings, but I had set the doors on fire.

I lobbed fireballs into the air, allowing them to fall willy-nilly around the circle, causing further pandemonium. The fiendish pack ran through the throng of brigands, ripping and tearing, spilling buckets of blood upon the cold and rocky street. They climbed the walls and jumped off, twisting in midair to pounce upon their unsuspecting prey. One sailed through the air, its vicious claws impaling one woman and slicing her from collarbones to hips. Another leapt upon the back of a fleeing man, digging its claws into his shoulders. His panicked screams ended in a gurgle when its iron jaws crushed his throat.

I prepared to dismount and do some killing of my own, but Dermot shook his head, a look of intense concentration on his face.

"Don't go out there," he said.

I stayed put.

The *Dobhar-chú* completed their slaughter in a matter of minutes, splashing apart into bloody puddles when the water elementalist released his magic. He swayed in the saddle, and Seth caught his shoulder to steady him.

"Sorry. I used a little too much magic." A dreamy expression crossed his face. "But it was *so fun!*"

"We're going to have to do something about his definition of fun," Seth muttered.

Duncan pulled something from his belt pouch and unwrapped it, then took Dermot's hand and made him take it.

"Fruit," he said. "Eat it."

"Can you do anything?" I asked, watching Dermot eat the candy. If he was too weak to ride, he'd have to ride with one of us, and that would slow us down.

The earth druid shook his head.

"Sorry," Dermot said again. "I got carried away, but I'm not tapped out. I'm okay. I can ride."

"Let's move."

We departed the circle of buildings, leaving the water reservoir at a fast walk, while I cast more elemental fire behind us to cover our trail. If nobody came out to see us moving away, they would just assume we were still in the tower circle. Dermot regained enough strength for a faster gait, and we trotted through the winding streets setting things on fire. We found one road that went due north for a few blocks, after which we turned east and were again set upon by our adversaries.

We repeated the tactic of Seth blocking with air while Duncan sent shockwaves through the ground before us, destabilizing both people and buildings. I laid down parallel lines of yellow-hot fire, creating a lane through which we could travel that would melt the bullets and maybe give Seth a break. As we rode through, however, the air elementalist gave them a lateral shove, setting the buildings on both sides of the street on fire.

Turning north once more, we found ourselves on the road that Martin's shield group had used to penetrate the bandit city. Several structures had succumbed to the violent rumbling of the earth, and the outer walls of the buildings were scored and blackened by Phelan's lightning strikes. The inhabitants seemed to have abandoned the area, so we were able to drop the air shields and increase speed until we reached the open area between the city and its northwestern gate.

We emerged from between the buildings just in time to see the three trail wagons rolling full tilt, back through the ruined gates, surrounded on all sides by Finns on horseback. Running after them were at least a hundred people on foot – slaves fleeing the city. What looked like two raid groups had mounted up and followed in hot pursuit of the captives who had bravely taken advantage of the breech.

"We have to help them!" Dermot yelled, pointing at the fleeing captives. Spurring Kelpie, he raced ahead with his full water bags flopping against his thighs. The blue roan stretched out in a full gallop, outpacing all our horses. Steel tried valiantly to catch up, but he was tired, as were Scarlet and Bucephalus. The best I could do was throw fireball after fireball, landing them among the raid group's ranks and slowing them somewhat. Several were unhorsed, either through direct hits or spooking horses, but it wasn't enough.

Still moving at breakneck speed, the water elementalist dropped his reins and uncorked both water bags. What looked like a hundred skinny ropes of crystalline water burst forth from the bags, reaching out and grabbing the raiders from behind, sometimes around the waist or arm, sometimes around the neck, and tossing them off their horses. Dermot decimated the raid group faster than a playful group of children could snatch laundry from a clothesline.

Now riderless, the bandit horses slowed and began to wander about aimlessly. I cast a ten-foot-high firewall behind us that stretched for a hundred yards east and west, then started catching horses for the escapees. Many of them managed to capture mounts on their own, and we advised them to ride due north until they reached Cypress Creek, then follow the creek east until they reached the garrison there. It took half an hour for them all to get up and go, but there was no immediate pursuit from the 'Ville.

As I watched the last of them ride north, Dermot's horse walked up with its head down and sides heaving.

"I think... that's... all of them," Dermot said, breathless. He slid out of the saddle and hit the ground. I jumped from my horse and ran to his still form, quickly patting him down in a frantic search for gunshot wounds and finding none. The others dismounted in a hurry and Duncan checked him over more thoroughly, pronouncing him exhausted and his water bags empty.

"I think he forgot he was almost out of magic," said Seth, shoving the water elementalist's limp form up and onto my saddle so I could carry him home. I was torn between worry over him and pride at what he had accomplished.

Wolfric was right – *nobody* could wreak havoc like Dermot.

* * *

The ride back to the Cypress Creek rendezvous point took

longer than expected due to the exhaustion of our horses. The temperature steadily dropped as the light faded from the sky. Dealing with Dermot's dead weight only made things more difficult. I didn't want to just toss him over Kelpie's saddle and tie him there because he'd probably freeze to death. Steel handled having to carry two as well as could be expected after the wild ride to and through the 'Ville, but even his endurance had limits. We ended up tying a rope around Dermot's chest to hoist him onto Duncan's spotted mare for the second hour of the ride, and then Seth's black stallion for the third. When I took him again for the last leg of the trip, his hands were like ice. Unsure if I had enough control to warm his body without boiling his blood, I superheated the air around us. The warmed air continually rose and cold air circulated in, so it required constant attention. Great relief accompanied the welcome sight of Cypress Creek's timbered walls; the even the horses perked up, trotting the rest of the short distance.

"Who goes there?" demanded the gate guard.

"We're druids," Seth replied and gave our names.

"Prove it!"

Before Seth could shout back an angry retort, I tossed a handful of fire darts at the guard. He ducked, and they sailed overhead, blowing out in midair. Moments later, the rattle of chains could be heard, and the gates opened.

"Was that really necessary?" Duncan asked as we rode inside.

"I'm tired and Dermot's cold," I said.

"He's only being cautious, as is prudent."

"Our names should have been good enough," I growled.

The guard ran up, apologizing profusely.

"There's no need to apologize," the earth druid said as he dismounted. "It was rude of Davis to throw that at you. He's the one who should apologize."

The man looked appalled at the very idea. "Oh, no, sir. I wouldn't dream of it."

I sighed, remembering where we were and how people here walked on eggshells around me. "He's right. I'm sorry, please forgive me."

"Begging your pardon, Master Davis, but it's completely understandable, you being cold and tired and all."

Behind him, Duncan rolled his eyes and started for the stable, leading Scarlet and Kelpie. Seth dismounted and came over to take Dermot while I did the same. A door banged open, and Conall ran out to greet us.

"What in Hel's name took you so long?" he demanded. The scowl was replaced with a look of horror when he saw Dermot's inert form.

"Oh, gods! Is he hurt? What happened?" The Norseman shoved past Seth. "He's ice cold! He's not... he can't be..."

"He's fine," I said.

"He doesn't look fine!"

"He overextended himself," said Seth. "He just used too much magic. Calm down."

"Don't tell me to calm down!" Conall shouted. "He looks *dead*!"

"He's not dead," I said. "Help me get him inside before he freezes to death."

Conall took Dermot from me and started for the door of the building he had just exited.

"You go with them," said Seth, taking Steel's reins. "I'll see to the horses."

I nodded, willing my tired legs to jog after them. I shut the door behind Conall and found myself in what looked like a large tavern. The sudden heat wrapped around me like a blanket, and I sighed in relief, but it didn't last long, for all conversation stopped as they stared at Dermot's pale face and limp body. The Finns stared at us in shock, unmoving as though stuck to their chairs, while several of the witches slowly rose, some of them with their hands against their mouths as though afraid of what noise might unexpectedly escape.

"Everybody relax. Dermot's alive," I said. "He overextended himself. Duncan said he should be fine by morning."

Nobody relaxed.

"Let's get him upstairs and into bed," I said.

Conall stomped up the wooden staircase, while the rest of the Finns crowded in behind us. The other three pure water elementalists slipped through the crowd and were hovering around the bed almost as soon as we laid Dermot in it. They'd always been a tight group, supporting one another in the biased and often unkind environment of Shitozaki's camp.

I warmed the room until everyone else began to sweat, then started pulling off Dermot's boots, socks, and coat. "Did everyone make it back okay?"

"Everyone is fine. No major injuries," Siorus reported. "We rescued fifty kids!"

"Everyone is fine but *Dermot*," Conall growled. "Why does he have a bruise on his face?"

"He fell off his horse."

The Norseman gave me a hard look. "He's a *good* rider."

"He passed out."

"How could he overextend with just one gallon of water?" Conall demanded, indicating the large water bags that hung on a belt about Dermot's waist. I unbuckled the setup from his narrow hips and pulled the canteens off. The water elementalist was so vibrant and energetic that it was easy to forget how young and skinny he was.

"The amount of water isn't what matters," said Nêreus. "It's the amount of magic expended. Technically you can overextend with a cup of water if you use it enough."

Mohinder nodded. "Yeah, remember last spring when Galen tried to irrigate the fields all by himself? He ended up face down in the dirt."

Galen frowned at him. "Thanks for the reminder."

I was grateful for their presence. I'd never experienced the limitations of an elementalist, having had full druid magic from the get-go. The severity of Conall's reaction was unexpected; more irate than concerned, he seemed annoyed with me in particular.

"We found a water tower," I said. Their eyes grew wide when I described it to them. "It's my fault. I let him do it."

"It wasn't the water tower that did him in," Seth said, entering the room. "It was lassoing all those bandits off their horses."

"What bandits?" asked Nêreus, moving aside to make room for Rhiannon and Maeve.

"Two raid groups were on your tail when the wagons left the city," Seth replied. "They nearly trampled their own runaway slaves trying to get at you."

"That reminds me," I said. "Did any of them make it?"

"Oh, yeah," said Mohinder. "Over a hundred. I wondered

369

where they all came from."

"Nice of them to mention us," Seth grumbled.

"Why would they have mentioned you?"

"Never mind."

"Such is the life of a hero," I said.

"Dermot has no physical injury," Rhiannon announced. "But he *is* low in spirit."

"He doesn't have spirit magic," said Galen.

"Spirit dwells in every living thing," the High Priestess replied. "It is that which gives us life and animates us. I can heal this."

"Duncan said there was nothing to heal," I said.

"Physically, that's true." She laid a hand on his forehead. "Spiritually, though, is something else entirely."

"Is it bad?" Conall tensed again.

"He'll be fine in a little bit."

"Duncan said he'd be awake by morning," I said.

Rhiannon raised an eyebrow at me. "Perhaps you could get everyone out of here and let me work?"

It was not a request.

"All right, everybody. Dermot's in good hands, so let's all go back downstairs," I said. The group thundered down the steps, and the sounds of drinking and conversation gradually resumed. Tiredness hit me like a hammer, and I collapsed into a chair across the room from the bed. I let my head thump back against the wall, struggling to stay awake. Duncan brought up plates of ham and eggs to Seth and me, after which my stomach woke the rest of me up.

"We missed supper, but Heath and Katarina made this for you," said the earth druid.

I looked up. "Did you eat?"

"I had the first plate," the earth druid replied.

"Good. Did anybody make coffee?"

"You don't need coffee. You need rest."

"Thanks, Mom."

"We all need to rest," said Seth, backing Duncan up.

"I'll rest when he's better."

Maeve stood up and looked at us. "There *are* four other beds," she said in a tone that clearly indicated we were idiots. I had noticed, in the way a Traveler always takes note of his surroundings but hadn't really paid attention. The three of us stood, but before we could take one step toward any of the beds, she added: "*After* you bathe."

"Sometimes I think she's worse than Angie," I grumbled as we stumped downstairs. Duncan snorted and nodded agreement.

"I heard that," Maeve called.

* * *

I woke to find Conall standing beside Dermot's bed staring out the window like an angry cat.

"How is he?" I asked, swinging my legs out from under the blankets and reaching for my boots. We'd been Traveling for so long, I'd almost forgotten what it was like to sleep in a real bed. Even a rope bed was a luxury.

"Better. Whatever Rhiannon did worked."

I yawned. "Good."

"After you guys sacked out, he woke up, ate, and went back to sleep. *Real* sleep."

"Have *you* slept?"

"No."

"Let me get some coffee, and I'll spell you," I said, shoving my feet into cold boots. "You should get some rest."

He neither responded nor turned around. Glancing back at the still-sleeping Seth and Duncan, I sat back down on my bed.

"What's going on, Conall?"

He let out a hard breath. "I should have been there. I should have gone with you instead of riding on the wagon."

"That wouldn't have changed anything," I said.

"It doesn't matter. I should have stayed with my pentacle."

"You couldn't have done anything about this," I said. "I tried to call him back, but he just took off on his horse like his hair was on fire."

"Twister can keep up with Kelpie. I could have taken part of that raid group out."

"He had his Mossberg," I said. "He just got carried away."

Conall made no reply.

"It's not the first time one of the Finns has overextended—"

"No, but it's the first time it happened in enemy territory,"

371

Conall snapped. "He could have been killed yesterday."

"We all could have been killed yesterday."

"'We all' aren't seventeen years old. He's just a kid!"

I sighed. "I know. I have that very thought every single time we do anything dangerous."

He looked at me. "And yet you still let him come."

"That's why he's with *us*. So we can watch out for him."

"But I wasn't there."

"Are you mad at yourself, or at me?" I asked. "Because I really can't tell."

"You. Me. Both." He shook his head. "Neither. What on earth could Shitozaki have been thinking, allowing us to drag a boy into the wilderness?"

"He knew I'd be fine with you guys," said Dermot, pushing himself upright. "Don't be mad at me, okay?" His face was still pale, red hair and freckles standing out in sharp contrast to his skin.

"I'm not mad," Conall said. "Just worried."

"I wasn't worried," Duncan said.

"I'm worried," said Seth, stretching and yawning. "You should have seen the monsters he created yesterday, Conall. I'm surprised I didn't have nightmares." He finished the stretch with a shudder.

"Oh, but it was *so* fun! And that tower had *so much* water!" Dermot said, falling back on his pillow with a blissful expression. "I can't wait until I'm a druid!"

Seth and Duncan exchanged a disturbed look, but I only smiled. "You're going to be one volcanic water druid."

"Druid or not, if you ever scare us like that again, I'm gonna kick your ass," Conall said.

Chapter 21 – The War Band Rides Again

If you are neutral in situations of injustice,
you have chosen the side of the oppressor.
~ Desmond Tutu ~

"That's everyone," Rhiannon said the next morning. Everyone who had been captured, she meant. No one could bring back the dead. We'd rescued fifty-seven children between the ages of two and ten.

"So who do all the other kids belong to?" I asked, watching Dermot play with the smaller ones, pretending to pull a button from one little boy's ear. He had started to use magic to entertain them, but Conall had nearly bitten his head off over it. The Norseman had been dogging his steps since he'd regained enough strength to leave the inn.

"Fortunately, all the ones who are too young to know where they are from were kept together with the older ones from the same villages," Rhiannon said. "Unfortunately, quite a few of them are from Watson, Bailey Lake, and Otto."

Those places had all been destroyed in the 'Ville's quest to expand its territory. We had heard that even the children of Bailey Lake and Otto had been murdered, so I was thankful that it wasn't true, even if they were now orphans.

"See those children with Ruth and James Reece?" Rhiannon said, indicating them with a nod of her head. "They're all from Faulkner."

"Were any of their parents among the people we rescued?"

"Sadly, no."

Five children encircled the two adults, playing ring-around-the-rosy while Ruth laughed and James Reece blushed. The smallest, who looked to be about three, fell and skinned his knee. James Reece scooped him up as he started to cry and kissed the boy's scrape. There was a sparkle in Ruth's eye as she looked at the man from Faulkner, who didn't seem to mind a bit that she carried a rifle and wore pants "like a man."

"I think there may be a rare and precious flower blossoming in spite of the cold," Rhiannon said with a knowing smile.

"One can only hope," I said. They both were kind, generous, and courageous people. They deserved better than what life had given them so far. "What about the rest of the kids?"

"They're from farther south and west – Conway, Mayflower, and a place called Blue Hill."

"Those will be our next targets, then."

"You don't have to save the whole world, Davis."

"No, just my little piece of it."

I didn't know when Dermot would be back to full strength, and nobody could tell me, either. Seth had merely shrugged and commented that everyone was different and the size of one's inner Well was the main determinant. An elementalist with a small Well would be refilled in no time; a larger one took longer. What Dermot lacked in size and strength, he more than made up for with elemental ability, so we'd probably be here for a few days. Maybe longer.

We built two large, druid-style apartment buildings where the old bandit barracks had stood, which gave us a little room to stretch out and relax. The invaders had thoughtfully stocked the garrison for winter, but I didn't want the rightful owners to go without in the winter months, so we fed ourselves by trapping and hunting. I waited until the next day to tell the Finns about the towns the orphan children had come from.

The only question was from Phelan:

"When are we leaving?"

"We've had a hard couple of days, so maybe in a couple more," Seth replied. "We'll go when everyone is at optimal strength."

What he really meant was that we couldn't leave until Dermot was ready, but we didn't want to make him feel singled out as the cause for delay.

"I don't know about anybody else, but I'm ready to go *now*," the water elementalist said.

"No, you're not," said Conall. "Just this morning you told me you were still down by at least a quarter."

"So? I still have my shotgun."

"We're not leaving until everyone has a full Well." I said, forestalling further argument. "Besides, my ass is sore from all that riding the other day." It wasn't, but it made them laugh and took the heat off anyone who wasn't ready to go and put it on me.

And as everyone knew, I could take the heat better than anybody.

* * *

Three days later found us on the outskirts of Conway, nestled on an arrowhead-shaped peninsula that thrust into a lake of the same name. While we had initially planned on making the journey alone, many of the witches accompanied us. Having been rescued from a dire situation themselves, Killian, Heath, Cullen, Toby, Ruth, and James Reece had come to me the night before we departed asking to join so they could help those who were still enslaved. Cullen still wasn't physically up to the hard riding we did, so I had to refuse his request.

Rhiannon had joined us, ostensibly to watch out for her people, but I sensed she was motivated by her own desire for vengeance. Shannon, Riordan, Tiernan, Weylin, and Maeve came along with their bows and rifles, while Ahearn and the Weird Sisters came to look after the horses.

Katarina and Elin had chosen to stay behind, having taken it upon themselves to care for the witchlings and help with the other orphaned children. While they were happy that Cullen was staying, Katarina was not pleased that both her brother and her lover would be in harm's way yet again and let me know about it in no uncertain terms. Heath confided in me that his choice stemmed from a desire to exact revenge upon those who had hurt her. Were our situations reversed, I would have felt the same and supported him in spite of her ire.

Thankfully, a few more of the Finns had progressed from

elementalist to druid in the intervening days: Ishkur, Skylar, and Westley. With the exception of Ingvar's, every pentacle had two or three druids now. Martin had two other druids beside himself, so I had the two pentacles ride together for safety. Since Alexandros was responsible for shielding his own pentacle, Phelan was to back up dualists Jasvinder and Tristan with spirit and air as needed. My own remained at a count of two druids, two elementalists, and one altered gunman.

"When will you be twenty-one?" I asked Seth.

"I turned twenty-one on October tenth," he replied. He still couldn't channel his element directly from the gods, but my understanding was that it could happen anytime during a person's twenty-first year. I could only hope that it would be soon.

"Quakes, I missed your birthday, too?"

"We've been a little too busy for cake and gifts," he said drily.

"My birthday is March fifteenth!" Dermot announced.

"Beware the Ides of March," Duncan and I said in unison, exchanging an amused glance.

"Not that it matters," Conall grumbled, "since you'll only be eighteen."

"Yeah, but at least then I'll be an adult."

"Age isn't what makes you an adult. Taking on adult responsibilities like you have is what makes someone an adult," I said. "When is your birthday, Conall?"

"Next month, but that doesn't matter, either."

"Why do you say that?" Dermot asked.

"Because the reason he's asking Seth about his birthday is to find out when we can expect to have a third druid in our pentacle. For what it's worth, I turned twenty-one last January."

Seth grinned at me. "I think we have your number."

"I wasn't going to throw you a party anyway."

"I think we've had enough parties lately," he said.

"Yeah, with too many uninvited guests," Dermot agreed.

"Speaking of uninvited guests..." Conall pointed at the expanse of denuded land that revealed itself as we rode out of the trees. There was nothing but bare earth, sawdust, and tree stumps from here to the palisade that surrounded Conway. The waste and outright desecration was abhorrent. Low muttering and grumbles of disapproval could be heard throughout the war band as they took in the wanton destruction of the sacred forest. At least it wasn't as extensive as the denuded area around the Faulkner fortress had been.

"Looking at this, you'd think the Rebirth had never happened," said Seth, frowning.

"Or that it *just* happened," said Dermot.

Duncan frowned, "have these people learned nothing?"

"They don't know the earth the way we do," I said. "To them, it's just a source of raw materials and a thing to be used."

"Kind of like how they view the people living on it," Conall said. Seth nodded in grim agreement.

Republic forces had indeed taken the town. As our reception was likely to be cool, I was ready to warm things up a bit.

"Remember that there are townspeople held prisoner in there," Rhiannon said.

"As we saw in Faulkner, that makes an attack difficult, but not impossible," said Seth. "How do you want to play this?"

"We could just tear down a wall like we did at Cypress Creek," I said.

"Or all the walls, for that matter," suggested Conall.

"How big do you think it is?" asked Dermot.

"Not as big as Faulkner," I said. "But I'd rather not destroy it." Cypress Creek had gotten pretty full from the influx of refugees.

"Agreed," said Seth. "It was rather inconvenient to ride here all the way from Cypress Creek. If we hadn't burned the garrison at Faulkner, we could have used it as a base of operations."

"Yeah, just like the bad guys did," Dermot said.

"We don't need a base of operations," I said, clapping my hands and rubbing them together briskly. "We're druids. We *like* sleeping outside."

"Speak for yourself," muttered Conall. Riding beside him, Cinna chuckled.

"It would benefit the townspeople greatly to have the wall as a defense once the bandits are gone," said Duncan.

"My sentiments exactly. Give the order to dismount and get ready," I told Seth. "Cinna, would you please have Ahearn, Toby, and James Reece move the horses back into the woods?"

"I'll tell them," she said, guiding her horse to the rear.

Before planning any kind of attack, we needed to know what

we could not see; namely, what was on the other side of that wall. Duncan knelt, placing a hand on the cold ground to perform a *seeking*, and I did the same.

"Similar layout to Faulkner," I said, thrilled to be able to perceive so much even at this distance. "What do you think?"

"Seems approximately half the size," the earth druid said, confirming my estimation. "If you don't want to destroy the wall, we could go under it."

The enemy certainly would not be expecting that tactic. "Can we move that much earth without destabilizing the wall?"

"With one earth druid moving the earth and the other seven holding it up while everyone goes through the tunnel, I don't think it'll be a problem," Duncan said drily.

"Wait a minute," said Conall. "They're going to see us digging and as soon as somebody pops their head out, it'll get blown off."

"I guess that means I'm going in first," I said. Seth groaned, and the look on Duncan's face suggested that he felt the same.

"Speaking of risking life and limb, how do you propose we keep from getting shot between here and there?" the air elementalist asked.

"I'll leave that to you," I said.

He wore a dubious expression but gave a nod anyway. "I'll get right on it," he said and started gathering the Finns with elemental air.

The plan he came up with was ingenious. Since we now had one druid triple threat, two druid dualists, and twelve elementalists that could either wield dual elements or pure air, it was possible to cast a narrow shield from the garrison wall all the way back to the tree line, approximately two hundred yards away. They created a vault of hardened air that all the Finns could safely stand beneath. We jogged from the tree line to the fort, making it halfway across the open expanse before the invaders got organized enough to do more than take pot shots. The air shields held until we were all gathered in the shadow of the palisade. The enemy began concentrating their fire, shattering one after another.

Seth had anticipated such a maneuver and directed the four air-wielding druids to take over the job of maintaining the vault of hardened air. Phelan, Ishkur, and Skylar took turns holding the vault in layers; as the top shield was destroyed, there were another two beneath it. They shuffled shields like cards, allowing the elementalists to conserve their limited stores of magic for the battle to come.

Emboldened by our recent victory over the Faulkner garrison and the successful rescue of the witchlings, a thrill of anticipation resonated through the Finns. Enthusiastic earth druids ran in and out of their underground tunnel, whispering excitedly to each other. To a man, they completely ignored the deafening ping and crack of bullets striking the air shields. Nobody paid attention when the enemy dumped a cauldron of boiling oil over us, for it merely splatted on the bulletproof archway of solid air and slid off to glop upon the ground. I smiled and waved at the frustrated invaders.

"You're going to piss them off," said Seth.

"Good. Angry people make bad decisions."

"Is that why you're letting them do that?" He pointed to Dermot, Mohinder, Nêreus, and Galen. They had dropped their trousers around their ankles and were shaking their bare asses at the furious defenders above.

I shrugged. Water elementalists were impulsive and easily bored. Seth sighed.

Phelan, who was standing in front of me doing his part to hold up the air vault, turned around to catch my eye. "If you're going in first, I want to go with you."

"Actually," said Martin, who had stopped to listen, "you're coming with me. We've decided to dig a rabbit hole for each pentacle. Then we can launch the assault in unison."

"*Volcanic*," I said. "Excellent idea."

"You like it?" The earth druid beamed.

"Absolutely! Since they can only see us digging one hole, they'll never suspect it."

"Genius," said Wolfric. Then, to me: "Where do you want me?"

I considered. "Go with Halldor. Barak has been channeling air so you can support them in case his Well runs low after he switches to spirit."

He nodded. "See you topside." He scooted down the long, narrow tunnel that ran beneath the palisade wall. Barely wide enough for a man to pass through sidewise, it connected each of the rabbit holes. Due to the narrow confines, it took several minutes for each of the Finns to disappear down his own pentacle's rabbit hole. Seth, Dermot, Conall, and I were the last to go down, where we met Duncan underground.

"Everybody good on weapons and ammo?"

They all nodded.

"I added another gallon of water," Dermot said. He now carried a one-gallon backpack and two half-gallon bags secured to his belt, increasing his mobility when he was out of the saddle.

"Pace yourself. I don't want a repeat of what happened at the 'Ville."

"I will," he promised. "Being completely drained feels *awful*."

"It was pretty awful for the rest of us, too," Conall said. "I thought you were dead when Davis brought you back. So don't fucking do it again."

"Aww, Conall, I didn't know you cared."

"It's going to be awfully hard for you to fight after I break both your legs, Dermot," the Norseman growled.

Seth eyed him critically. "You'll never make it up that ramp carrying all that extra weight."

"He won't have to," I said. "I'm going to launch us up."

"Launch?" Conall said.

"Yes. Each earth druid is going to raise the slope until it's level with the ground."

"Maybe you should let Duncan handle that."

"I can do it," I said. "It'll be fine."

It wasn't fine.

Before Duncan even had time to remove the thin layer of dirt hovering over our heads, I exploded from the ground like one of Dermot's many-tentacled water monsters. The force sent me tumbling through the air until I slammed into the nearest group of enemies while about twenty cubic feet of soil rained down upon us. I had effectively launched myself right into the teeth of danger.

Disoriented by my graceless flight, I came up on one knee with hands upraised and fire shield spinning, but facing the wrong direction, for the threat was behind me. I rolled sideways and threw a big, ugly, disorganized mass of flame at the group of enemies charging my way. They ducked and immediately returned to the business of trying to kill me. Restoring the spinning fire shield, I drew my sword and fell upon anyone and everyone who came close to the rabbit hole.

Duncan had reacted to my overuse of earth magic by cancelling out most of the thrust and rising at a rapid but far more reasonable pace while Seth kept them all safe from gunfire with an air dome. The earth druid had retained control of the rest of the rabbit hole, a fact that I had forgotten to take into consideration when expending my own energy.

I tried to use the same tactics I'd used at Samhain and when assaulting the garrison at Faulkner. While holding the fire shield, I cast two triangular walls of solid fire, into which my enemies might be funneled. They didn't take the bait. We faced each other in a standoff while they fired round after round into the fire shield, only to have the slugs melted and flung away like a dog shaking water droplets from its sodden coat. Undaunted, I dropped the flaming gauntlet and ran forward to engage them with the enchanted grey blade. The Morrigan would have trophies aplenty this day. Blood blackened and boiled on the sword's cold metal, sizzling in the frigid air as it swept through the swirling flames. They backed away in terror, fighting each other to get away.

I spun about as pinging sounded loudly in my ears: bullets ricocheting off an air shield overhead.

"We were supposed to stay *together*," Seth barked.

"We're together now," I said. "If you open a hole in the top, I can take out those snipers on the roof."

"Dermot's on it," said Conall. "He and Duncan are still underground."

As he finished speaking, silvery ropes glinting with the afternoon sun shot out of a small hole a few feet to our left. Streaking out in multiple directions, they picked off each of the snipers, sending one after another sailing overhead, most landing beyond the garrison walls.

"How'd he get over there?"

"Oh, I don't know," said Conall. "Earth magic, maybe?"

"That's a damned good idea," I said, and erased the ground under our feet, dropping them into a hole with me. Before either Seth or Conall had time to recover, I shunted us through a tunnel of

381

darkness until I sensed we were near the rear of the garrison, then channeled a pillar of fire upward through the dirt before propelling us upward again, using considerably less force than the last time.

I leapt out of the hole and landed on my feet in the southernmost corner. Luck must have been on my side, for we ended up with the palisade wall at our backs and about twenty or thirty bandits facing away from us. Conall's shotgun *boomed* and scattershot burst into the crowd, which made them mill around in confusion if not panic. Sword in hand, I plunged into the crowd of enemies, fire shield spinning and sparking in my left hand, while the grey blade flickered and danced in my right, severing limbs and heads and spilling guts with ridiculous ease. I could thrust with the sword and run a man through, then slash sideways out of that body and into the next without ever withdrawing it from bloody flesh.

Lost in a murderous trance, I ripped through them like a razor-edged whirlwind, never even noticing when they stopped fighting and abandoned the attack. When they tried to run, I raised a firewall to block their escape and cut them to bits as they screamed for mercy. Hearing their cries, more of the invaders ran to assist their comrades. I dropped the firewall and dove into them, the grey blade slicing through metal and bone, spattering the palisade wall with blood from the back of the garrison to the front. Reaching the rabbit holes, I looked around for more enemies to kill but found none. The earth warned me of a presence behind, and I pivoted, nearly taking Duncan's head off. He parried with his own sword and dodged. Something grabbed me around the waist and slammed me into a nearby building, knocking the air from my lungs. The grey blade fell from my hand, and I slumped to the ground gasping for breath.

The earth druid kicked my sword away before kneeling in front of me and placing his hand on my chest.

"Gods, I'm sorry!" I gasped. He gave me a chiding look and shook his head in exasperation.

"Quakes, Duncan, I nearly killed you."

"That is highly unlikely, seeing as how both my father and uncle surprised me with attacks on a regular basis," he replied, suppressing a smile.

"This isn't funny."

"No, it isn't, but I would be a poor swordsman *and* a poor

earth druid if I'd been unable to defend against *that* strike."

Meaning my swordsmanship had been was sloppy and my tactics obvious.

"Is he okay?" Dermot ran up, looking scared. "Are you hurt?"

"I'm fine. What hit me?"

A guilty look crossed his face. "I grabbed you with a big tentacle when I realized you didn't know it was Duncan behind you. I didn't mean to slam you against the wall, but the water turned to steam, and I couldn't hold you!"

"It's okay," I said. "You did the right thing."

"Maybe you shouldn't use this anymore," said Conall, bending down to pick up the grey blade. He dropped it just as quickly, hissing in pain. "It's *freezing*."

The early December temperatures were near freezing during the day and below freezing at night. The grey blade was far colder than that.

"As cold as the Phantom Queen herself," Duncan murmured.

I rested my head against the building. "Go make sure everybody else is okay."

Seth hesitated.

Conall said, "Obviously Dermot is more than a match for him if he misbehaves." Seth gave him a sharp nod and departed.

"Thanks," I said.

"No, I'm not!" The water elementalist sounded panicky. "I'm *not*! He just wasn't using magic to fight back!"

"Relax, Dermot," the Norseman said. "You've done nothing wrong. You did good."

He squatted beside Duncan and looked me over. "I've never seen you like that before. You fought as though possessed by Tyr himself."

"Or *Dagda*," Dermot said emphatically.

The earth druid changed the subject. "Is this similar to what happened after you rescued Maeve and the bandits were pursuing you?"

I nodded. "Maybe worse. I dropped the fire shield."

"You didn't drop the shield," Conall said. "It just got bigger and surrounded your whole body."

"Gods. I don't even know what's happening when I get like that," I said, then noticed Dermot holding his right hand up to his chest. "What's wrong with your hand?"

"Nothing."

"Let me see."

"It's fine!"

"Dermot," I said in a warning tone, and I pushed off the wall and staggered to my feet. My back was going to be black and blue, by the feel of it. Conall moved to stand between us.

"Be careful, or you might fall down," the Norseman said. The warning light in his eyes said that if I took another step, he was going to make it happen.

"Fine. *You* look at his hand."

With a rebellious expression, Dermot opened his hand and showed it to Conall.

"Well?" I asked, even though I already knew the answer.

"It's burned."

Of course it was. When Dermot had grabbed me with the water tentacle, my fire shield must have turned the water to steam instantly, burning his hand before he could turn it loose.

"Shit," I said.

"Why didn't you tell me?" Duncan said, taking his injured hand gently between his own. After a few moments the tension left Dermot's body, and he sighed in relief.

"I didn't want Davis to feel bad about it."

"Maybe he *should* feel bad about it," Conall said.

"I *do* feel bad about it!" I said. "Do you think I *wanted* to hurt either of them? Or Seth? Or you?"

"Come with me," he said.

I followed him, feeling sick to my stomach. We rounded the corner of the building, and the iron stench of fresh blood and the foul odor of burned hair and leather hung thickly in the air. There wasn't a square inch of ground that wasn't soaked with it. Cleanly sliced bone showed through hunks of muscle, while piles of slick intestines steamed in the freezing air. Unidentifiable pieces of gore and flecks of flesh were spattered on the blood-sprayed walls.

Bile rose up into my throat.

Conall gestured to the morass of blood, guts, and severed limbs. "Now, I know we're here to kill people, and these bastards certainly got what they deserved, but when you're in that berserker state, you don't know *what* you're doing. You can't even tell friend from foe."

"It's not the sword."

"You never lost control before the Morrigan enchanted it."

"Yes, I have."

"I'm not talking about that time I threw the scythe at you," he said. "Even then, you didn't go berserk."

"Regardless, I need it if we're going to win this war."

"Use either the sword *or* the fire," Conall replied. "But not both. Not at the same time. Not until you can control it."

"I can't fight with a sword if I can't shield myself," I said.

"Remember the day that Duncan was in a snit and you asked him to pull you back if your magic got out of control?"

"Were you eavesdropping?"

He gave me a sardonic look. "I have no magic to speak of, while you are both earth druids." Hence, if someone overheard our conversation without our noticing their presence, it was our own fault.

"Yes. He said he couldn't."

"Consider the possibility that *no one* can. Especially not when you're in a berserker rage." He nodded at the ruin of human flesh.

My first inclination was to reject the notion out of hand, but the wiser voice that sounded so much like my father made me listen. The first thing that came to mind was how frequently Wolfric voiced amazement by the sheer quantity of fire that I was able to channel. I'd believed it was due to his relative inexperience, assumed that he hadn't learned as much as he could have because he was forced to keep his magic hidden. However, his father Adalwulf was a man of honor and integrity who was unlikely to allow his son's training to be substandard or incomplete.

Next was the stunned look on Connor Shitozaki's face when I had taken away *his* fire, subsuming it within my own. He had quickly covered up his discomfiture by downplaying the event, but I'd never seen him thrown off stride like that. He was a former ArchDruid and a powerful fire elementalist who had seen it all and done it all. Nothing ever surprised him.

Nothing except *my* fire magic.

He had even told me that the power and control I had with fire was "as good as or better" than any druid he'd ever seen, including his own. Then, less than six months later, Duncan had told me that both of my elements had become dramatically stronger since Samhain, that he believed my power over earth to be even greater than his own.

What if the Morrigan's enchantment *was* at the root of this power surge? What if I *couldn't* control it?

I was hit with fear so intense hard that it made my hands shake. Today I had become the monster I'd told Rhiannon I was afraid of becoming. I'd burned Dermot. I'd nearly murdered Duncan. Trying to fight it, I wrapped my arms around myself, tucking my hands in tight to stop the tremors. The more I tried to control them, the more I shook. Soon, my whole body was taken with rigors.

Eian and Declan rounded the corner, spying us.

"Is Davis all right?" Declan asked.

"He's fine," Conall said.

"He's shaking," Eian replied with an expression of concern.

"Do you *see* this mess?" Conall snapped. "It's muscle fatigue. Get lost."

The twins departed with obvious reluctance, murmuring to one another.

"Relax," Conall said. "Just let it happen. The more you try and control it, the worse the shaking gets."

"I n-noticed," I replied through chattering teeth that had nothing to do with the cold. "If y-you want s-some of this f-fire, I'll g-gladly share it w-with you."

"Augmenting someone with foreign magic is very dangerous," he said. "Only a fool would attempt it."

"I was just k-kidding." Thankfully, the tremors were receding. "How did you know how to make the shaking stop?"

"Experience."

"This has happened to you?" Except for the grumpiness, frequent sullen silences, and occasional angry outburst, Conall was one of the calmest people I'd ever met.

"Having people shoot at me when I have no magic with which to defend myself was terrifying. So yeah."

"'Was'?"

"Now I rely on Seth or one of the other air druids. And if I do get hurt, I'll rely on Duncan to heal me."

"Then why were you ever scared?" I asked. "They've been

there the whole time."

"It wasn't their magic that I didn't trust," Conall said quietly. "It was *them*. I've never been with anyone I could trust before."

"And what about me?"

"I hated your guts after Shitozaki stuck me in your training group, but even then I trusted you."

"How could you trust someone you hated?"

He rose and held out his hand. I took it and allowed him to pull me up, hoping my legs stayed steady.

"Because no matter what happened or who you were dealing with, you were always fair. You proved that the day you picked me to come with you, when I was certain you'd shove me off on Shitozaki."

I didn't know why I had chosen Conall to join my half of the Finns, but I'd been glad to have him at my back ever since the bullets had started flying and a whole city of marauders had begun howling for our blood.

"You went to Duncan and asked him to pull you back if the fire magic got out of control," he said. "You didn't ask me, but as a member of your pentacle, this is it. This is me pulling you back."

Of all people, he was the last one I had expected to rely on for this.

"Which one do you think I should give up?" I asked.

"You are a druid with a birthright of elemental magic given to you by the Shining Ones," he said. "Which one do *you* think you should give up?"

Chapter 22 – Surrendering the Sword

War is mainly a catalogue of blunders.
~ Winston Churchill ~

I burned the remains of the unknown number of enemies I'd killed. There wasn't much I could do about the blood dripping down the palisade wall, but I scorched it, too, for good measure. I stood looking at the char for several long minutes. Prior to this moment, I had never been in a hurry to burn the bodies before any of the other Finns could see them. The fact that I had felt it necessary to do so only reinforced the idea that I had a problem.

Maybe Conall was right. Maybe it *was* the sword.

We returned to the foremost part of the garrison, where four of the earth druids were finishing up filling in the rabbit holes and the narrow tunnel beneath the palisade. I pretended not to notice the looks the Finns gave me as I passed, which ranged from subtle glances and double-takes to outright stares.

"You're covered in blood," Conall murmured. "It's natural for them to be concerned."

"I'm still on my feet, so there's no reason to be."

No doubt the rest of the Finns would put my gory appearance together with Eian and Declan's report of my episode of shaking and come up with a near-death experience that had frightened me badly. That was just fine by me, and much more preferable to them questioning my leadership – or my sanity – after the butchery I'd just committed.

Duncan and Dermot were standing where we'd left them, the

earth druid standing guard over my sword. He considered me silently for a few moments before stepping back. His sword was loose in its sheath, while one of Dermot's water bags was uncorked. It should have bothered me that they were standing ready in case the murderous impulse returned. Instead, it was reassuring. I stood looking at the grey blade for a few moments, steeling myself for the possibility that touching it would affect me again. Logically, it was the fire that enthralled, and there should be no danger since I wasn't channeling any elemental magic, but I still hesitated.

"Want me to get it?" asked Conall.

I shook my head. "No. I don't want anyone else to touch it."

If indeed the grey blade was the problem, no one else needed to be contaminated by it. He nodded understanding, appearing relaxed as though nothing was amiss.

Nope, nothing going on in this pentacle. Just another day of Davis slaughtering dozen of people with an enchanted sword and losing control over his fire magic, ho hum.

Snatching up it up, I thrust it home in its sheath. Then I peace-tied it with the leather thongs that had been sewn onto the scabbard for that purpose. Duncan quirked an eyebrow at this, but Dermot quit fidgeting. Without saying anything more on the matter, I proceeded to check on the rest of the Finns.

Seth was overseeing a group of prisoners, which caught me by surprise. We'd never taken prisoners before.

"What's the situation?" I asked.

"They surrendered."

"And?" No one had ever attempted to surrender before.

"Were we supposed to kill them after they threw down their weapons?"

After watching me do that very thing, I was surprised he'd even ask. Maybe he'd been distracted, or perhaps the firestorm had obscured his view.

"Any injuries?"

"A few gunshot wounds, all quickly healed."

My conscience twitched, warring over keeping the sword and possibly hurting someone unintentionally, or giving it up and seeing someone get hurt when I might have prevented it.

"You can't be everywhere," Seth said, misreading my silence.

"I know what you promised my father, but our lives are in the hands of the Fates. If Atropos decides to cut the thread of one of our lives, there is nothing you can do about it."

"I don't believe in fate," I said. "And I have no idea what we should do with a bunch of prisoners." We couldn't take them with us, and I sure wasn't going to send them back to the 'Ville so they could try to take over the world again. Perhaps we could obtain information from them, but I doubted they would willingly answer questions.

"So what do think we should do with them?" I asked, observing the townspeople coming out of the buildings, timidly emerging from the shadows of oppression and into the light of renewed independence. While I'd never met any of them before, the various expressions they wore – fear, shock, disbelief, anger – had become all-too familiar.

"Why don't we let the people they've wronged dispense justice as they see fit?"

"Sounds fair."

* * *

Once the prisoners were locked away, we informed the folk that we'd recovered several children who claimed to be from Conway. Even after listing off their names, there were no tearful parents rejoicing to hear it. It was disheartening but not as bad as finding that *no one* wanted them.

"Where do you plan to go next?" asked one man.

"We're headed for Mayflower and Blue Hill after that."

"Mayflower was doing all right, last I heard. Don't bother going to Blue Hill, though. Ain't nothin' left."

Just like Watson, Bailey Lake, and Otto.

"What happened?"

"They refused to surrender," the man replied.

"That had to have taken a lot of guts," I said.

"Not that it did them any good," Conall said.

"They died free," said Wolfric. "That's worth something."

"Nothing's worth anything if you're dead," the man said. "I'll fight, but I'll surrender every time if it means a chance at life."

"Then you are destined to live life as a slave," Wolfric said.

"Not if there ain't no slave masters," the man retorted. He

390

turned back to me. "You boys got any plans for that?"

I fixed him with a steely look. "You're not willing to risk your life for your freedom, but you expect us to?"

"Ain't nobody here got magic like you boys do."

"It doesn't make us immortal."

He wilted and drew away.

We spent the rest of the afternoon cleaning up the mess and repairing most of the damage we had caused. What I had scorched or burned couldn't be fixed. The townspeople offered to let us stay in the raider barracks. The Finns gladly took advantage of their hospitality, for it was getting colder by the day. It was nice to sleep in warm beds, even if the blankets were itchy wool.

That night, I sought Rhiannon's counsel. As second-in-command, Seth came along as usual. So did Conall, presumably because of the Morrigan's enchanted sword.

"How much longer do we have until we can return to Ward?" I asked.

"Eighteen days, after today," the High Priestess replied. "We've gotten quite a bit accomplished in just a week and a half."

"If we continue at this rate, we'll have wiped out the rest of their garrisons and outposts before we have to return," Conall said.

"It's doable," Seth agreed. "If I remember correctly, there are only three more garrisons and a single outpost remaining."

"Let's just take it day by day and see how things go," I said.

"Speaking of seeing how things go," Rhiannon said, "did you happen to find out if anyone here is missing their children?"

"They don't want the children back," I said.

She stared at me incredulously. "Their parents didn't want them?"

Seth said, "No one came forward to say they were missing children. Perhaps all their parents were murdered."

"No matter whose kids they are, they're the next generation," I said. "You'd think *somebody* would want them, even if only to preserve the future of their village."

"It may be that they have suffered so much that they don't feel capable of taking on that responsibility," Rhiannon mused. "We don't know the horrors these people have experienced."

"What are we going to do with them, then?"

She smiled. "We'll adopt them, of course."

"Even though they aren't witches?"

"Anyone can learn the Craft, Davis," she replied, lips quirking with amusement. "Even you."

"I think my plate's kinda full right now," I said, and she laughed softly. "Speaking of full, do you remember that favor I asked of you?"

"Regarding your magic? Yes, I do."

"It looks like this might be part of it," I said, holding out the sword in its scabbard, along with the broad belt upon which it was hung. "I need you to keep this for me and not give it back until Conall says it's safe to do so."

"Or until there is some cataclysmic disaster where we're all going to die unless he uses it," Conall added.

"The way things are going, that seems more likely than not," Seth said drily.

The High Priestess gave Conall a good, long look with her penetrating grey gaze before turning her attention back to me.

"Why give it to me?"

"Because you're used to handling a lot of power and I'm not. I'm struggling to control my own magic, and the addition of an enchanted sword is getting to be too much." I glanced at Seth. "Sorry, I should have mentioned it to you before now."

"I saw what happened today," he replied. "But I don't understand why you think the sword has anything to do with it."

Rhiannon took the scabbard but did not touch the hilt of the grey blade. "I sense enchantment within the sword, but it is not malevolent. Why do you think the sword is dangerous?"

Conall said, "Davis never lost control of his magic before the Morrigan showed up and enchanted his sword."

"The Morrigan." The High Priestess repeated. "When did she appear to you, Davis?"

"At Samhain." I told her the whole story, detailing my visit from the goddess.

"Remarkable," she said. "I am curious... How did you find our lady goddess?"

"Powerful. Beautiful. Cunning. Desirable. Terrifying."

"Everything a goddess should be," Rhiannon said with a satisfied air. "Having wondered why she did not appear at my ritual, I am glad to hear this story."

"You summoned the Morrigan at Samhain?" I said.

"I called upon the Goddess in the aspect of the Battle Queen for strength and protection," Rhiannon corrected. "One does not summon a goddess as though she were a mere demon or spirit."

"Honestly, I'd rather not deal with demons, spirits, *or* gods."

"Then what is the point of reciprocity?" she asked, looking just a little bit sly.

The give-and-take between druids and gods was expressed in the idea of reciprocity. We performed ritual and gave offerings, not only to honor the Shining Ones but also to establish and maintain a relationship in which we could approach them for aid.

"You have me there," I admitted.

Seth said, "Epicurus wrote that it is folly for a man to pray to the gods for something that he has the power to obtain by himself."

"That," I said. I could always count on his logic and knowledge of Greek philosophy.

"Agreed," said Conall. "Being under the influence of a death goddess has been detrimental. That's why he needs to give it up."

"It wasn't so 'detrimental' during the battle to take down the Faulkner garrison," Seth remarked.

It hadn't been a detriment in Watson, either, when the Morrigan brought me back to life. Remembering that made me reconsider giving up the grey blade, but I decided the fire shield would be enough to protect me.

"The Morrigan is not a death goddess," Rhiannon said. "She is an ancient Celtic goddess of war who is said to value cleverness, courage, and the will to win. There are many old tales relating how she rejoices in bloodshed, frequently inciting warriors and armies to valiant attack."

Conall frowned. "So what you're saying is that she likes to stir shit up."

"I suppose that is one way of looking at it."

"Then it stands to reason that the enchantment placed on Davis' sword might be making him go berserk."

She frowned. "Literally, or figuratively?"

"Literally," Conall said. "It happened today."

"What actually happened?"

"I killed a lot of people," I said. "And then I almost killed

393

Duncan."

"I find it difficult to believe that you would intentionally harm a friend."

"He was still *berserkergang*," Conall inserted helpfully.

"I see." Her grey eyes sought mine. "And what brought you out of it?"

"Dermot stopped me before I could do any serious harm."

"*Dermot* stopped you?"

Conall said, "The kid may not look like much, but he thinks on his feet and is a master of his element."

"And what if the Morrigan does not appreciate Davis rejecting her gift?" asked the High Priestess.

"If she doesn't like it, she can come back and tell him," he said, unmoved by the possibility.

"While I disagree with Conall about the sword, I see no harm in giving it up for a while," Seth said. "After all, we've already been given all the help we need from the gods – elemental magic."

"Speak for yourself," said Conall, but there was no rancor in his voice.

"Now that you mention it, I have given some thought to your situation, Conall, and that of the other altered ones," Rhiannon said. "I am not so certain that magic is forever beyond your reach."

"I assure you it is," he replied. "My mother severed the conduit to my magic as completely as if she had cut my throat."

"You can channel a little," said Seth.

"Barely a trickle," Conall said with a trace of bitterness. "It would be better to have none at all than just a taste."

Rhiannon laid her hand on his. "No matter who we are or how powerful we might be, in the end, we are still only human. Is your mother a deity, that she can deny the will of the Lord and Lady? No."

"And yet the gods have never seen fit to heal my spirit."

"Have you asked?"

He was silent for several seconds.

"No."

"Why not?"

"Why should I have to ask for that which is rightfully mine?"

"You shouldn't," she said. "But consider this: if you woke up tomorrow morning to find that your horse had been stolen and you lacked the means of getting it back yourself, what would you do?"

"I would ask Ahearn to lend me one of his, and then I'd ask my pentacle to ride with me to get it back."

"Exactly." She smiled. "You were given a gift by the gods, Conall, and it was stolen from you. It only makes sense to ask for their help in seeing it returned to you, especially since they are the ones who gave it to you in the first place."

"I'll think about it." He considered her words a moment, then turned to me. "Are you going to leave it with her, or not?"

The sheathed grey blade had somehow found its way back into my hands. "If she'll have it."

"While I agree with Seth that and do not think the sword is the source of your problem, I will keep it for you until Conall gives me leave to return it..." Her grey eyes glittered with mischief. "...or until Angie shows up."

"Are you expecting her?" Seth's questioning gaze went first to Rhiannon, then to me.

"I sent a fetch to find her," I admitted. "Hopefully, it will lead her to me."

"Davis, you are a *druid*," the air elementalist scolded. "It is dangerous for you to send a spirit animal, even to find your chosen."

"I know. Duncan told me." The knowledge that the earth druid was aware seemed to mollify him some. In the eyes of the Finns, Duncan Everlight could do no wrong.

Conall frowned. "What does the arrival of his chosen have to do with whether or not he possesses an enchanted sword that he can't control?"

"Nothing," she replied. "But it has everything to do with pulling him back, as you call it. I know in my heart of hearts that there is no one in all the world who can do that for Davis like she can."

* * *

We skirted Lake Conway all the way to the next town, and no one complained about the extra miles of riding that were required. Every member of my war band had developed a healthy appreciation for what a water elementalist could do in a fight, even Wolfric, so we were careful to stick close to water whenever possible. According to the map obtained in Faulkner, Mayflower was a town with land holdings about the size of Conway's, but whose town center was protected on an island connected to the mainland by two drawbridges. We stopped on the southeastern side of the lake, and I took a small group on foot through the trees to a spot where we could see the eastern part of the island and its drawbridge. Staying low to the ground and using reeds for cover, we quietly observed the far shore and the town that inhabited it.

The drawbridge was up and from the faded scorch marks on its underside, it appeared to have been that way for quite some time. Makeshift walls had been put up on each side. Upon further inspection with the spyglass, I discovered them to be made up of concrete blocks, barbed wire, plywood, and anything else the beleaguered residents had on hand when the bandits attacked.

The Republic forces had been unsuccessful in gaining access to island town, so they had laid siege. At least three raid groups were camped on the point of land leading to the east bridge, and I was willing to wager that the other side had as many or more. The map showed that the western shore was a much larger land mass unbroken by water.

"They're in a bad situation," Seth said when I handed him the spyglass. "There's nowhere on that island that a rifle round can't reach." He passed the spyglass to Rhiannon.

"The only things protecting them are the houses and the trees," she said.

"They also can't dig very deep because the water table is too high," Duncan said.

"With that many trees, I doubt they've ever farmed the island," Siorus put in.

"Probably can't fish, either," said Dermot. "Unless they're doing it in the dark. Even then, they'd have to be *real* quiet."

Madoc nodded. "They'll starve to death if they didn't have enough food put up before the siege."

"If we attack one force, the other will be on us in no time," said Conall, who had come to the same conclusion I had. "We'd be crushed in the middle."

"Not if they can't get to us," I said.

"What are you going to do?" Wolfric said. "Build a wall?"

"Give me that spyglass again?" I said, taking it from Rhiannon and examining the small army of raiders from the 'Ville holding Mayflower under siege. If we attacked that eastern force, we could raise a wall behind us to keep the western force from flanking us. It was only a temporary solution, for as soon as we finished with the first group, we'd have to turn right around and deal with the second. However, if we put up a wall preventing the eastern raid groups from leaving, and then assaulted the western force, we could take them out one at a time. I outlined my idea to the others.

Ahearn frowned. "That peninsula has got to be almost a quarter-mile across. Can you raise a wall that long in such a short amount of time?"

"A quarter mile is four hundred yards, give or take a few," I said. "We'd be spaced out about every fifty yards."

"That's closer than we were on Samhain." Duncan said.

Siorus nodded. "We can do it."

"While under fire?" Madoc gave his chosen a skeptical look.

Conall said, "The air elementalists can shield until then."

"That's a big shield," I said.

He shrugged. "It doesn't have to be continuous. But if you're worried about it, we can have the water and spirit elementalists keep them occupied."

"I could bring out the *Dobhar-chú*." Dermot grinned, and it wasn't at all nice. "Those assholes will forget all about that wall."

"That's not a bad idea," I said. "Be sure and teach that to the others."

"I told them about it, but they've already come up with their own water monsters." He grinned.

"Gods of Olympus," Seth muttered under his breath.

"Of course, the best thing to do would be to raise the wall in the middle of the night," said Conall. "We'll catch the eastern force off-guard without alerting the western force to our presence."

If there was anything I admired, it was someone thinking outside the box. The Norseman might not have had much magic of his own, but he certainly knew how to utilize the various elements of others.

"After the wall is up and you leave to attack the western force, what's to keep the ones over here from knocking down your dirt wall?" Ahearn asked.

"We can reinforce it with rocks," Duncan said.

Conall said, "Well, you can either reinforce it with rocks, or Davis can melt a bunch of rocks and coat the wall with them."

"Then it'll be rock solid," Dermot said, smirking at his own pun. The others groaned quietly.

"What's to keep them riding through the shallows to get around the wall?" Seth asked.

"My people can handle that," Rhiannon said. "We should be able to keep them pinned down with rifles and bows."

"Be sure to use the arrows in the dark," said Dermot. "That'll make it scarier."

Conall looked at him. "I don't think there's anything scarier than you. Unless we're talking about Davis and his Magical Sword of Death and Destruction, of course."

"Speaking of, do you think it will be needed?" Rhiannon asked.

"No," I answered before anyone else could speak. "Any other ideas or questions?" There were none. "Let's mount up and move on a little further until we're at the edge of the peninsula. Then we'll rest up until dark."

The moon was nearly full, but the weather had been cloudy for days. With any luck, our movements would be hidden in darkness, with just enough light to see by. As we made our way back to the main body of our war band – and our horses – Conall and Wolfric fell into step beside me.

"You *are* going to use fire, aren't you?" Conall asked.

"I'll have to if I'm going to melt rocks."

"You know what I mean."

"I think I'm going to stick with earth for now."

"Know what I think about that?"

"I can guess."

"It's enough that you've given up the sword," he said.

"What if it isn't?"

"Then I'll sic Dermot and his *Dobhar-chú* on you."

"Gods, anything but that."

"Seriously, though," he said. "We're going to need that elemental fire." He paused. "If it makes you feel better, we can tell everybody to back off if you start to fling fire like Surtr with his flaming sword."

Except I wouldn't have a sword.

Wolfric rolled his eyes. "Davis is powerful, but I hardly think his magic is great enough to bring about Ragnarok."

"What's a Ragnarok?" I asked. As much time as I had spent around Wolfric and Conall, one would think I'd have learned more about the Norse hearth culture.

"Ragnarok is the end of the world," said Conall.

"More like the end of the cosmos," corrected Wolfric. "The literal translation is 'Doom of the Gods'. It is the time when the people in Midgard – the realm where we are – forget their traditions, refuse to recognize their bonds of kinship, and devolve into chaos."

"The same thing happens in the realms of the gods," Conall continued. "Or so the stories tell."

Wolfric looked annoyed at the interruption. "Ragnarok is heralded by three consecutive winters without any summer at all, followed by The Great Winter, a long season of dark and cold."

It sounded like the Fracture after the years of storms and hurricanes, when thousands of volcanic eruptions had filled the sky with so much ash that there had been no sun for years on end.

"To make a long story short," Conall said, "Loki and his son Fenrir – who is a gigantic wolf – lead an army of frost giants into Asgard, the home of the gods, and Fenrir eats everybody and everything. Then the giant Surtr comes along after everyone is dead and sweeps his flaming sword over the earth, burning all of it until nothing remains but a fiery inferno. Then everything sinks into the sea."

"Oh," I said, finally getting the reference.

"It's not as bad as Conall makes it out to be," said Wolfric. "It's a cyclical ending. The gods return, and the world is reborn again."

"It sounds pretty bad for the people who get eaten by the wolf," I said.

Wolfric shrugged. "The point I am trying to make is that even with elemental fire and an enchanted sword, you are not capable of bringing about Ragnarok."

"Quakes, I should hope not!"

We rejoined the rest of our group, rode south for another hour, and picked a campsite. Then, while everyone else was setting up camp, I took the other earth elementalists on a little hike to find some rocks.

* * *

Luckily for us, the enemy had pitched their tents on the far side of the peninsula, close to the drawbridge. That meant we could trap them on a relatively narrow spot of land, and so we decided to carry out our plan in stages. The three water druids went ahead of everyone else, as only someone possessed of elemental water could move in it soundlessly. I was concerned that they would get hypothermia or frostbite, but each of the three druids hardened a small scoop of water – similar to Dermot's turtle shell shield – and stepped out onto the lake.

Mohinder and Galen took the southern and western points of the peninsula. Having newly acquired the full complement of elemental magic possessed by a druid, Nêreus headed for the north, waving farewell as he did. Dermot, forced to remain on land to preserve his limited supply of magic, frowned as they departed. I put a hand on the water elementalist's shoulder and squeezed lightly to say I understood. Four more years was a long time to have to wait for full druid magic.

In the dead of night, we eight druids slowly raised a giant wall composed of soil, mud, and clay, while the Finns with elemental air created an invisible wall that stretched across the peninsula. The barrier acted to dampen sound as well as to protect us, and the enemy never stirred. It worked so well that we decided to expand the wall everywhere that land touched the water, completely encircling the eastern force from the 'Ville.

This required us to link up, with four earth druids on each side of the peninsula, magnifying our magic so that we could extend our elemental ability farther. There was no air shield between the wall and our adversaries, so we threw caution to the wind and jerked the wall up and into place before any of them had a chance to react. We could hear shouts of alarm as the wall slid up to its final height of approximately twenty feet. Concerned that the sound might carry across the water, Skylar capped the wall with an air dome.

There was nothing we could do about the grinding noise caused by a ton of rocks rapidly rolling across the ground, but Halldor had the brilliant idea of masking it by creating a minor temblor. Earthquakes had occurred less frequently in the last fifty years, with big ones occurring once or twice a decade. Minor ones shook the world several times a year. We herded rocks ranging in size from pebbles to three-foot diameter boulders until they lay piled up at the base of the wall.

I began melting them by channeling pure fire, sweeping it back and forth across the pile until the rocks began to glow with a deep orange light.

"That's not fast enough," said Duncan, watching me work with his hands tucked into opposite sleeves.

Conall sighed. "Stop dicking around and just get it done."

"He's right," said Seth. "If you lose control, we'll handle it."

Releasing the twin flamethrowers, as I liked to call them, I went to the wall, kicked off my boots and pulled off my socks. The ground leeched the warmth from my feet almost instantly, but they wouldn't be cold for much longer. I closed my eyes and concentrated, feeling a oneness with the earth that calmed my fears. The rocks glowed with a flare of intense, yellow-white light before melting into velvety orange that swam up the side of the wall, coating it from bottom to top. Placing my hands into the lava for greater communication with it, I commanded it to spread laterally, until the entire outside of the wall was covered with a three-inch-thick layer of molten rock.

"Very nice," said Conall, when I returned to where I'd left my boots.

"What if they have ladders?" asked Wolfric. "Or ropes?"

"I don't think anybody will be touching that for a while," said Seth.

"It'll cool eventually, though," Wolfric pressed. "What then?"

"Same plan as before," I said. "Ruth, Maeve, and the witches will keep them pinned down with rifles and bows."

"I'm kind of disappointed," Gale said when he, Mohinder, and Nêreus returned. "We didn't get to do anything."

"Oh, I wouldn't be too disappointed, if I were you," said Dermot.

"Why?"

The water elementalist pointed upward. "The clouds are orange. And so is that great big, glowing wall."

"Oh, *quakes*," I groaned, feeling like an idiot.

The light of a single candle could be seen a mile away on a pitch-dark night. I knew this. Even on a night like tonight, when the moon was nearing full, fire could be seen at a distance. I couldn't account for what had made me fail to take this into consideration, except that I'd become accustomed to magic compensating for any strategic failings I might have. Our plan had been foolproof up until that point. Somehow, not one of us had considered the fact that the wall of radiant orange would be clearly visible to our enemies on Mayflower's western shore.

"Oops," said Galen.

"Galen, run tell everybody I said to mount up and get ready to fight," I said. "Wolfric, I'd like you to ride with Halldor tonight if you don't mind." Halldor's pentacle had three dualists, but only one was a druid – Skylar. He and Ciaran would have their hands full shielding with air, so their pentacle needed another elementalist capable of attacking at range besides Barak. The fire elementalist gave me a sharp nod and took off after Galen.

"We should take cover in the forest so they'll be between us and that lava-covered wall when they come to check it out."

"We'd better move fast," I said, whistling for Steel. "They'll be coming for us before too long."

Dermot grinned. "Might as well give them a warm reception."

That it would be warm, I had no doubt.

Chapter 23 – The Heart of Prometheus

The tree of liberty must be refreshed from time to time
with the blood of patriots and tyrants.
It is its natural manure.
~ Thomas Jefferson ~

Riding fast down the main road, we retreated southeast to a heavily forested area at the base of the peninsula. An assortment of witches and Finns lay prone in the underbrush, waiting and watching for enemy activity. Periodically I sent a burst of heat into the ground beneath us to keep hypothermia at bay, but also to prevent any noise from shivering or chattering teeth. A mere quarter of an hour later, a rider galloped past, heading the way we'd just come.

"Scout," said Seth in a low tone. I nodded.

"Good thing it's dark," Ruth murmured. "He'd have seen our tracks, otherwise."

"Should we stop him?" asked Yiorgos.

"No point," I said. "They already know we're here."

A few minutes later the scout passed us again, doubtless to inform the western siege army of the wall surrounding their brethren to the east.

"What now?" asked Martin.

"Now we wait for the main body of their forces to show up."

"And then?"

"Then we cut them off and smash them against the lava wall," Warwick said. "Easy peasy."

"Nothing is ever that easy," said Maeve.

"Have a little faith," Ingvar chided. "Davis hasn't led us astray yet."

"If I lacked faith in him, I wouldn't be here," she retorted.

"Easy now," said Halldor. "We're all in this together."

"Quite so," said Rhiannon. "In fact, there is so much togetherness right now that we're at risk of being discovered by the enemy."

"They're coming!" whispered Siorus. "Feel it?"

Stretching out with my senses, I detected the presence of about a hundred people and horses half a mile away. They were practically on top of us.

"Everyone move back," I said. "*Silently.*"

One by one the earth druids returned to their pentacles. The witches faded away without a sound, followed by Seth. Only Duncan and Ruth remained.

"What is it?"

"Just wonderin' why Rhiannon has your sword," Ruth said.

Neither of them was going to move until I did, so I began edging backward through the brush. "It's complicated."

"You ain't plannin' on holdin' back, are ya?"

"Magic is enough," I said. "Swords are no use against guns."

"That ain't what I heard. I heard you went through a hundred bandits all by yourself with that sword."

"I could have done that with fire magic alone. It's the fire that shields me from bullets."

"I know. Seen you do it before." She sniffed. "Just wanted to make sure you'll use the sword if the need arises."

"If the situation is dire, yes."

Ruth regarded me with an inscrutable expression. "Let's not wait quite that long," she said and rejoined the witches.

"How many counselors does one man need, I wonder?" murmured Duncan.

"Not this many, I'm sure."

"Especially when not one of them mentioned the light that would be cast by coating the wall in lava," he said. "Interesting that Conall did not seem to take that into account."

"Are you saying he did and chose not to mention it?"

"He *has* been the biggest proponent of eradicating the 'Ville."

I considered the possibility and decided it didn't matter. Everyone's magic was at full strength, and no one seemed particularly tired. It might be a good thing to have this battle tonight. We might even have the island town liberated by the time the sun came up.

Duncan and I kept tabs on the approaching force from the Republic of Jackson, which I couldn't help but think of as an army. It wasn't its size, for there were only about a hundred people and horses, but the fact that they were moving in formation made me perceive it differently. Instead of spreading ourselves thin across the peninsula to try and contain the Republic forces, I decided to place the pentacles in strategic locations with witches to assist with magic, longbows, or firearms. Ahearn, James Reece, Toby, Weylin, and Riordan were to stay behind with the horses and give warning if any bandits approached from the rear.

Once the enemy reinforcements had passed, I split the war band in half, sending three pentacles to the southern side of the road. Siorus' and Ingvar's pentacles moved to the edge of the lake, with Shannon and Heath to provide cover fire for Mohinder and Nêreus with their bows. Martin's pentacle was next, where Galen could access the large pond beside the road. It was also accessible by Phelan, who was capable of defending himself with air or unleashing damaging spirit or elemental water as necessary. Ruth and Maeve accompanied them for added protection.

My own pentacle would stand across the road from Martin, at the center of the peninsula, which was sure to be the most dangerous area. Rhiannon and Cinna were with us because they were powerful magic users and expert archers. Both women could take care of themselves in the event that I had to raise a ruckus to garner the enemy's attention. Dermot was a small distance back, by to Warwick's pentacle, which was to the left and behind mine. That put the water elementalist near the small pond that water/spirit druid Ridley and air/water druid Ishkur would be using.

Halldor would be stationed farther away, north of Warwick's position, alongside the stream that fed into Dermot's pond. His pentacle stood about three hundred yards from Siorus', more or less directly across the peninsula, with Tiernan's bow and

Wolfric's elemental fire to cover them.

Since Yiorgos had three dualists who could attack at range with spirit – Westley, Solon, and Wyatt – he took the position farthest north, close to an inlet of the lake. If the trapped enemy broke through the wall at our backs, it was an area guaranteed to see some heavy fighting, so I had Bébhinn, Ianna, and Rowena accompany them. Each of the Weird Sisters was skilled with water and spirit, and Rowena could put an arrow through a rabbit's eye at fifty paces.

Even with the strategic placement of pentacles, a third of the area was still undefended. To keep the Republic forces from flanking us, Halldor, Warwick, and Yiorgos were responsible for keeping that area racked with shockwaves and impassible by either man or beast. Duncan would assist as necessary, but he would be most useful helping me, Siorus, Ingvar, and Martin do the kind of earthmoving that would keep the enemy pressed against the smoldering wall imprisoning their allies. There, they would be in easy reach by bow, rifle, or elemental magic.

Moving stealthily, we came upon the restless army, its soldiers muttering to one another about the mysterious glowing wall. I signaled Yiorgos, Halldor, and Warwick to move into position, and shortly thereafter the earth on the northern shore of the peninsula began to roll and buck. There were cries of *"Earthquake!"* from the bandits, which covered any noise the rest of my war band might have made as they moved into position. Shouted into silence by their commanders, the soldiers fell into a semblance of order.

Once everyone was in position, I gave the signal to attack – a small fireball cast high into the air that exploded in an umbrella of sparks that showered down upon the siege army. Looking up in puzzlement, the enemy soldiers watched the glimmering embers drift down from the sky. When they reached head-high from the ground, each glowing cinder violently exploded, flaring with brilliant white light into a ten-foot blast radius that blinded men and sent frightened horses into a panic.

Phelan and Wolfric launched a volley of spirit orbs and fireballs into the crowd of confused bandits, causing yet more pandemonium. Horses bucked and reared, throwing their riders and running away in fear. Siorus, Ingvar, and Martin linked their magics and sent a surge through the earth that knocked men off their feet and drove the enemy horses to their knees. More raiders were unhorsed as their panicked mounts strove to escape the terrifying environment. We allowed the horses safe passage back down the main road, where Ahearn and James Reece could round them up.

In spite of the rolling and rocking ground beneath their feet, the Republic forces began to fight back. The air elementalists shielded against the gunfire, mostly to guard against stray bullets, for the enemy was silhouetted against the still-smouldering lava covering the earthen wall, while we were shrouded in relative darkness. There was far more running and screaming than retaliatory fire, especially after the water druids brought their magic into play.

The head of a giant snake emerged from the gloom beyond the land, followed by eight others. Nêreus had created a *hydra*, the scales on its nine heads glittering in the moonlight as they undulated over the battlefield in search of prey. The first head, opening its mouth wide and revealing a pair of massive fangs, plunged into the bandit army. The other heads followed in swift strikes, gulping down men and horses alike. I had no idea where they went inside the giant water monster, but one thing was clear – they weren't coming back.

Shortly after the appearance of the hydra, a great lumbering beast arose from the lake. Using its articulated fins to drag its scaly, fish-shaped body across the western part of the peninsula, Mohinder's *Makara* lowered its elephantine head and swept its trunk from side to side, violently smashing anyone or anything in reach into the still-scorching wall that enclosed the eastern siege force.

Compared to the other monsters, Galen's *Watcher in the Water* was a warm, familiar companion. Its sucker-covered tentacles scooped up the screaming Republic soldiers, shoving them down into its toothy maw or flinging them away to plunge into the depths of the dark lake. As the *Watcher* itself was in a small pond beside the road, sometimes they missed the lake. A couple of enemies sailed over the raised drawbridge and crashed down on the island.

Our surprise attack was going even better than I had expected – until a *BOOM* sounded from inside the containment area. The eastern force, it seemed, was not going to take this insult lying down.

"What was *that*?" Phelan yelled at me, flinging lightning bolts at any enemies the sea monsters missed.

"Cannon!" I shouted back. "They're trying to break the wall down!"

"Can't you stop them?"

While the outside of the wall had been covered in lava, it still hadn't cooled sufficiently to harden into igneous rock. Therefore, the enemy within was perfectly capable of blowing a hole in it with cannons or other types of explosives – unless I reinforced it with earth magic. I dropped to one knee, both hands making contact with the earth. First I drew all the heat from the lava, the rapid cooling changing it to a thick layer of obsidian. Next, I reached out to the damaged part of the wall, scooped up the piles of dirt that had been blown out of it, and packed them back in where they belonged. It wouldn't stop them from trying again, but they could only continue as long as they had cannonballs and gunpowder. With a Well of magic within me that would never run dry, I could continue forever, at least in theory. In reality, I would have to sleep and eat, but there were other earth druids who could spell me, so the bandits had no hope of breaking free while we were attending to the wall.

"Davis! *Davis!*"

It was Weylin. The witch galloped toward us, shouting my name and pointing behind him. The *crack* of multiple rifle reports sounded, and he jerked, back arching and arms flying outward. His horse screamed, falling to its knees and flipping forward onto its back, crushing the witch.

"*Weylin!*" Rhiannon screamed, running to him. "*No!*"

Beyond the bodies of the fallen witch and his horse, the hoofbeats of hundreds more horses could be heard but were as yet unseen. I knelt to touch the earth, horrified to find that there were three hundred horses approaching our rear. We were caught between two powerful armies with enough firepower to kill each of us a hundred times over.

"We're being flanked!" I shouted. "Finish this *now!*"

Accompanied by the thunder of shotguns, the barrage of spirit orbs, lightning, and fireballs increased in a dramatic cascade, but I was afraid it still wouldn't be enough. Leaving my pentacle and sprinting toward the wall, I laid down a wide swath of fire. Arms extended before me and fingers spread wide, I created an inferno so hot that it turned flesh to char in seconds, exploded ammunition inside of guns, and even turned the obsidian back to lava on a small area of the wall. Fighting to keep from losing myself in the flames that had destroyed the first division, I turned to take stock of the situation.

Siorus was frantically tending to Madoc, who had been caught in the volley of gunfire that had taken Weylin down. The gunman lay motionless in the dry, brittle grass. Fenris laid about with lightning bolts, and Eian shielded them all from the enemy gunfire coming from the rear. Shannon had somehow witnessed Weylin's fall amidst the turmoil and was firing arrow after arrow at the now-visible flanking army, offering what protection she could to Rhiannon as she crouched over his inert body. Mohinder had pulled the *Makara* back into the water and was running on the shoreline beside with the apparent intention of sending it into this new group of enemies. Noticing his change of direction, the pentacles commanded by Ingvar and Martin made an about-face and began a new barrage of spirit bolts and orbs. Phelan was at the fore, channeling chain lightning that shocked the foremost riders and their mounts into convulsions until they fell down dead. Behind him, Ruth and Maeve fired round after round into the oncoming horde.

Both Halldor and Warwick had taken steps to move their own people to face this new threat. Rather than stopping their earthquakes on the northern shore, the seismic activity increased and spread. The shock waves traveled southward along the peninsula, restricting the Republic forces to fighting on a narrower front. Nêreus's gargantuan hydra dove into the lake and came up beside the siege army, each of its fanged jaws opening wide before descending on them like an angry nest of snakes. Wolfric darted ahead, not only throwing fireballs but also spraying the enemy with a flamethrower born from his palms. Tiernan was close behind, picking off bandits one by one with his bow.

Closest to the host of raiders, Ridley held a water whip charged with flickering spirit, laying about with a ferocity that I'd never seen before. Beside him, Ishkur channeled long ropes of elemental water, lassoing bandits out of their saddles while Narinder protected them all with an air shield. Ianna stood behind Narinder with a hand upon his shoulder, somehow bolstering his magic with her own. Bébhinn and Rowena crouched over Rob, who was clutching his bleeding thigh and grimacing against the pain.

Dermot's deadly pack of *Dobhar-chú* streaked by me in a silvery flash and slipped like eels through the front ranks of marauders, and in moments screams and commotion erupted from the middle ranks, evidence of how deadly and terrifying they were. The water elementalist was standing in the pond with a snarl on his face, while Cinna fed her own magical energy into him so he could channel magic without restraint. Beside her, Conall slam-fired his Benelli at anything that even looked like it might be thinking of attacking them.

Seth had kept me covered while I was incinerating the remaining members of the first army we had encountered but was now protecting Duncan as he attended to Chester. The gunman was screaming and thrashing on the ground with blood spraying from one of his arms.

The situation wasn't dire, but it soon would be. I raised my fire shield and sent a tremor through the earth that made the enemy horses read and then sprinted for the battlefront. In spite of everything we threw at them, the Republic forces still kept coming. They screamed and died under a shower of fireballs and a blast of channeled fire, but inexorably they pushed onward. Rhiannon would be trampled if she didn't get out of the way.

An icy chill blew across the back of my neck, its temperature colder than any ever experienced on the mortal plane. The sounds of battle faded from my hearing as the High Priestess rose, standing before the oncoming legion with her head held high. Her appearance had changed, flickering so that my eyes were continually deceived. At times her clothing was of leather and wool; at others mail, fur, and cold grey steel that absorbed all light. Her hair was red but looked black as midnight in the darkness, and her face changed from a woman in her late thirties to the agelessness of a goddess. With queenly poise, she turned her back on the approaching army as though they were insignificant and unworthy of her attention. Her eyes found mine, and I saw it was the Morrigan, possessed of Rhiannon's body.

I dropped to one knee, bowing my head, and a hail of bullets whistled over my head. When I raised my gaze to hers, the Queen of Battle smiled with knowing delight. The fire within me begin to rise, and I struggled against it as it burned to erupt, to destroy, to *annihilate*. The Morrigan/Rhiannon drew my sword, raising it high, and I knew I was lost.

"Rise, my champion!" Her ruby lips quirked upward in a wicked, eager smile. Cutting through the air with the enchanted sword, she pointed toward the oncoming threat. All hesitation and doubt were carried away by the turbulent rush of pure, incandescent power that washed over me.

"Slay them."

At her command, I started for the enemy, paying no heed to the way they urged their horses forward to grind me down under their hooves. Their bullets melted, tossed aside like so much useless slag. With the fire shield glowing ever brighter, changing from orange to golden yellow, I channeled elemental fire into the enemy ranks, not caring whether it was men or animals that that were slain.

Conall's yelling and swearing for the others to get back faded into the background along with the roar of guns and the screams of the injured and dying as the power carried me away on a surging wave of darkness and flame. Streams of fire erupted from my hands, creating twin firewalls that cut between the army and my people. The hold I'd so carefully kept upon my element was swept away in the inferno that surrounded me. As I strode forward, invincible and unconquerable, bright orange elemental fire cut a swath of blazing destruction through the Republic forces as easily as the grey blade cut through flesh, and the whole world was engulfed in glorious, beautiful flame. They tried to run from the holocaust, but elemental earth brought them back, their bodies tumbling helplessly over each other as the last of them were burned and brutally crushed beneath rough waves of dirt and rock.

The touch of earth brought me back to myself, the wildfire within me sated by the lives upon which it had fed. By the glow of soft moonlight and burning embers, I took in the ruined landscape, blackened and charred from one side of the peninsula to the other. Mesmerized by the flames, I had traversed its entire length, burning an entire forest to the ground. Not one tree, bush, or blade of grass had survived. Looking back, I could see the still-hot section of the obsidian-coated wall that imprisoned the eastern siege force, still glowing like a furnace.

Turning in a slow circle, I surveyed the damage. Charcoal crunched under my feet. Puddles of molten rock were scattered here and there; steam rose from them into the cold night air. I didn't know whether to move forward and look for more enemies, go back and check on my friends, or just abandon them all and run away. There was nothing I could do for the ones I'd left behind. If they were alive, they'd be fine. If they'd been injured, they were either healed or dead of their wounds. The dead would stay dead, gone to join their ancestors.

The sound of a lone horse approaching pulled me from my reverie of despair, and I turned to face this new threat. Gentle moonlight shining on his dark grey coat, Steel stopped and nickered. Pulling the heat out of the ground beneath his feet, I approached and found find him still tacked up. Counting that as a sign from the gods, I patted his neck and swung into the saddle. Most of my gear was missing, except for the small bag that attached to the saddle horn, the one that contained a day's worth of rations. I counted that as a sign from the gods, too.

There was no going back, and no running away. I couldn't help those who'd died, but I could make damned sure nobody else did.

A job worth doing is worth doing well, my father would have said.

It probably wouldn't even take very long.

Turning the grulla stallion to face southwest, I headed for the western bridge of Mayflower and the enemy that was sure to be there.

Cloaked in shadows, I rubbed Steel's neck to keep him quiet while I studied the Republic forces left behind to keep the western bridge of Mayflower under siege. This rear echelon was fully three hundred strong if I was reading the earth right, divided into six camps that I estimated to be groups of fifty each.

It was a shock to see so many. Why had the Republic of Jackson committed close to a thousand troops to taking one small island town? Maybe they were making an example of Mayflower, but you'd think that the destruction of Otto, Bailey Lake, and Blue Hill would have been enough. Then again, news didn't travel very far or fast in a war zone, so maybe they wanted Mayflower for some other reason.

It didn't really matter. They weren't getting *this* town.

There was no one around who might be accidentally hurt, so it was an opportune moment to find out just how much fire I could funnel from the Shining Ones. Leaving Steel in a safe place, I hiked the last furlong and attacked the closest of the six campsites, hurling fireballs and igniting their tents. Ignoring the soldiers' shouts of alarm, I sent lines of fire zigzagging through the camp and launched more fireballs until all the tents were on fire.

While the enemy was distracted by the rapidly spreading blaze, I walked around their camp, encircling them in a wall of flame, and then ignited my fire shield. Captivated by its radiant luster, I was amazed that the wild swirl of flames madly spinning about my body actually protected me, for there were large gaps that contained only flickers and sparks.

The whirling, yellow-orange sphere attracted a roaring barrage of fire that sounded like it had been produced by a hundred guns. It probably *was* that many, for instead of being flung away, the melted droplets of bullets spattered my arms, face, and chest. None of it mattered, for nothing born of earth and flame could harm me.

As the last vestiges of control slipped from my grasp, elemental fire leapt forward, ready and eager to devour everything in sight. The bodies of men and women went up like torches, flaring brightly in the instant before each figure's tiny amount of energy was spent. The tents bloomed upward in a burst of pure, radiant light until the entire camp was resplendent with fire.

Captivated, I stood in the center of the inferno, where now only dancing flames lived, gracefully turning pirouettes and slow spirals with passion and fervor. A salamander ran over my boot, trailing sparks as it scurried about with its brethren, their sinuous bodies leaving intricate tracings of Celtic knotwork in their wake. Dragons winged overhead, borne aloft by rising thermals. I lay down in the lake of fire, looking up at them the same way that children gazed at clouds. The drakes departed and replaced by red-gold phoenixes soaring around the faces of the gods, Brighid and

Dagda and Lugh and the Morrigan. They gazed benevolently from above, sculpted of living fire and smiling in approval, larger than life as only gods could be. There was no sound but that of the roaring blaze, nothing to see but the spreading inferno, nothing to feel but the white-hot intensity of pure, beautiful fire.

Do not forget me.

I sat up and looked around to see who had spoken.

Do you so easily forget the mother who gives you life, who sustains you, who nourishes your body and soothes your spirit?

Recognizing the voice of the Earth Mother, I said, "No, of course not." The flames gradually darkened, changing from bright yellow to thick orange and clear cherry red.

You belonged to me first, and you are mine, Danu whispered. *Fire does not own you.*

A strong breeze blew in from the lake, carrying the residual smoke away. I rose and remained there dazed for an unknown length of time as the hypnotic power of flame slipped away. I took a deep breath and let it out, feeling as relaxed as if I'd soaked in a tub of hot water for hours.

Heal me, the earth mother commanded.

I looked down, noting the ash and char coating the ground. Reality slapped me in the face, hard. I'd done it again. I'd destroyed every speck of foliage in the area. The damage, however, was limited only to the campsite, where the winter grass had been trampled by the siege army. None of the trees or underbrush surrounding the site had been harmed. It was an improvement.

I got busy turning over the earth, like a farmer getting ready to plant in the spring. Reaching down to a depth several feet beneath the surface, I churned the earth an acre at a time, until all traces of men, horses, tents, and weaponry were gone – except for one pile of boxes and barrels that stood a couple hundred yards beyond the campsite. Curious as to what the bandits would have stored so far away, I strolled over to check it out, using my shield of swirling flames for illumination.

They were barrels of gunpowder and boxes of ammunition.

I say "were" because it exploded a split second later, ignited by the fire shield that I had neglected to extinguish. The force of the blast picked me up and threw me, and I tumbled helplessly

414

through the air until I landed hard in the dirt. Ears ringing and head pounding, I lay there for several minutes until the world slowed its mad whirl. The first few times I tried to get up, I staggered like a drunk and fell down again, so I decided to stay there awhile.

The vibration of hoofbeats roused me, providing the motivation I needed to get back on my feet. Picking myself back up in spite of severe vertigo, I coughed and waved my hand uselessly to get the thick, oily smoke out of my face. When it finally cleared, I was standing a couple dozen yards from a crater where all those barrels of gunpowder used to be. The explosion had catapulted me fifty feet away.

"Shit," I said, feeling like an idiot. "Quaking hells!"

We needed that ammunition. The safety of others aside, I was really, really glad that no one else had witnessed this. So of course, that's when my pentacle showed up looking scared to death and riding horses lathered with sweat. Duncan called to me, swinging out of the saddle before his horse had even stopped moving.

"What?" I took a few staggering steps toward him, stopping before I fell down. He repeated what seemed to be a question, but I still could not comprehend his words. I shook my head, as though that would dissipate the shrill ringing in my ears.

"I can't hear a thing!" I shouted.

Looking somewhat exasperated, the earth druid placed his hands over my ears, closed his eyes, and concentrated. The high-pitched ringing gradually faded, as did the throbbing ache in my head. Hearing returned after another minute or so.

"Thank you," I said, sighing with relief.

"Both your eardrums were ruptured, and you had a concussion," he said in a chiding tone. "What happened?"

"What are you doing here?"

"We got worried when you didn't come back," Seth said.

"We saw the fire from the other side and thought it might be you," Duncan added.

"Then we heard the explosion and *knew* it was you," added Conall with a smirk.

"You look a mess," Duncan said. "Are you injured anywhere else?"

"No." Even he couldn't heal injured pride.

"I told you he was fine," said Conall.

"That was one big explosion!" Dermot said excitedly. "Can you do it again?" Duncan gave him a dirty look.

"No, I can't do it again."

The water elementalist stood on the edge of the crater and peered over it, sniffing. "It smells like gunpowder."

I sighed. "It *is* gunpowder."

"You mean it *was* gunpowder," Conall said. "How'd you break the spell?"

"What spell?"

"The Morrigan's spell. The thrall of the elemental fire. Whatever it is that captivates you and makes you start creating Muspellheim on earth."

"Creating what?"

"The realm of Surtr the fire giant. It's a desolate land of endless fire."

I sighed. "Would you please stop bringing up Ragnarok?"

"After last night, it's kinda hard not to."

I decided to drop the issue and answer his question. "The first time, I ran out of people to kill and things to burn."

"The first time? Where and when was there a second time?"

"Right here," I said. "Not long after the first time. Steel showed up, and I rode over here. It was only about thirty minutes ago, I think."

"Davis, you've been gone for *hours*," Seth said with a frown.

I looked up. Sure enough, the moon had journeyed far in its course across the curtain of night. In fact, the sky held the grey coloring of pre-dawn light on the eastern horizon. Strange that I wasn't exhausted.

"Oh."

"You must have gotten lost the fire again," Seth said with a pointed look at Conall. "Confirming that the sword is, in fact, *not* responsible."

"That's not good," said the Norseman.

I understood his reasoning. If the enchantment laid on my sword had been the root cause of my loss of control, it would have been easily remedied. Now that we knew it wasn't, it seemed likely that *nothing* on earth could stop me.

Except for Danu, the earth mother herself.

"At least this time I didn't go very far."

"Only around the whole peninsula," Conall said.

"It was two separate battlegrounds, not the whole peninsula," Seth corrected. "Limiting the destruction to a smaller area is definitely an improvement."

"It's okay," said Dermot. "I can fix it."

"An improvement would be not destroying anything at all, or at least saving it for the enemy," said Conall. He looked at me again. "Are there more bandits around here?"

"There were."

"In that case, I take it back. Good job!"

I frowned. "Doesn't it bother any of you that I can end the lives of so many people without any effort at all?"

"It's not like they were out here knitting booties for their grandchildren," said Conall. "They've been raping, slaughtering, and enslaving people for at least the past six months and probably longer."

Seth nodded. "They deserved their fate."

Dermot paused in his task for a moment. "Remember what they did to Maeve and Ruth and James Reece's brother."

"Duncan?" Surely his would be the voice of reason.

"Our magic is a gift from the Shining Ones," replied the earth druid. "It would not be amiss to reason that they view our actions favorably."

"I know one that does for certain," Conall said.

Duncan inclined his head toward the Norseman. "My point exactly."

Seth nodded. "It stands to reason that if the other gods did not support the Morrigan's actions, we would see them acting upon the mortal realm as well."

I could only imagine what sort of devastation would occur if that were to happen. From the expressions of the others, I could tell they were thinking much the same thing – except for Dermot.

"That would be volcanic!" the water elementalist exclaimed. "Can you imagine getting to see Manannán mac Lir riding in his sea chariot? Or Dagda wielding his mighty club? Or Zeus, striding among the clouds casting thunderbolts!"

Duncan and Seth both looked at him like he was insane, but Conall just smiled at him. "I wouldn't mind seeing Odin riding on Sleipnir."

"Really?" I asked.

"Sure," he replied. "Who wouldn't want to see an eight-legged horse?"

"Exactly!" said Dermot. He dusted his hands. "I gave the land a good start in recovering, don't you think?"

Every inch of the area that I'd destroyed was now covered in green, with a variety of saplings scattered about. It was a pocket of spring, complete with flowers blossoming in spite of the cold.

I clapped him on the shoulder. "I can't wait until you're a druid. You're going to do some amazing things."

Chapter 24 – For Whom the Bell Tolls

The dead cannot cry out for justice.
It is a duty of the living to do so for them.
~ Lois McMaster Bujold ~

We shared a breakfast of what dried meat, fruit, and biscuits remained in our saddlebags and waited for the sun to come up. Leaving the horses grazing in Dermot's grassy field, we proceeded to Mayflower's western drawbridge. Across the neck of water that kept the island isolated, we could see thick wooden planks through the crisscrossed steel beams on its underside. A generous coat of white paint had been applied to the entire bridge to prevent rust and rot. None of the inhabitants were in view.

"How do you propose we get them to let down the drawbridge?" Seth asked.

"They might not know we're here," said Dermot.

"That's highly unlikely, given last night's bonfire," Conall said.

"I just hope they don't shoot at us," the water elementalist said.

"Considering that we have brought their siege to an end, they have no reason to do so," Duncan said.

"The enemy of my enemy is not necessarily my friend," said Seth, quoting some ancient piece of lore.

"I could slip over there and let the bridge down," Dermot offered.

"Too risky," I said. "I don't want you to get shot by an over-enthusiastic villager. We'll just make an earthen bridge like the aqueducts we built in Sanctuary."

Though either of us could have done it alone, Duncan and I worked together to raise a bridge of dirt and rocks over the narrow channel. We tramped across as if we hadn't a care in the world, keeping our hands away from our weapons in an attempt to appear non-threatening. Once across, we sent the mass of earth back where it belonged and proceeded down the main street of Mayflower, moseying down to the center of the island to give the inhabitants a chance to look us over. We halted at a crossroads. To the right, the road south ran down to the lakeshore, and to the left the road ran north, bordered by the thick trunks of trees, all barren of leaves.

"It's too quiet," Conall said, examining the buildings that stood around the intersection. The ones facing the water had all their windows boarded up.

"We've been in the open ever since we crossed the channel," Seth said. "I seriously doubt they'd have stayed in a place with no cover."

"Maybe they're all dead," said Dermot.

"Then who cleaned up the bodies?" Conall asked.

"If they starved to death, they'd probably have died in their beds," I said. The Norseman grimaced at the thought of dying in bed instead of fighting to the death.

"Let's go left," Seth suggested. "If I were trying to avoid being shot, I'd go to the place with the lowest visibility."

"That's a good idea," I said, "But that's not where they are."

Duncan gave the barest dip of his head to show that he had felt them, too.

"Get ready," I murmured to Seth.

"They're behind us, aren't they?" Conall muttered.

Dermot spun around. "I don't see anybody."

"I imagine they're rather proficient at staying hidden," Seth said. A ripple of air told me he had readied a shield.

"Why do I get the feeling they're not going to be very friendly?" Conall said, rubbing his hands on his jeans like they were itching for the feel of his shotgun.

We turned around and waited. I was prepared to stand there in the street until they developed the courage to show themselves, but

Dermot had other ideas.

"We know you're out there!" he yelled. "So grow some balls and come on out!"

If there was anything I'd learned about water elementalists, it was that patience was *not* one of their virtues. Since it worked and didn't get us killed, I didn't mind.

From cellar doors, ditches, sheds, and even a doghouse, a group of six men and four women emerged. Each one was armed to the teeth and dressed in heavy layers of clothing, including calf-length shearling coats like the ones I'd stolen from that very first outpost. Bandit coats.

"Heya," I called.

A man with iron grey hair and scars on the backs of his hands snorted. "There ain't no more Travelers, boy, so don't waste your time pretending."

"Good manners are never a waste of time," I said.

His eyes narrowed. "What do you boys want?"

"Just came to check and see if y'all needed any help after that siege."

"We're doin' just fine on our own," the man said. "Didn't need help breaking that siege, and don't need help now."

Dermot exclaimed. "What a bunch of ungrateful assho—"

Even though the rest of his words were silenced by the air dome that Seth quickly dropped over him, it didn't take a genius to figure out that none of them were complimentary and most were off-color.

Somehow, the grey-haired man's answer didn't surprise me. There was something wrong here, and while I wasn't one to judge a book by its cover, I was starting to think that the reason this group was wearing long leather coats like Republic soldiers was because they *were* Republic soldiers.

"Where are the people that lived here before?" I asked.

"Gone," the man said, raising his rifle. "It's our island now."

"What happened to them?"

"We gave them the choice to leave alive or stay and die, and the smart ones went across the western bridge." He paused. "Hopefully you boys are smart like they were so we don't have to kill you, too." The people behind him drew their weapons and aimed them at us.

Maybe the people of Conway were wrong about Blue Hill being destroyed; maybe they'd mistaken here for there. Stories had a way of changing over the miles, distorting with each telling. It didn't really matter. These belligerent folks had invaded a town that didn't belong to them and had taken everything from the rightful inhabitants.

"I don't take kindly to threats," I said, opening a deep pit under their feet. The earth slammed back together, leaving nothing remaining of them but the echo of their screams.

"Seth was right!" said Dermot, released from his dome of silence. "They *were* all enemies! Why would their own people attack them?"

"Mutiny," Conall replied. "The ones that took the island wanted to keep it for themselves."

"President Jackson must have found out they'd gotten too big for their britches and sent a thousand soldiers to get it back," I said. "Maybe this is where the two hundred other soldiers from the Faulkner garrison ended up."

"It's rather early in their conquest for that sort of infighting," said Seth. "It will work in our favor."

Conall looked at me. "I think Hel could use a little more company, don't you?"

I nodded. "Let's exterminate the rest of the vermin."

We tracked them all down using earth magic, and when we departed the newly uninhabited island, we left the drawbridges up. If the Mayflower folk still lived, they'd want their home back. If not, we'd find some other displaced folk to give it to.

* * *

The first thing I did upon our return was to check on Rob, Madoc, and Chester, who had been wounded in the attack. Madoc was up, and Siorus was following him around with a worried look on his face even though the gunman appeared healthy. Rob and Chester, however, had been settled in a tent, where each was being attended to by his own pentacle leader. It made me realize that no matter what other mistakes I'd made since we'd parted company with Shitozaki, I'd done something right in grouping my men into pentacles. It had bound them together like nothing else could.

"Hey, you're back!" said Rob. "Come tell me what's been

going on. I'm going stir crazy in here, and Warwick won't let me leave."

"Quakes," I muttered, kneeling beside him. "How bad is it?"

"I'm dying," said Rob.

"*What?*"

"I'm dying of boredom. Save me!"

I scowled at him. "Scare me like that again, and dying of boredom is the last thing you'll have to worry about."

Warwick rolled his eyes. "Your leg is broken, Rob. You *can't* walk."

"I saw you down, but not what happened," I said.

"Took a bullet to the thigh that broke the bone," Rob replied.

"Luckily Bébhinn got the bleeding stopped and helped me pull him out of the line of fire," Warwick said. "I never expected the witches to be any real use in a fight, but by the gods, they have courage! Every single one of them stood their ground."

Rob nodded agreement. "It makes me think Dermot has the right idea, you know? About living in Ward, I mean."

"I've heard some of the others mention that a druid and a witch would make an impressive dyad," Warwick said. The small grey shrike on his shoulder scolded him in a raucous tone. I couldn't remember him having it when we departed Ward, but I had enough to keep track of without worrying about spirit animals.

"I thought it was a good idea, too," said Martin, joining us. "Until we lost Weylin, anyway."

"So he is dead."

They nodded, and I heaved a deep sigh and bowed my head. I had assumed as much after seeing the witch gunned down and crushed under his horse, but inside there had been a tiny spark of hope that Rhiannon had managed to save him. My gaze turned to Chester, lying still except for the slow rise and fall of his chest. He remained unconscious, either from his injury or because Martin was keeping him down. From what I remembered, his wounds had been worse – at least, he'd bled a lot more.

"How is Chester?"

"He almost lost his arm," Martin replied. "He would have, too, if not for Duncan's quick action."

"Then why do you look so unhappy?"

"Because *I* should have been the one to help him. He's in *my* pentacle."

"Considering that Duncan's been with me for the past several hours, I'd say you *are* the one healing him."

"I should have gone to him the moment he was injured."

"Did you see it happen?"

He scowled. "No."

I ran my hand through my hair. "Believe me, Martin, I understand how you feel. It's hard to see your friends get hurt. But the fact of the matter is that you were doing the job that *I* told you to do. It was my idea to make big, loud earthquakes that hid the sound of enemies approaching. I wasn't watching behind us, and I didn't tell anybody else to watch, either. So if there is someone at fault here, it's me."

After a moment he nodded, but I could tell he wasn't convinced. That was all right; no matter how Seth tried to tell me that I'd done my best with the situation, I wasn't convinced, either. It was really hard to swallow the fact that we had lost Weylin and risked our lives, not because the Republic forces were after our friends, but because they were after another group of our enemies. The mass casualties we had inflicted didn't bother me half as much as my own injured ones.

And the one who was dead.

"Where's the High Priestess?"

"She's in her tent," Warwick said, "with Weylin."

"She won't come out," said Martin.

"All right." I rose and stretched my back. My body was begging for rest, but there was one thing yet I had to take care of.

Standing guard outside the High Priestess' tent, Ahearn stopped me.

"I am sorry about Weylin," I said. "It's a terrible loss."

"Thank you," he said. "And thank you for ending that murderous scourge."

"That's one of the reasons I'm here. I need to talk to her."

"She's doing spellwork," he said. He was a dreadful liar, but his loyalty to his mother was undeniable.

"Without candles, incense, or chanting?"

He dropped his head, defeated. Looking up after a moment, he laid a hand on my arm. "She grieves deeply. Maybe even more than after Ward was taken."

I nodded and entered her tent, intending to read her the riot act for whatever she had done last night to bring the Morrigan. I had planned to tell her that I was not the tool of her retribution and to warn her that it would be the end of our friendship if she ever cast another enthralling spell on me again.

Instead, I held my tongue. Seeing her sitting there slumped on the ground, no longer wearing the armor and ageless countenance of a goddess, my anger was replaced by pity. Her hair was in disarray as though she'd been tearing at it in grief, and her eyes were red and swollen.

"I trust the Goddess to lead me, no matter what face she wears," Rhiannon said, as though reading my mind. Her voice was hoarse, laden with the crushing weight of heartache and defeat.

I don't, I almost said, but it would have been a lie. My sword would not be enchanted if I hadn't put my trust in the Phantom Queen's word. I dropped to my knees beside her, staring at Weylin's pale face, his body held in the stillness that only death could give.

"They *murdered* him!" she whispered fiercely. Her grey eyes lit up with energy like winter clouds threatening a storm of ice and snow. "And my heart cries out for revenge!"

"You'll have it," I said.

"*They murdered him!*" Rhiannon wailed, grief winning out over rage. "He died trying to warn us of danger! He sacrificed himself so that *we* could live!"

"I know." I put my arms around her. "I'm sorry."

Rhiannon sagged heavily against me, and I could feel her shaking as sobs wracked her body. Pulling her closer, I let her vent her pain in safety, knowing that I was there to carry on as she faltered. She deserved a respite. She was the one who had to be responsible for all her people, the one who had to be strong for them, and she had fulfilled that duty until today. It was one of the burdens of leadership that there was no one she could turn to for comfort but me, simply because I understood what it was like to feel responsible for everyone and so terribly afraid of losing even one of them.

"I have to bury him away from home," she sobbed. "I have to leave him behind!"

"No you don't," I said. "I promise."

"But his body…"

"I'll take care of it."

Martin molded a simple jar of clay, and I fired it in a makeshift kiln of dirt and stone while Weylin's body lay in state. When the sun dipped toward the horizon, we placed his body on a pyre of stone. Duncan, our only druid priest, officiated the ritual and funeral ceremony. Wolfric and I ignited the funeral pyre and stood watch over it until the cremation was complete. In the morning, I placed the ashes in the clay jar and brought it to Rhiannon. She accepted the urn as though it was a priceless treasure, wrapping it carefully to stow in one of her saddlebags.

I debated on whether or not to leave the eastern landscape of the scorched and scarred, but in the end, we decided that it would keep until spring. Rob and Chester had recovered enough to ride, and I wanted to be away from here and off to Blue Hill as soon as possible. For another, that half a square mile of blackened ground might make any other marauders from the 'Ville hesitate before trying to take the island town.

"You got the sword back," said Conall.

"I did." I patted the hilt of the grey blade, happy to have it again. I'd already lost my shotgun; losing my sword too would be nigh unbearable.

"What's the plan?" asked Seth. He had to know we were less than a week's travel from there, but so far he hadn't mentioned anything about returning to Master Shitozaki. He seemed relaxed, showing no indication of feeling the need to return, or even wanting to. It made me wonder if he, too, thought that relocating to Ward was a good idea. Dermot had already asked Rhiannon if he could live there, and Conall's disdain of the grove and Shitozaki's plan to retake it was as likely to make him settle in Ward as much as his infatuation with Cinna. Duncan hadn't mentioned a preference one way or the other, but he seemed content anywhere so long as he maintained contact with the earth mother – which was all the time. As for me, I didn't care where I lived, so long as Angie was there.

"Now we start searching for survivors," I replied.

"From Mayflower, or Blue Hill?" Seth asked.

"Either. Both."

"It's a little like looking for a needle in a haystack."

Conall said, "Yeah, but it seems like a waste to win the town back and not try to find the people who own it."

I nodded. That had been my reasoning as well.

Wolfric asked, "Do you really think there are survivors? It's likely that those people were run out of their homes into the cold with nothing more than the clothes on their backs."

"That happened to us, and we survived," said Ahearn. Beside him, the Weird Sisters nodded agreement.

"And how long were you alone?" Wolfric asked.

"Almost a month. We'd have died of cold and starvation if you druids hadn't come along."

"And you have magic," said the fire elementalist. "A bunch of nulls wouldn't stand a chance on their own. Especially not for two months."

"On the contrary," Seth interjected. "They are not accustomed to using magic to solve problems or make their lives easier. Logic would suggest that a people accustomed to deprivation and hardship would be the *most* likely to survive."

"It's a waste of time," Wolfric said. "Time we could be spending on orchestrating attacks on the rest of the garrisons and then the 'Ville itself."

My doubts regarding our ability to destroy the 'Ville had returned. The Republic of Jackson's willingness to commit a thousand troops to recapture one little island town from a bunch of mutineers indicated to me that they had thousands more with which to defend their own territory.

"We're still working on a viable plan for that," said Seth.

"Besides," said Conall, "we have two more weeks to kill until the *Circitorium Fati* runs out, so we might as well make good use of it."

"Yeah, it would suck to attack the 'Ville and not be able to get back inside Ward," Dermot said. It was a possibility I hadn't considered, and from the way the others were looking at him, they hadn't thought of it either.

Ruth said, "That would be like kicking an anthill and then standing in it after you'd pissed off all the fire ants."

"We'd be trapped between the 'Ville and the Veil of Doom," said Seth.

"I will run through the *Circitorium Fati* of my own volition before I allow bandits to take me again," Maeve said with quiet fervor.

"After witnessing the extent of Davis' fire magic the other night, I doubt that will be necessary," Duncan said.

"We're not attacking the 'Ville until all coven members are safely back at Cypress Creek," I said, for Weylin's death had taken the fight out of them. Rhiannon wanted vengeance, but I wasn't taking anyone into battle whose heart wasn't in it. "So, let's focus on the current situation. Conall, let's have a look at the map you got from Faulkner."

The land area south of Mayflower was relatively small, approximately four miles wide, bordered on the east by a large stream flowing from Conway Lake and by the great river on the west.

"We could split up and search in a crisscross pattern," Ahearn suggested.

"If we split up, we might never find each other again," Ruth said.

"With earth druids around?" Wolfric asked, raising an eyebrow.

"There are distance limitations to *seeking*," Duncan said.

"What kind of limitation are we talkin' about?" Ruth asked. "Feet? Yards?"

"Currently, the eight of us are capable of sensing a range of distances from half a mile to a mile," Duncan said. Ruth whistled. "However, our ability to determine precisely what is there decreases as the distance increases."

"So, if we have a span four miles wide to cover," said Conall, "we could spread out the pentacles every half mile or so and just head south in a straight line."

"Except Duncan and I are in the same pentacle," I said. He had shown a decided reluctance to leave my side since I'd been shot at the Watson outpost. "Want to lead your own for a while?"

He hesitated a moment, then nodded. "I will until we've finished the search."

"Who else is going to be in it?" Wolfric asked.

"You, for one," I said.

"I'll go with him," said Ruth.

"I can go if his pentacle will be close to the stream," Dermot said.

"I'll be closest to the eastern stream," I said. "So you should stick with me."

"Okay."

"That's three," I said, realizing that we had only witches left to round out Duncan's pentacle. Ahearn remained silent, while the Weird Sisters had what seemed to be an entire conversation contained in a series of glances.

"We will also accompany Duncan," said Rowena.

"The High Priestess won't like that," warned Ahearn.

"Davis' fire magic will be between us and the enemies to the east," said Ianna.

"But—"

"It is decided," Bébhinn said, brushing past him.

"Six is an unlucky number!" Ahearn protested.

"Fine, then," said Maeve. "I'll go with them. That makes seven."

From the look on the horsemaster's face, he clearly felt that adding her to the group would please Rhiannon even less, but he said nothing more. It wasn't exactly a pentacle anymore, but that didn't matter. Maeve was good with magic and great with a rifle, and I had a feeling that we hadn't seen the magnitude of what the Weird Sisters could accomplish with magic.

"What about the rest of the witches?" Seth asked.

"Rhiannon can decide where she wants her people," I said. It was fine if they wanted to include themselves, but after losing Weylin, I was done with deciding how the witches participated. His death weighed heavily on my conscience.

Seth nodded and went to pass the word along to the rest of the Finns before going to speak with Rhiannon. He didn't relay their conversation when he returned, but I noticed the High Priestess riding westward with Ahearn, Killian, Cullen, Tiernan and Riordan, Heath, Toby, and James Reece.

I held my pentacle to the search line's point of origin beside the stream, while the other pentacles and Duncan's group first came together, then turned their horses' noses west and started off at an easy pace. Siorus's pentacle was slated to ride farthest west, beside the big river. They trotted after the witches and fell into an easy traveling pace beside them. Ingvar's was next, followed by Yiorgos, Warwick, Halldor, and Martin. Next in line was Duncan's group, and then mine, which now included Cinna. It was a surprise that Rhiannon didn't protest about her daughter riding so close to potential danger.

After about an hour, I received the ready signal. It had originated with Siorus and had passed from one earth druid to the next until reaching me. I gave the signal to go and began walking south.

"Aren't you going to ride?" asked Dermot.

"My reach is farther on foot," I said. Searching for the people from Blue Hill and Mayflower on horseback was doable, but I was also *seeking* in an easterly direction, on guard for the approach of enemies. A horse traveled about four miles per hour at an easy walk over flat terrain. We had about five miles to cover on our southern heading, so I reckoned the search would take no longer than a couple of hours, depending on how many times we stopped.

It didn't take nearly that long. We'd only been riding about half an hour when the earth carried a signal from Martin that could only be described as an excited flutter.

"Martin found them," I said, mounting my horse.

"You mean he's found *something*," said Conall. "He could be in trouble."

"It's possible, but it didn't feel like trouble," I said. "Let's meet up with Duncan."

Warmed up and well-rested, Steel broke into a trot, then transitioned to a smooth canter that brought us to Duncan, Wolfric, and the witches in just a few minutes.

"Why haven't you gone yet?" I asked.

"I was waiting for you," the earth druid replied.

Behind me, I heard Conall mutter to Cinna: "His chosen is going to *hate* Davis."

"Be nice," she whispered back. "You don't know that."

He was probably right. I hoped that Duncan's protective behavior toward me would only last as long as we were fighting bandits and risking our lives. Then again, my days as a Traveler had been frequently filled with dangerous events, and if wandering with Angie healing the earth was equally risky, maybe not. Considering how often the cousins had been at odds back at the grove, there was some question of whether Angie would even want him around.

For that matter, there was no guarantee that she'd want me around, either. Chosen or not, Angie and I had spent more time apart than we'd spent together. My year and a day would be up long before we returned to Sanctuary. I shared these doubts with no one, for it didn't seem fair for me to express worry about it when none of the Finns had even gotten to meet their own chosen. Some of them never would, if the continued absence of fetches was any indication.

We found Martin speaking earnestly with a pair of men in blue jeans, plaid flannel shirts, and boots.

"Davis!" Martin called. "Come meet Jeb and Jared Bommer! They're from Blue Hill!"

"Pleased to meet you," I said, dismounting so I could shake each man's hand in turn.

"That remains to be seen," said Jared, punctuating his remark by spitting on the ground.

"Don't mind my brother," said Jeb. "He's not convinced you ain't bandits yet."

"That's understandable," I said. "Is there anything I do to ease your mind?"

"We-e-l-l-l... If you're really druids, that means you have magic." He squinted at me. "So maybe I'd like a demonstration before I trust ya."

"All right." I squatted and picked up a small rock, holding it out so that both brothers could see. Closing my fingers around it, I melted it with a wash of intense heat that made them take a step back. I opened my hand again to display the molten rocky liquid sitting in my palm.

"That good enough for ya?" Jeb asked.

"That'll do." Jared nodded. "You ain't got no bandits on your tail, do ya?"

"Naw," said Dermot. "We took care of 'em yesterday."

"Good to hear," Jeb said. "What brings you folks this way?"

"We're out here looking for you," I said.

"Now why would y'all be lookin' for folks you ain't never met?" Jared asked.

"The people at Conway said your town was destroyed. And

431

then we heard that the folks at Mayflower had been run off."

Jared's eyes narrowed. "And who told you that?"

"The ones who ran them off," I said. "The ones that took the island decided to keep it for themselves, and the 'Ville sent a thousand soldiers to get it back."

"Unfortunately for them," Conall said, "we showed up and took it back."

"Well, I'll be," Jeb said.

"I hope you killed every last one of them bastards," Jared Bommer said, emphasizing his feelings by spitting on the ground again.

"We sure did!" said Dermot, looking proud.

"The bandits said that they allowed some of the Mayflower folk to leave alive," I said. "It's a long shot, but we were hoping to find them."

The Bommer brothers exchanged a look.

"It's colder than a well-digger's ass out here," said Jeb. "Let's go on inside so we can get warm and chit-chat a bit."

"Inside" turned out to be a small grove of trees with the topmost branches lashed together, with vines and branches interlaced between them to form a makeshift roof. The lower walls were made of short logs of firewood stacked up between the tree trunks, while more woven greenery formed the upper portion. A few small fires were lit; one was being used for cooking, and small people huddled in small groups around the others for warmth. The people inside jumped to their feet, clearly frightened by our arrival.

"Settle down, y'all," Jeb said, raising his hands and waving them down. "These folks ain't bandits. They're druids, and they're here to help."

The Bommer brothers took seats on the ground. We did likewise and listened to their story. They were the only survivors of the Blue Hill massacre, and the only reason they were still alive was because they'd been out hunting far from the town.

"They done burnt our village to the ground and built one of them big garrisons right on top of it," Jared said.

"We've seen it," I said, remembering the first garrison we'd come across, whose raiders had pursued us north. If we'd been there just a week or two later, we'd have been caught smack dab in between those raiders and the siege army headed for Mayflower.

The gods must have had a hand in that bit of good fortune.

The Bommers introduced us to Victor George, a man in his sixties who was now acting as the town elder for the Mayflower folk. Out of the island town's original population of five hundred, half had chosen to stay and fight. Of the ones that had chosen to leave, another fifty had died of exposure, leaving just two hundred survivors. Most people were still too fearful to approach us, but I met and shook hands with Victor and his niece, Shenae Lovejoy. We unpacked our saddlebags and shared what meat and vegetables we had so they could be added to the thin soup they were cooking.

"I'm sorry about your town," I said, "but I sure am happy to see at least some of you folks alive and well."

"Thank ya, son," Victor replied. "I'm pleased as punch to see druids riding the range again. You folks will have those bandits under control in no time."

It would take a lot longer than that, but I couldn't tell him that. The outside world didn't need to carry the burden of the problems of the druid community.

"We'll do what we can, sir."

"So tell us what's brought you here," he said. I started relaying a bare bones version of our journey until Conall interrupted.

"You're a terrible storyteller," he said. "This is what happened." He proceeded to spin a yarn worthy of a bard, describing how we'd spent days running from bandits until we learned to fight them. Dermot interrupted occasionally with sound effects and dramatic reenactments of our battles as Conall told of finding the witches, winning back Ward, and then attacking the enemy garrisons and outposts, traveling counter-clockwise around the 'Ville freeing people and diminishing the bandits' hold upon the area. Between the two of them, the tale drew the timid folk in and made them forget their fear.

"So, anyway," Conall concluded, "now that we've shoveled all the shit out of Mayflower, we thought we'd come find you and see if maybe you wanted it back."

There were tears in Victor George's eyes, and he shook my hand again, and then Seth's and Conall's. "We are much obliged to you young fellers," he said. "Thank you."

"We druids have neglected our duties for far too long," Seth told him. "It was the least we could do."

Victor and Shenae hugged each other, and together with the remaining survivors of Mayflower, moved around hugging or shaking hands with all the Finns. Several minutes of laughing, joyful tears, and excited talking dominated the atmosphere of the grove hut.

"This is so awesome," Dermot said happily.

Jared Bommer gave him a quizzical look. "What's it to you?"

"We've seen a lot of bad stuff, so it's nice to find people still alive," the water elementalist said. "Some of the towns around here were totally destroyed and all the people killed." His voice dropped to a whisper: "Even the children."

The Bommer brothers nodded. "Like ours," said Jared. "We lost a lot of good people. So did these folks."

"Not everybody would have taken in strangers after losing everything themselves," said Wolfric. "You have much honor."

"It was the right thing to do," said Jared.

"We didn't do it alone," Jeb said. "We couldn't have, not without that other group of druids."

"Another group?" Seth and I exchanged a puzzled look. "Are you sure they were druids?" the air elementalist asked.

"There ain't no mistaking that kind of magic," Jeb said.

"How many were there?" I asked.

"Five," he replied. "Two young men and three young women." He paused. "Come to think of it, one was just a girl. They said they was looking for ya. Tryin' to catch up, seemed like."

"They were looking for *us*?" asked Seth.

"No. They were looking for *him*." Jared pointed at me.

"Could have been Master Shitozaki," Dermot said.

"I don't think anybody would describe him as a *young* man," said Conall.

"Well," said Jeb. "It was really that pretty girl with the green eyes that was looking for him. Ain't never seen eyes like that in my whole life."

"What?" I nearly dropped my coffee. "Was her name Angie?"

"Yep, that's her."

Chapter 25 – Fires of the Heart

When the water starts boiling, it is foolish to turn off the heat.
~ Nelson Mandela ~

Angie had been there and was looking for me! I couldn't decide how to feel, my emotions were such a jumble. Joy that she was looking for me mixed with fear for her safety.

I asked Jeb, "Would you mind describing the others for me?"

"One of the men was dark-headed and had a smart mouth," he replied.

Jared said, "The other didn't talk much, but he had long, blond hair and a patch over one eye."

"White blond?" I asked, feeling uneasy.

"Sure was. Carried a shotgun and knew how to use it, too."

Quakes. Fear intensified and happiness faded.

"That can only be Niall," murmured Duncan. "Which means the dark-haired man is likely to be Darryn."

"Who?" asked Seth.

"Niall Ashcroft and Darryn Darkmane," Wolfric growled. "Both their mothers are in the ArchDruid's Tetrarch."

"Why would your chosen be with *them*?" Seth asked.

"Niall was who Sebrina had picked out to be Angie's chosen," I said. "I taught him to use that shotgun."

"Wow," said Dermot. "You trained the guy who replaced you? Harsh."

Conall glared at him. "Not nearly as harsh as having one of your friends point it out."

435

Seth asked, "How long ago was this?"

"Mmm… It's been about a month, I guess," Jeb said.

"That can't be right," I said, exchanging a glance with Duncan. The oath had broken when I was shot on December first; it was now the fourteenth.

Seth's brow furrowed in puzzlement. "She must have already known you were alive."

"And now she thinks I'm dead again."

"She *probably* just thinks you just got laid," said Dermot, rolling his eyes.

"Dermot!" Conall snapped.

"What? I'm just trying to make him feel better!"

"It's *not* helping," the Norseman growled.

"Can you describe the other two girls?" I asked. Maybe this wasn't as bad as I thought.

Jeb pondered a moment. "One girl had long, strawberry-blonde hair," he said. "She was their healer."

"Did she have big blue eyes?" I asked.

"Yep."

"That has to be Iriana Disney," I told the others. "She's an earth elementalist." Unless something had gone dramatically wrong, Iriana wouldn't have gone anywhere near Niall and Darryn.

"What about the other one?"

"The other one had red curly hair and freckles." He pointed skyward. "It was her that built this place, weaving all them vines and branches together to make the roof and walls."

"A water elementalist," said Seth, sounding vaguely surprised.

"She was a cute little thing, but she didn't look near old enough to be out with the rest of them," Jared added. "In fact, she looked even younger than *him*." He pointed at Dermot, and I started to get a bad feeling.

"Do you remember her name?" I asked.

The man frowned. "Annie… no. Arrie-Andy, or somethin' like that."

"Ariadne?" Dermot blurted, his face suddenly pale.

"Yeah, that's it."

"That's my sister!" he exclaimed, pulling at his hair.

"Is she cute?" asked Fenris.

"She's *fourteen!*" Dermot shouted, lunging at him.

"Whoa, whoa, whoa." Conall grabbed him. "Settle down."

"Sorry!" Fenris said, scooting away. "I was just kidding."

Dermot turned back toward me with wild eyes. "We have to find them!"

"Where did they say they were headed?" I asked.

"North."

"That's where *we've* been!" the water elementalist cried. "They *can't* have gone north!"

"They couldn't," said Victor George. "They showed back up here a couple of days after they left. Said they'd run into a big group of bandits."

"Probably the siege army at Mayflower," Seth said, nodding.

"Where'd they head after that?" I asked.

"Back southeast, the way they came from," he replied.

"Oh, gods! My mother will be *devastated* if we don't find Ariadne," Dermot moaned. "What if the bandits have her?"

"We'll find her," I said.

"*How?*"

I had no idea.

Seth raised his hands. "All right, everybody, let's cool off a bit and consider the situation logically."

I took a deep breath and let it out again. "Okay, let's break it down. Angie is a triple threat, possibly a druid. Niall has no magic but does have a shotgun. Iriana can't earthmove, but she can heal. Ariadne is a water elementalist who is clearly talented with plants. We just need to figure out who the second man is."

"We already know," said Duncan. "Darryn and Niall are close companions. Where Niall goes, Darryn follows."

I shook my head. "I don't think Angie or Iriana would want to be anywhere near Darryn Darkmane, much less take an extended journey with him." Wolfric nodded agreement.

Jeb rubbed his bearded chin. "I can't recollect the dude's name, but I'm pretty sure it wasn't Darryn. It wasn't a long name, either."

"Did the dark-haired man ever use any magic?"

He shook his head. "Not that I saw."

"What sort of weapons was he carrying? Did he have a shotgun like Niall?"

Jared snorted. "Damn fool had a sword. Like that's going to be any use against a gun."

I ignored the gibe; even though most of us carried firearms, we all still wore swords. The fact that this person only carried a sword – when he could have had a shotgun – indicated that he had magic.

"Duncan. Tell me again who else in the grove had magic besides Wolfric?"

"Haamid Parks and Lin Overholt."

"Which one came with Angie, do you think?"

He considered. "Lin, I should think."

"What's his element?"

"Air."

No wonder he hadn't been discovered. "That would have been an easy element to hide."

"Exactly," said Wolfric. "You can't see air."

"You can see its effects," Seth said.

"Most people don't pay that much attention," I said. "They see what they expect to see."

"Now *that's* the gods' own truth," said Conall.

"So," said Seth, "they have a triple threat, air and water elementalists, and a healer. That's actually not a bad pentacle."

"Ariadne works *plants*!" Dermot snapped, coming out of his sulk. "She probably doesn't even work with elemental water!"

"That might be an advantage," Conall said.

"How?"

"She won't need to carry water skins or be near a body of water. Plants are everywhere."

Dermot glowered at him. "Not in the middle of winter, they're not."

"Don't be ridiculous," Conall said. "You yourself grew a whole field of grass and flowers just yesterday."

The water elementalist fell silent again, but I could tell he was now thinking instead of panicking. I knew how he felt; part of me wanted to run around yelling and burning things, but at the end of it all I'd just be tired and still facing the same problem.

Then I remembered my fetch.

"I'll be right back," I said, heading outside. I didn't know exactly how to call the fire lion back, but I *did* know that having it appear in a tiny room constructed of dried logs and filled with

438

people wasn't a good idea.

"Where are you going?" Seth asked.

"Calling my fetch back. Stay there," I said.

At what I judged to be a safe distance from the grove hut, I sank to my knees in the dry winter grass, closing my eyes and focusing inward in the meditative practice that my mother had first taught me and that Duncan had expanded upon. Allowing a few minutes for my body to relax and my mind to open, I willed that separate part of my spirit back to me.

It was a good thing that I'd gone outside and away from the others because I'd also forgotten that my Well had fully compensated for the magic infused into the spirit animal. It was brimming full of fire even without the thirty percent or so that had contributed to the creation of the lion. So when all that extra magic tried to cram itself back inside my Well all at once, the force hit so hard that it knocked me flat on my back and held me pinned until I managed to wrestle a semblance of control over it.

Seth told me later that it looked like the lion was attacking me. The experience was not unlike an attack, but instead of fighting it, the best thing to do was try and relax. After all, it couldn't hurt me. If there was anything about which I had perfect clarity, it was that magic was my servant, entirely subject to my will. All I had to do was focus and control it, and if I couldn't absorb it, maybe I could change it.

Plunging my fingers deep into the lion's flaming mane, I envisioned a transformation that would suit its new purpose – to guide me to Angie, instead of bringing her to me. The accumulation of roiling flames coalesced in on itself, and I poured more and more elemental fire into it until it began to take shape. The creature of fire stretched out, unwinding into coiling lengths that gradually took shape. A serpentine head, sinuous neck and scaled body emerged from the amorphous mass, followed by four muscular legs, vicious talons, and delicate-looking, membranous wings. It towered over us, bigger than my parents' three-story house, its scaled hide shimmering like hot metal in a forge.

A dragon.

A glance over my shoulder showed Seth with his *zweihänder* pulled halfway out of its sheath, looking positively gobsmacked. Dermot and Duncan stood beside him with their mouths hanging open. The rest of the Finns – who had poured out of the green hut to see what I was going to do – were frozen in the middle of whatever action they'd been taking when the dragon appeared, most slack-jawed and wide-eyed. Only Conall appeared unimpressed.

Duncan recovered first. "Was the lion not good enough?"

"Lions don't fly."

"You could have made a phoenix."

I looked over the dragon, from its triangular head of ash and magma, down its neck and body of brilliant orange-yellow and blazing white sparks, to its wings of smoldering red and black tipped with pale yellow talons.

"This suits my frame of mind better," I said.

* * *

We escorted the Blue Hill and Mayflower folk back to the island, and while I would have liked nothing more than to find Angie as quickly as possible, we couldn't just dump them there. Many were weak and sick. The earth druids did what they could to bring them back to health while the rest of us worked to make the place livable again with repairs and supplies. It took a few days, but fortune favored us once again, for the Republic mutineers had prepared well for winter and possible siege.

We departed the morning of December nineteenth, taking leave of the witches as well as the Mayflower folk. They were a peace-loving people unused to conflict, and they'd had their fill of death and destruction. I couldn't blame them. Unlike druids, they had no history of patrolling the world and protecting the weak. Ruth and James Reece stayed with them.

"Be careful," I said to them.

"Be careful yourself," said Ruth. "And don't forget what I told you."

"I'm over it," I said. "If somebody doesn't like the way my magic works, they're free to find their own way."

"And if none of them like it?"

"I've been alone before," I said, smiling in spite of the sudden tightness in my chest. "I have a job to do, and I don't have to time to worry about who won't play with me on the playground."

The Finns were my friends and losing them would hurt, but

stopping the 'Ville from taking over the world was more important than one man's feelings.

"They ain't gonna leave you," Ruth said in her uncanny way of reading my mind. "So don't you waste time worryin' over it."

"We'll be prayin' for you," James Reece said.

"Thanks." Impulsively, I hugged her, and then hugged him, too. "You two take care of each other."

"We will," he said.

The Finns bade the witches farewell, each in his own way. I had thought that saying goodbye to Maeve would be the hardest, but she was still cold and distant. Rhiannon turned out to be the one who was most difficult to say good-bye to.

"Make sure you return by sundown on the twenty-eighth," said the High Priestess. "Spencer and I will be re-casting the *Circitorium Fati* on the twenty-ninth, just as soon as total darkness has fallen."

"With any luck, you won't have to cast it at all," I said with a confidence I didn't feel.

"Lord and Lady make it so," she replied. "Goddess watch over you, Davis." There were tears in her eyes as we embraced.

"We'll be all right," I said, and mounted my horse.

"We'll be better than all right," said Conall, sitting beside me astride Twister. Cinna stood by Rhiannon, her fists clenched and fighting tears. I was a little surprised that he was leaving her behind, but it was yet another sign that we were headed into increasingly dangerous territory.

"Merry meet and merry parting!" the witches called, waving.

"And merry meet again!" the Finns shouted with them.

Heading southeast, we followed the wide stream that wound its way southeast from Lake Conway to the Blue Hill garrison. I had planned on destroying said garrison, but someone else had beaten us to it. The outer walls were untouched, but the gates had been ripped off and remnants of vines dangled from their hinges. Investigating to ensure that no one inside was still living, we found the inner palisade covered in blackened zigzags that could only have been caused by spirit bolts. The buildings within had toppled like dominoes, and scattered corpses lay scattered about. A few had died to gunfire, but most had fallen to elemental spirit.

Phelan whistled. "Somebody was pissed off."

"Davis' chosen, no doubt," said Conall, indicating the lightning strikes.

Phelan whistled again. "I'd better step up my game."

"But what leveled the buildings?" Siorus asked.

"Looks like a tornado," said Madoc.

"It wasn't a tornado," said Seth. "It was an air push. A *big* one." He turned to me. "Looks like their air elementalist is a druid."

"*Five* people did this?" Martin said, wearing a stunned expression.

"Five *druids* did this," I said.

"You mean two druids, two elementalists, and a null," Conall corrected. "Even so, it's a good thing there wasn't a full complement of Republic soldiers here."

I nodded agreement. We had taken out the raid groups that had given chase when we were first passing through, and I was willing to bet that several others had been sent to Mayflower to take part in the siege.

"Let's tear it down," Seth said, and we set to work.

The garrison was burned and buried in no time and we continued onward. Luckily for us, the Republic had left the Blue Hill bridge undamaged, so we didn't have to take the time to devise a magical means across it. We didn't intend to come back this way, however, and destroying the bridge might slow or stop our enemies.

Just for fun, and to test the limits of my magic, I had the dragon fetch strafe the bridge, breathing fire down upon it. The flames from the mouth of the molten beast were just as effective as if I'd directed them with my own two hands.

"I didn't think a fetch could have an effect on the physical environment," Seth said.

"Neither did I," said Wolfric, frowning.

"Perhaps it is a creature of fire magic, as the *Dobhar-chú* are creatures of Dermot's water magic," said Duncan.

"It doesn't feel the same," I said. "It hasn't created a drain on my Well like when I first made the lion."

"You never actually drew the lion back into your spirit," the earth druid replied. "So it is unlikely that you would experience the same sensation as before."

Except that I had poured even more elemental fire into my fetch to transform it from lion to dragon, with no ill effects. I held my tongue, however, allowing the philosophical discussion to continue.

"Following that logic, it stands to reason that the dragon is, in fact, a spirit animal," Seth said, his expression laden with meaning. He was thinking about Kam Stone's prophecy, and how allowing part of my spirit to remain outside my body put me at increased risk of death by thunderbolt.

"All I know is, with that thing, we are going to fuck those bastards up!" Conall said, sharing a fist bump with Dermot.

"*Gods*, I wish I was already a druid," the water elementalist moaned. "Then nothing could stop me from finding Ariadne."

"Having an unlimited channel from the gods isn't everything," Duncan said. "It's how you use what you have that counts."

Seth nodded. "Spending time as an elementalist is how we learn to be creative with our magic. It teaches us to be precise. We learn how to do a lot with a little, and have that experience to fall back on when we're in situations that limit how much magic can be used."

"Exactly," Conall said. "Look how much you can already do."

"Even full druids have limitations," I said. "You still have to eat and sleep to keep your body strong."

"And meditate," Duncan said.

"Don't forget making offerings," Wolfric added.

Seth nodded. "All those things are necessary. Meditation teaches you focus, while ritual strengthens your faith in the gods and reminds them of your reciprocal relationship with them. Together, those things give you the will required to manipulate your element, but as Davis mentioned, said, your will weakens when you're hungry or tired."

"Speaking of," said Conall. "I'm starving. When's supper?"

* * *

I wasn't naïve enough to believe that burning one bridge would keep the western towns safe from the Republic of Jackson. The citizens of the 'Ville may have started out as mere thieves, rabble-rousers, and bandits, but they were a far from it now. The destruction of the 'Ville was the only thing that would ensure the freedom of all, and we were the only ones willing and able to carry out that task. I didn't know how we were going to do it, but the dragon gave me hope and my determination to destroy the 'Ville was renewed.

After the Blue Hill garrison, we ran across only one other enemy outpost as we traveled east. It seemed odd, and I wondered at the absence of strongholds to the south of the 'Ville. While the outpost burned, I discussed the possibilities with my pentacle and Wolfric.

"Beggin' your pardon, but I think I can be help with your conundrum."

I turned to see a half-drunk, skinny old man who had every intention of progressing to completely drunk if the bottle in his hand was any indication. Fenris was following him with one hand on the hilt of his sword. It hardly seemed necessary; the man looked as though he would topple right over if a stiff wind came along.

"Where are you from?" I asked, keeping my voice carefully neutral.

"Where? Why the Republic of Jackson, of course."

"You're one of them?" Seth asked, thumbing over his shoulder to indicate the outpost burning behind us.

"Ain't all Jacksonians warmongers!" the old man snapped. "Some of us *like* our peace and quiet. When the shootin' starts, the drinkin' stops."

"Now there's the gods' own truth," said Fenris.

I couldn't help but chuckle. "What can you tell us, friend?"

"The reason there ain't no garrisons down south is 'cause there ain't no need for 'em," he said. "We're protected by them uppity tree-worshippers." He cackled. "Them that call themselves *druids*."

"Druids," Seth repeated.

"Yep. There ain't no settlements between here and there, and as long as them treehuggers stick to the treaty, there ain't no reason to have a garrison."

Seth and I shared a look. I'd told him about the group of bandits I'd run into when Sebrina had sent me out with Darryn and Niall to "test" my shotgun on live enemies, and how they'd mentioned that our actions were in violation of a treaty. Worse, they had also known that the young men of the grove had no magic.

"There's a treaty?" Seth asked innocently.

"Everybody knows about that," said the dirty man. "I heard the President sealed the deal in a magical orgy with their leader, and that they danced naked around a fire in the moonlight."

Conall and Dermot wore twin expressions of disgust. I doubted that anything like that had *ever* happened and quickly shoved the thought away. I didn't want to think about Sebrina Silvermist at all, naked *or* clothed.

"Thanks for your help," I said.

"I don't suppose you got any food," the man said. "After all, you done went and burned down my home."

In fact, we had burned down the buildings only *after* emptying them of all useable food, supplies, clothing, and equipment. Siorus, Halldor, Yiorgos and their pentacles were busy going through everything and properly outfitting the people we'd rescued.

"Fenris, take him over and have Siorus give him whatever he needs."

"You're giving food to an *enemy*?" Wolfric protested.

"I *ain't* your enemy," said the dirty man, pointing a gnarled finger into his face. "I ain't *nobody's* enemy. Didn't nobody ever ask me before they took my woman and made me a slave. And they sure as hell didn't ask my permission before they stole my son and turned him into one of them."

"As they would have done with the witchlings," Duncan murmured.

I couldn't help but wonder if the drunk man's son was still alive, or perhaps dead at our hands. "This man has been wronged and deserves compassion, not criticism for trying to survive in the best way he knows how," I said, and the fire elementalist stiffened. No doubt I'd insulted his honor.

"Thank you, young man," said the dirty man. "My name's Carl. Used to be Carl Freeman, but I gave up using that name when I lost my family and my freedom."

"Davis," I said, shaking his proffered hand. "You're free now. You don't have to go back to the 'Ville."

"Don't have anywhere to go forward to, neither," Carl said.

"Come with me, Mr. Carl," Fenris offered. "We'll get you

445

something to eat." Clutching his bottle, he shuffled off after Fenris.

When he had wandered away, Seth said, "You were right about the treaty between the Republic and White Oak Grove."

"Sometimes things just add up."

"What if the druids at the grove hear about what we're doing and decide to get involved?" Dermot asked.

"I imagine they already know," Seth said.

"Then things are about to get very bad for us," Wolfric said darkly.

"Then we'd better get moving before they do," I said.

The others nodded solemnly.

Even though we had already ridden over a dozen miles that day, I had the Finns mount up and continue onward. According to Conall's map, we were only about five miles south of the 'Ville, and it was imperative that we catch up to Angie's pentacle before they wound up in hot water. I also wanted a place to scout out the 'Ville and start making a plan of attack.

Proceeding northeast for another few miles, we came across a long, narrow lake, the main body of which ran north-south, with a few fingers of water pointing to the west and fairly straight eastern border. Trees were scattered across the lake, indicating that it was fairly shallow, but it was still more than enough water for our water elementalists to use.

"We'll camp here," I said, calling a halt on the eastern side of the lake. There were a few clear acres of land near the shore, surrounded by forest to the north, east, and south. With the lake at our backs to the west, it would be a good place to stay the night.

The next morning I gathered all the water elementalists.

"I want you guys to find out everything there is to know about this lake," I said.

"Looks more like a swamp than a lake," Phelan said with a skeptical frown.

"That might work to our advantage," I said. "We need a place from which to conduct raids on the 'Ville. Someplace they won't find us easily."

"So we're looking for a place to hide," said Mohinder.

"Exactly."

"Why here?" asked Phelan.

"Because I want to be near water, and I think this is the last place they'll expect to find us." We'd carried out most of our attacks to the north and west of the 'Ville, so hiding out just south of the bandit city might be something they wouldn't expect.

"Are we splitting up?" Dermot asked, looking excited.

"Yes and no. I'm putting you in three groups, each of which will have offense, defense, and pure water."

"I'm my own offense and defense," said Galen. Mohinder, Nêreus, and Dermot all nodded agreement.

"I know, but I want your focus solely on the lake," I said. "First group is Nêreus, Ciaran, and Ridley. Second group is Mohinder, Skylar, and Barak. Third group is Galen, Westley, and Phelan. Phelan, that means you're shielding, not attacking."

"Understood," he said. He didn't look overly delighted with the prospect.

"Head out, guys. Be safe."

Assisted by the low temperatures and the dual wielders with both water and air, the scouting party formed thin, narrow sheets of curved ice and was soon zipping away over the surface of the lake.

"What about me?" Dermot asked, clearly upset at being excluded.

"You're staying here," I said. "We're going to hike around the southern shore to check out a couple of peninsulas."

"Why can't I go with them?"

"They're all druids."

"Ciaran isn't!"

I stifled a sigh. "Yes, he is. He got his full magic during the battle for Mayflower." With the obvious exception of our unmagicked gunmen, ten of the Finns were still elementalists.

"So are you afraid I'll get into trouble, or that I'll run off to find Ariadne?" he said, his voice low and angry.

"Neither," I said.

"Then why didn't you let me go? Surely I would be safe with a bunch of druids. Besides, I can channel more magic than any of them!"

"I know you can, and it's not only your safety that concerns me," I said. During our raid on the 'Ville to rescue the witchlings, we'd all seen just what he could do, and his Well was deep indeed. It had taken four days for him to get back to full strength. "I don't want your Well to get any lower than you can replenish overnight."

"You think I can't be trusted to mind my own magic? Thanks, Davis. Thanks a lot."

"Dermot—"

He held up a hand. "I don't want to hear it." He stalked off, took his horse's reins from Conall, and stood there sulking. The Norseman tried to pat him on the shoulder, but he jerked away and continued to glare at me.

Seth turned around as if inspecting the lake behind us. "Maybe you should have let him go," he said quietly. "As a sign of trust."

I did likewise so that we both stood with our backs to the Finns. "But I *don't* trust him. He overextended himself when we rescued the witchlings, and came close to tapping out at both Conway *and* Mayflower." All water elementalists tended to be led by their emotions, but Dermot's youth made him especially vulnerable to rash behavior.

"You're concerned that he'll get caught up in the moment."

"Or that he'll try to keep up with the big boys and do what the druids are doing," I said. "I can't afford to give him four days to recuperate if his Well gets depleted again."

The air elementalist nodded. "That is true."

I glanced back to see if Dermot was still glaring at me, but was distracted by the sight of Duncan, down on one knee with both palms on the ground. It was an odd sight, as he was fully capable of sensing and manipulating earth while standing – even with boots on. Other than going barefoot in warm weather for the sheer enjoyment of being in contact with the mother, an earth druid only made this sort of intimate physical connection with her when *seeking* over a far distance or exerting a tremendous amount of effort.

"Duncan?"

"Something is wrong," he replied. The rest of the earth druids – myself included – immediately dropped where they were, imitating his posture.

"I don't feel anything," said Siorus.

"Me, neither," said Halldor.

I, too, felt nothing, but that was odd in and of itself. At the very least, the presence of animals and trees should have been palpable. The others shrugged and shook their heads, looking at

Duncan, crouched motionless with his eyes closed.

"There's something, though," he said. "I can feel... I don't know what." He shook his head, frowning. "I've never felt anything like it before. It's like being blindfolded. Like something is keeping me from *seeking*."

It was a good description for what I myself was sensing, and I remembered the day Angie and I had met. My latent earth magic – which I had referred to as my 'sixth sense" at the time – had vanished. It was only later that I'd discovered the truth, that Angie's uncle Padraig, a fire-earth druid like myself, had used earth magic to hide both his presence and that of Angie's father, Liam.

"There's another earth druid out there," I said, immediately regretting having sent almost a third of our number away on a scouting mission.

Seth's head snapped around, and I knew we'd both come to the same conclusion: Sebrina must have taken action to honor her treaty with the 'Ville. She had sent someone to aid her allies.

"*Shields!*" the air elementalist roared.

Chapter 26 – The Battle by the Lake

Beware the wrath of a patient adversary.
~ John C. Calhoun ~

The Finns were stunned into stillness for the barest second, but it was more than long enough for disaster to strike. A burst of gunfire came from the forests on all three sides, taking down Eian, Declan, Alexandros - and *Seth*.

I watched in frozen horror as his body jerked, a fine mist of blood spraying from his chest before he collapsed. Duncan and the other earth druids laid hands on the fallen air elementalists just heartbeats later, and I prayed none of them had been killed outright.

Three raid groups exploded from the trees: one from the north, one from the east, and one from the south. My primary air elementalists were down, leaving me with air/spirit dual wielders Solon, Wyatt, Tristan, Barak, and Jasvinder and Narinder Chaudri, and *none* of them were full druids. Being in the same pentacle, Solon and Wyatt were accustomed to sharing the duties of offense and defense, as were Jasvinder and Tristan. It had made them well-balanced dualists who switched between their elements with equal expertise. In contrast, Narinder was accustomed to protecting his pentacle with air magic and occasionally attacking with spirit, while Barak played a primarily offensive role in his pentacle.

Indeed, while Tristan and Solon threw up large air shields to the north and south with Jasvinder and Wyatt backing them up, Barak went on the offensive and sprayed spirit lightning at the raiders to the east. A split second later, he spun around and hit the dirt, struck by gods knew how many bullets. He was screaming, though, so at least he was still alive. Wyatt stepped into the breach, raising his own air shield against the hailstorm of bullets that erupted from their guns.

Limited by the amount of magic contained in their Wells, they wouldn't hold out for long. Unlike Dermot's water shield, which could be repaired, a damaged air shield had to be dropped and reformed. As the air druids had done at the Conway garrison, the elementalists shuffled their shields rapidly, working in pairs, alternating holding a shield or readying to form a replacement as necessary. The odd number of elementalists hampered their ability to support one another.

I grabbed Conall and told him to get them to decrease the length of their shields as we dropped back. The less ground the air druids had to cover, the thicker their shields could be, and the longer they would last.

"Back up and move in tight!" he roared, somehow making himself heard in spite of the thunder of rifles and shotguns.

Wolfric raced to the front, arcing fireballs over the air shield to drop down among the bandits. Fenris followed his lead, lobbing spirit orbs by the dozens, sending the tiny blue-white balls to rain down upon them. Together they harried the enemy with fire and lightning while backing up behind the air elementalists.

Jasvinder and Narinder kept up rotating air shields with the others, alternating between them to maintain cover while simultaneously moving backward in a leapfrog pattern. As we retreated to the banks of the lake, the battlefront narrowed and the protective shields thickened. Quick glances were exchanged between five air dualists, followed by firm nods.

We're fine, their confident expressions seemed to say. *We've got this.*

I ran to the rear, where the gunmen had helped the earth druids drag the wounded, and knelt beside Seth. Holding my hand a couple of inches over his chest, I summoned the bullets from the deadly tunnels they'd made while Duncan healed his wounds one by one. Moving to Alexandros next, I tried not to look back at Seth's blood-soaked shirt and limp body. I went to each one's side and pulled the slugs from their bodies as quickly as the earth druids could heal them, then left them in their care and turned my attention back to the battle.

It was none too soon, for I felt that other earth druid, reaching out to take the ground beneath our feet. In a group with eight earth druids, we naturally claimed any ground over which we traveled, but we had all been focused on healing our wounded and had let it slip from our grasp. I stomped one foot, a symbolic move to reassert my control, and grabbed the battlefield as far as I could, stopping only when the other druid's magic bumped up against mine and made the earth tremble.

I shoved back with my own earth magic, causing a small but jarring quake. The Republic horses reared and bucked, some dislodging their riders and galloping away. Our own mounts merely snorted and pranced, long accustomed to fire, lightning, unstable ground, and the thunder of firearms. Each time the other earth druid struck, I hit back just a little bit harder, searching for her location.

It became apparent that the enemy druid's goal had been primarily to keep me distracted. Narinder screamed as he was struck down, shot in the back. Jasvinder would have gotten shot, too, had he not dropped to his knees to check on his brother. With a third of our protection gone, bullets whizzed by unimpeded. Solon took Narinder's place, risking his life to form another air shield.

I spun about to see enemies flanking us on the south and tried to construct an earthen wall while holding the ground against the enemy druid's attacks. It proved to be too many divisions for my attention. Even though I managed to get the barrier up, it crumbled as soon as we were assaulted by another enemy earthquake. I extended the firewall until it surrounded us on three sides and blazed it to a bright yellow heat. Intensifying my focus, I tried to create waves of earth to hold the Republic forces off. The enemy druid's magic thwarted my attempt, and the ground remained smooth beneath their feet. It was all I could do to keep the earth still beneath ours and maintain the firewall between us and the enemy.

"Hang on!" I heard Dermot yell. Ignoring the storm of bullets plunking into the water around him, he plunged his hands into the water and *yanked* it from the lake. A huge wave arced overhead and spread out into a wide dome that splashed down to cover us all in a giant version of his hard water turtle shell. Hundreds of bullets slammed against the water shield like a hailstorm, but Dermot repaired the cracks as soon as they formed. Standing in freezing water, the water elementalist shivered violently but never took his hands off the inner wall of the dome.

It was exactly the break I needed. Looking upward, I commanded the fire drake to dive. In a rush of bright yellow scales and smoking grey talons, it spread its scarlet wings and glided low over the ground, strafing the flanking Republic forces and breathing white-hot flame over them. I wasn't sure if the high-pitched noise outside the water dome was screaming or the sound of steam escaping the burning bodies. Angling its flight pattern slightly, it opened its jaws wider and incinerated the bandits to the south as they tried to run for their lives. A few flaps of its great wings brought it back to the raiders still attacking from the east, and it bellowed before enveloping them in an inferno that consumed every last enemy in the area.

All except one.

"*Find that druid!*" I snarled to the dragon. It banked sharply, eyes intent on the forest below. It found nothing after a few sweeps, but the enemy druid was still standing her ground, so I knew she hadn't changed position. If it couldn't find the druid, it would drive her out instead. The trees were sacred to us, but if I had to, I was going to destroy every last one of them to make sure she was either captured or charbroiled.

"Burn it down," I commanded through clenched teeth. "Burn it *all* down." With a roar, the dragon opened its maw wide, releasing a stream of pure flame that set the surrounding woods on fire. It glided over the trees, sweeping back and forth across the treetops, moving gradually closer to our position. The dragon made its final pass, torching the tree line. A lone figure burst through the trees as they combusted into a blazing wall of fire. Trailing flames, the enemy earth druid sprinted for the lake, dove into the frigid waters, and rolled around until her clothing was extinguished. As soon as I felt her stagger back onto dry land, I opened a hole under her feet. With a screech, she dropped inside, trapped.

I looked at Dermot, shaking with the effort of holding the dome, and gave him a nod. With a sigh of relief, he peeled back the water shield, starting at the forest side, then let it flow gently back into the lake bed. Smoke began to pour under the dome, but Solon and Wyatt got it under control and pushed it away.

The water druids came speeding back, racing over the surface of the lake on their narrow, concave platforms of hardened water. Leaping from its surface and onto dry land, they turned to putting out random fires around to the south and east.

Shotguns at the ready, Conall and Dermot flanked me as I walked over to the earthen prison I'd made. We were followed by Tristan, Solon, and Wyatt, all with spirit magic sparking at their fingertips. I squatted beside the hole, enjoying the irony of having trapped an earth druid in the dirt. Commanding the earth beneath her feet to rise, I created a bright fireball as soon as we were face to face and was rewarded when she flinched in fear. Holding it overhead to illuminate our quarry while remaining in shadow myself, the flames revealed a woman's frightened face, her wet hair and clothes plastered to her shivering body.

I blinked in disbelief.

Never had I expected the ArchDruid to send one of her own Tetrarch.

"Dianthe Aspen," I said aloud, as though saying her name would make her presence less fantastic, or less frightening.

"Who are you?" she demanded, standing with a regal pose and holding her head high, but the effect was spoiled by her chattering teeth. "How do you know my name?"

Her eyes were a pale blue – eyes that she had passed down to her son Orion. They were the eyes of a man I would never forget, a man who had been driven mad by his desire for magic, and perhaps also by his desire for his mother's love. They were the eyes of the man who had tried to kill me.

I drew back my hood and lowered the firelight to she could see my face, and she turned white with fear.

"I see you remember me."

"*Impossible!*" she whispered. "You're dead!"

"Oh, I am *very* much alive and *very* pissed off," I growled. "My second was one of the air elementalists your allies gunned down."

"Everyone lives," Duncan said as he made his way to my side.

"Good," I said, much relieved. "Thank you." I was thanking him specifically for saving Seth, but also for helping me keep my

454

promise to Master Shitozaki to bring everyone home alive.

"Pity," sneered Dianthe. "You should all be neutered, and if not that, *exterminated*."

Realizing who she was, Duncan gave a jerk, his dark eyes wide. The surprise was mutual.

"Duncan Everlight." Her sharp blue gaze flickered to me, then back to him. "I knew we should have neutered you, no matter what Sebrina said! She always was too concerned with the opinion of her First Warrior." Her tone made the title an insult. "A fat lot of good it did her now that he's gone!"

"Gone," I said. "Liam's dead?"

"If only that were true," Dianthe spat. "He broke his oath and severed their tie as chosen. And as if deserting the ArchDruid was not enough, he and his wretched brother abandoned the grove and took nearly half our people with them, the traitors!"

Though he showed no outward sign of it, Duncan's excitement at hearing the news thrummed through the earth. I sent a thrill of happiness back to him. Liam *had* left the grove with Padraig and Angie!

Dianthe's lip curled in a snarl as she continued to glare at him. "We should have known *you* were responsible for the disappearance of this filthy Outsider."

Duncan said nothing, but his dark eyes narrowed.

A sly smile slipped over Dianthe's lips. "Although, it would have been prudent to inform your family that you had done so. Then perhaps Liam would not have gone on a mad rampage kicking in doors and threatening people in his vain attempt to find him."

"I assume this was before leaving the grove?" I said.

"I will not demean myself by speaking with a barbarian," she hissed.

"My father and uncle – where did they go?" Duncan asked.

"I neither know nor care," she spat.

"No matter," I said. "It is enough to know that they are free of Sebrina's tyranny."

After a moment, he nodded. "That it is."

"You have your answers," Dianthe said. "Now release me."

I smiled. It was neither pleasant nor friendly. "Release you?"

"Yes! The only reason I have had any dealing at all with those barbarians from the 'Ville is because Sebrina demanded that I represent her in upholding our part of the treaty!"

"She sent you alone?"

A shadow of cunning crossed her face and was gone in an instant. I drew my sword and laid it against her neck. It steamed with cold in the bitter air and froze the neckline of her drenched garment, causing her breath to hitch.

"Do not waste your breath with a lie. Who else is with you? Your chosen?"

"I have no chosen!" she spat.

"That is true," Duncan said. "Her chosen abandoned her and quit the grove when he found out she had denied Orion his gift."

I pressed the grey blade harder against her throat. Frost spread from the neckline of her garment until the skin on her neck and face glittered with it.

"Who. Is. With. You."

"Laiken Birch, Shonda Cotton, and Poppy Braden," she whispered. "Blythe Hollander. Fiona Roughgarden."

"And their elements?"

"Laiken and Shonda are triple threats. Blythe has fire. Poppy and Fiona are earth/fire dualists. Druids, all of them."

"And?" I knew she wouldn't have left them alone – in the 'Ville or otherwise.

"And their chosen, of course!"

"Do they have shotguns?"

"No!" Her offended expression was so genuine that I believed her.

"Do they have magic?" Duncan asked. It was something I would never have thought to ask.

"Absolutely not! *Their* mothers are loyal supporters of the ArchDruid! Now release me!"

"Very well." I stepped back and withdrew the grey blade, sheathing it. The muscles in my arm trembled, rebelling at the thought of putting the sword away without blooding it. The Morrigan may have named me her champion, I was *not* her slave.

"Now release me!" Dianthe demanded.

"No one promised to let you go," said Duncan, drawing his own sword and advancing on her. "Dianthe Aspen, you are an offense to the Shining Ones and a blight to the Nature Spirits. You are a disgrace to your ancestors. You bring shame upon every druid who has ever lived."

"You should have died with your traitor mother!" she screamed, cowering from him. "You should have been thrown upon her corpse and burned alive!"

"The Earth Mother weeps at the touch of your feet," he said.

He never even asked who his mother was.

He just ran her through.

* * *

When the water druids had finished putting out all the fires and cooling the scorched earth, they demanded to know what had happened. Conall and Dermot started explaining, and I went to check on Seth.

Relieved to see his eyes open, I knelt down by him and took his hand. "How are you?"

"I'm still alive," he croaked. "My chest hurts like Duncan dug the bullets out with a knife."

"I got them out with magic," I said, "but it doesn't feel any better."

"You did that in the middle of a battle?"

"Can't use a knife to dig a bullet out of your lungs."

He sat up, grimacing. "You shouldn't have. You should have waited until it was over and everyone was safe."

"Maybe next time."

"I'm serious, Davis. You should not show me special favor."

"When I promised your father that I'd bring everyone back alive, that included you, too," I said drily.

"Funny." His dark eyes traveled over the rumpled earth along the battlefront and then took in the smoking forest, still burning in spots. "I think that Carl Freeman might have betrayed us for another bottle," he said.

"He might have," I said. The 'Ville was only about an hour away. Even a drunken old sot like that could have made it there by nightfall yesterday.

"Help me up."

I grabbed Seth's hand and helped him to his feet. The newly arrived water elementalists fell silent when they saw his disheveled state.

"This is my favorite shirt," the air elementalist complained.

"They were gunning for you and the other air elementalists."

"Dianthe Aspen must have educated them on druid abilities and tactics," Duncan observed.

Seth frowned in puzzlement. "Isn't she one of Sebrina's Tetrarch?"

"She was," I replied.

Following my gaze, Seth turned to see Galen wrapping vines about the chest of Dianthe's corpse so the other six earth druids could hoist her into the blackened hulk of the only tree in the area that still had branches. It seemed that they all shared Duncan's opinion when it came to keeping her from touching the earth. Denying an earth druid the privilege of being buried in her element and consigning her to the predations of carrion crows was a harsh punishment indeed.

One of her boots had fallen off, and she hadn't been wearing socks. It was like she couldn't be bothered with putting any on, either because she had thought her mission would be over quickly, or because she couldn't stand another layer of separation between her feet and the earth. For some reason I found myself staring at that one bare foot with its vulnerable toes and dirty sole.

We had killed a druid.

"This is terrible," Seth said, putting his hands on his hips and surveying the scene with a disgruntled expression. I sighed and got ready to explain why Duncan had killed the woman.

"We're going to have to put in a *lot* of work to bring this forest back," he finished.

"Oh. Right." Relief washed over me. "We'll get to that in the spring." Right after repairing Faulkner and Mayflower.

"After we destroy the 'Ville," Conall said as he and Dermot joined us.

Seth nodded. "Of course."

"At least something good came from all this," Dermot said.

"What?" I asked.

"The others found us a hideout," he replied.

Beside him, Phelan nodded. "There's a big swamp on the north side of the lake. As far as we could tell, there's only one easy way in or out."

"Anywhere to set up camp?" I asked.

"There's a narrow island to the north. There aren't a lot of trees, but the ones there are have pretty thick trunks."

"Galen says the entire lake is shallow enough for the horses to walk across and never get their knees wet," Dermot added. "Except for your horse, Davis. He'll probably have to swim."

"Sounds like exactly what we need," Conall said.

"We'd better get moving then," Seth said.

I looked around at the remaining air elementalists, still passed out on the ground with their pentacle leaders beside them.

"How are you even awake?" I asked him.

"I don't know." A sly expression came over his face. "Maybe it's because I got my full magic."

I whooped, startling half the Finns. "Praise the gods!" I cried, hugging him.

"Yeah," said Conall. "Because if there's anybody who needs an air *druid* to shield him, it's Davis."

Those that were able mounted up and started across the shallow lake on horseback. The druids with elemental water took charge of transporting the wounded. They created larger versions of the scooped hard water platforms for them to lie on and pulled them behind their horses with fluid ropes. We reached the center of the swamp, where the trees parted and the ground rose to a slightly higher elevation, revealing a patch of dry land just big enough for us and our horses.

"Excellent work, guys," I said. "This place is perfect!"

We unloaded and set up camp in the growing dark, settling the wounded together in the center. There they were more easily protected, and only a couple of earth druids at a time were needed to watch over them, allowing the others to rest. I solved the problem of hiding the dragon by digging down into the little island and burying it. Only its face remained visible, eyes burning like coals and nostrils emitting smoke. The radiant heat of its body was more than enough to keep everybody warm at night, killing two birds with one stone. As the light faded from the sky, ice formed at the outer edges of the lake, but not along the shore of the island. Within the camp, we were shielded from the bitter wind by the trees and their thick clumps of grey-green moss.

I was about to bed down for the night when I noticed Dermot standing alone at the edge of camp, staring off into the darkness. I went over to him, reminding myself once again that no matter how powerful this water elementalist was, he was still little more than a boy. He had been forced to grow up and become a man too soon, and while he had taken on that challenge with determination and courage, there was a fragile part inside of him still.

"I'm sorry about today," I said. "I should have let you go with the others."

"Gods, if you had, we'd all be dead," Dermot said.

He was right. The Republic forces had known to target the air elementalists to make us vulnerable, so the logical progression was that they would have taken out our healers next. Without earth or air for protection, the spirit and fire elementalists would have been sitting ducks, and the emotional water elementalists would have charged into battle to avenge their comrades. While my fire shield would have protected me, helplessly watching my friends fall one by one might very well have spurred me into a foolish action that could have resulted in my own demise.

"Thanks to you, we're alive."

"No offense," he said, "but I don't think sending out all the water druids was a very good idea."

"That's the gods' own truth," I said.

He added, "After all, the lake isn't *that* big."

"What's bothering you?" I asked.

"What if they were attacked like we were today?" he said. "Ariadne could be dead now, and I'd never even know it."

"It's possible that they are in danger, but Dianthe Aspen brought that army specifically to kill *us*." I put my hand on his shoulder. "Your sister will be all right. Angie will keep her safe."

"How can you be so sure?"

"Because she kept *me* safe."

He looked at me in surprise. "She did?"

I nodded. "Angie used air shields to keep me from getting shot, just like Seth does."

"I don't like the idea of people shooting at my sister."

"Nor do I, but I trust Angie. She's smart and brave and loyal to her friends," I said. "You can trust her to keep Ariadne safe."

* * *

We were stuck in the swamp until the wounded Finns were

fully recovered, but that didn't stop me from taking action. We discussed our options over stale biscuits and the last of the coffee the next morning. Ordinarily, I'd have included just the members of my pentacle and the other earth druids, but for this, I wanted everyone's input.

"We need to know what's out there for certain," I said. "We may have found a place to hide, but for all we know, we could be surrounded by enemies."

"Our choices seem to be limited," Seth said. "Should we send scouts alone, or in groups?"

"Going in groups would be safer," said Siorus.

Beside him, Madoc nodded. "Bandits won't think twice about taking on a lone man."

"If you're suggesting that there is safety in numbers, they haven't thought twice about taking on all *thirty-six* of us," Phelan argued.

"A single rider is more easily overlooked," said Duncan. "A person alone and on foot even more so."

"Can't run away from a horse if you're on foot," said Fenris.

"I do not need to run," the earth druid replied.

"Well, *woo-hoo-hoo!*" mocked the spirit druid. "Listen to the big, bad swordsman!"

"While I am considered a master swordsman," said Duncan, "I was referring to my ability to conceal myself quickly."

"It's simply amazing that anyone here would still be dumb enough to try and bait Duncan Everlight," Conall said, smirking at Fenris. "In fact, I'm pretty sure you're the only one."

"Shut up."

Seth cleared his throat. "Phelan is right," he said, returning to the topic at hand. "It doesn't matter whether we send one person or a dozen. In all likelihood, the risk of encountering danger is the same."

"I have to say I agree with Siorus, that pentacles would be better," said Wyatt. "But right now Davis has the only pentacle that's fully functional."

"He's right," agreed Solon. "That effectively takes pentacles off the table for discussion."

"Not necessarily," said Nêreus. "We could combine members of different pentacles."

I shook my head. "It's not realistic to throw five people together and expecting it to function as well as a pentacle that's been together for several weeks."

"We saw evidence of that yesterday," said Halldor. "We can't just assume that a dualist or triple threat will automatically know which element to use in any given situation."

No doubt he was referring to the way Barak had immediately chosen to use his spirit magic to attack our enemies rather than elemental air to shield his allies.

Yiorgos nodded agreement. "True. Even when instructed to take a certain action, the natural reaction when one's life is in peril is to fall back on what one knows best."

"Perhaps we should switch things up a bit," Phelan suggested.

"It's a good idea, and under different circumstances, I'd utilize your suggestion," I said. "I'm not willing to do that at this point, however. We're better off with everybody doing what they know best."

"Then in the future, I suggest that we not split up at all," Martin snapped. His bitter and angry tone resulted in a moment of silence while no few of the Finns looked up at the sky, down at the ground, or anywhere but at me.

Martin was mild-mannered by nature, rarely offering suggestions, and was generally content to follow the will of the group. In addition, outside of our pentacles, we earth druids were a close-knit group. The most likely explanation for his ire was that the injuries suffered by his air druid, Alexandros, were second in severity only to Seth's, and while *my* air druid was already up and about, his had not yet recovered.

"Point taken," I said. "My decision to send so many out scouting was a mistake. In the future, I will keep everybody together unless it is safer to do otherwise."

After a moment, Martin gave me a sharp nod of acknowledgement, while all the other earth druids looked relieved. Until that moment, I had not appreciated the stress they'd been under where keeping their pentacles healed was concerned. Evidently, we were not as close as I'd believed, possibly because I could dual wield fire and earth, or simply because I was in command. Regardless of the reason, after this scouting mission, I was going to ask for input before enacting any future plans. Things tended to go badly when I acted without the input of others.

"Have you tried looking through the dragon's eyes?" Wolfric asked, breaking the silence.

"Yes. I can't see anything." It was annoying and frustrating.

"He couldn't see through the lion's eyes, so why even ask?" said Ingvar, sounding irate.

"Because it is a different form," Wolfric replied tightly. "Things might have changed."

"You don't think Davis is smart enough to think of that first?" Ingvar shot back. His vehemence and the frowns on the faces of the other earth druids suggested that maybe it *was* my leadership position that had kept them from coming to me with their concerns. Perhaps dealing with the situation without complaining was their way of supporting me.

"Alright, alright," I said, interrupting before an argument could start. "As recent events have proven, the answer to that is: not always."

"That's just the overconfidence of elemental fire," Seth said. He had a tendency to attribute anyone's mistakes as a side effect of their particular element – usually the most powerful or dominant one. "I had some misgivings about sending such a large percentage of the war band away and should have spoken up."

"What if we go out in pairs?" Wyatt suggested. "If one falters, the other can support him."

I shook my head. "I don't want anyone seen, period."

"What difference does it make?" asked Mohinder. "The bad guys already know we're here."

"But not our exact location," Seth said. "Say we send out two people in each of the cardinal and intercardinal directions and four of the pairs are spotted. Theoretically, whoever sees them might happen to mention it to someone else, and word might get back to the 'Ville that there have been sightings of strangers in certain locations. It would allow them to pinpoint down our location."

Dermot piped up. "They might just assume a lone rider is from the 'Ville because nobody else would dare to go out alone."

Yiorgos said, "Whoever we send must be able to hide, and quickly."

"I believe that was what Duncan was getting at in the beginning," said Conall. "The earth druids are the only ones who can hide in seconds by dropping into a hole in the ground. I've even seen Duncan hide his *horse*."

"We're also the only ones who can perform a *seeking*," said Halldor.

"Or hide our tracks," added Warwick. The grey shrike on his shoulder chirped agreement.

"*Or heal!*" said Martin, clearly not over his anger. "Just in case any of you have forgotten, a third of our number has been wounded! *Someone* has to stay and make sure they recover!"

"How many healers do you need for this task?" I asked. "They aren't critical anymore, so how many healers really need to stay?"

Siorus shifted uncomfortably. "At least two, so they can take turns."

"That puts quite a strain on whoever stays here," Seth said. "Let's make it three so you can rotate every few hours. Siorus, Yiorgos, and Martin can stay if nobody has any objections?"

"Sounds good to me," I said. "That leaves five to explore the territory."

"Five?" Seth asked. "Who's the fifth?"

"Me. I can't heal, but I can play hide and seek with the best of 'em."

"That will leave us leaderless," he protested.

"No, it won't. You'll be here."

Ingvar, Warwick, and Halldor went west, south, and southeast, respectively. Duncan and I would scout closest to the 'Ville, with him going northwest while I headed east/northeast. Even if I hadn't been responsible for the Finns, we still would have been the logical choices for the riskier areas simply because he could hide faster than anyone, and I could defend myself with fire.

As Steel splashed through the shallow lake, I found myself looking forward to having some time alone. I loved my friends and the camaraderie I shared with them, but there were times when I missed the quiet lifestyle of a Traveler. And while this was a scouting mission and stealth was essential, the thought of engaging the enemy on my own was appealing.

This just might be fun.

Chapter 27 – Discovery

When in doubt, do it.
~ Oliver Wendell Holmes, Jr. ~

While my main objective was to discover the locations of any other outposts or garrisons in the area, finding another place to camp was also on my mind. Dianthe Aspen had led the Republic soldiers to us using earth magic, but the dozen or so acres I'd burned trying to find her had sent billowing black smoke into the air had announced our location like nothing else could.

Normally the air elementalists would have taken care of that, but so many of them had been wounded that the smoke had billowed into the sky unrestrained. Staying on the island was a risk, but I figured it would be fine for another day or two. Gearing up and provisioning more Republic forces for another campaign against us was likely to take at least that long.

Getting another member of Sebrina's Tetrarch to lead that army, however... that might take a bit longer.

I followed a winding stream out of the swamp, crossing open grasslands at an easy pace and sitting relaxed in the saddle like I had every right to be there – which I did, even if the Republic of Jackson didn't recognize that fact. If any hostile individuals wanted to challenge that right, I would be more than happy to oblige them. None showed up, however, and Steel continued his forward march across the plain. We crossed the flatlands and passed into a boggy area where the ground squelched under his hooves, and when I turned around to check my back trail, I could no longer see the plains.

Dismounting to touch the earth, I did a *seeking* to see if I could get an idea of how extensive the wetlands were. A water elementalist would have had an easier time of it because they could read the path of water the same way an earth elementalist could read the lay of the land. However, since I'd left Dermot behind with the others, I'd have to rely on my own magic and a little bit of cleverness. Earth magic couldn't tell me where the water was – but it could give me an idea of where the water *wasn't*.

For as far as I could *seek* – which was about a mile – the whole territory was a comprised of soggy islands of earth that had been created by the myriad rivers, creeks, and streams crisscrossing the land. Swinging back into the saddle, I guided Steel deep into the marshlands. Trees lined each of the channels and clumped together in the larger expanses of green swamp water. There seemed to be no end to it. I reckoned that anybody who was followed us in here would be quickly baffled and led astray by the many meandering streams. Even a druid would have a hard time finding his way around.

I couldn't have found a better place to stage raids on the 'Ville if the gods themselves had led me to it and was cheerfully congratulating myself on a job well done when I came across a man-made structure. Steel noticed its presence first, coming to an abrupt halt and raising his head with nostrils flaring and ears perked forward. Catching a glimpse of dark brown timbers between the pale trunks of the marsh trees, I patted the stallion's neck and praised him, for the early warning might very well have saved me from a bullet to the brain.

It was strange that the Republic had chosen a location like this for a fort when all the other sites had been cleared of trees, standing boldly in the open. Were they hiding it from their druid allies in the grove? Or was it a place to hide the their druid allies? Was this where Dianthe and her army had come from?

I frowned. No matter which it was, the best course of action was to find out and deal with it. Hopefully, it was just an outpost, because a garrison would take a long time to capture unless I was willing to burn it to the ground from outside – which I wasn't. Killing our enemies was one thing, but condemning to death the innocent enslaved people who might be inside was something else entirely.

The abundance of water confounded my earth magic, so I circled the fort, giving the palisade a wide berth. I rode as far away from them as I could and still keep them in view. Winding his way through the trees and up and down hillocks, Steel kept one ear on the fort while I kept both eyes on it. After one complete circuit, I decided it was only a little larger than the outposts we'd previously encountered. I could destroy it alone if necessary.

But should I?

Now that I knew where the fort was, it would be easy to avoid. What better place to hide than in the shadow of our enemy? After all, I'd stumbled across it by pure dumb luck. How much more difficult would it be for them to find us, a group of druids who lived as one with the land and who manipulated the elements according to our will?

If it had been just me, I'd have chanced it without a second thought. I had thirty-five other men relying on me, however, and I wasn't sure if I should ask *them* to take that risk. After all, one man could escape notice more easily than thirty.

Turning Steel east once more, I rode on past the fort, still pondering what the best course of action might be when events conspired to decide things for me. The crack of a rifle shattered the quiet morning, and I was showered by splinters when a nearby tree took the bullet meant for me. Now I *had* to do something about it. Working on the assumption that the rifleman had missed because the foliage had obscured his view, I left Steel in a heavy thicket and proceeded to the fort on foot.

Altering course randomly, I was able to avoid the next few shots but had a feeling the bandits would soon be leaving their hideaway to hunt me down. I wasn't too concerned about that, but the creeping suspicion that they might have grove druids with them was worrisome. For all I knew, Sebrina could have sent her whole Tetrarch to deal with us and not just Dianthe Aspen. Nualla Ashcroft couldn't hurt me since she was just a fire druid, but Pollona Morningstar and Betrys Darkmane were both triple threats. Either of them could bring me down with a single spirit bolt, effectively fulfilling Kam Stone's prophecy. Logic suggested that any druids inside would have come out to deal with me already, but perhaps the random gunfire was their way of luring me into a trap.

If it was a trap, it was an effective one, but it was too late for recriminations. Whether grove druids were present or not, I couldn't risk being followed back to where the Finns were holed up. Especially not with the air elementalists wounded and most of the earth druids away scouting. There was no sign of magic and my communication with the earth mother was unaffected by enemy opposition thus far, so I sprinted to the protective cover of the palisade wall. Moving without my fire shield was hazardous, but it seemed safer to remain unseen. I still had no protection against spirit magic, but targeting me would be awfully hard while I was standing in the lee of the wall.

Shouting erupted from the other side of the palisade, accompanied by the sound of guns being loaded and rounds chambered. There were a few more shots fired randomly into the swamp; I surmised they were intended to pin me down or draw me out. Running stealthily along the timbered wall with fire shield ignited and sword drawn, I rounded the northwest corner of the fort and came face to face with a trio of gunslingers. They fired without hesitation, but my spinning shield of flames melted the bullets. The liquid metal was flung against the wall, sizzling as it dripped down the blackening wooden timbers.

I took out the gunslinger on the left first, gouging deep into his shoulder with such force that the grey blade slashed through his collarbone and down through his ribcage. In the heat of a first engagement, I often forgot that I didn't need to swing with my full strength. Training demanded that I follow through on the strike and the grey blade exited his body just above the right hip, slicing him in two. Blood gushed from his torso like a fountain where the aorta had been severed, spattering on the ground and burning on the fire shield, filling the air with a foul metallic stench. Pivoting right, I severed the neck of the woman in the middle, who had been steadily firing twin pistols with a snarl on her face. Her guns and her head struck the ground in the same instant; it was one of the stranger things I'd seen happen. The last gunslinger, another woman, had dropped her empty pistol and was desperately firing the other while trying to run backwards. Panic made her keep pulling the trigger, even though the click of the hammer was the only result. She screamed when I lopped off her hand, falling to her knees and clutching her arm. She stopped screaming when I plunged the point of the sword through her neck. Her body fell right in front of the entrance to the fort, blocking the gate, but that didn't matter. A burst of earth magic punched the gates inward, snapping the crossbar in two.

The flame shield spread out to protect me as gunfire came in from all directions. It would have been easier to burn them all, but the smoke would have given away my presence. Resigning myself to the slaughter, I took them out one by one, keeping a tight rein on my mind and my magic. One man came at me from behind with an axe. My elemental fire was blazing an intensely hot yellow, melting the sharp edge to dripping sludge. Pain lanced all the way up to my skull when the thick part of the axe struck my spine, but it didn't kill or cripple me. I shifted my stance and turned sharply, the grey blade whipping about in an arc with a speed and power that remained undiminished as it passed through his neck, separating his head from his shoulders. I came back around, searching for the next enemy, the next target, the next victim, and soon found myself surrounded only by corpses.

The blood lust subsided as I caught my breath, and I sheathed the grey blade but continued to maintain the fire shield. Even if there had been someone here to heal me, I refused to repeat the mistake I'd made in Watson. Maybe I made foolish mistakes from time to time, but at least I learned from them. As my father often said: *That which does not kill me, makes me stronger.* He had always laughed when he said it, which I'd never understood until I had left home. It was gallows humor, the kind you get when you've cheated death a time or two.

I searched every room, closet, and cupboard of every single structure, searching for enemies but also keeping an eye out for signs of Angie. If she had continued her eastward journey, she might have stumbled across this place. The search effectively ensured my own safety but found I no trace of my chosen. Only one door remained, but I didn't have much hope since I didn't feel her through the bond we shared.

Dropping the fire shield, I opened the final door to find myself in a small room with only a single tiny window high up on one wall to let in light. Its furnishings were sparse and only included a washstand, a pallet of blankets on the floor, and a chair with a broken leg. It was both a disappointment and a relief to find no sign of Angie here.

A short, narrow object came at my face as I turned to leave. Quick reflexes saved me from a broken nose as fire blossomed forth instinctively, turning the stocky club to ash in an instant. I stepped toward this new enemy with stinging eyes and the intent to kill, but the sound of a familiar female voice stopped me.

"Davis, wait! I'm sorry! I thought you were one of *them*!"

Squinting through the ash burning my eyes, I could just make out a slender woman with light-colored hair. She was standing with her hands raised in the air – not in surrender, but in a gesture of calming.

"Who are you?"

"Don't you – Oh, wait, your eyes. No, don't move away. Let me help." Cool hands touched my face, and the eye irritation faded away. My vision cleared, bringing into focus the face of Iriana Disney.

"Iriana! What are you doing here?"

"By the gods, you *are* alive!" she exclaimed.

Back at White Oak Grove, Iriana had never seemed to like me much, merely tolerating me for Angie's sake. She surprised me by grabbing my free hand and squeezing it tightly. I stilled my impatience, realizing that she needed a moment to overcome her shock at seeing me alive or I wouldn't get the answers I desperately wanted.

"Where is Angie?" I asked. "Has she been captured?"

Iriana's face fell. "I don't know. The bandits were chasing us, and we got separated," she said. "I've been Dianthe's captive for three weeks, and she locked me in this room three days ago."

My gut clenched at this news. "Did they hurt you?"

She shook her head. "They haven't laid a finger on me."

"Good. Let's go before any more of them show up," I said, placing a hand on her elbow and guiding her out of the building. She stopped in her tracks when she caught sight of the blood-splashed walls and dismembered bodies littering the yard.

"Come on," I said, holding out my hand. "Let's find you a horse."

Iriana's wide-eyed gaze traveled over the dismembered corpses and puddles of blood before returning again to me, but all she said was: "Dianthe's horse is in its stall back there, behind the smithy."

She pointed out a building that was little more than a shed. It was constructed of sturdy posts in the front and walls on only three sides. Coals still glowed brightly in the blacksmith's forge, as though he had set aside the task at hand in order to deal with me. I drew the heat to me, and the coals went dark; a random spark could set the fort ablaze and attract unwanted attention. Drawing my sword, I told Iriana to stay behind me and in place called forth a burst of elemental fire to creating a forward shield. Hearing her gasp, I glanced over my shoulder and prepared to attack if an enemy appeared. There was nothing, so I raised an eyebrow at her.

"It's nothing," she said, looking embarrassed. "I was just... I've never seen anybody do that."

"It's a fire shield," I said. "If anybody shoots at us, it'll melt the bullets before they hit."

She nodded, and we proceeded around the corner of the building. All the other structures made use of the palisade for one or two walls, but this one had space behind it with an angled roof. Beneath the roof was a tall chestnut gelding with a star and four white socks.

"That's him," Iriana said. "He returned alone last night. I kept watching out the little window but never could find out what happened to Dianthe or the men she took ·with her."

I said nothing while I ran my hand over the horse's glossy coat, checking carefully for abrasions, cuts, and burns. He was completely sound and whole, a sign that Dianthe had cared for her horse enough to have kept him well away from the fight.

"I was so afraid that they'd found all of you," Iriana said. "The Finns, I mean."

"They did," I said, poking my nose into the tiny tack room behind the gelding's stall. It was more of a tack closet, really.

"Oh no!" she cried. "She had two hundred soldiers with her when she left! What happened?"

"It was more like a hundred and fifty," I said, backing out the door with a saddle. Someone had thoughtfully oiled both it and the bridle before putting them neatly away. There were also two large sacks of grain; I'd have to get those before we left.

"And you're the only one left?"

Hearing a catch in Iriana's voice, I looked over my shoulder at her, noting her distressed expression and the tears in her eyes.

"No, of course not," I said, placing the saddle and pad on the mare's back. "People got hurt because they took us by surprise, but nobody died."

"Oh, thank the gods!"

"Thirty men with elemental magic are more than a match for a hundred fifty bandits," I said, buckling the girth. "How do you even know about the Finns?"

Iriana slipped the bridle over the horse's ears and began fastening its various buckles. Druid bridles were more complicated than the one Steel wore.

"ArchDruid Shitozaki told us," she replied.

"*ArchDruid* Shitozaki?" Since when had he resumed using his former title?

"After you died and Duncan went missing, the Everlight family came together and tried to oust Sebrina. When that didn't work, they decided to quit the grove and promised to protect anyone else who wanted to come," she said. "We met Connor Shitozaki and the rest of the Finns about a week after leaving the grove, and he guided us to his secret sanctuary. Everyone was so astounded! The older generation wept to see so many boys who still had their magic. The vote to make him ArchDruid again was nearly unanimous."

The last pieces of what had happened in White Oak Grove fell into place. I wondered if the rest of the Finns would be happy for the opportunity to live among their own people, or resentful that they'd been outcasts for so long and choose to live with the Ward Coven instead. While Sebrina had spearheaded the movement to take their magic away, it had been the tacit approval of the rest of the grove that had sealed their fate.

"I always wanted a horse this nice," Iriana said, leading the red horse out of the stall. "But you have to be friends with the right people and my family wasn't, if you know what I mean."

"He's all yours," I said, picking up the bags of grain and laying them across the gelding's withers and saddle. "Dianthe won't be coming back for him."

"You killed her?"

"No, but I probably would have if Duncan hadn't."

"*Duncan Everlight* killed Dianthe Aspen?!" Her bewildered expression turned to one of dismay. "Sebrina won't like that. Once she finds out, it'll be *her* hunting you."

I shrugged. I was working under the assumption that she already was, with the members of her Tetrarch acting as her hands.

"Where is everybody else?" she asked, wrinkling her nose at the raw odors of iron and melted brass.

"Hiding," I said. "Come on. My horse is outside," I said, leading the way across the courtyard. Iriana led her horse, stepping gingerly over a decapitated head as we made our way out the destroyed gates. I wracked my brain, trying to decide if we should return to the Finns or try to find Angie first.

"Do you think you could take me to where you were captured?" I asked, thinking it likely that she would have tried to stay in the area to look for Iriana.

She made another sour face. "No. They captured me at night, and I was blindfolded."

"And you didn't perform a *seeking*?"

She looked down at her feet. "I can't."

"Sorry, I must have misremembered. I thought you were an earth elementalist."

"I *am* an earth elementalist," she said, frowning. "I'm just not a very good one."

"Oh."

"I can't earthmove, but I'm very good at healing."

So much for my idea for retracing her steps. If she couldn't do a *seeking*, she wouldn't be able to feel her way back to where she'd been captured.

"Healing is good," I said. She seemed to need some reassurance.

"Can you feel Angie through the bond?" she asked hopefully.

"No."

"She's too far away, then," Iriana said. "You shouldn't worry, though. She won't *ever* stop searching for you."

Her words stopped me in my tracks. While her lack of concern that Angie could be in extreme danger should have been what had garnered my attention, what gripped me hardest was her confidence in my chosen's dedication to finding me. Her eyes held only faith and honesty, bolstering my own trust in the connection

473

Angie and I shared.

Continuing onward through the marshy wood to where I'd left Steel, I wondered if she could be right. I reckoned Angie was pretty angry with me. After all, I'd abandoned her to save my own skin. Guilt assailed me, a guilt I hadn't felt since summertime. I shouldn't have come out here with the Finns. I should have gone to get her instead.

"You're lucky I came when I did," I said, changing the subject. "Republic soldiers are not known for treating women kindly."

"I think they were holding me hostage for ransom, or maybe to use as a bargaining chip."

I grunted. I might have bargained with the bandits to save someone, but it wouldn't have stopped me from killing them afterward. It wasn't in my nature to lie, but our enemies were duplicitous and not to be trusted. In any event, they'd have been on Iriana as soon as they realized Dianthe would never return.

"So they know we're druids." I had assumed as much.

Iriana nodded. "They don't know exactly who you are, but I heard some of the soldiers talking about capturing you."

I let out a grim chuckle. You'd think they'd have known better, but maybe news of the battle for Mayflower hadn't reached them yet. After all, no survivors had remained to carry the tale. Even so, I couldn't come up with a single reason for them to want to capture any of us. Even if the so-called President Jackson wanted to curry Sebrina's favor, all he'd have to do is present her with our heads.

"Dianthe told them to kill the lot of you and be done with it," she added.

"Considering what happened to her, I'd say that was good advice."

"What a dreadful thing to say!"

"It might be if you didn't know that we've been waging war against the Republic for the last few weeks," I said.

"You've been fighting a war?"

"It didn't start out that way, but that's what it became."

"Don't you think that will put a lot of people in danger?"

"They were already in danger," I replied. "You can't even ride through the territory without being harassed."

"We certainly found that to be true," Iriana agreed. "But I'm not sure that starting a war is the answer."

"*We* didn't start anything," I said. "As far as I can tell, every town and village within a day's ride of the 'Ville has been attacked and overrun, including Ward."

"Ward. Isn't that where you and Angie met the witches?"

"Yes. We'd only been out for a week or two when we came across them in the wilderness. They were just days from dying of starvation and exposure."

"You helped them get their home back?"

I nodded. "We did. We stayed awhile and defended it, and then helped them get their children back."

"Their *children* were taken?" Iriana was aghast.

"The Republic of Jackson has made quite a name for itself, kidnapping children, enslaving the people they conquered, and torturing the ones that rebelled." I gave her a knowing look. "Still think fighting a war against them is a bad idea?"

"No," she said quietly, shaking her head. "No, of course not."

"While we were hunting for the witchlings, we ended up liberating a few captured towns," I said. "There just wasn't any way around it."

"You couldn't just rescue some without saving them all."

"Exactly." I was surprised by her understanding. "I'm not quite the warmonger Angie makes me out to be."

Iriana gave me a puzzled look. "I've never heard her say anything like that about you. She always says how proud she is that you always try to do what's right and that you stand up for people who can't protect themselves."

Angie had accused me of being overeager to engage in fighting more than once, so hearing this was most welcome. I just hoped that I hadn't become some kind of martyr in her eyes. It was all very well and good to honor the dead for their bravery and good deeds, but I didn't want to become some sort of legendary hero in her mind. There was no possible way I could live up to it.

Steel bared his teeth at the chestnut horse when we arrived.

"No biting," I said, pulling the grulla stallion's head away. Removing one of the bags of feed from the gelding's back, I draped it over Steel's haunches. After giving Iriana a leg up onto the her horse, I mounted also and we silently made our way out of the swamp. The quiet allowed me to concentrate on *seeking* for enemies. None appeared, but I was still glad to be on more solid ground. We rode in silence until the ground became dry and the trees gave way to the open countryside.

"How long has Angie known I wasn't dead?" I asked finally, unable to contain myself.

"She *says* that she's known almost from the beginning. But how could she without seeing it with her own eyes?" Iriana said, regarding me intently. "And yet, here you are, proving that she was right all along."

"Shitozaki didn't mention it to her?"

"Oh, he did. He told us that you'd be back by Samhain, but when you weren't, she insisted on searching for you."

"I'm surprised Liam let her go."

"I was surprised she waited a whole week before sneaking away in the middle of the night," Iriana said. "It's just lucky that Niall knew she would, so we could get ready ourselves."

"Good for him," I said.

"We were in the middle of nowhere when your oath broke." There was no judgement in either Iriana's tone or manner. "When that happened, Angie panicked."

I winced. "Because she thought I was dead again."

Iriana nodded. "And then Lin had to open his big mouth and tell her it was just as likely that you had taken a lover." She rolled her eyes and let out a huff. "Air elementalists are *so* insensitive."

I chuckled, thinking of Seth's relentless logic. "They can be a bit straightforward."

"Anyway, it's not right, this jealousy of hers," she said primly. She looked down at her hands as if embarrassed to discuss the topic. "We are druids, and we share our love with whom we please. Without such liberty, we would not have individuals with multiple elements. Dualists would be rare and triple threats would not exist."

I nodded, having heard it all before from Duncan and Seth.

"I understand that's how all of you were raised and that's fine," I said. "But I was raised in a home where my parents were devoted to each other exclusively."

"But what if Angie desires another lover someday?"

"Then we'll cross that bridge when we come to it," I said,

wondering if she was trying to prepare me for that day to be sooner than later. "For me, there is no one but her."

"Except you broke your oath." As soon as the words left her mouth, Iriana slapped her hands over it. Air elementalists weren't the only insensitive ones, it would seem.

"That was a situation over which I had very little control."

"For what it's worth, Angie said she was going to break it anyway."

"Why?"

"She said that she shouldn't have let you swear such a foolish oath," Iriana said. "However, I hope you're finished sowing your wild oats or whatever you've been doing out here because she's still as jealous as she ever was."

I smiled in spite of myself.

"So you really *do* miss her."

It hit me that Iriana's line of questioning wasn't a challenge to how we had chosen to live our lives, but one born of caring for a friend and a desire for reassurance that Angie would not be left disappointed when we were finally reunited.

"I miss her like I'd miss air if I couldn't breathe."

"That's good." Iriana smiled and relaxed. "Just so you know, she's even more besotted with you than before, if that's even possible. You're all she ever talks about. Even when you were dead, she couldn't shut up about you."

I smiled all the way back to camp.

"We're almost there."

I'd given Iriana my coat, but the sun was setting, and she had begun shivering in spite of it. From the looks of her clothing, it appeared that she hadn't expected to be out in the wilds long. I was only warm by virtue of my elemental fire, but it took an annoying amount of focus and concentration. Annoyed was better than frostbitten, though.

Our arrival was noted, but nobody reacted much – until they noticed that I was accompanied by was a young woman. The island was small and crowded, so most everybody stayed put even though they were probably dying of curiosity. Of course, they could also have thought that I'd found Angie.

If only.

Seth came to meet us first. I swung my right leg over Steel's neck and jumped down to assist Iriana, but the air druid had already beaten me to it. She made no move to dismount, just sitting there on her horse staring at him with her mouth open.

"May I?" he asked.

Iriana nodded dumbly, and he put his hands around her waist to help her down. He wasn't going out of his way or treating her with special care; he had assisted the witches off their horses any number of times, whether he'd been sleeping with them or not.

For her part, even after he had set her on her feet, Iriana stood there as though enchanted, staring at him – or maybe it was the tiny hummingbird clinging to a single dreadlock come loose from the leather tie holding the rest of it back. Seeing such a tall, powerfully built man decorated by such a tiny shimmer of a thing was incongruous, to say the least. In addition, he towered over her by at least a foot and a half, so perhaps that was the reason she was standing there dumbfounded. He turned back to me, all business.

"Davis, all the earth druids are back, and we have a problem."

"Let's hear it."

"There is a large Republic force massing to the north."

I nodded. We were close enough to the 'Ville for them to have seen the smoke from our recent battle and figured out that we had destroyed their army.

"That's not all of it," he said. "Ingvar, Warwick, and Halldor each caught sight of a dyad. They seem to be waiting for something, but we're not sure what. I think it's likely that they're waiting for a signal to move on our position."

"If they were waiting on Dianthe Aspen, they'll be waiting a long time," Conall said.

"Sounds like they're going to try a hammer and anvil approach," I said. "The Republic will attack from the north, and while we're busy dealing with that, the dyads will try and flank us." It wasn't a terribly original plan, but with a fire elementalist, two earth-fire dualists, and a pair of triple threats at their disposal along with a host of well-armed Republic forces, it didn't need to be.

Seth nodded. "The triple threats are situated west and south. Yiorgos thinks the southeastern dyad will keep moving northward until it is due east of us."

"If the earth-fire druid went southeast, that means they know we aren't headed in that direction," I said. "Any idea where the other two dyads are?

"Unfortunately, no," the air druid replied. "It is possible that they are with the army. We think they'll attack tomorrow or the next day. Otherwise they risk losing the advantage of surprise."

"So we need to move soon."

"It would seem prudent."

Through it all, I couldn't help but notice Iriana was *still* gawking at Seth, having never once taken her eyes off him. His hummingbird was also suspiciously still and silent. He noticed her wide-eyed stare as well, finally giving her his attention.

"Are you all right, little one?" he asked. Then to me: "*Is* she all right?"

"She was perfectly fine before she saw..." The words trailed off as I realized that it was neither Seth's size and dark appearance nor the hummingbird in his hair that had struck her dumb.

"Before she saw what?" he prompted.

Holding up a hand to forestall further questioning, I turned back to the earth healer.

"Iriana, this is Seth," I said. "Would you like to say hello?"

"I don't know what I want to say," she said, sounding breathless.

Seth glanced at me with a raised eyebrow, but I just stood there with a big stupid grin on my face.

"Come to me!" Iriana finally said, holding out her hand with one finger extended. The little bird chirped once before releasing its tight grip on Seth's hair and taking flight. The tiny bird buzzed over to land on her finger, vanishing in a burst of red and green sparkles.

Iriana Disney's dyad partner, chosen for her by the Shining Ones and the Ancestors, was none other than Seth Starseeker.

Chapter 28 – News of the Grove

Only solitary men know the full joys of friendship.
Others have their family; but to a solitary and
an exile his friends are everything.
~ Warren G. Harding ~

It was rare for anything to throw the logical air elementalist off balance, but Iriana's revelation that she was his chosen had done just that. I grinned at the reactions of the others: Dermot was wide-eyed and giggling, elbowing Conall in the ribs. Duncan, who had gone completely unnoticed by Iriana, was standing behind them with his hands tucked into his sleeves and a satisfied look on his face.

"Hello, little one," Seth said, recovering quickly. He smiled broadly and offered his hand to her. Her lips spread in a wide smile and she reached out to take it.

"I am *so* glad to finally meet you!" Iriana said, her voice high and sweet. All trace of uncertainty gone, she moved to stand close by him. An intense longing for Angie's presence came over me. Loneliness and desire for her presence always struck at the most unexpected and inconvenient of times.

"This is truly an unexpected pleasure," Seth said, his large hands engulfing hers. "I only regret that we had to meet under such inhospitable circumstances."

"Hey, at least it'll make a good story to tell your kids," Dermot said.

"Dermot!" Conall hissed, and Iriana blushed.

As for the rest of the Finns, they'd been about as polite and reserved as they could stand, so Seth patiently introduced Iriana to each of them as they approached in pentacles to greet her. Siorus' group was the last and managed to linger for quite a while longer than the others.

"How is it that Davis always manages to find beautiful women in the middle of the wilderness?" Fenris said.

"I don't know, but I wish he'd go find me one," said Dermot.

"Cheer up. I found you another horse to take care of," I said, handing over the chestnut gelding's reins.

"Aww, man." Dermot dragged his feet as he led it away.

"You're so mean." Conall laughed, following with Steel.

I turned back to find Fenris placing a kiss on the back of Iriana's hand. She raised an eyebrow at me, and I glared at him. Seth rolled his eyes and snorted.

"Ignore Fenris," said Eian, pushing the spirit elementalist aside. "He's a braggart and fancies himself good with the ladies. I'm Eian Fitzpatrick."

"Didn't we already meet?" Iriana frowned in confusion.

"That was his twin brother Declan," said Mohinder, squeezing in between them. Some of the Finns, it seemed, were missing the witches' company a little more than others.

"Finding beautiful women must be a special aspect of earth magic," Fenris said, trying to garner her attention again.

"Well, I'm an earth elementalist, and I can tell you it isn't," said Siorus, giving her a respectful nod.

"You don't like women anyway," Fenris retorted.

"I like women just fine," Siorus said. "I just don't want to kiss any." He winked at Iriana, who laughed. "This is Madoc, my chosen."

The gunman gave her a sharp nod, eyeing her warily.

"There's already another dyad here!" Iriana exclaimed. "How wonderful!" Madoc relaxed upon hearing her obvious delight. Siorus gave him a look as if to say *I told you it would be fine.*

"Did you know that *none* of the histories have a single instance of dyads as exclusively male-female combinations?" Iriana said.

"I'd never heard that," Siorus replied, intrigued.

"I spent a lot of time in the grove library." She paused.

"Sebrina tried to force them based on some warped notion of balance."

"She always was trying to pound square pegs into round holes," Duncan murmured.

"Siorus and I chose each other," said Madoc.

"Oh, that's perfectly acceptable, too, according to the lore," she said, nodding. "Usually it was after two druids had lost their original partners."

"But what if someone has never even met the partner chosen for them by the ancestors?" the gunman asked.

"Oh, Madoc…" Siorus said, exasperated.

The gunman held up a hand. "This is important." He turned back to Iriana. "What if someone had a spirit animal for a while and then it left and never came back? What if someone never received a fetch at all?"

"I would think that situation fits within the lore," Iriana said with a small shrug. "I mean, if the partner that was originally chosen for you refuses to *be* with you, then you should be free to choose whomever you want."

"Feel better now?" Siorus asked.

"Yeah, I do," Madoc said.

"Thank you, Iriana," the earth druid said. "He's been fretting about this for weeks."

"It's important to follow tradition," Madoc replied.

"Well said." Iriana nodded with approval. "I heard Siorus say his element is earth, but I didn't catch what yours was, Madoc."

Those within hearing distance fell silent, but he just smiled at her and slipped his shotgun partway from the holster on his back.

"Steel and gunpowder," he replied with a wink.

Siorus laughed and put his arm around his chosen. "Come on, guys, let's give them some space." He and Madoc herded the other members of their pentacle back to their own patch of the island.

Moving to our own campsite, Seth gave Iriana a blanket and gave her water to drink. He had explained the origin and purpose of dividing the Finns into pentacles, and was discussing the development of the gunmen when Conall returned with Dermot.

"Speaking of gunmen, this is Conall, who is ours," said Seth. "And this is Dermot, our very talented water elementalist."

Iriana peered at him. "Conall! I hardly recognize you. It's

been a long time." She paused, her gaze flitting to me and back to him. "It's good to see you again. And with Davis?"

"Master Shitozaki took me in when I left the grove," he said, tensing slightly.

"And he's been a pain in our asses ever since," Dermot interjected, filling the awkward silence that followed their exchange. "But you know what a *real* pain is? Not knowing where my sister is."

"Dermot is Ariadne's brother," I said. "He's been anxious for news of her."

The redhead scowled. "I don't want *news* of her. I want to know where she is and why y'all took a fourteen-year-old girl into the wilderness with you!"

Iriana appeared stricken. "I'm sorry, Dermot, I don't know where Ariadne is. But she was fine the last time I saw her." She paused, turning to me. "How did you know she was with us? For that matter, how did you know we were even out here?"

"We Travelers have our ways," I said. If she wanted an answer to her question, she'd have to answer his first.

She rolled her eyes. "First off, we did *not* invite Ariadne on this journey. She just showed up a week after we left Sanctuary, and by then it was too late to turn around and take her home. She came because she's looking for you, Dermot."

"Like she'd be able to *do* anything," he grumbled. "She's just a stupid kid."

"She's actually quite good at combat magic," Iriana said. "I never thought elemental water could be used to fight, but she's proven everyone wrong on that score."

"Maybe she's not that stupid," Dermot allowed. "I wonder who taught her that?"

"Your mother, I imagine," said Iriana. "She refused to allow your sisters to be educated in the Elementalists' Third."

"Good for her," Dermot said.

"If only my mother had been as strong," she said wistfully. "I wish I could tell you more, but I've been separated from the others for three weeks after being captured by bandits. I kept begging Dianthe to tell me if they'd been captured, but she refused to tell me anything."

"Dianthe gave you over to the *bandits*?!" Seth exclaimed. In a split second the air druid had gone from relaxed to protective, while demonstrating a marked hesitancy to touch her. We'd all seen how being abused by Republic soldiers had affected Maeve, Elin, and Katrina, and how the slightest unexpected touch could startle them, often sending them away in tears.

She faced Seth, placing her hand over his. "They didn't hurt me. Dianthe locked me in a room and threatened them with dire consequences if they so much as laid a hand on me."

"She'll not be threatening or imprisoning anyone else," Seth reassured her.

"Davis told me!" Iriana said. "Duncan, I can hardly believe you did such a thing!"

I wondered what she'd say if she knew the Finns had hung Dianthe Aspen's corpse in a tree to allow the carrion birds to devour it so that as little as possible could pollute the body of the Earth Mother.

"She deserved to die," the earth druid said, and she stared at him with wide eyes. It must have been rather shocking to see the calm, quiet, unassuming earth druid as he was now, roughly garbed, bearded, and contentious.

"But that's… Duncan, druids do not murder one another!"

"That prohibition didn't stop *her*."

"Dianthe admitted that she was involved in the death of his mother," I said.

Iriana covered her mouth with both hands. When she had collected herself, she said, "Sebrina and her Tetrarch are evil, but we must not stoop to their level. You should have captured and imprisoned her!"

"You might ask your chosen how he feels about that," the earth druid replied cryptically.

"We have no way to imprison enemies," Seth said. "If we had released Dianthe, it would only have given her another chance to try and kill us in the future. Her death was regrettable but necessary."

Seth's usual penchant for engaging in a rational argument was not likely to convince her, but I knew what would.

"Dianthe's earth magic helped her army take us by surprise," I said. "And I've no doubt that it was she who advised them to shoot all the air elementalists first so we'd be defenseless. Her actions very nearly resulted in Seth's death."

"No! Are you all right?"

He nodded and smiled warmly at her. "I am well, thanks to Duncan's skill and quick action."

"Then I owe you my thanks, Duncan," Iriana said with a smile. "But hopefully it will be me healing Seth next time."

"Oh?" He raised an eyebrow, a glint of amusement in his eyes.

"Not that I want him to get hurt!" she said, flustered. "I just meant…" Her face flamed bright red. "I was merely referring to my ability to heal."

"No one thought you meant that," Seth reassured her, and tactfully changed the subject. "Your hands are cold."

"It is a bit chilly," she said with a shiver.

"Oh, sorry," I said. I touched the ground, channeling more magic into the fire drake.

"Better watch it," said Conall. "The eastern end is glowing a bit."

"I'll take care of it." The dragon burrowed down deeper, and the light began to fade. A few feet below the surface the clay and sand that made up the island was saturated with water, so it could only go so far.

"The eastern end of what? The island?" Iriana.

"Yeah."

"What's making it glow?"

"Davis' fetch," said Seth.

"Which part?" Her eyes shifted from the glowing rocks at our feet to the other end of the island, where the light gradually faded to darkness.

"All of it," I replied with a yawn.

"*All* of it? Your fetch is as large as the *entire* island?"

Her amazement should not have surprised me, but for the most part, the rest of the Finns treated my fire magic like it was nothing out of the ordinary. Perhaps Sebrina had felt threatened by male magic because it was more powerful. Even the older druid men had been discouraged from using their elemental power, so it was possible that Iriana had never been fully exposed to it.

"That ain't nothin'," said Dermot. "You should see me make waves." A tiny mermaid rose up out of the swamp water and performed an undulating dance in a circle before sinking below the surface once more.

"Don't waste your magic," I said.

"I knew he was going to say that," he said to Iriana. "I'm still just an elementalist."

She nodded. "Me, too."

"I have a big Well, though," he said. "It's almost as big as my—"

"Dermot!" I snapped. He grinned, unabashed.

"That's all right," Seth said, reassuring her before she could even begin to feel insecure. "I only received my full magic yesterday."

"Oh, I can't believe I forgot to ask! What *is* your element?"

"Air."

"Oh, just like your mother!" Iriana said, clearly delighted. Then she slumped again. "It wouldn't matter if I was a druid anyway. I'm terrible at earthmoving. All I can do is heal."

"Healing is important," Seth said. "As Davis said, I would be dead if not for Duncan's healing ability. So would he, for that matter."

"Please don't tell Angie that," I said.

"Hey, you aren't the only one Duncan has had to pull back from the jaws of death," said Dermot.

"No, he's just the one who has to be pulled back the most often," said Conall.

"Don't tell Angie that, either."

"Hiding things from your chosen, are you?" the Norseman jibed.

"No. Yes. But only that," I said. "She thinks I'm always looking for a fight."

Seth snorted. "I can't imagine why."

"Some battles need to be fought," said Duncan.

"That's what Angie says, too," Iriana said. "It must be an Everlight thing."

"I'd say Davis and his chosen are in good company, then," Seth observed with a smile.

Thankfully, the conversation regarding fighting and how often I'd been injured badly enough to require healing was interrupted by Wolfric, carrying a steaming pot of stew in his bare hands.

Iriana was clearly delighted to see him.

"Wolfric! You're all right! How is Onóra? Is she here?"

"Iriana! It's good to see you again," he said. "She's safe. I left her in Ward with the witches."

"But she is your chosen! She is supposed to be with you!"

I intervened. "Wolfric and Onóra had a rough time of it after escaping the grove. Sebrina sent druids to hunt them down until they entered the territory claimed by the 'Ville. After that, they were continually harassed by bandits until we found them."

"Goodness, Davis!" she exclaimed. "Do you find *everyone* who is lost?"

"Unfortunately not," I replied. I hadn't found Angie yet.

"You must be one of those beautiful women that Fenris was talking about, Wolfric," said Dermot. "I just *looove* your long, blond hair!"

Like most of the Finns, the fire elementalist's hair was tangled and unkempt, held out of his face with rough braids and leather ties.

"Shut up," Wolfric snapped, glaring at Dermot.

"Make me, fireballer."

"Hey, now—" I said, but it was too late. Wolfric thrust the big black pot toward Dermot, tipping it as he did so. Steaming hot liquid surged over the lip and would surely have splashed over the water elementalist's face, had he not taken control of it. A thin stream of water shot out of the canteen on his back and into the stew. With a few circular waves of his hand, Dermot made the stew turn sharply away from him and sweep around Wolfric. He held it in place, streaming through the air in a loop about the fire elementalist's body for a few seconds before allowing it to slip back into the pot. He grinned proudly, but soon deflated under Seth's glower of disapproval over the waste of magic.

"You wanted to meet the Finns," I said to Iriana in a dry tone. "I hope you're not disappointed."

"Not at all," she laughed. "Not at all!" She grew serious again. "So tell me, Davis – how *did* you know we'd left the grove? And don't give me that Traveler nonsense."

I chuckled. "We ran into some folks you may remember – Jeb and Jared Bommer."

"Yes! The brothers from Blue Hill!"

"They told us that the five of you had helped them save the

people at Mayflower after it was overrun," I said, then briefly related my history with Kam Stone and what she had discovered on her visit to White Oak Grove. I left out the parts about finding out she was the Oracle of Delphi and her prophecy foretelling my death.

"You didn't have magic when you were at the grove, did you?"

"No."

"So… you were altered?"

"The general consensus is that I was blocked."

Seth coughed.

"But if you didn't have any magic when you were in the grove, how could Angie have possibly known you were an earth elementalist?" Iriana frowned. "And why didn't she know you had fire as well?"

So she *had* known. And she hadn't told me?

Seth coughed again.

I raised an eyebrow at him. "Is there something you'd like to say?"

"No."

"It sure seems like—"

"There is nothing *I* need to say, but there is someone else who should speak." His expression was studiously blank.

Wolfric seemed puzzled, Dermot wore an air of innocence that *always* indicated guilt, and Conall was giving everyone that look that said they should have known better. Duncan, however, appeared resigned. He raised a placating hand.

"We suspected you might have elemental magic, nothing more."

"We? We who?"

"Angelina mentioned to my father that you seemed to have an innate ability to sense when other people were around."

My sixth sense. I had been *seeking* without knowing that it was my gods-given earth magic. "And?"

"And I confirmed it for him."

"The day we met," I said, feeling my temper rise. If there was anything I hated, it was people keeping secrets from me.

"Aye," he said. "How did you know?"

"I felt the magic," I snapped. "I'm not stupid, you know."

"None of us have ever doubted your intelligence," said Duncan. "Why are you angry?"

"I'm not angry!" It was true; I was *furious*.

"No, of course not," said Dermot. "Except the ground is steaming and the edge of the lake just started to boil." I glared at him, and the cattails behind him burst into flame and then exploded with little pops and puffs of smoke.

"Why don't we go check out the other side of the island?" Conall said, placing a hand on the water elementalist's shoulder and guiding him in that direction.

"Why? There's nothing over there. Just mud, reeds, and trees."

"Exactly," replied Conall. "And none of it is on fire."

"Right," the water elementalist agreed, and they walked away.

"I told you he'd be pissed that you didn't tell him sooner!" Conall called back over his shoulder.

"You didn't tell me, either!" I snapped. More puffball reeds burst into clouds of sparks.

Iriana moved a little closer to Seth. While my raised voice had attracted a few glances, the Finns were used to my flares of temper and largely ignored our discussion.

"We *couldn't* tell you," said Duncan.

"Why not?"

"For one thing, it would have put you in even more danger than you were already in," he said. "Think of how Sebrina would have reacted!"

"By the gods, Duncan, you're right! She might have actually tried to kill me!" I said. Then I glared at Seth. "What's your excuse?"

"While the master was certain that you possessed some sort of magical ability, you had never displayed any evidence of it." He shrugged helplessly.

"How was I supposed to discover something if I had no idea it is possible?"

"You were happy the way you were," Duncan said.

"What is *that* supposed to mean?"

"It sounds like it was something of a dilemma for both Seth and Duncan, and possibly Angie as well," said Wolfric. "Balancing the potential good versus potential harm that could have been done to you, Davis, the harm would definitely outweigh the benefit."

The irony of a fire elementalist bringing cool logic to the discussion was not lost on me, and I started to calm down. These were my friends. If I couldn't trust them to act in my best interest, who could I trust?

"No one said anything because finding out you're supposed to have magic and then *not* having it is devastating." Seth gestured toward the far end of the island, where Dermot and Conall were talking and skipping rocks on their way back. "We only wanted what was best for you," he concluded.

"You were happy the way you were," Duncan said again.

I took several minutes to calm down and consider the matter rationally. Knowing they had been denied the special gift given to all druids had resulted in terrible reactions among the young men of the grove. It had driven Orion Aspen insane. It had caused Darryn Darkmane to betray one of his childhood friends and murder the other. It had turned Conall and the other altered Finns bitter and angry. And while I'd have liked to believe that finding out I was supposed to have magic wouldn't have affected me much since I'd lived my whole life without it, I had to admit that eventually, it would have.

"All right, you have a point," I said. "It just doesn't seem right to hide something like that from somebody."

"The truth is, Davis, nobody said anything because we all secretly hate and despise you," said Conall, back from his stroll with Dermot.

"Why are we friends, again?"

"No one else will have you," said Conall.

"Yeah," said Dermot. "You're a grumpy loner, and you set things on fire when you're pissed."

"Then surely it is the great love we all have for one another," said Duncan in a sardonic tone.

"Yes," agreed Seth. "Only men who love one another like brothers could live in such caring, honest community."

"You're all a bunch of assholes," I said.

"I hate to interrupt this beautiful exchange," Iriana said, "but I am curious as to when your magic manifested, Davis."

"At Midsummer." Thankfully, no one mentioned that I'd come into my elements by falling into a volcano.

"You've only had magic for six months, and yet you attacked

a Republic fort all on your own today?"

I winced. Seth crossed his arms and narrowed his eyes at me.

"I was going to tell you."

"I'm sure you were."

"Hearing what the other earth druids found out was more important, so I don't expect me to apologize for not mentioning the fort," I grumped.

"And it had nothing to do with the fact that you ignored your own mandate to remain unseen by the enemy."

"I was in a swamp. I couldn't *seek* because of all the water, and I couldn't see because of all the trees, and then the people in the fort started shooting at me," I protested. "Besides, if I *hadn't* taken out that fort, I wouldn't have found Iriana." I scowled at him. "Quakes, Seth, it's not like I set it on fire and told the whole world where I was!"

"Perhaps we should all agree that there should be no more secrets among us," said Duncan.

"I don't have any secrets," Seth said.

"Do you not, Master Starseeker?" I prodded.

"Just because *you* didn't know about a particular thing, it doesn't mean that thing is a secret," Seth said, visibly exasperated.

"I bet Iriana doesn't know."

"What do I not know?" she asked.

Seth let out a sigh. "Connor Shitozaki is my father. Davis finds this fact important for some reason."

"Oh!" she said. "He did mention that his son was with Davis, but he never described you."

"Of course not," Seth muttered. It was the first time I'd ever heard him say anything remotely negative about Shitozaki.

"I didn't mean it that way," she said. "He didn't speak to *me*. He was talking to Angelina at the time. He mentioned that you were with Davis as a way to reassure her that he would be back by Samhain, safe and sound."

Seth sighed. "I have certainly failed in that regard."

I clapped him on the shoulder, grinning. "But not for lack of trying."

"He and Angie are two peas in a pod," Iriana said to Seth, shaking her head. "Once they set their minds on something, nothing is likely to change it."

"So I have noticed," he replied with a smile.

"There's nothing wrong with being dedicated," I said. "Or persistent."

"Do you know she said exactly the same thing to me?" Iriana shook her head. "And then she said she'd keep searching even if she had to go to the ends of the earth to find you."

"I'd rather she didn't."

"But I thought you wanted to see her again."

I wasn't sure, but I thought I detected a taunting note to her words. "I do! I'd just prefer it if she was someplace safe and warm, not wandering around in the bandit-infested wilderness with winter coming on."

She snorted and tossed her strawberry blonde hair back over her shoulder. "I have never known Angelina Everlight to make a single sane, rational decision where you are concerned," she said tartly. "She is utterly besotted."

There was nothing complimentary in her tone or her words, but still, they warmed my heart. If Iriana was to be believed, Angie still loved me.

"After all, *that* is how we came to be out here in these savage lands," she continued, mostly for the benefit of the others. "As soon ArchDruid Shitozaki told her that you had been living in Sanctuary, she wanted to run right after you, but her father talked her out of it."

"I'm sorry..." Seth held up a hand, saving me from further chastisement. "Did you say *ArchDruid* Shitozaki?"

She nodded. "As soon as we arrived in Sanctuary, the elders insisted on taking a vote, and he was elected ArchDruid again. Liam and Padraig were both nominated for Vice ArchDruid, but Liam said he'd had enough of governance and Padraig said that a fire druid needed someone without fire to balance the leadership out. So Herakles Crawford was elected."

"I'm glad the Everlights left the grove when everyone else did," I said. "Their family has been divided for too long."

"So true!" Iriana said. "Speaking of families, Seth, your mother came to Sanctuary also. Your parents' reunion was... interesting."

"I bet it was," he replied. "I've never lived with both of them under the same roof, but after living with each of them separately, I cannot imagine what my ancestors were thinking, pairing them as chosen."

I remembered Shitozaki saying that chosen should not be kept apart for long. At the time I had thought it a rule or tradition, never considering the possibility that he might be talking about his own situation.

Iriana turned back to me. "Anyway, when Samhain came and went without your return, even Liam couldn't keep Angie from chasing after you," she continued. "Fortunately, Niall knew she'd go anyway, which gave us time to prepare. You should have seen the look on Angie's face when Niall, Lin, and I showed up with our horses saddled and our bags packed!"

"I'm surprised Niall would leave the grove without his pet weasel," said Wolfric.

"His what?" Her brows knit in confusion.

"Darryn Darkmane," I supplied.

"That's what I said," the fire elementalist replied. "Niall's little weasel."

"Really, now, Wolfric," said Iriana. "It's not polite to speak ill of the dead!"

He nearly choked on his stew.

"He's dead?" I asked. "How?"

Her voice dropped to a whisper. "Liam Everlight *beheaded* him."

My brain crowded with multiple questions, but all that came out was: "When?"

"A couple of weeks after your mysterious disappearance," Iriana said.

"My uncle vowed to kill Darryn if he harmed Davis again," Duncan said with an air of satisfaction.

"Did he?" Wolfric said. "Can't say I'm sorry to hear he fulfilled that vow." Duncan acknowledged his words with a gracious nod.

"Darryn claimed that Sebrina had made him First Warrior, and called Liam out," Iriana said. "So in a way, he asked for it."

"I'm surprised the honor of First Warrior wasn't bestowed upon Niall," Wolfric said. "Darryn was always more of a follower."

"After what Orion Aspen did to Niall, he wasn't in any shape

493

to be First Warrior even if he had wanted to," Iriana said. "Which he did not."

"What Orion did to him?" I asked, my supper forgotten.

"Wait. I need to backtrack. Otherwise, you won't understand why he tried to kill Niall, or why Liam killed Darryn."

What in the name of all that was green and good had happened after my departure? Had the entire grove gone insane?

Iriana was peppered with questions, and she held up both hands for silence. "Just let me explain," she said. "Orion went on a murderous rampage against the grove's healers, slaughtering them in their beds. Hearing the screams, Niall led a small group from the Warriors' Third to help, but they split up so they could help more people. He was just in time to stop Orion before he could murder Halle Starseeker."

"That's my mother's sister!" Seth said. "Did she survive?"

"Oh, yes! Danica Harris got to her just in time. Orion fled when she and Padraig Everlight showed up. Padraig left Niall to keep watch over them and then ran to tell Liam what was happening. While he was gone, Shekhar Patel ran out of his house yelling for help, and Niall held Orion off so that Shekhar could get away."

"Hold on a minute," I said. "When did this happen?"

"The night you were… the night you were whipped." Iriana paused, regarding me with compassion. "Danica told me that she has regretted her actions that night ever since, and that if she had gone against Sebrina and healed you that night, Liam would not have done what he did and the grove would still be whole."

"I don't understand."

"It was Darryn who released Orion and put a blade in his hand," she said. "No one knows what lies he told, but whatever it was caused Orion to attack our earth druids. Niall said that he thought Darryn was there to help him fight Orion, but that he attacked the moment Niall turned his back on him. Then he had to face them both."

"That back-stabbing weasel," Wolfric growled.

"Once Niall was no longer a threat, Darryn cut Orion's throat and left Niall to bleed to death on Halle's doorstep. Then he went to Sebrina claiming to have stopped the massacre." She paused to take a deep breath. "Twenty-seven earth druids died at Orion's

494

hands that night, and by the time the sun came up, eighteen more had gone to join the ancestors."

"*Gods of Olympus*," Seth breathed. Dermot never uttered a word, wide-eyed and riveted by the story.

"Danica is lucky Darryn didn't try to kill her, too," I said.

Iriana nodded agreement. "It was a blessing that he didn't know she was already in the house with Halle when Niall fell. Unfortunately, since Darryn's betrayal led to Niall also falling under Orion's blade, and she was forced to heal them both at the same time! I heard it took the rest of that night, all the next day, and the next night, too." She gave me a look of sympathy.

"No one knew the truth until Niall woke up and told his mother what Darryn had done, but that was a week later," Iriana continued. "Angie said that his story only confirmed what Liam and Padraig had already pieced together – that Darryn had turned Orion loose to do all those horrible things simply to lure Danica away because she was the only earth druid willing to heal you."

I was stunned, but also felt a burden lift from my spirit. Danica and the Everlight brothers hadn't abandoned me. They'd been helping innocent people who had become the victims of a madman.

"By the gods," Duncan breathed.

"Angie says that her father killed Darryn in retribution for killing you to fulfill his vow. But I think it was really because Darryn's actions had caused her so much suffering."

"Not to mention putting the grove's healers to the blade," said Wolfric, shaking his head. "I should have killed him when I had the chance."

"Darryn's execution wasn't the worst part," Iriana said. "Liam swore an oath to his gods that he would discover the truth of what had happened to you. In front of his family and a hundred other people, he swore by land, sea, and sky, proclaiming that his offering was the blood he had just spilled – *Darryn's* blood."

"A blood oath?" I said. "That doesn't sound so bad."

"That was no blood oath," Seth intoned. "That was a blood *sacrifice*. It is strictly forbidden."

While my parents had raised me in the ways of druids, teaching me the legends of our gods as well as the prayers and the rituals used in worshiping them, the topic of blood sacrifice had never come up. Using wood from our orchard for the sacred fire, we sacrificed some of the ale or whiskey that my father had brewed, along with my mother's honey cakes and cornbread. I myself had made offerings of polenta cakes, herbs from my own garden, and various handmade objects over the years. Sacrificing a living being was something I'd never even imagined.

"Our ancient ancestors used to burn people alive in their wicker men," said Duncan. "Usually enemies or criminals."

"*Usually*," Dermot said with a shudder.

"Looks like your uncle decided to bring the *old* Old Ways back," Wolfric said with a savage grin. "I knew I liked him for a reason!"

"Our more recent ancestors, those who brought druidry back just prior to the Rebirth, did not practice blood sacrifice, and *this* generation will not, either." Seth's tone was firm.

"Of course not," I said. "It's barbaric."

"My uncle swore an oath," Duncan said. "Darryn's life was forfeit."

"I honestly thought it was just a threat," I said.

"Apparently, Darryn did, too," said Wolfric. "Either that or he thought Sebrina would protect him."

"My uncle would have allowed nothing to stand between him and his vengeance," the earth druid said, his dark eyes solemn. "We Everlights take our oaths seriously."

Chapter 29 – Divide and Conquer

There is nothing impossible to him who will try.
~ Alexander the Great ~

Before going to sleep that night, I dropped by Siorus'
pentacle. They were all still awake and keeping warm around
Wolfric's woodless campfire.

"How's everybody doing?" I asked.

"Fine," Siorus said, with the others echoing similar replies.

I looked at Eian, their air druid. "How you feelin'?" He'd
taken two bullets to the chest in the last fight, one of which had
narrowly missed his heart. His twin, Declan, had taken two shots to
the chest and one to the neck. I felt lucky to have them both with
me still.

"Right as rain," was the air elementalist's reply.

"Good. I'm glad to hear it." I looked around the campfire,
reading each man's expression: Siorus and Eian patient and
waiting, Fenris and Mohinder curious and excited, and Madoc and
Wolfric guarded.

"I'd like to send you on a solo mission."

"To do what?" Fenris asked.

"To take out the enemy dyads," Madoc said. If there was
anything that could be said about my gunmen, it was that every
one of them was sharp-witted and quick on the uptake.

"Just one," I said. "And I want them captured and not killed."

"Capture!" Wolfric frowned. "Why not just kill them?"

"Because I'd rather not start a civil war," I said.

They were silent for a moment.

Eian was the first to break the silence. "Davis is right. Think about all the damage that we've wrought fighting the Republic." He pointed to the southeast, where the acres and acres of burned, devastated forest lay under cover of darkness. The trees still smouldered and the scent of smoke hung in the air. "Can you even imagine what a war between two groups of druids would be like?"

Siorus nodded agreement. "We are here to heal the earth mother and her children, not destroy them."

"Capturing a druid is a tricky proposition," said Fenris.

"Dangerous, is what it is," said Mohinder.

"You're both right, but we've experimented with our own magics and have dueled each other often enough that I'm confident you can do it."

"Oh, I wasn't arguing against it," said Mohinder. "I'm in."

"Me, too," said Fenris.

"It's an acceptable risk to take," Eian said.

Madoc nodded. "We can do it."

"All right," said Siorus. "When do we leave?"

"There's one other thing," I said, pausing a moment before throwing the next and sure to be unpopular idea at them. "Madoc, I'd like you to consider staying behind."

"Why would you suggest such a thing?" Siorus said, frowning.

"Because I'm a *null*," Madoc said, his eyes blazing with anger.

"Look, just hear me out. Someone without magic is on equal footing with bandits or soldiers or anyone else with a gun. But going up against druids puts you at greater risk," I said. "We've been lucky so far. People have been hurt, but no one has taken a bullet to the heart or the brain. Alexandros, Seth, and the twins all came a little too close to joining the ancestors for my comfort."

"Your promise to Master Shitozaki means *nothing* next to the pledge between Siorus and me as chosen," Madoc said hotly. "I'll *not* stay behind while he rides into danger!"

"This isn't about my promise to Shitozaki," I said. *How long had that been common knowledge?* "You're all my friends, and I don't want to lose any of you."

Siorus gave me a reproachful look. "Do you honestly think your concern for Madoc's safety is greater than my own?"

"No, but that isn't the point," I said. "Since we have the time, it's only wise to stop and consider how much we're willing to risk in any given situation."

"Your lack of magic never stopped Angelina from putting *you* in dangerous situations," said Wolfric.

"She never asked me to face a druid in a combat situation."

"No, she dumped you right in the middle of a whole grove of druids, most of whom hated you simply because you were an outsider."

It was a low blow, but he was right.

Mohinder turned to me, looking somewhat apologetic. "I am sorry, Davis, but I don't think Madoc should stay behind. Truthfully speaking, he is in no more danger than Siorus or I."

"You can shield with your magic," I said.

"*I* can't," said Fenris. "And we've never tested whether a water shell can stand up to a spirit bolt."

"We aren't going to, either," muttered Mohinder.

Eian tilted his head to one side and said, "Honestly, I'm surprised you're not planning to take those dyads on solo."

Air druids and their intellectual prowess be cursed to the nine hells.

"I did consider it, but as far as risk goes, it wouldn't be smart."

Siorus smirked. "That means Seth and Duncan said no." The others laughed, elbowing each other and making comments along the lines of *Oooh, you got in trouble!*

I sighed.

Madoc grinned. "So which dyad do you want us to pursue? West, south, or east?"

"West," I said, giving in. "The six of you should be able to capture one measly triple threat."

"If it was up to me, we'd just kill them and be done with it," said Wolfric.

"That's why Siorus is in charge." I rose to leave. "I'm going to go talk to Yiorgos' pentacle about taking out the southern dyad."

"That includes both twins on dangerous missions," Siorus said.

The fact of the matter was that I had all five of Ma and Pa Fitzpatrick's children, and all three of Mother Chaudhri's sons spread out among the seven pentacles. The loss of any of them would be devastating for their families.

"I know," I said, "but Yiorgos has three dualists with spirit, and I want as many elements as possible out there." He also lacked a gunman, and I wanted only my very best elementalists out there hunting the druids that come from the grove with Dianthe Aspen. After Seth, twins Eian and Declan were the best with elemental air. Mohinder had more than adequately demonstrated his creativity with water back at Mayflower. Fenris was our only pure spirit druid. Westley was one of the best dualists with elemental spirit and water; he had taken Ridley's electric whip invention a step further, wielding one in each hand. Likewise, Solon and Wyatt had more than proven their skill and versatility with air and spirit at the battle by the lake. Siorus and Yiorgos were the most steady earth druids as well as the fiercest fighters, and Wolfric was the only other fire elementalist besides me.

"What's everyone else doing?" Siorus asked.

"The rest of us will head east, where I'm guessing we'll run into the other dyad," I finished.

"Rendezvous point?" Madoc asked, pulling out their copy of Conall's map.

"The fort where I found Iriana today," I said, showing them its location on the map. "Get some sleep. We leave before dawn."

* * *

We rose, geared up, and were on the move well before the waning gibbous moon had set in the western sky. The Finns rode in their pentacles as usual with the exception of mine and Siorus'. Iriana was now riding with us, and Wolfric rode with Siorus' pentacle to add to their offensive magic capabilities, giving them both fire and spirit with which to attack. Ideally, each pentacle would have all five elements, but no fire elementalists had taken refuge with Connor Shitozaki. Not for the first time, I wondered if there were any other men our age with elemental fire, or if Wolfric and I were the only ones.

"Are you sure about this?" I asked Seth as we watched Siorus' and Martin's pentacles head west and south.

"Am I sure it's less risky than you hunting them alone?" he said. "Absolutely." He regarded me with serious eyes and continued in a quieter tone. "While you don't seem to take the Oracle's prophecy seriously, I do."

That's because she's the oracle of one of your gods, I did not say, for it was only part of the truth. The other part was that while I did not believe in fate, I felt that a natural lightning strike – which ancient peoples believed really did come from Zeus' hand – was as likely to be the cause of my death as a druid with elemental spirit. In addition, Seth seemed to have completely ignored the last two lines of the prophecy:

> *"Beware the grey wraith, the spirit walker.*
> *Bargain well with the immortal and the dead."*

I hadn't seen anything that even remotely resembled a grey wraith yet, and the Morrigan was the only immortal being that I'd struck a bargain with. I suppose the Phantom Queen could have been considered a wraith, but when I saw her at Samhain, she was as solid and as real as the ground beneath my feet. Our pact was a simple one, encompassing only the enchanted sword and me standing as her champion. Until a wheeling-and-dealing spirit walker showed its face, I felt relatively safe.

"Either group is more than adequate for capturing one triple threat and her chosen," said Duncan, interrupting my thoughts.

"Are they? Chosen, that is."

"What do you mean?"

"Were they brought together by the Ancestors and the Shining Ones or were they assigned by Sebrina?" I said.

"You're pondering how solid their loyalty to one another is?" Seth asked. I nodded.

"As solid as quicksand," Iriana said, waving a hand dismissively. "Sebrina and her ilk know nothing of loyalty or honor."

"Eloquently spoken," said the air druid, smiling down at her. He squatted down, linked his hands, and offered her a leg up onto her horse. Once he had mounted his own, they started across the shallow lake, discussing possible names for Dianthe's horse. I followed on Steel, marveling at their complete acceptance of one another. These two perfect strangers had settled into their roles as chosen almost immediately, without once questioning if they were right for each other. It was something else I had missed by being reared outside the grove. Would I have accepted Angie this simply and easily if I'd grown up there? My reluctance had necessitated her approaching me multiple times. She'd had to admit that she was alone, and eventually, demonstrate her magic to prove she wasn't insane. Then again, relative to how quickly I accepted anyone, perhaps it wouldn't have been all that different.

The way Angie and I had come together was nothing like Iriana and Seth, but I couldn't make myself regret how events had transpired. After all, the overindulged protégée of the ArchDruid and the apple of the First Warrior's eye had been nearly intolerable for the first few days of our acquaintanceship. I smiled to myself, remembering the feel her long dark hair between my fingers. Her exotic green eyes revealed her every emotion: alight with joy, sparking with spirit magic in anger, soft and dark with love. For the first time in almost a year, the thought of Angie was unaccompanied by pain or a sense of loss. Iriana's arrival had changed that. My chosen had not given up on me; neither had she been disheartened by the broken oath. Instead, she had set out on a dangerous journey, just as intent on finding me as she had been the first time. Maybe even more so.

This time, however, *I* was going to find *her*.

But first I had a war to attend to.

The Finns crossed the shallow lake with my pentacle at the rear. As soon as the swamp island was completely clear, I summoned the fire drake from beneath the dank earth. Its bony, red-streaked face and twin spiral goat horns outlined in deep, glowing orange burst forth with a rumble. It shook like a dog as though relieved to be free of its prison of sand and clay. Grey scales, highlighted with brilliant yellow and orange, shimmered down its neck, across its shoulders, and along its sides. The spiked ridge along its back and tail had darkened to match the head, with vermillion fire peeking between scalloped ebony scales. The white heat of its underbelly set the grass alight and scorched the trunk of every tree it passed. Steam rose in great gouts from between the pale yellow-orange talons with each footstep until it cleared the trees and leapt skyward, born aloft by membranous wings of smoldering red and black.

"By the gods!" Iriana yelped. "That's not your fetch!"

"It is," Seth said.

"It can't be!" she said. "It's *huge*!"

"Hey, Davis," said Dermot, scratching his nose with a mittened hand. "Does it look bigger today to you?"

"Maybe. What do you think, Seth?"

Seth squinted up at the dawning sky. "It would appear so," the air druid replied. "The color has changed, too. It seems to be darker."

"It looks more solid," said Dermot, watching as the fire drake flew in a lazy circle overhead, trailing sparks across the greying sky. "You can't see through it anymore."

"Well, one thing that hasn't changed is that it gives our position away," said Conall. "So let's not waste time admiring the scenery."

"You're making an assumption that the bandits of the 'Ville will equate the dragon to Davis' presence," said Seth.

"Have you seen any other dragons around here lately?" Conall said. "Let's move."

"I'll take care of it." Bending my thoughts to the dragon, I gave it the same command I'd given the lion: *Find Angie. Keep her safe.* Then I added: *Guide her to me.*

The great beast straightened out, spread its wings wide, and shot away to the northeast like a fiery arrow.

"What happened?" asked Seth.

"I told it to find Angie."

"I thought you couldn't see through its eyes?"

"I don't think that matters."

"It doesn't," Iriana replied absently, still searching the sky.

"How do you know?" Seth asked.

"I didn't know where you were when I sent *my* fetch. I didn't even know *who* you were," she replied.

We rode cautiously through the fire-ravaged woodland, keeping the pace at an easy walk until the sun broke over the horizon. Once the forest was behind us and the flatlands stretched ahead, no one could resist galloping across the inviting expanse, as free and wild as the biting winter wind.

* * *

We arrived at the hidden swamp fort to find that it was inhabited once again.

"That was quick," I said, scowling at the repaired front gates, now closed and bolted. It was irksome, even if meant we didn't have to clean up the bodies.

"What if that island was really a fairy ring and it's really been like a week or a month that passed while we were sleeping?" Dermot said.

Sometimes it was hard to tell if he was serious or if he really believed the fairy tales his mother had told him.

"Maybe a patrol was out when you were here and then came back later," Duncan said.

"Or a caravan brought supplies," Seth said.

"What if it's Angie?" Iriana whispered excitedly. "Maybe they came back to look for me!"

"More like it's the dyad that Yiorgos saw heading this way," Conall said. "It's too quiet for there to be more than a couple of people here."

"Whoever it is," I said, "there's only one way to find out."

"Right." Seth clapped his hands and rubbed them together.

"Quietly. And without trashing the gate, please."

He looked disappointed for a moment. Maybe it was because he hadn't had a chance to do any big magic since becoming a druid, but it was probably that he wanted to show Iriana how he could blow those heavy timbered gates right off their hinges. I understood that feeling because I, too, wanted to show my chosen what I could now do. Angie would never see the full extent of my fire magic if I could help it, though. Things got scarily dangerous when I was mesmerized by elemental fire.

A chill wind blew past us and through the gate, lifting the bar inside from its brackets, tipping it on end, and setting it down. Then the gates silently swung outward until they lay flush with the palisade wall.

"Very nice," I murmured.

Seth just shrugged.

"Finesse is always more impressive than power," Duncan said.

Dermot snorted. "If you say so."

"All right, let's go see who's inside," I said, dismounting. "Ingvar, Warwick – dismount and get your people up here. Martin and Halldor, watch the horses and our backs."

"Remember," said Seth, "If there are any druids here, we take them *alive*."

I was halfway across the courtyard with the air druid a step behind when a dozen vines shot out, lashing whiplike about my body and trussing me like a roast for the oven.

"Don't move or by the gods, I'll squeeze him until his eyeballs pop out!" shouted a fierce female voice.

A light wind spun around us and the spectral crackle of electricity filled the air as Jasvinder, Tristan, Narinder, and Ridley readied their magic. Each one was an air/spirit dualist capable of attacking or defending as necessary.

"Wait," I said, knowing I could be free in under a second if I so chose. They did as ordered, while both Duncan and Seth cast concerned glances my way. "It might be Ariadne," I added.

"It might also be one or both of the triskelia Dianthe Aspen brought with her," Duncan warned. "The druids she named were the ones who became Sebrina's favorites after Angelina rebelled. Do not underestimate them."

"I really don't think that *vines* would be the weapon of choice for any of Sebrina's followers," Conall said, and I agreed. Grove-trained druids considered elemental water worthless as an offensive weapon, and I doubted they'd have threatened to squeeze me until my eyeballs popped out.

Raising my voice, I called, "We mean no harm. We're just tired travelers looking to warm up for a bit."

"Find someplace else!" a male voice shouted, followed by a mighty straight-line wind strong enough to knock us all off our feet and send us tumbling back through the gates, were we not protected by elemental air of our own.

The sounds of an urgently whispered discussion could be heard, then a brief scuffle, and footsteps running toward us. A slip of a girl with wild, curly red hair scrambled out from behind a building holding a flower pot in the crook of her arm. The plant in the pot was the originator of the vines entangling me.

"Ariadne!" Dermot shouted, bolting forward and embracing her so tightly that she dropped the flower pot.

"Dermot, is that you?" she cried. "You look so different!"

"It's this manly warrior physique," he said, posing to flex muscles that no one could see under his heavy coat.

His sister giggled. "You haven't changed a bit."

I cleared my throat.

"Oh, hey," said Dermot. "That's Davis you've snared, so you should probably let him go."

Ariadne Stoddard put her hand on one cocked hip and regarded me with the confidently superior air that only a teenager can possess.

"Why, can't he get out of it on his own?"

I flexed my arms, straining against the vines, and when she smirked insolently at my effort, incinerated them to ash. Her attitude vanished as quickly as though someone had slapped it off.

"He's only supposed to be an earth elementalist!" she protested, as though I had cheated at a game we'd been playing. She backed up a little when I approached but did not try to hide behind her big brother. Arrie Stoddard had raised herself some fearless children. Perhaps that was to be expected of a woman who had carried on alone with the five of them, continually defying the will of the reigning ArchDruid even after her chosen had died under mysterious circumstances.

"Who's here with you?" I asked.

"Lin Overholt, but he can't come out here right now."

"Why not?" asked Duncan.

"Oh, hello, Duncan! Angie's going to be so happy to see you!" Ariadne said, smiling broadly at him. Then she caught sight of Iriana.

"Irri!" she squealed, shoving past us to hug her. "We've been so worried about you!"

"I was worried about you, too!" cried Iriana. "Is Angie here?"

"No. She sent Lin and me to come look for you," she said. "But we found someone else instead!"

"Really, who?"

Ariadne smiled. "Poppy Braden and Edmund MacGregor!"

There was something familiar about the name of Poppy's protector, but I couldn't quite put my finger on it.

Dermot's jaw dropped. "You caught an earth-fire druid all by yourself?"

"No, of course not! Lin and I did it together," she said. "His magic has to have an eye-line, so he has to stay back there."

I scratched my head, wondering what she was talking about.

"Line of sight," explained Seth.

"Aye, that's what I said!" Ariadne said. "He's holding them

506

prisoner in a big air bubble."

"Line of sight must be maintained for control," Seth explained. "It's a limitation of using elemental air."

"I didn't know elemental air had any limitations," Conall said dryly.

"Don't be stupid," Ariadne said, rolling her eyes. "All elements have *some* limitation." She pointed back the way she had come. "Follow me. I'll take you to them." She grabbed Dermot's hand.

"Lin sent you out here to deal with an unknown enemy alone?" the water elementalist asked, frowning as she dragged him along.

"We thought you were Republic soldiers," said Ariadne. "I can handle *them* just fine on my own."

"It sounds like they made the best decision possible under the circumstances," said Seth, following them. Beside him, Iriana nodded agreement.

"How do you figure?" Dermot demanded over his shoulder.

"A dualist and her protector are far more dangerous than any non-magical enemy," Seth replied. "Leaving a druid in charge of them was the wiser course of action."

"How do you know he's even a druid?" Dermot asked.

"Wolfric mentioned they were the same age." Seth gave a slight shrug. "It seemed likely."

"Yeah, well, Wolfric's not a full druid yet, so save 'likely' for when your own sister is in danger," the water elementalist retorted.

We entered the building. I recognized Lin immediately, sitting in a chair tipped back against the wall with his eyes on a pair of sleeping people. His eyes were bloodshot and heavy with the need for sleep, and exhaustion was carved into the planes of his face.

The chair legs hit the floor, and he put his hand on the hilt of his sword. "Well, Ariadne?"

Something told me that dealing with a teenage water elementalist might have been part of the reason he was worn out.

"Help has arrived!" she announced. "The Finns are here, and Dermot, too!"

Amidst the commotion, his prisoners had stopped pretending to be asleep and were now sitting up. Together with Lin, they eyed us suspiciously.

"They look like bandits to me," he said.

"They do, don't they?" Iriana said, gracefully navigating her way through the crowded doorway. "I'm so glad you're both safe, but Lin, you look terrible! How long have you been awake?"

"I'm fine," was his terse reply. "The ArchDruid told Angelina that Davis would be among your number. Is he here?"

"Yes." I pushed back the hood of my coat.

Jaw dropping, Lin lost his cynical expression. "By the gods, she was right."

"Lin never believed her," Ariadne said.

"That's because I saw what he looked like after he was whipped and poisoned!" he shot back. "Nobody could come back from an illness like that without an extremely skilled healer, and there were none after Orion's massacre."

"You didn't believe the ArchDruid?" Seth asked, looking mildly offended.

"It could have been a trick." Lin gave a diffident shrug. "I've lived my whole life not trusting one ArchDruid, and I won't be trusting this one, either, until he proves himself trustworthy."

Seth scowled at him.

"I was lucky," I said, interrupting before an argument could start. "Duncan came back for me."

The earth druid pushed his hood back. "It is good to see you, Lin," he said.

"But Master Padraig said he couldn't find you! He searched countless hours, for days on end! Where were you?"

"I did not remain long in the grove," the earth druid replied, smoothly evading the question.

"How'd you catch 'em?" asked Dermot, poking at the air bubble with the toe of his boot and diverting Lin from pressing Duncan for a better answer.

"Ariadne kept Poppy distracted while I trapped her," he replied. "Edmund entered voluntarily."

"Voluntarily?" I said.

Lin shrugged. "He's a null," he said as if that explained everything. Conall made a disgusted noise and walked out. Dermot scowled mightily at Lin and followed.

"We do not use that term," Seth scowled. "It is derogatory and offensive. You should apologize."

"Sorry."

"To *him*," Seth said, pointing toward the door through which Conall had just exited.

"Who are you, exactly?" Lin asked.

"Seth Starseeker," the air druid replied.

"Seth is my chosen!" Iriana exclaimed, her delight evident. "Can you believe it? I found him!"

"That is why you came, isn't it?" Lin said, looking Seth over with renewed interest.

"No!" she said, a little too emphatically. "Well, it wasn't the only reason. I came to help Angie, too." She glanced up at Seth, emboldened by his warm smile. "And just so you know, he is the son of Nioba Starseeker and ArchDruid Shitozaki. So mind your manners."

"My lineage is no more special than anyone else's," he replied. "We are all equals here."

"The ArchDruid's son," said Lin. "I would have expected you to be in command."

"I was not a druid when we departed Sanctuary," Seth replied.

Lin eyed me. "If Shitozaki put you in charge, that means you're the big dog here."

Assuming that he was referring to the magnitude of my elemental ability, I said, "I prefer to think that I was chosen because I'm fair and reasonable."

Out of the corner of my eye, Poppy Braden's partner – Edmund MacGregor – slowly rose to his feet, eyes fixed on me as though I were a creature of legend – or perhaps a ghost. And no wonder, for my memories came together as soon as I saw his face. He had been one of my gunnery students, and I was supposed to be dead. Edmund recovered quickly from his shock, performing the gesture of druidic respect with all apparent sincerity. Though we could not hear him due to the solidity of Lin's air bubble, from the movement of his lips I gleaned that he was greeting me with the accompanying words, calling me *Master Davis*.

Poppy herself remained sitting, arms holding her knees tightly to her chest and watching him. Her head snapped toward me as soon as Edmund said my name, her dark eyes taking my measure.

Ignoring her, he turned about to show off the worn leather holster on his back, containing an Ithaca 37 replica. I inclined my head to him in respect, and he smiled grimly in return.

"Let him out," I said.

"What?" Lin said, brow furrowing in anger. "No!"

"He has no magic, so you have nothing to fear, correct?"

The fatigued air druid glowered. "He may lack magic, but he still has a shotgun."

"He'd be a fool for trying," I said. "Even if he was that stupid, do you really think I'm going to let him get a shot off? Let him out."

There was a gust of shifting winds as Lin altered his bubble, releasing Edmund. Left alone, Poppy leapt to her feet with a panicked expression, palms slapping against the solid air. Whether she was scared for him or herself, I could not determine. She looked like a frightened little girl, and I had to remind myself that she was a dangerous earth-fire dualist.

"Master Davis," said Edmund MacGregor. "It is good to see you…"

"Alive?" I couldn't help smiling.

"I was going to say *again*, but I have to admit that seeing you alive was something of a shock."

"I've been getting that fairly often these days." I clapped him on the shoulder. "And it's just Davis now. I'm no more a master than anyone else here."

"Davis, then," he said. "And you're a druid?"

I nodded.

"Is that the real reason Sebrina had you… punished?"

I shook my head. "I've only had magic since Midsummer."

"We believe he was blocked," Duncan said.

Edmund nodded. "I envy you."

I wanted to tell him not to envy me and that every person had something to contribute to the world, but when dealing with a person whose entire culture had conspired to deny him that which was his gods-given right, it would have sounded just as trite and meaningless as such words so often are.

"So this is your chosen?" I asked Edmund.

"No," he said. "When Dianthe Aspen asked for volunteers to accompany the ArchDruid's envoys to the 'Ville, I took the opportunity to see the world outside the grove. Will you let Poppy out, too?"

"We'll see after we talk."

"Poppy isn't like the others," he said. "She only went along with what the ArchDruid wanted because that was the best way to thrive in the grove. She has no brothers and so was removed from experiencing the pain of a loved one who was denied the gods' gift. She is a good person."

"Many have suffered at Sebrina's hands because 'good' people like her and her family stayed silent," Lin said angrily.

"Yes, and many of them left the grove with the Everlights!" Edmund retorted. He turned back to me. "You should treat me the same as Poppy, for when the time for choosing came, my whole clan silently followed the will of the ArchDruid to keep our home."

"*White Oak sap runs through MacGregor veins,*" said Duncan. In response to Edmund's look of surprise, he added, "That is your family motto, is it not?"

"It is," Edmund replied. "It's also how my grandmother justifies staying in a place where her grandsons are denied their gift."

"I'm sorry," Duncan said. Then to me: "The MacGregors were one of the founding families of White Oak Grove. They have a long history of noble deeds and a firm dedication to tradition."

"The grove's wretched state of affairs cannot be justly laid at the feet of *our* generation," Edmund said. "It was our parents and grandparents that allowed our magic to be taken from us for the sake of preserving a familiar ring of trees and the dirt houses surrounding it. Poppy was just trying to survive the best way she knew how."

"And you, Edmund?" Seth pressed. "If you don't believe in Sebrina or her politics, why did you stay? Why not leave with the Everlights and all the others?"

"And leave my family?" he replied. "If anyone should be imprisoned, it is I and not Poppy. Her family may have seemed like silent supporters of the ArchDruid, but when the Everlights left, the Bradens packed up and departed with them. They didn't even tell her they were leaving!" He shook his head. "After losing all her friends and family, she did what anyone would do – she clung to the only familiar people remaining in her life: Dianthe Aspen and Nualla Ashcroft."

"So that's it?" Lin asked, spreading his arms wide. "You're

both just innocent victims of circumstance?"

Help came from an unexpected source: Seth, ever logical and rarely swayed by emotion. He turned to me and said, "It sounds like they've both done the best they could, under the circumstances."

"*What?*" Lin fumed.

"My father was ArchDruid before Sebrina," he continued. "I could just have easily have been corrupted by his politics, had he continued in that position."

I told everyone else to leave except Seth and thought about what each of them had said while waiting for the room to empty. Lin remained, dog-tired but hanging on through sheer willpower.

"I want to talk to them alone," I said to Lin. "Why don't you go get some rest."

"If I go, the bubble goes," he warned.

"I am well aware."

"She has elemental fire!" He stabbed a finger at Poppy.

"You can do it now, or we can wait until you drop from exhaustion," I said. "What were you planning to do? Drag her around in a giant bubble forever?"

"*Fine.*" He threw up his hands and stormed out the door in a chaotic whirl of air.

I studied Poppy for a few long seconds. "Heya. My name is Davis."

"I know who you are," she said. "You're Angelina's chosen that supposedly died a year ago." She fluffed her curls, and then smoothed her split skirts. "And you are either very brave or very foolish."

"You're assuming I've been altered."

"You have to be a druid to have been altered." Her tone was more than a little condescending. "*You* are just a null."

"Correction: I *was* a null. I am now a full druid with elemental earth and fire."

"That's impossible. The ArchDruid said she made sure that all the boy babies with fire were neutered in the womb!"

Her words unraveled the mystery of why no fire elementalists had been sent to Shitozaki for safe-keeping. Adalwulf and Eireanne had hidden their son's gift, and the others had capitulated to Sebrina's cruel whim. It was quite possible that Wolfric and I *were* the only fire elementalists of our generation. Why focus on the ones with fire, though? Was it some convoluted way of retaliating against Connor Shitozaki since he was a fire elementalist?

"You forget Wolfric," I said. "And if the ArchDruid was hoodwinked by one mother, you must consider the possibility that she was tricked by more than one."

Poppy's expression told me she had indeed forgotten about Wolfric Rask. She'd start to wonder what other untruths she'd been told soon enough.

"Edmund told me about your family," I said.

"That was private!" she snapped.

"I'm sorry," Edmund said. "It was important to make them understand the situation we're in, and I knew you'd never tell."

"Be glad he did, or I'd not be giving you the choice I'm giving him," I said.

"And what is that, exactly?"

"You can stay and help us fight the Republic of Jackson, or I can send you back to your family with five of my men to escort you."

Her snotty attitude vanished. "You know where they are?" she asked, as though afraid to hope.

"I do."

She bit her lip, hugging herself.

"What if I want to return to the grove?" Edmund asked.

"Just because your family made a poor decision doesn't mean you have to follow in their footsteps," Seth said.

"And if I want to return to the grove?" Poppy asked.

"That is not an option," I said.

"We're both fire elementalists," she said. "You can't hurt me with fire, and I'll melt any weapon you try to use against me." She seemed to have forgotten the rest of my rough bunch, who were probably standing outside just waiting for an excuse to break down the door and start a fight.

"You won't melt this one," I said, drawing the grey blade from its sheath and laying its point at the base of her throat. Poppy gasped at the blade's chill touch but did not otherwise move. She met my gaze with fear in her eyes and a complexion gone ashen, but her spine was straight with courage.

"Did you give Dianthe the same choice?" she whispered.

"No."

"You've killed her?"

"No, but she *is* dead." I pulled the grey blade back. "Telling Duncan Everlight that he should have been burned alive on his mother's corpse proved to be a fatal mistake."

Sheathing the sword, I strode to the door.

"You have fifteen minutes to pick which side you're on. Choose wisely."

* * *

While Edmund MacGregor and Poppy Braden deliberated the choice that would govern their immediate future, the Finns got busy setting up camp. Martin and Halldor's pentacles brought in the horses, untacked them, and settled them in the back with several bales of hay they'd found. Ingvar's pentacle rummaged through the main building to find out what it had to offer in the way of vittles that would feed forty people. Warwick's pentacle scouted the perimeter before closing the gate and securing the fort, then started searching for supplies, weapons, and ammunition.

Lin had offered Conall an apology that was accepted with a rapidity that surprised us all, and we were standing outside the door talking when Poppy and Edmund came out.

"We have conditions," said Edmund.

"Conditions weren't part of the terms," I said.

"Please just hear us out?" Poppy asked. Since her arrogant demeanor had not returned, I acquiesced.

"All right."

She spoke first: "I realize that I've been misled. I think I've known it for quite some time but just couldn't admit that my whole life has been wasted on a lie. I was so blind that even my own family didn't think it worthwhile to try and make me see reason."

"Just because they thought you wouldn't listen is no reason for them not to try," said Seth. "They did you an injustice."

"It wasn't like I listened to them before that," she said. "But I *do* want to see them again."

"Are you aware that the reason the Republic of Jackson became powerful in the first place is that White Oak Grove made a treaty with them that druids would no longer interfere in their dealings?"

The pair exchanged a distressed glance.

"Why?" asked Poppy. "Why would Sebrina do such a thing?"

"She knew she wouldn't be able to defend the grove in the future," Seth replied. "Cutting all the male babies off from their magic for the last twenty-two years created a druid population in which eventually only fifty percent would have magic. She literally emasculated the grove, leaving it vulnerable to attack, so she made the treaty to ensure its protection."

"Unfortunately, that left all the small towns and villages near the 'Ville virtually defenseless," I said. "And when the Republic made its bid for expansion, most of those people were completely unprepared to defend themselves."

"Sebrina sacrificed them to keep the grove safe?" Poppy asked. She looked mortified.

"Exactly."

"If I had heard this earlier, it wouldn't have taken me even a minute to make up my mind!" she said. Edmund nodded agreement.

"If you were a true follower of Sebrina," Lin said, "you wouldn't have believed it anyway."

"Or you wouldn't have cared," Conall added.

"Liam Everlight was First Warrior," Poppy said after a pause. "He had to have known about that treaty."

"I'm sure he did," I said.

"Liam selfishly went along with Sebrina's plan in order to protect Angelina," Duncan said, sounding disgusted. "He should have realized it wouldn't work."

I nodded. "You can't eat your cake and have it, too." It was one of my father's favorite phrases.

"What do you plan to do when you see him next?" Poppy asked. "Him being your chosen's father and all."

"I haven't thought about it," I said. "I suppose that's *my* blind spot in this tangled mess."

"My father is not innocent, either," said Duncan. "He could have protested more loudly. He could have left the grove at any time. But like you, Edmund, he could not bear to leave his family."

"I want to join you," said Edmund. "I don't know what help I'll be since I don't have magic, but I'm willing. I just don't want to fight other druids. *I won't.* I don't want to fight a war and find out later that I've killed a member of my own family. I couldn't live with myself."

"I've no desire to start a civil war, which is why we didn't kill you on sight," I said. "A war between druids could cause as much destruction as the Fracture."

"That's a bit of an exaggeration," Lin said.

"Earthquakes, lightning, tornadoes, forest fires, and floods are all within the sphere of druid elemental magic," I replied. "The only difference is that it wouldn't be on a worldwide scale."

"This is not why we were given magic," said Duncan. "The Shining Ones bestowed it on our ancestors in order that they might heal the world, not ruin it further."

Poppy's face twisted wistfully. "It's been so long since I've heard anyone speak of the will of the Shining Ones or our true purpose in the world."

"I'm won't go so far as to say that fighting the Republic is the will of the gods," I said, "but I'm not above using their gift to free enslaved people and restore balance."

"That's a judicious use of it if anything is," said Edmund.

"Feel better now?" I asked Lin.

He nodded, his shoulders losing some of their tension. "I suppose everyone deserves a second chance."

Duncan checked Lin and Edmund over, pronouncing them tired but sound, as though they were a pair of horses that had been worked too hard. He offered Poppy the same, and after a couple of half-hearted refusals, she let him heal some minor wounds. I introduced them as new members of our war band and was humbled by the Finns' generosity in accepting them so readily.

I lit the cooking fire and sent Galen and Nêreus to fetch water while I thawed the meat. After a group of us chopped it up, I tossed it into a large iron cauldron to sear while Conall, Dermot, and Ariadne helped Jasvinder, Tristan, and Regnar chop the vegetables they'd raided from the fort's larder. While they worked, the fourteen-year-old updated her brother on how the rest of the family was doing, and he wore a happy smile for the rest of the afternoon and evening.

There weren't enough bowls to go around, but Warwick had

found a crate packed with wide-mouthed mugs that served well as soup bowls. Rob had found a small supply of freshly baked bread, an unexpected treat; he and Ishkur sliced it so that everyone could have a piece, while Ridley and Narinder smeared rich butter on each slide and laid it out on long trays.

Supper was ready by sundown. Lin helped Duncan and me ladle stew into each person's cup or bowl as they came through in a line. I had tried to convince him to rest, but he wasn't having any of it.

"It's remarkable that you've become the leader of this bunch," Lin said. "It's almost easier to believe you're not dead."

I chuckled.

"By the way, man, you need a haircut in the worst way. It looks like you haven't even seen a pair of scissors since Angie gave you that chop job last year."

"I haven't. I've been scared of them ever since."

Lin laughed. "Except for that, you look the same. Duncan, though… I'd never have recognized him with that moustache and beard if he hadn't spoken. He looks like a wild barbarian."

"He *is* a wild barbarian," Phelan said as I filled his mug with stew. He moved on and grabbed a piece of buttered bread. The earth druid rolled his eyes.

"We've lacked the niceties of civilization for several weeks now," Seth said, carrying out another tray of mugs.

"You mean you've all been running about in the freezing cold this whole time?"

"Yeah, most of it."

Lin's gaze traveled over the courtyard of the fort, where Finns were talking and eating around the various campfires. "That is a story I would quite like to hear."

"Wish granted," said Seth. "Iriana has been pestering me to tell our tale since yesterday, but I'm no storyteller." He rose and clapped his hands, garnering everyone's attention.

"The newcomers among us have expressed an interest in our adventures," he said, "and in the spirit of hospitality, we should honor that request. What say you?" The Finns cheered. "Conall, Dermot, would you do the honors?"

The water elementalist jumped up and ran through the camp and then hopped up on a woodcutting stump, followed by the gunman at a more sedate pace. As we ate our fill, they entertained us all with their storytelling skill. One would think that the Finns would be tired of hearing stories of events they'd lived through, but they only seemed to enjoy them more with each retelling.

Once they were finished, I relayed how I'd come to be with Connor Shitozaki and the Finns. I tried to gloss over our training, but Halldor, Warwick, and Nêreus gleefully told all about how I'd defied our master. Then Dermot interrupted everyone to blurt out that I'd come into my magic by falling into a volcano. He blamed it on Conall, who retorted that if the water elementalist wasn't such an annoying little shit, he wouldn't have tried to punch him, and they were off and running, exchanging ever more obscene insults describing one another's deficiencies, both real and imagined.

"It seems that you still have a penchant for finding trouble," Lin said with a small smile.

"I'm not the one who took a direct hit from one of Sebrina's spirit bolts," I said, keeping my tone light.

"That hurt," he said, rubbing his left arm.

"You were struck by a spirit bolt of elemental spirit and lived to tell the tale? Remarkable," Seth said. "Why didn't you put up an air shield?"

"And give myself away?" Lin shook his head.

The Finns demanded to hear the story, and Lin graciously complied, assisted in parts by Iriana, who had also been at the Autumn Moon gathering.

Liam nodded. "My heart would have stopped if not for Liam Everlight."

Edmund leaned around Seth to look at him. "The way you stood up to Sebrina made you a hero in the eyes of everyone in the Warriors' Third."

"I wouldn't have been so bold that night if I'd known she would actually hurt me," said Lin. "Liam took me to Danica Harris, but I still carry the scar." He rolled up his left sleeve, where a thick scar from an electrical burn ran from the back of his hand up his arm, disappearing beneath the fabric. "It goes all the way up my arm and across the left side of my chest."

"It's a good thing you're right-handed, then," said Edmund.

It was difficult to fight when your range of motion was limited by scar tissue. I had worked hard and endured a lot of pain to make sure my own flexibility wasn't limited by the lash marks on my back.

"I still had to switch from a two-hander to a bastard sword," Lin said. "Master Padraig helped me learn to fight one-handed."

"Some things even magic cannot heal," I said.

"You, too, hunh?" Lin asked, his mouth twisting unhappily.

"I am too lucky to be alive to complain about the scars."

"We both are," he agreed. "I only hope Wolfric and Onóra are content with the freedom you bought with those scars."

"Wolfric!" I threw my hands up. "I forgot to tell you – he's with *us*!"

"Where? I haven't seen him."

"Well, he's not here right now, but he's been with us for weeks," I said, pausing before adding, "I've sent him on an errand with some others, but they know to meet up with us here."

"If you sent him to track down Laiken and Shonda, you'd better have sent somebody with him," Poppy said. "They're not like me. They truly believe that drivel the ArchDruid spouts. They'll put up a fight."

"You don't seem happy too about that," I said.

"Onóra and I were friends as children," she said. "We grew apart because of her mother's open opposition to the Arch– to Sebrina's policies, but I still don't want anything bad to happen to her *or* her chosen."

"So you still believe in preordained dyads?" Seth said.

"Some fairy tales are hard to outgrow," she said softly.

"Have you tried sending out a fetch?" he asked.

"I've been a druid for over a year now," she said in a tone of finality.

"Perhaps a return to peaceful days will allow you to send one out," he said kindly.

"Would it be wise even then?" she asked.

"It can suffer no physical harm, and by that time there should be no danger for it from elemental magic."

"Davis has had his fetch out for weeks," Dermot said, grabbing another mug of stew.

"Have you really?" Poppy's eyes were large.

I nodded.

"Why would you take such a risk?"

"It was the only way I could find Angie."

There were a few moments of silence.

"I have to admit that I was curious about that," said Lin. "It was you who sent that lion?"

"A lion!" Poppy yelped, immediately covering her mouth with both hands in embarrassment.

"Then it *did* find her." I was pleased.

"Yes, and she was both thrilled and distressed."

"Oh?"

"It is dangerous for a druid to bring out a spirit animal, which I'm sure is why Poppy is reluctant to send one of her own," he said. "Your friends have done you a disservice by not telling you this."

"We told him," said Seth, ladling more stew into his bowl. "He decided the risk was worth it." He paused. "And now, after coming together with my own chosen, I have to confess that I will do the same, should the need arise."

Iriana made that cute little *Awww* noise that girls so often do when they are touched, gazing adoringly at him.

"Oh, did you come together already?" Dermot said, poking his head between them. Iriana blushed and giggled.

"Get outta here," Seth growled, throwing a chunk of potato at him.

"Clearly you still feel strongly about Angelina," said Lin, frowning. "I'm surprised you haven't asked about her."

"Iriana already told me what you've all been up to," I replied. "And since we're following my fetch, I expect to find her soon."

"There's no need for you to follow a spirit animal, or even have one out at all."

"Why is that?"

"Because I know exactly where she is."

Chapter 30 – Wolves in Sheep's Clothing

Good strategy even in failure often produces compensations.
~ Winston Churchill ~

"What?" I asked. "Where?"

"There's a township due east of here that's walled around just like this fort," Lin said. "Angie said you'd never find each other if you both kept wandering around in the wilderness, and that Lone Oak was the one place where you'd be sure to turn up eventually."

"Lone Oak!" I slapped my forehead. In the name of all that was good and green in the world, why hadn't I thought of going there? "Why didn't Iriana know about it?" I asked.

"We lost her before we got there." He made a sour face. "I don't think Angie mentioned the town's name until we arrived."

"How far is it from here?"

"Less than five miles, as the crow flies."

"If we leave now, we could be there and back by midnight," Duncan said.

Lin shook his head. "She won't leave. We've been there for over three weeks because Lone Oak is the last independent town to stand against the Republic of Jackson. She called it 'a bastion of light and hope against the forces of evil and darkness'."

"That sounds like Angie, all right," I said with a smile. "I wonder why Lone Oak and not Ward?"

"We heard that Ward had been taken," said Lin. "She was distressed about it, but said that it was more important to hold Lone Oak than to lose it trying to get Ward back."

"She sounds like quite the strategist," said Seth.

"She also said that once you were reunited the two of you would ride up and help them get it back," said Ariadne.

"Just the two of us, eh?"

Seth chuckled and said, "You and your chosen think alike."

At Lin's questioning glance, I said, "We've already liberated Ward."

"And most of the other settlements," Conall added.

"We heard that over ten companies of soldiers have been slaughtered defending the Republic's holdings," Edmund said, reminding me that he and Poppy could be an excellent source of information about our enemies.

"How many are in a company?" Seth asked.

"About fifty."

"That's what we've been calling a raid group," I said.

"We've taken out more than five hundred of them," said Conall. He caught my eye. "Guess they haven't heard about Mayflower yet."

"Mayflower..." Edmund said. "I've heard mention of that place. Something about how their own soldiers had turned mutinous and refused to leave the town or allow any other people from the Republic on the island."

"That's the one," Conall said.

"I heard they sent something like five hundred mounted troops there."

"It was closer to a thousand," said Seth. "Of course, we didn't stop to count. It could have been more."

Edmund stared at him. "You don't even have half the men a company does! And you destroyed them all?"

"There were about fifty of us at that time," Seth said. "We had some of the witches from Ward, along with a few people rescued from the liberated settlements who were still in good enough shape to ride and shoot."

"That is hardly less impressive," Edmund replied. "Fifty against a thousand? It's unbelievable."

"Well, we didn't take them all on at once," said Dermot. "The fifty of us took out maybe half of them."

Conall nodded. "Davis polished off about six raid groups by himself, then rode to the other side of the island and took out six more. That doesn't include the hundred or so that our pentacle 'removed' from the island."

"His elemental fire is pretty potent." Dermot yawned, as though bored by the topic.

"Having an enchanted sword doesn't hurt, either," Conall remarked, picking at his fingernails as though the possession of an enchanted blade was nothing special. Which, I suppose, by that time it was.

"Unfortunately, none of that will matter with two triple threats who each have an army of their own," Poppy said.

"What do you mean?" Seth asked.

"Lone Oak is where Shonda and Laiken are headed. Their soldiers are supposed to meet them there," she said. "I hope that's not where you've sent Wolfric."

"Quakes," I muttered. "They moved before we did."

"And what about your army?" Conall asked her.

"*Obviously*, they aren't mine anymore," Poppy said, sounding miffed. "But I doubt that will change anything."

"How many were each of you supposed to command?" I asked.

"Command?" She snorted. "None of us are in command of anything. The Republic wanted druids to ride with their armies to keep *yours* busy."

Seth gave her a skeptical look. "The Republic expects three druids to hold off over thirty? That seems… optimistic."

"I don't think Dianthe knew how many of you have elemental magic," Poppy said. "Either that, or she lied."

"And they *believed* her?"

"It's not like you left anyone alive to contradict her," she said.

"But why mislead her own allies?" I asked.

"Because having to admit that they missed cutting so many of us off from our magic would be embarrassing," Conall growled. "It might make President Jackson question the ArchDruid's competence."

"Now *that* reasoning, I can believe," said Seth. "What about the other two druids, Poppy?"

"There is a possibility that Blythe and Fiona might be at Lone Oak, too. Although, the last I heard was that their armies hadn't come back to the city yet." She paused. "They were supposed to send us with one company each, but that was before you wiped out Dianthe's army," Poppy replied. "They might send more now."

"That's at least three raid groups," Conall said. "Five if the other two druids show up."

"Time for a war council," I said, setting my cup aside.

Seth nodded. "I'll get the others."

I had Phelan and Alexandros take Poppy and Edmund to their pentacle's campfire while Seth rounded up the earth druids present. We met in the building farthest from the kitchen, which was an armory of sorts. It held the same kinds of small arms, longarms, and ammunition that we had found in various bandit outposts. As everyone got settled, I noticed that in addition to the grey shrike carried by Warwick, a ferret peeked out of the chest pocket of Halldor's coat, and Ingvar sported a copperhead. The snake was wrapped around his neck, presumably for warmth, which was odd thing for a spirit animal to need. Maybe a tenth of the Finns had fetches before we'd parted with Shitozaki. Maybe it was my imagination, but it seemed that over half had them now.

"Here's the situation," I said. "According to Lin, Lone Oak is the last free township that hasn't been taken by the Republic. Poppy has just informed us that this is where she and the other two triskelia were headed, and that each of them was supposed to be met by a raid group."

"So, roughly a hundred and fifty soldiers," Warwick said. "We can handle that."

"Two hundred fifty, if the other two triple threats show up."

"Maybe we'll be lucky and they won't," Halldor said.

"Either way, it's still doable," Ingvar said.

"Provided we don't send all the water elementalists away," Martin muttered. I stifled a sigh. He just wasn't going to let me off the hook about the disastrous battle by the lake.

"The enemy forces are not all we need to consider," Duncan said. "Davis' chosen is in that town."

"That shouldn't be a factor in whatever decisions we make," I said.

"Don't be ridiculous," said Seth. "Of course her presence there should be given consideration."

"I just don't want anybody to get excited and rush in there recklessly," I replied. "I also don't want to leave before Siorus and

Yiorgos rejoin us." While her well-being was important to me personally, what was good for the two of us might not be good for the group as a whole. Besides, as she had adequately demonstrated on more than one occasion, Angie Everlight could take care of herself. She had been raised and trained by a powerful ArchDruid and the First Warrior of White Oak Grove, and was a force to be reckoned with.

"How long do you think it'll take them to figure out they're not going to find the dyads?" asked Halldor.

"Since both of them planned a continual *seeking*, it is likely that they already know and are headed this way," said Duncan.

"It took us about four hours to get here," Conall said. "It will take at least three times as long for them to get here."

"They could very well be here by midnight," Ingvar said.

"*If* both earth druids accept that the dyads aren't there," said Seth.

Warwick nodded. "There's always the possibility that they decide to thoroughly search those areas. We're a stubborn lot, sometimes."

He was right. Earth druids were solid and dependable when they took on a job and could be expected to doggedly see it through to the end. However, they were also stubborn and slow to change both their minds and their plans.

"Wolfric is with Siorus," said Dermot. "I bet he'll get impatient and want to come back quick when they don't find anything."

"Westley, Solon, and Wyatt aren't known for their patience, either," said Halldor. "They'll hustle Yiorgos along."

"Either way, we probably won't know anything until dawn," Martin said. "What are we going to do if they're not here then?"

"I can send the dragon," I said. "Have it lead them back."

"That might also give away their position to the enemy," said Conall. "Especially while it's still dark."

Seth nodded. "We should wait until morning, then. If they don't show up by sunrise, you can send the dragon then."

Ingvar said, "If they don't show up and the dragon doesn't bring them, we'll have to go and find them."

"That's a lot of extra work for the horses," said Warwick. "Not to mention giving us less time to defend Lone Oak."

"What if we *don't* make it back to Ward before the High Priestess renews the Veil of Doom?" asked Martin.

"We'd better," growled Conall.

"Worst case scenario, we'll ride to Ward to make sure it's still protected and then return to Lone Oak to stay until the next new moon," I said.

Seth nodded. "We'll cross that bridge when we come to it," he said. "Is everyone in agreement that we wait for Siorus and Yiorgos until dawn?"

There were nods all round.

"Anything else?" I asked.

"Yes," said Conall. "I don't think we should trust our 'new members' just yet. They've shown too great a willingness to choose whichever side they think will benefit them the most."

"Agreed," I said. "No discussions of battle plans around them."

"Maybe we should put them into different pentacles," Dermot said. "We could just say it's too much for one group to show the ropes to two new people."

"Good idea," said Conall, giving the water elementalist one of his rare smiles.

"Any volunteers?" I asked.

Martin raised a hand. "I'm fine with keeping Poppy in mine. We could use a little extra firepower." With two air/water dualists and an air/spirit dualist, his pentacle would be well-suited to keeping her under control if she decided to switch sides again.

"All the other pentacles have gunmen except Yiorgos', so maybe he'd like to have Edmund," said Ingvar.

"An excellent suggestion. I'll ask him as soon as he gets back."

"All right, everybody pick a building and get some sleep," Seth ordered. "Dawn will be here all too soon."

* * *

I woke up late the next morning and found most of the Finns already up and preparing for departure under Seth's direction. Martin's crew was feeding the horses, giving them the last of the hay but also dividing up several bags of grain among them. They were too heavy to take with us, for we had to ride fast. Warwick's

526

pentacle divided up the weapons, ammunition, and extra supplies they had found the day before. The members of Halldor and Ingvar's pentacles were in charge of breakfast, and Regnar handed me a cup of chicory coffee as soon as I stumbled through the kitchen door.

"We found *bacon*," he said with a grin.

"Proof positive that the Shining Ones hold us in the highest regard," I said.

"There's a big plate of it already on the table, and we're just finishing up another batch of scrambled eggs. Do you want toast?"

"Please," I said.

"You got it," he said and went back to the stove.

I slid onto the bench beside Lin, who was so focused on eating that he didn't say a word. Even after a full night's sleep, he still looked exhausted. Conall was on the other side of him, making a bacon and egg sandwich, while across the table from me Seth sipped chicory coffee over an empty plate.

"Where are Duncan and Dermot?" I asked.

"Duncan rode out to go look for Siorus and Martin. To see if he could sense them near," said Seth. "He wasn't able to *seek* well, so he came back for Dermot. Apparently he can *seek* using water now?"

"Oh, yeah. When we were at Ward, he found out he could do it while we were on patrol. He discovered a group of bandits before I even knew they were there, just by *seeking* through the snow."

"Impressive."

"They took Ingvar and Nêreus with them," said Conall. "Something about trying to increase their range."

I nodded. Earth druids could link up through the ground to increase power and control. Nêreus and Dermot might be able to do something similar with their combined magics.

"How long have they been gone?"

"About an hour," Seth replied.

I'd just finished my last bite of toast when Alexandros burst through the door. "They're back!" he shouted, and then disappeared once more. Through the briefly open door, we could hear the jingling of tack and the hoofbeats of more than a few horses. Seth and I rose to see who had returned when first Yiorgos and then Siorus entered the building.

"We didn't find them," Yiorgos said without preamble, followed by Siorus: "Neither did we." The members of their pentacles all piled in after them. Regnar directed everyone but the earth druids into the kitchen to cut down on the noise. Then he and Tristan brought each of the earth druids a plate of eggs and bacon with mugs coffee.

"They moved faster than we expected," I said, but was interrupted again. Wolfric and Madoc were the last to enter, took one look at the crowded kitchen, and decided to grab some coffee first.

"Wolfric!" Lin exclaimed, jumping to his feet.

"Lin! Good to see you!"

They embraced, thumping each other heartily on the back and exchanging congratulations on escaping the grove alive. They ate while I explained finding Poppy Braden and Edmund MacGregor held captive by Lin and Ariadne, as well as the expected situation at Lone Oak.

"Angelina is there with Niall?" Wolfric asked. He frowned slightly, as though he couldn't decide whether to be pleased or annoyed.

"He's all right now that he's not an arrogant jackass anymore," Lin said.

"What's our plan of attack?" the fire elementalist asked.

"We don't have one yet," I replied. "I'm making this up as I go along."

"A lot will depend on whether or not the Republic forces have arrived, how many there are if they do, and how many of Sebrina's druids are involved," said Seth. "We'll have to see when we get there."

"So we're off after breakfast?" Yiorgos asked.

"Unless you need to get some sleep first," said Seth.

Siorus waved his hand dismissively. "We rode fast and figured out what was going on pretty quickly yesterday," he said. "We're rested enough."

Yiorgos nodded agreement. "Same."

"We'll leave right after breakfast, then," said Seth.

He was about to say something else, but both newly-arrived pentacles erupted from the kitchen – along with Dermot, who was sneaking a second breakfast – just as Warwick and Martin's guys burst through the door to warm up and get their own food. The once-quiet room was suddenly overcrowded and noisy, with each group shouting questions or hollering answers at the other, trying to catch each other up on current events.

"*Pipe down!*" Seth roared. "You sound like a rowdy bunch of bandits!"

"That's all right!" Dermot yelled back over the hubbub. "We *look* like a rowdy bunch of bandits!"

As I surveyed the room full of Finns, I realized he was right. Gone were our neat haircuts and shaved faces, replaced by wild, shaggy locks and, with the exception of Dermot and me, thick moustaches and beards. Raiding multiple outposts and garrisons had provided us not only with the armaments, holsters, and tools common to our enemies, but also the sweaters, blue jeans, and heavy duster coats in which they were always clad. Many of the Finns had also exchanged the small, lightweight druid saddles for the heavier, more comfortable ones like mine.

"I know that look," said Conall. "What is it?"

"I have an idea."

* * *

"If we keep adding people to our pentacles, we're going to have to call them something else," said Dermot.

"Theoretically, our number could increase to ten," said Duncan, meaning when each of us was joined by our chosen.

"Theoretically, our number could increase to eleven, assuming that Cinna rejoins us and Conall's chosen shows up," said Seth.

"That won't happen," the Norseman said. "Cinna might, but not the other."

"Why not?" asked Dermot.

"I've already been found by a fetch," Conall replied.

My mind on reuniting with Angie in Lone Oak as we rode, I'd barely been paying attention to the conversation, but his statement made me turn around in my saddle to see if he was joking. You could never rely on his tone of voice. His characteristic smirk was absent as he gazed off at some unknown point in the distance; he appeared disinterested, as though speaking about someone else.

"You have?" I couldn't help asking.

"Yep. Got it and lost it, all in the same week."

"When was this?"

"Right before I left the grove," he said.

It didn't take a genius to figure out that his chosen had discovered his identity and found him wanting, or that unbearable pressure had been applied to make whoever it was withdraw their fetch. I had figured that, as a male who had been magically neutered and therefore acceptable by Sebrina, it had taken something major to make him leave. I wondered if losing that fetch had been the straw the broke the camel's back.

The water elementalist snorted. "Her loss."

"Or his," said Duncan, clearly meaning that the mystery chosen could have been male.

"My mother says that dyads should be opposite genders for balance," said Dermot.

"My father says there was no precedent for it until Sebrina created one," the earth druid countered. "And according to Iriana, the histories agree with him."

Seth said, "My father says that if you ask ten druids about anything, you'll get ten different opinions. And if they spend all night drinking and talking, you'll get a hundred more and still nothing done."

Dermot and Duncan exchanged a look.

"Fire elementalist," Dermot said, as if that explained Connor Shitozaki's outlook.

Duncan nodded. "No patience."

"Anyway," Dermot continued, "What's the root word for ten?"

"Deca," Seth replied.

"Ten people would give us a decacle."

"Decacle isn't a word," said Poppy. "A ten-pointed star is called a decagram."

The earth-fire druid rode between Seth and me. If she showed any hint of treachery, I would counter her fire, and he would contain her. If either of us failed, Conall was riding behind her with a sawed-off shotgun that I'd modified for just this purpose.

Edmund, riding in the back with Yiorgos' pentacle, had been allowed to keep his longsword and shotgun, but Lin and Wolfric were riding at the rear with instructions to trap or kill him if he took a wrong move. I wasn't risking any of my people, even if it did cause a civil war.

"*Bor*-ing," Dermot said.

"You don't need a fancy word for it," Conall said. "There would just be two of them. Pentacles, I mean."

"A pair of pentacles," said Dermot. "I guess that'll do."

"That's not a bad idea," I said, "but what I've been thinking is that we have enough people for an eighth pentacle now. If Duncan wants to lead it, that is."

"Who else would be in it?" Dermot asked.

"Wolfric, Lin, and Edmund, for starters." That was only if I could take Edmund away from Yiorgos, which I doubted. When I'd asked the earth druid about the warrior joining his pentacle, he'd sounded slightly put out, saying: "All the other pentacles have gunmen except mine. Of course I want him!" I was genuinely pleased that our altered Finns were held in such high regard that the leader of our only all-magic pentacle had felt deprived because he didn't have a gunman of his own.

"*If* Edmund turns out to be reliable and not a liar," said Conall.

Poppy twisted around in her saddle and frowned at him. "Edmund is a good person," she said. Resuming a proper riding form, she murmured, "Unlike *some* people."

Pretending not to hear her, I said, "It's not fair to judge somebody based on what their family has done."

Conall grimaced and returned his gaze to the distant horizon.

Dermot continued the discussion on creating an eighth pentacle as if no one had interrupted.

"But they wouldn't have a water elementalist," he said.

"Ariadne could ride with them," I said.

His usually bright and cheerful countenance turned troubled. "I don't know. It's dangerous out here, and she's only fourteen."

"That's true, but look who she'll have to protect her."

"Well, who's going to heal for our pentacle?"

"Iriana."

"I don't know," he said again. "I *like* Duncan being in our pentacle!"

"As do I."

"You'd better," said Conall. "Sometimes I think he's the only thing keeping you out of Valhalla, or wherever you Celts go when you die."

"Donn is lord over the Land of the Dead," said Dermot. "But I reckon the Morrigan will come to collect Davis, seeing as how she likes him so much." Poppy looked at him as if trying to decide if she should believe him or not.

"Now *there's* a cheerful thought." Conall laughed.

"Hardly," I said.

"Shouldn't we be trying to be quiet?" Iriana asked, looking over her shoulder for the thousandth time since we had departed the swamp fort. The thinly populated forest to the east with its widely spaced tree trunks had allowed us to pass swiftly through to the road. This route took us farther north of our destination and would require a small amount of backtracking, but traveling the road was necessary if we wanted them to believe we had come from the direction of the 'Ville.

"It's quite impossible to be stealthy with a group this big," Seth said to his chosen. "Besides, we want them to see us. We want them to know we are coming."

"Why?"

"Because bandits don't sneak," I said. "They think they're the big dogs around here, so they come barking and howling."

"Unfortunately for them," Conall said, "*we* are wolves."

"I just hope it fools Laiken and Shonda," Iriana said, looking worried.

"A raid group is about fifty bandits riding together," Seth explained. "We're not far off that now."

"They'll be expecting more than one," said Poppy.

"Yeah, but we'll have taken care of them by the time they figure that out," I said.

"Are we there yet?" asked Dermot.

"Yes." Duncan pointed at the shape of a walled town, the top of its palisade clearly visible in the distance.

"Put your hood up," Seth told Iriana, flipping his own up as he did so. "You'll be a target if you're recognized."

Poppy stayed at the vanguard with us in full view to lend us credibility. As we came around a bend in the road, I could see at least three companies of Republic soldiers camped outside the gates of Lone Oak.

"They're under siege," I said, pulling the spyglass out of my coat pocket. The walls of Lone Oak had looked all right from a distance, but a closer inspection revealed the thick timbers to be charred by flame and lightning strikes.

"We might not be too late," Seth said. "Form up!" He shouted. "Air druids at the fore!"

"Are we going to fight?" Poppy asked. Her knuckles were tan from the tight grip she had on the reins, a sharp contrast to her dark skin.

"We are."

"Is it always this scary?"

I frowned at her. "You have magic. They don't."

"Oh, yes, they do," she retorted. "There are black marks on those walls. That means the others are here."

"Even if they are all here, four elementalists are no match for thirty-four," I said. I stood up in my stirrups and spun my horse about in a circle. "Finns! We ride!"

Seth's great black stallion leaped into a gallop, leading our pentacle at the vanguard. The rest of the pentacles followed suit, each air elementalist taking point to guard against magic and gunfire until we were close enough to engage the enemy. The air shields were hardly necessary; we had successfully caught the Republic forces off guard. Meeting little resistance, the war band plowed right through their camp.

As soon as we were close enough, I began throwing fireballs at enemy tents on both sides, while even more streaked overhead, courtesy of Wolfric and Poppy, setting half the enemy camp aflame. Seconds later, dozens of spirit orbs sailed overhead, bursting apart as they struck the ground and shocking anyone within with a five-foot radius. They had a limited area of damage but were effective even so.

My war band plowed through the fiery tent city, continuing to launch magical attacks. I glanced back once and saw Wolfric riding with his arms spread wide, outward-facing palms pouring elemental fire in twin continuous streams. I couldn't do that from the vanguard, so I focused on keeping our path clear of fire. When they reached the center of the encampment, however, the Finns split up and charged off in all directions.

Up ahead, water arced upward, high over the burning tents, grossly defying gravity to splash down and extinguish the flames.

Elemental water.

I urged my horse in that direction, hoping to capture the druid before anyone killed her. The air was thick with bursts of steam and billowing black smoke, and in my haste I lost track of the other members of my pentacle. Reining Steel around blazing tents and flinching at blinding flashes of spirit magic, I drew my sword and slew any Republic forces that got in my way. Fire darts distracted them and fireballs destroyed their weapons, allowing me to cut them down with the grey blade.

As my horse made a tight turn around the central tent, I came across Martin's pentacle. He was keeping the Republic soldiers away with periodic shockwaves while Chester took out any who came too close with his shotgun. Galen and Alexandros lent them all protection with their water and air shields. I couldn't figure out what Phelan was doing until he spun up a small whirlwind. A tornado could not survive in freezing temperatures, yet somehow he was doing it.

"More heat!" he yelled.

Poppy peppered the tiny whirlwind with elemental fire, and the flames spread rapidly through it. Galen swept his arm toward it, and a nearby mass of roiling steam turned the whirlwind into a landspout. Phelan spread his arms wide, and the landspout grew in height and breadth until it was a full-blown tornado. Poppy directed a stream of fire into it, and they scrambled up on their horses. Together with the rest of the pentacle, they rode pell-mell to escape the fiery coils of their destructive creation.

Trailing sparks and thick black smoke, the fire twister carved a path of devastation at least a hundred feet wide, plowing straight through the center of the camp. It tore tents, cots, blankets, and tables off the ground. Burning debris flew in all directions, bombarding the entire area with blackened wood and charred fabric. What had started out as a confusing turmoil turned into chaotic and mindless carnage. The tents and poles were transformed into luminescent beacons of light that shimmered in the intense heat. Streams of molten iron and steel twisted and coiled like living vines. The Republic forces were immolated as the cleansing flames consumed everything in sight. It was a nightmare straight out of Conall's story about Ragnarok, a hellish and terrifying world of flame. Waves of heat washed over me, caressing my skin like the hands of a lover, and slowly, inexorably, it drew me in.

Steel reared, whinnying loudly when the ammo dump at the southern edge of the camp detonated, bringing me out of the deadly reverie. Phelan's flaming cyclone sent barrels of gunpowder shooting up into the air. They exploded in a series of thunderous booms, raining flaming splinters and jagged shrapnel down on terrified people fruitlessly seeking shelter.

I spurred my horse in the direction of the explosions, settling the earth and extinguishing the fire ahead. The lethal child that had been born of Phelan and Poppy's combined elements was out of control. It was up to me to make sure none of the Finns were harmed by it. Reaching out with my hand, I stripped the fire twister of its lustrous light and beauty, depriving it of life and leaving it to spin itself into tatters.

A screaming girl crossed my path, flames streaming behind her like an extension of her golden hair as she fled. Recognizing her druid-style clothing, I snatched the flames away, but still she ran, stumbling and falling with each temblor that rolled the earth under her feet, never ceasing her frantic search for escape. She'd be gunned down, burnt up, or smothered if I didn't do something, and I couldn't allow that to happen. Even if we didn't mean to kill her, we'd still take the blame.

I ran her down with my horse, then dismounted to capture her, commanding the earth to bring her back. A great wave of dirt rose up under her feet, arcing up over her. She wailed in despair as it sent her tumbling back toward the inferno, but as soon as she laid eyes on me, she jumped to her feet ready to fight. Her hands clutched at the air, fingers curved like claws, and a spirit orb grew between them. Two words from Kam Stone's prophecy popped into my mind – *Zeus' hand!* – had me dodging to avoid her hasty throw. Her shriek of rage was cut off by the ocean of dirt crashing down over her. I rolled it into a hollow dirt ball ten feet in diameter, then brought the thousands of tiny rocks within it to the surface. Laying my hand against it, I melted them all, covering the dirt in a crust of stone through which she would not easily break. I sent it rolling in the direction of Lone Oak, and then slapped Steel's rump to send him that way, too. It had become entirely too dangerous a place for anyone but a fire druid.

I dropped to one knee, *seeking* for any others and finding another female druid, motionless on the other side of the enemy camp. She had to be alive still, or the earth would not have registered her presence. Running back into the red hot, dazzling chaos, I fought to stay in control of my element. Focusing on the Earth mother, I sought a deeper connection with her to keep me grounded.

When I found the other young woman, she was standing under an air shield with two black-clad warriors from the grove. Spying what had once been a pile of cannonballs, I summoned the thick, black liquid. As the molten iron coated the outside of her air shield, the druid pressed one hand against it, mouth open in a silent scream of terror. I pushed it ahead of me using a series of small, rolling temblors to bring it to Lone Oak. Rolling it would have badly injured the three inside, and this I avoided, more or less. I hoped they all had enough air to breathe because I had no intention of risking my life further.

Back at the front gates of Lone Oak, I found a few of the Finns arrayed in a protective line. The rest were fighting at the edges of the seething camp, taking out the last of the Republic forces. Halldor's pentacle was standing where the first ball of soil and rock had come to rest.

"What's with the giant balls?" asked Skylar, eyeing the large orbs covered in iron and stone.

"I caught two of Dianthe's druids. One of them is in the rock ball. The other girl is in the iron ball with two warriors."

Ciaran whistled. "What are we going to do with them?"

"Nothing, until the fight is over." I paused for a moment to catch my breath. "I'm pretty sure they're both triple threats, so I want you and Skylar to put air bubbles around them. If either of the men gets loose, Barak, you shock the shit out of them, but don't kill them."

"What if the girls get loose?" Uri asked.

I hesitated. No matter how itchy his trigger finger was, he'd still be slower than living electricity. I couldn't ask any of the Finns to take a risk like that, especially one without magic. As the only person who could keep the spheres intact and secure, I was needed more here than on the battlefield.

"Never mind," I said. "We'll just wait until the fighting is over."

"The hostilities have mostly ceased," I heard Seth say. The air druid approached with long strides, Iriana keeping pace beside him with quick, light steps. The rest of my pentacle trailed after them, with Dermot and Ariadne bringing up the rear.

"Well, Davis," said Conall, "That was some explosion. I think you may have outdone yourself."

"Don't look at me," I said. "That was Phelan's doing."

"Phelan doesn't have fire magic," Dermot said, looking confused.

"No, but Poppy does, and they cooked up that fiery whirlwind all on their own with no help from me."

"Are you certain?" Seth asked. "Phelan and Poppy?"

"I watched them do it. Ask Martin if you don't believe me." I paused. "I'm guessing it was Poppy's idea."

"We should probably do something about that fire before it gets much more out of control," the air druid said.

"I'll take care of it," I said. "Keep an eye on those balls for me."

Seth raised an eyebrow.

Dermot laughed. "Ha-ha! He wants you to look at his balls!"

"You're so stupid," Ariadne said, rolling her eyes.

Chapter 31 – Lone Oak

*I know of no higher fortitude than stubborness
in the face of overwhelming odds.*
~ *Louis Nizer* ~

I put the fires out in short order and returned to deal with the imprisoned druids. Seth had begun to address the matter of Sebrina's acolytes, and I got the impression that he wished I'd stayed away longer – not because he was grandstanding, but because he was genuinely concerned about Kam Stone's prophecy.

"Time to crack the eggs," I said. The rocky coating sloughed off the sphere containing the blonde druid. If she had suffered injury or severe burns, I wanted her out alone so one of the earth druids could heal her without having to worry about lightning strikes from the other girl.

"This one got burned in the fight," I said. "She'll need healing."

"I'll do it," said Warwick. The pale grey shrike hopped about on his shoulder, flapping its black-edged wings and peeping nervously.

"We'll cover you," Narinder said, drawing his sword. Elemental spirit sizzled down the length of his blade. Ishkur followed suit with his own longsword, while Ridley uncorked the water bags strapped to his thighs, ready to imprison her with water if she should attack. Either of the girls would expect an air shield, but a shield of hardened elemental water would catch them by surprise. Since Ridley was a water/spirit dualist, there was little

538

chance she could hurt him with magic.

"Rob, I'm not sure that's a good idea," I said as he drew his shotgun and moved to stand by his pentacle.

"*She* doesn't know I've been altered," he said.

"Still—"

"I'm staying."

I raised my hands in surrender and backed away to stand beside Seth and Iriana. Staying behind a shield was a good idea that I had no argument against, so I had Dermot, Conall, and Duncan stand with us.

"Why the bubble?" Dermot asked.

"Just in case either of the young ladies emerges throwing spirit bolts," the air druid replied. "None of you has a defense against it."

"The best defense is a good offense," said Conall, patting the stock of his shotgun.

"Only if your reflexes are faster than lightning," Iriana said.

"I think maybe he could use a little lightning," Dermot said.

Conall chuckled. "And here I thought we were friends."

"We are," Dermot said. "I was just thinking that what worked for Davis might work for you."

"I'd rather not find out that way," said Conall, "but I appreciate the sentiment."

"Davis was blocked, not altered," said Seth. "In fact, I'm not even sure the block was still in place when he fell in the volcano."

"He really fell in a volcano?" Iriana asked.

"Yeah, didn't you listen to my story?" said Dermot.

"I thought you just made that up."

"There's no need for embellishment with Davis around," said Conall.

"Hold up," I said. "Warwick's cracking the sphere."

It was less cracking or breaking and more along the lines of sifting or sweeping the dirt away. It was to keep from smothering the girl, I assumed. Once her head became visible, the rest of the orb slumped to an unformed mass around her feet.

"Oooh, she's gonna be pissed when she sees her face," Dermot said.

"The burn isn't that bad," Conall said. "It's mostly her right ear and neck."

"You wouldn't be so nonchalant if it was your face," Iriana

said.

"Aaand… She's out!" Dermot announced.

The blonde woman staggered to her feet, fists balled up and ready to fight. She must have been itching to throw a bunch of spirit magic around but wasn't crazy or suicidal enough to risk being killed by one of the somber young men surrounding her.

"That's Shonda Cotton," said Iriana. "She's a triple threat."

Shonda Cotton's lips moved rapidly, face twisted in a snarl. I couldn't hear anything, but she appeared to be listening when Warwick began to speak. When he held out his hand, however, she slapped it away. The earth druid shook his hand as though he'd been burned – or shocked.

"Drop the shield," I said.

"I really don't think—" Seth began.

"*Now.*"

Seth let out an irritated huff and did as I asked. I rarely used that tone with a member of my own pentacle, but it was more important to make sure Warwick walked away from this alive.

"Let me heal you." The earth druid gestured to her burns.

"Don't touch me with your filthy magic!"

"Well, it is *earth* magic," quipped Dermot. Conall thumped him on the shoulder to shut him up.

"It's a bad burn," Warwick said. "At best it will leave a terrible scar." His expression was earnest; he was concerned about her and showed complete disregard to the danger she presented. Duncan and I approached to back him up.

"Then I'll have something to remember you by when you're dead," Shonda snarled. "When you're *all* dead!"

"No one else is dying here today," I said. "Except maybe you, and that's only if you do something stupid."

"Do I look like a fool? I know you won't let me go!"

"If I wanted you dead, I'd have left you to smother inside that dirt ball," I said. "As it stands, I'm willing to send the lot of you back to the grove."

"Tell that to Dianthe," she shot back.

"Dianthe Aspen got what she deserved," Duncan said.

"*Abomination,*" she hissed. "Do not speak to me!"

The earth druid was shocked into silence. From his expression, I could tell he was seriously evaluating her accusation.

Seth raised his eyebrows. "You think he's been augmented?"

"How else would a *boy* possess the unlimited power of a druid?" she said.

"Because the Earth Mother favors him," said Warwick, frowning.

"Idiot. Padraig Everlight made up that story to protect him," she spat. "He has always been Shitozaki's tool!"

As Liam Everlight had been Sebrina's tool. No wonder Angie had been so desperate to break free of those crushing entanglements.

"How do you figure?" I asked, puzzled by her farfetched accusations.

"First Shitozaki got him to create that abomination, and now he's split the grove!"

"As I possess only a single element, your accusations are absurd," Duncan said. "Padraig is not my natural father, and even if he was, only the woman who bore me could have augmented my magical ability."

"You can't blame ArchDruid Shitozaki for that when he wasn't even there!" Iriana protested.

"He is *not* the ArchDruid!" Shonda screamed. Iriana ducked behind Seth.

"He is now," Seth replied, crossing his arms. "Return to Sebrina now, or stay and be destroyed. The choice is yours."

"You are the ones who will be destroyed! We'll not go back until we finish the task ArchDruid Sebrina gave us!" Shonda said.

"You will leave," the air druid said, "or you will die."

My second was done messing around. Connor Shitozaki's blood was proving true, and the rest of the Finns responded to it. Any protest or retort she might have made was drowned out by the metallic hiss of swords sliding free from scabbards and the clicks and clacks of rifles, shotguns, and pistols. I didn't want to kill any of Sebrina's minions, but I backed him up just like everyone else.

"You heard the man," I said. "Surrender and return to White Oak Grove immediately, or forfeit your life. Your choice."

A flicker of uncertainty appeared in Shonda Cotton's eyes, but it was overcome by arrogance and hatred. I drew the grey blade, its crimson etching bright in the late morning sun, and laid it on the blistered flesh of her neck. She clenched her teeth in defiance, but within seconds the killing frost had tears streaming down her face and whimpers escaping her lips.

"Will you leave peacefully?" I asked.

"Not without Laiken and the others," she managed to say, her voice quavering.

"They will be given the same choice as you," I said. "After you've made yours."

"I won't leave without them!"

"By the gods, I swear I will take your head as a trophy for the Morrigan."

I had no idea what gods Shonda honored, but clearly they weren't Celtic, for she looked horrified at the notion. The Phantom Queen certainly knew how to strike terror and dread into the hearts of her enemies.

Dermot grinned and said, "Look at the bright side. You won't have to pay the ferryman."

"I'll not abandon them!" she hissed. Her continued defiance in the face of death made me wonder if she was brave or insane.

Seth held up a hand. "It is a fair request," he said. "We'll let them out."

"Don't move," I warned her. "I might slip."

As I focused my attention on the spherical prison holding the other triple threat and the two warriors, the iron turned cherry red, then brightened to orange and melted away. Unwilling to waste more time, I cracked the hardened dirt in half. The men spilled out onto the ground with the young woman on top of them. She was knocked aside as both men came up ready to fight. She cried out in pain and curled into a fetal position on the ground, cradling her left arm to her chest with her eyes squeezed shut.

"That's Laiken Birch," Iriana announced. "She is also a triple threat."

I barely paid attention to the second druid, for the two warriors trapped with her were none other than Kurt Young and Stephen Brisbane. The last time I'd seen them together was after I'd been made the gunnery master. I had returned to my old barracks in the Warriors' Third to retrieve my belongings so I could take them to the new home that Padraig and Duncan had built for Angie and me. They had blocked the door and Kurt had made lewd and inappropriate remarks about her. My threat to inform Master Brion

– and the Ithaca 37 on my back – had made them back down without a fight.

The last time I'd encountered Stephen was during the Yule longsword competition. He had deliberately thrown the match (as had several others), allowing me to advance in the competition to the point where I would face first Orion Aspen, and then Darryn Darkmane. A chill raced down my spine, and I reminded myself that they both were dead.

"Remember that you want them alive," Duncan murmured.

"Right."

Warwick dropped to one knee before Laiken. "Here, let me see your arm," he said.

"It *hurts*!" she wailed, flinching from him.

"I know it does," he said. "I broke my leg a couple of weeks ago." He ran gentle fingers over her forearm. "Does that feel a little better?"

Finally, she opened her eyes. With an expression of pained confusion, she asked, "Why are you helping me?"

"I'm an earth druid," he said, giving her a gentle, boyish smile. "It's what I do." Again he held out his hand. "May I?"

Wincing and with obvious reluctance, Laiken allowed him to take her broken arm.

"I'll try to make this as painless as possible," he said. "Don't look at your arm. Look at the pretty bird."

The little grey shrike clutching the collar of his coat fluttered its wings and peeped as if trying to attract attention to itself, and Laiken's gritted teeth and furrowed brow transformed into slack-jawed, wide-eyed shock. Her eyes darted from the shrike to Warwick's face and back again. Pressing the splayed fingers of her good hand across her chest as though she couldn't quite catch her breath, Laiken seemed not to feel any pain at all as he reduced the fracture and set the splintered bones back into place.

Oh, surely not, I thought, feeling my heart sink. Praying to the gods that the grey shrike wasn't her fetch, I risked a quick look at Seth. He somehow managed to appear stoic and mortified at the same time, clearly having had come to the same conclusion.

Ridley and Rob shifted position slightly, while Narinder and Ciaran exchanged an uneasy glance. Warwick was truly a healer at heart, graced with kindness and generosity that few could match.

He didn't deserve to be saddled with one of Sebrina's hateful pupils as his chosen. I'd rather have him hate me forever for killing her now than watch him suffer a lifetime with someone who thought him inferior and unworthy of his druidic birthright.

"There, all better now," said Warwick, still unaware of the situation at hand. If ever there was a time that ignorance was bliss, this was it. Met with her stricken expression, his warm smile faded.

"Does it still hurt?"

"No," she whispered.

"Then what's wrong?" he asked, then shook his head. "Wait, never mind, stupid question. We're at war."

"No," she whispered again. "The fetch."

"Oh, right." He touched a finger to his shoulder, and the shrike hopped onto it. "Pretty, isn't she?"

Laiken nodded, blinking rapidly as though fighting tears.

"It's all right. We won't harm you," Warwick said. "You can go home."

"No!" she cried, lunging at him.

Several things happened at once: Narinder and Ridley raised their longswords to strike, Ciaran threw a water stream that tightened about her neck like a lasso, and Rob pressed the muzzle of his shotgun to her temple.

"Let him go!" the gunman growled.

"No, wait!" I yelled. They'd been so busy moving in for the kill that they hadn't noticed the tiny raptor vanish in a burst of white and silver sparkles.

"Back off," I said. "Now."

Entangled in the girl's arms, Warwick gave me an incredulous look, one that clearly said: *Help*?

"She's not hurting you," I said, completely unsympathetic.

Warwick and his pentacle looked at me like I'd lost my mind. Which I probably had. Conall hooked his thumbs together and flapped his fingers like bird wings, then pointed at Laiken.

"Maybe you should hug her back," Dermot said with a grin.

WHAT? Warwick mouthed, looking horrified to the point of near-comedy.

"Hug her back!" Iriana hissed. "She's your *chosen*!"

"Is she?" he said, putting tentative arms around her. "Are you?"

"You had my spirit animal," Laiken replied, her voice tremulous, still holding onto him as if for dear life. "Do you hate me?"

Putting his hands on her shoulders, he pushed her back to look at her face. "Of course not," he said. "We've only just met. How could I hate you?"

"We did just attack a town and try to kill you," she said weakly.

"Oh, well," Warwick said. He rose and helped her to her feet. "That was before you saw I had your fetch. No worries."

"WHAT?" Shonda shrieked, completely wrecking the magic of the moment. "You sent a *fetch*? You know how the ArchDruid feels about that! What in the nine hells were you *thinking*?"

"I didn't realize the kind of bargain Sebrina had struck!" Laiken cried. "The Republic soldiers have enslaved hundreds of people and slaughtered countless others... I can't be a part of that! Not anymore!"

"They're just a bunch of nulls!" Shonda snapped "What do you care?"

"They're still *people*!"

"Why didn't you leave sooner?" Warwick asked.

"I couldn't go back to the grove, and I was too scared to be out there on my own because I knew what the Republic soldiers would do to me. So I sent the fetch and prayed my ancestors would show me a way out." She smiled through her tears. "And it found *you*."

Shonda would have lunged at her if not for the grey blade at her throat. She settled for a verbal assault instead.

"You stupid, *spineless* bitch!" she screamed. "You *traitor*!"

Laiken cringed. Warwick, gentle earth druid and kind-hearted healer, moved to place himself between the two triple threats. It was the bravest and most foolish thing I'd ever seen anyone do.

"That's enough," I said, jerking my head toward the gate. "You're leaving now."

"So are you," Seth said to Kurt and Stephen. "Move."

"At least give us horses!" Shonda demanded after we herded them toward the road. "The grove is leagues from here!"

"Why don't you head over to the 'Ville and ask your friends for some?" Dermot suggested helpfully.

"I wouldn't stay too long if you do," Conall added. "We're

headed there next, and by the time we're finished there won't be much left."

"You've sentenced us to die of the cold," she said, shaking with fury.

"Lightning starts forest fires all the time," said the ever-logical Seth. "You'll manage."

"I swear by my ancestors, I *will* kill you!"

"Not today," I said with a smirk.

"One day, Outsider," she swore. "One day."

"I am no outsider," I said, flicking my sword to the side as flames raced down its icy length. "Haven't you figured that out yet?"

She bared her teeth at me one last time, let out a wordless scream of rage, and stalked away from the gate. Glaring daggers at us, Kurt and Stephen followed behind. I noted with grim satisfaction that they headed south and back to the grove, instead of west and to the 'Ville.

"You're just going to let them go?" said Wolfric. Lin was with him.

"I'm going to look for Angie," I said, turning around and starting for the downed front gates of Lone Oak. "You can follow them and make sure they don't double back, if you want."

"I *do* want," said Wolfric.

"Me, too," Lin said. As they mounted their horses, Siorus and Madoc ran to see what they were about, collected the rest of their pentacle, and rode out after our defeated enemies.

"I hope Wolfric doesn't decide to kill 'em," said Conall.

I felt reasonably sure he wouldn't; it was dishonorable to kill someone in cold blood. I wasn't wasting another moment worrying about Sebrina's emissaries. I'd spent enough time and energy on them and the Republic forces both. Getting to Angie was my priority now. Seth insisted that I allow him to shield in case the townsfolk of Lone Oak decided to shoot first and ask questions later. I agreed, but only because Duncan, Conall, and Dermot were tagging along and I didn't want to waste time arguing. We proceeded to the ruined pile of timbers that had once been a daunting obstacle.

There was a rifle shot and a PING as it bounced off the air shield. Two more shots rang out, pinging against the shield before they ricocheted away, and then the shooting stopped.

Projecting his voice with elemental air, Seth boomed, "You don't have to be afraid of us. We are not with the druids who have attacked you. We're here to help."

"Son, we ain't lasted this long by bein' stupid," a woman called back. "We ain't fallin' for that ruse." Her familiar, gravelly voice was music to my ears.

Seth frowned in consternation. "It is no ruse. We have spent the last two months assisting others in their fight against the bandits. If you allow it, we can help secure your town and rebuild your fortifications."

A nut-brown, weatherbeaten woman with frizzy grey hair poked her head up over the blackened timbers, rifle held at the ready.

"A year ago, that would have been just the thing to make us give you fellers a warm welcome," Chasity said. "Problem is, you just can't trust anybody these days. You're on your own, son, and so are we."

As they talked, I dropped to one knee and performed a *seeking*, looking for Angie as far as my earth magic could reach. I looked at Duncan, doing the same; he shook his head.

Quakes. My stomach started to churn. I tried to make myself relax, closed my eyes and tried to feel Angie through the bond. It was faint, but it was enough for me to know she was in trouble.

"Stay here," I said, skirted the edge of the air shield, and tossed back my hood. "Ms. Chasity?"

She squinted. "You seem to know me, but I don't think I know you."

"My name's Davis," I said. "I came here with a druid girl a couple of summers ago. She called up a thunderstorm to fill your wells, and you gave us shelter for a few days."

"The young Traveler!" she said. "Well, I'll be!"

"It's good to see you, ma'am, and I wouldn't mind to renew our acquaintanceship, but if you're not comfortable with that, I understand. I know this is a town full of capable folk and you'll do all right like you always have." I paused a moment. "Even if we can't help you, I'm hoping you can help me. Angie and me got separated, and I've been looking for her for a powerful long time."

"Hold on, son." Chasity disappeared and the longest, most

excruciating minute of my life passed before she pushed through the damaged front gates and came to stand before me with a grim expression.

"I'm sorry, Davis, but your girl's gone," she said. "Those other two druid gals took her and the young man with her."

"What happened?"

"They had us under siege, and we were doing all right until them gals with earth and fire showed up and tunneled under the wall. Angie was going to fight, but I figured they might be after her and made her go hide in the house," Chasity continued. "They started killing people with fire. Roasted them on the spot and watched them die screaming. Said they were going to kill everybody in Lone Oak one person at a time until she came out of hiding."

"And she gave herself up," I said, hanging my head in frustration. Of course she would. I would have chosen an action like flanking my enemies while they were busy torturing people, but I was neither present during the event nor vulnerable to another druid's elemental fire, so there was really no sense in second-guessing her decision.

"She knew you were coming for her, though, because she left something for ya," Chasity continued. "She asked me to make sure you got it."

Before I could ask, the grizzled woman turned toward the village gates and let out a piercing whistle. A young man ran out with an oilcloth-wrapped bundle. I thanked him, taking the heavy bundle. He bobbed his head in acknowledgment and ran back inside. Holding my breath, I unwrapped it with eager fingers, certain of what I'd find inside.

I was not wrong.

The oilcloth fell to the ground unnoticed, revealing the sleek black metal of my Ithaca 37, complete with its back holster and the bandolier Sinclair had given me, loaded with shells.

"*Volcanic*," I breathed. "Oh, Angie... You are amazing."

After adjusting the straps to fit over my coat, I shrugged on the holster and buckled it across my chest, and then slipped the bandolier over my head. "By the gods, I have missed this!"

Seth gave me a puzzled look. "It's just a shotgun."

"This is not just any shotgun," I said. "This is *my* shotgun."

Grabbing the pistol grip, I whipped out the Ithaca 37 with the fast draw that had beaten more than a few gunslingers. Nodding to myself in satisfaction, I holstered it, relishing the feel of its familiar weight on my back.

"How long ago did they take her?" I asked.

"Half an hour, maybe?" Chasity shook her head. "They ran as soon you boys showed up. I'm not sure, what with the battle and all. It could have been an hour."

"Thank you, Miss Chasity." I gave her a quick kiss on the cheek and headed for the road.

"I regret that we did not arrive sooner," said Seth, following me. "We could have stopped them."

"That's my fault," I said. "I thought we'd be here before they were."

"Dianthe deceived us," he said. "She told us they were coming for us when their target must have been Lone Oak all along."

"It's water under the bridge now," I said and whistled for Steel.

"What are you doing?" asked Seth.

"I'm going after her."

"Alone?" he asked.

The grulla stallion trotted up, followed by Duncan's chestnut mare with the spotted rump.

"Apparently not," I said.

"She *is* my cousin," he said, mounting his horse. I couldn't argue with that and swung into the saddle. "She may also be injured," he added.

"She'd better not be," I growled, reining Steel about to point his nose in the direction of the 'Ville. If she was hurt, I was going to burn the entire city to the ground, walls and all.

"Hey, wait up!"

We turned to see Dermot riding up on Kelpie and leading Twister. Iriana followed close behind with her chestnut and Bucephalus. Both Conall and Seth took their horses' reins and mounted without waiting for my approval.

"I should not ask this of you," said Seth to Iriana. "But I would like you to stay behind."

She hesitated, then nodded. "I'll stay this time," she said. "But after I master earthmoving, don't bother asking."

He smiled. "I wouldn't dream of it."

"Hey, keep Ariadne out of trouble for me!" Dermot said.

Iriana put her hands on her hips. "That's about as likely as keeping *you* out of trouble, but I'll try."

The water elementalist merely grinned at her.

"Warwick!" I yelled. The earth druid came running over, his new chosen close behind. "You're in charge until Siorus gets back."

"What's going on?"

"The bandits took Angie. We're going to get her back."

Warwick's eyes grew huge, while Laiken looked concerned.

"Just the five of you?" he asked. "And on tired horses?"

Ignoring the question, I said, "The rest of the Finns are to stay here and repair Lone Oak's defenses. The veil of death comes down tonight, so when Siorus gets back, tell him I said to make for Ward."

"I'll tell them," he said. "Be careful."

We reined the horses around to face the road again.

"Wait!" Laiken called. "I can help!"

Conall spurred his dapple grey forward, bumping Steel out of the way to get between her and me. The two stallions laid back their ears and bared their teeth at one another.

"Hey, watch it!" Warwick said. "You could have hurt her!"

"Yes, and she could have killed Davis."

The earth druid shifted uncomfortably, as if only just realizing that not everyone was going to accept his chosen as readily as he had. Laiken stared up at the Norseman with big dark eyes.

"You can try that out on me first," Conall said, looking down at her.

"I'm not going to hurt anyone!" she protested.

"See that you don't," the Norseman said.

Warwick glared at Conall. Meekly, Laiken nodded and took his proffered hand. Conall stiffened in his saddle and gasped for air before relaxing again. He smirked at her.

"That'll do nicely," he said, reining a dancing Twister away.

"Sorry about that," I murmured to Laiken when she approached me.

"He's right to be suspicious," she said, laying a hand on Steel's shoulder. A ripple of invisible spirit magic ran through his body and into mine, invigorating us both. The fatigue of hard riding and fighting faded to nothing, replaced by a burst of energy. The little stallion shivered and then shook his head, prancing and pulling at the bit. I knew how he felt – her magic had left me feeling as though I could take on every soldier in the 'Ville by myself. Moving through the group, she laid hands on each of our horses, finishing with Kelpie. The blue roan shook all over, nearly dislodging Dermot from his saddle, and reared, whinnying loudly. The water elementalist let out a loud *WHOOP!* and took off at a gallop. Twister and Conall were next, and the rest of us moved out in a bunch.

Overfull of energy, Steel's hand gallop became an all-out run as he lengthened his stride. I loosened the reins, and he stretched out his neck, catching up with the long-legged Kelpie and Twister in a couple dozen strides before passing them with ridiculous ease. He kept his lead for about half a mile before the bigger horses caught up.

The snow that had begun to fall again when we'd arrived at Lone Oak grew thick in the air, reducing visibility to a hundred feet ahead at most. The race became even more hazardous, for shod hooves tended to slip easily on slush and ice. The horses were so tightly bunched that if one stumbled or fell it was likely to bring down the rest, but they were so full of elemental spirit that there was no holding them back. The best any of us could do was sit tight in the saddle and guide their headlong rush down the road.

I didn't care about the risk; the sooner we reached Angie, the better. If she'd been taken half an hour ago, we had a chance of catching them before they were back inside the protective walls surrounding the 'Ville. If it had been an hour, we'd be too late. The bandit city was only four or five miles from Lone Oak. Even at a walk, our quarry would arrive long before we did, and I doubted they were walking.

If they took Angie behind the walls, I would tear down every single barricade, destroy each rampart, and demolish any building that lay between us. I would unleash so much destruction with fire, earth, steel, and gunpowder that not one citizen of the Republic of Jackson would have time to even think about laying a hand on her.

Laiken's phenomenal boost of spirit had so energized the horses that they never tired or broke stride for an incredible five miles. Their breakneck pace brought the southeastern wall of the 'Ville into view in less than a quarter of an hour. Just ahead, a small group of riders was coming to a stop in the shadow of the massive gates. The inner doors of the gate swung open, and the portcullis began to rise.

Three cloaked women stood amidst a small group of Republic soldiers. The entire party, whether wearing cloaks or coats, had their hoods up and it was quite impossible to solidly identify Angie, but I guessed she was the one in the middle. As they became aware of our approach, the soldiers hurried to get through the gates while two of the women gestured dramatically. I kept my eye on the only motionless person of the group. When she turned to look over her shoulder, the wind blew her hood back, rewarding me with a view of her face.

It was Angie.

Her worry transmitted clearly through the bond. I sensed it with the same clarity as when she'd been kidnapped from the caravan by bandits. Thankfully, it lacked the intensity of when she'd nearly been burned at the stake in Searcy. She knew she was in trouble, but that danger of death or physical harm wasn't imminent.

The portcullis was only halfway up, but the druids who had kidnapped her wasted no time dragging her off her horse and toward the gate. In her struggles against Sebrina's adherents, she stumbled and nearly fell. Spirit magic flashed, shocking the other druids and sending them to their knees. Niall lashed out with his fists, knocking two of the Republic soldiers to the ground. He and Angie tried to run but only managed a few steps before sinking to their knees in the ground, trapped by the earth-fire druid. One of the grove druids grabbed Angie by the hair and yanked her head back, so she was certain to see the shotgun muzzle rammed up under Niall's chin. She capitulated and they shoved her back toward the gate after Niall, who they herded with the muzzle of a shotgun placed squarely between his shoulderblades. They were inside and through in moments, taking Angie beyond my reach. The portcullis dropped and the doors slammed shut just as we slid to a halt in the deep snow. The horses snorted, their hot breath smoking in the frigid air.

"Shit," Conall said.

That about summed it up for me, too. Resolute, I dismounted and started toward the forbidding southeastern gate of the bandit city. Beyond the portcullis, the heavy wooden door was reinforced with thick iron spikes that had been driven into the planks in a diamond pattern. Instead of rounded or flat, the heads of these nails were pointed. It might deter an attack by axe or natural fire, but neither fortification would be the least bit effective in stopping me.

"What are you going to do?" asked Seth.

"I'm going in. Alone."

With no time to waste, I grasped the latticed grill of the portcullis and funneled a burst of heat through it. It was glowing hot in moments, and snowflakes hissed when they struck the burning metal. The horizontal bars began to sag, while the vertical bars melted and ran like candle wax. The entire portcullis melted into a puddle of iron within a couple of minutes. The walls enclosing the space between portcullis and wooden doors were dotted with murder holes, so I coated the inside of the gate with a layer of metal and cooled it, covering them up.

"We're not going to go through this again, are we?" Conall said. "Because you know Duncan would follow you even if both his legs had been lopped off at the knees and he had to crawl."

The earth druid snorted. "I am indeed unwilling to allow Davis to face such a danger alone or abandon my cousin to the enemy, Conall, but I assure you I am not so great a fool as that."

"Maybe you aren't, but I am," Dermot said with a grin. "I'm coming, too."

"As am I," Conall said. "Coming, that is. Not the fool part."

Seth gave me a reproving look. "Did you really think we would ride all the way out here and then leave you to fight this battle on your own?"

I looked back at them sitting confidently astride their horses without a hint of fear on their faces. It made me grateful for their company, their courage, and their skill in battle, for there was no one I trusted more. But I was also afraid for them. I was responsible for them, but more than that, I loved each of them like brothers.

I sighed. "No, but you should." At least I could tell Shitozaki that I'd tried – *if* we made it out of this alive. The rough wood beneath my fingertips burst into flame, dropping its protective iron spikes impotently to the ground as it turned to ash. Seth blew the thick, greasy smoke away with a steady stream of air.

When the smoke dissipated, I examined the huge walls of concrete and stone stretching far on either side of the gate; Duncan made a visual inspection of his own before nodding in agreement. Better to take it down now and give ourselves a wider area through which to escape once we rescued Angie. We knelt on opposite sides of the gate and pressed our palms to the ground, joining our earth magics to make them exponentially stronger. The entirety of the earth beneath the southeast-facing wall was ours, ready and eager to accede to our wishes. It trembled at first, like a prisoner afraid to believe freedom is near, and then roared to life with a vengeance, as if awakened to anger after decades of oppression.

One with the earth's energy, Duncan and I rode out the jarring waves. The huge bastion of metal, stone, and concrete shuddered and groaned with the effort of trying to hold itself together, but the surface of the wall shattered with a series of loud cracks. Chunks of concrete sloughed off and crashed to the ground. Screeching filled the air as metal was ripped from the body of the bulwark, warping into twisted shapes. Like a massive dying animal, the entire expanse gradually collapsed inward, one long segment after another. Dust rose into the greying sky as the deafening sound of a thousand thunderstorms rolled across the land.

I turned around to see Seth with his arms in the air, supporting an air shield against the falling pieces of debris. Duncan slowly rose to his feet and backed away as the rest of the gate came crashing down.

"Was it necessary to destroy the *entire* wall?" Seth said, giving us a reproachful look.

Duncan returned his gaze with aplomb. "Aye. It was."

Incredibly, when the dust settled, a man was standing amidst the ruins of the gate. Shoulders hunched and arms covering his head, he was perched on a pile of rubble just inches above pooling molten iron. As the earth stilled and the rumbling ceased, he slowly raised his head and looked around. Upon seeing the five of us standing before him, he bolted. Scrambling over broken and jagged rocks, he didn't get far.

I was remounting my horse when a snowball zipped by and struck the gatekeeper in the back of the head, knocking him off his feet. He tumbled down the pile of debris and did not get up. Riding past, I looked down at the gatekeeper's inert body, blood and brains splattered all over the pristine carpet of snow.

"Didn't your mom ever tell you not to put rocks in your snowballs?" Conall said.

"Yeah, but she never said anything about ice," Dermot replied.

Chapter 32 – Into the 'Ville

Courage is poorly housed that dwells in numbers;
the lion never counts the herd that are about him,
nor weighs how many flocks he has to scatter.
~ Aaron Hill ~

"If they didn't know we were here before, they certainly do now," Seth said.

"Even if you know death is coming, that doesn't mean you can outrun it," Conall said, cocking his Benelli.

"Let's move," I said, urging Steel into a canter. We had to find Angie fast. The heavy snowfall was rapidly filling the enemy horses' hoofprints, and the temperature was dropping along with the sun. If we stayed out in the wind and heavily falling snow, we'd be in danger of frostbite, not to mention freezing to death.

Angie might be a triple threat with full druid magic at her disposal, but it was damned hard to defend with air and attack with spirit at the same time – even without trying to protect someone else. That was why Phelan and the dual wielders had learned to switch between their elements with alacrity. An air shield could be felt but not seen, leaving an enemy unaware of its absence until a spirit bolt came streaking toward him. I had no idea if my grove-trained chosen was experienced in switching rapidly from element to element like the Finns were.

We were going to need every bit of help we could get, so I called my fetch. Within minutes, the dragon streaked over our heads, so close that the heat of its passing brushed us with a warm

556

breeze. Its black head, ashen scales, and wings the sullen red of banked coals stood out starkly against the white and grey backdrop of the wintry world.

Find Angie, I willed the dragon. *Lead me to her.*

The great beast, now as much metal and mineral as fire, rose higher into the air. It made a slow, searching circle before leveling out and shooting through the air like an arrow toward the northwest. The bond pulled me in the same direction, toward what I feared was the center of the bandit city. Our raid to get the witchlings back had been challenging enough, and it had been on the outskirts. Rescuing Angie would be more difficult by several magnitudes. Going deep into the heart of the 'Ville with a single pentacle might be a suicide mission, but I could not ignore the bond pulling me toward my chosen.

The earth mother told me that there was a wide expanse of open ground with no manmade structures and few people for a half-mile ahead of us. Still full of spirit-fueled vigor, the horses were more than eager to run again. Plowing through the snow that muffled their hoofbeats, they brought us swiftly across the distance to a collection of small outbuildings. I squinted through the snowfall, barely able to make out larger structures in the distance.

A small group of Republic soldiers tried to ambush us as we were passing the small structures. The druids holding Angie must have alerted them to our pursuit, but there were only a dozen of them so they didn't slow us down much. I drew the Ithaca 37 and began slam-firing right into the middle of the insignificant group. Conall and Dermot followed my lead, each firing upon the left and right, dropping the rest in their tracks.

We holstered our weapons and continued onward; I hoped we didn't have to stop to fight every quarter mile. We didn't have the time or ammunition for that. The goal was to find Angie fast, rescue her with as little fighting as possible, and make a quick escape. The early winter night was fast approaching, and the last thing I wanted to do was try and fight our way out of unfamiliar enemy territory in the dark.

My fetch glided ahead of us, keeping my chosen in sight. As we plunged down the street in the dragon's wake, other small groups appeared from doorways at random, rushing out at us with whatever weapons had been close at hand, only to be cut down as we rode past. Most of them weren't dressed for the weather or wearing armor. The smaller one-story buildings were replaced by two-story structures as we pressed forward. The way ahead was clear, but faces began to show at upper story windows and heads poked out of doorways to investigate the sound of gunfire. Our horses charged down the street shoulder to shoulder, deterring the curious from venturing out. The rest of the people we encountered were milling about, shouting at one another in a useless attempt to get information. Our passage was disregarded by a great many, probably due to our manner of dress. With the colossal barrier surrounding their city, I doubted they'd ever anticipated any sort of attack at all. After all, who would be crazy enough to attack a fortified stronghold in the dead of winter with a fearsome snowstorm brewing?

With the exception of a perceptive few who recognized too late that we were outsiders, we were unimpeded in our progress until we skirted a large building to avoid a group of Republic soldiers. They had had put up a barricade of wagons and wooden barrels across the road. Swinging back around toward the street, we nearly collided with a posse of defenders, and what they lacked in cold weather gear, they made up for in firepower.

"Whoa!" Dermot shouted. Kelpie reared, neighing loudly. Even before the horse had all four feet on the ground again, the water elementalist's shotgun was up, and he was shooting into the crowd. Steel slid on a patch of ice that landed us right in the middle of our enemies. Three went down beneath his hooves while a few others were knocked down or thrown off-balance. The rest tried to take aim but did not shoot for fear of hitting their companions.

Sword in hand, I slashed at the enemies still standing on my right, slicing through three in one blow with the grey blade. Once they were down, their compatriots threw caution to the wind and began shooting. I formed a flame shield out in front that would cover both me and my horse as pistols thundered and bullets whizzed all around. The stallion spun in a tight circle, allowing me to catch them unawares with a sweeping slash. It was a maneuver that would have been impossible with a mundane sword, but the Morrigan's enchantment had given the grey blade a finely-honed edge that went through bone and sinew as easily as a scythe cut grass.

The fallen bandits had regained their feet and were taking aim again when Duncan created a temblor that ruined their aim and saved my skin. Steel spun about again, surging away from the posse and returning me to relative safety. As soon as I was out of the way, the earth druid sent a shockwave that knocked them all off their feet again, allowing Dermot, Conall, and I to fire a volley of scattershot that made sure they never got up again.

"*Fire in the hole!*" came a yell, followed by an explosion that rained dirt and debris down upon us. Dozens of tiny wood splinters and tiny pieces of sharp metal sliced through clothing and skin. Twister and Kelpie, who had been closest to the blast, screamed in fear and pain, bucking Conall and Dermot out of their saddles. Bucephalus and Scarlet, reacting to the fear of their herd-mates, spooked and threw Seth and Duncan. Even Steel, who was used to the thunder of gunfire, being surrounded by flames, and rumbling earth beneath his hooves, scrambled to join them in their mad dash from danger. I somehow managed to jump clear without breaking my neck.

Rolling in the dirty snow to break my fall, I regained my feet and spotted three bandits, each holding a piece of metal pipe with a skinny piece of rope poking out one end. Before they could light the wicks, I hurled a spear of flame that ignited all three pipe bombs. The resultant explosion tore the men apart and damaged one wall of a nearby building. A barrage of fireballs set the roof of that building ablaze, along with the two on either side of it. Seth used an air punch to blow a hole in the damaged wall, and we scurried inside.

They wouldn't expect us to take shelter in a burning building. It allowed us to catch our breath and gave Duncan time to heal our minor injuries. I ordered the dragon away to keep it from giving away our position, sending it winging away to the east. Taking a moment to focus on the bond, I sensed that Angie was close. With any luck, I wouldn't need the fetch to seek her out again. The enemy druids had stopped running, and she was less than a furlong away.

The pull toward her was so strong that it was all I could do to remain calm and listen to intellect rather than emotion. Setting aside my apprehension regarding her safety and my eagerness to see her face again, I took stock of the situation. There were no enemies visible, but we would have to cross terrain that was completely devoid of cover in order to reach her location. If our horses hadn't run off, I might have tried to make a mad dash for the building, but it would be a suicide run on foot through calf-deep snow.

"What now?" asked Seth, breathing hard.

I pointed to the one direction not engulfed in flame, "They've taken her there."

"So close and yet so far away," Dermot said. "It looks quiet."

Conall frowned. "Too quiet."

My thoughts exactly.

"Can we tunnel through the earth to reach the building?" asked Seth.

Duncan shook his head. "The water table here is too high. We could make a tunnel, but it would have to be at such a depth that it would completely fill with water before we crossed the distance."

"Water, hunh?" Dermot said.

"Think you can keep a tunnel of that size dry?" I asked.

He squinted at the distant building through the haze of smoke and falling snow. "If I only had to keep the water off our heads, I might be able to do it," he said, sounding frustrated. "But having to keep the whole tunnel dry all at once..." He shook his head. "My Well would run dry before we were even halfway across."

The best thing to do would be to leave them here while I went ahead alone. There was always a risk that they'd be discovered, but Seth and Duncan should be able to keep up secure defenses of air and earth until I returned with Angie. They would never allow it, though, so I didn't waste time presenting the idea as a plan of action. And while I could go without their assent, they'd only follow and get themselves killed in the process.

"I'm going to have a look and see what's out there," I said.

Rather than sticking my head out or surrounding myself with a bright shield of swirling flame that would immediately attract the enemy's attention, I dropped to the ground and low-crawled through the snow, creeping under burning bushes until I had a decent view of the street. There I discovered three things:

First, that our horses were nowhere to be seen, dashing all hope of grabbing Angie and riding out of here. *Second*, that the

560

path to my chosen was clear, but would almost certainly lead to our demise because *third*, they had left a wide open corridor between our position and Angie, protected by a group of defenders the size of two raid groups on each side.

Quakes.

I eased backwards several feet and then plopped down on my ass in the snow, allowing my head to fall back against the charred wood in frustration. I was out of ideas and running out of time. The day was dying and the grey, wintry sky above was darkening in the east. It occurred to me that without horses our escape would be painfully slow and that we would be forced to fight every step of the way...

Unless we slipped out under cover of darkness.

That meant finding a place to hide until it was full dark. It also meant increasing the chance that Angie might be harmed, for the longer she was in enemy hands, the more precarious her situation. Faced with a choice between our own imminent danger versus the potential threat to her, I had to choose reducing our own peril. Dead heroes rescued no one.

I returned to the others and explained the situation, along with my possible solution. "If any of you have other ideas, now is the time to speak up."

Seth said, "We could backtrack and circle around. They're not likely to expect that."

"We could try heading west and attempt the same tactic," suggested Duncan. "There's a street that runs north-south. If we cross it and proceed north behind the buildings, we might be able to avoid their trap entirely."

Conall nodded. "If things get hairy, we can always create a smokescreen or distract them with an earthquake and hole up somewhere until dark."

"If we do that it will take longer to reach the place they're holding Angie," Duncan said.

"True, but it should be completely dark by the time we get there," Seth said. "That aligns with Davis' plan to withdraw with minimal enemy engagements."

"You mean hide and run away," Dermot said.

"That's exactly what I mean."

"Will not remaining in enemy hands expose her to increased

danger?" Duncan pressed.

"Not as much as if we don't make it there at all."

My pronouncement was met with several moments of silence.

"I am not one to tempt the Fates," Seth said.

"She'll be fine," Conall said. "Fiona and Blythe won't allow anyone to harm her."

I hoped he was right. "Let's move. Everybody stay close."

Directly to the west of our position was a pair of buildings, still burning brightly in the aftermath of the fireball barrage. Through the narrow walkway between them, I could see people moving up and down the street with purpose. We needed to cross without being seen.

"Everybody, get behind me. Seth, drop a dome over everyone else."

"What are you doing?"

"Creating a diversion."

As soon as he gave me a thumbs-up, I took several seconds to build up an immense amount of elemental fire before bringing it forth in the shape of a small sun. Dividing it in half and then enlarging each to the size of the original sun, I firebombed the house on the left. The already-ignited structure exploded outward, propelling splinters, broken glass, metal shrapnel, and entire wooden timbers into the street ahead. When struck by the second blast, the bottom half of the building on the right burst out into the street where two of the raid groups lay in wait to ambush us. Its roof and second story shot upward in an eruption of fire. Trailing smoke as it tumbled end over end, it crashed down upon the roadway, effectively creating twin roadblocks of scorching debris on both sides of the route we needed to take.

With any luck, the Republic forces would think the destruction had resulted from the initial explosion, or perhaps that the buildings had been demolished by flammable materials within. I gestured for Seth and the others to follow, and we jogged through the fiery ruins, leaping over burning piles of wood and dodging falling embers and debris. There were few people around to see us, and no one paid any attention to five men in local garb running away from danger. We crossed an open area and ducked behind what appeared to be someone's house before turning north once more. There was another street to cross and no cover to conceal us from the enemy. Boldness was the only ally we had. As we sprinted across the street, I fervently hoped they would assume we were fellow citizens running for our lives.

"*There they are!*" a female voice shouted.

According to Poppy, the women who had kidnapped Angie were the only two druids that remained – the ones who had kidnapped Angie. One was an earth-fire elementalist named Fiona Roughgarden; the other, Blythe Hollander, possessed only elemental fire. I had truly believed that both of Sebrina's bootlickers would stand guard over Angie. She was, after all, a triple threat and their overlord's original protégé. The Republic soldiers must have thought we were more than they could handle if they'd called upon one of them to help track us down.

A minor earthquake rumbled our way, confirming the enemy druid's identity as Fiona Roughgarden. Duncan shrugged off the baby temblor and sent his own bigger shockwave speeding back at her. While Fiona's quake had been limited to an area barely as wide as the street due to the approach of her allies, Duncan and I were under no such restraint. The bucking earth tossed her head over heels into the snow and threw the soldiers with her into a pile of tangled arms and legs, buying us a few precious seconds. Shouts and bellows of anger followed her cry of alarm, along with the metallic clicks and clacks of guns being readied to fire. Bullets began to ping off the lateral shield Seth had raised, rapidly increasing to a hailstorm of metal. Dermot splashed a thick water shell behind it a split second before it shattered. We ran faster, seeking shelter behind a building that stood on the corner of the intersection, thinking it might be another empty house.

It wasn't.

Over a dozen armed bandits poured out the back door, and more could be heard shouting as they exited the front of the building. I slipped on a patch of ice, escaping harm only because my fire shield had blossomed out of defensive reflex. I drew the grey blade; my footing improved as the ice and snow melted from the warmth of our enemies' blood. Conall let out a battle cry, emptying his shotgun into the crowd of aggressors coming from the front. As he ducked behind Seth's air shield to reload, Dermot took his place with his own shotgun, preserving his elemental magic for when we really needed it. I reloaded my Ithaca 37, and the three of us took turns firing and reloading while Seth warded us against gunmen taking random potshots from the upper story windows of the next house down. Duncan kept the enemy off our backs with a series of minor earthquakes. We couldn't fight effectively while the air druid had us shielded, however, so we gave ground and moved to the south side of the barracks, seeking better cover.

We were in trouble. We knew it, and the Republic soldiers knew it, too. It wasn't so much that we were outmatched by a couple dozen gunmen. The danger lay in the way they had us pinned down at the intersection while the four companies of defenders we'd worked so hard to avoid charged down the street with the goal of ending our lives. We had to get through the soldiers from this barracks and past the snipers – and possibly more melee combatants – in the next one.

Ducking around the air shield, I lobbed several fireballs through the open second-story windows, forcing the snipers to withdraw and setting both buildings ablaze. Fire spread to the rooftops, burning out of control. Glass windowpanes shattered in outward explosions of murderous shrapnel. Determined to retake the ground we had, I destabilized the earth beneath the barracks bucking, causing it to collapse in upon itself. Conall followed my lead at first, but then pressed the attack, driving a wedge through the enemy. His ferocity caused him to become separated from us, and he was soon lost to sight.

"We have to get him out of there!" Dermot cried.

"I'm trying!" I yelled. I was as likely to kill him as save him using elemental fire. "Use some magic or something!"

He looked at me helplessly, on the verge of panic. "What do I do?"

In a stark moment of clarity, it hit me that we'd brought a seventeen-year-old boy on a rescue mission into enemy territory that had erupted into a war zone. We were so accustomed to taking him everywhere with us that even Seth hadn't suggested leaving him behind.

"Use your imagination!" I shouted.

The red-haired water elementalist backed off, just out of sight, while Seth and I plowed forward in the direction Conall had vanished. Terror appeared on the faces before us, and we attacked with renewed vigor, enemies falling to our blades. They gave way before our assault with unexpected ease, and I realized that their goggle-eyed shock was because of something else – a giant made of snow, brandishing a club of solid ice. The Republic forces quit targeting us and began shooting at it instead. The thing roared and brought its ice club down upon the mass of aggressors, smashing several. They tried to dodge but were so closely packed together that there was nowhere to go. The ones in the back retreated to a safer distance to shoot at it some more, and Seth and I threw ourselves to one side to get out of the snow monster's way as it plowed through the sea of bodies.

"What *is* that?" Seth yelled.

"He made a… I think it's an abominable snowman!"

The twenty-foot-tall golem of ice and snow waded into the thick of the fray, taking out five or six enemies with each swing of its club. Heedless of being peppered with gunfire, it paused a moment and reached down with its free hand, picking something up and tossing it backward in our direction. Conall flew through the air yelling obscenities and rolled for several feet before landing gracelessly in a heap besides us.

"What in Hel's name is *that* thing?" he demanded. "It looks like a fucking frost giant!"

I told him.

"You gotta be fucking kidding me," said Conall.

"At least it's not the *Dobhar-chú*," Seth muttered.

"Keep him going as long as you can!" I yelled to Dermot.

The water elementalist, down on one knee with one mitten off and his hand plunged into the snow, gave me a thumbs-up, grinning fiercely.

Wanting only to get Angie and get back out, the last thing we needed was to become embroiled in a battle, but now we had no choice. As I pressed the attack with blade and blaze, I began flinging darts and fireballs all around us. Seth protected us from a sudden rain of bullets from a group of riflemen that had climbed on the roof of a building across the road, but when they threw a pipe bomb, his shield shattered and the resultant concussive burst drove us all to our knees. Another pipe bomb came sailing toward us, and I managed to hit it with a small fireball and detonate it overhead. Several large fireballs took out both building and attackers.

"Seth! Give me an opening!" I shouted. "Fire wall!"

I laid down a line of fire, and he pushed it forward into the enemy line with a powerful burst of air while still shielding us on the other three sides. I'd never seen any of the other air druids manipulate their element in multiple directions like that before. That random thought crossed my mind that, if he wanted to impress Iriana, *that* was the move to do it with. I laid down fire lines again and again, as we sent wave after wave of fire into the enemy ranks, killing them or driving them back.

Duncan intensified his efforts. The earth rose and fell all around us, shaking violently as ripples spread out from our circle of stable ground like water after a stone has been thrown into it. Unlike water, however, these ripples grew stronger and their amplitude larger the farther they traveled. Buildings on both sides of the street – those that hadn't burned to the ground yet – began to tremble and then shudder. One by one they slowly crumbled in upon themselves or collapsed onto the street, scattering sparks and ashes. Some of them fell onto people outside who didn't get out of the way fast enough.

I glanced at the marauding snow monster, its legs and feet stained with bright red blood, still stomping around and smashing the 'Ville's defenders with its icy club. The five of us were fighting an impossible battle on three fronts, both attacking and defending with our magic. Seth, Duncan, and I had virtually limitless magic channeled directly from the gods, but the others were not so blessed. Dermot would not be able to continue wielding those massive amounts of elemental water forever. Conall's bloody enthusiasm made him a force to be reckoned with, but he would eventually tire. We all would.

Searching for any remaining elevated positions from which Republic soldiers could snipe us or throw pipe bombs, I located a man standing atop the one remaining corner of a building and hit him with a small, fast fireball. Screaming in pain and terror, he mindlessly fled – straight off the edge of the roof.

"How are we doing?" I asked.

"Is that a rhetorical question?" Seth shouted, looking at me like I was insane.

"I'm down by three-quarters," said Dermot. "That's ammo *and* magic."

"Conall?"

"Let's send those bastards to Hel!"

About what I had expected.

"Duncan?"

"We can lay down a series of earthquakes to collapse the buildings on either side of any road before we pass between them," he said. "But it comes with the risk of hurting innocent people."

"I'm past worrying about that," I said, rubbing the back of my neck.

"Any noncombatants are likely to have run away—"

A fresh barrage of gunfire interrupted Seth.

"Collapse the buildings behind us so they can't flank us!" Conall yelled.

Duncan's expression was grim as he touched the ground; mine couldn't have been much different. Together we rocked the surrounding area with earthquakes, violently shaking those buildings still standing until the walls gave way. As we raised the ground beneath our feet, the decimated buildings crumbled, tumbling down the slope in a wave of dirt and debris, creating a rampart to cover our southern flank.

"Split air wall!" I yelled, laying a thick firewall before us. Seth thrust a column of air into the enemy ranks, forcing the flames outward. I used the time we had gained for another massive internal ignition of elemental fire, razing the front ranks of the closest defenders between us and Angie's prison with another scorching firebomb. Following it up with a tremendous fireball, I created an incendiary path of safety for us. Conall ran its length first, longsword in his hands. He was out of shotgun shells.

A group of brave defenders at the end of the firelane set upon him. The actinic blue of elemental spirit zigzagged along the length of his sword. It was enough to make them hesitate, and he drove into them, laying about wildly. He blocked a couple of gunshots with an air shield that shattered almost immediately, and I waited for him to move so I could step in and create our next passageway, but he refused to give ground.

Conall was tired of fighting without magic. Veins bulged in his face and neck as he laid about with his sword, taking heads, hacking off limbs, and spilling the entrails of all who came close, crying aloud the names of Odin and Tyr. He recharged the blade a few times and managed to create another air shield, but those weak magical efforts ceased within a few minutes. When the lightning on his blade fizzled out for good, the Republic soldiers attacked with renewed ferocity.

In spite of having little magic left, Dermot sent a swarm of water tentacles shooting over our heads. They plunged into the fray, at first tossing aside those who approached Conall. When that did not deter the marauders, the crystalline appendages formed hard, sharp points and speared them through. The ground behind and to either side of the Norseman was scattered with bodies in pools of blood. Only the enemies directly in front of him dared approach.

Lost in a berserker rage and bleeding from multiple wounds, Conall refused to give ground. We were hemmed in by the bulwark of wreckage we'd built to the south, the main body of the defending Republic forces was breathing down our necks from the east, and we couldn't continue north until the Norseman was out of the way. I was yelling at him to stand down when he fell. One second he was on his feet, red-faced and screaming at Odin about his birthright, and in the next something flew screaming through the air and hit the ground, exploding in a burst of fire, smoke, and flying shrapnel. Duncan reacted first, rolling the earth all around us and knocking the enemy combatants flat. Using Wolfric's flamethrower technique, I blasted the oncoming threat, holding off any who would try to come at us. Seth raced forward and grabbed Conall; the rest of us followed to cover him.

"In here!" Duncan called. Under cover of smoke, he kicked open the door to a burning building and charged inside. Seth followed with Conall slung over his shoulder, unconscious. I slammed the door behind us and leaned heavily against it, closing my eyes. After a few much-needed deep breaths, I opened them again and examined the room. Seth was squatting with his back against the wall with his eyes closed, much as I had done. Conall was lying on the floor, where Duncan was attending to him.

Someone was missing.

"Guys," I said. "Where's Dermot?"

Chapter 33 – Running the Gauntlet

What matters most is how well you walk through the fire.
~ Charles Bukowski ~

Seth jumped to his feet, eyes darting around the room. "He was right behind us!"

"When did you see him last?"

"I don't know."

"Think, man!"

"*I don't know!*" Seth shouted. His shoulders slumped. "Oh, *gods*, we left him behind!"

"I'm going back out there. He can't be far." I turned to Duncan, kneeling beside the still-unconscious Conall. "Stay here and take care of him."

"I'll come with you," Seth said, collecting himself with a visible effort.

"No. They'll need you here in case the enemy figures out you're here." Or if the fire spread and the building collapsed, which was a distinct possibility.

"You can't go out there alone!"

"The only reason we're in this situation is because I *didn't* come alone!" I snapped.

"But the prophecy…"

"Angie is the only druid with elemental spirit in a five square mile radius, and I don't think *she's* going to hit me with a spirit bolt!" Seth looked away.

"Be careful," said Duncan.

"Sit tight," I said. "I'll be back as soon as I can."

Unshielded and alone, I stepped out into the twilight frost and extinguished the burning upper story. Once I was clear of the building, I raised the level of the earth surrounding the wrecked barracks building nearly as high as the second story. Duncan would be able to move it easily; our enemies would not.

"They've gone underground!" I heard the earth-fire druid yell, sounding some distance away. "Find them!"

Let her not see me, I prayed to Danu. Not wanting Fiona to recognize my presence the way I had discovered Dianthe Aspen's before the battle by the lake, I willed myself invisible to *seeking* but limited it to the earth directly beneath my feet.

Creeping around the corner of the building, I spied the Republic forces running about searching for us. Most of them had moved south, further down the road. Drawing the grey blade, I retraced our steps to the place where Conall had fallen. As I'd told Seth, it wasn't far. It was also easily identified by widespread bloodshed and bodies with gaping holes. The ground beneath my feet was steady but uneasy. Because of the violence and sheer numbers of people in the area, I couldn't sort out where Dermot was with elemental earth. I risked an infusion of elemental fire that made the grey blade glow just enough to allow me to see tracks, or perhaps some other sign of Dermot's passing. I told myself that I wasn't looking for his body. I simply could not accept the thought that he might be dead because of my negligence.

The ground had been so torn up by booted feet and tumbled earth that a trail was difficult to find, but I finally spotted a bulbous leather lump half-buried in snow and mud. It was one of Dermot's canteens. I picked it up and examined it; the thongs that bound it to his belt and thigh had been severed, leading me to surmise that he had left it behind for us to find. Sweeping the sword in an arc over the area, I found his boot knife a few feet away.

There was blood on the blade.

From there, a striated depression in the mud began, indicating that something heavy had been dragged away, and my gut clenched. I told myself that they'd knocked him unconscious to put an end to his resistance and so he could no longer use magic. Refusing to give in to despair, I followed the drag-trail. It meandered a bit but straightened out, heading in the direction of the building where Angie was being held. With any luck, they'd be holding Dermot captive in the same place. A feeling of blessed relief washed over me as the bond was finally allowed to lead me toward my chosen. Walking in a slow crouch, I was so utterly focused on following the trail and searching for any other sign Dermot might have left that I'd progressed to the middle of the street without realizing it.

"Foul abomination," I heard an unfriendly female voice say. "You will come no closer."

I rose, coming face to face with a young woman that I assumed was Fiona Roughgarden. Standing just beyond the reach of my sword, she clenched and unclenched her fists, flickers of flame dancing across her fingertips.

"Over here!" she called to the soldiers. Booted feet thudded from nearby streets in answer to her call.

It would be easy to employ my fetch in laying down a swath of fire that would destroy the morass of defenders as easily as it had scorched the forest by the swamp. The question was, could it discern one person from another? Could it avoid including Angie in the firestorm, or would it indiscriminately roast her along with everyone else? What if Dermot got caught up in its attack?

With all our lives in imminent danger, there was little else I could do. The water elementalist might have enough magic left to turtle under a water shell to keep the flames at bay. Angie was smart and well-versed in the use of all three of her elements; if caught in a burning building she would protect herself from the dragon's attack with air and then douse the surrounding flames with water.

"Get out of my way," I growled.

Fiona put her hands on her hips and smirked. "You can't hurt me. I, too, possess the elements of earth and fire."

"Don't tell me what I can't do."

"Fool! You are only one man, and I have an army!"

"You may have an army," I said. "But I have a dragon."

Coming in from the west, the fire drake glided over the middle of the intersection, opened its jaws, and breathed living fire, immolating everything in its path – humans, horses, weapons, structures, *everything*. Slack-jawed and wide-eyed, Fiona stared in shock. Her hold upon the ground relaxed, allowing me to take control. In response to my respectful request of the earth mother, a wave of mud rose up and washed over the arrogant girl, knocking her to the ground. Even if I had wanted to kill her, using elemental earth to do so would have been an affront to Danu. While Fiona struggled, I tossed a few red-hot, half-melted firearms over the glop of mud, cooling them rapidly to pin her there. It was likely that she could work metal, but for now, she was out of my way.

"I will kill you!" she howled, struggling fruitlessly to free herself.

"Not today," I said, stepping over her.

Fiona jerked one arm out of the morass and lashed at me with elemental fire in the shape of a bullwhip. Catching it in my fist, I held it for a moment, smiling at her – and then I took it from her, drawing her fire into myself.

She screamed in rage, drawing the attention of defenders newly arrived to the intersection. Having been drawn by the newest eruption of flame, they came running with guns booming. My fire shield blazed white-hot, fending off the barrage while I waited for the dragon to return. It wasn't long before it appeared north of the intersection. Its maw a roaring furnace, the dragon sailed overhead, releasing another incendiary stream of fire, encompassing the cross-street in a wide swath of purifying destruction all the way to the southern barrier wall of the 'Ville. I reveled in the river of fire, enraptured by its destructive beauty. My only desire was to see it spread the lovely radiance as far as the eye could see.

"*Davis.*"

The grey blade swept about my body as I turned to see who had spoken. No one else could withstand the destructive potency of elemental fire. So who had spoken?

"Careful now, someone might get hurt."

Peering into the icy darkness, I spied a figure draped in a dark cloak. At first, I thought it was another druid, but I was unable to sense him through the earth. The last time that had happened, a goddess had approached me. Was this a god? His very presence made the hair on the back of my neck stand up.

"I mean you no harm," he said, displaying empty hands.

"Who are you?"

"A friend." He paused. "One who knows that there are more

important things than annihilating your enemies."

"Oh, I don't know about *that*."

"Is indulging yourself in wanton destruction more important than your heart?" he said. "Is it more important than your chosen? Remember why you are here."

Everything came crashing back in an instant: Seth and Duncan watching over Conall in hiding, Dermot lost, and Angie held captive nearby. The bond between us reasserted itself, gripping me more tightly than my own elemental magic and releasing me from its mesmerizing effect. The dragonfire ceased, and the inferno died down. I shivered all over, suddenly aware of the bitter winter wind.

"By the way," he said when the flames had died down. "Your spirit animal is too big."

I stared at him dumbly. "What?"

"Do not disregard the words of Apollo's Oracle."

"Who are you?" I demanded. "How long have you been following me?"

"Long enough," he replied cryptically. "Your friends are waiting."

I glanced back at the wrecked structure providing shelter for Seth, Duncan, and Conall to make sure I hadn't accidentally burned it to the ground. Thankfully, it was still standing, the earthen berms having provided added protection. When I turned back to face the cloaked figure, he was gone. There was no telling who or what he might have been, but there was no point in wasting time trying to find a ghost.

"Davis!"

The call was followed by a blast of arctic air that blew past me with such force that I struggled to stay on my feet. I turned around to see Seth, Duncan, and Conall leaving the house in which they'd been partially buried. All looked hale and hearty – even Conall, thanks to Duncan's skill with healing. After running across the snow-covered ground, they stopped at the edge of the street, which was radiating immense heat and a pretty orange glow.

"Look!" Conall yelled, raised his fist in the air... And fired off one of the biggest spirit bolts I have ever seen. Static electricity crackled all around us in the frigid winter air.

"How are you doing that?" I asked stupidly.

He laughed again. "Can you believe it?" Hands outstretched,

he delivered another rush of freezing air. Beside him, Seth and Duncan were grinning from ear to ear.

"You can work air now, too!"

"And water! I never even knew I *had* elemental water!"

Combined with his ability to channel spirit and air, that would mean–

"I'm a triple threat!" he crowed. "The gods healed me! *I'm a druid*!"

Geysers of snow launched into the air and came pounding down on the hot street, sending steam billowing into the air. It completely cooled the surface of the road and solidified all the melted little pebbles that had been setting it aglow. The three were across and we were hugging each other even before the steam dissipated.

"This is amazing!"

"I didn't scare you with the thunderbolt, did I?" he asked with a grin.

"Conall, you've always scared me," I laughed.

"Now that I have magic, we might actually make it out of this shithole alive!" he said.

Considering how long it had taken me to gain control over my own elements, I wasn't too sure how much help he would actually be. Then again, he had been raised in the grove and had received a wealth of education in magic – albeit theoretical – that I had not.

The brand new triple threat put his hands on his hips. "So what happened?" he said, surveying the crossroads where at least four raid groups' worth of smoking and charred bodies lay. The streets were lined by the skeletal frames of burned buildings, with structures on the verge of collapse or in ruins further down the road.

"Looks like you got a good start on destroying the place," he added. "Why'd you quit?"

"I still haven't found Dermot," I said, "And then there's *her*." I pointed at Fiona, or more accurately, the pile of metal and mud where she was supposed to be.

"Who?" asked Seth.

"Fiona," I said. "The earth-fire druid."

"There's still the whole rest of it to burn," Conall said, rubbing his hands together as if about to enjoy a hearty meal.

"Right now we need to find Angie and Dermot and get out of here."

"I think the whole rest of the city is coming for us, anyway," Duncan said. No sooner had he spoken than the rumble of a thousand boots could be felt, headed our way from the west. We bolted across the street, but before we'd gotten very far, a wave of enemies charged around the building where Angie was being held. Our way was blocked by a group of thirty or forty bandits brandishing pistols. This had to be the longest amount of time it had ever taken anyone to cross a street.

"These people must be insane!" Duncan said, throwing a shockwave at a group who'd gotten a little too close. "One would think they would see their fallen comrades and try to avoid meeting the same fate."

"That's not how these people think," I said. "They see the corpses and want revenge."

"We *have* invaded their home," Seth said.

"Only after they invaded everyone else's!" said Conall.

Duncan and I held at bay the Republic forces with waves of earth that rolled and bucked all the way to our goal – the building where Angie was being held. Seth shielded us to the rear and sides with a semicircular barrier of air. Conall threw clumsy, erratic spirit bolts at the defenders, raising his own shield of air when Seth's was damaged. It was only for few moments at a time, for he clearly preferred to fight offensively, but he was starting to get a handle on using his magic.

The door popped open, and a man stepped out into the night lit with fire and lightning, his long, white-blonde hair giving away his identity: Niall Ashcroft. With one of the replica Ithaca 37s at the ready, he led the way down the steps, firing into the backs of the enemy crowd. Angie followed, her dark hair whipping in the wind. Catching sight of her, everything else faded in importance. My heart leapt while my gut clenched with fear for her safety. I need not have worried, however, for none of the soldiers' gunfire penetrated her protective dome of air. She and Niall must have worked out a system that allowed him to fire, for the shield did not seem to hinder his shooting.

Niall pointed the shotgun's muzzle upward and drew back to stand beside Angie at the bottom of the steps. She raised her hands, and the interior of the dome began to glow, increasing in intensity until it was painful to behold. Determined to keep my eyes on her, I squinted through the pale blue brilliance with watering eyes. A blinding flash of light exploded outward in a torrent of spirit bolts that hammered the bandits surrounding the dome. The tightly pressed enemy bodies provided the optimal situation for the electricity to travel. Spirit bolts jumped from foe to foe, spreading wide to encompass the entire corner of the intersection.

I smiled, taking genuine pleasure in her power and skill – until the crooked fingers of spirit magic headed our way. I grabbed Seth's arm just as he raised his own protective dome of air. Forked lightning crawled all over the exterior.

Conall whistled. "That's impressive."

"If by impressive you mean terrifying, then I agree," said Seth. "What *was* that?"

"Chain lightning," said Duncan. He knelt and sent a small ripple through the ground.

"Hey!" I frowned at him. "What are you doing?"

"I'm letting her know I am here," he said. "Remember that we look like bandits."

"You'll break her focus!"

"It is merely a bump," he said. "Father uses it to communicate with Uncle. She should recognize it."

Indeed she did, for the actinic light show faded away, vanishing in a shower of sparks. Seth waited until every last twinkle of elemental spirit was gone before lowering his shield.

He gave me a look of chastisement. "Warn me a little sooner next time." He shook his head in disbelief. "That was a nasty spell."

"She *is* an Everlight," Duncan.

To anyone who had ever known Liam and Padraig Everlight, I supposed it was explanation enough. Even other druids gave them a wide berth when they were on the warpath. Tales of the two brothers, with all five elements between them, had been popular after-dinner entertainment, not only in the Warriors' Third at the grove but also among the Finns. Connor Shitozaki's many tales had led me to believe that he must have spent quite a bit of time with the brothers in his youth.

Republic soldiers were rapidly approaching from the west.

Random rifle shots punctuated the sound of something heavy and metallic being dragged over the cobblestone streets. I wasn't sticking around to find out exactly what that was.

"Split fire wall!" I shouted at Seth. Thrusting both fists before me, I created a thick line of fire that ran straight toward Angie and Niall, incinerating everything in its path. Elemental air sliced right through the middle and divided it, creating a path of safe passage. We raced down the fiery lane with Duncan directing earthquakes on either side while Conall tossed spirit orbs back over his shoulder to cover the rear.

"Get in!" Niall yelled, jerking his head toward the open door.

"Come on!" Angie cried. "Hurry!"

Niall charged inside first. As he was a null, I could hardly blame him. Duncan, Seth, and Conall thundered up the wood steps and through the open door. At the rapid *chunk-chunk-chunk* of a large-caliber gun, I spun about, free hand outstretched to push Angie behind me. The spinning barrel of the heavy gun discharged heavy rounds that tore chunks of wood out of the building's wall, stitching a pattern of holes toward us in a murderous search to end our lives.

"Charlie!" she cried, pulling on my arm.

"Get inside!" I shouted. Palm outstretched toward the incoming threat, I brought forth a fire shield larger than any so far. The spinning flames sparked from orange to white hot in the blink of an eye, and the melted rounds struck the walls around us in fat globs. Creating a second fire shield with my other hand, I poured more energy into it, making it thicker and doming it outward until it was half a sphere. As with the miniature suns I had created to help us escape earlier, I focused my will in the direction of the big gun, took a deep breath, and *shoved* it forward with all the power I could muster. The barrage ended, and there was a split second of silence before the roar of an explosion. A flaming cloud mushroomed above the intersection, revealing people running in all directions and searing pieces of shrapnel and ammunition shooting into the sky. Debris rained all around, trailing bright yellow ribbons of fire in the darkness.

Angie was no longer tugging on my arm and was now gripping it tightly in openmouthed shock. I ushered her inside and slammed the door. With my arms around her, I leaned against the door, breathing hard. She sagged against me.

"This door isn't going to keep them out," I said.

"I've got it," Seth said. Wind gusted in through the gaping bullet holes and spread to all four corners of the room, effectively blocking all the doors and windows. There was a barrage of gunfire from the east, in the back of the building, and a couple of explosions that shattered the windows on the western side of the building, followed by silence.

"Are you all right?" I asked Angie, and she turned to face me.

"Never better," she said, her eyes glistening. "I can't believe you're really here!"

Caressing her cheek with gentle fingers, I slipped my hand behind her neck and drew her in for a kiss that was tender at first but soon became heated. She met my ardor with equal passion, clutching at my back. My hands slid over her shoulders and down her back, pulling her body closer to mine. Dizzy with the nearness of her, intoxicated by the scent of wild honeysuckle, I wanted nothing more than to lose myself in her exotic green eyes.

"Davis!" Conall shouted. "Turn the heat down, man, you're roasting us alive!"

He was right. It was sweltering.

"Oh. Sorry," I said, and lowered the temperature of the room. I was tired and hungry, we were surrounded by a howling horde of enemies screaming for blood, and there was no safe way out. Even so, I felt immensely better for having her in my arms again.

"Gods, I've missed you," I said, kissing her again and holding her tightly.

"I was so afraid I'd never see you again!" Angie replied. "And then I was afraid that when I did see you, you wouldn't want to see me."

I frowned. "Why?"

"Were I in your place, I'm not sure I would." She paused, her brow furrowing. "I've put you through so much!"

"You can't blame yourself for what others have done," I said. "We both made mistakes."

She seemed about to protest, but said, "Your hair is so long!" and brushed an errant lock out of my face.

"You were the last person to cut it." Padraig had actually been the last, but I didn't count being scalped almost bald.

A pained expression crossed her face. "Another example of how you suffered because of my pride."

"It's only hair, Angie. And you had to learn sometime. When we're on our own in the wilderness, there won't be anyone else around to cut it."

"Is that what you want?" she asked with the barest tremor in her voice. "I mean… after everything that's happened… Are you sure?"

The one possibility I had not anticipated was that she might be afraid of the same thing I had been: rejection. And while I had received complete reassurance in her loving embrace, she was still uncertain.

"Angie. When I heard you were roaming the wilderness searching for me, I created a fetch to seek you out and followed it for miles through the freezing cold, risking my life and the lives of thirty-five other men, battling every Republic soldier and rogue druid that dared stand in our way," I said. "As soon as I heard that you'd been captured, I chose to invade a city of brigands, thieves, murderers, and slavers for one thing and one thing only: *to have you back.*" I took her hands in mine. "Do you honestly believe I would do those things for someone I don't want? For someone I don't love? *Yes*, I want you with me, a thousand times, *yes*. I have never been more certain of anything in my life."

Her chin quivered, but she did not shed a tear. I pulled her close again, wishing that simple physical touch could take away all her fears. The events of the past eighteen months had toughened her; it grieved me that she had endured so much heartache.

"I couldn't believe my eyes when I saw you ride up on Steel. I honestly wasn't sure you would come."

"Well, you *did* bring me my gun."

Angie laughed softly, but her smile still held a touch of sadness. I caressed her cheek with the back of my fingers.

"I will always come for you," I whispered. "*Always.*"

Chapter 34 – The Long Night

It ain't as bad as you think. It will look better in the morning.
~ Colin Powell ~

"They've stopped firing," Seth said.

"I guess they remembered they were shooting their own property," said Conall, throwing back the hood of his coat.

"Conall?" Angie said. "Is that you?"

If I hadn't known better, I'd have thought she was just as happy to see him as me. It should have come as no surprise to me that Angie and Conall knew each other, but they obviously shared a connection akin to that of long-time friends.

"It's good to see you again, Angie. And you, too, Niall, even though you look like shit."

"Thanks," Niall responded dryly. "It's good to see you, too."

"Sorry it took us so long to get here," I said, turning back to Angie. "We kept running into problems."

"Speaking of problems," Seth interrupted. "Where is the fire druid that accompanied Dianthe Aspen?"

"Blythe?" Angie said. "She saw Fiona bested in combat and ran to help her get away." She turned back to me with an expression of confusion. "You have elemental *fire*? *You* defeated Fiona?"

I raised an eyebrow. "You're surprised by the fire but not by the fact that I'm a druid?"

She had the grace to look chagrined, and her eyes flickered briefly toward Duncan. If he was trying to hide his amusement at

580

her discomfiture, he wasn't doing a very good job of it.

"We suspected," she admitted.

"He already knows that," Conall said. "He's just putting you on the spot because he's pissed everyone hid it from him."

There would be time later for explanations, so I let the matter drop. Besides, I had plenty of things to account for myself, not the least of which was the broken oath and the fact that I'd never gone back for her.

"You'll have to learn to control your magic better than that," Angie said with a impish smile, referring to the unintentional temperature spike.

"That might be easier said than done," I said, giving her a wink.

"I missed you so much!" She hugged me tightly.

It was a tremendous relief that she had accepted me so readily, with the broken oath still unexplained between us.

"I know we have a lot to talk about, but…"

She nodded. "It will keep until later."

"Yeah, like when nobody's trying to kill us," a weak voice said.

"Dermot!" Conall bolted over to a couch, upon which was sprawled our lost water elementalist. Duncan and I were not far behind. The redhead was pale, more so than usual, and his eyes were dull. His vulnerable appearance made him look even younger than his seventeen years. Seeing Seth mortally wounded was one thing – he was an adult and a fully-trained warrior. Seeing Dermot that way was something else. He was a seventeen-year-old kid who might not make it to eighteen because I hadn't been watching him closely enough.

A kid whose mother might suffer yet another grievous loss.

A kid whose friends' hearts would be so much darker without the light of his enthusiasm for life and his gift for making people laugh.

A kid whose world would suffer for lack of his skill with elemental water.

"I'm fine," he said, chest heaving. "I'm just out of magic," he said, closing his eyes. "*And* shotgun shells."

I couldn't help but chuckle even though my eyes were burning and my vision blurred. He looked terrible.

"I'm no healer, but I think he's bleeding internally," Niall murmured. With a worried frown, Angie nodded agreement.

"Luckily, we have the best healer in the world with us," Conall said, squeezing Dermot's shoulder. "Stay with us, buddy." The water elementalist didn't answer. "Duncan, do something!"

"Move." The earth druid ran his fingers lightly over Dermot's chest and abdomen and began listing off the damage. "The right side is undamaged, but the left…" He shook his head. "Some ribs are broken, but the lung's not punctured." He pushed up Dermot's shirt to reveal a huge purple bruise that covered his lower ribs and upper abdomen. "I think his spleen might be ruptured, but I need to see inside to fix it. Davis, give me your skinning knife."

"You're going to cut him open with *that*?" Conall said as I handed over the razor-sharp blade I used both for skinning animals and filleting fish.

"It's the sharpest one I have," I said.

"I don't care how sharp it is! He'll get an infection!"

"He won't live long enough to *get* an infection if I can't stop the bleeding," the earth druid said tightly. "I need light."

I created a small, brilliant yellow fireball to illuminate the area, and Angie cast a trio of spirit orbs into the air. Dermot looked even worse in the light than he had in the dark.

"Why can't you just heal him from the outside like you've done with everybody else?" the Norseman demanded.

"Internal injuries are different!" Duncan snapped. "I don't know what a spleen looks like! I don't even know if it *is* his spleen! I need to *see* what's wrong to fix it!"

"Come on," Angie said, taking Conall by the hand. "Let him work." He resisted for a few moments, but she spoke to him quietly until the angry spirit magic in his eyes faded.

Tension riding his shoulders, Duncan sliced open Dermot's abdomen just below his left ribs. Dark blood poured out, running over the leather couch cushions and onto the floor. The earth druid pried the incision apart, peering intently into the wound.

"Hold that," he said. "Wide as you can." I did as instructed while he poked around in the wound. He pressed deep inside until bright red blood began to show and heaved a sigh of relief. "I found it." The fresh bleeding stopped almost immediately, and he pushed around on Dermot's abdomen until he'd removed most of the dark blood. "You can let go."

I watched as the wound edges, held in alignment between Duncan's hands, sealed themselves together. The broken ribs rippled beneath the water elementalist's flesh and snapped back into place.

"He needs an infusion of spirit," Duncan said to Angie.

Leaving Conall's side, she nodded and placed a hand on Dermot's forehead while I used a towel to wipe the blood off his skin and mop it off the floor. Pulling a crocheted blanket off the back of the couch, I tucked it around him to keep him warm. I sat back on my heels, staring at Dermot's blood on my shaking hands and trying to breathe through lungs that did not seem to want to accept air. Until that moment, I never appreciated how hard it must be for a healer to repair a severe injury on those he knew – especially when failure meant the death of a friend. Duncan had healed me time and again, and I'd never once thought about what it must have cost him.

Angie placed a comforting hand on my arm. "He'll be all right," she said.

"I know."

"He's special to you?"

"Yeah." I nodded. "He's also Arrie Stoddard's son."

Her features registered surprise, and she ran affectionate fingers through his shaggy red hair. "She'll be happy to see him again."

I nodded again. "I'm going to go clean up."

Duncan had found a pitcher and washbasin and was finishing wiping his fingers clean when I approached. "Here," he said, picking up the pitcher. "Wash your hands."

"I need to apologize," I said, as he rinsed cold water over them.

"For what?" He did not look up.

"For putting you through this so many times," I said.

He said nothing and handed me a towel before giving my shoulder a comforting squeeze. I could well understand why he'd taken refuge in the earth mother after Watson; just then I felt like burying myself deep and never coming out.

"Mother Oyá..." Angie murmured. "Somehow he managed not only to deplete his Well but also..." She trailed off, frowning.

"What?" Conall asked.

"I think he somehow donated his life force to fuel his elemental ability beyond its natural capacity," she said. "He must have done it trying to get away."

Seth and I exchanged an uneasy look.

"He was trying to help us escape," said Seth.

"No, he wasn't!" the Norseman snapped. "Don't lie for me." He shook his head. "He wasn't defending *us*. He was defending *me* when I went berserk. It's *my* fault he's hurt."

"We've all been there," I said, thinking of the moments when I had literally lost myself to the heat of battle. As a direct result of my inattention or bad decisions, nearly every one of the Finns had suffered grave injury, and Weylin was dead. "It's not your fault."

"I'm going to give him an infusion of my own elemental water, too," Angie said. "I think it'll help bring him around sooner."

"There's no rush," the air druid replied, looking out a north-facing window. "We're surrounded, but the three of us should be able to maintain an air shield at least until morning."

Tucking the blanket more snugly around Dermot, Angie looked up with a puzzled expression. "'The three of us'?"

"Yes," Seth replied. "You, me, and Conall."

"But Conall doesn't..." She trailed off as the Norseman produced a spirit orb, and her features lit up with delight. "Your magic's been restored!"

"Less than an hour ago, and I've no idea why."

"It would seem that the Norse gods respond positively to mortals who scream curses at them about reciprocity and debts of blood and honor while in a berserker rage," Seth said drily.

Conall had the decency to look chagrined.

"Of course," continued the air druid, "nearly ending up in Valhalla might have had something to do with it as well."

"If almost dying is truly a catalyst, then mine would have been restored as well," Niall said, pointing at the patch over his eye.

Recalling the story Iriana had told about Darryn's treachery and Orion's mad rampage, I looked him over carefully for the first time since entering the building. Where his shirt was open at the throat, a mass of scar tissue the width of a longsword's blade rippled at the juncture of neck and shoulder. Someone had gone for the jugular and missed. A thin scar cut through his left eyebrow, disappearing beneath the patch over his left eye and reappearing to carve a furrow in his cheek. The backs of his hands were scarred, and the fourth and fifth fingers of his left hand were missing. The only thing that looked the same about him was his long, platinum blond hair, pulled back in a ponytail that hung between his shoulderblades.

"It sounds to me like you were blocked rather than altered," Niall said, naked envy on his face.

"I wasn't," Conall replied. "You of all people should know better than that."

"Perhaps you deceived everyone just as Lin and Wolfric did."

"Are you calling me a liar?" Conall asked softly, the spirit orb in his hand glowing more brightly. In the past, such an accusation would have sent him into a fury that would have resulted in a fistfight at the very least.

"Like mother, like son," Niall said bitterly. "It wouldn't surprise me if everyone else's son was altered while that two-faced, conniving bitch placed only a block on her own."

"*I have no mother*," Conall snarled, hand moving to the hilt of his sword. Moments later, he extinguished the orb and took his hand off the hilt with visible effort. I wondered if the only thing keeping him from violence was the knowledge that a fight between a druid and a null was unfair and therefore dishonorable.

"Does it matter whether Conall was blocked or altered?" Angie said. "He didn't do either one to himself."

"He could have hidden it from you," Niall said.

She faced him with a solemn expression. "I swear by my ancestors that I have never seen him channel more than a spark of spirit or a puff of air."

"You don't know everything about Conall just because he was the first one picked to be your chosen," Niall shot back.

"No, I know everything about Conall because he is my *milk brother* and we were raised together!" Angie countered. "He had about as much chance hiding magic from me as Duncan did!"

While I'd known that Angie's mother had died shortly after giving birth, I had never considered who might have nursed her. No wonder she'd been so glad to see Conall. He was her brother in every way but blood.

"Why would you even bring that up?" she snapped.

"Because he wants everyone to doubt me," Conall said tightly.

"Just clearing the air," Niall shot back. "Seeing as how you're not a liar. Lies of omission count, you know."

"Just because Sebrina thought she could pick a partner for me doesn't mean that either of you were truly my chosen," Angie snapped. "It can't be a lie of omission if it were never true."

"Everyone in the grove thought it was true, so for all intents and purposes, it *was* true," Conall said. "But that's not what he's talking about."

Niall scowled at me. "Does it not bother you that you ride with a man who is less than honest with you? You do not know whose blood runs through his veins!"

Conall's sword flashed and was at Niall's throat in a heartbeat.

"I swear by Odin's missing eye, if you utter one more word on the matter—"

"What can you do to me that has not already been done?" Niall sneered at him.

"I can finish what Darryn and Orion started!" Conall growled.

Niall leaned into the blade. "Do what you will. I do not fear death when all that lies before me is a useless life devoid of magic and purpose."

Angie's urgent look clearly said that she wanted me to intervene.

"All right, everybody settle down," I said. "We'll never get out of here alive if we start mistrusting one another."

"Some do not deserve to be trusted," said Niall.

I sighed. Fatigue had enfolded me like a heavy blanket. We'd been traveling hard and fighting harder since early morning, in a string of days filled with long rides, intense battles, and nights of little sleep. We hadn't eaten since breakfast, and all our supplies were in the saddlebags on horses that were probably miles away by now.

"I'm too damned tired to care about your death wish *or* Conall's lineage. I don't give a shit if Sebrina Silvermist is his mother. I just want to get some sleep."

Angie's eyes went wide while Niall and Conall slowly turned their heads toward me in unison. Seth folded his arms across his chest and began intently examining the ceiling. Duncan, who had

586

been cleaning and oiling his sword, paused and gave me a significant glance.

Oh.

"Yet another thing that everybody knew but me." I said with a shrug. "I still don't care," I told Conall.

He sheathed his sword. "You don't care."

"No."

"The woman who gave me life had you beaten within an inch of your life, and you don't care."

"Well, I feel bad that you had to suckle at that particular poisoned tit, but other than that, no."

"Hey, so did I!" Angie said, clearly perturbed.

"Yes, but it saved your life and ruined his."

From their matching flummoxed expressions, it was clear that neither of them had considered the matter in that light.

"You're only saying that to please Angelina," Niall said angrily.

"No, I'm saying that because Conall has proven his loyalty a hundred times over. He is my friend, and I trust him," I said. "You're just angry because his magic was restored and yours wasn't. Stop acting like a child."

"I have a right to be angry!" Niall shouted. "I, too, was denied my birthright!"

"Yet he has given up his anger and resentment, whereas you have not," I replied. "Adults don't allow children to play with fire. Perhaps the gods are waiting for you to grow up and become a man before they return your gift to you."

Niall went for his shotgun, but it fell to the floor when he was slammed against the wall and held there by an invisible hand.

"Release me!" he demanded, struggling uselessly.

Seth strode across the room to where he held Niall prisoner. "I will release you when you are calm," he said.

"You will release me *now*!"

"I would like to do so, but unfortunately you have threatened two druids who have come into their magic relatively recently," Seth replied. "And while both Davis and Conall are capable of raising a defense, each is far more likely to respond to violence with violence."

"Hey, I have better control than that," I protested.

"Says the man who treated us to a sauna earlier," Conall said.

I frowned, concerned that Angie might think I was completely ruled by elemental fire. While that might be true on occasion, those occasions were rare. Or they would be, if I wasn't in the middle of a war.

Seth continued. "As you said, Davis, you are tired – as we all are – and fatigue is known to impair both skill and judgement."

"Who are you?" Niall asked, calmer but still challenging.

"Seth Starseeker."

Niall raised his chin, his one eye narrowing. "Don't you mean Shitozaki?"

"For reasons that should be obvious, my mother decided I would carry her family name," Seth replied. "If you give me your word that you will refrain from violence, I will release you."

Several long seconds passed, and I wondered if our air druid would have to hold him there all night.

"Fine," Niall said through gritted teeth. "You have my word."

That would have been good enough for me, but Seth seemed to expect something more. A full minute passed before Niall relented: "In the names of Brighid and Lugh of the Long Hand, and of all the Tuatha de Danaan, I swear I will do no harm to anyone present. May the sky fall upon me, the sea drown me, and the earth swallow me whole if I break faith with you."

"Very well." Seth released him gently to the floor. Niall grabbed his shotgun and holstered it. "Aristotle wrote that patience is bitter, but its fruit is sweet. Do not give in to despair."

"You're assuming it will eventually happen to me as well," Niall replied with a grimace. He collapsed in a chair with a defeated expression, the anger in his remaining eye wilting away.

"You should demand it of your gods like I did," Conall said.

Like Dermot, Duncan, and I, Niall was of the Celtic hearth culture that honored Danu, Brighid, Dagda, Manannán mac Lir, Lugh of the Long Hand, Donn the Lord of the Dead... and the Morrigan, Queen of Battle.

"I'm not so sure that's a good idea," I said, thinking of the Morrigan's blood red lips and merciless ice blue eyes. Duncan's skeptical expression indicated he agreed.

"Regardless of the manner in which it might occur, logic would suggest that what happens to one can happen to all," Seth said. "Besides, as Conall was the first to lose his magic, it is only right that he be the first to have it restored to him."

"I'd give it up right now if it would help Dermot get better," Conall said, pulling up a chair to sit beside the sleeping water elementalist.

"He will be well," Duncan said, giving the Norseman's shoulder a squeeze before gracefully settling into the other armchair beside the couch.

"We would all do well to rest while we can," Seth suggested.

"Teach me how to shield the room and I'll take first watch," Conall offered. "I can't sleep now, anyway."

"Focus on making it the same thickness as the ones you made outside. The important thing to remember is that air molecules are widely spaced apart. So in order to make something as solid as a shield, you need a lot of them," the air druid said. "Rather than holding it in midair, however, you just press it against the walls. It's easier that way."

"I never even thought about making a square shield."

"It can be any shape you want it to be." Seth paused. "Just remember to draw the air from *outside* when you condense it. Otherwise, you'll create a vacuum that will kill or severely injure everyone in the room."

Conall nodded. "Good to know."

"You didn't already know that?" Niall said, looking horrified.

"How could he?" Seth gave him a puzzled frown. "His gift was restored less than an hour ago."

Appalled, Niall gestured at Seth. "And you're going to let him cast a shield?"

"He has to learn sometime."

"I think I'd rather be gunned down by bandits."

I stopped paying attention to their conversation when Angie moved to speak with Duncan. The earth druid took a deep breath, as though steeling himself for a confrontation.

"I have something to say before you talk to Duncan," I said, stepping between them. "He's the reason I'm alive and is not to blame for my continued absence. He may have taken me to Sanctuary, but no one made me stay. I made that choice of my own free will."

"My father exerted pressure on you to stay," said Seth from

across the room. "I know he did. Every time you mentioned going back for your chosen, he talked you out of it."

"It was still my choice," I said, forcing myself to hold her gaze. "I alone bear the responsibility for your continued suffering. If you have any feelings of anger and betrayal, they should not be directed at anyone but me."

"Angry? At you?" she asked, giving me an incredulous look. "What right would I have in blaming you? What would I be if I felt that way?"

"Human," I said.

After a moment's consideration, she nodded. "That we are," she said. Taking a seat on the ottoman in front of Duncan's chair, she reached for his hands in a gesture of amity. "I am glad to find you well, cousin."

"It is good to see you, too," he replied, eyeing her warily.

"I admit, I *was* furious when I found out that you've been with him all this time," she continued. "But I've come to realize that you were right about Sebrina. You warned me about the danger, but I did not listen. You had the wisdom and courage that I lacked, and I cannot thank you enough for saving his life."

Duncan was speechless for several seconds. When he finally found his tongue, he said, "Sometimes we want things to be a certain way so badly that we fail to see situations as they truly are." He gave her a rueful smile. "We are Everlights, Angelina, and so are accustomed to privilege. We are used to having our own way and getting most everything we want – and so we do not always recognize the futility of pursuing those wants."

"That's the gods' own truth," she said, looking a bit sheepish.

"I apologize if my actions caused you anguish," he said. "That was not my intent."

"It was my own mistakes which caused me pain," she said. "Your actions kept me from far greater sorrow. For that, I can never repay you."

"We are family. There are no debts between us."

They hugged each other tightly, and neither had dry eyes when they separated.

"You look a wild man," Angie said, affectionately scrubbing her knuckles in his rough beard. "I don't think even your father would recognize you."

Duncan gave her a wan smile. Padraig had been a touchy subject with him since we'd left the grove, but I'd never been able to pry the reason out of him.

"We've all changed a lot in the last couple of months," I said.

Angie looked over the members of my pentacle, her gaze including the still-unconscious Dermot.

"You risked so much for me," she said. "All of you."

Seth left off instructing Conall and settled in the chair across from Duncan. "In all fairness, he did try to make us stay behind."

"Twice," the new triple threat added.

"And you came anyway?" she asked.

"Of course," Conall replied. "What are friends for?"

Chapter 35 – Hard Water

Water, taken in moderation, cannot hurt anybody.
~ Mark Twain ~

"*Manannán mac Lir!*"

I jerked awake to see Dermot sit bolt upright and grab his side. A quick glance around the room revealed Conall sleeping in the big chair behind the desk with his feet propped up on it, Niall wrapped in a blanket slumbering in a far corner, and Angie awake and maintaining the air shield. Still asleep in their armchairs, Duncan and Seth never stirred. There had been no attack during the night, but it wasn't surprising that the Republic forces hadn't wasted the bullets. All they had to do was wait us out.

Angie walked over to Dermot to check on him.

"Are you all right?" she whispered.

"Yeah, now that my stomach doesn't hurt anymore." He eyed her warily. "Do I know you?"

"I'm Angie. I was here when the soldiers dragged you in last night."

The water elementalist peered around her. "Everybody is sleeping so I guess that means you're not one of the bad girls."

Angie's lips twisted in an effort to hide her amusement.

"Sebrina's acolytes fled shortly afterward."

He frowned. "I don't remember that."

"The Republic soldiers beat you up pretty badly, but Duncan healed you last night." After a pause, she continued: "I'm pretty sure you'd have died if he hadn't."

"He's brought almost everybody else back from the brink of death," Dermot said. "I guess it was my turn." He tried to stand and then sank back down again, his face as white as new-fallen snow.

"Are you all right?" Angie said.

"Just dizzy."

"You lost a lot of blood. Maybe you should take it slow."

"We're surrounded by an entire city of people who want to murder us," he replied. "We don't have time for me to take it slow." He stayed put, however.

"If it means the difference between you leaving under your own power or being carried, we have time," she said.

"Especially since we lost our horses."

"If they're druid horses, they won't have gone far."

"Maybe Duncan or Davis can do a *seeking* and find them," he said.

"That's a very good idea. We'll have to ask them when they wake up."

The room was grey with the winter dawn's light, so I closed my eyes again, only to be roused by their conversation what seemed like a few minutes later. If the sun's brightness was any indication, an hour or two had passed.

"What are you looking for?" I heard Angie ask.

"Water," he said.

"I can get you a drink if you're thirsty."

"I'm a water elementalist," Dermot said. "I can get my own water." Somehow, he was up and rummaging around in the next room.

"Ah-*ha*! I knew there was a water tank around here somewhere," he said. Through the doorway, I could see him uncork the two large waterskins that hung on his back harness, then grabbed the tank's hose and began refilling them. I wasn't sure if he was filling them like that because his magic was still low, or because it was expedient.

"I could have told you that," Angie replied.

"Oh, are you a water elementalist, too?" he asked.

"It's one of my elements, yes."

He turned his attention from the water tank to take a good, long look at her. "What did you say your name was again?"

"Angie."

"Wait… Aren't you Davis' chosen?"

"Indeed I am." I couldn't see her face, but I could hear the smile in her voice.

He whistled. "Now I understand why Davis won't sleep with anybody else." He held up a hand. "Don't get me wrong – I still think he's crazy because you guys have been apart for a *really* long time – but I understand."

"Are you good friends with him?"

"Aye, we're friends – the five of us, I mean," he said, corking the skins again. He reached for the canteen hanging at his left hip and began to fill it. Once it was full, he reached for the one that should have been on the right – the one that I'd found in the mud – and discovered something else missing as well.

"My sword!" Dermot cried. "It's gone!"

There would be no more sleep after that. I rose and approached them, rolling my shoulders to loosen tight muscles. Angie slipped an arm around my waist and smiled at me.

"Did you notice if he had it last night when they brought him in?" I asked Angie.

She winced, knowing the value of a good blade. "I'm sorry, Dermot. Your scabbard was empty."

"That sword belonged to my dad! I have to get it back!" the water elementalist cried, bolting for the door and flinging it open before I could stop him. An array of Republic soldiers standing in the yard halted his headlong rush.

"Well, lookie here! The wolf pups have finally decided to leave their den!" called one. Perched atop the roof of the building across the street, he manned a multi-barreled gun mounted on a tripod. I'd only seen its like in books but recognized it as a machine gun. If the gunner focused its fire on a specific target, it could chew through even one of Seth's air shields in seconds. A quick look around revealed several such rapid-fire weapons mounted on the rooftops of various buildings. We were lucky they hadn't brought them into play the night before.

A stocky bandit sauntered forward and leered at the young water elementalist. On his hip was Dermot's sword, hanging naked from the man's belt.

"A bunch of little bitches is more like it," he taunted.

594

"Give me back my father's sword, you fucking asshole!" Dermot yelled.

"Why don't you just come and get it, big man?" The man put his hands on his hips and grinned. He was as tall as Seth and looked fifty pounds heavier; a skinny seventeen-year-old kid stood no chance against him.

"I'll get it," I said, taking a step forward. Dermot stopped me, the back of his hand thumping against my chest.

"No." He lowered his head like a charging bull, a thick lock of tousled red hair fell over his bruised and swollen eye. "I'll get it myself." He thumbed the corks out of the canteens on his back and stood in the doorway like a gunslinger.

"Last warning," Dermot said. "Give it back."

The bandit laughed, his hundred-plus compatriots joining in.

"I usually just give one warning," I murmured.

"Good policy," he said.

Twin streams of water shot out of the canteens and plunged through the man's chest. They held him there for a single frozen moment of silence as he gasped for breath and his comrades watched in uncomprehending shock. When Dermot jerked the water spears out, great gouts of blood poured out onto the ground, followed by the man's corpse. One wrapped around the hilt of Dermot's sword and brought it back, slipping it neatly into his scabbard. Our enemies' laughter became angry swearing and alarmed exclamations, followed by the shouting of orders and the chambering of rounds.

Igniting a hasty fire shield to cover our retreat, I jerked the water elementalist inside. Angie had the door shut and the room shielded by the time the thunder of gunfire began hammering the exterior walls of our shelter. Something crashed to the floor behind me, and I spun about to find Conall on his feet with his chair overturned on the floor behind him. Above it was a scorch mark on the ceiling from the spirit bolt loosed when he was startled awake. Niall was scrambling for his shotgun while a bleary-eyed Seth was up and bolstering Angie's shield with one of his own. The gunfire lasted only a few seconds, but the door was chewed to bits.

"I found your other canteen," I told Dermot, pulling it from one coat pocket and a spool of leather lacing from another. "Hold still, and I'll tie it back on your belt."

Duncan stretched and yawned. "Feeling better?" he asked Dermot.

"I do! Thanks for healing me! What was wrong with my belly?"

"Ruptured spleen," the earth druid replied. "I had to cut you open to fix it."

"Whoa, really?"

"Yes, and he made *me* help," I grumbled. "So stay out of trouble. I don't *ever* want to see your guts again."

"You saw my *guts*?" He tugged at his shirt and pulled it up to look at his abdomen. His wriggling messed up my attempts to refasten the waterskin, and it flopped to the floor.

"You didn't leave a scar?" he complained when he saw no trace of the surgery. "Women love a rugged man with scars!"

"I could cut you open again."

"Duncan!" said Angie, appalled. He chuckled.

"You have a black eye," Conall said. "I'm sure they'll like that, too."

"I guess." Dermot wore a hangdog expression.

"There, you're all set," I said, tying the last knot attaching the canteen to the right side of his belt. He perked up and returned to the side room to fill it.

"There's nothing like waking up to gunfire," Seth said. "I feel like I could sleep for a week."

So did I. Whatever Laiken had done to us with her spirit magic, the effects had worn off. I wasn't sure what was worse, the sore muscles or the extreme fatigue. It looked like several weeks of hard riding and waging war were starting to take their toll.

Seth yawned hugely and stretched. "What happened?"

I told him. He frowned at the water elementalist. "There's no point in filling your bags if you've no magic left."

"I have plenty of magic," Dermot said, appearing a bit puzzled by the air druid's statement.

"I thought you said he was tapped out last night," I said to Angie.

"He was," she replied.

"*Was* seems to be the operative word," Conall said, studying the young water elementalist with a keen eye.

"Well, I'm full up today," Dermot said.

Seth frowned. "The last time you emptied your Well, it took four days to be renewed."

"Yes, but a druid's Well fills much more quickly than that of an elementalist," said Conall.

Angie gave him a skeptical look. "He's much too young to be a full druid."

"So was I," said Duncan.

"I'm a druid?" Dermot's face lit up with realization. "I'm a druid!" He danced around the room, water bags flopping. "I'm a druid! I'm a druid! I'm a druid! I'm a druid!"

"I'm proud of you, Dermot." Conall, smiled affectionately at him. "You're going to be a great water druid."

Dermot beamed, but his smile faded quickly. "But it's so unfair."

"What is?" Conall asked.

"I got my full magic early, and you've never had any at all."

"That's okay," said Conall. "I've got a surprise for you."

"What?"

"This." From behind his back, Conall produced a palm-sized spirit orb. For a second, Dermot gaped at it like he'd never seen one before, his eyes widening to comical proportions.

"You got magic!" the water druid crowed. He clapped his hands excitedly. "I'm gonna call you zinger!"

"I'll zap you every time you do it, too, water boy. Wolfric may take that 'fireballer' bullshit, but don't think for one minute that I will," Conall threatened, but he was smiling when he said it.

"Wolfric!?" Angie exclaimed. "Are he and Onóra with you?"

"He is," I said. "She's in Ward. We found them about a month and a half ago."

"Thank the gods," Niall said, exhaling in relief. "It probably sounds ridiculous, but I've worried about them."

"Wolfric did all right," I said.

"He still has a stick up his ass, though," said Conall.

Niall snorted. "He wouldn't be a Rask if he didn't."

"That's the gods' own truth," Conall agreed.

"However in the world did you find them?" Angie asked.

"*That* is a long story, and one that will have to wait for another time," Seth interrupted. "We need to escape the 'Ville as quickly as possible and return to Ward. The *Circitorium Fati* should have come down last night, and the High Priest and Priestess will be renewing it *tonight* in the full dark of the new moon."

"The what?" Angie asked.

"The *Circitorium Fati* is the magical barrier that Rhiannon raised around Ward to protect the coven members," I said. "She said it means *veil of doom* or *curtain of death*."

"We'll never get back to Ward in time without our horses," Conall said. "We might as well go back to Lone Oak."

"One thing at a time," I said. "Let's get out of here first."

"Wait," Angie said. "Let me give you a boost."

She took my hands, and a tingle ran up my arms and throughout my body. All my fatigue washed away in the wake of her spirit magic and energized me, just like when Laiken Warner had touched me yesterday. She moved around the room, touching each person in turn.

"Wow!" Dermot exclaimed. "I hope my chosen has some spirit magic because that shit is *amazing!*"

"Everybody ready?" I asked, receiving eager affirmatives from the members of my pentacle.

"Now we just have to survive getting out the building," Niall said, his expression foreboding.

"I got this." Dermot started for the door, moving easily in spite of what had to be at least twenty extra pounds of water in his canteens. He might have been young and skinny, but he was tough and possessed a wiry strength.

"Can you make me an air shield?" he asked Angie.

She smiled. "I certainly can!"

"Volcanic!" he said. "Cover me while I clear the street."

Niall let out a sound that was half-snort, half-laugh.

"What's so funny?" The serious expression had returned to the water elementalist's face.

"You can't use elemental water for combat," Niall said. "Everybody knows that."

Dermot gave him a cocky grin, uncorked all four water bags, and jerked the tattered door open. He threw his arms out, fingers splayed, as though inviting the street full of Republic soldiers to come inside. Before the enemy could turn and shoot, however, twin jets of water burst from the canteens on his back. Each one split into half a dozen transparent tentacles that swarmed over them. Writhing like a nest of snakes, the multiple appendages lashed out and scooped up enemies, sometimes two and three at a time, and flung them screaming over buildings and trees. The air shield seemed to pose no trouble for the water druid; the crystalline feelers merely found their way around to its edges before snaking onward to their deadly mission.

Seconds later, loud, rapid gunfire pulsed through the air, and he splashed a gallon of water from his leg bags across the back of Angie's air shield, reinforcing it just in time. She flinched as her shield splintered and fell apart, but the turtle shell held fast against the multitude of rounds furiously pounding on it. Growing thicker, it cracked and chipped and repaired itself over and over under the assault of the Gatling gun.

The appendages from the canteens on his back merged into one, forming two great serpents that stretched out, undulating as they twined about the big gun with the spinning barrels sitting atop the building opposite our position. They lifted the still-firing gun and its operator, holding them dangling over the massed Republic defenders crammed between the two buildings. The gunner screamed in terror, clutching at the Gatling gun. He held tight to the trigger, heedless of the fact that he was raining death upon his own people. The rapid-fire weapon mowed them down as only a gun firing two hundred rounds a minute can. When the thing ran out of bullets, the twin serpents slammed the gun down, smashing it to bits, and moved on to the next one.

Once the machine guns were no longer a threat, Dermot dropped his water shell and turned all the hydra-like tentacles to keeping the remaining defenders busy. Liquid projections darted among the fleeing forces in rapid succession, spearing this one and that until the ground was covered with corpses lying in half-melted, bloody snow.

Finished with his bloody handiwork, Dermot summoned the tentacles back into their bags. He turned around to face Niall Ashcroft with a smug smile, twirling a length of water as though it were a rope.

"Like Davis' dad always says: Just because people think something is true, that doesn't mean it is."

* * *

We headed north but had only made it a couple hundred yards before Duncan announced that more enemies were coming from the south and west. Thankfully, they arrived in smaller numbers than before – only two raid groups this time. As soon as Seth raised a protective dome, rifle rounds ricocheted off its smooth surface. The pinging increased in volume and intensity, like a spring rain that begins as sprinkles and progresses rapidly to a downpour.

"Where's the dragon?" Conall asked.

"The what?" Angie said.

"Somewhere south of here."

"Why in Hel's name did you send it away?" he shouted over the hailstorm of metal.

"Because the shadow figure told me to!" I replied without thinking.

"The what?" Seth asked.

"It was more of a who." I paused, momentarily perplexed and trying to remember. Time and details became jumbled when I was mesmerized. "He said he was a friend, but it wasn't anyone I remember ever meeting." Angie frowned slightly, looking at me askance.

Conall scowled and shook his head disparagingly.

Dermot frowned at him. "Don't be an ass. Davis can't help it when he gets lost in the fire."

I couldn't help but hope she didn't realize what he was talking about, but her look of alarm said that she was aware of how serious it was when a druid became enthralled by elemental fire. Niall looked equally uncomfortable, and I remembered that his mother was also a fire druid.

"Look, it was incinerating everything in sight, and I didn't know where Dermot and Angie were!" I said, feeling defensive.

"I'm sorry, did you say 'dragon'?" Niall asked.

"Speaking of incinerating everything in sight," said Conall. "How about you call it back and do some more of that to the bad guys trying to kill us right now?"

"I already have!" I snapped, exasperated.

Angie broke in. "What are you talking about? A dragon?"

"It's Davis' fetch," he replied.

"A fetch will be of no use!" Angie said, rolling her eyes. "A spirit animal cannot affect the natural world. You know that!"

"Whatever you say," Conall smirked at her.

"We don't have time to wait for the dragon," the air druid warned. "The dome is failing. We need to move!"

"Don't worry, Seth, I've got your back!" Dermot directed his water upwards, coating the underside of the air dome with water. "This is going to be the best water shell ever! I wonder how thick I can make it?"

Seth dropped his shield as our view of the outer world became wavy and distorted, growing to a thickness of a few inches. Bullets struck the water shell, marking it with cracks and pockmarks which were rapidly smoothed over and filled out.

"This is amazing!" Angie exclaimed, running her hand over the turtle shell dome. "Where did you learn this?"

"I just thought it up," Dermot replied. "It was when we were playing around with different shields. Davis was trying to make one out of fire."

"All right, people," I said, ending that conversational thread before it could unravel me further in Angie's eyes. "The dragon's almost here, but the enemy is too close to us for it to flame them." I turned to my chosen. "I need you to help shield."

"I can fight!" she insisted.

"We noticed," Seth said, meaning our near-death experience with her spirit magic the day before. "Speaking of, can you repeat that spell?"

"The chain lightning? Of course." She paused. "Better to do it under an air shield, though. Spirit magic might travel though even hardened water. And I'll need a hole at the top."

"Conall, be ready to reinforce or replace the dome as necessary," I said.

He gave me a sharp nod. "Understood."

Seth covered the water dome with one of air, while Dermot siphoned the water back into his canteens.

"Will you be able to run with those?" I asked.

"Sure," he said. "Maybe not very fast, but I can run."

"We need to move fast. Empty the leg bags and keep the ones on your back," I said. "And don't give me that look. There's more than enough snow and ice out there to keep you entertained."

"Everyone cover your eyes," Angie ordered.

The hair on the back of my neck rose as the dome filled with static electricity and the smell of ozone. In spite of my closed eyes, I could still see a ball of dazzling blue-white light grow, illuminating the lidded darkness. The light burned upward in a beam, the light becoming so bright that I had to squeeze my eyes shut. They watered painfully even after I covered them with my hands, and I pulled the hood of my coat down over my face.

"It's safe to look now," she said. "You can drop the shield."

Freezing wind brushed my hot cheeks; the air dome was gone. I blinked rapidly to erase the afterimages created by her brilliant light while my eyes adjusted to the normal wintry light. We stood alone in the middle of the dirt road, surrounded by a hundred or so corpses killed by chain lightning. Angie stared straight ahead, as though afraid to see the reaction on any of our faces. The lines of her body were fraught with tension.

Dermot whistled. "Wow, you're really good at this."

"Taking lives isn't something to be celebrated," she said quietly. "Especially not with magic."

"Oh, I know," he said. "All I meant was that you didn't kill all the plants and trees, too. When Davis takes out that many bad guys all at once, and there's *nothing* left when *he's* finished."

As if on cue, the dragon soared overhead, its cinder-red wings spread wide to reveal a belly that had deepened in color from bright yellow to smouldering gold. Smoke streamed from its spiked reptilian head and billowed in a trail across the pale clouds of the winter sky.

Niall dove to the ground with a yell. Mouth hanging open, Angie tracked the dragon's flight as it passed over us in a gust of warm air. It arrived at the crossroads to the west at the same time as three more companies of Republic soldiers, come to reinforce their comrades. They began shooting at it, doing no harm whatsoever. The dragon banked in a tight circle, one wingtip just yards above their heads as its supple neck bent down in a graceful curve. It turned its head at an elegant angle, as if displaying its dangerous beauty for all to admire. Its jaws widened and it spewed a river of flame that enveloped them in bright incandescence. Still sailing along in that lazy, graceful turn, it flew in ever-widening circles, spreading the conflagration further.

Seeing the rest of us calmly watching and not screaming in

terror, Niall quickly climbed to his feet, looking sheepish.

"Dragon one, bandits zero," Dermot said.

Angie spun about and stared at Conall accusingly. "That's not a fetch! It can't be!"

"There is no doubt, cousin," Duncan said. "We all saw him make it."

Dermot nodded enthusiastic agreement. "It was a lion before that, but he changed it to a dragon."

"The transformation *was* rather startling," Seth commented. "Quite unforgettable."

Angie wasn't letting Conall off the hook, however. "I can't believe you let him make a fetch the size of a lion, much less a dragon!"

"First off, it's *Duncan* you need to be yelling at, because he's the one who taught him how to make it," he said. "Secondly, have you ever tried to tell that man he can't do something? It doesn't go over well."

Angie was taken aback for a moment. Then she chuckled ruefully and said, "Yes, I have, and no, it doesn't."

"The dragon was an *accident*," I said. "I didn't mean to make it that big. I know full druids are not supposed to make spirit animals – especially not big ones – but I needed something that could fly so I could find you."

She gave me a soft smile, warm affection in her eyes. I didn't know how she could be irritated with Conall for "allowing" me to make a big fetch but feel tenderly toward me for making it, but I was grateful all the same.

"We should get moving," I said, jogging across the wide track and into the shelter of some nearby trees. It was tempting to follow the road due east, for it would take us back to the downed eastern gate by the fastest route, but that meant crossing open territory and increased danger. I led the way north, heading into a forest whose pristine condition was a pleasant surprise.

"Don't get too far ahead of me," Angie called. "I want you close so I can shield when I need to."

Behind her, Seth raised an eyebrow at her insistence, but Iriana hadn't shown any signs of being demanding – yet.

Just you wait, I thought.

"Davis doesn't need a shield," Dermot said. "He has his own."

"Isn't earth a bit unwieldy when you're on the move?" she asked, picking her words carefully.

"It is," I said, suppressing a sigh. "He's not talking about earth."

"He has a fire shield." Dermot frowned at her. "I already told you that, remember?"

"There's no such thing as a fire shield," she said, trying not to sound condescending.

"There is now," said Conall.

"That's right. Because *we* invented it." They bumped fists.

"I don't understand," said Angie. "Why would you even need a fire shield if you have elementalists who can create one out of air or water?"

"Mostly because he won't stay behind them," said Seth.

"That and he kept getting shot," Duncan added.

I grimaced. I should have known there would be payback for making him worry so much.

"Wow, way to throw him to the wolves, guys," Dermot said. "Even I know better than to say something like that in front of *her.*"

Conall was uncharacteristically silent, watching us with a twinkle in his eye and a smirk on his lips.

"Dragons and fire shields," my chosen said, eyeing me thoughtfully. "Anything else I should know about?"

"Quite a bit, actually," I said, thinking of the Morrigan. "But for now we need to focus on getting out of here." While Angie accepted my decision, she was the only one.

"About last night and the dark figure," Seth said, pushing through low tree branches. The man was like a dog with a bone when he was fixated on a problem to be solved or a mystery to investigate. "Do you usually hallucinate when you're in thrall?"

"No," I said automatically, then thought about when the fire had enraptured me at Mayflower. "Well, maybe. Sometimes I see shapes in the fire."

"What kinds of shapes?"

"Knotwork designs and spirals. Salamanders. Fire-dancers. Phoenixes. Dragons." I sighed. "The faces of the gods."

Duncan frowned. "Which gods?"

"Brighid and the Dagda. Lugh of the Long Hand." *The*

Morrigan.

"Are you sure they weren't really there?" he pressed.

"Why would you ask that?" Angie demanded. "Of course they weren't really there!"

In my peripheral vision, I saw Dermot open his mouth and then shut it again. It was lucky that he'd held his tongue, for it saved him from Conall's fist, ready to deliver a sharp jab to his shoulder.

"Exactly what did you see?" Seth pressed.

"A man in a dark cloak," I said. "He wasn't a creature of elemental fire, I do know that."

"Are you sure he was a man and not one of the Shining Ones?" Duncan asked. Angie gave him a scornful look, as if he was an idiot for asking such a question.

"Well, no, since he was standing in the middle of a lake of elemental fire and I couldn't feel him through the earth," I said.

Again I explained what I had seen. Seth and Duncan exchanged a glance, and I knew they were thinking of how the Morrigan had appeared to me on Samhain.

"A shaman could appear solid but actually be sending out his spirit," Duncan said, delicately steering the conversation away from the dangerous topic of my recent close affiliation with the Phantom Queen.

"Can't the High Priestess do that, too?" asked Dermot.

"No," said Angie. "She walks on the astral plane but would be intangible and appear as a translucent form, if you could even see her at all."

"If he's a shaman, then he knows that the dragon is a manifestation of your spirit," said Seth. The expression on his face said: *Remember the prophecy.*

"What else could project an image like that?" I asked.

"A wizard? Maybe a sorcerer?" Niall shrugged.

"Wizards and sorcerers," I said. "Next you'll tell me necromancers are real."

Niall and Conall exchanged a look but said nothing.

Great.

"Maybe it's an animancer," Dermot said.

"What's that?"

"It's someone who can harness life energy, or even someone's

605

inner spirit after they die."

"In other words, a necromancer that lies to himself about the nature of his magic," Conall grumbled.

"You mean like a spirit elementalist?" Niall said, giving him a pointed look.

"No," the Norseman retorted scornfully. "Spirit druids are honest about the destructive nature of their element."

"It's not like that," the water elementalist protested. "A true animancer can create life, not just trap spirits and souls."

Almost as one, the members of my pentacle turned to look back at the dragon. It had left off circling the crossroads and was now laying down a line of fire along the east-west road to cover our flank. I'd never heard of animancy before, but it made me wonder about the dragon, too. It had been created from my own life force and the elements of earth and fire, and while it usually did what I wanted, there seemed to be resistance at times, as if it desired to be free. Or maybe that resistance merely reflected the divided aspects of my own will: the one that wanted to completely and utterly destroy the 'Ville, and the one that wanted to protect the lives of innocent people.

"In a way, healing and relieving pain with earth magic could be considered a form of animancy," Duncan said. I could have kissed him.

"Did this shadowy figure say anything else?" Seth asked.

"Yeah. He said my fetch is too big."

"It *is* too big," said Angie.

"It's a dragon. It's *supposed* to be big," Dermot said.

"Like anybody's ever even seen a dragon before," said Conall. "Now everybody's an expert all of a sudden."

"Oh, hey, speaking of big things…" Dermot said. "Remember the big water tower? The one where I made the *Dobhar-chú?*"

"How could we forget?" Seth said with a barely suppressed shudder. There was just something about bear-dog-seal water creatures with fangs and claws that the air druid found especially disturbing.

"You made a *Dobhar-chú?*" Niall said, looking as though he hoped the young water druid would admit to teasing. Between the talk of dragons, necromancers, and water monsters, it was a wonder his face had any color at all.

"I made a whole pack of 'em," Dermot said. "Anyway, it's really close – only half a mile south."

"That's too far and in the wrong direction," said Seth. "We need to go east."

"But it's my one true love!" he whined. "I dream about her luscious curves every single night!"

Angie giggled.

"Please don't encourage him," Seth muttered.

"We're not going that way, and the dragon probably destroyed it anyway," I said.

"Oh, well in that case…" the water elementalist said with a sly look. "There's another one about a quarter mile ahead, and it's even bigger."

Chapter 36 – Havoc

Cry 'Havoc,' and let slip the dogs of war!
~ William Shakespeare ~

We crossed a dirt track that was little more than a game trail before bounding downhill into a wide ditch and stopping at the bottom to let Angie catch her breath. While the rest of us were energized by her donation of spirit magic, she herself had received no benefit from it.

Duncan used the stop to perform a more thorough *seeking*, turning in a slow circle as if facing a distant horizon that only he could see. "Do you feel that?"

"All I feel is this stitch in my side," Angie wheezed, flopping back against the embankment.

Going down on one knee, I brushed aside a few inches of snow until I could touch the frozen ground. The barest of vibrations could be felt, but they were increasing in intensity.

"Stay here. I'm going to have a look," I said, climbing up the opposite embankment.

"You don't need to see!" the earth druid protested, scrambling up after me. "You can feel it!"

"Wait!" cried Angie as she hastened to follow.

"How far to the water tower?" I called to Dermot.

"Another hundred yards!"

I took off through the woods with the water elementalist at my heels. He quickly outpaced me, racing ahead through the trees. Seth caught up with me moments later, courtesy of his long stride,

608

while Conall and Niall kept pace with Angie. The forest gave way to a man-made clearing with not one, not two, but *three* gigantic water towers. They looked to be about fifty feet high and at least seventy feet in diameter. Each was easily twice the size of the first one we'd encountered in the southernmost part of the 'Ville, the birthplace of the *Dobhar-chú*.

"By the gods, who could have known there were three?" Dermot said when we had caught up to him. He was grinning like a maniac. "All that water and me a druid. What serendipity!"

I would have commented on his deception if the rumbling of the ground had not diverted my attention. "Stay here," I ordered. Grasping the rungs of a ladder bolted to the closest tower, I started to climb. The shaking intensified as I approached the top, but I gripped the metal more tightly and did not stop. Once I could see above the treetops, the tower offered a view of the northeast gate, set into the protective wall surrounding the 'Ville. It looked to be no more than a quarter of a mile away.

The frigid air cut straight through to my skin as though I were naked, but I forgot all about it as I discovered that we didn't need to go east. The northeastern gate was much closer and the territory between here and there more sparsely populated. Feeling bolstered by this revelation, I started to climb back down when I began to feel narrow-band vibrations crisscross the length and breadth of the 'Ville, seeming to come from all sides. I froze, trying to read them. They were no ordinary rumbles. Tightly focused temblors like that came from only one force: druid magic.

"What is it?" called Seth.

"It's the Finns!"

They seemed to be coming from each of the six gates – the earth druids from the other six pentacles, communicating for the sole purpose of coordinating an attack. After the flurry of vibration, the earth went completely still. There was nothing for several seconds, and realization struck – this was the calm before the storm.

"Davis, get down!" Duncan cried.

A shockwave hit before I had time to begin my descent and the ladder jerked loose with a screech of metal, nearly throwing me to my death. Angie's cry of alarm reached my ears as I hung on for dear life. The tower rocked ponderously back into place, allowing me to hook one leg around the ladder and grip one of the rungs with the crook of my arm. I pulled the spyglass from the inner breast pocket of my coat. Hampered by working mostly one-handed, I focused it on the northeastern gate. Snow slid from the top of the wall, and cracks emerged in the forbidding concrete, spreading rapidly east and west. It collapsed with a screech of twisting metal, followed by the roar of broken stone thudding to the ground. After another brief moment of stillness, the iron gateway fell slowly with a crash.

From both west and east came the sound of rocks cracking like thunder, followed by the shriek of rent metal. The western wall and its northwest gate were out of sight, but the eastern gate and what little remained of the wall Duncan and I had destroyed collapsed in a puff of snow and mist. I turned my attention to the south. By hanging off the ladder with my back pressed against the tower's icy metal, I could just make out where the southern wall rose out of the rubble of the southeast corner. Though I couldn't see much of the south wall and its gate because of the winter haze, snowfall, and billowing smoke from the still-smouldering crossroads and east-west thoroughfare, I could clearly feel the fracture of stone and concrete, followed by the faint groans of twisting iron.

The smoke reminded me that the dragon was still out there burning up the 'Ville and possibly endangering the Finns as they brought down the north, northwest, and western gates. I felt them destabilizing the ground beneath the bulwarks surrounding the 'Ville, bringing them tumbling down like giant dominoes. Starting back down the ladder, I sent the dragon on a fast flight over the remnants of the 'Ville's protective walls as a signal to the Finns that we were alive and had seen them.

Putting the lives of innocent people – the prisoners, the slaves, and even the children of the Republic – troubled me, but their safety was no longer in my hands, if indeed it had ever been. An image of Maeve's face when she said she'd run straight into the *Circitorium Fati* of her own volition before allowing them to capture her again came to mind.

Maybe Wolfric was right, and death *was* preferable to slavery.

Maybe those who had been forced into bondage inside the 'Ville felt the same.

As the city walls fell one by one, I realized that the other earth druids had deliberately started the destruction in the locations farthest from the area of densest population. They could give little warning without giving away their intent and exposing themselves to danger, but they were doing what they could. Collapsing the ramparts in this manner would prevent the Finns from getting trapped in a corner. It would also give any prisoners the opportunity to escape, while keeping our enemies off-balance because there was no way to anticipate the next direction of attack.

I headed down the ladder, skipping the last few rungs, and had just returned to earth when Siorus' pentacle arrived from the northeast gate. While I was happy to see them safe and sound, I was also furious that they'd risked their lives to come after us.

"What are you doing here?" I yelled. "You're supposed be in Ward!"

"Repairing Lone Oak's defenses took until after dark," Siorus replied. "It would have been too dangerous to leave then. One of the horses might have broken a leg."

"Then you should have ridden there at first light!" I snapped. "Either way, you shouldn't be *here*."

"The whole western sky glowed orange last night," said Madoc, backing up his chosen. "You wouldn't have been throwing around that much fire if you weren't in trouble."

"That doesn't mean I wanted you to come get into trouble with me!" I protested.

"We were worried about you, man," said Mohinder. "You can't be mad at us for wanting to make sure you were okay."

"Well, we didn't really think *you* were in any danger," Eian said. "Mostly we came to make sure everyone else was all right."

Siorus rolled his eyes, Mohinder threw his arms up in the air, and Madoc glared at the air elementalist.

"You weren't supposed to tell him that!" blurted Fenris.

Gods, I loved the practicality of an elementalist with air and the honesty of one with spirit.

Madoc looked around. "Where are your horses? There's a group of Republic soldiers right behind us!"

As if summoned by his words, a small group of mounted soldiers burst through the tree line to the north, taking potshots as they headed across the clearing at a gallop. Aiming with any accuracy from the back of a galloping horse was almost impossible, but Seth raised a shield just in case any of them got lucky. Eian backed him up. I began tossing fireballs to keep them at a distance, while Angie threw spirit orbs.

"We lost them!" Conall yelled over the gunfire. "As it turns out, horses don't like explosions very much."

"Imagine that!" said Ariadne.

"What are you doing here?" Dermot yelled from halfway up the ladder of the second water tower. "Siorus! You brought my sister into a war zone?!"

"She's safe with us," the earth druid replied. "Besides, we have to get back to Ward *tonight*. Everyone double up so we can get out of here."

"We don't have enough horses for everyone to ride double," Madoc said.

"That's okay. I don't need a horse!" Dermot said. Heedless of approaching enemies and flying bullets, he sped up the ladder like a squirrel, saying: "She's beautiful, and therefore to be wooed; She is woman, and therefore to be won!"

"Quit fucking around and get down from there!" bellowed Conall.

"Was that Shakespeare?" asked Angie, pausing with a glowing orb in her hand to peer up at him.

"He's stupid, not uneducated," said Ariadne.

"He's a fucking idiot, is what he is!" said Conall. "Get your ass back down here before you get shot!"

"I can't see from down there!" Dermot shouted back.

Still holding the shield that kept death at bay, Seth turned his head sharply. "What is he doing?"

I halted in the middle of lobbing another fireball, exchanging a look of concern with Conall. Whatever the water elementalist was planning, there was only one reason for him to need to be that high up – it was going to be *big*.

"I don't know!" I shouted back. "But get ready to move!"

Dermot poked his head over the top of the standpipe. "Davis! Get all the brick off!"

"Surely you're not going to do what he says?" Fenris said.

"Nobody else has any ideas," I said, slapping my hand against the brick. The mortar cracked, and bricks came crumbling down. The outer covering above the brick was made of wood, so I carefully burned it from the bottom up. Ash mixed with the light snowfall.

The water tower uttered a low, sonorous moan as I peeled back a section of metal plating. Water gushed out, spilling down its chill white surface, collecting in a slushy pool at our feet. It stopped and then began flowing back the way it came, against the pull of gravity. The deep, mellow groans altered in pitch, interspersed with grinding vibrations and grating screeches. The tower began to emit the high-pitched squeal as I peeled the shorn metal back farther. The wall of water quivered like a live thing, fully half a million gallons held in place by the will of one young water druid.

Dermot stamped twice on the rounded top of the standpipe, thrust his fist in the air, and bellowed:

"RELEASE THE KRAKEN!"

A multitude of tentacles burst through the wall of water, scrabbling for purchase on the ground beyond the protective air shields that surrounded us. A pair of clawed hands emerged and gripped the shorn metal of the standpipe, tearing it open further to reveal a squashed-lump face with small, beady eyes and a mouth full of razor-sharp teeth.

It was a colossus of myth and legend, brought to life by the imagination and will of a seventeen-year-old water elementalist with full druid magic and a tendency toward reckless behavior.

It was astounding.

It was awe-inspiring.

It was *terrifying*.

"*Gods of Olympus*," breathed Seth, his usual cool composure having abandoned him. I felt his air shield swirl away in a gust of winter wind, but it didn't matter because the soldiers were no longer paying us any attention at all.

"We are all going to die," said Conall, gazing upon the monster with aplomb.

"Do you think you'll go to Valhalla if you've been fighting in a battle but end up being drowned by a friend?" I asked, backing away from the monster.

"No," he said. "I don't."

The Kraken came tearing out of its steely womb, its claws

shredding the metal to ribbons. The myriad appendages protruding from its back and shoulders whipped about in the air as it slithered free on its thick, snakelike body.

"Move!" I yelled, grabbing Angie's hand and taking cover behind the first standpipe. The others scattered, darting to the left and right to escape certain death beneath the massive bulk of the Kraken. Siorus, Madoc, Eian, and Ariadne spurred their mounts a quick distance away to keep from getting crushed. Fenris' horse spooked and followed them. Mohinder's horse looked half asleep as it walked away, having long ago acclimatized to the madness to which a water druid's mount was regularly subjected.

A ferocious, metallic roar filled the air as the monstrosity ripped the standpipe asunder. Dermot lost his balance, pinwheeling his arms wildly in a desperate attempt to stay upright. The metal beneath his feet crumpled, tossing him off the structure. His shout of alarm was abruptly cut off as one swift tentacle snaked out to catch him in midair. It curled back in on itself, gently placing the water elementalist securely upon the Kraken's shoulder. Dermot let out a loud *WHOOP!* of triumph.

As the leviathan surged forward to the water tower we were hiding behind, Angie and I bolted for the third one with Conall scrambling behind us. One massive arm reached out and ripped off the wood paneling around the top. Its merciless claws rent the metal standpipe within, and it shoved its hideous head and writhing tentacles inside, drinking deeply. Within moments the Kraken had doubled in size, its head and shoulders towering a hundred feet over our heads. Its body, now over fifty feet thick, furrowed the ground as it slithered out to take on the enemy.

"I take it back!" Conall shouted. "He's not stupid – he's *crazy*!"

"He's a *genius*!" Angie said. "Look!"

No longer riding on the Kraken's shoulder, Dermot had wisely submerged himself in an air-filled chamber inside the monster's head. Safe from harm, he was free to attend solely to the business of attacking our enemies. It slithered over a group of Republic soldiers that were closely massed together, crushing them beneath its bulk, and slaughtered the rest by lashing out with its tentacles as they fled.

Siorus returned with his pentacle and Ariadne. Duncan

emerged from a bolt hole he had created, followed by Niall and Seth.

"Here!" Ariadne dismounted and thrust her horse's reins at Angie before sprinting to the remaining standpipe. I raced after her, tearing off the bricks as she raced up the ladder. Once she had attained the heights, I burned the wood panels and placed my hand on the freezing metal pipe.

"Ready?"

"You're just going to let her go?" Angie cried, running after us with the horse. "She's only an elementalist!"

"Mohinder!" I shouted.

"Way ahead of you, Davis," he said, dropping his horse's reins and scaling the ladder.

"I'm going too!" Fenris clambered up after them. At the top of the tower, the three put their heads together and conferred for a moment. Mohinder gave me a thumbs-up, and I split the metal down one side. A sea dragon emerged from the tank, its head gracefully arcing over the top of the water tower. It opened its toothy jaws wide, and they filed through the maw and up into the head. As soon as the trio was settled, the serpent took off after a raid group that had appeared from the northeast. The Republic soldiers wheeled their horses about in a mad dash for safety, but the sea dragon's eyes glowed bright blue and blasted them with a thick lightning bolt.

"I can't believe you let those three go off alone together!" Conall exclaimed.

"*Somebody* had to go with Ariadne," I said. "She's only an elementalist."

"Spirit and water elementalists on their own?" said Eian, shaking his head. "Prepare for pandemonium."

"Trust me," Seth said. "We are *way* past pandemonium."

"Niall!" Madoc said, noticing him for the first time. "Is that you?"

"Am I so difficult to recognize?" the blond said through gritted teeth. In spite of Lin's assurance that Niall wasn't an arrogant jackass anymore, it seemed to me that he had an even bigger chip on his shoulder than he'd carried around at the grove.

"You know each other?" I asked.

"Of course I know him," the gunman said, dismounting. "He's

615

my brother."

"You're no brother to me." Niall backed up a step. "You abandoned our family."

"You would have me be loyal to the family that defied the will of the gods and denied you their gift?" Madoc replied angrily. "To the mother that took our magic away?"

Niall looked away.

"I can't tell you how many times I wished that you had come with us," the gunman said in a softer tone. His expression changed to one of compassion and regret. "You are the only family I have left." He reached out and touched his brother's face, tracing the scar that ran from forehead to chin with gentle fingers. "Iriana told us what happened. It was courageous, standing against Orion the way you did."

"If courageous is another word for stupid, then yes, it was," Niall said in a voice heavy with bitterness.

"Don't be ridiculous. How many lives did you save? How many families did you spare mourning the loss of a loved one?" Madoc shook his head. "It's not your fault that Darryn turned out to be a false friend. What you did was brave. And noble."

"And it didn't make a bit of difference!" Niall snapped. "It changed *nothing*. The grove still broke apart."

Madoc laid a hand on his shoulder. "Sometimes things fall apart so that better things can come together," he said. "If the grove hadn't split, we might never have been reunited."

"You'd only been gone a day when I wished I'd gone with you," Niall said. They embraced tightly, and when they separated, Madoc kissed his forehead and smiled.

"I *missed* you, little brother. We will not be separated like that again," the gunman vowed. "Do you still have Charger?"

"I did until yesterday."

"We'll find him." Madoc remounted his horse. "Ride with me until then?" Niall took his hand and swung aboard.

Conall was already astride Fenris' horse, and Seth was about to mount Mohinder's when Iriana showed up with Ingvar's pentacle.

"Seth! Seth! We saw the fire in the sky, and I was so worried!" she cried, jumping off her horse and running to him. The air druid caught her up in a hug, smiling hugely.

"Everyone is well and accounted for," he said. "For now, anyway." She hugged him again and then spun around to Angie, her strawberry blonde hair flying.

"Thank the gods they found you! I was so afraid that something bad had happened!"

Angie smiled. "I'm fine, Irri."

"Look, Angie!" Iriana pointed at Seth. "I found my chosen."

"That's wonderful! I'm so happy for you!"

Iriana whirled back to Seth. "Did you lose your horse?"

"Yes, but I have Mohinder's at the moment." He helped her back onto her own gelding and was soon astride the water druid's bay.

That left Ariadne's blue roan mare for Angie and me. I figured it was of the same bloodline as Dermot's horse Kelpie and hoped she wasn't as unruly. I mounted and helped Angie up behind me, noticing the scabbard that banged against her thigh as she swung up. I turned to look over my shoulder at her.

"How long have you been using a sword?"

"Oh, um…"

"Only since forever," said Conall, halting his mount beside us.

"It hasn't been *forever*," Angie said.

"No, only since you were about seven."

"I was *ten* when Father began teaching me," she replied primly.

"Oh, that's right. You started jousting at seven."

Angie gave him a murderous look.

"Why didn't you bring your sword on the road?" I asked. We could have used another weapon on the perilous journey from Kingston to White Oak Grove.

"Because that was the deal I struck with Sebrina," Angie said. "No offensive magic and no weapons. Only water."

"Are you good with it?" I asked.

"Do you honestly think my father would permit anything less than excellence?"

Of course not; they were Everlights.

"So, Conall's your milk brother and was supposed to be your chosen before Niall, and you're a blademaster," I said. "Anything else I should know about?"

"Very funny." She pretended to be annoyed but sounded

amused instead. As Angie slipped her arms around my waist, it felt as though everything had fallen into place. True, we had lost our horses and were in the midst of enemy territory fighting a war, but with her by my side, I felt as though there was nothing we couldn't accomplish.

"What's the plan?" I asked when everyone had mounted.

"Uh…" Siorus cleared his throat. "Bringing down the walls and creating enough chaos for you to escape was as far as I got."

The Finns had definitely accomplished that. What with the casualties we'd already inflicted upon the defenders of the 'Ville, it was unlikely that they would be able to mount a defense on multiple fronts.

"To be perfectly honest, I was hoping to find you fairly quick so you could take over," he added.

"All right, then. Let's ride for the northwest gate and catch up to Dermot and the others," I said. Seth reined Mohinder's horse over to his usual place on my right, and Iriana moved hers beside him.

"Halldor's pentacle is there with Poppy," Siorus said, moving his horse alongside Conall's on my left.

"Excellent," I said, but Angie had a different opinion.

"Poppy!" she exclaimed in dismay. "You can't trust her! She came up here with Dianthe Aspen!"

"We know," I said. "She chose to join us, as did Laiken Birch and Edmund MacGregor."

Angie took a breath as if to speak again, but exhaled and said nothing. She was unhappy, but there was nothing I could do about that now.

"Don't worry," Conall said. "We don't trust any of them *that* much." She nodded but didn't look any happier.

"What about everyone else?" I asked.

Ingvar replied, "Martin is at the west gate with Wolfric and Lin, Warwick and Laiken went to the southwest gate, and Yiorgos is at the south gate. He has Edmund still."

Siorus said, "We figured those places would be the toughest, so we made sure each of them had extra firepower, so to speak."

"Excellent choices and brilliant tactics," I said. Seth nodded agreement. Each of those pentacles had an extra druid with offensive magic: Wolfric and Poppy's fire and Laiken's spirit.

Having Wolfric and Lin would help Martin's pentacle a great deal, as they would be traveling through the most densely populated part of the bandit city. Likewise, Laiken would be able to offer extra shielding to Warwick's.

"Might as well make the circuit and collect everybody," I said. "We'll start at the northwest and continue counter-clockwise. If anybody gets separated, just head for the next gate."

"And what else?" Conall asked. "Free the prisoners?"

"They've had time enough to escape," Seth replied in an iron tone.

I wasn't ready to give up on them just yet. "Help those that need it, if it can be done without risk," I said.

"And the rest?" Conall pressed.

"Raze it," I said. "Leave nothing standing."

* * *

We followed the rough road that had been carved out by the Kraken's destructive passage. It was far from ideal, crisscrossed with broken limbs and downed trees. It would have been easier to burn it clear, but the firelight would have attracted unwanted attention. I sent the other two pentacles ahead to clear us a path using earth and air, and then dropped to the rear so that Angie and I could speak privately. Duncan turned around with a questioning expression, and I gestured that he should continue onward. He nodded once in response and faced forward once more.

"Speak your mind," I told her, keeping my voice low.

"It's nothing," she said softly. "I'm sure you know what you're doing."

"That's debatable." I chuckled. "If there's something about Poppy or Laiken that I need to know, tell me."

She was silent for a few moments. "I could be wrong about Poppy," she said. "No one in her family supported Sebrina. It's possible she sided with the ArchDruid just to improve her own status in the grove."

Poppy herself had confessed as much.

"And Laiken?"

"She's the ultimate bootlicker. If Sebrina or any of the Tetrarch said jump, she'd ask how high." Angie shook her head with obvious disgust. "She's too timid to go against them." She paused, considering. "Then again, she also lacks the backbone for subterfuge."

"Apparently she has a little," I said. "She sent a fetch out just a few weeks ago. She partnered up with Warwick, one of our earth druids."

"*Laiken* sent a fetch?" Angie exclaimed.

"I *know*!" said Iriana, turning her chestnut horse. "I couldn't believe it, either!" She and Seth dropped back to walk beside us, followed by Conall and Duncan. So much for having some time alone.

"She's such a… shrinking violet," Angie said.

"It's hard to be brave when you've been discouraged from independent thought and action your whole life," I said.

"That's true," she said.

"Not everyone has your strength of spirit."

"My bullheadedness, you mean."

"Well, shit," Conall interjected. "I was hoping that at least one of you had some common fucking sense, but I guess that was just too much to ask for."

Angie tensed and drew a deep breath, but Duncan chimed in before she could tear into the Norseman.

"Chosen are supposed to balance one another," the earth druid said. "But in this case, I fear the Ancestors may have erred."

"Faint heart never won fair lady," I said with a wink. She gave me a slight smile in return, but it never touched her eyes. "Don't worry about all this," I said. "I've been running and gunning with these guys since before Mabon. We've been in a lot of dangerous situations, but we always manage to come out on top. Trust me, we'll get out of this one, too."

"I trust you," she said, but the worry never left her eyes. I wanted to reassure her further, but mere words would not assuage her fears. Only action could do that. The proof is in the pudding, as my father often said.

Duncan called: "Davis, the horses!" Arm outflung, he pointed toward a clearing visible only for a moment through a gap in the trees.

"Whoa…" I reined the blue roan mare, turning her about. She carefully picked her way through the splintered wood littering the forest floor as I guided her back to the gap in the trees. It was little more than a game trail, and it led to the main road that ran east-west through the 'Ville – the one from which we'd narrowly escaped death twice already. I wasn't looking forward to crossing it again.

"How did you see that?" I asked.

He rolled his eyes. "I didn't. I've been *seeking* for them since we entered the forest." He waved to Siorus and the others. "This way!"

As we proceeded down the trail at a slow walk, I joined my earth magic with Duncan's to strengthen the range and power of his *seeking*. There were no enemies in front of us or near our horses, but it was the possibility of them to the east and west that concerned me – mostly the west. With any luck, Halldor's invasion through the northwest gate would keep the Republic forces occupied while we retrieved our horses.

"Everybody stay in the trees," I said, moving out into the street. To the east, thin grey smoke mixed with steam was visible, but thankfully the charred corpses giving it off were not. To the south, thick black smoke still billowed from the buildings I'd firebombed the night before.

"There is no one else here," Duncan said, ignoring my order as usual. The others followed his lead.

"There are still two rogue druids out there, and one of them has elemental earth," I reminded him.

"I seriously doubt she can hide from *us*," he said, but what he really meant was that she couldn't hide from *him*.

When we were halfway across the road, Ariadne's mare stopped short, snorting and shaking her head. The other horses danced sideways a few steps and were quickly brought back under control by their riders. Their heads were up and their ears pricked, showing that something to the west had captured their attention.

Assuming it was escalating hostilities, I clucked at the mare and had her moving forward again when the Kraken hove into view above the treetops a quarter-mile distant. It disappeared momentarily and then reappeared holding one of those big machine guns. A mass of water shifted over the mythical monster's head to form a giant cowboy hat, and it held the machine gun in one clawed hand like a pistol. Like the gunner we'd encountered this morning, this one's panic and fear of falling caused him to grip the trigger tightly, resulting in a continuous hailstorm of bullets. The Kraken aimed its rapid-fire weapon like a gargantuan gunslinger, sweeping it back and forth. When its ammunition was depleted, it tossed the gun away and began smashing things with its clawed fists again.

"Now that's something you don't see every day," said Jasvinder.

"Sometimes I wonder about Dermot," Nêreus said with a frown.

"So do I," said Conall. "I wonder why a seventeen-year-old kid is smarter and better at using his element than the rest of you assholes."

"You don't have to be so rude," Nêreus retorted.

"I do when somebody's talking about my friend behind his back," the Norseman snapped. "So shut your mouth."

"All right, all right," Ingvar said, giving his guys a warning look. To his credit, Conall only scowled at the earth druid and said nothing more.

We crossed the road without further incident and stopped beside the pasture fence, where I tied the blue roan mare. At my whistle, a familiar black head popped up with his ears pricked and a clump of hay hanging out of his mouth. As the horses milled about, we could see they were all there: Bucephalus, Twister, Scarlet, Kelpie, Charger, and —

"Magic!" Angie cried. She was off in a flash and running across the field. The palomino mare whinnied in response and trotted right to her. Seth, Conall, and Niall dismounted and followed us into the pasture.

"I think she's happier to see her horse than she is to see you," Conall said.

"Wouldn't you be?" I said.

"Damn straight. Your face looks like the horse's ass end."

We climbed the fence, each approaching his own horse and greeting it with soft speech, petting, or a welcome scratch. I was checking Steel's feet and legs when a gruff voice yelled: "Hey! What're you boys doin' there?!"

I looked up to see a skinny old man emerge from a shack just south of the pasture. After passing through the gate, he came closer and peered at me. It was Carl Freeman, the man we had encountered at the Sherwood outpost. He was slightly less dirty and a lot more sober.

"Oh, it's you," he said, shoulders relaxing. "I figured you boys might be the cause of all that ruckus."

"Mr. Freeman!" I was glad to see he'd made it back home safely. The feeling was immediately replaced by a sense of guilt because we were about to make him homeless again.

"It's just Carl," he said. "I found your horse." He laid a gnarled hand on Steel's neck and stroked it gently. "He's a good boy. Well-mannered, for a stallion." He nodded, as if to himself. "Reckoned you'd be by for him when you got a chance."

"You put them here?"

He nodded. "Found the lot of 'em running scared yesterday, so I rounded 'em up and penned 'em in here. Their bridles are hanging on the branches of that tree over there. I'd have taken off their saddles, too, if not for this damned rheumatism." He closed and opened his hands, their knuckles gnarled and swollen.

"Thank you for caring for them," I said, touched by this unexpected boon. "It was mighty generous of you to keep them safe."

Carl said. "I have a soft spot for horses. Always have had. Besides, you did me a kindness."

"I was happy to help," I said.

"Something tells me you ain't here to help this time," he said.

"I wasn't there to help last time, either," I said. "Honestly, I wouldn't be here today if they hadn't kidnapped the girl with the palomino mare."

Carl looked Angie over. "Pretty gal. Yours?"

I glanced at her, then met his eyes again. "Yeah." She might not like it, but outside of the druid world, men frequently claimed ownership over women.

"She the reason you've been raising hell all over the territory?"

"One of them," I said. "She's just the reason we're here now."

"You and I both know it would have happened sooner or later."

"Yes, sir, it would have," I admitted, feeling Angie's eyes on me. "Just didn't plan on it being today, is all." I didn't have it in me to lie, and I was a terrible liar besides.

He nodded. "Greed and Pride never served anyone well, and from what I hear, President Jackson has both qualities in spades." He shrugged. "He done waved a red flag in your face one too many times, I reckon, and when you mess with the bull, you get the horns."

"He had some help from some of those druids you mentioned before," I said. "The ones from down south."

Carl squinted at me. "You talk like you boys ain't druids, too."

"We *are* druids," Angie said, stepping forward. "The old kind. The ones that helped people and tried to protect them. The ones that worked to heal the earth."

"There'll be a whole lot of healin' needed after this."

I nodded, looking away.

"Don't be ashamed that you're standing up for what's right," Carl said. "A great many people have been hurt by the bloodthirsty warmongers of this city. When evil deeds are done, there's always hell to pay afterward."

The others were astride their horses and ready to go. Conall held Kelpie's reins and those of Ariadne's mare, while Siorus had taken charge of Mohinder's. Duncan brought Steel's bridle to me, and I put it on him, feeling torn. Was it right to destroy a city even if there were only a few righteous people in it?

Carl backed away. "Mount up, boy. You got work to do and daylight's a-burnin'."

"I'm not sure I want to anymore," I said.

He nodded understanding. "That's because you're a good man. But what you got to remember is that good men sometimes do things they don't want to do, simply because it needs doing."

"We will return to mend what's been destroyed," said Duncan.

"There are a lot of places that need set to rights," I said. "We'll be back to restore this place, too." It didn't make me feel much better. With a heavy heart, I put my foot in the stirrup. The sight of Mohinder's empty saddle, however, gave me an idea. I put my foot back down on the ground.

"Why don't you come with us?" I said.

"Me?" Carl laughed. "Boy, ain't no way an old codger like me can keep up with the likes of you boys – horse or no horse."

"You don't have to. We'll be leaving by way of the northeastern gate when we're done. If you head there now, you can take it slow and easy."

"You mean the gate that ain't there anymore? Gonna be awful hard to get past all that rubble."

"We left a clear path," Siorus said. "There are spots where you can shelter from the wind and keep warm until we get there."

The old man was shaking his head, but it was clear he was thinking about it.

"You said you were only coming back here because you didn't have anywhere to go forward to," I said. "We can take you to a place where you'll be welcome."

He shook his head, his features hardening. "Ain't nobody got any use for a crippled old drunk like me."

Duncan took the man's gnarled hands in his. Carl winced, but then amazement crossed his weathered features.

"My hands," he whispered, holding them up and staring at them in wonder. "They don't hurt no more."

"I cannot repair the damage that has occurred over time, but I can relieve your pain," said Duncan. He placed a hand on the old man's shoulder. "Come with us. Live out the remainder of your years in peace and comfort."

Carl Freeman nodded, tears trickling over the deep wrinkles in his cheeks. "I'm gonna do just that," he said, taking a small bottle of whiskey out of his pocket and throwing it on the ground. "I'll never have to drink that poison again."

"Here," I said, holding Steel's reins out to Carl. "Take my horse. He'll see you safely there." Lacing my fingers together, I helped him into the saddle.

"Come on, boy." He reined Steel about and exited through the gate, held open by Madoc.

"Ride safe, Mr. Freeman!" I called after him.

"You can call me that when we're well north of that wall," he called back with a wave. Then, sitting as straight in the saddle as a man half his age, he cantered away to the north.

Chapter 37 - Annihilation

Once you are so unfortunate as to be drawn into a war,
no price is too great to pay for an early and victorious peace.
~ Winston Churchill ~

We hadn't come to destroy the 'Ville, but it was happening all the same. For all the talking and planning we'd done, the reality of what we were doing with our magic – mine in particular – was far more grim and ghastly. I reminded myself that these were the brigands who had pillaged Ward, who had driven the witches from their home, who had murdered their elders, and who had stolen their children. They were the monsters who had brutalized Maeve and Ruth, who had tortured Cullen, and who had thrown James Reece off a twenty-foot wall. They were the marauders who had utterly destroyed entire towns. They were the raiders who had deprived countless people of their homes, plundering their goods, enslaving them, and murdering their families. While their fellow citizens may not have had a hand in it, they gave their tacit approval by not putting a stop to it.

The people of the Republic of Jackson were evil in every sense of the word and deserved no mercy.

When we arrived at what remained of the northwest gate, the thick body of Dermot's Kraken could be seen in the distance, plowing southward through building after building. Slithering after it and collecting snow and ice as it went, the sea dragon had tripled in size. Spirit magic glimmered along its body, sparking brightly between its scales and shimmering in the dim winter air. It craned its head, seeking out targets that Dermot might have missed, discharging spirit bolts from its eyes. What remained of the defending forces fled before them in a fruitless effort to escape.

The northwestern wall lay in ruins. Every single structure in the quarter-mile area between the field where we found the horses and the crumbled wall had been flattened for as far as the eye could see. The demolition continued to the south. The water elementalists and their colossal creations had been so effective that Halldor's pentacle hadn't done much fighting at all.

"By the time we made a path through the rubble, they'd already done all the work," Halldor said as we rode south in the wake of the monsters' destruction.

"It was a bit disappointing, really," said Poppy. Angie hadn't said a word, but if looks could kill, the earth-fire druid would be dead on the ground.

"Don't be so eager to take the life of another," Uri said, not unkindly.

"That's not what I meant," she replied. "After hearing the stories of how you liberated all those towns, I just had this image built up in my head – you know, people cheering and happy to see us when we came in."

"Oh, well, that never really happened anyway," said Skylar. "Most of the time they were too beat up or scared to come out."

"Of course, Davis *did* spend most of yesterday afternoon setting the city on fire," Conall said. "So that might have made them a little reluctant, too."

"You forgot to blame me for what the dragon did," I said.

"I was getting to that."

"While you're at it, Conall, be sure and take your fair share of the blame," Seth said, defending me because once again he had forgotten that the Norseman's ribbing was just his way of letting off steam. "After all, you slaughtered no few bandits yourself with spirit bolts."

The members of Siorus', Ingvar's, and Halldor's pentacles slowly turned in their saddles to look at Conall with varying expressions of confusion and disbelief. Conall scowled at the air druid and then let out a huff of irritation.

"What is he talking about?" asked Madoc.

"Nothing," the Norseman replied, shooting Seth a dark look.

The air druid ignored him. "His magic was restored yesterday."

"That's not possible," said Uri.

"That's what I thought," Niall said. "But it's true."

"What element?" Regnar asked, looking shocked.

Conall let out a huff, clearly angry.

"Spirit, air, and water," he said.

"You're a *triple threat?*" Regnar blurted.

"If it makes you feel any better, he almost lost his life in the process," I said.

"Kind of like when you got *your* magic," said Madoc.

I winced as Angie turned sharply toward me with a stricken look on her face. I prayed they wouldn't say anything else about it, but didn't have much time to worry about it. Our gunmen were about to go rogue.

"Right." Uri's face reflected the understanding that was dawning upon him. He, Regnar, and Madoc exchanged glances loaded with meaning.

"Let's not go off half-cocked," I said, knowing that nothing I said would make a bit of difference. As Niall had pointed out earlier, risking one's life in the pursuit of magic would seem preferable to a long and frustrating life denied one's birthright.

"Are you thinking what I'm thinking?" Madoc asked, ignoring me completely.

Uri and Regnar nodded.

"Not to burst anyone's bubble," Niall interrupted, "but I, too, nearly died and have not received a similar restoration."

"Two with and one without," said Regnar. "I find those to be acceptable odds."

"As do I," said Madoc. *"YAH!"* He spurred his horse forward with a yell.

"Madoc, wait!" Niall cried, urging Charger after them.

"No!" yelled Siorus, followed by similar cries from Ingvar and Halldor. The three gunmen paid them no heed, racing ahead to the next side street. Then, instead of continuing along the relatively safe path laid out by the leviathans, they turned and galloped for the center of the 'Ville. The earth druids gave chase, followed by the other members of their pentacles.

"This is sure to end well," said Conall. He gave Seth a

withering look. "Which is exactly why I *hadn't* told them."

"I didn't know they were going to do that!" Seth protested.

"That's because you weren't denied your birthright," the Norseman replied. "Do us all a favor and don't mention it again."

"Did you think they wouldn't notice when you started hurling thunderbolts like Thor?" Seth snapped back.

"We'd better go after them," I said, a completely unnecessary statement in light of the fact that everyone in the other two pentacles had already charged off pell-mell after their rogue gunmen. I really hoped that Angie didn't think we usually operated this way, even though sometimes it felt like we did.

They were blocks away by the time we rounded the corner. Several pipe bombs flew through the air, launched by persons unseen. The explosives landed in the middle of the next intersection, just behind the hindmost galloping horses of the three pentacles, but I was too far away to control the resultant explosion. The Finns ahead scattered in multiple directions and were soon out of sight.

So much for that idea.

"What now?" Conall asked.

"Let's try to meet up with Martin's pentacle."

As we continued another couple of blocks, the Kraken's head and wildly waving tentacles were visible above the treetops. I didn't catch sight of the sea dragon, but from the bright blue-white flashes reflected by the heavy clouds above, I knew it was there, too. Turning down a side street, we met token resistance in the form of snipers shooting from second-story windows. Duncan's shockwave shattered windows on both sides of the street and ruined their aim. Conall lobbed spirit orbs through the ground floor windows to ward off threats from that direction, while a few well-placed fireballs wet the upper story blazing.

The merrily burning buildings reminded me of my fetch, flying back after fulfilling its mission. The Finns were scattered throughout the 'Ville so bringing it to the fight was too great a risk – but it could strafe the area along the remains of the northwestern wall and wipe out any remaining enemies, weapons, or ammo dumps. If we were going to eradicate the Republic menace and eliminate the threat once and for all, the annihilation of the city had to be complete. We could not leave a single stone stacked atop another or even the remnants of structural support materials, lest our enemies rebuild and rise again. I commanded it to return to the northwest gate, and it responded by dipping low and spewing flame over the entire area. The dragonfire acted as a blast furnace, turning glass, metal, and stone to slag. Back and forth it went, strafing over the ground and obliterating anything manmade that remained.

We went all the way to the wrecked western gate without meeting up with Martin's pentacle. Even though we met little resistance from the enemy, I was forced to concede that events were well and truly out of my control. The best thing we could do was to work our way across the 'Ville, leveling the buildings and burning the remains. It would accomplish our end goal of destroying the bandit city, and also help herd the rest of the Finns northward.

"It looks like you've already gotten a head start on this area," Seth remarked.

"Yeah…" I watched as Angie looked around at the blackened husks of once-inhabited buildings, burned to bare bones by dragonfire. "I may have gotten a little carried away last night."

"Might as well finish it up, then," said Conall.

Duncan and I dismounted and knelt down, each of us placing our bare hands on the frozen earth. Even though we agreed that none of our allies were within the planned destruction zone, we still sent a few tremors through the ground as a warning, then released a major temblor. It spread out in a cone as it headed west, its surface vibrations causing several weakened structures to collapse.

"Shockwave?" I suggested. Duncan nodded.

Linking our elemental magics increased the power available to us, resulting in a series of abrupt jolts that raced from our location to the remnants of the northwestern wall. Instead of the rolling waves we used to keep enemies at bay, these waves were rough and jagged, shaking the buildings in their path down to their foundations. All the remaining structures collapsed, one after another. When the grassland was once again visible on the horizon, I called the dragon to eradicate the signs of human habitation on the western side of the 'Ville.

Starting with the crumbled remnants of the southern wall,

Duncan channeled long, narrow shockwaves in an easterly direction. Keeping in mind that Martin and Warwick's pentacles were somewhere ahead of us, I pushed the falling bulwarks outward and away from the few remaining city structures. Conall and Angie rode ahead to eliminate any enemy resistance, while Seth and Iriana watched our backs.

From there we moved eastward, and I sent the fire drake west. It soared back and forth, obliterating the remnants of the western wall and the rubble of buildings. We had made it back to the central portion of the 'Ville and were a few blocks south of the building where we had sheltered the night before when a series of disjointed earthquakes struck at rapid, irregular intervals from several different directions.

I managed to keep my feet until one particularly strong pulse flipped me into the air. I tried to tuck and roll but the earth didn't cooperate and I landed hard on my back with the wind knocked out of me. If that wasn't bad enough, the glowing sea dragon was gliding menacingly toward me. Even though I managed to roll out of harm's way, I found myself in the path of the Kraken. It made an eerie *shhhshhhshhh* noise as it bore down on me with those violently waving tentacles. I scrambled out of the way and slapped my hand against its thick, ugly body. It was a surprise when it passed through into gel. The monster wasn't as solid as it seemed, and was quite a bit less so after I channeled a flare of elemental fire through it. Bubbles and steam churned upward, rocking the monster sideways. Opening up the bubble inside its head, Dermot leaned out and peered down.

"Watch where you're going!" I shouted up at him.

"Sorry!" called Dermot.

"Go north!" I roared. "Get out of here!"

"What?" he hollered back. "Why?"

For an answer, I pointed at my fetch, coming around for another flaming pass. Instead of following my order, the Kraken's tentacles began waving crazily at the sea dragon. Unable to attract Ariadne's attention, he drove the leviathan onward to catch up with her. I looked around for Duncan and saw him dodge the end of the monster's tail.

More erratic earthquakes pummeled the 'Ville. It was like every single earth druid in the Finns had suddenly gone mad, casting shockwaves in every direction in a completely chaotic fashion. The ground shuddered and shook for at least five minutes, which is an eternity when you're trying to stay upright – or even on your hands and knees. At the very least, I should have been able to calm the earth beneath my feet, but it continued to dip and buck like a wild horse. I pulled myself to the edge of the cracking earth, intending to drop onto what I hoped was solid ground. Instead, I was shocked to see the rest of my pentacle and Angie some twenty feet below.

"Something is wrong!" I yelled over the rumble of the land and the crashing of buildings. "The Mother isn't listening to me!"

"We've upset the balance!" Duncan shouted from below. "She has awakened in anger!"

Translation: we had destabilized the earth's crust, and were about to get a taste of what the Fracture was like. There had been no earth druids to quiet it then, and the earth's crust had folded, warped, and buckled in its wild risings and fallings.

All the Fracture stories ever written couldn't have prepared me for this. The ground soared, carrying the two water monsters and me rapidly upward, our ascent only interrupted by occasional short, shallow dips. The rising plateau shot up another ten feet, then twenty, and then fifty or more before shuddering to a halt. Dangerously close to the edge of a hundred-foot drop onto terrain I could no longer control, I struggled to hold onto the heaving ground. It buckled, billowing upward and back like a sheet that some giant was trying to lay over a bed, and I slid toward the precipice.

As I was groping for purchase, just inches from the edge, the plateau collapsed, plunging sharply and sending me tumbling backwards. A yell escaped my lips when a quick glimpse revealed a drop of at least two hundred feet and growing. With a burst of elemental fire, I melted the rocks beneath me and plunged my hands inside, drawing the heat out just as quickly. I was still going down, but with my hands secured in the consolidated rock beneath the soil, I wouldn't be flung out into empty air to crash into the bone-breaking bottom of the sinkhole.

The slope steepened to nearly vertical, allowing me to see the entire horrifying scene. Dermot and his Kraken had fallen halfway down into the pit, halted only by the iron grip of its monstrous clawed hands. It hung there a few moments, and then started to climb, gravel and loose scree falling far beneath it. The sea dragon thrashed helplessly on a ledge above the Kraken and then burst apart with a splash. I watched the serpent's water shower down into the crater, even though I knew I shouldn't. Tearing my eyes away, I searched for survivors. Ariadne, Mohinder, and Fenris were all still alive, standing precariously on the ledge with their backs pressed against the loose rock wall. One good earthquake and they would be thrown to their deaths.

I looked back down at the Kraken. Its tentacles were gone, absorbed into its body, and it had grown hind legs. Claws sprouted from its paws and dug into the crater wall. After a fall that should have killed him, and under extreme duress, Dermot had morphed the legendary sea monster into a giant *Dobhar-chú*. Its sinewy body and thick, powerful legs provided the perfect form for climbing the walls. I held my breath as it climbed, slipped, and climbed again, making its way up to the narrow ledge with painful slowness.

Steam rose into the air, obscuring my view of the opposite side of the pit. Looking down again, I saw a long, jagged crack at the bottom. Now that the violent motion of the earth had ceased, I could perform a *seeking* and was stunned to feel an enormous magma chamber. This was no mere sinkhole that had opened up beneath our feet; this was the developing caldera of a soon-to-be-active volcano. Lying below the 'Ville, it had been quiescent until our seismic activity stirred it up; the million or so gallons of sea dragon that had just fallen into it was further stimulating its unrest. Some of the water had landed directly in the vent, causing thick steam to rise. The rest had landed in the rocky soil around it, and was percolating down to the chamber below. The high water table that Duncan had mentioned yesterday was sure to have a negative effect as it ran downhill into the crater.

Dermot needed to move faster – *much* faster – but the loose rock and tumbled soil made it impossible. Every step the *Dobhar-chú* took had to be chosen with care and tested for firmness before the next could be attempted. I looked down again, feeling the magma starting to boil and wondering what could be done about it.

"Davis!" Seth called from above, his voice amplified by air. "Hang on, we're going to—"

"No!" I shouted. "Get everybody away from here *now*! Ride for Ward!"

"I'm not leaving you!" Angie cried. A water rope fell beside me, striking the rocks with a thick, wet slap. "I'm pulling you up!"

The crystalline rope slipped around my torso and I positioned it around my chest. Her magic had lifted me halfway to the lip of the crater when a tremor rolled outward from the center of the pit, traveling up the walls. Ariadne's scream echoed against the rocks, eerily muffled by the steam. A quick glance over my shoulder showed the Dermot's monster was nearly to the ledge where she, Fenris, and Mohinder were precariously perched. Another few labored steps and the monster's maw opened wide. Three tiny figures – Ariadne, Fenris, and Mohinder – made their way past its teeth and into its throat, just below where Dermot stood in the head. I breathed a sigh of relief. We were all going to get out of here.

Another quake hit, stronger than the last, and scree rained down on me. Angie cried out and the water rope grew slack, slamming me against the pit wall. Sliding down the gravelly surface, I looked up to see her dangling from the pit's edge, boots scrabbling for purchase. When the rope ran out of slack, my weight would yank her right off it.

"Hang on!" I shouted.

Plunging my fists into the talus, I superheated it enough to plunge both arms into the molten rock. Flushing the heat out into the surrounding area, the rock rapidly cooled around my arms and stopped my downward slide. Earth might not respond to my will, but elemental fire gave me control over the stone within it. I drew chunks of hot rocks to me, consolidated them, and directed the mass up to where Angie was hanging. Guiding the flow of melted rock upward and outward, I created a small ledge and cooled it until it was only warm to the touch to retain control. The layers beneath were successively hotter, and I built them up until they were actually lifting Angie and pushing her back up toward the ledge.

Another aftershock hit so hard that the teeth rattled in my head. Or maybe it was my face smacking against the rocks. I spit blood and dirt out of my mouth. Angie screamed, and the water rope splashed apart. She had fallen onto the ledge, but it was slowly slipping downward. The earth shook again, knocking Duncan, Seth, and the others backward.

On the other side of the massive hole, Dermot was faring better. The ledge upon which the others had taken shelter had provided the *Dobhar-chú* with a good place to grip with its claws. It was again progressing toward the lip of the caldera, only a few yards above the tip of its nose. As it climbed higher, the wolf-bear-seal-thing shrank to half its original size, letting go of thousands of gallons of water that sealed our fate. It slithered over the edge of the pit, leaving its tail behind in an additional shower, carrying Dermot and the others to safety.

Watching him gave me inspiration. If Dermot could make water run uphill and a million gallons defy gravity, then I could do the same with molten rock.

I channeled a massive amount of elemental fire into the rocks beneath me until I was standing in a small pool. Sweat pouring down my face, I willed the melted stone to flow upward. It was slow going, more like flowing mud than water, but it was working. Firing a blast of heat up into the rocks below Angie, I halted her descent and then rose up to her level on a wave of molten rock. While I wanted nothing more than to grab her by the waist and pull her over to me, she would be burned to a crisp in the heat.

"Oh, thank Obatalá—" Angie breathed, leaning heavily against the rocky pit wall.

"Don't move," I said. Any movement – sudden or otherwise – could send us careening toward the bottom of the crater, ripping the clothes off our bodies – and the skin as well.

"Ang."

"Yes?" Her response was a bare whisper.

"Look at me. No, don't look down. Look at me." Her eyes met mine, and I decided that if I were to die today, those beautiful green eyes were the last thing I wanted to see.

She looked away again, down, down, down into the depths of the crater, and stiffened. "Charlie! The lava!"

I didn't have to look; I already knew that the roof of the magma chamber below had fallen and that boiling rock was seeping into the caldera. A fierce pillar of lava jetted a few hundred feet into the air and spattered the opposite side of the crater. It would not be long before an eruption occurred, and I

635

wasn't at all sure I could protect Angie from the fire and extreme temperature.

"Aganjú be merciful!" she whispered.

She was afraid of falling but had not yet grasped the real danger – the rapidly rising, boiling lake of molten rock and the poisonous, sulfuric gases it emitted. We had to move fast.

"I told you not to look down," I said, gently chiding.

Her attention snapped back toward me, an indignant look on her face. That was better than fear. Frightened Angie would hesitate, second-guess, and falter. Angry Angie could solve any problem, get out of any situation, defeat any enemy, and face any danger.

"I know we've been apart for a long time," I said, "but I need you to trust me."

"I never stopped trusting you," she said.

"Things are about to get really hot," I warned. "If the rock starts to burn you, let me know."

Angie was trembling, but she nodded understanding.

"Okay," I said, sending a rush of elemental fire into the rocky debris above us. "Here we go."

I commanded it to liquefy into a glowing stream that pushed us upward with a gentle surge. She gasped but didn't move, even though it must have looked as though a river of hot rocks would pour over us at any moment. Our progress was painfully slow, but I was afraid that if I increased the temperature, Angie's ledge would be too hot for her to stand on.

"Can you make an air bubble thick enough to keep out the heat?"

"I think so," she said. "Why?"

"We can go faster if I can raise the temperature." It would also keep the toxic fumes rising from the volcanic vent below from suffocating us.

"Do it!" she said, and I stepped over to her ledge, careful to shake off any residual rockmelt before coming closer. Angie formed an air bubble so thick that it distorted our view. Reassured of her safety, I propelled more elemental fire into the ground. Everything around the ledge melted into a river of glowing rock, and Angie squeezed up against me.

"Let me know if it gets too hot." I chuckled. The situation was serious, but the idea that it wouldn't get too hot was laughable.

"Are you *laughing*?" she demanded. "This isn't funny! This is the worst situation we've ever been in!"

"Oh, I don't... I don't know," I said, trying to concentrate on keeping the rock ledge cool and the surrounding pit wall hot. My body was drenched with sweat, and it wasn't from the heat. "I think the grove... might have been worse." Whether or not it was true was irrelevant; the fact of the matter was that my elemental magics protected me from the extreme heat of volcanic emissions.

"Worse than being boiled alive in lava?!"

"Oh, yeah," I said. "Way worse." After all, lava couldn't hurt me. The only risks were suffocation from the fumes or dying of dehydration.

"Charlie Davis! I simply cannot believe that you think—" she began in a scolding tone. Then: "Oh! We're at the top!"

The lava stream glopped over the cliff's edge, carrying the bubble onto safer ground. I shunted the heat away, down through the earth, and Angie let the air shield dissipate. I wanted nothing more than to collapse and take a few moments to catch my breath, but we needed to get out the 'Ville fast.

"Get off this volcano!" I said, waving the others ahead of me.

Iriana bolted, running down the hill. Seth hesitated a moment before following his chosen. Nobody else moved, except for when the ground shook and we slid a few feet down in the scree.

"What are you waiting for? Go!"

Conall crossed his arms over his chest. "We've been together a little too long, Davis. I know you're not planning on leaving with us."

"What?!" Angie exclaimed. "You can't stay here! You'll *die*!"

"Actually," Conall said. "He's the only one who *can* stay here."

"I'm sorry," I told her. "I have to stay. This thing is going to blow at any minute, and I have to make sure all of you get away safe."

"Exactly," Conall said. "Let's go."

Duncan rounded on him. "We are *not leav*—!"

Conall kicked his feet out from under him, sending him sliding down the hill on his backside. Seth caught him at the bottom, scowling at the Norseman.

"I won't leave without you!" Angie shouted in a voice hoarse with threatened tears.

"If you trust me, you'll go," I said.

Fists clenched and face screwed up in a mixture of anger and fear, Angie whirled away from me and half-ran, half-skidded down the hill. Duncan caught her at the bottom and helped her keep her feet.

Conall stayed a moment longer. "I guess now is when we find out."

"Find out what?"

"What an augmented druid can really do."

Recent events and the dramatic increase in my fire magic had made me wonder if I might have been augmented, but I had convinced myself that it couldn't be true because no other augmented child had survived. The dragon, though… that was hard to rationalize. There was no longer any doubt in my mind that I was of druid stock, and that my parents had fled the grove after Sebrina had come to power.

He smirked. "Don't worry. Your secret is safe with me."

"How long have you known?"

"Since you fell in the volcano. Poppy was right when she said no one could have survived that."

That bastard Shitozaki. He must have known from the beginning. And Wolfric almost certainly knew, simply because no matter how many times he had tried, he'd never been able to create a fire shield.

"The Finns are going to hate me when they find out."

"Davis, they already know!" He let out a harsh laugh. "Except maybe for Seth. I thought maybe the dragon had convinced him, but…" He shrugged. "I don't think he wants it to be true."

Couldn't say I blamed the air druid. *I* didn't want it to be true.

"Don't worry about the guys," he continued. "They like having you on our side."

That was a relief.

"Don't be too long. The new moon is upon us."

"I'll be there on time. Keep Angie safe."

"That's *your* job!" he yelled over his shoulder as he skated down the hill to join the others. I turned my back on them, ignoring Angie's cry of protest.

Another temblor rumbled through the caldera, and a sulfurous plume of steam billowed skyward. A stiff winter wind from the north carried most of the sulfurous fumes away, allowing me to breathe in the toxic environment. There was a surge from beneath the earth's crust. The millions of gallons of water that had spilled into the crater along with an untold amount of snow, ice, and groundwater were dramatically increasing the pressure. The magma was boiling just below the surface and eruption was imminent.

I might not be able to commune with the earth and calm it down, but I could still control the hot molten rock. Scrambling back from the crater's edge, I called the dragon to me and had it spew bright dragonfire all around me until the rubble and talus were glowing and the rock was the consistency of mud. The earth mother may have been too wild to master, but I still possessed the power to harness and control this volcano.

A geyser of bright orange shot into the sky in a pillar of burning light with a deafening roar. As soon as it cleared the hole, I called a tentacle of lava to me, thereby gaining control through direct contact with the churning magma beneath the crust. Lava gushed through the fissure, creating a lake of immolating fire. I only had to keep it contained for fifteen minutes – half an hour at most. If they rode fast, the Finns would be well outside the ruined perimeter wall within that amount of time.

The lava rose faster than I expected and would soon be brimming at the crater's edge. Knowing I had to keep it from flowing north for as long as possible, I sent the dragon to the south side of the caldera, where it perched on the lip of the volcano. After breathing fire all around and softening the rock until it was the consistency of mud, it dug a deep channel down the length of the volcano's slope and past the rubble of the southern wall. By the time it was finished, a thick sea of simmering liquefied rock had completely filled the caldera. Rather than overflowing its banks on all sides, however, it gushed into the mouth of the trench and streamed down the slope in a glowing river of fire. Dragonfire kept the thick liquid hot enough to flow freely, and soon it was pouring out over the ground beyond the wall. There, however, the basaltic flow slowly oozed over the frozen earth, melting snow and ice in a curtain of steam as it traveled southward.

Tension within the earth spoke of building pressure within the magma chamber deep below. Digging furiously, the fire drake created several more trenches around the southeastern edge of the caldera, while I carved out more on the southwestern side. The level of the lava lake dropped, but even with the greater spillage, instinct told me it was not going to be enough.

The 'Ville had been constructed on a wide, flat plain that stretched as far as the eye could see. And after traveling the ninety or so feet down the side of the volcano, there was little to encourage the flow of lava away from it. The cold complicated matters, for the flow cooled rapidly as it coated the ground, developing a dark grey crust over it that halted the flow in a matter of minutes.

Feeling the imminent eruption, I skidded down the northern slope, and the dragon took to the air again. Back on level ground, I looked back and saw the upper slopes had begun to crack and fall inward. I sprinted away, not daring to look but unable to help sensing the wave of unstable earth behind me crumbling into the caldera. I might be able to survive being immersed in molten rock, but there was no guarantee that I'd escape it. I ran almost all the way to the building where we had sheltered for the night, nearly two hundred yards, before it felt safe enough to stop. Breathing hard and clutching the stitch in my side, I turned around to find that the caldera was twice its original size, turbulently boiling and bubbling with lava. Geysers of molten rock shot into the air, splashing into the fiery lake or arcing over its jagged shore to spill out over the ground.

I started to walk away, but something stopped me. Dropping to one knee and placing a palm upon the rubble, I felt the continued turmoil of the earth mother, still distressed at the damage wrought by her chosen ones.

"Forgive us," I said. "Forgive me."

We had not been given this power by the Shining Ones to wound and destroy, but to create, and to heal. While the original abuse of the earth had not been propagated by me and mine, it *was* my hand that had struck the first blow leading to the ruin of this place. And as there was no one else left to make amends, it would be my hand to make the initial effort in repairing the damage.

I just hoped Angie wouldn't be too upset with me, because I

definitely wasn't going to be back inside Ward before Rhiannon and Spencer re-cast the *Circitorium Fati*.

Surveying the violently seething lake of lava before me, I decided that not only did I have an obligation to begin the restoration of this place, but that I had also been given an opportunity to erase all evidence that a horror such as the Republic of Jackson had ever existed. None of the people who lived in the towns within a day's ride of the 'Ville would ever feel safe as long as any remnant of it existed.

What better medium to construct a new environment than liquid stone? Fortunately, there wasn't a single building standing, so that would make covering the rubble over a whole lot easier. As my father would have said, a good start is half the work.

Squatting on the banks of the churning lake, I marveled at its beauty, jetting fountains like amber on fire. I plunged my hand into the lava and encouraged the viscous liquid to overflow its banks. Sloping sides gradually formed, and I permitted it to spray upward and outward, adding height to the rocky matter surrounding the hole. All the snow and ice in the surrounding area vaporized into mist.

Only cold air and frozen ground were available to aid me, and neither were enough to cool the liquefied rock into a solid form. A crust formed over the top, but beneath that layer, the lava continued to slowly ooze over the flat ground. I backed away, gradually giving ground as it spread out. Even though I directed the lava to cool quickly, I was limited by how much I could focus on at any particular moment and could not release the heat as rapidly as I wanted. I tried to diffuse the heat laterally through the earth, but it had already extended nearly to the maximum distance my magic could reach. What I really needed was –

A frigid blast of air swirled around me and swept over the lava flowing over the ground. It became more sluggish as cooler black spots appeared, spreading as it rapidly cooled. I looked around, trying to find out who had called this wind, and saw Angie walking toward me, her dark hair whipping in the wind.

Standing in a glowing puddle of lava with an iridescent rope of it in my hand, I felt like a kid caught misbehaving.

"I can explain," I said.

"I don't need an explanation," she replied.

"You were supposed to ride to Ward."

"And you were supposed to meet us at the northern gate."

I sighed. "I'm sorry. I just couldn't leave it like this."

She smiled. "Of course not. You're an earth druid."

I chuckled. "I guess I am."

"Can I help?"

"I could use a hand," I admitted. "I can't cool the rock fast enough, but between the two of us, we just might contain this catastrophe." I grinned, feeling a surge of renewed hope. We might even stop it by nightfall.

"You have that much faith in me?"

"Absolutely."

She looked uncertain, half hopeful, and half scared.

"I hope *you* enjoy living up to his expectations," said Conall, appearing out of the steaming mist. "The rest of us certainly have."

"It's not so bad," said Dermot, following him. "I wouldn't have tried even half the things I've accomplished otherwise."

"Dermot's right," said Seth, "there's nothing quite like having someone believe in your abilities."

"As we believe in yours," said Duncan.

"I told you all to get out of here!" I said. Didn't *anybody* listen to me anymore?

"The rest of the Finns are riding for Ward as we speak," Seth announced. "We left our horses at the gate."

"Are all of you *insane*?"

"Obviously," Conall said. "Only a madman would stand this close to an active volcano." His expression became focused, and again a glacial blast of air swirled around to cool the jetting lava that had landed on the freshly cooled rock.

"So what are we going to do?" asked Dermot. "Looks like you're building a mountain."

I took another look at my inadequate stab at controlling the situation, and realized he was right. The simplest thing to do would be to change its structure. Instead of allowing it to be wide and flat, we could build it up.

"Dermot, you are a genius," I said. "That's exactly what we're going to do."

Seth cracked his knuckles. "Let's bury this place."

We backed up a respectable distance and got to work. If we

were to create a true mountain, spreading the lava around the rim of the caldera would make a more solid foundation; its root would develop as the magma chamber below cooled over time. Energized at the prospect, I shaped the jetting lava to rain down in a circular pattern on the ground. It was a veritable geyser that sprayed glowing orange lava a thousand feet into the air.

Conall set to piling fresh snow on the rocks and sent cold winds circling about the oozing lava. Before long, there was more black rock than orange. The earth continued to tremble, frequently jolting us off balance; more than once it sent everyone but Duncan and me to their knees. It was a good sign that we had enough influence over the earth to keep our footing, but it would be a long time before the mother settled down to peaceful sleep again.

The already powerful wind picked up in speed and energy as Angie added her elements to the mix, and the hot rocks cooled even more quickly.

"It needs more substance," said Duncan. "Something from which the lava can take support."

"I'm on it," said Angie. "Seth, you and Dermot keep cooling the rocks. Conall, follow my lead." She moved away a few steps, looking out over the remains of the 'Ville. With two fingers raised and quick, lighter flicks of her wrist, she created a tiny whirlwind and moved it over the volcano to allow it to draw in heat. It grew in size and power, a full-blown tornado rising up to the clouds, and she sent it off to scour the land. When she brought it back, it was laden with debris from the destroyed Republic buildings, and we all backed a safer distance away from our volcano in the making. When the tornado was close enough, she slowed the wind speed that powered it, allowing tons of debris to rain down around the mouth of the caldera. I directed thick streams of lava to spray all around its edge, completely coating the half-melted steel and chunks of concrete. Spinning it up once again in the heat of the volcano, Angie sent it out to gather more wreckage.

"Your turn," she said to Conall.

"Challenge accepted." He raised his fist above his head and began rotating his arm in a circular motion, slowly at first, then faster and faster. The clouds massed above our heads, and the hook of a tornado appeared, then dropped down toward the ground. His tornado traveled south to the ruins of the nearest wall, where it zigzagged around gathering broken concrete and twisted metal.

"I've got the perimeter," he told Angie. "You take the center."

The two cyclones grew in size and strength, consuming the remnants of human habitation with a vengeance. The two triple threats directed the tornadoes here and there, scouring the 'Ville like giant sweepers, gathering the rubble for our man-made mountain. Periodically one would approach, dropping its load before moving away again. I poured fresh lava over the entirety of the mess, binding it together while Dermot sprayed snow, ice, and water onto it, Seth used straight-line winds to cool it further, and Duncan shifted and compressed the cooled materials for greater stability.

We worked together like well-trained druids with years of experience, even though Conall hadn't had magic for even one whole day and none of us had ever done anything like this before. The rocky ring around the crater's rim grew back to its original height and then higher still. We gave ground as the base of it continued to spread outward and the slopes grew higher and higher. As long as I could feel the intense pressure rising up through the earth's crust, I continued to bring up the magma through the main vent at the volcano's center. It jetted into the air and over the lip of the caldera, the basaltic flow gradually cooling as it slid down the mountain slope.

As the hours went by, we moved steadily away from our creation until we reached the birthplace of the Kraken, where the water towers had once stood. It was a good two-thirds of a mile from the city center. Whereas the initial sinkhole-turned-caldera had initially been maybe a tenth of a mile across, the base of the volcano was now over a mile and a half in diameter. Sulfurous smoke billowed from the volcanic peak, releasing the angry energy of the earth mother. The snowfall had stopped, but the temperature was steadily dropping as the sun made its way to the horizon. It would have been too cold to tolerate if not for the residual heat from our druid-made volcano. Angie and Conall's tornados were returning with less and less debris and I was thinking that maybe we should move the horses when Duncan knelt and pressed his palms to the ground.

"Quieter now," he said.

I joined him, seeking out the consciousness of the recently

wakened earth. The mother was still rumbling and uneasy, but had vented much of her wrath. The pressure within the magma chamber had been steady for the last couple of hours.

"Think it'll be okay to leave it?"

He nodded.

"Thank the gods," I said.

Dermot flopped onto his back in the snow. "It is *so* nice not to run out of magic!"

Conall joined him. "It's nice to have magic, period." A wave of mushy slush lifted up and poured over the water druid.

"Hey!" Dermot protested, shivering. "I'll sic my *Dobhar-chú* on you."

Our brand-new triple threat just smiled. "I'll just call up a Kraken. It's from Norse mythology, you know. Not Greek."

"We can have monster battles and see who wins!" Dermot said excitedly, and they bumped fists.

Once again I was struck by how remarkable it was that two people who were so different – and who had initially hated each other – could have become such close friends. They rose, draining all the water from their clothes and hair, and I sent a wash of heated air over them to stop their shivering.

The six of us took a few precious minutes to admire our handiwork. The smoking volcano was huge, bigger than any solitary mountain I had ever seen, bigger even than the volcano beside Sanctuary. It was also hideously ugly. Someday, when it cooled completely, the rocks would break down into soil, and scrub brush and then trees would take root on its surface. Then it would have the beauty and majesty of any other mountain.

"Shall we go?" Seth said. "We have a long ride ahead of us."

We had thirteen miles to travel through knee-deep snow and less than twenty-four hours to do it. Ordinarily, the horses could accomplish this within a day, but the fierce wind and knee-deep snow could make the journey take twice as long.

"We'd better hurry, or we're not going to make it," Conall said.

"We'll make it," I said, surging to my feet and melting the snow to slush for an easier passage back to the horses. Walking quickly, we reached them in under a quarter of an hour. Carl Freeman must have taken a different horse when he'd left with the

Finns, for he had left Steel at the ruins of the northeast gate.

"The rest of the Finns should have arrived in Ward by now," said Seth. "We'll have easier passage if we follow their tracks."

"I hope we get there in time," said Dermot.

"We will," Conall said. "Rhiannon will wait for us until the last possible moment."

"How do you know?" I asked, giving Angie a leg up on her palomino mare.

"Because Cinna told me she'd *make* her wait," Conall said with a smug smile.

"I'll take point," I said, swinging aboard the grulla stallion. The dragon soared overhead, breathing fire to melt the snow and ice, laying out a path that would speed our journey back to Ward.

"Epona give us speed!" cried Dermot, leaping on Kelpie.

"And Odin guard our journey!" said Conall.

"Let's ride!"

Epilogue

As we rode north, I couldn't stop looking back at the inconceivable expanse of destruction that had been wrought by earth and fire. Steam rose from the scorched earth and smoke billowed from the mouth of the volcano in the center of where the 'Ville used to stand. It was still erupting and had begun to spew volcanic ash. When we were a couple of miles away, the ground rumbled ominously. I looked back just in time to see a pyroclastic cloud exploding violently into the sky.

How many innocent people had died in the fighting? How many were now homeless, doomed to die of exposure or starvation?

I had chosen to go to war with good intentions, aiming to deliver people from the threat of bondage and oppression. I had wanted to ensure that all could live in peace and free from tyranny. Yet when faced with the choice of hurting innocent folk and rescuing Angie, I had chosen to lay waste to every obstacle separating us scarcely a thought for those that might dwell within.

Every person that I'd ever read about in all of history who had done such a deed as this had been vilified and labeled as a malevolent psychopath.

How would history remember *me*?

The End

Watch for the stunning conclusion of the druids' struggle for freedom in the next installment of The Druid Chronicles:

CHOSEN

Book Four of the Druid Chronicles

Finally reunited, Angie and Davis face the challenge of helping rebuild the communities devastated by the war of expansion waged by the 'Ville, and the newly freed territory looks forward to a new era of peace and prosperity. However, remnants of the Republic forces continue to rape and pillage lands and peoples, necessitating druid intervention.

Now that the 'Ville is no longer a threat, the druids of White Oak Grove are free to travel the same roads as their expatriate brethren and the Finns, resulting in clashes that are becoming all too frequent and instigating a series of events that could very well lead to a conflict between the grove and Shitozaki's splinter faction of magic-wielding young men.

Davis continues to struggle with control of his fire magic, leading newly inaugurated ArchDruid Connor Shitozaki to insist on meeting his parents – with or without his cooperation. Rumors abound concerning a holy war led by Sebrina Silvermist for the sole purpose of hunting down and destroying those they believe to be augmented druids.

Fighting a war against bandits with no magic was one thing.
A civil war between druids would be something else entirely, a conflict likely to bring about cataclysmic disasters on a scale unseen since the Fracture.

Will Davis and Angie continue to hold their belief that they should not fight against other druids? Or will events conspire to challenge that decision, fighting side by side… as Chosen?

Continue to read a brief exerpt

CHOSEN

Book Four of the Druid Chronicles

My heart was beating so hard that each beat felt like a sledgehammer to the chest, making it hard to catch my breath. Clutching my chest and unable to see for the burning in my eyes, I stumbled. Throwing my arm out to catch myself, my hand made contact with the dragon once more, allowing me to steady myself. It sat back on its haunches, horned triangular head thrown back, muzzle pointed toward the sky. It filled the air with a dual-toned keening that was nothing like I'd ever heard, deep alto notes of mourning blending and twining with a sharp, high-pitched discordance.

Its cry became a scream of pain and it reared up on its hind legs, talons plowing great furrows in the dirt. I was tossed aside, or perhaps I just fell. Tormented by some unseen agony, the dragon shook its horned head back and forth, spewing fire. It convulsed in great, sinewed coils like a dying snake, shuddering and curling in on itself. It was horrible to witness, and I could neither bear to watch nor look away. The bright elements of fire within the dragon began to dim, as the white-hot talons turned a pale gold and then deep red. Its body darkened as the flames dissipated, then paled as it became translucent. Within seconds, little more than smoke remained, punctuated with sparks and occasional flickers of fire. The winter wind blew and snuffed what remaining warmth it possessed, scattering smoke and ashes.

Then there was nothing left.

I had only one thought – to get the hell out of there and run away, but I could barely walk, let alone run. Only sheer willpower got me back on my feet. I tried to whistle for my horse but couldn't get enough air. The pain in my chest had burned my lungs to nothing, leaving only an endless gaping cavern inside.

"Davis!"

Seth grabbed my shoulders. I tried to push his arms away so I could keep going, because if I stopped I wasn't sure if I could start again. My limbs were as rubbery as if I'd been on a three-day bender.

"Davis!" he shook me a little and my knees nearly buckled. "What happened to you? Where's the... What happened to the dragon?"

"It needed air," I rasped. "Fire needs air."

His hands gripped me tighter. "What's wrong?"

Behind him, Dermot asked, "What's he saying? What happened?"

"I don't know!" Seth shouted. "He's not making any sense?"

"Fire needs air and I don't have any air. Earth needs water and I don't have any water."

"I think he's talking about his elements," Dermot said.

"That's stupid!" Seth snapped. "You don't need elemental air to make elemental fire! One person cannot have both!"

"Fire needs air."

"Davis, snap out of it!" Conall demanded. "Iriana, find out what's wrong with him!"

"I've already tried," she said. "I can't find anything."

"Duncan!" the Norseman screamed. "Get somebody else to watch those fucking brats and get your ass over here!"

"You don't have to shout," I said.

"Thank the gods, you're starting to make sense," Seth said. "What happened? Are you hurt? Where is Angie?"

Zeus' hand. The eagle's strike.

"Spirit sustains us," I mumbled. "We can't live without it."

"He was fine before we left him alone with her," said Seth.

"What are you saying?" Iriana demanded. "Angie would never hurt her own chosen!"

"She doesn't want me anymore," I said, feeling reality come dangerously close before it receded to a safe distance again.

"You were saying?" Conall muttered to Iriana.

"We saw you talking," said Seth. "Who were you talking to?"

"Chasity," I said. "She's damned good with a rifle. Crack shot."

"Did she shoot you?" He ran his hands through my hair, feeling for blood. "Gods! Conall, help me check for bullet wounds!"

They yanked my coat off and I immediately started to shake from the cold. It was like all the warmth within me had fled forever. Of course it had - my chest was hollow and I couldn't breathe the air anymore.

"Fire needs air," I whispered, but no one was listening.

"He's shivering," Conall said quietly.

Reality faded away again and I was warm again when it returned. My coat was back on, I was leaning back against a saddle covered in blankets, and someone had lit a fire – Poppy.

1"Thank you," I said.

She laid her hand on my forehead. "I'd give you some of my fire if I knew how."

"Fire needs air," I whispered.

"Yes," she said. "It does."

She drifted away

"Let me look at him."

Seth released me and the calm of Duncan's presence flowed into me.

"Iriana says he's fine," Conall said, still speaking quietly.

"Physically, he is."

"Then why is he talking crazy?" Seth snarled. It was the snarl of a fearful dog, not an angry wolf.

Fire needs air, I thought.

But what did air need?

"Why are you afraid?" I asked him in a moment of lucidity.

"What?" Seth whispered. The others fell silent, as though speaking would break the spell. Unfortunately for me, the spell had already been broken.

What does air need?

It didn't need anything.

"You're perfectly capable of leading the Finns and making all the decisions that need to be made," I said. "You're a good leader. You just have to remember one thing."

"What thing?" he asked, but the thought died in the middle of being born and my mind drifted away again. "Davis, what thing?"

"Earth needs water," I said. Iriana's face swam into view, pale and tearful. I took her hand and placed it in Seth's. "Earth needs air, too."

"*Fuck.*"

"Davis. Davis, look at me." Duncan took hold of my chin and made me face him. "Was Angie there?"

"Yes."

"Did you speak with her?"

"I talked to her."

"What did you say to her?"

"I told her I was sorry."

"Sorry for what?" His brows knit together.

"For not coming back sooner. For abandoning her."

"You were sick, Davis, and it took a long time to heal," he said soothingly. "You didn't abandon her."

"She has a right to be hurt and angry," I said, too lost in my own thoughts to hear anything else. "I told her that. I told her it's okay for her to be angry. She should yell at me. I was wrong to letting her go on believing I was dead. Yelling at me would make her feel better. I told her I should never have left her alone for so long."

Duncan squeezed his eyes shut, like he sometimes did when wrestling for control of his emotions. I waited for my thoughts to drift again but the pain came back instead and breathing became difficult again.

"Fire needs air," I rasped, gasping for breath and wishing I could stop breathing so the tearing pain in my chest would go away. Not having any lungs would be so much better than having the air ripped out of them over and over again.

But air didn't need anything, and neither did water or spirit.

"Davis, what did Angie say to you?" the earth druid asked.

"Nothing."

"No, look at me. Tell me what she said."

"Nothing."

"I don't understand." He was shaking his head slightly, confusion evident in his eyes. It puzzled me; how could I know what he was feeling if I couldn't even follow my own thinking?

"Davis, answer me. She didn't say anything?"

"No." I tried to shake my head, but it made me dizzy – especially since the earth was shaking under my feet. "Earth needs water," I said. "Then maybe it wouldn't shake so much."

Duncan put his hands on my face, stroking one cheek with his thumb. "I'll go talk to her," he said. "I'll get this straightened out, I promise. Do you hear me? I promise. I will fix this."

I didn't know what a promise was anymore, but I nodded

654

anyway.

Their voices reached my ears in a mixed-up jumble: Seth's voice high with fear, Duncan's clipped and angry, and Conall, calm, soothing and logical. I thought that surely the world must be ending, but the ground quieted again and the voices went away.

"Seth!"

"I'm here."

"Do chosen go crazy when they've been apart too long?" I asked.

"No," he replied. "They're not happy, but they don't become insane."

"I don't think we're chosen anymore."

Stark silence fell, creating a world as devoid of sound as it was of heat. Duncan took my hands and broke the silence.

"Chosen are for life," Duncan said. "The bond cannot be broken while you both still live."

"*While they both still live!*" Conall said with urgency. "Something has happened to Angie!"

"Stay here," Duncan said. "Stay here with Seth, and Conall, and Dermot. Stay with your friends."

"I will," I said, then sat bolt upright as another thought came to me clearly. "Duncan!"

"What is it?"

"Did Padraig go crazy when Dragana died?" I asked. "Did Liam when he lost Angie's mother?"

Duncan's face went blank. "I don't know."

A thrum went through the ground, summoning the other earth druids. Wolfric, Fenris, Phelan, and the dualists with elemental spirit showed up with them.

"Seth, you and Iriana stay with Davis," Duncan said. "Everyone else, make sure the prisoners are secure."

I slid one hand from under the blankets to touch the earth, comforted by the presence of the Earth Mother.

Fire needed air to breathe.

Earth needed water to sustain life.

Spirit bound and sustained it all.

Without Angie, I no longer had any of it.

CHOSEN

Book Four of the Druid Chronicles

Coming in 2020!

Pronunciation Guide

Added per reader request. These are close approximations (without proper pronunciation marks) for the sake of simplicity.

Adalwulf: AD-al-wolf

Ahearn: airn (one syllable, like "air" with N tacked on)

Ariadne: air-ee-AD-nee

Arrie: AHR-ree

Bébhinn: BAY-vin

Betrys: BEHT-rees (I pronounce it BEHT-riss) *

Billé: bill-AY

Ciaran: kear-in

Dianthe: dye-AN-thee

Eian: variant of Ian (EE-an)

Elin: AY-lin

Fenris: FEN-riss

Galen: GAY-lin

Heracles: HEHR-a-kleez

Ianna - EE-ahn-nah

Ingvar: EENG-vahr

Iriana: ear-ee-AN-nah

Jasvinder: jus-VIHN-duhr *

Liam: lee-um *or* lee-ahm

Madoc: MAD-ock

Maeve: rhymes with "brave"

Mohinder: muh-hihn-druh *

Narinder: nuh-RAIN-druh *

Nêreus: NEAR-ee-uhs

Niall: nye-all (one syllable)

Nioba: NEE-oh-bah

Nualla: noo-AL-lah

Onóra: oh-NOR-ah

Orion: or-EYE-un

Padraig: PAH-drig

Phelan: FAY-lun

Pollona: Pole-LONE-uh

Riordan: REAR-dun

Rhiannon: rhee-AN-nuhn

Rowena: row-EE-nah

Shitozaki: shee-toe-ZAH-kee

Solon: SOH-lun

Tiernan: TEAR-nun

Toby: TOE-bee

Uri: YU-ree

Weylin: WAY-lun (variation of Waylon)

Yiorgos: YEE-org-ohse (the second O is long)

* Pronunciations obtained from PronounceNames.com

Author's Note

So you're probably thinking, "Hey, wasn't *this* book supposed to be the 'stunning conclusion' of the Druid Chronicles?"

Well, yes. It was.

When I started the rewrite of Druid, it was already 189,000 words. In comparison, Traveler has close to 108,000 words, and Warrior has just over 164,000. Thus, I thought that all I needed to do was make sure there weren't any plot holes, correct the grammar and typos, and call it done.

Davis and the boys had other ideas.

In the original version, the first thirteen chapters are pretty much the same as this one. The main difference is that Davis and the Finns stuck around in Ward to defend it, and he and his pentacle rescued Angie and destroyed the 'Ville shortly afterward.

Apparently, Davis didn't care for that version much. Probably because it was too easy. He started wondering if the bandits had attacked Lone Oak and if the people at Lake Pickthorne were okay. And wasn't it just a little odd that only a few witches were kidnapped, and wasn't it just a little too convenient that they were all in the same place when they were found?

Thus, the Wild Hunt was born, the search for more witches and the liberation of the settlements around the 'Ville. It was fun and exciting, and before I knew it, it was HUGE. This wouldn't have been a problem, except for one thing. Books printed through Amazon's print-on-demand service are supposed to be pretty durable as long as they are under 700 pages, and it would have gone way over. Way, way, way over.

This put me in a quandary. Should I curtail the writing and keep it at three books, or cut a big chunk off the end and use it to make a fourth novel? As a reader, my natural response to this would be a resounding "MOAR BOOKS," but as a writer, I wasn't at all sure I could make that into a decent story. I kept writing but wrestled with the dilemma for weeks. I drove myself crazy and probably drove my family crazy, too. They'd probably have packed me off to the looney bin if it wasn't for Jessica, my #1 cheerleader. During one late-night conversation, Jess casually commented that she would not be sad at all if there was a fourth book, and that settled the matter. Who could say no to that?

After that, writing got a whole lot easier because I was no longer trying to shoehorn the plot into an existing ending. I just let it rip. Chapters 14 - 37 are all brand new – approximately 130,000 words, for a grand total of 230,390.

Now you know why it took so damn long to get the book finished (other than 3 years of grad school and endless hours and days of editing).

I'm not worried about book 4 being a decent length anymore, seeing as how giving me a rough outline and then later adding a metric ton of detailed material is just going to be how Davis tells his tale. And honestly, it's super fun that way.

While I plan for some kind of showdown between White Oak Grove and Shitozaki's Sanctuary, I'm not sure it'll happen because of some other things that might need to be explored, like what the surviving citizens of the Republic of Jackson will do, or how Sebrina will respond to Dianthe's death. And what will Shitozaki and the Everlight brothers will do when the kids don't come home? But most importantly: how are the druids newly settled in Sanctuary going to react to finding out that Davis is an augmented druid, the horrifying specter they've feared for so long come to life?

Thank you for reading my book, and if you are one of the steadfast and loyal readers, thank you even more for waiting so patiently for it. I truly hope it lived up to your expectations.

Would you please take a moment to share it on social media or leave me a review at your favorite retailer? You don't have to write a review; I'm happy to receive star ratings.

Until we meet again in the post-Fracture world…

May you have warm words on a cold evening,
A full moon on a dark night,
And the road downhill all the way to your door.
May the saddest day of your future be no worse
than the happiest day of your past,
and may your home always be too small to hold all your friends.

August 18, 2018

~ * ~ * ~ Stay Updated ~ * ~ * ~

Where to find me on the web:
http://www.DruidChronicles.com

Facebook: Author J. Paige Dunn
http://www.facebook.com/jpaigedunn

Twitter: @jpaigedunn

Instagram: @jpaigedunn

Blog: 365 Days of Night
http://jpaigedunn.wordpress.com

J. Paige Dunn has traveled in Europe and the UK while living in Germany for a few years. She now dwells happily in Geektopia, a little-known realm in the New Madrid fault zone. She lives with her husband, three kids, one grandkid, four cats, a dog, and some fish in a house that looks like it's losing a game of Jumanji. A former ER nurse, she is fascinated by with apocalyptic events and is certified in basic disaster life support. Now that she's got a horse, she's going to do some trail riding and eventually some Traveling.

www.ingramcontent.com/pod-product-compliance
Lightning Source LLC
Chambersburg PA
CBHW030737030726
47497CB00001B/25